THE OWENS CHRONICLES

THE COMPLETE TRILOGY

AMANDA LYNN PETRIN

CONTENTS

PROPHECY

THE OWENS CHRONICLES
BOOK ONE

AMANDA LYNN PETRIN

PROLOGUE

I can still remember the very first time I met Embry and Gabriel, two mysterious men who came out of nowhere and inserted themselves into my life. The details were fuzzy, more like a dream than a memory, but I knew they were important. I always felt special when they came to see me, even if I didn't know why. I was so young that I didn't understand the gravity of the situation, or how these men would eventually become my dark knights in shining armor, keeping me safe from all the scary characters from my nightmares...

I was five years old and Grams had just died. She had been the one taking care of me ever since 'the cancer' took my mom away. I used to make Grams look under my bed almost every night because I thought 'the cancer' was a monster, like the boogeyman. They always talked about it in hushed voices, and I knew it was the reason my mom left me. Instead of admitting there was nothing that she or anyone else could do to protect me from it, Grams humored me with a flashlight and some herbs that she would leave under my bed, to make sure it wouldn't come while I was asleep. She would go through different phases, sometimes putting salt by the windowsill as a protective barrier, other times hiding garlic in the closet. The smell was terrible, but it made me feel safe. Grams convinced me that burning sage to cleanse the house and all of her other tricks could help ward off 'the cancer' and other misfortunes. I didn't realize they were old wives' tales until 'the cancer' ripped Grams from me as well.

I hadn't counted, but it looked like there were hundreds of people gathered in the manor I grew up in. It was unnerving when I had never met a single one of them before. The manor was big enough that every curious mourner could lurk in their own room and I would never run into them. However, the East and West Wings were roped off, so everyone was crowded in the parlour. Mr. and Mrs. Boyd, the groundskeeper and his wife, were in charge of me until someone else could be found to take me in. Neither my mother nor my grandparents had any siblings or relatives to mention, and I knew nothing about my father, other than a blurry picture of a man whose face you couldn't see.

Mrs. Boyd was always vocal about her opinions, such as how horrible it was that the townsfolk were using Grams' funeral to gain access to our elusive manor. There were real estate agents and lawyers wandering as far as they could, trying to get lost on their way to the restroom, sniffing around for clues as to who was inheriting the property and whether they were likely to sell. Mrs. Boyd made certain none of them felt welcome, and a few of them literally retreated from her steely gaze. She had always been fiercely protective of us, and her fiery red hair, though slightly graying, made it clear she was not the type of person you wanted to mess with. I was grateful it meant no one dared come near me, but I could still hear their whispers.

I would never have called Grams suspicious or eccentric, but that was how the strangers in my home described her. They spoke as though they knew her and her crazy old woman behaviors, but they didn't know about half of the odd things we did. I could only imagine what they would say if they knew we ate strawberries and jumped into the creek for summer solstice, had soul cakes instead of trick-or-treating for Halloween and filled the house with fresh cowslip. Not to mention the bonfires. Or the locket. In movies, girls wore lockets with pictures of people they loved, whereas my locket was incredibly old and sealed shut. Grams had wanted me to wear it all the time, but it smelled funny, so she said it was okay as long as I wore it around the end of October. She never elaborated on the purpose of the locket, or what she was protecting me from, and she did get most of her information from books and movies, but she ingrained in me from early on that something terrible would happen if I didn't follow these practices. When she died, I saw it as proof that none of it was real, but then again, maybe I just hadn't tried hard enough to do everything she taught me.

The townspeople knew none of that. They only knew that Grams was a recluse who never mingled with the outside world. A few people had come to visit us once or twice over the years, but we never left the manor and after my mom died, there were no more visitors. Mrs. Boyd did our grocery shopping and her husband took care of any errands we had.

Whenever Mrs. Boyd suggested I needed playmates my own age, Grams would remind her that I had Samuel, Mr. and Mrs. Boyd's fifteen-year-old-son. Sam had none of his mother's fierceness, and tended to make me laugh more than anything, particularly when he got angry, which was rare. His hair was ginger and reminded me more of a carrot than of fire, which suited his personality perfectly.

In an attempt to avoid the strangers, I secluded myself on the stairs, past the velvet rope Mrs. Boyd used to show our 'guests' where they weren't welcome. I was perfectly content there, playing with Grams' antique dolls. They lived on a shelf in my bedroom, too high for me to reach, because they were old and fragile. As Grams would say, "They're meant to be looked at, not played with." Sam had taken them down for me that morning as a special treat. On occasion, Grams would bring them down as props for the stories she would tell me about the lives they had lived. I loved these stories about adventures and courage, even though they never ended with the dolls living happily ever after. "It's not about that," Grams would tell me. "It's about the kind of women they were, the things they overcame with their strength and bravery." She made sure my heroes wouldn't be princesses whose sole ambition was to marry the prince by the end of the story, then live happily ever after.

Other than Beth, whose hair barely reached her chin, the dolls all looked the same, with big green eyes and lots of curly brown hair. I had to look at their clothes to tell them apart; Annabelle looked like a pilgrim with her bonnet, Rosalind had the big, poofy bottom to her dress, Cassandra wore a straight gown in bright colors with white gloves, and Elizabeth had a flapper dress. Grams said you could recognize them by their smiles, but I assumed she was teasing because the smiles all looked the same to me. They were strong and confident, but also a little sad.

My favourite part was that each doll had a crescent moon birthmark on the back of her neck, right below the hairline. You had to lift up their hair to see it, so Grams didn't know about it until I showed her. I liked it because I had one too, in the exact same spot. Mr. Boyd tried to rub it off once, when Grams put my hair up in a high bun for a ballet lesson, but Mrs. Boyd told him it was just something that ran in my family.

"Does that mean the dolls are real?" I had asked Grams *excitedly.*

"They're just dolls," she brushed it away.

"But they look like people who are related to me," I specified.

She looked at me in that way where she tried to be stern, but failed miserably. "They're made to look like your ancestors," Grams reluctantly agreed.

"Did you know them?" My eyes grew wide.

"They all died long ago," she sounded sad.

"That means that all of their adventures..." My brain tried to remember every story I had been told.

"They're just stories, Luce."

I WAS LIFTING up their hair to see the birthmark when a man, dressed all in black, knelt down in front of me. His sandy blond hair was still wet, as though he had tried to make it look presentable, but it was sticking out all over the place. Mine always got really frizzy, which made Grams think I hadn't brushed it when I had.

"That's a pretty doll you have there." He picked up the white bonnet I dropped when lifting her hair and handed it back to me. "What's her name?" His voice was kind, with the hint of an Italian accent, but his eyes were dark and intense. Not exactly scary, but unlike anything I had seen before.

"Annabelle," I answered, which made him smile. "And this is Beth and Cassie and Rosie," I introduced him to the others. The isolation I grew up in at the manor meant that I hadn't encountered enough strangers to be warned not to talk to them. Although even if I had, I would have made an exception for him. He made me nervous, not that he gave me any reason to be, and he felt familiar, as though I had met him before.

"And what is your name?" he asked me.

"Lucy." The shyness in my voice led him to turn around and see the other man who had caught my attention. His hair was dark brown and straight, but his eyes, that he hadn't taken off me since he came up the staircase, were the same as the first man's. He was listening intently to our conversation, but made no attempt to join it.

"It's nice to meet you, Lucy," the first man continued, turning back to me. "I'm Embry Dante and this is my friend, Gabriel Black." He said 'friend' in a way that told me they weren't.

The introduction provided an opportunity for the other man, Gabriel, to come closer. He also knelt down to my level and extended his hand, so I could shake it. Up close, his eyes were even scarier, but I wasn't afraid.

"I've never seen her so young before," Gabriel told Embry, looking me up and down. The statement confused me, as I had only ever been younger.

"How did you know my Grams?" I asked, sensing these weren't townspeople looking for access. They had gone past the velvet rope, but instead of looking like they got caught while exploring, they acted like I was the one they were looking for. They must have been Grams' friends. Or more likely my mom's.

"We're old friends of the family," Embry explained, not looking all that old to me. He was older than Sam, but younger than any adult I knew.

"Did you also know my mommy?" Grams knew so few people, that anyone who knew her would have known my mom as well, especially if they were friends of the family. I remembered so little of my mom that I was always asking people to tell me stories, but it made Grams sad, and the Boyds insisted they had already told me all the stories they knew.

"Of course I knew Marilyn," Embry told me while someone in the hallway caught Gabriel's eye.

"Lucy, you need to eat something." Sam came over and extended his hand, expecting me to follow him to the room where the food was set out. He had looked at the men with curiosity when he walked by them, but focused entirely on me once he got close.

"They knew my mommy," I argued with him, not ready to leave.

"This area is off-limits to guests," Sam told my new friends. "I'll bring you to her room later if you come with me now," he tried to bribe me. It was a tough decision. I could stay there and talk to men who might know stories I had yet to hear about my mother, or I could take Sam up on his offer and spend hours going through my mother's things, wearing her clothes and possibly hiding something in my blankie to treasure later. I carried it with me everywhere, so no one would suspect anything if I slipped a photograph or some jewelry into the creases of the pearl-colored material. Grams was always worried I would break things, which was why the dolls lived on the shelf that was too high for me to reach.

"Okay," I reluctantly agreed, taking Sam's hand to get up from the steps. "Will I see you again?" I asked Embry, looking around, but Gabriel had vanished while I was talking to Sam.

"I'll be around," he assured me before Sam brought me to the dining room, where his parents were waiting.

"Come here sweetie, I made a plate of your favorites." Mrs. Boyd motioned me over, took me into her lap, and handed me a plate with deviled eggs, Swedish meatballs, hot dogs wrapped in bread and bacon, as well as little cheese cubes. I knew she had also bought a tub of cookie dough ice cream for me to have later, once all the strangers were gone.

"Where was she?" Mr. Boyd asked Sam. He was tall and fair and usually wore dirt-stained overalls, but now looked uncomfortable in the stiff black suit his wife made him wear.

"On the stairs, talking to some guys I've never seen before. I got the feeling they were hiding something," he told his father, stealing one of my cheese cubes with a smile, knowing I would forgive him.

"Everyone here today is hiding something. None of them have seen the inside of this house in years, if at all," Mrs. Boyd added her two cents.

"They knew Grams. And mommy," I inserted myself into their conversation.

"What were their names, sweetie?" Mrs. Boyd asked me, playing with my hair. Sam didn't have any siblings, but she liked having a girl around, and I definitely didn't mind.

"Embry and Gabriel," I said with my mouth full. "I like them."

Mr. and Mrs. Boyd exchanged a glance before she took me off her lap and asked Sam to watch me while she went to take care of something.

I TRIED to ask Sam where they were going, but he didn't seem to know any more than I did, so he let me finish eating, then brought me to the backyard. His girlfriend, Deanna, showed up not long after and played hopscotch with me. Sam wasn't biologically my brother, but he had been there my whole life. Grams had rarely let him have friends over because they were always too loud or 'had a look about them', but even she had liked Deanna. Her auburn hair was cut just below her ears, but she still knew how to do French Braids, and would do mine sometimes when Sam had homework to do. Grams liked her because she was always smiling.

Eventually, Deanna and Sam snuck out to the garden swing to do 'grown-up things' which I knew meant kissing, leaving me alone.

I SAW Embry and Gabriel by the fountain, so I went over to try and talk to them some more. I was sure Embry would answer questions about my mom, and maybe even tell me some stories. Unfortunately, Mr. and Mrs. Boyd had found the men as well, so I stayed close enough to hear, but far enough that I wouldn't be seen.

"My family has been taking care of Lucy's for a long time, Mr. Dante, and I know who you are." There was a warning in Mrs. Boyd's tone, like when she was yelling at the animals that ate out of the garden.

"Then you know why we're here." Embry sounded serious, like it was important business that had brought him to the manor. Everyone seemed to know what was going on, but I didn't have a clue.

"Martha, you can't believe your father's stories? He was a drunk." Mr. Boyd didn't trust the two men, or believe their story, whatever it was.

"I never believed them before, Curtis, but he is not a day older than in the painting from the East Wing, or the picture from Miss Helen's bedroom." That was where I knew him from.

The manor had four wings, but I couldn't tell you which one was which, except for the East Wing, because I wasn't allowed to be there. This meant I had been dozens of times and seen the life-size portraits of my two new friends. Miss Helen was my great-grandmother, who died before I was born, so I never felt the urge to explore her bedroom, which was also in the East Wing.

"That painting could be of anybody. It's hundreds of years old," Mr. Boyd argued.

"It could, but it isn't. We understand that it's difficult to fathom, but we are exactly who we say we are, and we're here for Lucy." He didn't sound mean, but I could tell that he was going to get his way. I didn't think they were going to hurt me or anything, but at the same time, I didn't want to leave the manor, or Mr. and Mrs. Boyd.

"You'll take that girl over my dead body," Mr. Boyd said

with anger, but it still made me smile. He was strict, and often talked to Sam and I like we were soldiers in his army rather than children, but deep down, he was a softy. He was the one who would sneak me a cookie when Grams said I wasn't allowed to have dessert.

"We don't want to take her," Gabriel said as if it were preposterous. "What would we do with a five-year-old girl?"

"We want to come by every once in a while and make sure she's safe," Embry spoke calmly, convincingly, until he used the wrong words.

"She'll be perfectly safe with us." Mr. Boyd sounded hurt by the accusation.

"Of course she will. We don't doubt that you are fully capable of raising her with as much love and affection as her own mother would have, but we want to stop by sometimes and see how she's doing. We made a promise a long time ago, to look after this family, and it is imperative that we stick to our promise," Embry implied they would keep coming whether we liked it or not.

"I don't trust you," Mr. Boyd said before I heard his footsteps drifting away. I was about to go back to Sam and Deanna, but Mrs. Boyd wasn't done.

"What are you exactly? I mean…are you demons? Angels? Warlocks?" she asked, intrigued.

"You read way too many novels," Gabriel laughed, sounding bored.

"There's no name for what we are, though there are some historical references to The Gifted. Some people like us live normal lives and die just as they would have without it."

"I thought you were invincible, or immortal?" she inquired.

"We just stick around until our job is done. We linger until our unfinished business is taken care of, like purgatory. We have something to live for, something we need to accomplish, so we live," Embry explained. "There are some people like us who don't even know what their purpose is. Leonardo da Vinci kept making invention after invention, waiting to discover the one that would finally let him join the ones he loved."

"And you live to protect the descendants of the woman you loved?" she verified, unimpressed by whoever he'd mentioned.

"It was her dying wish that we take care of her daughter," Embry explained, the emotion clear in his voice.

"And she said she would come back," Gabriel spoke up, letting everyone know why he was still hanging around.

"There's no such thing as vampires and demons and werewolves and goblins and all of those things?" Mrs. Boyd sounded disappointed.

"Not that I've encountered." Embry laughed warmly, but Gabriel looked like he wasn't so sure.

"We should have this conversation when Lucy isn't listening in." Gabriel looked right to where I was standing.

I stepped out of my hiding spot behind some bushes, and he looked at me in a way that let me know I had done something wrong, but then he smiled. It was the tiniest of smiles that barely lasted a second, but I was sure I saw it. Like breaking the rules might be something he approved of.

"I thought I told you to wait in the kitchen with Sam?" Mrs. Boyd asked me in her motherly tone, trying to determine how much I had heard.

"Deanna came so they went to the yard, but I wanted to see Embry and Gabriel," I explained.

"Come here sweetie, we'll get you back inside." Mrs. Boyd picked me up so she would be sure I went with her. As she walked past the fountain, she paused. "We're taking care of her until, or unless someone else comes around to claim her. I don't mind you coming as long as Lucy still wants to see you, but the minute I start feeling about you like my husband does, you won't be invited back," she warned.

Embry nodded as we walked away. I tried to look back and wave at them, but we rounded a statue and they were gone.

"How much of that did you hear?" Mrs. Boyd asked me while we made our way back to the guests.

"All of it, I think," I said, letting my head rest on her shoulder. She smelled clean, like soap, but also like cookies and food. Being up in her arms made me feel safe. As long as she held me, Embry and Gabriel wouldn't have to worry, because nothing bad would ever happen to me. I knew I was wrong, even then, because Mrs. Boyd held me in her arms for most of the time that my grandmother was sick, and she still died, just like my mom.

"One day this hiding and sneaking around is going to get you in trouble," she said, rubbing my back so I would fall asleep. She didn't sound mad, and she usually found it funny when I snuck up on her in the kitchen.

"I can't believe our little girl is graduating." Deanna helped me fix my cap over my long brown curls, which she tried to tame for the occasion.

"You're not even 10 years older than me," I reminded her. We celebrated her twenty-seventh birthday a couple of months before my eighteenth.

"And I'm your little girl!" five-year-old Clara pointed out, barging into her parents' bedroom and putting herself between me and Deanna at the mirror. You wouldn't think we were related if you saw us individually, with Deanna's platinum pixie cut and Clara's strawberry blonde pigtails, but when I looked at the 3 of us together in the mirror, we were a family.

"Lucy is our big girl and you're our baby girl," Sam explained, making me roll my eyes. His mom died when I was twelve, then his father three years ago, making Sam my legal guardian. He was an amazing dad to Clara, but I still saw him as a big brother.

"But who is your favorite girl?" Clara was all about favorites these days, ever since Deanna went back to work. It was only part time, a day or two every week, but she loved being a social worker and helping people. Clara wasn't used to sharing her mom with anyone but me, and kept making sure she was still the favorite. I found it adorable.

"I love all three of my girls more than anything else in the world," Sam answered without answering, which got Clara to sigh loudly for effect, oozing attitude. I appreciated his sentiment, but it had been thirteen years since I was anybody's favorite, and I was okay with that. Most of the time.

"You're my favorite sister." Clara turned to me. She knew we weren't really related, but I had been there every single day since she was born.

"And you're my favorite little sister," I assured her.

She pouted at that, but I shrugged and looked up at Deanna, who became my big sister long before she became Sam's wife and, ultimately, my guardian. "I'll put this back on after lunch," Deanna assured me, gently removing the cap now that we knew how it would look.

"What time are we eating at?" I asked.

"I told everyone 12," Sam shared. He literally meant everyone, but no one would show up. A few kids used to come to my birthday parties when I was little, so their parents could explore the manor and see if the rumors about us were true, but they gave up when they realized the eccentricity died with Grams. Keisha was the exception. She moved to town halfway through sixth grade, when everyone else already had their best friend, except for me. I wasn't bullied, but people rarely went out of their way to make me feel welcome or accepted. Neither did Keisha, to be honest. She just showed up with so much confidence and strength that when she said we belonged, I believed her.

"I better start making the cake." I got up and followed Sam and Deanna out of the room.

"Do you want to play hide and seek?" Clara asked, following me.

"I can play now, and she can come join us?" Deanna offered on her way down the stairs.

"Does that mean I'll have to lick the spoons all by myself?" I pretended that was a daunting task.

"I can lick the spoons?" Clara asked in a whisper, looking over to her mom. Deanna liked to warn us about the salmonella we could get from cake batter.

"Of course," I told her with confidence. I was barely allowed to leave the property as a child, but the house was always stocked with cookie dough to deal with heartbreaks.

"Let me get my hat." Clara stopped midway down the stairs and ran back up.

I followed her to her bedroom, decorated with princesses and unicorns, and waited while she sorted through her toy chest to find a baker's hat. She loved playing dress-up and helping us cook, so it was the perfect birthday gift for her. Embry nearly replaced me as her favorite when she opened it.

I MADE the cake batter with Clara and let her lick all the spoons and mixers, but I saved a few spoonfuls from the bowl for myself.

"Now cookies?" Clara looked up at me, her face all sticky with chocolate icing from when she tried to lick the middle of the mixer spoons.

"Now I go set the table while you wash up," I corrected her. "We can make cookies next Sunday." I never understood the harm in a 'sugar rush' until we introduced Clara to chocolate.

I went to the dining room and set seven places for my Graduation Party. Sam, Deanna and Clara were a given, and Keisha said she would come for an hour or so between her two parents, who divorced a month into our sophomore year. Gabriel would run off with something important to do as soon as the cake was done, but Embry would make up for him by staying an entire week to hang out.

By 12:30, Sam, Deanna, Clara, Keisha and I were sitting at the dining room table, waiting while the smell of delicious food kept wafting in, making my mouth water.

"You did invite them, right?" Clara asked like maybe her dad had been silly and forgot to tell the other guests about the party.

"I did," he assured us.

"And?" I asked.

"Embry said he wouldn't miss it for the world. Gabriel looked at me like I was talking a foreign language and said he would see."

"Sounds accurate," I conceded. Gabriel was like that brooding teenager whose parents forced him to attend an event about 90 percent of the time, while Embry was the big brother I would run to whenever he showed up. Which was often.

"Maybe you told him the wrong date?" Keisha ventured after I tried Embry's cell phone again and was sent straight to voicemail.

"Or they thought this was a dinner party?" Deanna played along, but we hadn't had dinner celebrations since Clara was born. She had a tendency to fall asleep at the table if anything started past 6 o'clock.

"I'm hungry." Clara looked around the table to her parents, then back to me when they shrugged to let her know it was my party, so my decision.

"We can heat some up when they arrive," I assured her, letting Sam and Deanna know I was okay with us eating without them. There were a million reasons why they could be late or unable to come, but few that explained why they hadn't told anyone and weren't answering their phones.

Sam, Deanna and I went to the kitchen and made five plates of Sloppy Joes. The table was decked out with hot sauces and chili for Deanna, ketchup and relish for Clara, who treated it like a hamburger, and mountains of shredded cheese for Sam and I. Keisha ate hers as is, with a fork and knife, opposed to the 'sloppy' part of the meal.

I smiled at Clara, who loved being able to make a mess of herself with food, but my mind was on the two empty chairs.

"You okay?" Sam asked while we brought the empty plates to the kitchen.

"Gabriel never said he was coming," I said as if I hadn't expected him to.

"True," he agreed, but no matter how unenthusiastic Gabriel was sometimes, he was always there for milestones and big events.

"And maybe Embry doesn't like the idea that I'm growing up, or that I'm going off to college instead of staying here forever," I shared what had originally been a fear, but was now a better alternative to something bad happening to them.

"You think he didn't show up just to spite you?" he questioned my logic.

"Do you have a better suggestion?" I would take disappointing them over 80 percent of the scenarios running through my mind.

"He forgot the date. Got a new phone and couldn't figure out how to use it. He was speeding and the cop brought him to the station because he couldn't provide a valid driver's license. He got held up on his way because he stopped to rescue orphans from a burning building and his phone was lost in the fire," he gave me a list of somewhat plausible explanations where Embry wasn't hurt or mad at me.

"Thank you," I smiled at the last one, because it was very Embry.

"Anytime," he assured me.

"I hope it's a simple misunderstanding." I let out the breath I was holding and tried to release some of the tension that wasn't letting up in my shoulders.

"How many messages under the table?" he let me know I hadn't been as sneaky as I hoped.

"A million texts and three calls," I admitted. "But I'm sure they're fine," I brushed it off.

"They always make it back to you," he reminded me.

"Exactly," I agreed with absolutely no conviction. Even if I was worried about them, I didn't want Sam to worry about me.

"We're ready for you!" Clara and Keisha called.

"Let's go, High School Grads." Sam ushered me to sit beside Keisha, where they put the candle-lit cake.

"For they are jolly good fellows, for they are jolly good fellows…" Clara and Deanna sang. Sam asked, "Really? That's what we're going with?" before joining in.

"This is so unnecessary." I shook my head at them, but I was grinning ear to ear as Keisha and I blew out the candles.

"You girls are going to be amazing," Sam said, locking eyes with me so I would know he meant it.

"You'll knock them all dead," Deanna encouraged.

"Then bring them back to life." Sam looked pointedly to his wife, reminding her that I was going to be studying Medicine in the fall, where the hope is that I keep people alive, not kill them.

"Obviously." She rolled her eyes and smiled.

"I love you guys." I ignored the tears.

"Yeah, thank you Mr. and Mrs. Boyd." We all inadvertently

cringed when Keisha thanked them. Ever since the first time she came over, she insisted it was impolite for her to call them by their first names, but Mr. and Mrs. Boyd were Sam's parents, so it sounded weird to us.

"We can do it all over again once Embry and Gabriel get here," Deanna assured me when my eyes ventured to the empty chairs again.

"We'll try to come up with a more fitting song for round two," Sam agreed, getting a playful slap from his wife.

"I'll have to pass on round two. My dad is taking me for ice cream." Keisha got up from the table.

"How long is he in town for?" I asked. He moved to Providence after the divorce so his visits, though few and far between, were always extra special.

"He's moving me into MIT after prom, then traveling for the rest of the summer."

"How's your mom taking it?" Deanna asked.

"Me leaving or him being there?" Keisha asked in a way that told us neither of these were suiting her mom so well.

"It's a 15-minute drive," Sam pointed out.

"How are you feeling about the 30 minutes to Harvard?" Deanna shot back.

"Point taken," he agreed.

"And it won't be 15 minutes. She got a grant to go do research and dig stuff up in England."

"She finally said yes?" Her mom was always being asked to lead research expeditions all over the place, but she always said no to opportunities I would have jumped on.

"She says you can come with me at Thanksgiving if you want."

I turned straight to Sam, but all my hopes died when I saw his expression. "We'll have to talk it over," he told Keisha.

"You've got time," she assured him before Clara and I walked her to the door.

"Will you be at Lucy's graduation?" Clara asked.

"I kind of have to be. I'm giving a speech," Keisha shared.

"How come?" Clara looked at her like giving a speech was the last thing anyone should want to do.

"She's smarter than everyone else." I rolled my eyes before smiling at my best friend.

"By like half a percent," she argued.

"It still counts," I assured her.

"All that to say I will see you both later," she told us. "And thank you Mr. and Mrs. Boyd!" she called back to the kitchen.

"Anytime, sweetie." Deanna poked her head into the hallway.

"CAN WE PLAY TAG NOW?" Clara asked once we were back in the dining room, wolfing down her last few bites of cake.

"Of course," I sighed while Deanna smiled at me, knowing I was only pretending it was a chore. I loved hanging out with Clara and would miss her dragging me out for adventures once I was on campus in the fall.

"You're it!" She touched me before running off as soon as I opened the door to the backyard. I used to have to run at a snail's pace and pretend I couldn't catch her, but she was getting better, and sometimes I only barely caught her.

"Do you think Embry is okay?" she asked once I had her up in my arms, having trapped her in the maze that used to be our apple orchard.

"Of course he's okay. He's Embry," I told her as if she had nothing to worry about, but my heart had been tight in my chest ever since Sam suggested we sit at the table instead of waiting for them in the doorway. Gabriel usually showed up right on time, but he was never late, and I couldn't remember the last time Embry wasn't hours early for a party. Something was off.

"You're not worried at all?" Clara asked, making me feel terrible, because I knew she would trust me if I told her there was nothing to worry about.

"Nope. I'm thinking about all the cake we can have if they don't come," I teased, tickling her before running off.

"You're so fast today!" I said when she caught me. I wrapped my arm around her shoulders so we could head back to the manor to get ready.

"I'm always fast." She ducked under my arm and ran ahead of me to prove her point. If only I'd had her confidence at that age, I would have spent a lot less time worrying, and a lot more time doing things. Like standing up for myself and making friends, things I didn't do until Keisha showed me how. Clara had her grandmother's fierceness, her dad's kindness, and her mother's social skills. She was what I wanted to be when I grew up.

Once inside, I changed into the gorgeous yellow dress Deanna got for me to wear underneath the gown, and let her put the cap back on. Sam often said the luckiest day of his life was when he was the first person Deanna met when she moved to town with her dad, and it was one of mine as well. Sam had always been one of my favorite people, but Deanna had quickly become the best friend/sister I never got to have. Because Sam lived at the manor with my crazy family, a lot of the kids at school didn't take the time to find out how awesome he was. Deanna walked into the grocery store when he was helping his mom out, literally fell into his arms in the produce aisle and left with his heart. Luckily, he'd made an impression on her as well. I was still waiting for someone new to move to the neighborhood and stumble into the manor, which might be the only way I could meet him before he found out that I was 'that weird Owens girl' to everyone in town.

WHEN WE GOT TO SCHOOL, Sam and Deanna took Clara to get seats while I found my graduating class in the library. There were eighty of us, mostly the same students I met on my first day of kindergarten. I was amazed at all the kids my age I had as friends, until they went home and their parents told them to keep their distance. Mrs. Boyd would say, "People are afraid of what they don't know," which wasn't very comforting, even back then.

"We made it." Tennison came over to me while someone from administration tried to line us up alphabetically, leaving behind the cheerleaders he'd been talking to. Other than Keisha, who came much later, Tennison Montgomery was the only student who talked to me when the teachers weren't requiring it, which they rarely did. He had been my best friend on that first day of class, when I showed up all nervous because of so many new faces. He said he liked my curly hair, but I always thought it was the homemade brownies Mrs. Boyd sent me to school with. He sat with me at snack time until around second grade, when he became the boy every girl had a crush on. He would still volunteer to be my partner for school projects, with other kids acting like he was taking one for the team, but we would meet up way more than the projects required. Sam recommended I ditch anyone who was only nice to me when other people weren't around, but his dad used to tell me that not everyone could be brave and fearless. Some did the best they could, until they got brave enough to act the way they felt inside. I was all for giving him a chance as long as he wasn't mean to me, and he never was.

"Was there any doubt? It's not like we went to war." Keisha was utterly unimpressed, and felt the same as Sam about him.

"It's something you say. I just meant congratulations. To both of you. You guys slayed it," he said before one of his teammates called him over.

"We slayed it?" Keisha asked me. "You're literally the only person who signed my yearbook."

"I'm the only one you asked," I reminded her. "And you're valedictorian. I'm the runner-up. Academically, we did good."

"Academically, we slayed it." I shook my head at her before falling in line.

WE WENT OUT onto the football field once we were in order, with families in the bleachers. It took forever before they called out my name, and I was only two-thirds of the way down the list.

"Congratulations Ms. Owens." Our principal, Mr. Higgins, handed me my diploma before shaking my hand, while I scanned the audience. It was easy to find Sam and Deanna, who both stood up and cheered, with Clara on Sam's shoulders, looking like she had just woken up. It was also easy to find the empty space beside them, for Embry and Gabriel, who didn't show.

"LEFTOVER CAKE?" Sam asked, wrapping an arm around me once the ceremony was done and we were able to go home.

"I think I'm good," I told him.

"Did Lucy say no to cake?" Deanna pretended to be shocked. It wasn't that I had it all the time. We tried to limit the sugary and unhealthy foods, but if there was cake, I was always going to have some.

"I'm tired, and I'm helping Keisha pack tomorrow." She got

accepted to a super intense program at MIT, designed for people who were going to become astronauts or cure cancer or something equally impressive. This meant they expected her to spend the summer taking extra courses, so she could start off on the first day smarter than 99.9 percent of the population.

"You still need to have dinner," Sam pointed out.

"I will. I just don't need the whole round two thing," I explained.

"Sounds reasonable," he agreed, but he was mostly playing along so we could pretend the lack of celebration was because I was tired, not because half the guests never showed up.

CHAPTER TWO

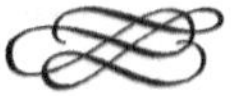

I spent the next week enjoying the beginning of summer holidays. For me, this meant reading books that were on my college syllabus rather than the high school curriculum. It may not have been entirely due to the manor and Grams' eccentricity that I had so few friends.

Like clockwork, Clara would come to my room every day at 3 and ask if I could come play outside. The one time I tried to say no, she reminded me that I was leaving her in September and it might be our last chance to play before I forgot all about her. Come Saturday, however, she didn't even bother to ask.

Part of me wanted to stay home and enjoy the weekend with Sam, Deanna and Clara, or spend one last day with Keisha before she was off to dorm rooms and college, but another tiny part of me, that I usually kept buried deep inside, was excited. I watched movies and read books about the high school experience. If they taught me anything, it was that prom was a night that could change everything. I didn't expect it to make a difference for me in the long run, but for one night, I wanted to get dolled up with my hair all fancy, wear a pretty dress and be like everybody else. I didn't even need the fairytale ending of finding my prince at the ball, I just wanted to be invited. Not that I admitted any of that while Deanna, Clara and I sat in the living room, doing each other's nails.

"Make sure your phone is charged. I want a million pictures," Deanna warned me, adding a second coat to my right hand. The color was called Blush, and it was the perfect amount of pink to be elegant without reminding you of Barbie.

"I'm surprised you decided not to chaperone," I called her on how overprotective they liked to be. I also knew that she'd filled out the application, but we came back from the shopping trip with a dress for me and nothing for her.

"Mr. Higgins implied that I was better at breaking rules than enforcing them."

"That's completely..."

"Accurate," she cut me off before I could come up with a lie. "But I'm old now and way more responsible and it's a volunteer position. You don't turn people down."

"He hurt your feelings," I understood.

"Only because I voted against setting his toupee on fire as our senior prank, and I can't go back and change that."

"What's a toupee?" Clara asked. We were letting her use a super cool nail polish stick that peeled off, in case she got it in the wrong places. Unfortunately, she insisted on wearing the green one, which left the slightest green tinge, just enough to make her fingers look infected.

"It's something people wear on their heads when they don't have hair. Like a wig, but only for one spot," I explained to her, because Deanna's eyes went wide, like she forgot her daughter was in the room when she made that statement.

"Wouldn't it hurt if you put his head on fire?" Clara looked up at her mom, so innocent, that Deanna's face went red instead of answering.

"I'm sure they weren't going to do it while he was wearing it," I assured Clara, making Deanna's face go even redder. After spending four years with Mr. Higgins, I couldn't exactly blame her, but I wasn't the type who was invited to or consulted on the senior prank. Deanna, on the other hand, had been a wild child, once upon a time. She was still a free spirit who didn't always follow conventional rules, but she did have her own lines that she would never cross.

Once my hair was dry, Deanna helped me put it up into the most gorgeous bun I have ever seen. My hair was curly, which I loved, but it was also unruly, so any updo usually came with a halo of fuzz around my head. She managed to tame it so there was no frizz or flyaways, just beautiful twists that met in an elegant knot at the back of my head.

"The finishing touch," Deanna said, taking something fragile and dainty out of a black velvet box.

"I think the tiara is a bit much," I argued once she opened it to reveal a delicate silver band encrusted with diamonds and indicolite. According to Grams, her great-great-many-times-great-grandmother had worn it when she met the Queen of England.

"But you're a princess!" Clara argued, overruling me.

"It's bad enough you convinced Sam to let you skip the Debutante Ball and your introduction to society. Your grams would never forgive me if I didn't at least make you look the part of a lady at prom." She slid the tiara into my hair, so it rested on the top of my head. I rolled my eyes like it was annoying and embarrassing, but Clara was right; I looked exactly like a princess. And I wasn't even wearing the dress yet.

. . .

MAKEUP WAS interesting because I never wore any. I dabbled with BB creams and foundation whenever I got a breakout, and used mascara the few times we went to a restaurant in town or if there was an event, but that was it. Deanna didn't need makeup with her perfect complexion and miles of eyelashes, but she had been a teenage girl once and now referred to my face as her canvas. I vetoed the use of the torture device she called an eyelash curler, but she only agreed when I didn't respond well to the eyeliner or mascara or anything that went close to my eyes.

She had me facing her instead of the mirror, so by the time I saw myself, I got the full effect of looking at a face I could tell was mine, but didn't look anything like me. I teared up, trying to stop it because I knew it would ruin Deanna's work, but I looked exactly like my mother. Or at least the version of her that lived in my head and was a combination of actual memories, the dolls and an older-looking me.

"It's perfect," I smiled up at her expectant face, which broke into a smile as well.

"I didn't want to do much. You never wear anything, but I thought it would be nice to bring out how beautiful you are," she told me.

"You have to say that," I reminded her.

"Nope, me being related to you is entirely voluntary, therefore I am not biased. I could even be mean to you and make you do all my chores because evil stepmothers are socially acceptable."

"In fairy tales," I pointed out.

"Either way, I think you're awesome and 100 percent the belle of the ball."

"I have an overwhelming urge to lock you in the basement until you're forty-five, so I'm gonna say she's right." Sam came in with Clara, who wasn't interested in the makeup if she wasn't the one wearing it.

"Let her out when she's thirty. I want grandbabies," Deanna teased.

"You guys are ridiculous," I pointed out.

"Aren't you glad you're stuck with us?" Deanna smiled at me.

"Overjoyed," I agreed, pretending to be sarcastic, but I loved them and was grateful for everything they did for me.

"Ready for pictures?" Sam asked, holding an old camera we'd had since I was a child.

"Just missing the dress." I looked to Deanna. We had all gone shopping together, but Deanna was the only one in the store with me when I found it, and she insisted it should be a surprise for everyone else until tonight.

I WENT UP to my room and took the garment bag from my closet, catching a glance at myself in the mirror. I looked different than I had ever looked before, and yet so familiar. Like someone I had met in a dream…

"Need help?" Deanna walked in and pulled me from my thoughts. I was holding the deep blue material in place, but hadn't secured it yet.

"With the zipper," I agreed, giving her my back. She did the clip before pulling up the zipper, which went effortlessly.

"So?" I asked, turning to face her.

"Clara was spot on. All this time you've been a princess," She told me.

"It's prom, this is what everyone looks like," I argued.

"You're mesmerizing," she refused to let me dismiss the compliment.

"You're like a Queen!" Clara exclaimed, coming close. "Can I hug you?"

"Of course," I assured her, but I could see where the uncertainty came from. The gown was gorgeous and intricate. I wouldn't know where to touch it.

"Babe, we're ready!" Deanna called, so Sam appeared in the doorway.

"Any chance you'll stop growing up if I ask?" he tried.

"In my head, you're still fifteen, and you better not tell me otherwise," I let him know I understood.

"I can still see you as the little six-year-old with the pigtails and the blankie you carried everywhere. Whenever something went missing, it was always hidden in there."

"Because you wouldn't let me take things away from where I found them," I defended myself.

"Even then you were a rule-breaker," he said with a smile.

"Let's get this over with." I shook my head at him. We all knew I followed the rules and curfew. The most rule-breaking I did in high school was read ahead in textbooks and write longer assignments.

"All the pictures." Deanna had a mischievous grin before they took pictures of me alone, then pictures of me with Clara, with Deanna, with Sam. We went downstairs and took more of all those pictures before Sam set the timer and we made about a dozen attempts at a full family photo before we succeeded.

"Am I good to go now?" I looked at my phone and saw I had 20 minutes before I was supposed to meet Keisha outside the yacht club.

"Come on, I'll drive you." Sam handed the camera to Deanna.

"I can drive," I argued.

"Not in those heels." Deanna shook her head, knowing I had very limited experience wearing high-heeled shoes.

"I'm sure you can, but I'll drop you off and come pick you up whenever you want."

"I can also take my car and drive home whenever I want," I pointed out.

"If I remember correctly, the best way to leave prom is either on the school bus to the Foundry, or in the limo to the house of some cool kid whose parents are out of town."

"And you're endorsing those options?" I asked, knowing that Tennison's parents left for Belgium right after graduation. I was pretty sure I could get Keisha and me an invite, but I doubt we would be welcome.

"I trust you more than I trusted myself at that age," he shrugged his shoulders. "I want you to have fun and enjoy your last moments of high school before the real world comes in."

"You're like every high school movie that thinks prom is some magical night?" I asked, eager to hear his take on it.

"No, I'm someone who was a teenager and knows there's nothing magical about prom." He looked over to Deanna with a knowing smile. "But this is your last night to hang out and have dance parties with Keisha before you both go to separate schools. And you look amazing in that dress."

"Magical proms," I shook my head.

"Confidence looks good on you," he told me.

"If only I had more," I agreed.

"You're perfect the way you are," he assured me.

WE SPENT the drive talking about his prom, which was a fiasco, except for the 5 minutes at the end. "And then she said 'yes'," he finished as we pulled into the yacht club, explaining the earlier smiles.

"On the night everyone else is worried about prom king and queen, you were asking Deanna to spend the rest of her life with you?" I shook my head at him, but I also loved it.

"No, I knew she wanted to spend forever with me, it was

asking if she'd marry me that was terrifying. My parents were hardcore Catholics if you remember, and Deanna was a free spirit who didn't want to be tied down."

"How did you get her to say yes?" I asked.

"I told her I never wanted to own her or tame her, I just wanted her to take me along for the ride."

"I had no idea you were this romantic," I smiled at him.

"I have many surprises you'll have to stick around and see," he said mysteriously.

"I'm still living on campus. I need to get out there," I warned.

"I know. This is me making sure you'll come home for Thanksgiving and Christmas and Easter and…"

"I wouldn't miss them for the world," I assured him.

"Not even for England?" he asked in a way that implied he felt the same.

"Would you let me go?" I turned it on him. I had never been anywhere further than our Beach House in my life.

"Have fun tonight, Luce." He knew the question was rhetorical. "Show them what they've been missing." I used to get so upset when I realized that the kids at school were mean to him. He was the coolest kid I had ever met, and they had no idea what they were missing out on.

"OH MY GOD! YOU LOOK AMAZING!" Keisha exclaimed when I got out of the minivan. Not the most glorious mode of transportation, but she was one of the only kids standing outside, and my reputation was non-existent to begin with.

"Look at you!" I reciprocated. "Did you get lost on your way to the Oscars?"

"I thought I'd pop in before going to my real party," she played along. Whereas my dress had volume and screamed princess, hers was long, black, sleek, and showed off a lot more skin than she usually did.

"I really appreciate it. I would be lost in that jungle without you."

"It's senior prom. We have to go, or we'll regret it forever, telling ourselves it could have changed our lives, and all of our dreams would have come true, if only we had gone."

"No regrets," I smiled at her, pretending she was doing this only for potential regrets, rather than because we secretly dreamed of fitting in and being a part of it all.

"Let's do this," she smiled back.

We headed into the yacht club and found the dining hall had been converted into a combination of a movie set and a Royal Ball for our theme of Once Upon a Time in Hollywood. It looked like everyone else chose Hollywood over fairy tales for the dress code, meaning gowns with swooping necklines and side slits, but I in no way regretted my dress.

I was lucky that people at school tended to ignore me more than the bullying I saw in most high school movies. Keisha had decided I was all she needed friend-wise, but it wasn't because anyone had been mean to her. She wouldn't have allowed it. She had a heart of gold, but also a tendency to put you in your place if you tried to belittle someone. I loved watching the shocked faces on some middle graders when they tried catcalling her, but it was less fun when I said something negative about myself and she launched into a lecture. Still, I absolutely loved her for it.

When the meal plates were cleared, they put the music louder. We loved dancing, even if we had no idea how to do it. Grams had taught me ballet when I was little, before she got sick, but that was the extent of dancing lessons I'd received. Any other dancing experience came from Keisha and I hanging out in each other's rooms, usually using a hairbrush to pretend we were singing along to songs from the 60s, 70s, 80s, and the occasional one from Spice Girls or Britney Spears. All this to say we looked like a trainwreck on the dance floor, but I couldn't care less.

"Not him again." Keisha turned away when Tennison walked towards us.

"He's nice, stop it," I warned. She was not a fan of how all the girls were into him, or how he played into it. I appreciated the way he never let popularity dictate how he treated me. Sure, we hung out less, but he was always nice to me.

"Hey Lucy, Keisha," He greeted both of us with a smile.

"Hey Tennison," I acknowledged him, nudging Keisha to do the same.

"I was wondering if you wouldn't mind dancing with me, just for a song?" he asked me, more nervous than I had seen him since our Spanish oral presentation last year.

"Sure," I accepted, getting a slight eye roll from Keisha, who went back to our table.

"We don't have to dance," he told me once she was gone.

"Is everything okay?" I asked. They weren't playing a traditional slow song I would dance with him to, but it would be less weird to dance than to stand in the middle of the dance floor.

"I need your help," he admitted. "I want to ask Keisha to dance with me once there's a slow song."

"Then why didn't you ask her instead of me?" I asked.

"Because she thinks I'm annoying and full of myself." I couldn't argue with that statement, so I let him keep going. "When she turns to you and asks if I'm serious, tell her yes. When she asks if this is a Carrie prank, tell her no, that she is beautiful inside and out and she's funny and strong and fierce and smart and keeps people on their toes and is exactly the dream girl I described to you on our first day in kindergarten."

I was about to tell him I wasn't going to lie to my best friend, when I remembered the conversation he was referring to. "You were talking about Buffy the Vampire Slayer," I argued.

"Yes, but other than actually slaying vampires, is there anything that wasn't accurate?" he asked. I thought about it, comparing his description of Buffy to how he had just described Keisha. Beautiful, funny, fierce, smart…

"You said you wanted a girl who kicks ass," I called him on it, but I was fully on board. I had a suspicion she hated the way he was with other girls and the way they fawned over him because she thought he was better than that. And they liked him for his hair rather than his brain.

"Were you not there at the spelling bee? Or debate meet? Or when Mr. Baltrek called Tiny Tim a cripple?"

"All this time?" I asked him with a smile. The Tiny Tim incident was a week after she arrived in our sixth grade class.

"Do you see anyone else who is anything like her?" he asked.

"Nope," I agreed, trying not to smile so much. I didn't know if Keisha was watching and didn't want to spoil it for her.

"You'll help me?" he asked.

"I'll do what I can," I agreed.

"Thank you," he smiled, looking relieved before taking me in for a hug. "It's kind of full circle, you being my sidekick on the first and last day of school."

"I feel like I have to mention it though; break her heart and I will kill you."

"I know," he assured me.

· · ·

"You too?" Keisha asked when I got back to the table, before wiping the smile off my face.

"For old time's sake. He's nice," I reminded her.

"Sometimes," she agreed. "Other times I think he's a babbling idiot."

"Most guys are," I teased before we went back on the dance floor.

Tennison moved off and on the dance floor, with different groups of friends, but always gravitated towards us, waiting for them to play a slow song. I was about to suggest he go and request one, when the music to 'You and Me' by Lifehouse began.

"I love this song," Keisha said, hinting that she wished we could stay and dance to it.

"Could I have this dance?" Tennison came over and extended his hand.

"Luce?" She turned to me when I didn't answer, annoyed that she was losing her dance partner.

"He's asking you," I argued.

"Making the rounds?" she asked like this was the exact behavior she had come to expect of him.

"More like building up the courage," he shrugged it off, but I could tell he was nervous.

"Is this a Carrie prank?" she asked me, figuring he was nervous because he was about to do something huge and terrible.

"Nope," I told her, smiling. He had known that was exactly where her mind was going to go.

"But he danced with you," she pointed out.

"So that he could dance with you," I agreed.

"That makes no sense."

"Give him a chance," I told her before retreating. She still looked like she wasn't sure, but she trusted me enough to go with it. They looked awkward at first, dancing with a lot of space between them, until she looked up and asked something. His answer took a long time, but by the end of it, they were both smiling and talking while dancing.

"They're cute," Danny Kinks commented, coming to stand beside me. He was a few years ahead of me and had quite the reputation. He brought our school to State every year he was on the team, but took his Junior year off. The official story was a torn ligament, but Tennison said something once that made me think it was an attitude problem that got him benched.

"They are," I agreed, wondering who he came with.

"Danny," he said with a smile, putting his hand on the wall behind me. Guys leaned onto lockers to talk to girls all the time on TV, but I didn't like how he was towering over me.

"Lucy." I gave him a polite smile and spotted his name tag. It made a lot less sense to have him chaperoning than Deanna, if you asked me.

"But now who are you going to dance with?" He came closer, so there was only an inch between us.

"I can wait my turn," I assured him, slowly inching away.

"Doesn't make sense, a pretty girl like you all alone on the sidelines. I'll dance with you," he said as though he was doing me a favor.

"I'm not much of a dancer," I argued, trying to get by him.

"Of course you are." He abruptly brought his other hand up to the wall, making me flinch. There was an arm on either side of me, the wall behind me and him in front of me. All I could smell was the whiskey and cigarettes from his breath. I scanned the room, but couldn't see any teachers or other chaperones, and Keisha had her eyes closed while she leaned into Tennison.

"I really don't feel like it, I..." I tried to stay polite and act normal, but he was making me incredibly uncomfortable.

"This might loosen you up," he offered, pressing his flask to my mouth, but I managed to turn away. It had the same notes of whiskey as his breath, minus the cigarettes.

"I would really like to get back to my table," I tried, but he leaned his forearms on the wall, bringing himself a lot closer.

"I'll bring you back when I'm done with you." He had the kind of smile that was reveling in my discomfort.

"Please let me go," I asked as politely as I could, trying to sound confident and strong, but I was terrified, and he knew it.

"What will you give me if I do?" He took a swig of his flask. I took advantage of the space that created, moving before his drunken faculties could react.

"I need to use the ladies' room," I told him, sliding under his arm and rushing to the one place he couldn't follow me into.

"I'll be right here," he called after me. I could hear the smile in his statement. He knew I was trying to escape and he wanted to let me know I wasn't getting away that easily.

I HAD LEFT my clutch on the table while I danced with Keisha, so I couldn't call her. Once my heart slowed to a normal rhythm I remembered that she was dancing with Tennison, her fairytale prom moment, and I would kill anyone who took that away from her, even if it was me. I could borrow the phone of the next person who came in and call Sam or Deanna, who would be there within 15 minutes. I was fairly certain Danny chose me because I was alone and friendless, so even if Deanna was the one to get me from the washroom, he wouldn't dare do anything. But that would mean bothering them, being the damsel in distress, and letting my entire graduating class watch me get escorted from prom by my guardians. That was not going to happen. Not tonight.

All I wanted to do was go home, change into my pajamas and curl up with a warm tea and a book on anatomy or systems. There was the possibility that Danny would get bored and leave, but I had no way of knowing without going back out. There was also a chance that the alcohol in his flask was strong enough to convince him to come into the washroom to get me. Which was not a chance I was willing to take.

I saw the window was open to let in a breeze and remembered how I used to sneak in and out of our kitchen window, so Mrs. Boyd wouldn't know I was gone. At the time I thought I was so smart for tricking her. I never considered that sneaking out to play in the mud brought damning evidence of its own.

I sighed and looked at myself in the mirror before going back to the window. We were on the ground floor. It didn't look like it would be difficult to take out the screen. The manor was only about an hour's walk from the yacht club, meaning I would be home long before curfew, but close enough that they wouldn't ask questions and be concerned.

"I'm really doing this," I said out loud to myself, looking around to see if there was a better option, but the bathroom offered no solutions. I shook my head at myself before removing the bug screen and leaning it against the side of the window.

I did not feel like a princess as I bunched up the bottom of my dress and hoisted myself onto the ledge of the window. Luckily, it was big enough that I could turn to get my legs through, because I would have fallen on my butt otherwise.

Once I was out, with my heels sinking into the muddy ground, I reached in to get the screen and place it back. I couldn't put it in properly, but at least it looked a lot less suspicious if Danny sent anyone in looking for me.

I was looking back at the yacht club to make sure I hadn't been followed, that Danny Kinks was still in the hallway waiting for me, when I collided with something a lot softer than a tree, but much harder than the clear path I was traveling towards.

CHAPTER THREE

They were here. Or at least one of them was, but Gabriel never came by without Embry.

"Get in the car," he said with his serious intensity. He acted like there was nothing unusual about me climbing out of a bathroom window in a prom dress, but I still felt like I had done something wrong.

I followed him to a beat-up Tercel, which was not a car I had seen him driving before. I had barely shut the door when he put the car in drive and started moving. He wasn't going more than a couple of miles over the speed limit, but he was clearly in a hurry.

"I'm sorry," I told him, assuming I had done something wrong by the look on his face. I had no idea if it was talking to strangers, climbing out the window, or going to prom in the first place...all I knew was that something was upsetting him.

He turned as if he was going to say something, then went back to the road for the rest of the drive. He barely even glanced in my direction, except to make sure I was okay after he made a sudden stop to avoid a raccoon.

I tried to hurry behind him as he walked straight into the

manor, looking over his shoulder like he expected Clara to jump out at us from the bushes. He opened the door without knocking and waited for me to go in first before calling, "Samuel!" in a tone that suggested he might be in trouble as well.

"Embry!" Clara called, rushing down the stairs to us. She was disappointed when she realized it was only Gabriel, but kept coming until she saw his face. Gabriel would sometimes let her jump into his arms, but tonight she didn't even try.

"Where is your father?" Gabriel asked her, making it sound like an interrogation rather than a question.

"Where's Embry?" she asked, suddenly small.

"He'll be here shortly," he placated her with a quick answer. "Where is your father?" he repeated.

"What's going on?" Sam asked, coming down the stairs.

Gabriel gave him a look before they both went to the kitchen.

"Aren't you supposed to be in bed?" I turned to Clara when they made it clear I wasn't welcome to follow.

"I thought Embry was here," she defended.

"You still have to sleep." I pointed my finger at her, knowing she would laugh.

"Gabriel looks mad," she told me.

"I'm sure your dad will calm him down," I said hopefully.

"Do you think Embry will be here when I wake up?" she asked.

"Gabriel said shortly," I shrugged my shoulders to let her know I didn't have any extra information.

"Maybe we can play hide and seek with him," she suggested through a yawn.

"I'm sure he would be happy to." I gave her a smile I only half-believed. *Gabriel wouldn't lie to her,* I told myself, but the uneasy feeling came back when I remembered that I had spent the past week lying to Clara because I didn't want to worry her.

ONCE CLARA WAS TUCKED in bed, hopefully sleeping, I called Keisha from the house phone to let her know I was okay and Gabriel brought me home. I could hear Tennison in the background, as well as the smile in her voice.

"You can come see me anytime at MIT. And we can do lunch every week."

"It's a 20-minute walk. We'll have study sessions and sneak into each other's libraries. It'll be awesome," I assured her before Tennison asked who she was talking to.

"I so would have regretted not coming," she told me before we said our goodbyes.

I WENT BACK DOWNSTAIRS and waited in the hallway to be allowed into the conversation of the kitchen. Gabriel had looked intense and scary at the yacht club, which was the only reason I was waiting in the hall instead of barging in and demanding answers. I was shaken when he showed up, but he had no reason to be mad at me. I had every right to know why he missed my graduation and ignored my calls. I spent an entire week thinking something terrible had happened to them. I still wasn't sure if that was the case or not. He was mad, or upset, which told me he either didn't agree with me going to college in the fall (even though I chose the closest one), or something serious was going on that he thought I was too young to handle.

After what felt like an eternity, the voices stopped, so I decided that was my cue to come in. They were both standing by the kitchen table. While Sam at least glanced in my direction, looking apologetic, neither of them said a word.

Gabriel was solemn, like the first day I met him almost fourteen years ago. It was definitely not good news. I also got the feeling it had nothing to do with my going to Harvard.

"Gabriel?" I asked, going closer to him, trying to catch his eye.

"Why don't you go see Deanna in the studio for a little bit?" Sam suggested when Gabriel stayed silent.

"What is going on?" I asked Gabriel, not at all impressed with his game. I hadn't seen him in months, he hadn't come to my graduation and now he was avoiding me. "Where's Embry?" I hoped he might answer if the question wasn't about him. Embry didn't usually go this long without a visit, and he always texted or called when he couldn't make it. Until last week.

"He's coming," Gabriel said with so little conviction, I worried that he might not be avoiding me so much as trying to find the words to tell me my death magnet struck again. It was the most likely explanation. That something happened to Embry. It explained him not coming to my graduation and ignoring me. Why else wouldn't Embry be here, apologizing profusely?

"Lucy, could you please give us a moment?" Sam asked of me. There was a pleading desperation in his voice. That, paired with me no longer knowing if I wanted to know what was going on, made me oblige.

I was on my way to the back door when Gabriel spoke, stopping me in my tracks.

"She shouldn't go outside. I'll bring her to the plantation. We can't let anyone else in." His talking showed an improvement, but he was talking to Sam as if I wasn't even there, and not making much sense.

"What do you mean?" I asked at the same time as Sam.

"Shouldn't Deanna and Clara go with her?" He looked worried, which I liked about as much as Gabriel's aloofness. I kept my hand on the door because if there was something dangerous out there, we should get Deanna back inside. The studio was basically a gazebo, and I doubt paintbrushes would be useful in a fight.

"I don't think they're at risk once Lucy is removed, but you could set them up at the beach house if it will make you feel safer," Gabriel offered.

"Once I'm removed? What the hell are you guys talking about?" I let go of the handle and focused on my anger, not wanting them to know how annoyed and hurt I was. Not to mention terrified.

"Not like that," Sam tried to reassure me.

"Like what?" I asked.

"We need to leave the manor and take you far away, where you can't be found," Gabriel said like it was supposed to make sense, looking down at his hands instead of up at me.

"Found by who? For how long?" I asked the first of dozens of questions that were forming.

"Indefinitely."

"No," I flat out refused. "I have college and orientation and a chance to start over as something other than the weird Owens girl and…"

"You're going with Gabriel," Sam overruled me. "You can defer and go next year, or once it's safe, but I am not losing you so that you can feel normal," he added when I looked at him with shock, but that only made it worse.

"Lose me?" I asked. "Neither of you are making any sense."

"A long time ago, I made a promise to protect you and keep you safe. Up to recently that meant checking in on you and making sure you were okay, but now it means taking you away from here." Gabriel looked up to me at the end.

"Who did you promise?" I asked him, trying to understand.

He and Embry had shown up out of the blue at Grams' funeral and inserted themselves into my life. They said they were old friends of the family, but there had to be more to it.

"Annabelle," Gabriel said simply.

I looked to Sam before coming back to Gabriel. "My doll?"

"She was a person before she was a doll. I'm sure Evelyn told you."

"My ancestor," I agreed. "Grams told me fairy tales about her from an old book."

While most girls were raised on Cinderella, Snow White and Sleeping Beauty, my grandmother had recited stories from an old, leather-bound book. My mom might have read me the normal stories before she died, because I knew enough to ask my grandmother why her princesses never found their princes or lived happily ever after. "There are much more important things than finding a prince," she'd say before continuing her tales. She would open the book to the right page, but she'd tell me the story like she had been there, or rather like it had been told to her a thousand times. She would tell me about Rosie saving soldiers from a mudslide, Beth singing on stage at a speakeasy, Cassie meeting the Queen and Annabelle bravely crossing oceans...I knew them all, but Gabriel couldn't have met them.

"The Chronicles," Gabriel agreed.

"Is that what the book was called?"

"No, it's what it is. Annabelle started it when she left England, and the major events have been recorded in it ever since."

"And I guess Rosie, Cassie and Beth filled in the rest?" I rolled my eyes, naming my other ancestral dolls.

"Some more than others," he agreed. "Rosie's was mostly stories she told us because she never had to deal with the dangers..."

"What dangers, Gabriel?" I cut him off. "The Annabelle my

doll was named after lived in the 1600s. Rosie was there on the first Independence Day, so I doubt she told you anything." Gabriel looked at me like he was wondering how much he should tell me, while Sam didn't look confused or surprised about these tall tales Gabriel was telling. It was like he took it all as fact.

"I was born here in 1662. I met Annabelle the day she arrived and have loved her every minute since. Before she died, she asked me to keep her daughter safe, so that is what I have been doing for centuries," Gabriel emphasized the last word. "Most of the time I stay in the shadows and watch from a distance, but every once in a while, one of you will look like her and then we do what we have to, so he can't get you."

"He?" I needed clarifications.

"The Big Bad who is after you," Sam shared.

I turned back to Gabriel. "You and Embry have been protecting me and my dolls from a guy who wants to hurt us…" I tried to sum it all up.

"The women the dolls represent," Gabriel corrected, which made the story even less plausible. He looked relieved that I was getting it, whereas I was trying to point out how crazy he sounded.

"They lived centuries ago," I reminded him, not believing that he was born in 1662 and had been hanging around for centuries to keep me safe.

"Correct," he stuck to his story.

"And you believe him?" I turned to Sam. It didn't make sense that he was going along with it.

"My mom did," he admitted. "My dad hated them, but even he told me that if ever a time came where you were in danger and they showed up, I was to let them do whatever they needed, because keeping you safe is why they're still alive."

"You're my guardian angel?" I asked Gabriel. I still found it ludicrous, but while Sam might have gone along with a prank,

Gabriel had rarely been anything but completely serious. As far as I knew, he didn't even have a sense of humor.

"Cassie tried calling us that, but I'm no angel."

"What are you then?" I was still skeptical. "A vampire? Do you have horns that sprout at night? Do you ride around on a broom?"

"This is serious Lucy." Gabriel wasn't yelling at me, but I could tell he was on a short fuse.

"You're the one who's implying you're immortal."

"I'm not immortal. I'm sticking around because I have a job to do," he argued.

"Protecting me."

"Yes," he agreed. "Which is why we have to leave. Now."

I was about to argue, but Sam spoke before I could. "Why don't you go upstairs and pack up some things." I wanted to say no and keep asking questions, but he gave me that look, where he was pleading and needed me to do it, so I sighed before reluctantly going up the stairs, shaking my head at the two of them.

"Pack light, but for a long time," Gabriel advised, which was much easier said than done.

My room, like me, had changed a lot since I used to beg Grams to show me the dolls and read me their stories. The teddies and costumes were replaced by books, and the walls held posters of skeletal structures and anatomy instead of Beauty and the Beast decals. The dolls were still up on a shelf that was no longer too high for me to reach, but it had been ages since I had taken them down.

I tried to imagine Gabriel interacting with them, the women from my family who died centuries ago, but that was a lot easier when I was a child who believed in magic. I wondered where the old book had gone. I had asked for their stories at first, but Sam said he didn't know any, and Mrs. Boyd ran out of them pretty quickly.

I figured the best way to comply with Gabriel's instructions would be to limit myself to whatever I could fit in my backpack. I packed it like I would for a sleepover at Keisha's, the two times that happened, then added my tiny old photo album. I doubted Gabriel would see the point, but it had all the pictures I had of my mother and Grams, the one picture I had of my father, as well as a few of Mr. and Mrs. Boyd. It wasn't something I took out frequently, but if we were going to be gone indefinitely, just the two of us, I got the feeling I might be homesick. Gabriel had been popping into my life sporadically since he showed up when I was five, but he had always been more reserved than Embry.

I put the copy of Gray's Anatomy that Sam had given me for graduation and some medical journals into the part that was for laptops. I was scanning the room to make sure I hadn't forgotten anything when Deanna walked in. She used to knock, even when the door was open, and wait for my permission to come in, but eventually she decided I was family, and family doesn't need permission. She never once acted like my mother, and I wouldn't want her to, but I appreciated having something like an older sister since she married Sam. She hadn't expected to have to raise a fifteen-year-old a couple of years into her marriage, but she stepped up to the plate like there was nothing she wanted more.

"I finished the laundry while you were escaping through bathroom windows." She gave me a look while putting a pile down on my bed. She must have seen the guys before coming up. "I didn't want you to forget this." She took my old blankie from the top of the pile and handed it to me. It was thin and white, made from a bamboo-like material, the kind that keeps you cool if you wear it in the sun, but warm if you're cold. It had a purple threaded border and my name in eggplant on the corner, with a pink heart underneath.

"I don't…" I was about to tell her that I was basically a grown woman and didn't need my blankie anymore, but she looked at me like she wasn't going to believe it.

"I'm not going to remind you that I was already dating Sam when you went through that phase where it never left your sight, or that it lasted two years and only ended when you thought you lost it and Martha suggested you keep it on your bed," she said, doing exactly what she said she wouldn't. "But if you're going somewhere far from those of us who love you, I want you to have it."

"Did they tell you what's going on?" I asked her, putting the blankie into my backpack.

"Sam filled me in," she agreed.

"And?" I waited for her to be the voice of reason.

"Years ago, when Sam first told me about it, I thought he had gone mad. Then I talked to Embry and…I'm glad they're looking out for you."

"Embry confirmed Gabriel's story of them being over three-hundred years old and put here to protect me?" I asked, hoping she would crack and admit it was all a joke.

"They don't get any older, Luce." She could tell I was having trouble accepting it. "Ask Embry about it when he gets here. He spent hours answering my questions."

"Is he even coming?"

"I don't think Gabriel would lie. About something like that," she added when I raised my eyebrows.

"Are you afraid?" I asked.

"I have it in my mind that Embry and Gabriel are invincible and the best at whatever it is they do, so I'm going to go the Beach House, make sandcastles, eat seafood, then hopefully come back and help you pack this all up for a dorm room."

"That's it?" I asked. The boys were way more scary and serious about it.

"That's it," she agreed.

"It was never because I needed a blankie. I knew it wouldn't keep me safe or any of those foolish kid reasons," I defended myself from her earlier comments. "My mother made it for me when I was a baby."

"I know," she assured me, like she understood, before going back to her own packing.

"I WANT TO GO WITH LUCY!" Clara was pleading as I came downstairs with my backpack. The ears from her bunny onesie flew as she shook her head, pouting through all her freckles.

"Sweetie, you, me and mommy are going on a trip of our own. You're going to have all kinds of fun!" Sam tried to calm her down and act like this was an exciting adventure.

"Please Lucy, please!" She ran over and wrapped her arms around my legs.

"Clara, if you let go of my legs, I'll make you chocolate chip cookies," I offered as a bribe, knowing they were her weakness.

"But how will I get them?" she asked, wise beyond her 5 years of age.

"I'll give them to your daddy and he'll bring them to you," I promised, looking to Sam for confirmation. He looked to Gabriel, who didn't look convinced, but nodded anyway.

"Promise?" she asked her dad, knowing he had more of a say than I did.

"I promise," he agreed. Clara let go of me and ran into his arms, but there was a guilty look to him that made me doubt his keeping his word, at least not for a while.

"I'm ready," I told Gabriel, who had stayed quiet

throughout this whole debacle. It wasn't just me he was acting indifferent to…he was a lot nicer to Clara the last few times he came.

Without saying anything, Gabriel effortlessly picked up an oversized suitcase I had never seen before. He walked to the garage while I said goodbye to the people who had long ago become my family. I knew Sam was bringing his wife and daughter to the summer house and Gabe was taking me to the old plantation, things we did every year, but I felt the same as Clara.

"The black one," I told Gabriel once I got to the garage and found him trying to decide which vehicle to take. We had a collection of expensive vintage cars from my great-grandfather, but Sam bought me a newer one when I got my driver's license, making sure it had all the best safety features, like the mini-van he was strapping his daughter into.

I watched Deanna's minivan drive out, then punched in the alarm code, got into the passenger's seat and let Gabriel take me to the plantation. My family had lived there for generations, until Cassie married Alan Roosevelt and we moved into the manor. I still spent a couple of weeks there every summer with Embry, but I hadn't been since it was remodeled last Fall.

"Speak," I said while we drove through the wooded trails. Most people would feel safest near a city, or in a place where you could walk to your neighbor's without it taking you an hour, but the plantation was completely isolated. There was the forest between the plantation property and the manor, then acres of land between it and any neighboring fields. It would be easy to keep track of any incoming visitors, but outside help would be extremely hard to come by.

"There's nothing to talk about," he dismissed me, keeping his eyes on the road.

"How about, 'Hi Lucy, it's been a while! How was graduation? It's good to see you too?'" I gave him suggestions.

"It's best if we stay quiet," he warned, still not looking at me.

I leaned over and turned the radio on to whatever station annoyed him the most. I didn't particularly enjoy the techno station either, but I could practically see the vein pulsing in his forehead while he forced himself to keep on ignoring me instead of making me change it. I would find it funny if I wasn't so worried and annoyed with him.

WHEN WE GOT to the house, he parked and got out of the car.

"What are you doing?" I asked. It could have been some prank to leave me alone in the middle of nowhere, but he left the key in the ignition.

"The house was retrofitted in case something like this ever happened. They had your DNA so you have free roam of the house, but everyone else needs to be given permission for each room."

"Like vampires need to be invited into your house? Or like booby traps and trolls?"

"With a high-tech computer security system. Embry and Sam know more about what happens if someone isn't invited in, but I got the impression it was more like loud noises and laser beams." He wasn't amused by my question, but it sounded just as reasonable as the rest of his story. I wanted to point out that getting dissected by laser beams was way more intense than being yelled at by an alarm, but Gabriel walked away from the car and motioned for me to drive up.

I tried to move into the driver's seat as gracefully as I could in my prom dress, but there was a lot of tulle and it was tight in places that made this incredibly difficult.

I stopped in front of the garage and wondered how I was going to get it to open. I was about to try 'Open Sesame' when a dark grey box came out of a hole in the ground, adjusting itself to be at my eye level.

"State your name," a computer-animated voice rang out.

"Lucy Owens," I said, but nothing happened. "Lucine Suzanne Owens." It was on my birth certificate, but no one ever called me by it. Except when Mrs. Boyd had been upset, or wanted to make sure I listened to her.

"Vocal Recognition Achieved. Move closer."

I saw the screen had switched to a handprint, so I put mine down and waited for it to say, "Digital Imprint Approved. Look here."

Here was a vague description, but the handprint was replaced by a red dot, so I moved closer and stared into the screen.

"Welcome Lucy, please proceed."

The garage door opened, and the inside looked the same as it always had. It was big enough for two cars, but half the space was taken up by bikes and toboggans and junk that hadn't been used in my lifetime. The major difference was a grid made from tiny green lasers. I bit my bottom lip as I drove through it, half-expecting it to chop me into tiny pieces like in Resident Evil.

I looked back to Gabriel, who called out, "I'll patrol tonight. Shut the door and get some sleep."

IT WAS EASIER SAID than done. He watched as I shut the garage door, but once I was in the house, other than the little computer screens that showed an analysis of every ChapStick and pack of gum it found when scanning the car, everything was dark.

I was always more afraid of the unseen than of the creatures that lurked in the night, but I was currently wishing that whoever put me into the system would have put Embry and Gabriel into it as well. Yes, it made sense to not let other people in if there was some evil guy trying to kill me, but the guys protecting me should be allowed to follow me in.

I tried to find the light switch, so I could look for a user's manual that would allow me company, but they moved the switches when they remodeled. I knocked over what sounded like a vase, and the crash nearly made my heart stop. For the third time tonight, I was terrified. I didn't like not knowing things and Gabriel's ridiculous story made me feel like it was just as likely that a zombie would crash through the window as a burglar or a ninja assassin.

I found a light switch just as something else fell, either from the wind or some side effect of my stumbling around, but my heart felt like it was going to leap out of my chest. I quickly walked to the front of the house, turning on every light on my way. As soon as I got close, I ran to the front door and wrenched it open, calling out to him, "Gabriel!"

He had been off in the woods, but got to the porch before I even finished his name. "What's wrong?" he asked, looking into my eyes with all of the intensity I could remember from his visits. He used to come every time Embry did, or at least summers and most holidays, but I either did something or he got bored and stopped coming right after my eighteenth birthday.

"I understand that you want me to stay here alone, but is it really breaking the rules if you stayed on the balcony tonight?" I asked of him, suddenly nervous. Embry was the easy-to-talk-to one who would understand that the last thing

I wanted to do after being ripped from my home because my life was supposedly in danger was to spend the night in a huge, mostly unlived in house, alone. I would prefer Embry or Sam or Deanna, but Gabriel could do the trick if he stopped running away.

He looked angry that I had made him worry and rush to my side for nothing, but I think he understood, though he hated it. If he didn't want me to imagine the worst and scare myself into a heart attack, he either had to give me more information, or stay close.

"Just tonight," he warned before walking away.

"THANK YOU," I told Gabriel, handing him sheets and pillows through the French doors that led to the balcony from my bedroom. The thought had occurred to me that he agreed because the balcony could be a liability otherwise, but I was comforted all the same.

"You should get some sleep," he said dismissively, keeping his eyes on the bundle I had given him.

"Gabe, could you please just tell me who this Big Bad is? And why you're being cold and distant? Are you going to hurt me? Will I hurt you? Are you keeping a secret and you're worried I'll get you to tell me? Give me a reason," I asked, putting a pillow and blanket for myself on the bean bag near the balcony. This wasn't the first time I'd had someone camp out here, although last time it was Embry who stayed on the balcony with me. At the time, he'd said he wanted to see the stars, but now I was thinking it might have been to keep an eye on me, like Gabriel was doing now.

"He knows you're here," he told me simply, like it was something I should understand.

"I've always been here. Grams kept me locked up in the manor. The Boyds let me get out sometimes, but they still keep me close. We've been here for generations," I reminded him, starting to take out the bobby pins that kept my prom hair in place.

"He checks in on your line every once in a while, but a lot less than we do. I knew the moment I saw you, even if you were younger, that he would come after you. Because you look like Annabelle."

"Like all the dolls," I realized. One for each of us the Big Bad hunted.

"We've kept an eye on every woman in your family, but you, Beth, Cassie and Rosie were the only ones who looked like Annabelle."

"Because we're related." I knew the dolls looked the same, but Grams could always tell them apart. She liked to call it a family resemblance.

"Identical," he argued. "Down to the very last freckle. The only differences are the ones you make, or don't. Scars, haircuts, tattoos…but every dimple, everything about you is her." He looked at me with a different kind of intensity, filled with pain.

"He's been hunting her since the 1600s and now he's after me." I nodded like this made sense and wasn't terrifying.

"He hasn't made a move yet, but he will."

"How do you know he knows?" I pressed.

"He's recruiting."

"An army?" I could picture those old Uncle Sam posters shouting, 'We Want You!'.

"He has the ability to control people who are like me and Embry. If he touches you, it forms a bond and he can manipulate you, even if he's far away. People like us are disappearing."

"What do you mean by people like you? Immortals?"

"Some people like us live a normal life and then die without coming back. It's only if you die before you accomplish what you're meant to do. There's no official name, but some call us The Gifted." He revealed that he wasn't invincible, he just came back to life whenever he died.

"And they're all protecting people?" I asked of The Gifted.

"No, but we all have something to do. Some of them are poets or authors or great figures in history. Scientists and explorers. It's an insurance policy to make sure the world doesn't go without whatever their talents are. Embry likes to tell it like they all had great tasks to accomplish, but Einstein also created the hydrogen bomb, and Hitler did a whole lot of shitty stuff before he finally got it right."

"Einstein and Hitler?" I asked, to which he nodded. "I'm pretty sure Hitler didn't get anything right."

"He lost his way and became the dictator he was born to defeat, but he did accomplish his task eventually." I waited for him to smile, or tell me he was teasing.

"When he committed suicide?" I asked, making sure that was what he was implying.

"There are many ways to get something done, and not all of it is pretty. The pharaohs turned their people into slaves to get the pyramids, we used nuclear power as a weapon instead of an energy source...not all contributions are worth it." He sounded bitter, but I couldn't tell if it was over the horrible things that happened on the way to discoveries, or the pointlessness of his contribution.

"And if my Big Bad controls these people, he can use them forever, making them commit murders, as long as they never do what they were supposed to?" I verified, not liking it one bit.

"It won't work forever. Once you discover what it is you need to accomplish, the drive is almost impossible to say no to. Some people tried to avoid their calling so they could live forever, but it doesn't work."

"Is he like you? The guy who is after me?"

"Yes."

"And what he needs to accomplish is to kill me?" I confirmed. There had to be a worthwhile reason for me to die if the universe was giving him an insurance policy for it. How horrible was I going to become?

"I don't know what he needs to accomplish. I don't know if he's working on something else and happens to want revenge over some slight from Annabelle…"

"But he's definitely trying to kill me, and you and Embry are staying alive to protect me from him?"

"Among other things," he agreed.

"Is Embry okay?" I asked, worried that maybe he was one of the people being recruited, which would mean the end game for me. Even if Embry and Gabriel weren't exactly friends, they would still lay down their lives for each other, which meant that if Embry was sent to kill me, both of us would let him. Or at least I would.

"He's on his way," he assured me. "He hasn't been recruited, he's just taking his time to be safe. We believe the bond breaks and has to be re-established every time you die, so Embry would be a prime target. And in case it doesn't, we can't risk getting too close to you." He implied that they'd been under his control before.

"Do you know why he wants to kill us, or what Annabelle did to him?" I asked, taking advantage of him answering me, but it was one question too many, as he sighed.

"Get some sleep, Lucy." He let me know the conversation was over.

I let out a loud sigh, to let him know I was annoyed too, and wasn't happy with everything he was keeping from me.

Still, I wasn't going to press after he had conceded to partially explain it to me.

I WENT over to the walk-in closet and managed to untie the bow at the bottom of my back, which loosened the gown enough that I could wiggle and step out of it. *Magical proms*, I thought to myself, though this was not at all what I had imagined. I found a pair of sweatpants and T-shirt and put them on, still trying to wrap my head around everything I was supposed to believe now. True, Embry and Gabriel didn't look any older, but neither did Sam. Younger me would have believed all of it. She believed in fairy tales and magic, but the only way my life compared to a fairy tale was the castle-like manor and people dying around me. Which was cancer, not magic.

I WENT BACK to Gabriel and tried to get comfy on the beanie bag, playing with my pillow and blankets, but I knew I wasn't going to sleep anyway. I was used to losing people after my mom, my grandmother, Mrs. Boyd and Mr. Boyd, but Sam had always been there for me. He was like a big brother before his parents took me in, before I even met Gabriel or Embry, and now he felt so far away, with his family possibly in danger, because of me.

I kept glancing at Gabriel, who wasn't moving, but couldn't be comfortable on the ground like that. I wondered if he had old bones and a bad back, even though he didn't look to be older than his early twenties. His skin was tanned, but otherwise flawless; no wrinkles, no cuts, and no bruises. I was wondering if he was sleeping, which was almost impossible, when he said, "You could always sleep in the bed," with his eyes still closed.

"I'm fine," I assured him, deciding to lie on my side. It wasn't exactly comfortable, but I didn't want him to make me leave if I moved around too much.

I concentrated on watching him sleep for a while. He was the more intimidating of the two. The one who never warmed up to most people, but asleep like this, with his dark hair a mess, his face peaceful…it almost made you forget how he could get when he was awake.

CHAPTER FIVE

Annabelle held her daughter close and walked into the church with purpose, her head held high. This was not a defeat, she reminded herself, this was coming home. She had waited until the last of the stragglers had gone inside to make sure that no one would try and talk to her. She was slightly surprised, but also expecting it when her usual spot was empty, even after she hadn't attended in years.

It was only once she sat down and placed Margaret on her lap that she allowed herself to look up, just a quick glance, barely a second, to see if he was there. As soon as she lifted her head, her eyes locked on his, and she had to turn away. That little moment was enough to make the emotions rush back, and the tears threatened to overwhelm her. Whether out of habit or simple inattention, when turning to avoid Gabriel, her eyes rested on Embry, who looked so happy to see her that she had to turn away from him as well.

Annabelle could feel eyes on her during the entire service, with the hairs on the back of her neck sticking up, but she managed to convince herself that it wasn't them; the boys she had loved. She knew that the entire congregation had reason to be staring at her, gossiping about how she had returned after five years, without a husband, but *with a daughter. They would be wondering what happened to bring her back, why she left in the first place, if there ever was a husband, if he deserted her, died or was coming with the rest of their household.*

*W*HEN THE SERVICE *ended and people made their way outside the church, Annabelle followed Father Brown to the side of the altar.*

"I was surprised when you asked to see me, Miss Owens," he said, eying Margaret, waiting for her to correct him on her name.

"It's Mrs. Hathorne now," she assured him, noticing that he exhaled and smiled, the relief obvious on his face.

"Your letter mentioned a baptism?" he asked.

"Yes, for Margaret," she agreed, looking down at the sleeping child, who smiled when her mother kissed her forehead.

"This has not yet been done?" Father Brown inquired, worried about what kind of heathen his parishioner had married. She had perhaps left town, but a shepherd never gave up on his flock.

"Yes, she has, of course," Annabelle assured him.

"I'm afraid I don't understand what you're asking of me."

"There were some rumors about the priest in the town where we were raising Margaret. I would hate to think my child would not..."

"Of course," he understood, cutting her off, not wanting to hear about any rumors that would tarnish the reputation of the church. It was enough to have rumors of witchcraft floating around, he didn't want to dignify them with a denial, or even admit to their existence. "Will your husband be joining us?"

"I'm afraid he is no longer of this world," she said, bringing her hand to her heart.

"I am glad you are turning to God for solace in your time of mourning. The baptism can be as soon as next Sunday."

"I appreciate it, Father," Annabelle said before making her way out of the church. A few women had stayed to eavesdrop on the conversation, and others were waiting to speak to the priest as well,

but most people had gone back to their fields, or Sunday activities. She knew better than to expect that Gabriel and Embry would have gone home after she returned to town without so much as a word to either of them.

Embry was to the right of the door, playing with his niece and nephews as if he hadn't a care in the world, though he glanced up almost as soon as she walked out, and smiled. He kept playing with the children, but it would be rude if she didn't go see him now, and no matter how things had ended when she left, he was still one of her closest friends.

"You're like a vision after so long in the dark," he said dramatically after whispering something to his niece once Annabelle was in front of him.

"You haven't changed at all." She had been nervous about seeing them again. The warm smile Embry offered made her want nothing more than to let him take her in his arms and tell her everything would work out. Embry was so optimistic that he would believe it, and she would be forced to do the same.

"You have," he said. "I mean, you're as beautiful as ever, but this little lady and I have yet to be introduced."

"Margaret," she smiled. "My daughter and the absolute love of my life."

Embry nodded, then said, "She's beautiful," but looked at Annabelle in a way that made her heart beat faster than normal.

He continued to smile at her, and she got the feeling he could keep at it all day, but she could feel herself blushing. She could only imagine what her mother would say if she could see her. Of course, her mother wouldn't have approved with the direction she took the conversation in either. "I'm sorry I left," she told him, hoping he understood how truly she meant it.

"We don't have to get into that," he assured her, but he looked away, and she knew it was because she had hurt him, and he didn't want her to see that.

"I have felt terrible about it. I should have explained myself and..."

"I wouldn't do well to pine over a married woman anyhow." He resumed his smiling, but there was a question to the statement.

"A widow," she corrected him a moment before realizing life here would be so much easier if she had said her husband was on a ship back to Europe or some excuse that left her unavailable.

"Then we might effectively have some talking to do." The happiness this brought him nearly broke her heart, but she couldn't bear to mislead him either.

"I would love to have you and Gabriel over for some tea this afternoon, but you must understand that Margaret is my priority."

"As it should be," he assured her, but not in a way that implied he understood her meaning. "And I would love to join you for tea this afternoon. Although I'm afraid Gabriel might not be so inclined." He nodded to a spot behind her, so she turned around and saw a young woman openly flirting with Gabriel under the watchful eye of who must be her mother. Her heart literally stopped as she watched them, or at least it felt like it did. Gabriel was the perfect gentleman, smiling and making her laugh, this young girl who was smitten with him, but Annabelle consoled herself by deciding that the smile did not reach his eyes. Those beautiful brown eyes that she was convinced followed her the moment she turned away.

"He can bring his friend if he likes. It's simply an afternoon among my oldest and most beloved friends." Annabelle hoped she managed a polite smile, but every time she heard that girl laugh, it felt like a knife was being twisted around inside her chest, eviscerating her heart.

I WOKE UP WITH A START, a feeling of fear and heartbreak overwhelming me. I'd been having a dream that felt so real, but I knew I wasn't me. It was like I was experiencing it from inside the person it was happening to. This wasn't the first time.

While I had long ago resigned myself to them, I now knew that Sam and his parents were wrong to tell me they were just dreams, nothing to concern myself with. The dreams were memories. Not mine, of course, but my ancestors'. I used to think it was my brain revisiting the stories Grams had told me; elaborate masquerade balls, romantic entanglements and European adventures. Given everything I found out yesterday, I knew I was visiting Annabelle's memory. They had always been so vivid and exhilarating, but this time the memory wasn't so pleasant.

I TURNED to the spot where Gabriel had spent the night and only saw the blanket and pillow, neatly folded as if they hadn't been used. I brought them inside, then stepped onto the balcony, knowing he wouldn't be too far.

This was one of my favorite spots on the plantation. It was high enough that you could see everything. If I went to the left side, I could see the meadow leading to the creek, with the little row boat I always begged to go out on. I had convinced Sam to take me out once, but I spent the whole time telling him about the scene in the Notebook with all of the swans. He spent his time laughing at me, until the rain came down in buckets, like in the movie. He swore, which he wasn't supposed to do in front of me, but it only made me laugh harder while he tried to row us back to the dock. We were both soaking wet. He told me I would have to do the rowing next time, but we never went out again.

In front, all you could see were trees. Big, weeping willows I used to associate with Pocahontas. For years after Grams died I would go out there and talk to the biggest one I could find, pretending that she was talking back. Embry found me once. I knew Grams wasn't really in the tree, but I wasn't ready for him to tell me that. Luckily, he was the type of grown up who understood those things, so he sat with me and pretended he could hear her too. By the end of it, I was wondering if maybe she actually was in the tree. Embry also used to pretend he could see our manor from the balcony, even though it was at the other end of the forest. I thought he had way better eyesight than I did. I would test him, asking what color the curtains were, how many windows…he would squint really hard as if he was trying to see further, then would answer the question. I was amazed by him. It never occurred to me that he had been coming to the manor for years, and knew these details about it, just like I did.

The view to my right held less pleasant memories, but the cemetery was still beautiful. I vaguely remembered my grandmother bringing me there to see my mother's grave, but after she died, Mrs. Boyd only brought me there once or twice, saying I could pay my respects without having to spend the day in a cemetery. Still, every time I found myself in this house, I would come out here and look upon the big white marble statues of angels and saints. Even from my balcony, I knew exactly which one was my mother's, and my grandmother's, but I didn't know most of the others. It was our family plot though, so they were all from the long line of women I came from.

Most cultures value male offspring, putting so much stock into heirs that would carry on the family name. In my family, whether by choice or by design, we were all women. I couldn't tell you how far back it went, but so much as I could tell, it was only ever the daughters who went on to continue the line, keeping the name of Owens and passing it on through generations. The only men who had tombstones in our cemetery were either their husbands or their sons who died in infancy, sometimes a little older, but never having children of their own. I tried to ask about it, to see if there was a reason or if we were a long-lasting fluke in nature, but the closest I got was Mrs. Boyd telling me the women in my family were stronger than most men. Considering how all the women I grew up with were buried in that cemetery, I wasn't sure how accurate she was.

It didn't surprise me that the cemetery was where I spotted Gabriel, standing solemnly in front of one of its oldest tombstones. I had followed him to it once and asked him who Annabelle was. I was maybe eight, and it hadn't occurred to me that it was the woman my doll was named after. That was when I found out that if I wanted to know about the past I could ask Embry, but never Gabriel. He was upset that I asked, shocked that I didn't know, and looked at me in a way that made me feel like I had no right to even utter her name. That should have tipped me off that when he said he was an old friend of the family, he meant long before my grandmother, but I never expected him to be from the 1600s like Annabelle.

Gabriel had come to me that night and apologized, stiffly, making me think Embry was the one who told him that I was just a child who didn't know any better and that he should make amends. It was a long time before I would ask him anything else.

I HAD PACKED SOME CLOTHES, but I knew the closet here was stocked. We stayed at the plantation when Embry came every summer, to give Sam and Deanna a break from me. I quickly changed into a blue polka dot halter dress and tried to wrestle my curls into a bun before going to see Gabriel. He was still standing in front of Annabelle's tombstone.

Her name was starting to fade, but the crescent moon carved into the stone on top of it was as clear as day. Even with my hair in a bun it was still long enough, and the elastic low enough, that you couldn't see my birthmark. He hadn't mentioned it when he was going on about freckles last night, but I got the impression he knew a lot more than he was sharing with me. Under the faded name were the years she lived, 1664-1692, and a golden plaque to cover where it used to say she was a criminal who was burnt at the stake. It now read, "Beloved mother and dearest friend, my heart is yours until we meet again."

"When was the plaque added?" I asked, fishing for information. I had always assumed the plaque was put there by someone who loved her, like her husband, who meant that he would be with her once he died. Now, with all the information I was learning, I got the impression Gabriel added it. He probably believed that she was going to come back to him some day, and they would be together in this world. Just pick up where they left off. Except Embry liked to hang out by the tombstone as well. It wasn't exactly going to work for the both of them, but I guess you wouldn't dwell on how she could only come back to one of them when there were bigger obstacles in the way. Like how she had been dead for centuries.

"You shouldn't be out in the open like this," Gabriel warned, turning away from the stone and walking to the opening in the wrought-iron fence, knowing I would follow even though he didn't so much as glance in my direction.

"We would hear if there was anyone within a mile of this place," I reminded him, looking around and seeing nothing out of the ordinary, only hearing animals and leaves dancing in the wind. Even squirrels would have sent the birds into a flying frenzy.

"If we heard them, would you have time to run to the house, get inside and lock yourself into the bunker before he got to you?" he asked, like he trusted the ultra-modern security system about as much as he trusted my athletic abilities. From what I could tell, the plantation house was safer than the White House. Still, Gabriel sounded like he trusted the trees and secret hiding places better.

I hadn't seen the remodeling yet, but 'the bunker' used to be a huge room in the basement that was made of some incredibly strong metal and installed generations ago as a bomb shelter. It also had all kinds of religious symbols and protective drawings on every inch of it, which Embry had told me were blessed. As a child, I thought Embry was teasing. Now, I wouldn't be surprised if the pope himself had blessed the metal sheets. I accidentally locked myself in it once, and although it took less than 20 minutes for someone to let me out, I still thought of the bunker as more of a tomb than a safe haven. Hopefully the danger would never come close enough for me to have to go in it.

"You haven't been back in a while, but I was on the track team this year," I tried for some of the banter we had in the past, but his face was a mask, emotionless.

A few summers ago, Embry would have smiled and asked "You?", teasing me for my lack of athleticism, while Gabriel would have sat there, pretending not to listen or care, with a smile spreading, until we would finally get him to participate. Today, all he managed was, "Get inside and try to figure out how to let me into the house, but not Control or your bedroom. I'll make sure no one has breached the perimeter."

"Be careful," I warned him as he set off. He walked around and made sure no one could get close, but anything with the perimeter was also code for spending hours in the woods. Either to be alone with his thoughts, or to get away from me, I couldn't be entirely sure.

I went back to the house and finally took a look at the renovations that had been done. Most of the rooms looked the same, albeit with a tiny black computer screen, except for what used to be an empty office. It now looked like the command station for a space launch. I assumed this was the 'command' Gabriel had warned me not to give him access to.

It took me a while to find the manual for the system, mostly because I had expected it to be a book instead of a computer file. My biggest issue was figuring out the pass-words, which seemed to have been chosen by Sam, as well as coaxing myself into the pin prick on my finger to confirm my DNA. The ocular scan, my fingerprint and all of these security measures were absurd. I still wasn't sure the entire thing wasn't an elaborate and expensive prank.

Once I figured out how to give other people access to specific rooms, I made the Control room and my bedroom off-limits to anyone but me, no matter what. Then I went to the kitchen to see what food I had to work with. The fridge was full of water with some coffee and Gatorade, while the pantry had a whole lot of canned goods and granola bars. It would do for now, but one of us had to go to the store.

I opened a can of fruit salad and went to wait for Gabriel on the porch. I was eating the last spoonful when he showed up, his face not revealing much, so there probably hadn't been any sign of Embry.

"I figured out how to let you in. I need some of your blood to give you access to the house, then your fingerprints and an ocular scan to get you past the foyer," I said offhandedly, giving him the second fruit salad I'd brought out. "It's not bad," I told him when he looked at it with confusion.

"I'll have to get groceries," he said, surprising me by sitting beside me on the porch swing.

"I can make you a list. I got a lot better at cooking since the oatmeal." I once made him the most pasty, chunky combina-tion of oats, milk and god knows what. I was eight at the time, so he couldn't hold it against me. "Clara says my mac and cheese is the best she has ever had." I noticed a small smile creep across his face before he remembered to hide it. "I was thinking, if you keep acting like you're mad at me and pretending you don't care, then I won't be able to tell if ever he does take over you, but if you're nice and we go back to our friendly banter, then I'll realize that it's not you when you start being mean," I suggested, hoping I had found a way to use the threat of my safety in order to con him into being nicer to me. Or at least to acknowledge me when I happened to be in the same room as him.

"Or it might be easier if you don't get close to me, either way," he said, getting up although he was nowhere near done his fruit salad.

"How come it's always one step forward, ten steps back with you?" I asked, getting upset instead of being quiet and letting him go, like I usually would have done. I didn't generally like confrontation, as you could tell from my escaping prom through a bathroom window. Plus, Embry was usually there to fight my battles for me.

"Lucy, why are you so bent on being friends? I'm not Embry," he said, half self-deprecating, half to hurt me.

"No, but if you're going to keep acting like this, then maybe I would rather you get controlled. He might at least pretend to be nice." I wasn't entirely sure why I was so mad at him. He wasn't being as distant as yesterday, and this was how he always acted. Gabriel usually hung around while saying nothing, but Embry would talk. If you sit around people having a conversation long enough, you can't help but participate every once in a while.

After 'lunch', I programmed Gabriel into the house. I enjoyed stabbing his finger to get DNA more than I should, especially when he disappeared to 'secure the perimeter' as soon as I was done. I got a book from the library and spent the rest of the day reading on the balcony, which was as close to reading in the field as Gabriel was going to let me.

CHAPTER SIX

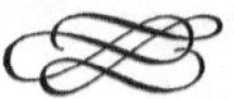

Over the next couple of days, we got into a routine, where Gabriel would spend most of his time reading old books from the library, or going to 'check the perimeter' and disappearing for hours on end.

While he was gone, I also read books from the library. Most of them were non-fiction, and in addition to medical textbooks, there were some on aviation, fashion, photography, biographies…I could read all day, every day, for the rest of my life, without running out of books. Gabriel would come back for most of the meals I made, politely thanking me for it before going off on his own again, but he hadn't been at breakfast Sunday morning.

I didn't like it, but I took advantage of his absence to do a little science experiment I had been planning. I was still mostly convinced everyone was overreacting about this Big Bad, but in case they weren't, I might as well help out.

There was a tiny, dilapidated shed on the property that held turpentine, rusty gardening tools, an old, defunct lawn mower Mr. Boyd used for the cemetery when I was little, and fertilizer. It was an old fertilizer you couldn't find in stores and people were supposed to have returned ages ago, but Mrs. Boyd had a stockpile she would use for her garden.

I wasn't comfortable having those levels of ammonium nitrate in such high quantities next to the house now that we were possibly expecting an invasion, so my first thought had been to get rid of them. Then I remembered what Mrs. Benson taught us in Physical Science, when someone asked how you can make a bomb with something that's 'just dirt'. She hadn't given us a recipe, but it couldn't be that hard to figure out.

One by one, I took out the bags and spread them along the edge or what we considered the plantation house yard. Beyond it was still our property, but it was mostly fields that hadn't been worked in at least a century.

I had enough to make a thick line all around the house, except for once I got to the creek. The meadow surrounding it was still in its wet stage, which meant it shouldn't light up anyway.

Once I was done, I brought the bags of evidence and buried them in the bottom of the garbage bins, underneath the household waste.

"You're back," I said, surprised when I walked into the kitchen and found Gabriel there, making himself a sandwich. I quickly slipped my dirty hands into my pockets and hoped he wouldn't notice.

"What do you mean?" he asked. I had the hardest time not smiling when I saw he was cutting off his crusts. Mrs. Boyd used to do the same for me, until her husband told me I could be as strong as him if I ate them. I eventually found out that wasn't true, but at the time, the lie had worked.

"We're the only two people for miles. I notice when you leave in the middle of the night, or pretend you're 'searching the perimeter,'" I pointed out, using air quotes for the last part before burying my hands back into the pockets.

"I'm keeping you safe," he defended his intentions, oblivious to my mistake.

"I have no doubt about that, but you're still running off all the time and I don't know where you are."

"Did something happen?" he asked, concerned.

"No," I admitted, sort of wishing something had, so he wouldn't leave again. "But what is going on? You're not leaving long enough to get out of town, so where are you going?"

"That's none of your business."

"Gabe…"

"Stay in your parts of the house. No more roaming around outside." He gave me what felt like a punishment for asking. "I'm going to check the perimeter," he said before going off without looking at me.

I watched him head off into the woods, the least likely route anyone would take to come and find us. He went past the cemetery, so I knew he wasn't going to see Annabelle. If I wasn't so worried he would be mad and yell at me for being reckless, I would follow him to figure it out.

WHEN I FIRST MET THEM, I was used to this. Embry would play with me and talk, answering any questions I thought up, while Gabriel would lurk in the background when he visited, mostly acting like he didn't care.

It wasn't until I was about seven that I first saw the side of Gabriel that made all of this ignoring me so hard. I had spent the day in the yard with Embry, who never complained about playing tag or hide and go seek for hours. Gabriel had gone off to the East Wing when he arrived to find Embry already there, and I hadn't seen him since. When Embry finally decided he had to go take care of something that wasn't me, I decided it was time for me to find out what Gabriel did with his time at the manor.

As a child, I thought the house was made specifically for me, because there were all kinds of little hidden passages between the walls for me to play in. Of course, the house was built hundreds of years before I was born, but I still made use of the passage ways every chance I got. They came in handy that day as I weaved through the rooms of the East Wing, trying to find which one Gabriel was hanging out in.

He was in what looked like a study, with a huge painting of a woman on one of the walls. Her hair was long and brown and curly, exactly like what I imagined my mother's to be when I tried to remember her. Of course, I now knew the painting was of Annabelle, and if I took out my mother's picture, I could point out all of the differences, but going off of memory alone, I often pictured them as one and the same.

I couldn't see what he was looking at, so I ventured into the next room. It had once been a bedroom, but was now used mostly for storage, based on the mountains of furniture covered with white sheets. I could make out a couch against the wall, underneath the weird grid thing you could slide to see into the other room. My bedroom used to be next to my grandmother's, so when I would have nightmares, she would keep it open and talk to me when I woke up in the middle of the night. Gabriel left his side of the grid open, so I could see him once I managed to open my side as quietly as I could.

He was looking at a book of old drawings. By old, I meant they were so faded that it took me a few minutes before seeing it was the portrait of a woman, Annabelle again by the looks of it. He was tracing the lines of her face with his fingers as if it could bring him closer to her.

He looked nicer and more vulnerable than I had ever seen him before, but there wasn't much else to see, so after about ten minutes, I got up and abandoned my 'spy' mission. I figured I would find Embry and convince him to play with me again. I moved the metal grid back into place as slowly as I could to ensure it wouldn't make a sound. I thought I was safe, until my knee bumped into the coffee table, and something under the sheet fell over.

Gabriel and Embry could be paranoid about strange noises, so he was definitely going to come and check. I debated for a second whether I would have time to get back to my passageway, before deciding to go back on the couch and pretend to be asleep, just as the door opened and Gabriel came in. I knew I wasn't allowed in the East Wing, but I didn't think he did.

I had grown up playing this game with Sam, of pretending to be asleep, so I knew my breathing would be convincing, but I was worried. Gabriel and Embry always knew things there was no possible way they could know. I concentrated on my breathing like my life depended on it. He had never been violent or punished me, so I wasn't afraid of what he would do if he found out. But I was worried he would like me even less than he already did.

Instead, I heard his footsteps stop in front of me, before his hand brushed the hair out of my face, to make sure my eyes were closed. I passed his test, but I was so nervous I almost stopped breathing when he picked me up in his arms and carried me all the way to my own bedroom. He put me down on top of the sheets, then he put my blankie over me, tucking it in at my sides.

I could feel him, standing in front of me, before he bent down and kissed my forehead. When I opened my eyes to peek, he was gone. I couldn't tell if it was me he didn't want knowing he had a heart, or if it was everyone else, but that was when I found out he did, and that as long as he didn't think you were watching, he would show it.

I NEVER USED it against him, or let him know I knew, but every once in a while, if Embry had been gone for a long time or I was feeling particularly vulnerable, I purposely curled up on a couch where he was sitting and tried my best to fall asleep. I couldn't be sure, because actually falling asleep meant I didn't know how much of what happened was real and how much of it was a dream, but I think he liked it too.

Sometimes, even when I was sleeping in my bed and had no idea Gabriel was even in the country, I would wake up convinced that he came to talk to me. I could remember snippets of conversation that it would be impossible for me to make up. Whenever I confronted him, to see if the conversations were real or figments of my imagination, Gabriel acted like there was nothing out of the ordinary and made me feel like I was losing my mind.

I TRIED to ask Embry about it once, to see if he thought it was possible that Gabriel might sneak into my room sometimes and talk to me while I was sleeping. After reassuring him multiple times that all he did was talk, Embry told me it wasn't likely.

"Unless he talks to you as someone else, and does it when you're sleeping, to make sure you can't hear," Embry proposed.

"No, everything I can remember him saying was to me," I argued, having expected him to either tell me I was imagining things, or that Gabriel was weird sometimes. I did not expect an inquisition.

"Long conversations?" he asked.

"No. Mostly sitting in silence, then saying a few words, then more silence."

"And you're not dreaming it?"

"That's what I'm asking you," I reminded him.

"Well, he is socially awkward. Maybe he thinks this is bonding," he said as a joke, but I felt there was more to it.

AT THE PLANTATION, there was no chance of him visiting me at night without my knowing. He was making me sleep in my bedroom, with all doors locked and barricaded, while he slept somewhere else. If he so much as tried to open my door, a bunch of alarms would go off and alert everyone within a five-mile radius. And possibly slice him to pieces. The plantation had its fair share of spare bedrooms, but I didn't think he was sleeping much these days. When I got up in the morning, there was no trace he even slept at all.

CHAPTER SEVEN

After a few weeks at the plantation, Gabriel was getting annoyed with me, or worried, which meant he had to spend as little time as possible in my vicinity. I had stopped asking questions and tried to pretend this was like any other visit, but apparently being nice and normal also unnerved him, so we settled into the most annoying silence. He might find that easier than arguing and bickering, but I felt a fight would be a welcome distraction.

That might be why I went to read on the dock instead of the balcony. Gabriel had gone off into the trees, pretending he was running security instead of running away from me. There was a possibility I would be back inside by the time he returned and none would be the wiser, but it was equally likely that he would come back and find me gone, panic, see me on the dock, come yell at me, then maybe understand that he couldn't lock me up and ignore me. I hadn't quite decided which outcome I was hoping for when I heard footsteps on the worn wood behind me.

I pretended I didn't hear, as though I hadn't been anticipating this moment all morning, waiting for him to say something first. It wasn't until the footsteps stopped and no words came that I wondered if maybe this wasn't Gabriel. If maybe he was paranoid for a reason and their Big Bad was on the dock, watching me, seeing I had nothing to defend myself with and Gabriel was nowhere in sight. I was cursing myself for not bringing a knife or a baseball bat or anything useful, when I heard it.

It was someone clearing their throat, with a slight cough that would have chilled me to the core if I hadn't recognized it. I stopped pretending to read my book and turned around excitedly, finding Sam a few feet away from me, his goofy smile in place. He looked tired, and for the first time, I saw he was no longer the teenager I always pictured him as.

"Sam!" I exclaimed, jumping up to go and hug him, leaving my stuff abandoned on the dock.

"I thought you were supposed to be in the house," he chided, but the smile told me not to take it too seriously.

"I was going stir-crazy," I lied.

"Don't try to upset him, Luce. He has your best interest at heart, but I think he also has a dark side," he warned, knowing me better than I wanted him to.

"You have no idea how awkward it is. He doesn't have you to talk to while ignoring me, so he just doesn't talk. Asking questions annoys him, so I stopped, but I had no idea if you and Clara and Deanna were okay, I still don't know whether Embry is on his way or dead or..."

"Can't they not die?" he cut me off.

"They die and come back. But I don't think it's an exact science. And from what I gather, if the bad guy takes over, they'll be worse than dead. He can make them do whatever he wants. Even Embry wouldn't have second thoughts about ripping my throat out."

"Well, I can't vouch for Embry's well-being, but I think Deanna has Clara convinced this is a fun summer vacation at the beach. She doesn't understand why you can't be there, but I figure you'd rather she be mad at you than in danger."

"Of course," I assured him. "Now that you're here, I should go make those cookies."

"A double batch might be good." He smiled before helping me grab my stuff and walking back to the plantation house.

"DID he tell you any more than he told me?" I asked Sam once I had programmed him to be able to access the house. We were in the kitchen, with me gathering cookie-making ingredients and him pretending to help.

"Probably less. Before my mom died, she told me to listen to them, no matter how crazy it sounds, because they're keeping you alive. I do as I'm told, but they don't tell me more than 'there's danger, we're taking her'," he explained.

"Gabriel didn't give you a time frame of how long he thought this would last?"

"He implied it was the biggest danger he has ever faced; the real one he's been waiting for all these years."

"Like their reason for being alive?" I asked, realizing this was bigger than I thought. I didn't know if I was more terrified because this guy was terrible enough to warrant making two men immortal in order to protect me, or because if they did somehow defeat him, they would both die.

"Protecting their descendants," Sam agreed.

"What do you mean?" I asked, confused.

"Isn't that why they care? You're either Gabriel's or Embry's great-great-great-great-granddaughter."

"No," I argued. "I think they both loved her, but I'm pretty sure someone would have mentioned it to me," I said, my certainty decreasing as I thought of all the secrets no one had bothered to tell me until a couple of weeks ago.

"One of them has to be." He stood his ground.

"No, I think they both loved and dated Annabelle, the first one, but she left town for years before she came back with a child. She died so they took care of her daughter. And then her daughter and so on." I pieced it from the memories and what Gabriel had said on prom night, but I only knew for sure that it wasn't Embry.

"That's a bit obsessive, no?" Sam asked.

"They loved her." It made sense in a tragic love story kind of way.

"But love isn't…"

"I'm not your daughter but you've been raising me and keeping me safe," I cut him off, knowing I had him. After losing all of my blood relatives before my sixth birthday, I had to rely on people loving me, or I would currently be being raised in an orphanage.

"That's for the money," he teased, which would have hurt if I hadn't known it absolutely wasn't true.

"You think that's funny, but it's just mean," I pointed out.

"Come on Luce, we grew up together. For all intents and purposes, you're my sister. I love you to death and would do almost anything to keep you safe. If you have kids I'll love them too, but I don't think I would spend lifetimes protecting your line," he argued as if just the idea of it were insane.

"I look like her," I reminded him. If ever I someday met someone who looked exactly like my mom, or Mrs. Boyd or anyone I had lost, even if I absolutely hated that person, I still couldn't watch them die. It would be like losing my person all over again. I couldn't imagine how hard it had been on Embry and Gabriel to keep having to watch Annabelle die over and over again. Plus, it wasn't like they could spend years protecting Beth, Cassie and Rosalind without caring about them as well.

"That's still weird," he acknowledged. "Especially if they both loved her. If she only loved one of them, the other is wasting his time, and if she loved them both, then she was playing them."

"I'm not saying it makes sense, it's just what they do," I defended, knowing from the memory that she had loved them both, and wasn't playing either of them.

"Well, I'll be happy when all of this is over, and this weird danger is no longer trying to find you," he said, sticking his finger into my mixing bowl to eat some of the cookie dough.

"When you said to make a double batch…"

"Yes, I want half of it raw," he agreed with a smile.

"It's not good for you. Raw eggs and all," I repeated what Deanna kept telling us, but I didn't believe a word of it.

"I've seen how much dough you leave in that mixing bowl when you make them. Deanna thinks it's sweet that you always offer to make the cookies and do the dishes after, but I know it's because you like eating the raw cookie dough and muffin mix and cake batter and…"

"Who doesn't?" I asked, taking a spoonful myself, before Gabriel came in and found us laughing and sticking our fingers into the mixing bowl.

"Is everything okay?" Gabriel asked Sam. He looked relieved that he wouldn't be forced to deal with me for a few hours.

"Yeah, we're all good. The beach house is great, Clara loves making sandcastles, and you know what they say, 'Happy Wife, Happy Life'." Sam smiled as if Gabriel knew what he meant. Or even cared.

"Has there been any trouble? Anyone casing the house, approaching you, watching from afar?" he asked, implying this Big Bad might be going after them as well, or using them to get to me. I thought they went to the beach house to be safe, so I wasn't exactly thrilled.

"Are we worried about spies, or an attack?" Sam verified, but at least he seemed to have been expecting the second option. It was the spies that worried him.

"An attack. But he'll most likely send someone ahead to find out where she is," Gabriel explained.

"Unless he has Embry," I pointed out. I liked how Sam was getting him to talk, but Sam might not think to ask about Embry, and Gabriel wasn't being forthcoming.

"Embry is taking longer to get here because he thought he was being tailed and has to mislead and avoid them. He should be here within another week or so," Gabriel answered my question, but directed the answer to Sam.

"And why is this guy so interested in Lucy?" Sam asked like it was the millionth time and he still didn't understand. We were rich, so he understood the threat of kidnapping for ransom or blackmail, but he couldn't wrap his head around villains wasting their time to acquire me. Neither could I, to be honest.

"It's a long story," Gabriel said dismissively. "And you have to get back to your family."

"Lucy is my family too, remember?" Sam pointed out. He didn't appreciate being left out when I was in danger.

"I understand your concern," Gabriel agreed, his jaw set. "But this isn't about Lucy, this is about ancient history, which I see no benefit in sharing it with you. Why isn't important. All that matters is that he wants her, and we can't let that happen."

"Because he loves me so much, you know," I said sarcastically, reinserting myself into the conversation.

"If he gets you he wins. And that wouldn't be good for anyone," Gabriel spoke to me that time, but it did not make me happy, or feel like a victory. A chill ran down my spine and I was a little relieved when he went back outside.

"And you say he's always this fun and bubbly?" Sam gave me an apologetic smile.

"I think he might be friendlier when he doesn't talk and pretends I'm not there."

"If he keeps you safe, I can't complain," Sam said, kissing the top of my head before eating another scoop of dough. I laughed, because I knew it was what he was trying to do, to make me smile, but all I could think about were Gabriel's words, and how as soon as the cookies were done, Sam would be gone, and I'd be alone with Gabriel again.

We kept almost half of the dough, so while the cookies were baking in the oven, we took the bowl out to the porch swing and Sam dug in while I stared blankly off to the creek.

"Earth to Lucy," he said after a while, moving his spoon up and down in front of my face.

"I'm just thinking," I defended, curling up into a ball and leaning my head onto his shoulder.

"About what?" he asked with his mouth full, putting the spoon down to wrap an arm around me.

"I never wanted you guys to be in danger," I admitted. "If something happens to you or Deanna or...Clara." I had to swallow before the last name, and couldn't finish my sentence. The faceless danger hadn't been real to me the other night. At least not real enough to be able to hurt the ones I loved, but Sam looked worried.

"You never wanted any of this," he reminded me. "You were born into this messed-up world, just like I was. And contrary to what I said earlier, I am not here for the money."

"But you have a family."

"I do," he agreed. "And it includes you. When my dad died,

they explained it all to me. I understood that they weren't exaggerating about your life being in danger and people wanting to kill you. I told Deanna she could leave with Clara. That I couldn't abandon you, but I couldn't stand putting them in danger either."

"Why didn't she go?" I asked.

"Well, aside from the fact that she loves me and doesn't want to live without me, she said that if I wanted her to leave, I shouldn't have made you part of her family too."

"Are you guys safe at the beach house?" I asked, looking up at his face, so I could see his eyes and know if he was lying to me.

"We are," he told me. "The house is almost like this one. As long as we don't go out, we're safe."

"But you do go out," I argued. He had mentioned sandcastles, and every time we went to the beach house before, Deanna and I spent half the time shopping at the outlets.

"But we're not the ones being hunted. You are." He tried to make it sound comforting as opposed to reminding me I was the root of all of this evil.

"They'll use you to get to me," I said, knowing it was true and hating myself for not realizing this earlier, when I was upset about missing orientation and having to defer university.

"Which is why keeping us safe keeps you safe. No matter how hard we try to stop you, if they got Clara, you would try to give yourself up," he said, looking at me like he was trying to convince me not to do that, although he was never going to ask. As much as he loved me, none of us were ready to sacrifice Clara for me. Except maybe Embry and Gabriel.

"Your point is that they won't hurt her or Deanna or you, they'll just dangle you in front of me to make me do whatever they want?" I summed it up.

"That is what I'm saying," he agreed, holding me close. "Smells like the cookies are ready." The smell was wafting outside, an overwhelming scent of home that reminded me of his mother more than anything else, but he was also trying to change the topic of our conversation.

"I could forget about them, so they burn, and you'll have to stay while I make more," I suggested.

"I have to get back to my daughter," he said, making no effort to get up, letting me decide if he would get his cookies or not.

"Well, I promised Clara," I said, sighing as I stood up.

"We'll be back at the manor before you know it." He stood up as well and wrapped his arm around me while we walked back to the kitchen. I didn't look into his eyes for that lie, deciding I'd rather not know the truth.

My egg timer went off as we walked into the kitchen, so I took the cookies out of the oven and prepared a basket while they cooled. I took my time lining the wicker basket with a checkered cloth, then some wax paper, before piling the cookies in.

"Do you want to keep some for you and Gabriel?" he offered.

"He doesn't deserve cookies," I said, realizing I sounded like a spoiled child. "I'll make more if he decides he wants some," I amended, hoping I wasn't coming off as bitter, considering what Sam was giving up, and the danger he was putting his own family in to keep me safe. I didn't have a right to complain or be upset that I had no one to talk to.

"Clara thanks you," he said, kissing the top of my head.

"Give her and Deanna a hug and a kiss for me," I said, so he held me tight one more time before leaving.

. . .

I WATCHED him go until his body melded with the trees and I could barely tell where he was. Gabriel came out of nowhere, silently and without showing any signs of hurrying. Still, he caught up with him effortlessly. He escorted him out, and I hoped Sam might remind him that I am a person in addition to being Annabelle reincarnate.

CHAPTER EIGHT

Two days after Sam left, Gabriel hadn't improved in the talking department, but he was making a slight effort to not roam the forest so often. He made it clear that he was not interested in conversations, but he didn't object to my sitting and reading in the same room as him.

We were both sitting quietly when I finished my chapter, my arbitrary timer to go stir the spaghetti sauce I was making for dinner. It was bubbling, so I lowered the heat, but not before it sprayed onto my shirt. I put it on low, then headed upstairs to change.

I was just going to put a different shirt on, but I had a closet full of clothes I never wore, including a lot of pretty summer dresses. I was going through some bright and vibrant ones when I spotted my beige lace dress. When Embry saw me in it last year, he stopped mid-sentence and said I looked like Annabelle. At the time I thought he meant I looked like a doll, but now I knew it was his first love he confused me for. I didn't want to make Gabriel sad, but I decided it was time to try and get some answers. I was going to put the dress on and hopefully convince Gabriel to talk to me like he would her.

. . .

THE DRESS itself resembled a lot of my other summer dresses, but there was something about the lace detailing and the unassuming color that made words like romantic and vulnerable come to mind when I looked at myself in the mirror wearing it. I left my hair loose, like Annabelle did in her portrait, then walked slowly down the stairs, taking my time so that if Gabriel happened to look up, he would see me and get the full effect.

It took me until I was on the before last step to realize he was no longer in the library, so I gave up my slow, elegant walking and was going to grab my book and go read on the balcony when I felt it happening again. I barely had enough time to sit down on the couch before slipping into the seventeenth century…

"I'm glad you came," Annabelle said when she found Gabriel in the parlor, looking out to the grounds. There were men working the field, animals grazing and a million things he could be seeing through the window, but every time Annabelle looked out, all she saw was the past. Running through the tall grass with Embry and Gabriel while her mother called after them, warning that she'd be sorry if she ruined another dress in the mud. Annabelle had always pretended she couldn't hear her. More than anything, she could close her eyes and see the scene of years ago now, when Gabriel had brought her to the edge of the field, acutely aware of her parents watching them, and asked her to marry him. Her father had consented already, of course, but Gabriel had asked like her answer meant more to him. Like as long as she said that she did love him and wanted to spend the rest of her life with him, then nothing could ever be wrong in the world. It was because of that memory that she tried her best not to look out at the field, or to ever close her eyes.

"She was beside me when Embry extended your invitation, and

she admitted she would love to meet you and take a walk in your gardens. They're still the talk of the town, I'm afraid," Gabriel explained why he came, as well as why he brought his laughing lady-friend.

"You didn't want to come." She understood, of course she did, but that didn't make it hurt any less.

"Would you?" he asked instead of denying it.

"Gabriel..." she fumbled for words, but it was the hurt in his eyes that stopped her, not the anger his tone had implied.

"I am glad to see you're well and happy. Your daughter is beautiful and my condolences about your husband, but this is the last place I want to be right now." He was talking in a harsh whisper, each word cutting into her.

"I deserve that," she said, bowing her head before looking up into his eyes.

"Don't. Please," he told her, holding her gaze for a moment before turning away and avoiding her.

"You left. You were gone, and it took a year before I believed them that you weren't coming back. I would have waited until the end of time..."

"Then why didn't you?" he cut short her excuses.

"What you made me promise before you went. I told you I couldn't, that ours was the love stories were written about, that I would spend my life loving you whether you came back or not... but you made me promise that I would find someone else, get married and try my best to be happy, so I did."

"With my best friend?"

"With the only other person in the world who understood my pain. I made a promise I had to keep, and Embry was the only man I knew who would let me spend forever finding reasons to talk about you."

"You loved him." He wasn't buying her excuses.

"I did. I do. I've always loved Embry. You and he were like my brothers when I got here, you took me in as one of your own and I

can't imagine my life without the two of you. But I fell in love with you and death wasn't going to change that. I would have married Embry and had a family and pretended to live happily ever after, but I have never, not for a second, stopped being in love with you."

"I came back," he reminded her. "And you still left."

"Embry was like a brother to you, and I knew the only way to mend what I had broken was to leave."

"And what if I would have chosen you? Did I not have a say in deciding which relationship I needed to mend?"

"You loved me, which made it the hardest thing I have ever done to leave, but I knew you needed Embry. I was just going to go while you two forgave each other, but then..."

"You got married."

"No. When I left there was no room in my heart for any others. I met someone and discovered things about myself, things that make it better for everyone if I stay away."

"I can't imagine anything about you that would make me not want you here," he contradicted himself, but the way he reached for her, then had to remind himself not to, told her this most recent statement was the truth, not the first one.

"It was safer for you with me away."

"Then why did you come back, Belle? To drive me crazy, wanting someone I can't have, loving someone I can't even touch though every part of me is aching for it?" he asked, reaching out for her, then dropping his hand midway to her face, making her have to close her eyes and take a deep breath to regain her composure.

"It wasn't safe for us anymore, and I had nowhere else to go," she admitted, the tears filling her eyes this time.

Gabriel didn't even take a moment to determine whether or not it was proper, he bridged the distance between them and took her in his arms. "I won't let anything hurt you," he promised.

"I told Embry, but...I didn't come here to tear you apart, or start anything. It is going to take every ounce of willpower I have to stand

back, but I need my best friends right now. I need to raise my daughter, to make sure she's safe and happy. This is the only place where I could think to do that."

"I'll do whatever you need me to." He kissed the top of her head, understanding there was a lot more to the story she wasn't sharing, but after waiting years, he figured he could wait and be there for her until she was ready...

I woke up in the library, expecting Gabriel to be there, kissing my forehead, but I found the sun had set and I was alone. I hugged myself and walked to the kitchen, where the spaghetti sauce was still in a pot on the stove. I turned the heat up again and boiled some water for the pasta, wondering if Embry knew Annabelle hadn't loved him. Or at least had chosen Gabriel. In a way, it made sense that I knew so little of this love triangle. Embry was the only one who answered my questions about his friendship with Gabriel, and he wouldn't want to admit he fell in love with his best friend's fiancée.

I set two places at the table and had just put the sauce on the noodles when I turned away from the stove and saw Gabriel in the doorway, staring at me. I was confused until I remembered I was wearing the dress.

"The spaghetti is ready," I said as if I hadn't noticed his gaze, bringing the plates to the table.

"I came back inside and you were asleep, so I made the rounds," he said, looking at me more than he had since we got here, purposely turning away before drifting back. "This sleeping in the middle of the day, are you having trouble sleeping at night or is this place boring to you, or..."

"I'm getting memories," I admitted.

"From your childhood?" he asked.

"From my ancestors."

"It could be dreams that you're making up," he dismissed me before hearing what I saw.

"The other day it was Annabelle coming back to town with a baby. She wanted Father Brown to baptize Margaret," I said, getting a reaction from the priest's name.

"And this time?" he asked in a way that made me think he didn't want to know.

"Do you forgive Embry for being in love with Annabelle because you know you were the one she really loved, the one she would have chosen if she could?" I went where I definitely wasn't supposed to.

"This is not something I want to get into, Lucy." He looked down, but wasn't completely shutting me out. He stayed at the table.

"Okay, then tell me where you went? I've been going over everything I knew about Annabelle and I assumed you both loved her, she dated both of you, then there was a big fight and she left...but you left for a year to make her go to Embry."

"Does it matter?" he stalled.

"It might." After all, I wasn't asking for these dreams, so they had to have some purpose.

He sighed, and I thought he was going to tell me to eat quietly, or leave. Instead he answered my question, "My brother had left searching for an adventure. He was supposed to return by a specific date, but hadn't yet. My mother was terribly worried and begged me to find him and bring him home, so I went off to do so."

"I never knew you had a brother," I stated, realizing I didn't know much about him, or Embry, before they showed up. I was still surprised to have seen Embry with a family, and made a mental note to find out what happened to those descendants; whether he was looking after them as well.

"Patrick. He was three years younger than me. A dreamer,

but also the nicest, most innocent kid you've ever met." He smiled, shaking his head and remembering him.

"Do I want to know why it took you two years and you never wrote home?"

"I found him, if that's what you're asking. He had settled with a small community in New York. He had a girl, Katherine, that he fancied…he promised me he would come home once he finished building the church. Then he wanted to bring the girl to meet my mother." I wanted to press him for more details, ask questions, but he had never shared a story about his past, and I was worried he might stop if I reminded him I was there. "I wrote home to let them know I found him and would bring him home soon, but letters took forever to get around back then, and it was common for them not to reach their destination. I figured I would help out with the church, so we could leave faster, but fate had other plans."

"You didn't finish it?" I asked, figuring the church was the part of the story he would be the least attached to.

"No, we finished it. You can still visit it if ever you find yourself in Sleepy Hollow…"

"With the headless horseman?" I couldn't help myself.

"That's a story, written in the 1900s, and set a hundred years after I was there," he argued.

"You're saying there is nothing supernatural about Sleepy Hollow, no headless horsemen?" I verified, slightly disappointed. I found it hard to believe The Gifted exist, but magic and fairy tales don't.

"I'm saying he wasn't in Sleepy Hollow when I was," he said, waiting for me to interrupt again, but I pressed my lips together. "The headless horseman is fiction, but Washington wasn't completely off in suggesting something supernatural was at work in Sleepy Hollow. Within a couple of weeks of the church's completion, all eight of us who had helped build it had died of seemingly natural causes and faultless accidents, without warning, after having been in perfect health."

"Patrick…" I asked, not sure I wanted to know.

"He drowned the day before we were supposed to leave. I wouldn't have suspected anything if it weren't for all of the others."

"When you say all eight of 'us'…"

"I got sick. So sick that no one understood how I survived. I know some people are immune to certain viruses, but this wasn't an immunity. I got sick, I was fading away, and I slipped into a coma. Katherine, who was taking care of me, swore I died, but it was winter, there was a blizzard, and it was days until she managed to go and get the priest. By the time they found me, I had made a full recovery and was as good as new."

"That was the first time you died," I understood.

"I promised Annabelle I would come back to her," he said simply.

"Which is why you believe she'll come back to you?"

"I was brought back to life so I could be with her. It stands to reason that she will come back too," he agreed, implying he wasn't sticking around to keep me safe, but rather protecting me so he would have something to do while waiting for Annabelle's return.

He said it with a finality, letting me know it was not up for discussion, and he was done sharing. He got up and went outside, so I cleared up the table, did the dishes, and realized there were worlds of questions I needed to ask Embry that I had never even considered before.

CHAPTER NINE

I woke up and it was pitch black outside. Being in the middle of nowhere meant we had no streetlights and couldn't see any other houses. If we didn't count the stars, there was absolutely no light. I knew something had woken me, because it was not like me to be up before dawn. I quietly got out of bed and headed towards the door. I put my ear against it to see if I could hear Gabriel's footsteps in the hallway, but all I got was silence. I was working on convincing myself it had been him going out, but then I heard it. Or rather them. Muffled voices coming from outside, somewhere near the balcony. The hairs on the back of my neck stood up, and I brought my hand up to protectively rub the birthmark, before I recognized Gabriel's faint southern drawl.

I rushed to the other side of the room and put my ear to the patio door and strained to see out into the yard. I needed to figure out if he was talking to someone I knew, or if someone evil had managed to get in. Then I heard the hint of an Italian accent.

I slid open the balcony door and quietly walked down the stone steps with my bare feet, not even bothering to put a robe over my nightgown. Gabriel saw me once I rounded the corner, but he rolled his eyes instead of letting Embry know, so I could jump from the bottom stair, onto Embry's back.

"Missed you, Bambolina," Embry called me one of his many Italian terms of endearment, like he had since I was a little girl. Bambolina, Principessa, Tesoro...each made me feel special and loved. He turned around so he could properly take me in his arms and give me a hug that felt like home. He sounded tired and worn out, but I couldn't tell if my arms encircled him easier because I was older and bigger, or because he was thinner.

"It has mostly been a borefest without you," I went along with the pleasantries, allowing myself to be happy he was finally here. I didn't want to complain about Gabriel being mean when he had been forthcoming yesterday, and there would be more than enough time to grill Embry on everything in the morning.

"I'm here now," he assured me, but he wasn't smiling and making everything okay like I had expected him to. "I'm sorry I missed your graduation. I hope someone took a lot of pictures?" he asked, so I nodded.

"Did you lose the people who were following you?" I fished for information.

"I did." Embry sat on the steps with me, while Gabriel disappeared into the darkness.

"I could have used you these past few weeks," I told him once we were alone.

"I think we all wish I was the one to tell you instead of him," he agreed.

"Why didn't you? You had a million opportunities over the past thirteen years..."

"You were a kid," he said simply, before noticing my reaction. "Not as in you were young or immature or couldn't handle it, but until the danger was concrete...I wanted to give you as much of a childhood as I could after everything you had already been through."

"I've been eighteen for months. Lots of them," I pointed out.

"I wasn't ruining your birthday with this, or Christmas. And Keisha and Clara are always there whenever I visit..." We both knew they were excuses.

"Maybe you should come more often then," I called him on it. He didn't tell me because he didn't want to tell me.

"I would give anything for your happiness Lucy, anything but your safety."

"Even the truth?" I asked, looking at him expectantly.

"I have been as honest with you as I could. There was no benefit to telling you all of this when you were younger."

"You could have trained me. Like John Connor." I tried to be serious, but we both laughed.

"What would be the point in saving you if I had turned you into a robot?" he asked.

"A badass, not a robot," I argued. "And I would have believed this a lot easier when I was five. The whole, we're Gifteds who don't stay dead while we wait for your dolls to come back to life."

"I wanted to tell you the supernatural parts when you were younger, so it wouldn't be so much of a shock all at once..."

"Then why didn't you?" I asked when he stopped himself.

"Your Grams," he said simply. "Evelyn knew everything and told you nothing about that stuff. She changed the stories to take out anything paranormal. She wanted you to be strong and confident, but she did not want you to be a part of our world."

"Did she know I was like Annabelle? That I would be hunted?"

"I think she suspected it," he gave me a sad smile. "But she didn't want you to know enough to be able to go looking. Neither did Martha."

"Will you answer everything I ask you now?" I verified.

"Anything I know the answer to," he agreed, looking worried, but I believed he meant it. He wouldn't volunteer anything, but he would answer whatever I thought to ask.

"J'ai trouvé un homme dans la forêt," Gabriel interrupted us, talking to Embry in a language I did not understand.

"Un des siens?" Embry answered with a question. My money was currently on French.

"Je pense. Il va à l'école avec elle, mais il a l'air louche."

"Louche comment?"

"The thing you're not telling me now is…" I knew I had a much better chance of getting information with Embry, especially after he told me he would answer all of my questions. Not only was Embry usually more likely to share, he was a terrible liar. Gabriel was already giving him an angry glare, knowing exactly what was coming.

"Gabriel found a guy in the woods," he told me in a tone that implied it was absolutely nothing to worry about. Just a precaution.

"Embry," Gabriel warned, nodding over to me. It was this that let me know there was danger coming, way more than Embry's slip.

"You realize I'm not a child anymore? You've already told me there's someone trying to find me whose main purpose in life is to kill me. Letting me know the details of how he's trying to accomplish this won't make much of a difference to my fear level. It just might let me prepare myself for what's coming, maybe see danger before it's right in front of me." I was mostly pretending to be so brave and unaffected. If I knew exactly what was going on, I could make a plan and figure things out. If they kept me in the dark, I not only had to fear the Big Bad that was after me, I also had to contend with everything my imagination was making up to fill in the blanks.

Gabriel shook his head before walking a few feet away, so Embry could fill me in. He knew exactly what was going on, but if he stayed away and wasn't a part of it, he could tell Embry 'I told you so' when things inevitably went wrong. It gave him plausible deniability.

"There was a guy creeping around in the woods. When Gabriel found him, he said he goes to school with you. We think he's harmless, regular townsfolk, but he might not have come of his own free will."

"Someone I know?" I asked, confused. No guy from school would come looking for me. Other than to do me harm.

"We think he's being possessed by the men who were following me," Embry admitted, exchanging a glance with Gabriel. I understood that was the secret part they didn't want me finding out.

"I don't really have friends who would come here otherwise," I confirmed their fear.

"He said his name was Tennison Montgomery."

"Then it isn't just people like you that he can..." I concluded, trying to find a nicer way of saying he takes over and makes you do what he wants you to, even if it hurts you or someone you love.

"It is. But there are more people like us than you realize. I don't know how he finds them, because most people..."

"Just die like they're supposed to," I finished for him, so he knew I was listening and understood the concept. It was an insurance policy, which most people didn't end up using, they were just nice to have, in case. "You think him being here means the Big Bad knows where I am, which is why you guys are talking French and Gabriel is angry." I was relieved it wasn't at me.

"We're trying to figure out our next move," Embry agreed.

He made it sound like we were playing chess. The other team moved a pawn at the other side of the board and we were trying to decide if we wanted to jump two squares to meet it, or sneak over from the side. Gabriel's face, however, suggested we were in check and figuring out if we should take their bishop or move our king.

"Would it help if I talked to Tennison?" I offered. "He's the only guy in the world, other than Sam, who would possibly visit me."

"Really?" Embry got into overprotective parent mode.

"He's a friend," I argued.

Embry and Gabriel had a full-on conversation with nothing but shrugs, raised eyebrows and looks before Gabriel said, "He's in the shed.".

"Tied up?" I asked, knowing that even an innocent person left alone in our shed would take a pair of shears or something to defend themselves.

"Alive," Gabriel said like I should be grateful, before I followed Embry to the other side of the house.

"Lucy!" Tennison called out with relief when I got close.

"Tennison, are you okay?" I asked, seeing he was tied to a chair inside the shed. He didn't look roughed up, but he was terrified.

"What's going on? I came to see you and this guy knocks me out and locks me in this thing." He looked to Gabriel.

"I barely hit him," he defended himself.

"What are you doing here? Did you try my house first?" I asked, remembering that I wasn't staying at home, and this wasn't like peeking into the windows when someone doesn't answer the door. It was at least a forty-minute walk from the manor to the plantation. I don't even think Keisha had ever been before.

"You weren't there. No one was there, which was weird. You're always home." He had a point. "I got worried."

"Why were you coming to see her in the first place?" Embry asked, worried I wasn't being objective.

"You disappeared on prom night. I missed my sidekick. I missed you." He turned on the charm, but not in our usual banter way from when we crossed paths. This was how he talked to the girls that were all over him, the thing that annoyed Keisha. "I knew you had another property, so I figured I would look around and find my Buffy."

"Just friends?" Embry turned to me, not impressed with me lying to him. He looked like he was about to knock Tennison out like Gabriel had. I pointed my finger at him in warning, then walked away from the shed, knowing he would follow.

"That's not Tennison," I told him. "He must be skimming over the memories or they come in all messy because those googly eyes are not aimed at me. I was his sidekick when I helped him get Keisha to dance with him at prom. She's his Buffy," I stopped any further reproach.

"Our Keisha?" Embry asked, and even Gabriel perked up, though one was excited for her and the other worried.

"She left right after prom for a summer semester at MIT. Cops would be all over this place if she hadn't shown up; I'm the first person her mom would reach out to if she went missing," I warned Gabriel's look, not letting myself think that way. "And it was so cute," I told Embry.

"He knows you're here then," Gabriel stated.

"Maybe he sent him here to see? This could be one of many places he sent people," I suggested.

"You just said that isn't Tennison, so even if he is one of many, the person who is controlling him knows you're here," he argued.

"We knew this was going to happen. This is your home, he

was always going to come, we just needed a safe place for the two of you to wait for me," Embry assured me like it was nothing to worry about, all a part of the plan.

"If they know where we are, that means we're leaving, doesn't it?" Tactical plans and defensive plays were not my strengths, but it seemed logical and straightforward to me.

"Ultimately, yes, but I think they might try to stage an attack while they think we don't suspect it. You're safer in here than leaving when they could be watching." What Embry meant was that we had to leave, but he didn't know which way to go, in case we were surrounded. Or so said my paranoia, that I only got because Embry's eyes didn't participate in the comforting words that told me everything would be fine.

"We're just sitting here and waiting for them to try and attack us?" I asked in a way that hopefully told him I thought this was a terrible plan.

"I'm pretty sure he's still at least a day's travel away. They didn't know for sure where you were, so it'll only be the men he had following me who will come at first," Embry continued to act like it was no big deal, when I knew it was.

"And you can handle them?" I verified. They were staying alive so they could protect me, after all.

"We will try our best," he assured me with his confident smile, making an effort for the eyes to play along, so I momentarily believed we would win.

"Did your best work for the others?" I asked delicately.

"Rosie died of an illness, Cassandra was mugged, and Beth was in the wrong place at the wrong time when a theater caught fire," he let me know none of them were killed at the hands of the Big Bad, though they didn't tend to die peacefully in bed either.

"What do we do with Tennison?" I asked, looking back to the shed. I didn't feel like dwelling on how my doppelgangers died, so I elaborated. "When he's not possessed he's not evil.

He's even friendly. Not to mention, he has apparently been in love with Keisha since the sixth grade, and I don't want to take that away from her."

"I'll take care of it," Gabriel said, exchanging a look with Embry.

"What is that supposed to mean?" I asked Gabriel, but quickly turned to Embry for backup.

"He'll be fine," Gabriel assured me.

"Because he'll come back to life?" I asked, not sure how far they would go to protect me…how far they would need to go to keep me alive.

"We don't know if he would," Gabriel reminded me, which did nothing to make me feel better. "I'll bring him to the highway and call him a taxi."

"My car's in the garage. The keys are…Where did he go?" I asked, looking around, but Gabriel and Tennison were gone.

"Gifteds often have a Gift," Embry explained.

"Hence the name?" I offered.

"Gabriel is a lot faster than your average human." He smiled at my smart-alecness.

"The Flash fast?" I questioned.

"He's not a superhero. It's just heightened speed, no stopping time or moving faster than speeding bullets," he explained.

"What's your gift?" I asked. Questions about them and their past was a lot less scary than our future at the moment.

"I can change the mood of people around me," he shared.

"That's a weird gift."

"I was good at talking my way out of situations, or convincing people to lay down their arms…"

"You were a charmer," I simplified.

"You could say that," he agreed with a sly smile. "When I was alive, I was good at negotiating and making people feel at ease, or safe, so that carried on."

"I would have found that made sense, but you're not helping much today." I wondered if he wasn't using it on me now that I knew about it.

"Your powers tend to grow stronger the longer you're alive, and it takes a while to come back in each new life."

"You died?" I asked, my heart beating fast again, the complete opposite of calming me down.

"It happens," he tried to dismiss it.

"That's why it took you so long to get to us. You were lying dead somewhere." I was horrified at the idea. I pictured him on the ground, dying alone, clutching his wound and feeling helpless.

"You're making it a lot more dramatic than it really is. I was injured and knew I wasn't going to recover so I got myself a nice hotel room, put up the 'Do Not Disturb' sign and got a nice long rest before heading here, with lots of detours, so I wouldn't be followed," he said simply.

"You said you wouldn't lie," I warned.

"You're not the one who is supposed to be worried, Tesoro. Especially not about me. I'm tougher than I look," he assured me.

"Why don't you two stay in the house with me? They can't get in and we can let the house protect us," I suggested. That was my Plan B to whatever their Plan A was. To bring everyone I cared about into one of these fortified houses, lock us all up in the bunker, then let the Big Bad grow bored and eventually give up.

"That can work for a little while, but then we're stuck. It's fire-resistant, but I don't know how long that would last. We don't want them to keep us in the house while they wait for reinforcements. We want to get rid of this search party and leave before the others get here."

"How long do we have?" I asked, looking around as if I

would be able to see them coming. This was why I wasn't the one making plans.

"I would say an hour if we're lucky, or a few minutes if we're not." At least he was honest this time.

"I need your blood then," I said before rushing inside to get the bloodsucking device from Control, so I could program him into the house.

I CAME BACK and pricked him, just as Gabriel hurried over in the dark, without making a sound.

"They're here," he said, all business. "Get inside," he added, turning to me when I took a deep breath to brace myself for their arrival.

I nodded before running back inside with the drop of Embry's blood. I knew Gabriel wanted me to run straight to the bunker and lock myself in, but I didn't see the point of that until someone defeated the two of them and managed to get inside the house. I still didn't know how the house would react to being breached by someone without access, but I felt certain it would put up a good fight. Otherwise I was poking everyone for a placebo effect.

I decided my time would be better utilized in Control, giving Embry access so he could rush inside if ever the fight wasn't going our way, which I hoped wouldn't happen.

I knew I would be a distraction and would get in trouble if I watched from a window, but I couldn't imagine not knowing what was going on. I was already in Control, so I played around with knobs and buttons until I managed to get the screens to show me the view from the cameras outside.

AT FIRST ALL I saw was Embry and Gabriel standing out in the open, no cover whatsoever, waiting for the others to show up. I switched to a few different camera views until I found the band of men that had been sent to spy on us and kill me. I watched them pass the gate at the end of the property and effortlessly go over the bridge that normally terrified people who hadn't crossed it before. Deanna had to watch me, Sam, and Mrs. Boyd cross it before she believed us that it was safe. The entire bridge looked like a well-placed gust of wind could make it crumble to the ground. Tonight, there were four of them, but only two of the strangers looked like they had any type of training and would know what they were doing in a fight. One of them had a leather jacket and combat boots, long greasy hair, and arms the size of my waist, while the other was basically a tattooed thug in a wife beater with a spiked-up Mohawk. Even in the dark, far past the point of accuracy for the camera, I could tell he had washboard abs, and arms that could lift cars. My money was on the other two being newly possessed, rather than voluntary recruits. They looked relatively tough, each one tall and wide, but their muscles were replaced by beer bellies. One had a red, plaid shirt on, like he was about to go out and work the fields, and the other had a really old, torn t-shirt. The type of guys who had wives at home who would wake up in the morning wondering where they were. Still, they definitely worried me when they finally fit onto the same screen with Embry and Gabriel.

For a few minutes, it looked like they were just talking, and after playing around with all of the buttons, I condemned the expensive system for not having something so pivotal as a microphone, to hear what they were saying. I considered going outside to figure out what was going on, but then the talking stopped and they drew their weapons.

I knew from experience that both of my protectors could shoot, as they'd used an old can as target practice once. I got to try a few rounds and had so much fun, as long as I was shooting at a cardboard box. I had no interest in hunting, or shooting people. Still, I was not surprised at all when it was knives and swords that everyone pulled out tonight. Now that I knew how old they were, it made sense. Big, heavy ancient weapons that were probably forged and blessed by priests, but looked so out of place with the modern day clothes. I would have found it funny if more than half of these medieval weapons weren't currently trying to chop my people into pieces. I was right in my original assumptions about the strangers. The main fight for Gabriel was with the biker, while the farmer occasionally butted in every couple of minutes, only to get pushed back with the handle of a sword, or a well-placed punch. The same was happening on the other side with Embry, the thug and the guy in the ratty t-shirt. They could tell the civilian types didn't know what they were doing, so the intent was to get rid of them, not to kill.

Embry and Gabriel were outnumbered, which terrified me, as proven by the nail marks in my palms, but they had also been training for this for hundreds of years. Their reflexes were outstanding, and I could barely keep up with them while watching, so it was hard to believe the other guys were still standing.

I would be able to breathe easier if Embry and Gabriel got rid of the farmer and the guy in the old t-shirt for once and for all. They were more than capable of it, but I understood why they weren't. Finally, Gabriel butted the handle of his sword into the head of the farmer, who had been rushing at him, effectively knocking him out. He then slid his sword into the biker's stomach, barely waiting for him to fall before he went over to help Embry. He put the guy in a ratty shirt in a chokehold and held him until he passed out. Gabriel was lowering his unconscious body to the ground when I saw the biker he had just stabbed getting back up.

· · ·

"Gabriel!" I screamed as I rushed out of the Control room, down the hall and pulled open the heavy front door. "Gabriel!" I yelled again, this time with a chance of him hearing me, but the biker had already made his way to him and plunged a dagger into his back. Embry had finished his thug, slicing the guy's carotid artery by the looks of it, and hurried to take care of the dying biker. I decided it was safe enough for me to run out of the house now, not that I could have stayed back at this point, even if it wasn't. The fact that Gabriel wasn't yelling at me to stay inside scared me more than anything else.

"I need something to stop the blood," I told Embry once I got close, putting my hands over the wound and applying pressure like they show you in movies, everything from my textbooks and first aid classes completely forgotten. I could feel the warm tears falling down my face, mixing with the blood on my hands, but Embry watched on without moving. "Why aren't you helping me? He's hurt, we need to save him." He always had my back. Usually.

"He's not going to make it," Embry said, his face a mask of anger and fear and adrenaline.

"There has to be..."

"You have to let him go," he cut me off with authority, and the lack of emotion at losing his only friend of the past few centuries reminded me that unless these four attackers were the Big Bad Gabriel was protecting me from, he shouldn't really die. Or more specifically, he should come back.

"We can't leave him outside," I decided, wanting to get away from the two dead bodies, and to be far away when the other two woke up.

"I'll bring him inside." Embry handed me the weapons they had used before carrying Gabriel over to the house. I had watched Sam carry Clara like that hundreds of times, and could remember Embry doing it for me too when I was younger. Watching Gabriel be the one who was limp in someone's arms made me have to struggle for air as I walked behind them.

Embry paused in the doorway, then cautiously stepped in when I nodded to let him know it was safe and the house wouldn't attack him. He put Gabriel down on the couch in the drawing room off the foyer, with his head on the pillow as if he was sleeping. It was then that Embry finally took me in his arms and let me cry.

CHAPTER TEN

Embry insisted I go upstairs and wash the blood off of my hands and arms, so I took a long shower, trying to let the stream of hot water melt the chill in my bones. I nearly scalded myself the whole time, but I was still cold when I got out. I twisted my hair up into a bun, put on some leggings and a big cream-colored sweater before going back downstairs, ready to sit and wait.

Embry kissed the top of my head before going outside, most likely to take care of the bodies and leave the other men far away from us. I was more concerned with the body in my drawing room.

The wound had stopped bleeding, leaving sticky, red goop in place of the warm, flowing liquid I still felt on my hands, though I had scrubbed them clean. Gabriel's eyes were closed, and his skin was already taking on that sickly, bluish white color of corpses. I could see the veins sticking out of his pale skin when I sat on the floor beside him and held his life-less hand in mine.

I understood that Embry and Gabriel were special, that he

would most likely come back, but I had never seen anyone go through it. Gabriel's story from the other day implied it took days to wake up, although I couldn't imagine Embry wanted us to travel with him like this, and it wasn't like we could leave him behind.

It was nearly an hour later when Embry came back and found me still sitting on the floor, still holding Gabriel's hand, still far from being okay.

"It won't happen instantaneously," he shared. "You should go back to sleep."

"Would you be able to sleep now?" I shot back at him. Even with him telling me Gabriel would come back, even though I knew it should be true. Looking at his dead body, I couldn't imagine leaving him alone, or going on with my life as if he hadn't died on us.

"Then why don't you go make us something to eat while I get washed up?" Embry suggested. I knew it was mostly to distract me from Gabriel's corpse, but he had been travelling and must be starving, so I nodded before going to reheat the leftover spaghetti and put the kettle on.

By the time his food and my tea were ready, Embry was back in the drawing room. He didn't waste time standing under the water for ages like I did.

He grabbed his plate and I followed him over to the other, unoccupied couch in the room. I didn't drink the tea, but held it for warmth while watching Gabriel, waiting for him to wake up.

"You still have a few hours," Embry told me, shovelling the noodles into his mouth.

"How do you know?" I asked.

"It has been taking less and less time as we go along, and last time he died on me it took him about eight hours to come back," he said with his mouth full, swallowing when he finished.

"And how are we sure this time won't be permanent?" I voiced my fear and tried not to think about how many other times they had died on me, without my ever knowing it.

"We're never absolutely sure," he conceded. "But our job isn't done yet."

"How did you figure this out?" I asked, cuddling closer to him, keeping my eyes on Gabriel just in case.

"Didn't Gabriel explain it all to you?" he asked.

"We're talking about Gabriel," I reminded him.

Embry sighed, putting the plate down, and wrapped his arm around me. "We lived normal lives, with the usual attempts at happiness, until Annabelle was accused of witchcraft."

I debated calling him out on how he breezed over the love triangle that made them both so invested in my ancestry, but his last words shocked me. "Annabelle was a witch?"

"No. She was accused and found guilty of witchcraft, but she was innocent," he said with conviction, as if that made it better. "She was sentenced to burn at the stake for her supposed crimes. Once someone spoke up against you, guilt didn't matter so much. She knew that and accepted her fate to ensure they wouldn't come after Margaret."

"She sacrificed herself for her daughter," I understood.

"She made the most of a horrible situation she saw no way out of," he specified.

"And she left her daughter with you when they took her?" I asked.

"No. When the inquisition started, before anyone even suspected her, she and Gabriel went to New York, but came back without Margaret. They told everyone she died on the journey and was buried in New York."

"She wanted her to be safe from any accusations of witchcraft," I understood, suspecting that I knew who watched Margaret until Gabriel and Embry got her back.

"She was convincing," he agreed, mostly hiding it, but I could hear a hint of bitterness that Gabriel had been in on it while he had believed Margaret died.

"But she told you the truth," I ventured, convinced they would never do that to him. I knew Annabelle chose Gabriel in the end, but I couldn't imagine anyone not turning to Embry if they were in trouble.

"Not at first, but when she realized she would be named, she came to Gabriel and I under the cover of darkness and confessed."

"To the witchcraft?" I asked. Magic was the next logical step in their fantasy world of people with powers.

"She confessed to hiding Maggie, but she also knew she would be accused and found guilty of witchcraft. We offered to prove her innocence, but she believed the outcome was inevitable. She told us she was going to die, and made each of us promise we would do everything in our power to keep her daughter safe. She suggested having my sister raise Maggie, as she was married and already had children of her own. She knew it was a big commitment, but she needed to make sure Margaret would be taken care of."

"And the promise bound your fate?" I asked, thinking of Gabriel's confession.

"I promised that her blood would be mine, and I would protect her child as if she were my own," he agreed, which explained why he would still be here, protecting me.

"What about Gabriel?" I asked, knowing he had already died and come back years before this promise.

"Gabriel was upset that she was accepting her fate instead of fighting so she wouldn't die in the first place. When she said that even if he didn't understand it, he had to accept it, for her, he reluctantly made the promise, and added that he would find her. Always."

"That sounds like a goodbye. Why is Gabriel convinced she's coming back?"

"She promised us she would. That night we made the promises, she said death was only temporary, and she would be back someday. That she would find us, and we would have the happily ever afters we all deserved."

"I know you loved her, but you didn't think she was crazy when she said that? Or you didn't suspect that maybe she really was a witch?"

"I would have, but you didn't see her. It wasn't the ranting of a mad woman, she wasn't trying to soften the blow of losing her by promising we would see each other in the afterlife. She looked us in the eyes, completely sane, and believed it when she told us she would be back. She promised, and if you knew Annabelle, you would know that she…a promise was a promise."

"You were going to say she would rather die than break a promise," I called him on it.

"And you would have thought that made it less powerful than it was. We both believed her without the shadow of a doubt."

"You were there when it happened?" I asked, not saying it, but he knew I meant when she burned. He got this faraway look, like he was seeing it, and made me regret asking.

"She didn't scream. The others all did, but she got this determined look on her face, and for a second I was convinced she truly was a witch and the flames weren't burning her, that she was going to wait for the ropes to burn, then she was going to walk over to us and we would run off, leaving the town stunned."

"But she didn't."

"No. She just didn't let them win. She bore the flames

without making a sound, she closed her eyes and let them take her."

"Then you went to Sleepy Hollow, got Margaret from Katherine and gave her to your sister?" I asked without thinking.

"How do you know about Sleepy Hollow?" he asked instead of answering.

"I did manage to get one story out of him," I admitted, looking over to Gabriel and remembering when my biggest problem was him not talking to me.

"That was the plan," he agreed, still shocked that I got Gabriel to say anything about Sleepy Hollow. It definitely wasn't the kind of story Gabriel had ever shared with me before.

"What part didn't work out?" I asked.

"We didn't realize we were being followed. We didn't know what the men wanted from us, or if it even had anything to do with Annabelle, but it made us uneasy. We took detour after detour, finally losing them when we got to the hallowed ground of the cemetery where Patrick was buried."

"Gabriel's brother," I nodded to let him know I knew who Patrick was, which he had expected when I knew about Sleepy Hollow.

"You would think it would make us feel safe, finding out they couldn't follow us into the church, but what men can't walk on hallowed ground?"

"They were possessed?" I guessed.

"All but one. The man leading them was the same man we stay alive to protect you from."

"The Big Bad." I expected as much. "Did you know he wanted Margaret, or did you think he was after you?"

"We were convinced he was after us, so Gabriel sent word

to Katherine through a priest, and she brought Margaret to my sister while we kept sanctuary."

"But he killed you, right? He killed both of you and that's how you found out the promise made you not able to stay dead?" I struggled for a word to describe what they were. They weren't immortal, and could be killed just as easily as anyone else. They simply didn't stay that way.

"A woman was a few feet beyond the gate, crying for help, so I went to her. I was unaware that she was possessed and put there solely to lure me out. Once I was far enough from the church, the man came and asked me where Margaret was. I told him I'd rather die than tell him, so he laughed and pushed his dagger into my heart. The pain didn't register so much as the fear when I saw Gabriel running towards me, knowing the man would kill him too. The next thing I knew I was waking up in Katherine's cabin with Gabriel."

"You had both been killed and come back."

"Katherine wasn't surprised, she said it was nothing she hadn't seen before. Although she confessed that the woman who had lured me out had given her bread and some honey for Margaret as they were setting off the week before. She worried the man got what he wanted and left."

"Did he?" I asked. No one had ever gone into what happened next, although I was under the impression that Embry and Gabriel raised Margaret together.

"He found my sister." Embry had that look on his face again, like he was seeing something terribly painful. "My niece, my nephews, my brother in law..."

"Is this why you never mentioned you had a sister, like Gabriel never mentioned his brother?" I asked, putting my hand on his arm.

"Time numbs and dulls pain, but it doesn't erase it. I have lived for centuries and can tell you that the pain of loss, it never goes away," he confided, then took a deep breath before continuing, stating the rest of the story like it was nothing but a bunch of facts. "Gabriel's mother had taken Maggie for the day. She was extremely devout, and happened to be in church when the man arrived in town. I don't know if he didn't go himself, or if he couldn't sense her because she was in the lord's house, but my niece was the same age as Maggie and looked quite similar, so they did their business and left town. We were long gone with the real Maggie by the time he realized his mistake and came back."

"Do you even know what he wants with me?" I kept asking this question, but never got a satisfying answer. "End of the world, apocalyptic things?" I volunteered when he stayed quiet.

"Which we won't let happen." He looked at me imperatively, like convincing me was the first step to making it be true.

"You know, when I think about everyone Gabriel told me is like you, the only conclusion I can reach is that you are good. It's like God put an insurance policy on some people who were supposed to do incredible things, to make sure they couldn't die for good before curing some disease or inventing something or painting the Sistine Chapel or winning a war... Even if they used terrible means to achieve their purpose. Everyone he mentioned has made incredible contributions to the world. Why him?"

"I don't know Tesoro. Maybe it's the balance of good and evil, maybe he's a fluke, maybe he isn't dying because there was something good he was supposed to do, and the evil is getting in the way of him doing it. I don't have all the answers."

"What if you can never kill him? And he keeps coming after me and everyone I love until we're all dead?" I asked, walking back over to Gabriel, not-so-living proof that my fear was rational.

"Luce..."

He was saved from answering when Gabriel woke with a start, like when you fall in a dream and it wakes you up.

"Morning sleepyhead," I said, the relief bringing back the tears as I smiled, unable to contain how relieved I was. "You're okay now. You're back," I said, getting him to calm down.

CHAPTER ELEVEN

*R*osalind *went from bed to bed, offering water, offering her time, offering whatever it took for one of them to be Roger. Every once in a while, someone would tell her they had seen him. Weeks ago. Or was it months? Maybe a year. They all told her incredible stories in which Roger had been a hero and saved hundreds of lives, but still, none of them ended with him coming home.*

It was a busy day at the plantation house she and her husband had shared, which had become a make-shift hospital. There wasn't much to set this day apart from every other day since she had offered her house up for the wounded soldiers. Not much, except for a man with a pair of the most intense eyes she had ever seen.

They had found him in the fields, badly injured, but not quite dead yet. He was placed with the others who had little to no chance of recovery, as nobody expected him to ever wake up. They were letting him die in peace in a bed, until he surprised them all. He had barely stayed awake a minute, just long enough to look up at her intently, as if he'd known her forever. He had said, "Annabelle?" questioningly before slipping back into the comatose state he had been in since his arrival. She knew it was more likely that it was a spasm, or a last moment of strength before he would die and hope-fully be reunited with this Annabelle. Still, the intensity with which he had spoken to her made her believe that maybe he was one of the miracles who was going to pull through.

It wasn't until late the following morning that he woke up and managed to take a small sip of water. When he kept down a few bites of porridge, they decided it was time to move him into another room, with other men who were not on their death beds. He wasn't entirely out of the woods yet, but they no longer expected to walk into the room and find him dead.

Once he was able to sit up in the bed, Gabriel took to watching her; the nurse who looked like Annabelle. He had been watching her for a couple of hours, without letting anyone know. She hadn't recognized him, so this couldn't be what Annabelle had meant when she promised to come back to him. But the women were practically identical, so he needed to find out everything he possibly could about her. So far, he had learnt that her name was Rosalind, this hospital was her house, and the little monster who kept trying to 'kiss people better' was her daughter.

The girl, for one, looked nothing like Annabelle, or Margaret, or even Margaret's daughter, Adaline. Her hair was a pale blond, the color of straw, and her eyes were a deep, dark grey. Gabriel found himself wondering what the father looked like, or if this Rosalind had simply taken in a stray. Although he had made sure that no one had seen him watching the woman, her daughter made no effort to hide that she was watching him. Ever since Rosalind rushed off to treat a new arrival, the girl had been sitting on a desk in the corner of the room, her eyes fixed on him.

He did the mistake of returning her stare, which got her giggling, and apparently implied that she was now allowed to walk over, sit on the edge of his bed and start a conversation.

. . .

"WHAT IS YOUR NAME?" she asked, curiosity winning over her shyness.

"Gabriel," he shared, deliberately giving her a thorough once over. "And who might you be? You're much too young to be my doctor."

"I'm not a doctor." She laughed, one of those innocent, childish laughs that he hadn't witnessed in years. He had been traveling a lot, but always came back to Massachusetts to check on Annabelle's descendants. This was the first time he had been this close and interacting with them, rather than just making sure everyone was safe and happy from a distance. "I'm Molly," she told him, looking around. "This is my house."

"I appreciate you letting me stay," he told her, deciding that although her looks were nothing like Annabelle's, the way her boots were covered in mud and her fingernails caked with dirt hinted that she might enjoy the same pastimes at least.

"We let everybody stay," she told him. "At first it was just daddy's friends, but then they brought their friends and now we have all kinds of people. My mommy helps them," the little girl said before looking around again.

"Your mommy is..." he pretended he didn't know exactly who her mother was.

"Her name is Rosalind, but daddy always calls her Rosie. He says she's beautiful, like an angel. I think so too. Do you?" Talking about her mother gave him back her full attention.

"Maybe more so," he said, thinking of Annabelle. "I haven't met your daddy." He hoped the girl wouldn't realize he was prying for information.

"He's not here," the girl shared, her smile disappearing for the first time. "They lost him. But we're trying to find him. That's his picture. Have you seen him?" She pointed to the small lithograph on the desk she had been sitting on.

"I have not, but I can keep my eyes open for him."

"Do you normally keep them closed?" she inquired.

He was about to explain that it was an expression when Annabelle walked back into the room and his heart stopped in his chest. Rosalind, he had to remind himself. This wasn't Annabelle, although he couldn't wait to get her alone to figure out what was going on.

"What is going on?" Rosalind asked her daughter. "I hope she isn't bothering you." When she turned to him, for a moment he couldn't speak.

"She's been lovely company," he assured her.

"The doctor tells me you're making an impressive recovery," she told him. He could tell the way he was looking at her now was making her nervous, but she was too polite to comment on it, and as hard as he tried, he couldn't help himself. "I was here when they brought you in. None of us thought you'd even last the night."

"Guess I had something to live for." He made sure to smile instead of sounding bitter. He had lived the first few years convinced Annabelle was coming back to him, but after he buried Margaret, and Margaret's grandchildren, he believed it less and less. He was still too good of a catholic to do the act of killing himself, but he didn't see the harm in joining the army and brazenly rushing into the thick of it. Unfortunately, his suicidal heroism only brought him trouble and pain. He kept waking up after the bullets ended his life, and then he would have to change towns. It got to the point where he couldn't tell if he had died and come back to life while he was there, or if he simply recovered. He had recently developed a phantom wound syndrome, where he could still feel the bullet holes and stab wounds, even after he came back. He would have to check under the bandages to be sure, but until he was ready to leave, he didn't want to reveal himself.

"Well, I'm glad you pulled through," she told him, and he was sure she didn't like people dying in general, but the way she looked at him made him think she had especially wanted him to make it.

"I had an excellent nurse," he smiled.

"You should get some rest," she suggested, beckoning for her daughter to leave his bedside.

She wasn't Annabelle, because there was no way she could have gone through that conversation without revealing herself. Still, it was incredible how much she looked like her. He had known Annabelle's face better than he knew his own, as hers was the one he saw every night as he fell asleep, and Rosalind's face was an exact copy, without even a freckle out of place.

That was the last time Gabriel had woken to the face of an angel and believed he would finally be with the woman he loved again. He had died many times and woken to many faces, both friends and foe, but it wasn't until he woke up in the dim light of the drawing room to Lucy saying "You're okay now. You're back." That he finally felt that relief again, that at least for a moment, he could believe her. That everything would be okay.

CHAPTER TWELVE

Gabriel wasted no time once he was back from being dead. Embry said they were always hungry when they came back, so I went to get him some food. By the time I brought his reheated pasta to the drawing room, he was sitting up and making plans with Embry like nothing had happened and he hadn't been dead less than twenty minutes ago.

"We have to go soon," Embry looked up to fill me in when I walked into the room.

"Now. Before they come back," Gabriel urged, taking the plate I was holding in front of him and putting it on the couch beside him without looking up. I saw a blood stain on the white material beside the plate and had to turn away from it. Blood didn't normally make me queasy. As a future doctor, I had trained myself to be used to it, but wounds that killed my family were not something I liked to look at.

"Where are we going?" I asked, sitting with Embry on the other couch.

"I have some friends in Asia," Embry suggested.

"What about your cousin in Italy?" Gabriel finally looked

up and turned to Embry, back to acting like I wasn't in the room. Or maybe it took a while to adjust to coming back to life and me constantly staring at him wasn't helping.

"Won't he be expecting that?" I argued.

"No, he won't, because he knows we know he knows about him," Embry defended Gabriel's idea, which didn't make any sense.

"I can finally go to Italy," I looked on the bright side. I had been asking to go for ever. Sam and Deanna were going to take me a few years ago, before she found out she was pregnant with Clara. We were still going to go, with me tagging along for their babymoon, but the day after I told Embry about it, the trip fell through. At the time I didn't think anything, but looking back, Embry probably discussed it with Gabriel, decided it wouldn't be safe and told Sam I couldn't go. We spent nearly a month at the Beach House that summer, which was a lot of fun, but it wasn't Italy.

"Not for fun," Gabriel argued, finally acknowledging me and knowing exactly what I hoped to do in the land of pizza and tortellini.

"Oh, I'm assuming you won't let me see the light of day while we're there, but I'll still be in Italy. Psychologically, it'll make being locked up way more bearable," I explained, seeing him roll his eyes.

"I'll be sure to sneak you some gelato," Embry promised. He was born in Italy, before his family came to America, which I now understood to have been in the 1660s. He was only a little boy when he left, but he had been back enough times that he spent so much of my childhood raving about the food, the architecture, the paintings, the culture and the weather. It was in large part his fault I was so eager to go, and he knew it.

"And pasta," I said with a smile, getting Embry to smile as well, but Gabriel was impassive.

"Maybe Terrence's will be safer while we're both recovering," he suggested.

"It is closer," Embry supported the idea. The possibility of bringing me to his cousin wasn't so exciting when he knew I was a death magnet being hunted by the Big Bad.

"Who is Terrence?" I asked.

"A friend of Gabriel's," Embry filled me in.

"We would have to fly," Gabriel said it in a way that hinted he was okay with that, but Embry might not be.

"Whatever's best for her," he sighed.

"You need to pack," Gabriel turned to me, getting down to business.

"You need to eat," I countered.

"Go," he said, unimpressed with my attempt at making him do something, but he did at least pick up the plate and take a fork twirl of spaghetti.

"Clothes for a week or…" I tried to get an idea of how long we would be gone for.

"Light on clothes, they don't matter. Bring the Chronicles and shadow book," Gabriel requested.

"What?" I asked. These were not items I ever had in my possession.

"He means the Book of Shadows," Embry clarified, as if that was my issue with Gabriel's statement.

"Like in Charmed?" I asked.

"It is what witches call the book they put their spells in, but Annabelle's is mostly remedies and useful information about the Big Bad," Embry used my terminology.

"Then she really was a witch," I concluded. "I thought she was innocent?"

"She didn't do any of the crimes they accused her of," Gabriel said with finality.

"And remember, we're travelling light," Embry reminded me as I headed for the stairs.

"Like suitcase, carry-on and a purse, or fit as much as I can into my backpack?" I asked.

"Like riding in the back of a truck full of chickens and roosters through a countryside in the middle of nowhere," he shrugged. I smiled at him, until I realized he was serious.

I TRIED to make my backpack something we could grab and run if the situation called for it. I didn't know how computer-savvy the Big Bad and his army were, but I figured we were on the run from now on, so cash would be better than credit cards, and I shouldn't bring any electronics. Not that I'd ever gotten my cell phone back.

I was also getting the impression we would be using the sketchiest truckers and private planes to hitchhike from place to place. The stuff normal parents would warn their kids to never do.

I packed the essentials, like a toothbrush, underwear, a pair of shorts, some shirts, a dress...I hesitated at the photo album, knowing I wanted to bring it, but it was too heavy to be worth it if they made me walk for days, which sounded like a possibility. My blankie, however, I packed. It was the size of a scarf, so I could justify it as something to keep me warm in the cargo hold, or in case we had to sleep outside. The truth was that Deanna was right, and I couldn't bear to leave it behind when I had no clue where I was going or when I would be back.

ONCE I WAS DONE, I went back down to the drawing room, noting a pile of books on the ground, with Gabriel pouring over another one at the coffee table.

"These are them?" I asked, motioning to the pile.

"These are books we're not bringing, but that should not be left in the open," Embry came in and explained.

"Isn't the house just a bigger bunker?" I asked, finding it unnecessary.

"We can never be too careful," he shrugged. I understood these would be extremely dangerous in the wrong hands.

GABRIEL HEADED off to the garage, but Embry helped me bring the pile of books down to the basement. The bunker extended past the house, under the creek if my sense of navigation served me right, but the only entrance was through a small door along the steel wall in the basement.

"You realize this is insane," I said after having to try three times before getting the bunker open, then having to take the books from Embry and carry them over to put them in the chest by myself. I maybe understood why Gabriel was so insistent that I wouldn't have time to run into the bunker if I was out in the field when someone evil came. I still thought they went way overboard as far as security was concerned.

"After devoting my life to keeping girls like you safe, I can confidently say that you can never be too safe. We have to keep trying new ways to keep you away from him."

"Unless the real solution to all of this is to let him have me," I suggested.

"No." He looked as angry and severe as Gabriel got sometimes. "I don't presume to know everything, but I will never, ever let that man have you. And when I say I would give my life to keep you safe, I mean many lives. All of them."

"We're never going to win then. Eventually, if we can't defeat him somehow, he is going to get me, or the next version of me."

"Not if we can help it," Embry said, as if that were a valid answer. "Could you grab that case and the dagger please? We don't want to keep Gabriel waiting."

"What's in this?" I asked, lugging the extremely heavy case across the room to him.

"Guns," he said as easily as if it were socks.

"Neither of these are making it through security," I pointed out, picking up the sapphire-encrusted dagger that I assumed was to slit my wrists if I was in the bunker and the bad guys were making their way in.

"I'm sure you've figured out that we won't be flying first class." He let me climb the stairs first, staying behind to shut the lights. That way he was the one who had to find their way up in the dark.

"Even the passengers in coach have to go through security."

"I think you have a too fancy idea of the planes we use." I could hear the smile in his words and hoped he was teasing.

"But no boats, right? I hate boats," I warned, but this time I looked back at him and saw the smile that made absolutely no promises.

"Try crossing the Atlantic Ocean in a boat with hundreds of people, before indoor plumbing was a thing."

"Was it an experience you would like to recreate?" I asked.

"No," he agreed. "But if we have to..." he stopped talking when he bumped into me. I stopped before reaching the top of the stairs. *Something was wrong.* I couldn't see outside yet from where we were, but I could feel it. I faintly heard the birds flying off in the distance and knew they had breached the perimeter, even before all the little screens in every room of the house warned us.

"Get in the garage. Tell Gabriel," Embry warned, looking like he was ready to fight.

"You're not going out to them," I argued.

"I'll hold them back while you get away," he told me, determined, before softening. "Don't worry, I'll find you."

"You want to create a diversion, so we can drive away," I called him on it.

"I do," he agreed. "The faster you leave, the more of a head start I can give you."

"Or we can all go together. I have a better idea," I told him.

"WHAT ARE YOU DOING?" Embry followed me up to my bedroom, but couldn't come inside.

"Getting these." I came out with the box full of bottles I had carefully prepared for this moment.

"This is cute. But Molotov cocktails are not enough of a diversion for me to come with you. I need to stay behind," he was apologetic.

"These are filled with fuel. The shed had bags of old fertilizer that were recalled for dangerous levels of ammonium nitrate. I poured those along the perimeter Gabriel loves to patrol. As long as I shoot these far enough, the fertilizer will explode, and we will be cut off from anyone trying to get to us."

"How would we get through?" he asked, looking confused, impressed and a little uncertain about my logic.

"The meadow," I said simply. "You don't put these fires out with water, you need flooding. I didn't bother putting any there because it wouldn't catch, or would go out right away."

"Your car will make it?" he asked, putting the pressure on me.

"Or we make a swim for it," I teased, but neither of us was laughing. "It'll work," I told him.

"I'll throw," he decided, sounding worried, but at least he was giving it a shot. "Go to the garage and set the alarm. If I'm not with you by the time the beeping stops, you tell Gabriel to go," he said in a way that left no room for arguing.

"One good throw should set the whole thing off." I wanted to make sure he would have enough time to get to us, and not waste time throwing more bottles than he needed.

"Go," he told me.

As I RUSHED DOWN the stairs, there was a huge bang at the front door. By the time I ran past it, the person on the other side, a 7-foot-tall boulder of a man, had moved on and managed to plow through the unbreakable glass windows. For a moment we just stood there, staring at each other. My face probably reflected the fear that had me frozen in place, but he looked at me like I was his winning lottery ticket.

I tried to make my legs run, either to the garage or the bunker, anywhere, but before my brain even considered screaming for help, the boulder tried to climb through the window to get to me. As soon as his fingers moved past the point where the glass had once been, a grey dust appeared out of the cracks, coating both of his hands. The substance was either a very powerful glue, or paralyzing him, because his upper body was not moving.

"Is this a friend?" the house asked me as the screens began to count down from five.

"No," I managed, my voice sounding foreign. The boulder and I looked into each other's eyes one more time before the grey dust activated and his arms turned to ash in front of me. He was determined to keep coming, but it was like an invisible barrier had settled where the window once was, covering anything that touched it with the grey dust. He got more and more of the dust on him, until there was nothing left.

. . .

I REALIZED I was still standing in the living room, watching the spot where he had been, so I shook it off and went to the garage.

"What's wrong?" Gabriel asked, already sitting in the driver's seat. "Luce?" he asked when I put my backpack on the seat, but didn't go in.

"They're here," I admitted, hoping my altercation gave Embry enough time to come down before Gabriel made us leave. I also couldn't get my mind off the guy at the window. I now had my answer as to what the house would do, but I didn't know if he had been one of the evil ones, or simply possessed.

"Get in," Gabriel ordered, pulling me from my thoughts.

"I'm setting the alarm." I shut the door to the SUV and went to the pad near the wall. I didn't expect it to make a difference, now that the house was already on high alert and murdering intruders, but I didn't want to risk leaving without Embry.

"Warning!" the box yelled once I put in the code. "Fire hazards surrounding location. Follow current route," she said as Embry barged in.

"Come on Lucy," he told me, so I followed him into the SUV and let Gabriel drive us out of the garage.

"Go towards the lake," Embry and I both told him. It was a good thing Gabriel spent so much time patrolling the perimeter, because a circle of fire surrounded the yard, bringing a thick cloud of smoke that hopefully obscured us. We drove through the meadow, turning left before we hit the creek, following the beach to another tiny road in the forest.

"What the hell was that?" Gabriel asked once the smoke cleared.

"The kid used science to create a diversion," Embry told him, looking back at the fire and smoke through the tops of the trees. "I can't believe that worked."

"Of course it did. You added fuel to the fertilizer she lined the woods with?" Gabriel looked to the both of us, fuming.

"How did you…"

"I worked Oklahoma City," Gabriel cut me off, saying the place like I should know what it meant. "That was a risky move. There's a reason those aren't in circulation anymore."

"But you left the bags of dangerous explosives in the shed next to our safe house?" Embry gave him a look.

"I figured they might come in handy," Gabriel said sheepishly. "If they know what they're doing," he added.

"Not as dumb as I look." I gave a small smile, but the adrenaline hadn't worn off yet, so I was slightly shaking.

"No one ever thought you were dumb, Luce, we just want to protect you," Embry gave me an encouraging smile before we drove through the woods in silence.

CHAPTER THIRTEEN

"Nice wheels," Embry told me, looking around the inside of my SUV once we drove out of the small town I grew up in. He nodded appreciatively as he touched the leather and played with the settings for heated seats and sun roofs. We didn't usually leave the estate when he came over, and I would never be the one driving. "Way nicer than my first car," he added.

I could tell he was trying to get my mind off what we just escaped. "You mean your horse and buggy?" I teased, noting the tiniest of smiles on Gabriel's face before he suddenly had to adjust his side mirrors.

"You know, being cute will only get you so far until you have to start relying on your personality. And that was mean," Embry said, putting on his shades and placing his boots on the dash. When he leaned his chair back and folded his arms behind his head, he looked like the lead singer from a rock band of the 90s. He had the leather jacket, black t-shirt, blue jeans and Ray Bans. Looking at him you'd think he hadn't a care in the world, not that he was hundreds of years old and on the run for my life.

"Is it still mean if you really are as old as I'm implying?" I caught Gabriel's smile in the rear-view mirror before Embry turned back to me.

"For your information, I didn't say the first thing I drove, I said my first car. And either way, yours is still nicer."

"Sam chose it because it was the safest. If we crash, we have more of a chance of killing the passengers in the other car than of dying," I explained, cringing like I had when Sam excitedly told me that fact.

"Comforting." Embry's sarcasm and our back and forth made this finally start to feel more like old times, before dangerous people were looking for me. Embry would come in the summers to keep an eye on me, then Gabriel would show up and even he would be singing along with us to the radio...

WE DROVE FOR HOURS, with Gabriel eventually putting on the radio to drown out Embry and my singing a cappella. I think he was tempted to join in for our renditions of classic rock songs, so he switched it to some radio talk show. Embry and I had to find other ways to entertain ourselves, such as reading the car manual, to show Gabriel how even that was more interesting than discussing the lives of reality stars none of us knew.

AT SOME POINT, Embry and Gabriel switched drivers, but I was in that land between sleeping and being awake, where your eyes are closed but your ears are listening. When I woke up, it was light again and we were stopped in the middle of a corn field.

"I thought you said we had to fly to Terrence's?" All I could see for miles was a rickety old barn.

"We do," Embry agreed with a smile.

"This isn't an airport," I pointed out.

"No, it is not." His smile got bigger. "We can't risk you being on the manifest and in the system. He would know where we were going."

"Is it an invisible plane?" I asked, looking around and not seeing anything that could possibly take us up to the sky.

"It's right over here." He walked to the garage and pulled on a tarp to reveal what was once a bright yellow airplane circa Amelia Earhart, but now looked like a rusted pile of junk.

"That doesn't fly," I decided.

"Oh, but it does."

"Maybe a few lifetimes ago, but…"

"It's a cropduster, Luce. It goes out all the time."

"For short trips. Close to the ground. Because of the multiple times it crashes. It can't take us anywhere."

"It'll take us to Terrence," Embry was way too confident.

"Where's the pilot?" I asked. The barn looked as abandoned as the crop duster.

"Right here." Gabriel walked past us to the plane and stuffed his duffle bag into a compartment meant to hold the water. Or the seeds? Whatever you dust the crops with.

"Since when can he fly?" Even before I finished the question, I knew it was silly. All I knew for sure since Gabriel found me at prom was that I didn't know anything about him and Embry.

"The first world war? Maybe before, but we weren't always in touch," Embry said like trusting Gabriel to fly us was no big deal.

"Where's my seat?" I asked once we got close and I saw one seat in the first cockpit and another in the second cockpit, but nothing else.

"Do you want to go on an adventure or not?" Embry asked like this was a fun activity I had wanted to be a part of.

"I don't want to die, so this is the lesser of two evils," I corrected.

"Let's make the most of it." He took my arm and led me to the second cockpit. I couldn't tell if his constant smile was just him, or if it was all for my benefit, to keep me feeling safe and happy all these years. Either way, I followed suit.

"Is it a short flight?" I asked once I was as buckled in as I could be while sharing a seat with Embry. We were travelling so under the radar that Embry and Gabriel were more likely to kill me than the Big Bad was.

THE FLIGHT FELT like it lasted days. I was so cold by the end of it that even with Embry lending me his jacket and wrapping his arms around me, I couldn't feel any of my extremities. We landed on what looked like an old baseball diamond. I could make out the white bases, but the lines had long ago disappeared, possibly around the time the grass yellowed and browned. Our makeshift runway became a cloud of dust once we got close, but it soon cleared to reveal a ranch in the distance. Big, brown cows and horses were grazing, but I didn't see any fences or dogs to keep them shepherded.

"Are we sleeping in the barn?" I asked, judging by our method of transportation.

"I'm sure we can find you some room in the attic," Embry teased before helping me out of the cockpit. The ground felt weird after spending hours up in the air. It was like my legs were still vibrating.

"You're a sight for sore eyes," a man, most likely Terrence, said when we walked up to the house with a large, wraparound porch.

"And you're as charming as ever." Embry went to take him in for a hug.

"I was talking to Miss Owens. The two of you look like

death." They did both look exhausted, but that expression meant something different now that I had seen one of them lifeless.

"This is Lucy." Gabriel went and got a hug as well, making sure they both forcefully slapped the other's back as a cover for it lasting so long.

"Nice to meet you, Lucy. I'm Terrence," he told me, extending his hand once they pulled apart.

Terrence had maintained a thick Irish accent, but looked like a cowboy with his hat and boots, plaid shirt and jeans. I would put his age somewhere around thirty, but wouldn't be surprised if he popped up in a John Wayne setting.

"Thank you for letting us stay here," I said, not sure how much he knew. Neither of the guys had called to warn him we were coming, but he didn't look the least bit surprised to see us on his field in the middle of nowhere.

"Any time," he assured me.

"Five settings for dinner?" a woman asked, coming out in fitted jeans and a cream-colored sweater with gold accents, her long white hair neatly braided.

"Thank you, Angela." Embry smiled, but she didn't return it.

"You're always welcome," she said with a slight reluctance.

"You three can go get cleaned up, then you can tell me about the new pickle over dinner," Terrence suggested.

I FOLLOWED the guys through the house, walking like they had been through this many times before and knew exactly where to go.

"What did you do to Terrence's mother?" I asked Embry, somehow making Gabriel smile.

"I didn't do anything to Angela," Embry said in a way that implied he was only right on a technicality.

"That's not the vibe she was giving," I argued.

"He's telling the truth," Gabriel told me before slipping into the second room on the right once we got up the stairs.

"Explain." I stepped ahead of Embry and blocked his way. He had promised to tell me everything, and this didn't seem like something he would have to lie to me about.

"Angela was sixteen the first time I met her, and her father didn't explain it all to her until many years later."

"That's Terrence's daughter?" I cut him off.

"That's why it's a curse. We still look the same, so you see us as this age, but I've raised children who've had children who had children...I've loved generations of kids who have all grown up, gotten older than me and died," he said, putting a damper on what I thought was a teasing conversation.

"He's eventually going to watch his daughter die. He'll take care of her and do all the things parents shouldn't have to do," I understood.

"It's a fate I wouldn't wish on anyone," he agreed.

I nodded, feeling bad, before I realized what he was doing. "You're making me feel like a horrible person to deflect from whatever you did."

"I did nothing," he stood his ground before sighing. "She had a crush on me. I didn't see her that way. I talked to her, I paid attention to her, I asked her about her life..."

"You fed into her infatuation," I summarized.

"I did," he agreed. "But I didn't realize she saw me that way."

"Until..." I pressed, but his face had gone red, which I had never seen before.

"She...made a move." He was careful with his words, but the shade of his face told me her move was a lot bolder than simply telling him she liked him, and possibly involved minimal clothing. "I turned her down, she was deeply embarrassed and never forgave me, even after her father told her how old I was and how it was never even a possibility in my mind."

"Does that mean you see me as more of a granddaughter than a little sister?" I asked, because I thought of him sort of like Sam. A big brother who always had my back, but would also play with me and tease me and stuff.

"I would have to say a niece, or a daughter. A sibling bond is similar, but you're on a more even playing field, where you still fight. You shouldn't be expected to raise your siblings unless a tragedy occurs. Keeping you safe and happy has always been my priority."

"It's unbelievable what you guys go through," I shook my head at all of the realizations going through my mind.

"With great power comes great responsibility," he teased before we got to the end of the hall. "This is your room."

"Not the attic?" I asked.

"Even Gabriel isn't allowed in the attic," he hinted that it held Terrence's secrets and treasures.

Cozy and welcoming would be the best words to describe the room I walked into. There were throw pillows and blankets in warm colors of the softest materials. Most of it looked like it had been knit or crocheted by Angela, or maybe her mother. There was a pile of towels at the foot of the bed, and some simple toiletries in the en-suite bathroom. They either knew I was coming, or were used to people showing up unannounced and in need of assistance.

I showered less forcefully than I had when I was covered in blood, but took the same amount of time, enjoying the warm water after the freezing plane ride.

I put on some of the clothes I had brought, but appreciated the warm wool socks and flannel jacket that were left on the bed, hopefully for me.

. . .

When I came back downstairs, Gabriel was talking to Angela while Terrence showed Embry something in a book. It was strange to see Embry be the unwanted one, while Angela's face lit up talking to Gabriel.

"Does it fit okay? I thought you might be cold, now the sun's gone." Angela was the first to notice me.

"It's perfect, thank you," I assured her. "Do you often take in strays?"

"It's my granddaughter's. That's the room she usually takes when we visit, but she didn't come this month."

"You don't live here?" I asked, realizing I had no idea where 'here' was.

"No, we live in South Carolina, but I try to come check on the old man every month or so. My husband's a pilot of real planes, so I flew in with him and he'll come get me in a few days."

"The Boeing-Stearman Model 75 is a real plane," Gabriel argued. This wasn't the first time they were having this conversation.

"You should have seen how beautiful she was when we first got her," Terrence agreed.

"It's both of your plane?" I asked.

"No, Gabe had his own." Terrence had a look that told me there was more to the story.

"Had?" I asked.

"There was maybe an incident," Terrence shrugged like it wasn't worth mentioning.

"I knew the plane wasn't safe," I shook my head at the guys for having taken me up for such a long flight in an unstable machine.

"Come and get it while it's hot," Angela called from the dining room as she brought dishes from the kitchen. I went over and helped her carry everything out.

"Did you know we were coming?" I asked. Even though my shower was long, she didn't have enough time to go get groceries, then prepare and cook everything for three extra people. Plus, Terrence called me Miss Owens when I arrived.

"Visitors are not unexpected here," she smiled. "But I always overdo it when I visit my father. I know he can take care of himself, but I don't think he ever learnt how to cook. If you're going to eat something frozen, it better be homemade."

"You remind me of the woman who raised me," I declared, seeing Mrs. Boyd in her.

"Is that a good thing?" she asked.

"The best," I assured her with a smile.

"Then I will take it."

We put all of the dishes in the middle of the table and let everyone help themselves. I opted for the chili, then added some corn and shredded cheese to it.

"Have some corn bread. Angie makes the best I've ever had," Gabriel encouraged.

"That's saying something," I smiled at her while the others agreed.

"More likely they're going senile in their old age," Angela dismissed the compliment.

"She's modest," Terrence told me. "And mean."

It was interesting watching the two of them interact. Angela still teased her father about being old and behind on the times, but she was the one who was older-looking and getting frail. I couldn't imagine what it would be like to stay young and healthy while watching your child eventually wither and die. I could understand why Embry never had kids, and Gabriel always tried to avoid attachment.

. . .

WHEN THE MEAL was done the men offered to do the dishes, so Angela took me out onto the front porch.

"How are you holding up?" she asked me, like she understood a lot more than she let on, and infinitely more than anyone told her.

"I'm okay," I told her. "How are you?"

"I'm old, but I'm not daft yet," she told me. "Uncle Gabe comes by pretty often, and as far as I knew, you were unawares of any of it and he wanted to keep it that way," she told me.

"Uncle Gabe?" I asked. This could explain how Terrence knew who I was earlier, but I couldn't picture Gabriel taking my picture from his wallet to show all his friends.

"He's my godfather. The only family my father has ever had, and the reason I got to have one," she shared.

"A family?" I asked.

"I didn't know any of this until I was in my twenties or so, but my father and Gabriel got close during the war, even before they found out my dad was like Uncle Gabe."

"They met before your dad first died," I understood.

"They fought battles, saved lives and my father spent 99 percent of the time he wasn't listening to other people's problems talking about how much he loved my mother and couldn't wait to get back to her. When he got shot in the head and woke up unscathed a few days later, he left his dog tags and helmet on another fallen soldier. He knew they would assume it was him, notify my mother and give her his last letter and her picture."

"It would be hard to explain surviving something like that," I ventured.

"True, but he could have been MIA rather than dead." I could sense some bitterness.

"He waited until the war was over to find her?" I asked.

"No, he meant it when he said goodbye to her in that

letter. The war ended and he came to America, bought a piece of land and planned to live out his days as a hermit. Uncle Gabe confronted him as soon as he found out, and my dad told him that he had to leave her because he loved her, and knew this was no life for a mere mortal, and he didn't think his heart could take losing her later. He felt she was better off moving on with her life and finding someone new."

"The Gabriel way of no attachments," I agreed.

"No, Uncle Gabe talked sense into him. Told him there's no use in living forever if you never go after the things your heart wants. If you don't have someone to share it with, you're not dying, but you're not living either. He said he would take any kind of torture if it meant he could have a lifetime with the one he loved. His Annabelle," she rolled her eyes like she'd heard enough about this character. "My dad came back to Ireland, hoping to woo back my mum and found out he had a daughter. She'd only found out she was pregnant after he went to England and he supposedly died before she could tell him. He never would have known about me and I never would have met him if Uncle Gabe hadn't interfered."

"He always seems so distant and disconnected." I tried to picture Gabriel waxing poetic about true love.

"I'd be slow to grow attached if I lost everyone I ever cared about," she defended him.

"If you keep letting more people in, you can't lose everyone," I argued, thinking how I frequently lost people, but was never alone because I kept letting new people in.

"I didn't mean…of course I know you've had a hard go of it as well," she assured me. I couldn't help wondering what Gabriel had told her about me. Was he complaining about me trying to be friends with him? Feeling sorry for me because I only had Keisha?

"I'm used to it now," I assured her, sort of answering her initial question.

"It's incredible what humans can get used to," she sighed. "But it doesn't mean we should," she added before the others finished in the kitchen.

TERRENCE AND GABRIEL had a night cap while the rest of us enjoyed a tea Angela made from leaves Terrence grew and dried himself. It had hints of lemon and honey and berries and I couldn't tell you what was in it, but the first sip warmed me to the bone.

"We should get an early night if we want to be out by sunrise," Gabriel told Embry once he was done his whiskey.

"Where are we heading now?" I asked.

"You're staying here," Embry corrected.

"What do you mean? I thought you were supposed to protect me?" I did not like this new plan at all.

"We'll be gone a couple of days, a week tops."

"Where are you going?" I asked.

"We need supplies and information."

"On what? From who? You said we were travelling light, but we had tons of supplies at the plantation. And at the manor."

"You'll be safe with Terrence. I promise," Gabriel told me, so I understood this was one of those things they weren't going to tell me. I wanted to remind them I was an adult now and keeping secrets wasn't cool, but that would have been the perfect ammunition to prove they were right and I was too young to understand.

CHAPTER FOURTEEN

When I woke up the next morning, Embry and Gabriel were gone, but Angela made toast with eggs, bacon and hash browns.

"They left that," Terrence said as I came and sat beside him at the table.

"The Chronicles?" I recognized the leather-bound book my grandmother used to find my bedtime stories in.

"Thought you should know where you come from." He gave me a smile before we ate.

AFTER BREAKFAST, I set myself up in the living room and read some of Annabelle's entries. The first was from 1671, when a seven-year-old Annabelle took the Arabella to America with her parents. You could tell it was a child writing from the way she mentioned dolls and her pet cat, but I knew I was going to like her. She mentioned her fears, and all of the unknowns she was facing, but she carried on as if she didn't have any.

. . .

"Are you sure they wanted me to read this?" I asked Terrence when he came and sat in his armchair the following day. Annabelle was quite the writer. So far, the book was her diary, recounting her school, her family, her friendship with Embry and her love for Gabriel. He had just proposed to her in her father's garden.

"It's your history, isn't it?" he pointed out, but I got the feeling he was purposely ignoring my question.

"I don't think Gabriel would want me to see him like this," I argued, coming to sit on the end of the loveseat beside him.

"How is that?" he asked.

"Sweet and romantic."

"It doesn't show anymore, but back in the day, I believe Embry was a player and Gabriel was the hopeless romantic."

"Player?" I asked.

"My great-granddaughter teaches me the lingo," he explained.

"That's nice." I could picture Mr. Boyd using a phrase Clara taught him in the same way, had he still been around. "It's hard to picture either of them like that."

"You should have known them when they were younger," he told me with a winking smile.

"Did you know them back then?" I wondered if Angela didn't know the whole story about her father's origins.

"No, I met Gabriel on the battlefields of the Second World War. But I have heard stories. From both of them, about themselves and about the other. It's a shame they haven't figured out that they've forgiven each other yet."

"You mean it's a shame that they haven't forgiven each other."

"No, I meant what I said," he assured me. "They think it's easier to pretend to hate each other. Old habits die hard."

"They're both still in love with the same woman. That they

think is coming back to them. If she does, them being friends would make it awkward all over again," I pointed out.

"Nonsense. People don't come back to life after being burnt at the stake centuries before. And if she did, she would be with Gabriel."

"How do you know if you've never met her?" I was intrigued by his convictions.

"They talk a lot when they're drunk," he said simply before deciding I needed more information. "If she comes back, hypothetically speaking, Gabriel will let her go with whomever she chooses. He loves her in that way where he wants her to be happy above all, even if it isn't with him," he shared, letting me know he did not see this ever happening. "Embry, on the other hand, will tell her to go with Gabriel. He knows that she loved him first, and was only ever with him because she thought Gabriel was dead. If she hadn't left town, he would have told her it was okay."

"You're all assuming she would choose Gabriel."

"They both say he's the one she's in love with. Majority rules," he told me.

"Have you tried explaining this to them?" I asked.

"They're stubborn as mules." He shook his head at what he saw as their stupidity, before changing the subject. "You just graduated from high school, right? Valedictorian?" he asked.

"Second in class," I corrected him. "My best friend was valedictorian." I thought of Keisha in her dorm room, completely oblivious to all the madness going on in my once semi-normal world. She always told me the others were crazy to think I was weird. How wrong she was.

"What are your plans now that school's done?" he asked.

"Not dying?" I shrugged.

"Not dying doesn't matter if you're not living," he told me. "My granddaughter went to art school. She paints like Van

Gogh." He said it proudly, but I cocked my head, wondering… "Way before my time," he answered.

"I'll leave the painting to her and Embry," I turned down his art school suggestion. "Are you all artistic?"

They'd mentioned Da Vinci and Hitler as examples, and I knew Embry painted. I was also pretty sure Gabriel drew the portraits he had of Annabelle in the East Wing…it explained calling them Gifted.

"I can play the fiddle if need be," he smiled. "My grand-daughter says it's amazing what you can see in the most mundane objects when you try to paint them."

"I'll take her word for it."

"Before all hell broke loose, what were you going to study in the fall?"

"I was going into pre-med," I admitted.

"After my own heart." He brought his hand to his chest. "I was miserable at it. Hated the sight of blood, but couldn't stand the thought of carrying a weapon," he shuddered.

"Still?" I asked.

"Nah, I got better," he assured me. "At both."

I lost him for a moment before he shook it off. "Gabriel was better. He took me under his wing. Even talked me through stitching him up once. When I said I had no idea what I was doing, he said it was fine as long as it lasted until he found a better place to die."

"Was that when you already knew?" I asked.

"That he was going to come back to life and give me a heart attack?" he answered my question. "No, that's when I found out. Saw him die half a dozen times before I found out I was like him, then I understood that the stitching doesn't matter."

"Wounds disappear when you come back?"

"From the outside, yes," he agreed.

"What did you study outside of the army?" I asked.

"I wasn't one for books. I've taken a few classes here and there if I find them interesting. Lots of history ones, to hear all the facts they get wrong." He smiled, and I could picture him sitting in the back of the class, getting into debates with teachers who couldn't compete with someone who lived through it. "I'm not one for the college experience."

"Me neither," I smiled, knowing there was little chance I would be going to parties and drinking kegs if ever I made it to college.

"So doctor is your dream? Saving lives or prestige?" he asked.

"Saving lives," I answered like the question should have been rhetorical, but he caught on to my slight hesitation.

"But doctor isn't your dream." He saw right through me.

"It's my dream career," I amended.

"Is it something embarrassing or are you afraid talking about it will stop it from coming true?" He wasn't letting me off easy.

"It's just silly," I tried to dismiss him, but he kept his eyes on me, knowing me better than he should for a stranger. "I love school. And learning. I am so excited for all the classes I'll take and things I will learn in med school..."

"But..." he pressed.

"But more than anything, what I want when I finish school, all of it, is to fall in love with an amazing guy, get married and have a bunch of kids. I want them to go to school and make friends and be confident and never be afraid and not lose everyone they care about," I said it quickly, like he wouldn't understand as long as I spoke fast enough.

"You want to give your children the childhood you never had," he finished for me.

"It's terrible, and I hate myself for it, but I am so jealous of Clara. She's like a sister to me, because her dad is my guardian, but she has her mom and her dad and a grandfather on her mom's side and she goes to the park and makes friends with complete strangers and...I want that," I admitted.

"Someday you'll have it," he told me.

"I'm hiding out at your ranch in the middle of God-knows-where because there's a guy, who basically can't be killed, who is hell-bent on killing me," I reminded him.

"You also have two men who will fight to their last breaths to make sure you get your happy ending. And many more of us who will do everything in our power to help."

"I wasn't complaining. I don't want to sound ungrateful, I just..."

"You don't want to get your hopes up because the most likely scenario is that it never happens," he understood. "You should try knitting."

"To defeat the Big Bad?" I asked, confused. He said it so seamlessly with the rest of our conversation.

"You're nervous and you're picking at your nail polish because you need something to do with your hands. Knitting gives you something to do and you get something cozy out of it."

"Is that what your wife did whenever Gabriel brought you into something?" I asked, looking around at all the knit blankets and pillows.

"She did," he agreed. "But I did as well. She made socks and sweaters, but all the pillows and blankets are my handiwork," he shared.

"You're full of surprises, Mr. Terrence."

"Most people spend their time showing you who they are, we're just too busy to pay attention."

THE NEXT MORNING when I came down for breakfast, Angela was knitting on the couch, what looked like a sweater dress in beautiful rust color. A pair of knitting needles and a ball of yarn sat on top of the Chronicles, waiting for me.

"I can teach you if you'd like," Angela offered without looking up.

"He likes solving problems," I said of her father, coming to sit beside her.

"He likes helping people," she corrected.

"He's good at it."

"My dad and Uncle Gabe stayed close for a reason," she told me with a smile, that I returned, but I couldn't wrap my head around her calling him 'Uncle Gabe', or how smiley he was with her.

"What's your dad's...um...gift?" I asked, not finding a better way to say it.

"You tell him the truth," she said simply.

"Like a lie detector?"

"No, it just comes spewing out, which was not cool when I was a teenager and didn't know it was basically magic," she said like she could name many instances where it got her in trouble and she shared way more than she wanted to with him. "He'll tell you he was bad at the medicine, but he was an incredible medic. People tell their secrets on their death bed, and he went from soldier to soldier, listening to their biggest confessions, aspirations and regrets. He listened and gave them peace."

"Like a priest," I ventured.

"No, my family stopped believing in God a long time ago," she said like she had no interest in a false savior.

"Was your mom like them?" I pried.

"Nothing like it," she shook her head with a smile. "She made the rule that us kids were not to know. I think she only agreed to tell us the truth because my brother had no tact and pointed out that she was getting old while dad looked as good as ever."

"Do you have a lot of siblings?" I asked, fascinated with the idea of someone like them having kids. It either had to be a family secret or you would have to keep abandoning them.

"My parents adopted twins when I was ten. My sister died when she was little…"

"I'm so sorry," I gave her my sympathy, but she waved it off, like old wounds you don't want to think about.

"And my brother was in Africa last I checked, taking pictures of lions or giraffes or something."

"That sounds like an incredible adventure." Africa was high on my list of places to visit. Everywhere was, but I wanted to work for Doctors Without Borders and take safaris on my days off.

"He bought into all of my father's adventures and still hasn't figured out that dad spread his experiences over multiple lifetimes with the knowledge that he wasn't going to die if his parachute didn't open when it was supposed to."

"He's given you a lot of heart attacks," I understood.

"Don't be the oldest," she told me.

"How come?" I asked, thinking how Clara basically made me an older sister, though I was the younger sister to Sam.

"You worry. So much. And you put this burden on yourself, like you're responsible for anything that goes wrong. All the pain, all the tears, as if you could prevent it." I got the feeling it was her sister's pain that kept her up at night.

"Isn't that where you try your best and that has to be good enough?" I said it more because it was what I was told than because I believed I would be able to tell myself that if something happened to Clara.

"But how much of yourself can you lose before your best becomes more than you had to begin with?"

CHAPTER FIFTEEN

The Chronicles turned out to be an excellent insight into the lives of my ancestors. After Angela left the ranch, I took it out with me to the barn and read on the upper level, that someone had converted into a tree house type of reading nook. Annabelle used the Chronicles as a diary, with near-daily entries up until she left town. She left the book behind, along with her heart.

To sum up the years she spent away, as well as the short time she was back for, someone had written a single paragraph:

"Annabelle married Henry Hathorne on January 8th 1690 in Salem, Massachusetts. Margaret Hathorne was born to them on December 22nd 1690. Annabelle returned to Boston in June 1691 and was burnt at the stake on July 19th 1692. Margaret Owens was then raised by Embry Dante and Gabriel Black."

Rosalind had a few entries after Embry explained everything, but she clearly wasn't inspired and didn't see the point to the Chronicles. She shared a couple of stories from encounters she had with soldiers during the war, and took down pages of remedies and medical procedures. Every page had a child's drawings in the margins. From what I could tell, she lived a mostly quiet life and died of consumption shortly after America won its independence.

Things got interesting again when I got to Cassandra's stories. I gathered that Embry and Gabriel kept her in the dark about her ancestry. She was many adventures in by the time they told her the truth. The first dozen pages were her trying to remember incidents that happened years before, when she had no idea about Gifteds, or Annabelle. It wasn't until Embry and Gabriel came clean to her that they became friends rather than distant relatives.

I had taken my time with Annabelle's entries. Each page felt like I was spying into the private lives of men who might not appreciate it. Cassandra's, on the other hand, was incredibly easy to pour through, like a novel. She had double the entries Annabelle did, but I was getting through them twice as fast. She made the most fantastic stories of guts and courage sound like run of the mill, everyday occurrences. She had a group of friends who kept popping into her adventures, especially Teddy, Lorie and Gen. I was surprised that a lot of her crusades weren't supernatural at all. She fought for labor laws and against abuse. I was reading about her arrival at Seneca Falls for the first gathering of the Women's Rights Movement when I flipped the page and felt myself going again…

"WHAT DO YOU MEAN, *he found us?*" Cassandra asked, the terror apparent in my voice. I knew I was her because Rosalind would never have worn such a beautiful dress in this vibrant yellow. Cassie was the ancestor who married into the money that bought us all of the cars and houses and most of my inheritance. Based on her doll, I always pictured her as the type of woman who walked around with an umbrella in the sun, smiling and making sweet tea. The Chronicles had since proven that she was a lot tougher than I gave her credit for.

"Gabriel saw him in town this morning. He's trying to get us passage on one of the ships, but we don't have a lot of time," Embry told her in that calm, soothing voice I mostly loved. Except when I had a valid reason to be upset and didn't want to be told everything would be okay. Especially now that I knew it was his Gift.

"I can't leave Corinne. Alan already doesn't understand why we keep leaving without notice and I can't go without them," she argued, and I reminded myself that Corinne was her daughter, and Alan was her husband. So far, she was the first of my ancestors who looked like me to never love Gabriel or Embry. Her heart always belonged to the man she married.

"We can send for them once we are somewhere safe, but for now, you're the only one who is in danger," he was apologetic, and she knew it wasn't his fault, but she was still upset.

"Because I look like Annabelle," she said, exasperated, as if she had been told many times but still didn't quite understand. I got the feeling that if she ever found herself face to face with the Big Bad, she would tell him to just get over it.

"He wants you, and I made a promise that he would not get you," Embry said in a way that made you believe him, even if you knew he had no way of keeping his word.

"I think your promise ended a century ago," she argued before everything got foggy.

WHEN THE FOG CLEARED, it was nighttime. Neither Gabriel, nor Embry were anywhere near. I could feel Cassie's fear. Although I wasn't in any real danger, I knew she was, and my heart was pounding in her chest. I was convinced you could hear it from miles away, which was probably how the man found us. He wore a nice, dark grey suit and looked like a proper gentleman, except for the murderous look on his face, and his eyes. Embry and Gabriel's eyes were black, which I had frequently pointed out when I was younger, but this man's eyes were so dark that I wasn't even sure if they were eyes at all, or if they were just dark holes.

"Run and catch, run and catch, the lamb is caught in the black-berry patch," he said, taunting her with a smile. He enjoyed seeing her like this, terrified, and knowing nothing she could do would stop it. "No bodyguards tonight?" he asked, tilting his head and coming closer, dangerously close, so I could smell his breath. A mixture of pipe tobacco and strong alcohol.

"If you have me, you stop? No more coming after my family?" The words shocked me, but they were the first she said with purpose.

"Of course, love. Once we get you, there's no more family for us to come after," he said with a laugh that curdled my blood.

"What do you mean? What do you want with me?" she asked, having not accounted for this. She came out in the middle of the night, alone, knowing he would find her, because she thought it would be the end of their hunt for the women of her family.

"You don't only carry your essence in that lovely little shell of yours. You carry the essence of your entire line. Past, present and future." The joy in his laugh would haunt me, as it would have haunted her, if she hadn't taken off, running surprisingly fast for the high heeled shoes she had us wearing.

She ran through streets she knew well, turning before I even realized there was another street, or alley. We were getting away, and she became more and more confident as we got closer and closer to where I could only assume Embry and Gabriel were.

I recognized the cliff from one of the paintings in the manor. You could see a lighthouse in the distance, and I remembered noticing a cottage at the base of the cliff, when a searing pain shot through my side.

I had never expected the men who hunt us to use guns, and I doubt Cassandra had either. We stopped for a second, for her to put her hand to the wound and see from the crimson on it that she had *effectively been shot in the back, through her lower abdomen, and the warm blood was pouring out, running down to her leg.*

She looked back and saw that he was gaining on her, so close now and so sure of himself, of his win. She had to know there was no way she could outrun him like this, but she kept going, slower than before, and in excruciating pain, as he laughed, no longer worried because he knew he had her. She stumbled, and his laughter grew louder, until she got to the side of the cliff. She inched away from the wooden railing that hid a staircase, closer to the jagged rocks you could hear the waves crashing into.

"What..." I heard him start, afraid for the first time, before I felt us jump. I was falling, the air like ice against my face, but a calm rushed over me, like I was finally at peace. He wasn't going to get me. We were safe.

I WOKE up with a start on the edge of the upper level of Terrence's barn, confused as to why a pair of strong arms encircled me. I tried to break free at first, terrified that the man had found some way to follow us off the cliff and get us. Then I saw that it was Gabriel's arms, and they were the only thing that kept me from jumping off the second floor of the barn.

I looked up to him, trying to catch my breath, aware that tears were running down my face. He was breathing heavily, like he'd had to run around before finding me up on the landing, about to jump to my death. While I was terrified, he looked furious. As soon as he gave me a once-over to make sure I hadn't been harmed, he released me to the side of the room that didn't have a twenty-foot drop.

"What the hell do you think you're doing?" he asked. I thought he was using this fury to disguise how he was just as scared as I was.

"Cassie wasn't shot in a robbery. She jumped," I said, trying to process the lie I had been told when I asked about the others. Burned at the stake, consumption, robbery, fire. That was what I had been told. He looked at me, shocked, before spotting the Chronicles on the floor by the couch. He looked at me with a mixture of anger and guilt, but also like I was the one who had done something despicable, before walking off without another word.

I brought my arms around myself in a hug, and looked over the edge, wondering for the first time if the dreams might not be a warning from my ancestors, like I had thought, but a game of this evil person's, to see if he could get to me without even lifting a finger.

CHAPTER SIXTEEN

I brought the Chronicles with me back to the house, where Embry was waiting on the porch. "What happened?" he asked.

"You lied to me," I said, torn between wanting to let him take me in his arms and comfort me, and being mad at him for yet another lie after he promised it would be the truth from now on.

"I can count on one hand how many times I've seen Gabriel that upset, and I wouldn't need three of my fingers," he implied Gabriel was the more pressing matter.

"Cassie was shot in the stomach and jumped off a cliff so the Big Bad wouldn't get her," I stood my ground.

"You read it," he understood, seeing the leather-bound volume in my arms. His body language immediately changed, going from being tense and upset to guilty and defeated.

"I started to. Did you put the truth in the book, or did you lie in the Chronicles as well?"

"Saying she was shot in a mugging isn't entirely a lie—"

"That isn't the point," I cut him off even as he tried to

diffuse the situation. "Was Cassandra shot in a mugging or did she jump off a cliff so the Big Bad couldn't have her?"

"Getting shot would have killed her. She just sped up the process by jumping," he said as if it was a technicality issue, as opposed to him lying to me about why she died. "It's all in the Chronicles that you somehow felt you had the right to read."

"It's my history," I defended myself, deciding not to incriminate Terrence.

"And their diaries," he reminded me. "You can't just read the Chronicles and assume you know everything. They're one-sided and…"

"I didn't," I argued. "I mean, I did read them, but I didn't get to the part where Cassie dies yet. I lived it."

"What do you mean?"

"I was inside her while it happened. I felt her heart pound against my chest, the bullet pierced my back…I was her." I kept bringing my hand to my stomach, expecting it to come back bloody like hers had, but I was fine.

"Has this happened before?" he asked, concerned rather than defensive.

I nodded before admitting, "I used to think they were dreams, but then I realized they weren't. I was sure it was them, my ancestors, giving me clues or warning me. Now I think it might be the Big Bad attempting to kill me from a distance." A shiver ran through me.

"How?"

"I woke up in Gabriel's arms, because he caught me when I jumped off the cliff," I explained.

"He was controlling you?" Embry looked horrified.

"No, I was Cassie. She jumped, and I was inside her, so I tried to do the same."

"Did that happen the other times too?" he asked.

"No, but I haven't died as the others yet." When he looked at me, he could tell I was shaken, but it was dying as Cassie and almost dying as me that bothered me more than the lie at the moment. Although that wasn't cool either.

"It's okay," he told me, coming close.

"I don't want you to calm me down now," I argued. "I want answers."

He sighed before admitting, "She left while we were recovering. There was a confrontation and we managed to get the upper hand, but I died and Gabriel got hurt. He was holding on until I came back, so she wouldn't be completely exposed, but we were in no condition to protect her." I could hear all of his guilt for not being with her when it happened.

"You were waiting in the cottage at the bottom of the cliff." I had figured as much, from how fiercely she tried to get to it.

"She could see we were no match for him, even when we weren't lying half-dead in her Summer house, so she got the idea that giving herself up would somehow protect Cory."

"It wouldn't," I shared. "If they'd gotten her, she and Cory would have died."

The confirmation of his suspicions, or the fact that I knew this information, surprised him for a moment. That part wouldn't have been in the Chronicles, as he was never privy to her final conversation. "Almost losing you, then reminding him of how we lost her..." he tried to defend Gabriel's reaction.

"He needs to grow up."

"He was never great at dealing with emotions," he agreed. I gave him the tiniest of smiles, because I knew it was what he was trying for.

"If he doesn't want anything to happen to me, you guys shouldn't leave me like that."

"We needed information and Terrence would have defended you as fiercely as we would," he stood by their decision. "But we're going together this time."

What information?" I asked, but he got a look that raised another question. "We're leaving?"

"They found us," he admitted.

"They're coming here?" My heart beat faster and I suddenly felt sweaty.

"I don't think they know where the ranch is, but they landed at Houston Intercontinental." He used what must have been the old name for the George Bush airport, but at least it gave me a better idea of where we were.

"Where are we going?"

"An old friend's."

"You have a lot of those," I pointed out.

"I'm very old," he conceded with a smile.

"If you can't defeat him, what are we even doing?" I brought it up even though I knew he didn't want me to. I assumed that as my protectors, they could protect me, but if the bad guy won every time… "What's the point?"

"We are keeping you alive," he said like it was the only justification needed.

"We spend the rest of my life hiding, running away every time he finds us, hoping we never have to go up against him? That doesn't sound worth it," I pointed out.

"Your life is always worth it," he told me. "And we can't let the alternative happen."

"What happens if he gets me?" I pressed. "The guy with Cassie said something about my essence?"

"I don't know exactly what he wants with you Tesoro, I just know it's bad and that Annabelle let them burn her alive to prevent it," he said with finality, so even though I had more questions, I went upstairs to put everything I brought into my backpack. I also found room for a misshapen pair of socks I spent an embarrassing amount of time on.

. . .

WHEN I GOT DOWNSTAIRS, the guys were waiting for me in the kitchen.

"You have been a wonderful, yet nervous house guest and it was a pleasure having you." Terrence got up from his chair to take me in for a hug.

"Thank you, so much. For everything," I said, trying to let him squeeze the fear and nervousness out of me.

"Don't forget this." He picked up the knitting needles and ball of yarn I had been working on.

"I don't have room for it," I argued.

"Taking care of great adventures is perfectly fine, but you need to take care of yourself as well," he insisted.

"Thank you," I said again, hoping he knew how much I meant it.

"You can come back anytime. We will always have a room for you."

"Same goes for you at my place, once it isn't so dangerous," I assured him.

"You take care of yourself now."

"You too." I gave him another hug before going outside and waiting for the guys to join me.

"WHERE TO?" I asked, looking at the expanse of land with only the crop duster and Terrence's truck to get around.

"The River," Embry told me, while Gabriel was quiet. Silent was his default setting, but today he was doing it on purpose.

"I don't see a river," I pointed out, looking around. I also didn't remember seeing one from above.

"Didn't you say you wished we could do more hiking?" Embry smiled, trying to pretend this morning hadn't happened, as we followed Gabriel to the wooded part of Terrence's land.

"When I was eleven and we played the survival game in the woods," I agreed, realizing as I said it that some of the 'games' Embry did with me when I was growing up were more like training for this eventuality.

"It'll be fun," he said with a smile that told me it would not be fun, but we would get through it and have stories to tell someday.

"What happens to Terrence when they show up looking for me?" I asked, taking a look back at the ranch that was as peaceful and quiet as when we arrived.

"He'll talk his way out of it," Embry told me confidently.

"You don't believe that," I argued.

"I do," he said naively. "If he doesn't, then he'll wake up in six to twelve hours and we will make it up to him," he assured me.

"Will he try to get information from them?" I asked.

"I don't think he has the upper hand against…"

"Not like that, but with his power."

"Oh…he told you?" Embry was surprised, and I could tell that Gabriel was listening in, even as he walked ahead.

"Angela did. Although I'm pretty sure he used it on me."

"It's not like that. A Gift like Terrence's is always running in the background, whether he wants it to or not. If he encounters someone with mental defenses, he might have to concentrate and work at it, but otherwise it just happens."

"And you're sure he hasn't done whatever he was supposed to?"

"Unless his purpose was to harbor you. We never would have gone to him if he had," he assured me.

CHAPTER SEVENTEEN

We spent the rest of the day in the woods, not exactly hiking, but walking through sometimes treacherous paths to get to this river they implied was out there. I usually lived in flip flops all summer long, so I was happy I opted for hiking boots instead. Not so thrilled we hadn't taken any of Terrence's horses.

"Are we there yet?" I asked Embry expectantly, getting him to laugh.

"Soon," he assured me.

"Is it really this far or are we lost? Or is this our new technique, where we wander the woods, lost, and hope they can't find us because we can't find us either?" I asked, more to make conversation than because I thought it was true, but I could see the back of Gabriel's shoulders tense up with his annoyance.

"We know where we're going," Embry assured me without any hint as to how far it was, or if we were taking a round-about route to get people off our tracks.

"Should we play I Spy or…"

"This isn't a game." Gabriel stopped and turned to face me,

unable to contain what I thought was annoyance, but could now see was anger.

"Wandering through the woods, or the adventure you've taken me on?" I asked. He didn't know it yet, but I knew exactly what was going on.

"Both! We took you away from the manor and are trekking through the woods right now because someone evil is after you. They want to kill you, or worse." He tried to scare me into seeing the seriousness of my situation.

"Gabriel," Embry tried to warn him.

"I know," I said simply, with a heaviness I hadn't used for the banter with Embry.

"Then why are you acting like a child?" Gabriel brought his hand to the pulsing vein in his forehead, which I usually found funny, but not today.

"Because you're treating me like one. I just felt Cassie's last moments. I didn't see them, I felt them. Then I woke up and I was hanging over a ledge. I would be dead if you hadn't caught me. And that's not even the bad guy you're warning me about, that's just me. So yes, I get it. This isn't a game. But I'm not a child. And lying to me won't make this easier. Tell me where we're going and tell me what I'm up against, but don't leave me somewhere for a week with the promise that I'll be safe when no one can promise that." I blew up at him, cursing the tears that made me feel weak and vulnerable when I wanted to convey how wrong it was to keep lying to protect me.

My words gave Gabriel pause, but his anger was ever-present.

"None of the others had the dreams," Embry filled me in. "It's new for us too."

"Do you think it's from him? Or from them?" I asked of the Big Bad and of my ancestors.

"I hope it's from them, but I don't like how far you went, or how close you came to…"

"She was off the ledge," Gabriel shared through gritted teeth. I got the feeling he believed the memories had less friendly origins.

"Any of the others jump to their deaths?" I asked, a terrible attempt to lighten the mood, but it did the trick.

"No," Embry gave me a desolate smile.

"Can we stop being mad at me and hiding things from me now?" I asked.

"We will try to include you." Embry looked pointedly to Gabriel for confirmation.

"If there's a benefit to you knowing it," he reluctantly agreed.

"What about the location of the river?" I got a small smile.

"We're not walking in circles, we're avoiding a canyon, which is why you didn't see the river from the plane," Gabriel shared. I was starting to understand that Embry didn't know where we were going either.

"Will we get there before it gets dark?" I asked.

"You'll have a roof over your head to sleep," Gabriel assured me, kinder than he had been all day, but I still wasn't sure what that meant.

It was nearly 9 o'clock by the time we got to what I would call a mudslide. Branch-like-roots grew from the ground, which was slanted in a way that would be dangerous to climb, even in the best of conditions, but especially today, when everything was slippery.

"Can we get around it?" I asked as the sun began to set, leaving us more and more in the dark.

"Nope."

"We have to go through it," Embry shrugged.

"Not through it, into it. This hill…"

"Landslide," I corrected.

"…takes us down into the ravine, which we can follow to the river," Gabriel continued like I hadn't said a thing, though I did get a stern look.

"Where we have…" I asked, dreading the answer, but anything else would be worse.

"A boat. It's much too far to swim," Gabriel told me.

"I did tell you guys I hate boats, right?" Both of them had gone back to the mudslide. "Rowboats and canoes on the creek are fine, but anything else is…" I didn't want to go into details about the time my class took a tour of the Boston Harbor, but it was far from being pretty, and not an experience I ever wanted to repeat.

"It won't be like your field trip," Gabriel assured me, so I turned to Embry, knowing I hadn't told Gabriel about it.

"You'll be fine," Embry assured me before we got down to the muddy ravine floor, with the tiniest of streams, and followed it to the bed of the river.

"How far is your friend?" I asked Embry, seeing nothing but a single kayak on the smooth rocks surrounded by trees.

"We wouldn't make it in that," he told me, shaking his head.

"Do I get to spend lots of time on your big ship?" I asked with fake enthusiasm, remembering how horrible I felt on the rough waters of the Harbor.

"I would call it lots of things, but big isn't one of them," Gabriel said, moving some branches and moss off an old tarp, to reveal a tiny fishing boat, about half the size of the one from Jaws. All I could remember was that line…

"We're going to need a bigger boat," I said to myself.

"It's perfect," Gabriel argued. "Small enough to stay under

the radar of anyone looking for people travelling long distances, but big and powerful enough to get us to our destination."

"Which is how far, exactly?" I asked, not a fan of our means of transportation.

"A night or two, depending on if the current cooperates."

"There's no motor?" I asked, shocked.

"There is, but it's small. A strong current would tire it out, but we should be fine," he assured me. Embry didn't look any happier than I was, but he wasn't complaining.

The boat consisted of a tiny glass cabin from which Gabriel could steer the boat, and what I might call a 'crevice' below deck. The deck itself had to be walked by one person at a time and even then, Embry's football player frame found it tight. Gabriel offered me his hand to get on board, where I immediately went below deck with my blanket, hoping it would be better if I couldn't see the water.

I GOT LULLED into a false sense of security, thinking I had been wrong and boats weren't all as terrible as the one from my class trip, until the calm, stream-like river turned into River Rapids. The boat rocked so violently I was convinced we were going to tip over and be lost at sea.

"We're fine," Embry assured me, sensing my fear.

"It feels like we're tipping," I argued.

"You'll be better up on deck," he suggested, as I gripped the sides to brace myself and closed my eyes in an attempt to not throw up.

"Seeing it won't help," I argued.

"It does," he promised. "When we came to America, it was terrible. Our boat was bigger, but there were so many people and the stench made me feel like I couldn't breathe," he reminded me of his past experience with ships.

"Didn't half the passengers die during those crossings?"

"Not half, but a fair amount," he agreed.

"I think the only reason I'm not sick is because I would die if I had to spend the rest of the trip in a closed space with vomit all over me."

"That's smart," he humored me. "But I've always felt it's better out than in."

"Not helping," I warned him.

"Do you want me to distract you?" he offered.

"Yes please." I closed my eyes tighter. "Tell me about you."

"You know all about me," he argued.

"I know the lies of omission," I corrected.

"I know we kept things from you, and you have every right to be upset, but that doesn't mean that what I told you before was a lie," he got defensive.

"But it wasn't the truth," I called him on it.

"You didn't find it strange that we never got older?" he tried to put the blame on me for not noticing on my own. Deanna had also pointed out their youthful looks, but people in my world tended to leave before getting noticeably older.

"Neither did Sam," I argued. It took me until this summer to realize my big brother wasn't fifteen anymore. "And I trusted you. I had no reason to doubt you."

"Without fail, every single one of you has been way too trusting," he sounded exasperated.

"If I couldn't trust you and the Boyds, I had no one," I defended myself.

"I'm not saying you shouldn't...I'm saying you should question things, no matter who tells them to you."

"Do you plan on lying again?"

"I want you to know the difference and catch me on it if I do." His words stopped the rest of my rant.

"You might want to brace yourselves," Gabriel poked his head down.

"Why aren't you driving?" I asked, not appreciating the sight of our captain in a place where he had zero visibility of where we were going.

"The boat can't be steered right now, the storm is going to take us wherever it wants to," Gabriel said calmly.

"Why am I the only one panicking?" I asked, looking to the two of them. Embry was bracing himself for something unpleasant, but Gabriel was entirely unconcerned.

"We aren't going to crash or sink, but it might take us a little longer to get where we're going," Gabriel shrugged before going above deck. Before he closed the latch, I could see the sky was a ghastly shade of black, with lines of white when lightning tore through it. This was not the time to be on a boat.

"Why don't you try to get some sleep?" Embry suggested.

"Sure, we're about to be torn apart by the ocean, so why don't I go take a nap." I looked at him like he was crazy.

"You've been hiking all day, it's nighttime, and there is absolutely nothing you can do. Might as well get some rest rather than stay up worrying about it so you're tired and useless to us tomorrow."

"Could you sleep?" I turned it on him.

"I could if you did," he shrugged. "Come on." He motioned for me to come over, so I reluctantly let go of the side of the boat and sat beside him. He immediately wrapped an arm around me so I had something anchoring me down.

"I don't think this is going to work," I warned even as I yawned.

"At least your eyes are closed," he pointed out.

"That's not the same thing," I argued, cuddling closer.

"Rest your eyes then. I've got you," he told me, and even with his warning about not trusting people, I somehow believed him and managed to fall asleep.

CHAPTER EIGHTEEN

When I woke up, I could hear the storm still raging outside, but the water felt calmer. Embry was asleep with a tiny pool of my drool on his shoulder. I would have been embarrassed, but the more awake I got, the more I felt sick. I decided to try Embry's advice and went onto the deck.

The sky was still dark, with grey clouds and rain, but it looked bluer. It was like this rain was trying to wash us clean while the other had been trying to drown us.

"Everything okay?" Gabriel asked, putting away a telescope as he came over to me in his bright yellow raincoat. He opened the door, so I could follow him into the glass shelter.

"Are you using the stars to navigate?" I asked. "We have GPS and satellites now."

"I'm making sure we're going the right way." He rolled his eyes at me.

"Where are we going?" I asked.

"It's a safe house for people like us."

"Whereas that was Terrence's house-house," I understood, having stayed in the room his great-granddaughter usually sleeps in.

"If the safe house gets compromised we just find a new one. No one gets discovered or is in danger."

"Do you think he'll find us there as well?" I asked.

"Eventually," he admitted, causing a shiver to run down my spine. "But we will hopefully have moved on by then. We'll try it for a couple of weeks. If everything is safe and quiet we will stay longer. If we hear whispers or rumors about you, we'll find somewhere else."

"And that's our game plan?" I asked, not very reassured. "Keep running, making sure we're one step ahead so we can leave by the back door when he knocks in front?"

"You don't want to be lied to anymore, right?" he verified before answering.

"Right," I agreed. I was certain that I wanted to know what was going on instead of the lies they had been giving me, but I was also aware that I would regret the decision.

"Right now, it's all we can do. We can protect you and keep you safe, but hiding and running are our main defenses. In open battle, against him and his army all together, we don't stand a chance."

"So we always need to escape before he reunites with his army," I said like it was simple rather than terrifying.

"Exactly," he agreed.

"Forever?" I asked.

"From my experience, he usually gives it his all for a few months, then leaves us alone for a while."

"How long is a while?" I asked. I could deal with this for a few months, but I wasn't sure I trusted the possible calm before what would definitely be the storm.

"Months, years…it depends. I'm just saying this isn't what the rest of your life will look like."

"We just need to keep me alive long enough for him to give up for a few months," I summed it up.

"Exactly." Compared to the alternative it was good news, but it still painted a pretty bleak picture.

I STAYED in the cabin until it stopped raining, right before the sun peeked through the clouds to light the horizon. It would have been absolutely beautiful if the waves hadn't threatened to pull us to the ocean floor. I went out onto the deck at that point, holding on to the rail for dear life. Embry was right that being outside helped. He joined me not long after the sun claimed its spot in the sky, then took over in the glass cabin so Gabriel could get some sleep.

BY THE TIME Gabriel woke up from his nap, I was starving, and my empty stomach liked the rocking of the waves even less than my fed stomach had.

"Perfect timing," Embry said when he saw him.

"Why?" I asked, spotting what looked like a shipwreck graveyard in the distance. Some of them looked like old pirate ships, some were fishing boats, and there was even a rowboat by an orange buoy. I told myself its occupants had jumped ship, rather than imagining that something from the water came out and got them.

"We're here," Gabriel explained.

"I think I'm safer with the minions," I voiced my concern.

"You're better at this part," Embry told Gabriel, leaving him the wheel in the glass cabin so he could maneuver us through jagged rocks, coral and ship carcasses. I spotted an eel and possibly a crocodile, but refrained from asking them if the kraken and inferi were real, deciding I would rather not know until we were out of this particular area.

. . .

"WHAT WAS THAT?" I asked, bracing myself when the entire boat shook.

"Not what, who," Embry said with a smile.

"Caleb," Gabriel explained like he'd had the same reaction once upon a time.

"I was worried you wouldn't make it." The voice belonged to 6 feet of pure muscle, but he had the kindest face when he smiled over to Embry.

"How does everyone know we're coming?" I asked, figuring the Big Bad would find us as easily.

"I heard what happened at Terrence's. You were either heading to me, or to Rosenberg, and he's better at confrontation." They exchanged a look that made me feel like I didn't ever want to meet Rosenberg.

"Is Terrence okay?" I asked of our last host.

"They were using Silas, so they didn't even bother sending him into his next life." Caleb didn't sound happy about it.

"Really?" I was relieved Terence was okay, but it did not make sense to me that this evil person who was hell-bent on killing me would get their hands on someone who harbored me, and let me escape, but just let him go.

"Silas is similar to the man who's hunting you. He won't control you, but if he touches you, he can read your mind. Even after he's gone, that touch is a bond and it's like he's right in front of you," Embry explained as if he'd experienced it before.

"If Terence eventually found out where I was, Silas would just have to check in sporadically so the Big Bad would know as well?"

"Yes. Which is why Terence is now persona non grata and won't be checking his messages until The Big Bad or Silas enter the next life," Caleb assured me, adopting my name for him.

"We don't always come back and we're not always the

same when we do. It's a last resort," Gabriel answered the question I didn't ask.

"I wasn't…"

"It's a valid question," he assured me. "If you get hurt, why not finish the job and be good as new? Eli lost an ear during a drunken duel in Marrakesh and stayed half-deaf for three decades because he lost half his powers in a previous life and didn't want to risk it." I was equally fascinated by their stories as the fact that they had friends and lives outside of protecting me and mourning Annabelle.

"You must be starving," Caleb broke from the conversation he was having with Embry to address everyone. He was looking at me like Sam did sometimes.

"Food would be welcome," Gabriel agreed.

"Etta here?" Embry asked, looking over to a lighthouse, the only building on the island. The remnants of ships in the peninsula told me it wasn't doing its job.

"She likes to come a week or so when I'm stationed at the safe house, but I think she enjoys running things when I'm gone," Caleb smiled.

"She runs things when you're home as well," Embry pointed out with another smile.

"100 percent. But this is when she gets to remodel and throw away the stuff I never use."

"Didn't she already enact the Two Lifetimes rule?"

"I think that's more for hats and shoes she swears will be making a comeback." He even smiled while he rolled his eyes at her.

"You don't live here?" I asked of the island while Caleb crouched down beneath a row of bushes. There had been a faint humming, but then I heard a click and it went silent. He emerged with a pebble, but Gabriel beat him to it and threw a rock at the wooden fence ahead of us. When it hit the wood and fell without getting electrocuted, Caleb went ahead and opened the gate for us all to go through.

"This is a refuge for The Gifted," Caleb answered my earlier question. "If you get discovered, if you're on the run, if something terrible is going to happen and you need to contact someone…We each do our time."

"Even you?" I asked Embry. Gabriel had some extended absences, but Embry always came by.

"You can trade if you find someone who is willing, or who loses a bet," Caleb shared.

"But the last time I was the guardian was 1841, back when it was in Argentina, and I'm not supposed to be back until 2086," Embry told me, explaining why Gabriel was the one who knew how to get to the island.

"How can you plan that far ahead?"

"People move on, others step forward…Corbett will step in for any no-shows because he enjoys being here all by himself," Caleb shrugged.

"How do people find you?"

"It's not like all The Gifted are enrolled or on a mailing list. We don't advertise, so a lot of them will never know we exist. Most of them fly under the radar so we don't know about them. Lola can track Gifteds once they're in their second life, but no one is ever forced to be a part of our club."

"We need a treehouse," Embry teased.

"Does everyone like fish?" Caleb polled when we got to the back of the lighthouse. Spears of fish were roasting atop a tiny campfire, surrounded by wooden logs and Adirondack chairs. An interesting setup for a mostly deserted island.

"It smells delicious," was my answer.

"Then dig in," he invited us.

Caleb handed us all a plate and fork, then brought the

spear around so we could each take a fish. Once the first spear was empty, he scooped some sauce from a pot in the fire onto our plates and gave us each a tin foil-wrapped potato.

"No electricity on the island?" I asked of his primitive cooking practices.

"I like a little outdoors every once in a while," he corrected me with a knowing glance at the guys, before going inside.

THE FOOD WAS DELICIOUS, and Caleb re-emerged with a stick of butter and a bag of shredded cheese.

"No onions?" Embry asked.

"Or sour cream?" Gabriel looked around.

"This is perfect," I voiced.

"The garden has some onions you can dig up, but I don't even know what sour cream is made of." Caleb shrugged his shoulders apologetically.

While I dressed and ate my baked potato, I took the time to look around and explore the island, and the lighthouse. In addition to the fire pit and garden, there was a potato field, a forest and a lake. Unfortunately, the lighthouse, however beautiful, didn't look like it could fit even one person comfortably.

"Are we camping?" I asked.

"Because of the campfire?" Embry asked me.

"And you're taller than the lighthouse is wide," I explained.

"It has a basement," Caleb shrugged.

WE STAYED at the fire until it got dark, with Caleb offering everyone coffee from an iron pot, which only Gabriel accepted.

"You caught me on a cowboy day, but I can Martha Stewart like nobody's business," he let me know.

"No judgment," I assured him.

"Ready to call it a night?" Embry turned to me in a way that told me the others would be staying up. I wanted to say no and be a part of whatever conversation they were about to have, but a yawn escaped. I felt exhausted.

"Sure," I agreed instead.

I FOLLOWED Caleb inside the lighthouse, which looked as rustic as I had expected, but with a shiny fridge in the corner that looked out of place.

"Etta?" Embry asked.

"If the water isn't ice cold, she won't drink it. She forgets that she used to drink from a well, but it's either this or she leaves me for Clyde." He winked at me before lifting up the rug in the middle of the room to reveal a latch.

"A basement?" I asked. The lighthouse might be like the manor, that held more secret passageways than I could count.

"Isn't that what you call the town-like tunnels under your house?"

THE 'BASEMENT' was like a submarine with huge iron doors that could lock off sections.

"Is the new plan to lock me up in here until he gets tired or I run out of food?" I asked, thinking it might be their endgame.

"This has been the Safe House since 1918. That's when we made a sturdier version of the tunnels. Bringing trench warfare home," Gabriel explained the décor.

"Your very own bunker tomb," I commented.

"Not everyone gets a head start like you," Caleb pointed out. "Some locations have been exposed, but others were destroyed when their Big Bads caught up with them…it's only a safe haven for as long as it's safe."

"I appreciate it," I said, feeling the guilt. I wasn't a fan of my situation, but I was incredibly grateful everyone I cared about was okay.

"It's what I'm here for," Caleb assured me before explaining the system. "Pick a room and write your name on the chalkboard, so people know it's yours. Erase it when you leave."

"Thank you," I told him before going off and doing as I was told.

From what I could tell, all of the rooms were identical, with a bunk bed, a desk and a small wardrobe. There were communal washrooms at the end of the hall, but I had no idea how many rooms this place held. The first chalkboards had names on them, but we were the only ones on the island at the moment. Delia had a heart beside her name, someone else drew a top hat on Jacob's and there was a note that read 'food stays in the kitchen!' on another one. I chose the first empty room on my right, not wanting to venture too far into the maze and get lost. The guys went off, either to explore or to reclaim their own rooms. I put my bag inside the wardrobe and sat on the bed. At first, I was just going to look around and organize my thoughts, but then I got so tired that I fell asleep on the bed, without even bothering to get under the covers.

CHAPTER NINETEEN

I woke up without knowing which rooms everyone else took, so I couldn't tell if the guys were up yet. I went to the underground kitchen and found Caleb making what looked like a dozen-egg-omelette.

"They're bigger here," he defended himself.

"Does living on this island make you part-farmer?" I asked.

"We have essentials delivered every month or so, but there's a chicken coop on the other side of the woods and some animals I try to tend to," he said, putting his omelette on a plate and cracking more eggs into a bowl. He was right, they were much bigger than the ones we got back home. "Mushrooms, peppers and any cheese that isn't blue or from a goat, right?" he asked me.

"Which one did you know?" I understood exactly how he knew, and what some of last night's looks meant.

"Cassie," he said with a warm smile. "I met Beth a couple of times as well, but Cass was family."

"As in…" I wondered if the men in my family hadn't died so much as become Gifted.

"Some ties are stronger than blood," he shook his head.

"Embry introduced you?" I guessed.

"No, Etta did."

"She's your wife?" I assumed.

"My heart and soul," he agreed.

"Did Etta help them protect her?" I asked, trying to remember if anyone else had popped up in my dreams of Cassie.

"No, but Cass tried to protect Etta. In her first life," he said pointedly.

"I know that's supposed to mean something, but..." I raised my shoulders to let him know I had no idea what he was getting at.

"Your first life is before the first time you die and come back. Most of us don't know we're Gifted until that happens, so knowing someone before their second life is a big deal."

"It makes you family?" I asked.

"In some cases," he agreed.

"Is Etta short for something?" I asked, the wheels turning in my brain.

"Loretta," he shared.

"You're Teddy and Lorie," I clued in.

"We are," he smiled. "If Etta were here right now, she would have smothered you in hugs the second you arrived."

"You wanted to," I called him on it, remembering the look.

"I did," he agreed. "But I held myself back when it was Cassie as well. Back in the 1800s, it was considered improper to sweep a woman up in your arms if she wasn't your wife."

"If history serves, that wasn't common either," I pointed out.

"No, it wasn't," he agreed with a laughing smile. "Etta was extremely proper, so it drove her mad, but she also loved it."

"What was Cassie like?" I asked, having nothing more than her accounts and a couple of dreams.

"When I met her, according to society, she was the perfect, docile woman every mother-in-law dreamed of."

"A bore," I smiled to show I got his meaning.

"She knew how to fit in," he defended her.

"Did Alan know the truth?" I asked, ever curious about my ancestors. I was fascinated by the women who came before me, but so intrigued by the men that I never had the chance to encounter. Grams had explained that the women in our family were simply stronger, but it seemed more like the men were cursed.

"When I met her, he knew everything. He was the most progressive and supportive husband I had ever seen. He traveled for business and he would bring back elaborate protective devices from Asia and Africa for her, because she always insisted on getting into trouble."

"He was the Lucius Fox to her Bruce Wayne," I smiled.

"Batman references?" he sounded surprised.

"I grew up with an older brother."

He was mid-nod when he decided my answer made even less sense than the reference. "A full-brother?" he asked.

"All my 'full' relatives died when I was little, but the couple that raised me had a son who was a few years older. He's my guardian now." I was aware that as an eighteen-year-old I didn't legally need a guardian anymore, but Sam liked to say parents didn't stop being parents when the kid turned eighteen, it was a lifelong adventure.

"I'm sorry."

"It was a long time ago," I said awkwardly. I didn't often meet new people, so it rarely came up.

"Still hurts," he told me.

"Why were you shocked at the idea of me having a brother?" I asked.

"Cassie had three brothers who all died in infancy, and she

suffered miscarriages before Corrie," he looked uncomfortable, like he wasn't sure he should be telling me.

"Could the protective devices help against this man who is hunting me?" I changed the subject for him, figuring I would ask Embry about it later.

"The ones from Africa might have. They had voodoo or shaman powers or something, but most of them were leather gauntlets or spiked purses, heels with blades that sprung out…"

"That sounds like super cool spy stuff," I pointed out, impressed.

"It was. I think she freaked out with excitement when he brought them home to her, but we never saw that. By the time she used them with us, she acted like it was completely natural for a woman to shoot spikes from her umbrella."

"Seriously?" I was in awe.

"She was the coolest," he told me, placing the second omelette in front of me.

"I have none of that," I shared, accepting the fork he handed me.

"The gadgets?" he asked with his mouth full.

"The confidence, the skills. All I can do to defend myself at this point is run and hide."

"Do you want to change that?" he asked instead of the reassurances Sam would have given me.

"Is that your magic power?" I asked.

"My Gift is my strength," he filled me in. "I can teach you how to box. I mostly do it for fun now, but there was a time when I was training or sparring against the best the field had to offer."

"I would love that." I didn't realize how much I meant it until I said it.

"Then finish your breakfast and meet me in the gym," he smiled.

"Where is that?" I asked. This place was huge, but it didn't have any signs.

"Take a left out of here, right at the theatre and straight down to the end," he told me like it was the simplest thing ever. "We keep meaning to put signs, but we don't usually get visitors who don't already know their way around," he explained.

"I'm sure I'll figure it out."

I FINISHED my breakfast and went to the room where I had left my bag to change into shorts and a t-shirt. I tied my hair up into a ponytail and tried to retrace my steps back to the kitchen, then from there to the gym. The 'theatre' looked like the inside of a movie theatre, with about fifty seats. I was surprised to find the gym had at least a dozen exercise machines, and a section with every weight imaginable. The machines looked like they had never been used before, while the heavier weights had the most wear and tear on them.

"Over here." Caleb poked his head through a door behind the row of treadmills.

The room he was in had a boxing ring and punching bags, but it looked like everything came from the 1920s, when you would sew your bag back together rather than using duct tape.

"This came with the building?" I teased.

"It used to have mats for wrestling, which was pointless because we were never two people. A week into my first time as Guardian I had Etta come join me with my stuff."

"And it stays here?"

"Etta was more than happy to get rid of the dusty old bags."

"She sounds..."

"She's amazing. I just like to pretend complain about her,"

he assured me. "You can take Etta's wraps and gloves." He nodded to a pile of thick strings and well-worn pink gloves.

"Wraps?" I asked, totally clueless.

"Let me help you." He smiled to himself before coming over and taking one of the thick strings. He put a tiny loop from the end of it onto one of my thumbs, then proceeded to wrap the rest of the material around my hand and wrist.

"Wraps. I get it," I told him.

"Everyone has to start somewhere. You're way ahead of everyone who sits on their couch and doesn't try anything," he pointed out.

"You're very glass half-full, aren't you?"

"Eternal optimist," he agreed. "I know that bad stuff happens, but I've been lucky overall. And Dale had a point. When you act enthusiastic, or happy, you can't help but be."

"I like it," I assured him, wondering if he had only read the book, or had actual conversations with Dale Carnegie.

HIS FIRST LESSON consisted of showing me the proper stance for boxing. He placed my feet shoulder width apart, then had me jump a few times to figure out my left is my dominant side. At least for balance and boxing. I brought my right leg back, then Caleb nudged me a few times, with increasing strength, to make sure my base was strong. It was only then that we moved on to my arms, which needed to be high enough to defend my face, but not close enough to get punched into it...it was a lot to remember just to be able to look the part.

"Your feet," Caleb called me on my stance while he taught me how to jab.

"I seriously doubt my footwork will give him pause," I argued.

"You won't knock him out with it," he agreed. "But the

stance was made for a reason. It's to help you move and pivot and…" as he spoke, he gave a demonstration, punching into thin air, but he looked fierce and powerful doing it. Graceful even, when he pivoted on the right hook.

"Don't worry, Cash didn't get it the first time either."

"You taught her too?" I asked.

"Her?" he was confused. "Oh, Cassie."

"Who were you talking about?"

"Cassius."

"Clay?" I knew enough about boxing to know Muhammad Ali's real name.

"He was a sweet kid," he agreed.

"You trained him?" It made sense that if you lived for centuries you met a lot of cool people, but there was a lot of subtle name dropping going on.

"Of course not. I trained at his gym for a couple of years when we settled down in Louisville. He would use me as a training partner sometimes."

"You guys should all write books about all of your adventures."

"No one would believe it," he waved me off.

"Fiction, obviously."

"Fiction has to make sense. Reality is the one that doesn't," he told me.

"I'm thinking you don't read a lot of fiction," I argued.

"I'm thinking you're stalling," he called me on it.

WE STAYED in the boxing room until 2 o'clock, when the watch on his wrist flashed with a fireworks display. He went off to his room and I went upstairs to the outside world.

It was weird being on an island with no one else, especially when it didn't look abandoned. I figured I would rather get lost looking for them up here where I could always find the lighthouse, than down below where I could wander for days before being found.

I spotted the chicken coop Caleb mentioned, as well as some cows grazing by the woods, before finally encountering another human being. Embry was jogging on the sandy beach at the other end of the island.

"Have a good lesson?" he took out an earbud and asked me.

"It was practically a two-hour lunge, so my legs will hate me tomorrow, but it was a lot of fun," I agreed.

"It's hard not to follow along whenever he gets excited about something," he understood.

"Did you meet him through Cassie?" I asked.

"No, I fought with him in the Texas Revolution. But she introduced me to Etta," he shared.

"Do you box?" I asked. I knew he could shoot, play sports and run a lot faster than me, though nowhere near as fast as Gabriel, but I didn't know what his other skills were.

"Caleb taught me, so we do spar sometimes, for fun, but I prefer kickboxing and he gets insulted by that."

"Can you teach me the kicking part once I figure out the boxing?"

"I'm not a teacher but we can take a class sometime," he smiled, as if my new interest in martial arts confused him.

"I'm not gifted, so I need to have something to not feel so useless," I explained.

"Luce," he reproached me for being hard on myself.

"No, Embry, I have lots of talents. I know I'm book smart. But if this big scary guy shows up, I have nothing. I either run and hide or stand frozen like a deer in headlights and neither of those sound appealing." I thought of the plantation and what would have happened if the house hadn't attacked.

"It's not like you can defeat him in a boxing match," he said delicately.

"I said I didn't want to *feel* useless," I got him to laugh. "And I know we don't stand a chance against him, but maybe I can defend myself from someone he takes over to try and get to me."

"I'll see what I can do," he assured me.

THAT NIGHT, Embry made us Spaghetti e Olio to go with the seared scallops Caleb prepared. The guys paired it with a nice wine, but I didn't join them, although I doubt any of them would have stopped me for being underage. I figured one of us should be sober and alert if ever the Big Bad managed to find us.

WE GOT into a new pattern on Caleb's island, where I would spend my morning boxing with Caleb, then have a quick lunch before Embry or Gabriel, or both of them, would teach me simple self-defense.

"What about S.I.N.G.?" I asked Gabriel during his first solo lesson.

"I don't think your singing is terrible enough to send him away," he teased, so I pretended to be offended.

"I mean from Miss Congeniality."

"I have no idea what that is."

"Here, try to grab me from behind," I told him.

"I haven't taught you how to defend yourself from that."

"I won't hurt you for real, I promise," I said, which he possibly felt attacked by, because he obliged.

"I grab you from behind and…"

"Solar plexus, instep, nose, groin!" I showed him the steps and yelled them out at the same time. "Would that work in real life?" I asked, smiling at the absolute shock on his face.

"That's from a beauty pageant?" he asked.

"A movie about a beauty pageant," I agreed.

"Life isn't a movie Lucy. The force you would need to elbow me with, the chances of you inflicting any pain in my foot through my boots..." he shook his head. "If you manage to break my nose you'd have a tiny window to maybe get the groin, but..."

"I'm sorry. It was just an idea."

"It's great that you want to defend yourself. I'm glad you're taking this seriously. But he isn't a drunk guy at a bar who won't take no for an answer," he said more gently.

"I get that," I assured him. "Are you saying it's pointless and I shouldn't do anything?"

"No, you should never be complacent, or powerless in your own life. I want you to be confident and know how to defend yourself. But I never want you to argue when we tell you to run, or to hide. No matter how well-trained you are, these aren't fair fights and I can't lose you." His eyes were as intense as I had ever seen them.

"I'm not delusional."

"Okay." He picked up one of the pads Caleb had lent us. "Let's try some krav maga."

CHAPTER TWENTY

On the fourth day, after Caleb's boxing workout, he brought me to the kitchen for a cooking lesson.

"Croque-Monsieur?" I verified after he told me what we were going to make.

"The key to a man's heart is through his stomach. This gives you the stomach," he agreed.

"Maybe a man should be cooking his way into *my* heart." I resented the implication that my goal in life should be to find a man to marry me, then remembered that he was from that time period, even if he didn't look it.

"Etta loves fancy French things. Or simple things that are fancy because they're French. She grew up with a bit of Paris-envy." I thought he was ignoring my comment, but then he said, "And he does need to woo you, and be worthy, and you should have an equal partnership, but on his birthday, or times when he's amazing and you want to let him know you appreciate him, this is a meal that can do that."

"I was mostly teasing. You're incredibly old, so you can't help it," I assured him with a smile.

"You're right, I am very old," he agreed. "But I have also been a huge feminist for over a century."

"To impress Etta?" I asked, sensing a trend.

"Because society was implying that she didn't have the same rights as me. That she was somehow less than human," he said like he found the entire concept unfathomable.

"I'm sorry," I apologized for my assumptions.

"She likes to call me her giant teddy bear. I'm big and strong, but I'm a bleeding heart. We went to marches and demonstrations, but if we weren't Gifted, she never would have lived to see any of the things we fought for come true."

"She sounds incredible," I gave him a smile.

"You think I'm biased, but she's amazing. She's stronger than me in every way but physical. She's fierce and vulnerable and caring...she's perfect."

"Why do you come here to be the guardian then?" I asked.

"I figure a year every couple of centuries is enough to make her miss me," he smiled.

"I hope I get what you have someday," I told him.

"I hope everyone does," he agreed. "Now are you ready to learn?"

"Yes, chef." I gave him a salute and got a nod in return.

"Two pieces of bread, ham, butter and cheese," he told me the ingredients while whisking away in a frying pan.

"What are you making?" I asked.

"Béchamel sauce. It's butter and flour, a little milk, then some mustard and nutmeg to be fancy," he said while combining the ingredients.

"Is this a ploy so I can make it for you every day as a thank you for the boxing lessons?"

"This is out of the kindness of my heart. If you feel so inclined to practice on the daily, that's your prerogative," he played innocent.

"I see." I looked at him skeptically while he finished making his sauce.

WE PUT the béchamel sauce on the first slice of bread, then we layered it with cheese, ham, cheese, another slice of bread, more cheese, ham and topped with cheese.

"This is really decadent," I said while he put them in the oven for all the cheese to melt.

"I told you. Simple, fancy, French," he put words together that didn't form a sentence, but I completely understood.

WE STAYED in the kitchen to make sure we didn't burn them, then went outside to eat them on the Adirondack chairs out front.

"The view is gorgeous," I said of the island, biting into my Croque-Monsieur. "And this is delicious."

"Why thank you," he said with a head tilt and a smile.

"You guys lived in Paris?" I asked.

"We've lived all over."

"What's your favorite place in the entire world?" I thought of all the magical places he could name.

"Wherever Etta is," he smiled. I should have expected it.

"If she was with you wherever you went," I amended.

"Texas," he said after a while.

"Really? I've heard Europe is gorgeous, Iceland looks amazing...what does Texas have?" I asked.

"Nothing anymore." He took a bite that encompassed at least half of his sandwich. "It's where I'm from. They say home is where the heart is, and Etta is my heart, but Texas is my home. If I go back, I know none of them are there anymore, but it's where I feel closest to my mom and my sisters and brothers..."

"I get it," I assured him. My whole life, I wanted to travel and see the world, especially since I was always confined to the manor, but the more time I was spending away from it, the more I missed the rooms and hallways that smelled like home.

"What are we talking about?" Embry asked, coming out with one of the Croque-Monsieurs we had left on the counter for him and Gabriel.

"Home," I shared. "Yours would be Italy?" I guessed.

"Italy is home," he agreed.

"But that wasn't your first thought," I called him on it. "Boston?" I asked.

"That is where you are," he smiled.

"Where is your favorite place in the world?" I asked, rolling my eyes at his answer.

"Anywhere can feel like home, depending on who is with you," he gave a cop out. "I spent so long speaking of Italy like it was the home I lost, that I didn't realize home had changed until it was the Boston from my childhood, or a villa in New Orleans that I missed."

"You don't realize what you have until it's gone." Gabriel stepped out as well, so the four of us sat in Adirondack chairs eating fancy grilled cheeses.

"I know exactly what I have," Caleb assured them.

"Not if you're sitting here with us you don't," Embry argued.

"Or I also know what's at stake."

"Are there a lot of Gifted who are hunting other Gifted?" I asked, figuring my life wasn't the only thing at stake.

"Not a lot, considering how many of us there are, but enough to warrant places like this," Caleb told me.

"Not all of them are hunted by other Gifted. When you look twenty-three and your driver's license says you should be eighty-six, people start by assuming it's a forgery, but eventually they take notice," Embry added.

"This is like an FBI/CIA hideout too?" I asked.

"Law enforcement have been an issue," Caleb glanced at Gabriel, who did not look happy.

"But scientists and armies are usually the bigger concern. Subjects that don't die are exactly what mad scientists and ruthless generals want to study and replicate," Embry sent a shiver down my spine.

"Have any of you been caught?"

"I have my doubts about Area 51." I could tell Caleb was teasing to lighten the mood, because he smiled instead of looking worried.

"No one I've known has been caught and tested against their will for longer than a night or two, but we've had doctors we trust run every test in the book and medically, there is nothing wrong with us," Embry told me.

"It's like we're frozen in time," Gabriel shrugged. "We don't age, and we heal back to however we were before we first died."

"What happens if you accomplish your—"

Before I finished my question, an alarm went off inside the lighthouse, as well as on Caleb's watch. "What does red mean?" I changed my question, knowing red lights weren't good.

"This doesn't make sense." Caleb stood and looked around as if he expected and army to rush at us from every direction.

"Which part?" I asked.

"We have different colors for different warnings. Blue when someone enters the airspace, green if a boat is nearby. Yellow means a threat is attempting to breach, like when we were coming through the rocks and the coral with the abandoned ships," Embry explained to me while we went underneath the lighthouse.

"Red means they're already here?" I guessed.

"It means they've made it past all of the defenses and breached the final perimeter," Caleb explained.

"The electric wooden fence?" I asked, remembering how he had to turn it off for us to come in.

"Exactly."

"What happened to the other alarms?" I asked, thinking we missed a few.

"They can be turned off, like if I know a cruise ship is going by or an air show is coming up and I don't want to be bothered. They were on when I checked last night, but lower level alarms are something you could disable by hacking into the computer system."

"He hacked us?" I asked.

"It's a high-level encryption, especially remotely. I assume he got someone who knew the codes."

"You don't change them?"

"We do, but the Gifted can always find them so they can get help," they implied that the Big Bad was using one of the people who knew the access codes. Or that someone switched sides.

"Red can't be disabled though. Every time a new person sets foot on the island you need to manually turn it off with the current guardian's fingerprint, or the alarms go off," Caleb explained why we got at least that much warning.

"How long will this hold?" I asked of our underground haven.

"Against nuclear attacks or human enemies, we can stay months or even years until we run out of food and water," Caleb said proudly.

"But against a Gifted who knows how to get in?" I asked of our current situation and got nothing in return. "How long do we have?" I asked again, knowing that them not answering meant things were bad.

"It depends on what they want and who they have with them. We have six sections down here and each one has reinforced steel doors. They can withstand an explosion, so we can hide you at least three doors deep and—"

"If the Big Bad is up on the island with his magic and an army of Gifteds, and what he wants is me?" I cut him off.

"We're not going to wait here long enough to find out how long we have," Embry told me. "We're leaving."

"How do we do that?" I asked as the alarms got louder. As far as I could tell, the only entrance on the island to get down here was in the lighthouse, which wouldn't take long to breach.

"There's an escape in the theater. The tunnels are tight, but it will bring you to the buoy," Caleb shared.

"The one with the rowboat?" I asked.

"Exactly," Embry tried to be reassuring, which worked as long as his attention was on me, rather than figuring out our next move with Gabriel.

No one but me seemed concerned with us escaping via rowboat after we barely survived coming here with a much sturdier vessel. "Won't they know about the escape? Or see us rowing away?"

"Only guardians know about the escape and only people who have used it would know where the escape ends up. A lot of tunnels leave from different rooms and let out at different locations," Caleb sounded sure of himself, but it had to be for my benefit. "And we can use a distraction to make sure they're not looking at the water while you row away."

"Any more fertilizer?" Embry turned to me with a smile.

"I happen to be a life-size distraction, so I'll go give them the guardian schpeel while you leave by the theater. Hopefully I can give you enough time that they won't be able to catch up," Caleb decided.

"I don't like this plan," I voiced.

"You don't have a choice," he told me.

"They'll kill you," I pointed out. They kept saying I wasn't taking this seriously, but Caleb was about to face them on his own to cause a diversion.

"I have a few tricks up my sleeve," he winked at me before turning to Embry. "I've got this," he assured him, leading to a long look between the two, which ended with Embry nodding.

"Have you accomplished your purpose?" I asked Caleb. It might be naïve, but with my limited knowledge of the Gifted, as long as he hadn't done what he was meant to do, he could lose his powers or gain new ones, but he wouldn't die.

"I don't think so." He was honest, but it didn't reassure me.

"You heard him, let's go," Embry ordered before I could comment on the admission. I looked to Caleb, horrified, but he nodded in a way that told me to leave, so I did.

At first, I thought Caleb was exaggerating. The tunnels behind the screen of the movie theater were big enough for the three of us to crawl through comfortably, with Gabriel leading and Embry tying the rear. Eventually though, they got smaller. Much smaller. I took off my backpack and had to keep my body flat and pull myself along, wiggling through, but unable to stay on my knees. I was having trouble, so I could only imagine how hard it was for them.

The alarms turned off suddenly, which I feared meant we lost Caleb. It took what felt like hours after that before I saw the light at the end of the tunnel. The buoy was hollow, and while it looked like it was floating from the outside, it was held in place by the tunnel it was attached to. I had to roll my body onto my back so that I could hoist my upper body through, then stand inside the buoy, which was wider than usual. I put my hands on the top of the rim and jumped up, like you do on a pool ledge. Gabriel was on the other side, in the rowboat, to help me over.

I could see the island off in the distance, but we were on the other side of the forest. Other than the lookouts, who were facing away from us, no one could see our tiny boat. They had me lie down on the bottom and covered me with a blanket before Embry rowed us further and further away from what was supposed to be a safe haven.

CHAPTER TWENTY-ONE

We took the rowboat in the opposite direction we had come from, and I completely rethought my theory about being more comfortable in smaller boats. The open air was nice, but the small boat rocked and added a deep element of fear to the queasiness I felt on our first ship. Once they let me out from the blanket, Gabriel suggested I focus on a point in the distance that wasn't moving. Unfortunately, watching the island go up in flames brought on a lot more uneasiness than relief. Can a Gifted come back to life after their body is eaten by fire?

By nightfall, all I could see was a tiny speck in the distance, that I assumed was the island in flames, but it could have been anything. I gave up on asking the guys where we were going, or if Caleb was okay. The consensus was that they knew absolutely nothing about our next move. We traveled mostly in silence, with directions the only thing that broke it. Gabriel took over rowing for a while, then they switched a few times before we let ourselves float. I felt like this was a terrible idea, letting the water take us wherever it wanted to, but they both pretended they had a plan and knew what they were doing.

IT WAS dawn by the time our rowboat hit sand, waking me with a tiny thud.

"Where are we?" I asked, trying to get my bearings.

"I was aiming for Mexico, but it could also be Cuba," Embry shrugged. It didn't matter where we were, as long as it wasn't where the Big Bad was.

"And where do we go from Mexico-slash-Cuba?"

"We need to keep moving," Gabriel said simply. I hoped he was right about the Big Bad giving up after a few months. For many other reasons, but I would not be able to spend the rest of my life on boats.

"Towards Italy? Or towards a cave in the middle of the amazon?" I tried to figure out what my life was going to look like for the next little while.

"Off the grid, but safe," Embry told me. "We will stay in remote places and travel under the radar, but we will also try to bring you to friends and find bunkers where we can keep you safe."

"Until they burn the island to the ground," I pointed out.

"You're the only person who didn't have an opportunity to not be a part of this," Gabriel reminded me.

"What happens if Sam and Deanna need help? How can they contact us if we're off the grid?"

"You're forgetting that we were around long before cell phones and the internet. If Sam needs our help, we've taught him ways that he can reach out. Even if we're off the grid and don't see it, someone will, and someone will help him," Embry reassured me, either through his confidence, or his Gift.

"Today is a beach day then?" I made an attempt to lighten the mood, to show him I was okay.

"No, today is a hiking adventure through beautiful scenery with wildlife all around us," Embry sold it like a super fun excursion to unsuspecting tourists.

"Let's go," Gabe was all business, heading straight for the line of trees that bordered the beautiful, abandoned beach we shipwrecked onto.

"Aye, aye, captain," I sighed before following him. Embry was right about it being absolutely beautiful. I would have loved to go on an adventure vacation last year, but now that it was a rushed and intense trek through wilderness to hopefully avoid the army that was trying to kill me, it wasn't all it was cracked up to be.

FOR THE FIRST HOUR, we had no trail to speak of. It took forever to advance even a little bit, because Gabriel and Embry had to move the overrun vines or help me climb over fallen trees. Eventually we came across an abandoned hiking trail that hadn't been cleared in a while, but at least I could tell where we were going. Fallen trees became an obstacle to get over, rather than the norm.

"I don't want to ask how much longer, but..." I asked after my stomach made a growl that could rival a lion's roar.

"But we haven't eaten since the grilled cheese yesterday," Embry let me know he understood.

"Normally when people say something was so good that they don't have to eat for the rest of the week, they don't mean it literally."

"You can eat the nuts," Gabriel said of one of the trees we had passed.

"How many lives would you bet on that?" I asked. The tiniest of smiles cracked through Gabriel's serious façade.

"If memory serves we're an hour from a little farming town. We can get something there," he softened.

"You've been here before?" I asked before the trees opened up to reveal a gigantic waterfall.

"One of Caleb and Etta's many weddings," Embry smiled at my expression.

"It's beautiful," I remarked, taking it all in.

"Beautiful enough to make you forget—"

"Still hungry," I cut him off without taking my eyes off the view. "But if we're going to take a break, this place is perfect."

"Maybe a few minutes to get organized," Gabriel gave in, removing his backpack and pulling out something thin and pointy.

"Do you think someone will be waiting in the small farming town?" A shiver ran through me.

"Of course not, they would have no way of knowing where we ended up."

"So that's just in case?" I asked, nodding my head to his weapon.

"In case someone happens to be in town on vacation, or the villagers don't take too kindly to strangers, or if there's a wild animal. Lots of variables." Gabriel was either trying to reassure me, or to remind me that the world at large could be dangerous even if you weren't on the run.

"It's just a precaution, but it's better to be safe than sorry." Embry put his hand on my arm and I couldn't help but relax.

"I hate that you can do that," I said, smiling in spite of myself.

"Even if I tried not to use my Gift, I would still be trying to make you smile," he explained why it was nearly impossible for him to turn it off with me.

"I guess there are worse things than having someone who wants to see you happy," I conceded.

. . .

WE WERE able to stay a few more minutes at the waterfall before we continued our hike, encountering some monkeys along the way, before finally meeting our first human.

"Hola," I told the little boy from behind Embry and Gabriel, who each had their arms out to protect me from the child. "Estas solo?" I had been waiting years to put what I learnt in Spanish class to good use.

The boy, who looked to be about six, stared at me, making no effort to communicate, or to get back to whatever it was he was doing on the path.

"Do you know another dialect he might understand?" I asked Embry.

"He understood," Embry assured me, looking distrustfully at the boy, who pulled out what I thought was a toy, but saw was a gun just before Gabriel pounced.

He used his speed rather than force, removing the bullets and emptying the chamber while the boy looked on in wonder.

"Superman?" he asked with a heavy accent.

"Not even close," Gabriel said before carrying the boy over to one of the thicker trees and tying him to it.

"I'm sensing this isn't a quiet, friendly, farming town," I confronted them.

"It is. But there's also a cocaine farm on its outskirts, the kind that is heavily guarded, illegal, and will shoot witnesses rather than finding out why you're on their property."

"Even little kids?" I asked. The boy was barely older than Clara.

"Sometimes," he said simply before we kept moving.

EVENTUALLY WE MADE it to a clearing with tall grass and tiny houses in the distance. At least a dozen men worked the field, but not a single one of them approached us or reacted in any way when we walked past them to get to the closest house. We stayed along the forest line, in case we had to retreat.

"You've got this?" Gabriel asked Embry once we found cover.

"You know the drill," he agreed, giving me a smile before walking off, as Gabriel put out his arm to hold me back.

"What's the drill?" I asked him.

"He's going to ask if we can borrow a truck or buy passage to the border."

"And if he says no?"

"We run."

"Gabriel." I didn't find it funny, but he wasn't laughing.

"Embry is highly trained, and he knows how to control the room."

"I'm not sure how helpful it'll be to make them happy and calm," I argued.

"People don't usually want to shoot you when they're calm and happy, but those aren't the only emotions he can summon."

"Is he going to make them love him?" I realized that would be a way to buy him time to escape, but it also made me rethink my relationship with Embry.

"Love doesn't work like that. We can't make someone feel it, or take it away. Even Etta can heal anything, but she can't mend a broken heart."

"Interesting." I liked the idea that the Gifted had limits to what they could do.

"Embry uses his Gift to make people happier whenever he can, but he can also use it to make them feel small, helpless, depressed, suicidal...you can fight it if you know it's coming, but if you suspect nothing..." he let the thought linger, but shook himself out of it when he saw my face. "He usually convinces people with words and a smile," he assured me.

. . .

I was stressed out and staring at the house for another five minutes before Embry came out with a smile on his face, giving us the thumbs up.

"A car?" Gabriel asked.

"Horses?" I saw a bunch of them galloping in the distance.

Embry shook his head for both of our guesses. "Oscar can take us as far as Albuquerque, but if we get stopped at the border, he'll pretend he doesn't know us."

"I have my passport." I reached into my backpack to try and find it. This would be my first chance to use it since I convinced Sam to let me have one. And to renew it when it expired. All without ever leaving Massachusetts.

"We won't be needing it," Embry shook his head. "And if we did, we wouldn't use yours."

"Right. Under the radar."

"Way under," he agreed.

"I thought you were joking," I looked over to Embry, involuntarily jumping when the rooster beside me pecked at my head. Embry had talked our way onto the back of an old pickup truck, filled with hay and poultry, covered with a grey tarp.

"I thought they'd be in cages," Embry apologized. "You get used to it."

"Do you do this often?" I leaned as far away from the rooster as I could without exposing myself to the chicken on my other side.

"Once with Cassie," Gabriel surprised me when he spoke up, a fond smile on his face.

"And once before it all began," Embry added.

"Before what began?" I asked.

"Before she left," Embry said simply. "When my biggest concern was finding someone my father approved of, and we all knew Gabe and Annabelle were going to get married and live happily ever after."

"My bachelor party," Gabriel said like he had completely forgotten up to that point.

"You guys traveled like this voluntarily?" I raised an eyebrow at them.

"We mistakenly trusted John, my older brother, to be the sober and responsible one," Embry explained. "Halfway through the night he decided we were having a lot more fun than he was, so he joined in."

"And the chicken truck came in…"

"We left the local watering hole and each stumbled towards home, but Embry and I took a nap on the way. We hit the hay," Gabe recalled. I couldn't help but smile at the way they were both remembering a time when they were happy and the best of friends.

"We woke up in a neighboring town, to a surprisingly unhappy friend of my father's," Embry shared.

"He was friendly when I offered him the rest of my ale," Gabe shrugged with the hint of a smile.

"I'm sure," I smiled, picturing it with difficulty. Gabe never let loose, so I couldn't imagine him pass-out drunk and making a joke.

"How did you get back?"

"We helped him deliver the rest of his eggs, then we convinced him to drop us off at home."

"Embry was the best at getting you out of trouble," Gabriel smiled. "I wish you'd been at dinner when I explained to Belle what happened."

"She was upset?" I asked.

"We'd had plans for the afternoon and I showed up smelling like chicken and manure," Gabriel said before he caught himself, realizing he'd shared too much.

"I bet she forgave you." I wasn't sure where it came from. I didn't know much about her, but I could see Gabriel pulling away, and I wanted him to talk about her. About a time when no one was special or in danger and they were just young and in love. Or, in Embry's case, trying to find love.

"It took tea with her aunt as well as letting her father give me a tour of the gardens," Gabriel confirmed my suspicions.

"I thought her gardens were the talk of the town?" I asked, remembering her memory.

"They were, the first hundred times we saw them. After growing up in them and having to give the tour a million times, to every new person who came to see them, we sort of got tired of them," Embry explained.

"Mr. Owens never tired of them. He loved explaining how the garden was enough to sustain them, and it represented his family, and they brought some of the plants with them from England… Annabelle usually saved me from the tour, but that night she did not."

"Well, you deserved it," I sided with her.

"I deserved a lot worse," he agreed.

"At least you got a couple of decades of fun before thirty-five or so miserable ones."

"They weren't all miserable," Embry argued, looking to Gabriel to back him up.

"We had a few good ones," he agreed, somewhat reluctantly.

"A year every other decade?" I asked.

"Most people are miserable," Gabriel shrugged.

"So being semi-immortal is more of a curse than a gift?" I asked.

"Yes," Gabriel agreed while Embry said, "No."

"Sometimes," Embry relented.

"No one wants to live forever alone," Gabriel said simply.

"I'm sorry," I apologized.

"It's not your fault," Embry assured me.

"Some things are worth it," Gabriel added.

"Like getting to meet you," Embry teased.

"That's really sad if I'm the highlight of your last three centuries," I laughed at how pathetic that would be, which got Embry to join in, and Gabriel, after trying to get us to quiet down.

"I'm glad I met you too," I said. "Not only because I'd be dead without you, but I'm glad we were friends before all of this happened."

"Me too," Embry agreed.

CHAPTER TWENTY-TWO

After what felt like weeks in the chicken coop, driving through the middle of nowhere, we made it to Albuquerque. The most eventful part of our border crossing was when the immigration officer asked Oscar if he was okay. He was sweating bullets, so the officer proceeded to offer him some water instead of investigating the back. I suspected it had more to do with Embry's Gift than the officer's good-heartedness, but Oscar was impressed. He let us off at a truck stop where we got ourselves some food, then continued our journey on foot.

When it got dark, we stopped at the most rundown, disgusting, rent-by-the-hour motel I had ever seen. If this were a movie, I would be yelling at the screen for the characters to get back in their cars and turn around. It was the kind of place only serial killers and psychopaths would stay at. On second thought, the psycho would probably kill their victims, dissolve the bodies in the bathtub and then drive off to sleep somewhere more inviting.

The three of us went together to the front desk to check in, but it would have been safer for me to wait outside, alone. If I still had hopes of it having cable or a swimming pool, they vanished when I saw that the front desk hadn't been touched by anything but dust since the eighties. The carpet was orange shag, the walls had lime green wallpaper, and there was even a lava lamp in the corner.

"Can we have a room please?" Embry asked the old woman who was sitting behind the counter on a Chesterfield. She was about 300 pounds, noisily chewing her pink bubble gum, and looked about as happy to be there as Gabriel did.

She gave us a once over before asking, "King bed?"

The way she raised her eyebrow with the hint of a smile almost made me sick.

"Two beds and a cot," Embry specified, as pleasant as ever, while Gabriel inched closer to me.

"If you say so," she lost all interest in us. "No cots, so one of you can take the floor."

We got an actual key for the door, and wouldn't have been able to pay with a credit card even if we had wanted to. Her registry was paper, and she saw nothing wrong with Embry saying his name was Cesare Borgia.

"Do you think the Big Bad is busy checking hotel registries and credit card statements? Would he ever know if we paid cash to stay at a hotel that didn't have bed bugs?" I imagined the Big Bad as an ancient, demon-like guy in a travelling cloak who was baffled by computers and possibly even electricity. If he could rule ancient magic, I was going to remove his current technology, at least in my mind.

"We might be old, but we still adapt. If the two of us have been able to figure it out, he will too," Embry warned, not wanting me to underestimate my foe. We unlocked the door and got into the musty room that while relatively clean, hadn't been used in the past ten years or so. I would be amazed if the television even turned on. It was one of those huge boxes with a tiny screen, and a knob that you had to get up and physically turn in order to change the channel. Even Embry, who had been around long before the invention of television, was eying it with apprehension.

"Rock, paper, scissors?" I suggested as a way of determining who would get a bed and who had to sleep on the floor. I wasn't sure which option was preferable.

"Are we vying for the bed bugs or the blood-stained carpet?" Embry was hopefully just trying to get a rise out of me, but it worked as I rushed over and turned on the lamp to see if the ground truly had blood stains.

"Maybe we can pitch a tent in the parking lot. If anybody miraculously figures out that we're here, they'll barge into the motel room and we can drive off in their car. Safe and sound with clean seats and air fresheners," I offered. Embry nodded, still looking to the stained carpet between the two beds, but Gabriel had a horrible look on his face.

"Gabe?" I asked, wondering if he had discovered a dead body. It wouldn't surprise me at this point.

"I'm with her." Embry turned to face Gabriel and realized, like I had, that it was something outside the window that was troubling him. Not like the stains were troubling us; he looked scared. Unless it was regret I saw etched onto his face. Either way, I didn't like it.

"They're here," Gabriel told us, remaining calm, but I could see the electricity coursing through his body as he prepared himself for what was to come.

I had less than a second to react before the door behind me burst open, with a man entirely dressed in black barging through it. I was closest, and my hand was still beside the lamp, so I picked it up and smashed it on the top of the intruder's head with all my might. He fell to the floor immediately. I looked over to the guys, childishly expecting praise, but he hadn't been alone.

"Behind us, now," Gabriel yelled as Embry took my arm and placed me in the corner of the room, so anyone would have to go through them to get to me. It also meant that I had nowhere to go if ever that happened.

LUCKILY, the men and women who barged in had no weapons, or at least they didn't have time to take them out before Embry or Gabriel overpowered them. They were all dressed like civilians, and their hand to hand combat was mediocre at best, which made me think they were being controlled rather than voluntarily trying to kill me. I knew it was an arbitrary system, that evil people could be dressed like normal people, but it was reassuring for me to think that the majority of the Big Bad's army would disappear if someone managed to kill him. One person was easier to fight than an entire army.

I was inching closer to the fighting, wanting to help as I saw my guys growing tired and making mistakes. The steady stream of assailants was never-ending. Before I could attempt to make a difference, a chilling voice called out from the middle of the parking lot.

"Stop!" it called, making the hairs on the back of my neck rise. Even scarier than his voice was how every single member of his army froze without question. Whether they were hunting me by choice or being controlled, they were terrifying.

CHAPTER TWENTY-THREE

Embry and Gabriel waited expectantly for the fight to resume, but when it didn't they turned to the window, to see where the voice came from. They both looked straight at me, horrified.

I made my way over to see what they were seeing, then ran for the door half a second after Gabriel's arms wrapped around me. He held me back so that all I could do was scream "Sam!" over and over again, as I tried to fight my way free from Gabriel, as if I could do anything to help Sam.

"Let go of me Gabriel, I have to help him," I argued, fighting and twisting to try and shake him off.

"Do you promise not to go out to him?" he asked, holding on to me as if I weren't moving at all.

"He has Sam." He knew there was no way I would stay in the room while Sam was being held by a man with a knife to his throat.

"Sam's dead if they get you," Embry was delicate, but I wanted them to stop focusing on me and start helping Sam.

"It's Sam," I repeated, giving up the fight. I looked at them pleadingly, so they finally agreed.

"Stay behind us. If you have a chance, run, then find a car and drive," Gabriel let me know not to stay and wait for them if anything happened. His eyes were as intense as I had ever seen them, letting me know that there would be hell to pay if I didn't listen.

"Okay," I said, knowing I could never leave the 3 of them behind. I didn't mind staying out of sight as long as I could listen. I went to get my backpack from the corner and slipped the dagger into my boot.

"I know you're inside, and you see I'm alone. You have no reason not to come out," the man called.

"Lucine Suzanne Owens you stay inside!" I heard Sam use my full name, to show me he was serious. The man chuckled, not at all concerned by his outburst, knowing it wouldn't deter me in the slightest.

Embry and Gabriel looked at me like they would rather I listen to Sam as well, but I stood my ground. Gabriel opened the door and stepped out first, followed by Embry, then me.

The man who held Sam was a couple of inches shorter than my brother's 6 foot 3, with blonde hair slicked down to his head. His eyes were the same color as the men in front of me, but while theirs came off as intense, his were dark and scary hellholes. He smiled at us, making him even more ominous, but it was the knife to Sam's throat that solidified him as a horrible, evil person in my book.

He kept his smile while Embry and Gabriel came into his view, but the look he gave me made my blood curl. I had been the victim of catcalling, and guys looking at me like they wanted to do ungodly things to me, but he looked at me like I was a piece of meat, something to be butchered for the parts and then discarded.

"You must be Lucy," he said, bowing to me. Sam had to go down as well, to prevent his neck getting sliced by the ever-present blade. If his goal had been to show me deference and respect, he failed. All I did was cringe until I saw Sam come back up, unharmed.

"What do you want, Donovan?" Gabriel asked as if he was completely unfazed by the way he was handling Sam. I had hoped knowing the Big Bad's name would make him less scary, but so far it did not help.

"Bypassing the formalities?" Donovan's amused smile made me want to punch him, had I been able to reach him. "You both know what I want. It has been the same for centuries. I want the girl." His look told me that if I gave myself up, I would not be making it out alive, and they would never find what was left of my body. Still, I wouldn't be able to not go to him if the price of keeping me safe was someone I loved.

"Our answer has been the same since you came after Margaret. We will die before we let you have her, and even then, we still won't let that happen," Gabriel said.

"I expected as much. But you brought the girl out with you. Do you think that she will stand back and watch as I slice into her big brother, the man who has been raising her?" Donovan moved the knife so it glistened in the moonlight. Embry took a step back to put his arm on my shoulder, ensuring I wouldn't fall for it and run to my death. "Will you still be able to hold her back when it is his daughter I eviscerate? When I cut every freckle off of that fire-kissed little girl?" Sam's hands were balled into fists, and if the knife hadn't been so close to his jugular, he would have used them.

"I'll lock her in a cell and throw away the key if it means you can't have her." I had expected it to sound like a lie coming from Embry, but he was just as convincing as if Gabriel had been the one saying it. He meant it.

"Will you drain her blood and incinerate her to keep her from me? That is what you did to Cassandra, right? She thought that if she could just get to you, she would be safe. Do you still value the mission more than their lives?" Donovan was playing with the knife, making me incredibly nervous. I wanted to yell at him to stop when I saw a speck of red on Sam's neck, but I also didn't want to remind anyone that I hadn't made a mad dash for the highway yet.

"If necessary." Gabriel's face was stone, and it shocked me that I believed him. I knew Cassandra would have been dead before they did anything to her, but the conviction in his eyes made me realize for the first time that I wasn't their mission. Sure, I was the promise they made, but protecting me might not mean my life so much as whatever it was of mine that this man wanted. I loved them like family and I knew they loved me too…but if I ran out and let the man take me, would they be fighting to save me, or to stop him?

WHETHER BECAUSE HE saw what I was thinking, or to keep me in place, Embry gave my shoulder a squeeze. My first instinct was to shake him off, but I knew that even if they would sacrifice me to stop him, they were still all I had.

"See dear, you think they care about you, but they would slaughter you faster than I would. Come to me so I don't have to kill the boy," Donovan addressed me. I got his logic, but loving and caring about someone wasn't something you could turn off. Which was why I tried to go for Sam, causing both Embry and Gabriel to put themselves in front of me.

"If I can't go to him, what is our plan for saving Sam?" I asked without taking my eyes off of my big brother.

They exchanged a look that implied they had no intentions of letting me turn myself in, or of putting me at risk while they saved Sam.

"We either come up with a plan or you will have to carry me over your shoulder for the rest of this trip," I warned, letting them know that I wasn't kidding either. I just didn't have the same bargaining chips that they did.

"Luce, he knew what he was getting into. We all signed up for this," Embry tried to talk me out of it.

"He didn't. He maybe knew that this was a possibility, but I was dropped into his lap when his parents died. You two chose to love Annabelle, and to dedicate your lives to this, but Sam just feels like he has to take care of the girl he grew up with."

"He made his choice when he agreed to take you," Gabriel said calmly, but I could see the vein pulsing in his forehead.

"If I'm going to die either way, I'd rather it be saving Sam than whatever else you have planned."

"We don't plan on you dying at all," Embry assured me, sensing a slight edge to my voice.

"Feel free to continue talking as if I don't have a knife to his throat, but if the girl isn't walking towards me within the next five minutes, I am slicing until I reach the bone," Donovan sounded more annoyed at the prospect of having to slit Sam's throat than anything that would imply he had some humanity left in him. Assuming he had any to begin with.

"We have five minutes to come up with a plan," I turned to Embry and Gabriel expectantly.

"We have five minutes to get you as far away from here as possible," Embry argued.

"Or we could waste it all debating," Gabriel was exasperated.

"Have the two of you ever taken him on alone? Is it a possibility that while I walk over and he releases Sam, you could fight him and win?" I asked, looking from one to the other. "Wouldn't it keep me safe if while he was dead, we locked him up in a steel box and tossed him to the bottom of the ocean?"

They looked at each other, weighing the situation and

deciding whether or not they had a chance of managing that. Two of his men still hovered a few feet away from us, but I felt like it would be easy enough to get past them. Then it would be my two guys against Donovan, but I got the feeling Donovan was older and more powerful somehow, especially with all of the freaky magic stuff. I took it as a good sign that he hadn't used any of it against us, but the guys were not as optimistic.

"This isn't the entire army. This is just Donovan's scouting crew," Embry said before a bunch of men and women dressed in black showed up. They came from every possible hiding place, surrounding us so that other than barricading ourselves back in the motel room, there was absolutely nowhere we could go. Any hope I'd had of being able to fight Donovan to get Sam back disappeared. We would be lucky if any of us made it out alive, which was an issue, because once I was gone, I was not coming back.

Sam was mouthing for me to run, resigned to his fate, but not only could I not leave him, I didn't have anywhere to go.

"Like Prom," Gabriel told me, reaching for his bag.

I barely had a moment to realize he meant escaping through the bathroom window before they all pulled swords and guns out of nowhere, prepared to fight to the death. I stayed there, frozen in place, before making eye contact with Sam, who once again mouthed that I should run. I reluctantly rushed back into the motel room and locked the door. I was shocked when no one followed me, but one look back through the window showed me Embry and Gabriel wouldn't let them. I grabbed my bag and locked myself in the bathroom, which was a bright pink I attributed to the seventies. The lock on the door might hold if you tried to turn the handle, but one good push or some jiggling would get you in.

The window was right on top of the toilet, so I was able to stand on that to pry it open. It was harder than I expected, due to a layer of rust and mildew, but my arms were used to lifting Clara and had spent hours boxing with Caleb. I threw my bag out into a bush, then hoisted myself through the opening, trying my best not to get tetanus or some other infection from the ledge.

I expected an army in black to be there waiting for me. They were everywhere on the other side, but the woods were completely deserted. I could hear the busy highway, with its constant flow of cars that could take me away. It was what the guys wanted me to do, but I had nowhere to go, and I wouldn't last long without Embry and Gabriel. So, instead of doing the smart thing like I had promised, I spotted a tree I could climb and found cover, just as a woman poked her head out of the bathroom window. I tried to convince myself that she got past Embry and Gabriel because they calculated how much time I needed and knew I would be safe, but I saw how many people they were up against. It was more likely that my line of defense was lying dead in the motel parking lot.

CHAPTER TWENTY-FOUR

Luckily, the woman who came looking for me thought I would have done the smart thing and gone to get help, as opposed to making myself a sitting duck, just waiting to be found. A couple of the guys who followed her walked around the edge of the tree line, but the forest wasn't dense, and the trees weren't thick enough for me to hide behind. I would have been discovered if they had bothered to look up, but they were satisfied that I was gone when they couldn't see me running off in the distance.

I tried to get settled into the branch I was on, wondering how long I should wait before going to check on the guys, when I felt my eyes drooping. All I could think was that this was the worst possible time for this to be happening, before the forest disappeared, and I was someone else…

"I love you truly, truly dear, life with it's sorrow, life with it's tear, fades into dreams when I feel you are near, for I love you truly, truly dear! Ah, love 'tis something, to feel your kind hand…"

Beth sang to the great bulge of her stomach, one hand rubbing it while the other flipped through the pages of an incredibly old volume. Even older than the Chronicles. The pages had turned brown and looked frail, which she reflected by carefully bringing up each page and gently putting it down on the other side. The right pages held incredible amounts of text, the fancy kind that makes it hard to understand with all of the extra legs, but the left had beautiful pictures of people, places and things. There were happy families, smiling men and women, lakes, small towns, great towers... all of them warm and bright.

She was more focused on the child in her womb, that I could feel moving and pressing on my organs, especially my bladder, than on the happy pictures.

*"Ah yes, 'tis something, by your side to stand, gone is the sorrow,
gone doubt and fear, for you love me truly, truly dear!"*

Her singing became distracted when she got into darker images of two towers with smoke billowing out, a giant wave taking over buildings, a forest on fire...

She stopped suddenly when the page revealed nothing more than a crescent moon on the back of a woman's neck. It was completely harmless, but I would have stopped even if she hadn't.

I could feel the words and hear them coming out of my mouth, but I would not have been able to decipher what was written on the page otherwise. "Prophecy of the Crescent Moon," she said before looking around, as if to make sure no one was there.

"The earliest historical account of the Crescent Moon Prophecy was in the fevered rantings of Saint Malachy, shortly before his death in 1148. 'She who is marked by the Crescent Moon brought forth the Coalescence, and the world was bathed in light. It was miraculous to behold such a blessed sight of angels in white.'
The next was from the accounts of Ioanit, trusted historian of Talina and Zeke, who ruled the earthly realm from 1385 to 1460. Though

he did not bear witness to the ritual, he recorded part of the
incantation here:
'From the kindling of Emmanuel's Betrayal
burns the soul of his untouched child.
Let the tears of Isis fuel the flames
in the arms of Yggdrasil.
As the blood of the incumbent quells the fire,
may the heart of the Bearer of the Crescent Moon
originate the Coalescence.'
Without the completion of the ritual, the powers granted through the
Coalescence could not be passed on, so shortly after 1460, they
returned to the source. It is said they lie in wait for the Bearer of the
Crescent Moon, so they may be claimed."

Beth flipped through more pages, then found another book and
looked up 'Bearer of the Crescent Moon'.

"Little is known of the origins of the Bearer of the Crescent Moon in
regard to the Prophecy. Most historians agree that it refers to the
line of Talina and Zeke, who ruled over many tribes for nearly a
century, though some have attempted to create her."

The page was covered in drawings of these attempts, including
knives, fire, actual crescents...The next page was even worse, with
an amateur surgeon listing the steps to remove a heart from some-
one's chest while it is still beating. I wanted to turn away, but Beth
kept reading.
"Mommy?" A tiny voice came from outside the room, making us
jump. A girl, maybe three-years-old, cautiously walked in.
"Helen." Beth's face lit up as she gently closed the book she had
been reading from. I had assumed Beth was pregnant with her
daughter, Helen. As far as I knew, my great-grandmother didn't
have any siblings.
"What are you reading?" the little girl asked, coming close.

"Just some nonsense, love. What have you been up to?"

Helen tried to look at the book once more before giving up and answering the question, "Daddy's making dinner."

"Pasta again?" Beth asked with a smile, like she wanted nothing more.

"The baby's favorite!" Helen said excitedly, putting her hands on our stomach. The baby kicked, and I swore it was like it recognized its big sister and was saying hello.

"You know what the baby really wants right now?" We got up from the chair and brought the little girl out of the room, leaving the old book behind.

"Ice cream?" Helen asked with a smile, sharing what she wanted.

"Maybe after dinner," Beth humored her. "Right now, he would love for you to play the piano and sing for him. Mummies lullabies aren't doing the trick and his soccer match is all over my organs." The way she referred to the baby as a 'he', after my conversation with Caleb, made me think I might know exactly why I never heard about this child, and I felt sick. Part of it was Beth's morning sickness, but a huge part of it was feeling this baby inside me, feeling how much she loved him, and knowing he was never going to grow up.

"Do you know what song he wants?" Helen asked as she took her seat in front of the piano. "Clair de Lune?"

"That would be perfect." Beth took a seat beside the piano and the little girl played and sang us the French folk song. "Au Clair de la Lune, mon ami Pierrot..."

We rubbed the stomach and smiled for the girl, but while this should have been a perfect, happy little moment in time for Beth, who might not know she was cursed, but all I could feel inside her was dread...

I WAS BARELY HANGING on to the tree when I woke up, so opening my eyes gave me the tiniest of jolts and I fell, trying my best to spread out the impact like Sam had instructed when he caught me jumping off the boat shed when I was little.

Hitting the ground knocked the wind out of me, but I was still reeling from the shock of what I had seen.

I was trying to figure out a different way the prophecy could be interpreted when two men, dressed all in black, with eyes as dark as coal, came and stood on either side above me.

"Well, well. Look what we have here. Not so great at hiding, are we?" They both leered down at me.

This was not good.

CHAPTER TWENTY-FIVE

The two men each grabbed one of my arms and half-dragged, half-carried me around to the front of the rundown motel, to where their boss was waiting. As soon as we rounded the corner, I saw that Sam was now being held by a few of Donovan's henchmen. He looked like they might have beat him to find out where I had gone, but I breathed a sigh of relief. He was alive. I took it as an excellent sign that he was standing on his own, even if they had him restrained.

It wasn't until we were about twenty feet away from Sam and Donovan that I had my suspicions about Gabriel and Embry confirmed. To make sure I had no doubts about it, Embry was in a pool of blood. I would have told myself it was someone else's, but I could see that it was coming from the large gash on the side of his head. Gabriel, my last defense before the woman managed to come after me, was lying in the doorway of our motel room. There was an axe on the ground next to his chest, which was covered in red. I had to turn away so I could catch my breath.

"Miss Owens, I am so glad that you finally decided to join us." Donovan came over as his minions let go of me. They stayed on either side, and more of them were all around us, so I knew I had no chance of escaping, even if I had known how to hotwire a car.

"That is the last thing I would ever want to do." I made sure I was standing straight, looking right into the dark holes he used as eyes while I said it. I was doing my best to appear confident, and in control, even though it couldn't be farther from the truth.

"Lost your nerve?" Donovan asked with a smile. "No longer rushing to save poor Sam now that you don't have your lap dogs to keep you safe?"

"I stayed, didn't I?" I pointed out through gritted teeth. His relishing of Embry and Gabriel's deaths upset me more than the way he mocked me.

"That, you did. I am still trying to decide if that was out of bravery or stupidity." He looked me up and down, sizing me up in a way that made my skin crawl. Unlike prom night with Danny Kinks, Donovan didn't have any desire in his eyes.

"You had my people," I explained. As soon as I saw Sam through the window, there was no way I was leaving.

"Stupidity then." My answer bored him. He was talking slow and walking around as if he had all of the time in the world. True, it did look like he had won and no longer had anything to worry about, but I still had a dagger strapped to my ankle, and my guys were going to wake up eventually.

"Or decency," I said it under my breath, but with conviction. He heard, but instead of being offended, he looked back at me with the tiniest of smiles.

"But I digress; I have not called you here to taunt or insult you, my dear. I apologize if I have made you uncomfortable or scared. You'll find I can be a very accommodating host." He was still gauging my personality, figuring out which buttons to press to get what he wanted. Was I hot-tempered? Would threatening me work? Or was his original assumption right, that the easiest way to get me to do what he wanted was to threaten to hurt my family? I had made the answer clear, but he wasn't accepting it.

"Why? Are you planning on entertaining my heartless body after you bleed it dry?" I knew he needed my heart, and chanced a guess at the rest. I got the feeling that my death wouldn't interfere with his plans, but Cassie had thrown herself off a cliff so he wouldn't have access to her dead body. That the guys then burnt. Blood seemed like an ominous equivalent to my 'essence' for an occult ritual.

"Your friends should have told you that vampires don't exist," he smiled at me.

"Then what is it you want to do with me?" I asked. "What do I have to do for you to let Sam go? To leave him and his family alone?" I chanced a glance in Sam's direction. He looked disappointed that I had come back rather than running off to ensure my own safety.

"That's quite simple Lucy; all you have to do is join us."

"Join you?" I knew this was a trap, but him killing me would probably be better than what would happen if I joined him.

"I want you to decide, of your own free will, that you wish to be a part of our organization." He raised his arms and looked around at his followers, who all stood at the ready. I wondered how many of them were here of their own free will.

"I have a lot of trouble believing that all you want is for me to be one of your minions," I argued.

"You would not be a minion. You would have an honored spot at the side of the king," he said as if this were a seductive idea I should be tempted by.

"I would rather die," I said with a courage I was only pretending to feel.

"Of course. Your death would be the first step, but eventually, it would be an incredible reward."

"I would be dead," I reminded him. I had seen horror films with necromancy, and it churned my stomach.

"You are so blinded by your ideals of good and evil that you're not even considering the whole picture," he sighed.

"Then enlighten me. Tell me exactly what I would be getting myself into, so I can make an informed decision as to whether or not I want to willingly join you," I said, partially because I did want to know what he planned to do with me, but also because the more time he spent talking, the closer we got to Embry and Gabriel waking up, and the longer Sam stayed alive. I wasn't naïve enough to think we could talk for the eight hours Gabriel and Embry would need, and I knew help wasn't coming, but I needed to keep him talking long enough to come up with a plan.

"For centuries we have been collecting a variety of items for a ritual. There have been many attempts since the beginning of time, but few of us are still searching. Most of them gave up when they kept trying and failing." He had a gleam in his dark eyes when he mentioned the ritual, and pride when he spoke of the others who gave up while he forged on.

"What makes you think yours will work?" I stalled him.

"We have yet to attempt the ritual, because we are missing a pivotal ingredient." The way he looked at me made me feel extremely uneasy. "You see, over a few centuries, you can collect most of the essential ingredients. Splinters from the cross Jesus of Nazareth was nailed to, soul of a virgin…a lot of religious or supernatural paraphernalia I won't bore you with. The issue comes with the heart of the Bearer of the Crescent Moon," he gave weight to each word, waiting for me to understand his implications.

"You want my heart," I stated. It was the one thing I knew for sure from Beth's memory. He waited, possibly for a reaction, but I didn't know what he wanted me to say. At this point it wasn't my life I was going to plead for. If I died, Donovan's quest ended, and everyone else would be okay. I didn't have a daughter to worry about like Cassandra had.

"Precisely. For centuries, men like us have been branding their slaves, their wives and their children with crescent moons. Some believed it had to be the virgin, some thought an innocent child. Hundreds tried, but none ever succeeded. It was not up to us to brand someone with the Crescent Moon, we had to find the women who already had it."

"Annabelle had it, so you've been tracking her descendants, waiting to get your hands on another one who has her birthmark," I concluded.

"We have everything else," he agreed. It bothered me how he spoke of himself as a collective.

"Then why am I still standing? Shouldn't you be slicing into me and letting Sam go?" I asked. It was cruel to torture me if he was ultimately going to rip my heart out.

"You need to give it willingly," he reminded me.

"Did the virgin willingly give you her soul?" I shot at him. I normally only talked back to Embry and Sam, sometimes Gabriel, because they felt more like friends or older siblings than parents or elders. With Donovan, I figured he was going to kill me anyway, although I didn't like how much he was enjoying it.

"She did, believe it or not. Magic, whether dark or light, has precise nuances. One virgin's soul over another's can make a world of difference in a spell. Combining powerful elements such as those required for this ritual…it takes more than finesse, it can go terribly wrong. A heart given willingly will always be more powerful, and easier to control than one taken by force." His eyes lit up as he spoke, which was extremely hard for them to do. This was his life's work. I was the final element to his masterpiece.

I was going to tell him he could have my heart if he let everyone else go, but I was still hoping we could hold out until Embry and Gabriel came back to life. Then we could defeat the monster and all live to see another day.

"You want me to rule, metaphorically, because my heart will be…what? Your source of power? What does the spell do?" I pressed to keep him talking.

"Everything." The holes he had as eyes grew wide with excitement. "The one who succeeds in completing the ritual will be powerful above all others. You have seen how easily we control those who are like us, those who do not die until their business is done. Once the ritual is completed, we will be able to control the entire planet in that way. Kings, presidents, armies…no one would be immune to obeying our commands. Our power would be unimaginable. We would rule the world."

"And everybody wants to rule the world." I rolled my eyes at how cliché it was. I knew the song and could hypothetically see the attraction, but I would wish for a million other things before ruling the world ever crossed my mind.

"You don't agree?"

"Do you realize how crazy it is that you basically can't die, and instead of taking advantage of the past…I don't know how many hundreds of years, you have been tracking down a line of women and trying to kill them? You could have travelled the world for pleasure, gone to every church and museum in Europe, learnt every language, painted, written novels, read every book ever published…you could have accomplished so much."

"I stay alive so the ritual can be completed. If all I wanted was to write a few poems, I would have died."

"It's not just culture. You could have found someone to love and be happy with, raise a family, instead of becoming this monster hell-bent on killing my family. Isn't it lonely knowing you're killing the only person who isn't under your control?" I knew it was pointless, but if he did have a heart somewhere deep down, it couldn't hurt to try and reach it.

"You're not controlled, but you aren't a willing participant either. That's why I want you to see that we are not entirely evil. When we take over the world, we will have order, and go back to a simpler, less forgiving way of life. Society has become much too tolerant of late. And best of all, we can bring you back, Lucy. True, we need your heart in order to complete the ritual, and you will die. But once it is done and we have all the power, we will be able to bring you back to life. You will be able to rule at our side, a coveted position," he offered as if he were doing me a favor.

Something in the dark way he smiled had me worried. "What exactly is your plan for the rest of the population, once you can control everyone?"

"Those who are useful can join our society and contribute. The weak and the poor, who exist solely as leeches or parasites will be eliminated, as was suggested millenniums ago. We haven't worked out all the details yet, but the gist of it is… anything we want."

I knew better than to expect his new world would be a utopia, even a dysfunctional one. Judging by how he treated me, Sam, and even his minions, I got the impression that not many people would survive his reign, especially not caring, selfless people like Deanna and Sam, or sweet little girls like Clara. I looked to Sam, who was still standing about ten feet from me, with tape on his mouth and his hands tied behind his back. It was determination and irrepressible sadness that he found in my eyes once we made contact. I saw the same emotions in his as he nodded. He knew what I had to do. Even if I willingly gave up my heart, he would still meet the same fate.

"I would be glad to enlighten you further on the ride, but

we must get going. We have a long drive ahead of us." Donovan extended his hand, still expecting me to follow and willingly let him murder me to protect the ones I loved. I would have, if there was even a possibility it would work, and they would get to live happily ever after. But we all knew they wouldn't.

I looked back to Sam and mouthed "I love you," which got a tiny nod, before I used my fingers to count down.

Three...

Two...

One.

When all of my fingers were gone and my hand was in a fist, Sam bopped his head back to knock out the man behind him, who had loosened his grip on the knife. I grabbed my dagger from my boot and planted it a few inches to the right of Donovan's heart. The element of surprise was the only way I managed to get that close. He was fast, and strong, and threw me to the ground with a force that knocked my breath out.

Sam managed to incapacitate two of the men charged with holding him, but more of them took their place. One of them now had his knife dangerously close to Sam's jugular, as Donovan used his boot on my windpipe to pin me to the ground. I tried to push it off, but gravity and biology were on his side.

"I take it this means you won't be coming willingly," Donovan concluded. "That is a shame. For you, at least. The challenge of an uncooperative heart is one we have been expecting since that slut got away," Donovan's voice had taken back its bored quality, except when he referred to Annabelle, my ancestor, as 'that slut'. Pure hatred laced those words, and I feared what he might do to someone who looked exactly like her.

My refusal of his offer and trying to escape disappointed him. Any victory I might have felt from learning that he could still be hurt, that I had hurt him vanished the instant he nodded to the men holding Sam. I barely had time to turn my head before the blood was pouring from Sam's neck and he slowly fell to the ground.

"Sam!" I screamed, rushing to him as soon as Donovan let me go. He knew he had me now, so it didn't matter if I cried from a distance, or leaning over Sam's lifeless body.

I CRUMPLED onto the ground next to my big brother, taking his head into my lap, running my fingers through his carrot top head. He hated the color of it when I was younger, until he met Deanna and found out she liked it. All I had known growing up was my mom, Grams, Mr. & Mrs. Boyd, and Sam. As the warm blood continued to flow from the wound on Sam's neck, onto my jeans, all I could think was that every single one of them was gone now.

The tears poured freely, which blurred my vision, so I didn't notice that the army of men and women that made up Donovan's army had diminished. I looked to Donovan, waiting for him to mock me for crying, or to taunt Sam for being dead, but he was on the ground, right next to where he had been crushing my windpipe.

I couldn't even summon any excitement over my stab costing Donovan one of his unlimited lives. All I wanted to do was lie down beside Sam until he woke up and told me it was all a horrible nightmare and we could go home now. Sam's death would be in vain if I didn't figure out a way to escape before Donovan came back to life, but I didn't have any fight left in me.

ALTHOUGH MOST OF the people who followed Donovan had been under his control, some of them did so by choice. These were the men who now recovered Donovan's body and put it into the large Hummer they had found us with. They could see from my catatonic state that I wasn't going to run or put up a fight, so they let me be. Even if I had tried to escape, it wasn't like I could reach anywhere before the dozen or so of them that remained caught up to me.

I knew I didn't have long, that they weren't forgetting about me, just dealing with more pressing things, but it took everything in me to focus on a plan rather than the crushing pain around my heart. It was like I couldn't breathe, and I was breathing too much, all at the same time.

I needed something to make sure Embry and Gabriel would find me, so they could stop Donovan from using my heart to end the world as we know it. I was relatively certain no one would make an executive decision to kill me until Donovan woke up, so I had a bit of time. Unfortunately, I had no more weapons, and everything I brought was in the backpack Donovan's minions took when they found me at the foot of the tree. Not that I could think of anything in my backpack that could help me. I could see Sam's car keys sticking out of his pocket, but I didn't see the mini-van anywhere. Unless I could find it, get in, start it and drive off before one of the minions could get to me, the keys weren't going to help. The key wasn't even the type that you could use to scratch someone's eyes out or stab them. It was a small, rounded, rectangular shape that you just needed to have in your pocket for the vehicle to let you in. I was reproaching us for buying fancy cars instead of the ones with weapon-like keys, when it hit me.

I made sure no one was watching me, then reached into Sam's pocket to release the standard dealership keychain, the one where he put our Onstar stickers, so we would always have our numbers. I looked around again and saw that they were still huddled around Donovan's body, doing god-knows-what. I threw Sam's keychain as far as I could in Embry's direction, slipping the actual key into my pocket. I breathed a sigh of relief when the keychain landed on Embry's stomach, his shirt muffling the sound. Hopefully, Embry would see it when he woke up and remember how to work the Onstar.

THE MINIONS FINISHED their task and remembered me, so two of them came over and lifted me by the arms when I refused to leave Sam. They pulled me towards the side of the vehicle, both of them dressed like they were in special ops, all in black, with matching cargo pants and side arms. The taller of the two was the muscle, not saying much other than occasional grunts, but the shorter one kept barking orders when the others looked to him for confirmation. He had his brown hair slicked back with way too much gel and was clearly in charge now that Donovan was out of commission. He was about to open the door for me when one of the other men called him over.

"Tie her up while I teach Miguel how to discard," Slick commanded Muscles, who was still holding on to me.

"You could have had it all," Muscles told me, shaking his head like I had torn up the winning lottery ticket. His knots weren't stellar, but they were too tight for me to be able to do anything. He helped me into the backseat, then let me sit alone and wait for another fifteen minutes while they figured out what they were going to do. Or maybe they talked about the weather, because they still didn't know what they were doing when they got into the car. They had me move to the middle seat, with a minion on each side. Muscles took the passenger seat while Slick had the wheel. I saw the other guys following us in another car as we turned to get out of the motel parking lot. All I could do was hope Embry and Gabriel had time to wake up and find me before Donovan came back to life and killed me.

PERHAPS I HAD SEEN TOO many movies, but I was fully prepared to get a burlap sack put on my head and spend the next few hours counting turns and how long we drove so I would be able to escape and find my way back, or help someone find me if I got my hands on a phone. The fact that none of that happened, that they let me know exactly where we were, told me they were either terrible kidnappers, or that no one expected me to be rescued, so they didn't care what I saw or heard.

We drove for hours, making lots of elaborate detours, and sometimes driving in circles. I didn't know if they were worried someone would come and save me, or if they had other enemies they were trying to avoid, but either of those options would give me a chance to escape. The first hour was in almost complete silence, and I would have sworn we had been driving at least three hours if the dashboard clock hadn't let me keep track of time. It wasn't until Muscles turned the radio on that they all loosened up. They talked about past road trips, some with their families, while others had been traveling together for a long time. The driver, who I nick-named Slick, didn't talk much, except to admit that his first road trip with 'the big guy' was before cars even existed. Then they got to teasing each other about how old they were. I tried to listen to everything, just in case one of them would slip and mention something I could use to escape or bribe my way out. The only useful information I got was that Slick was loyal to the mission, but the rest of them were waiting for the riches and the glory that was promised to them as soon as Donovan got what he needed.

CHAPTER TWENTY-SEVEN

After a little more than five hours, we stopped at a gas station of the run-down variety. The machines hadn't been updated in decades, so the pumps had meters with needles instead of display screens. Either because we were on an abandoned road in the middle of nowhere, or because it was so late, the station only had one employee working inside. He looked so engrossed in his cell phone that were they to hold him up for all the cash in the register, he would probably hand it over without looking up. He wasn't going to be the one to save me tonight.

Slick was in charge of filling the tank, Muscles went inside to get snacks and the guy on my left went to the washroom. This left me alone with the guy on my right, who they had called Jim, if I wanted to fight my way out of the car. However, that would also involve me having to outrun Slick once I made it outside. Luckily, the tank was on the left side, which was also where the other vehicle had parked. I was considering whether or not I could hit Jim hard enough to knock him out, when I noticed his leg was shaking, which it hadn't for the rest of the drive.

"I know you guys are going to kill me, so you probably don't care, but I really need to pee, and we are sitting on the same seat," I shared, hoping I hadn't misread the situation.

"You too?" he asked, looking to me and considering it. He was the one who had seemed the least dedicated to the cause in earlier conversations. He was a nervous nail-biter who dreamed of writing the next Great American Novel, but couldn't make it past the prologue before ripping it all to pieces.

I nodded, pleading with him, before he got out of the Hummer and stepped aside so I could follow. I sighed with relief and made sure to look extremely grateful as he helped me get out with my hands still tied behind my back.

"What do you think you're doing?" Slick asked from the other side of the car.

"She's about to pee all over the seat," Jim complained about me, without mentioning that he was about to do the same.

"Be quick," Slick warned before we headed towards the building.

THE RESTROOMS WERE around the side of the station, so Slick and the others wouldn't see what was happening once we rounded the corner.

"Do you think you could untie me?" I asked Jim, playing into the innocent little girl image as much as I could.

"That wouldn't be cool," he shook his head, looking over his shoulder towards the others. He struck me as someone at the bottom of the totem pole.

"It's really awkward with my hands behind my back. Even walking is hard when I have nothing to balance me."

Lucky for me, Jim was more interested in using the men's room than in doing anything inappropriate to me, so he liked the idea of making it easier for me to go in on my own and not take a million years.

"What if your hands were in front?" he offered.

"That would be amazing. Thank you," I told him, swallowing hard, both to show him my fear, and because I was having second thoughts about what I might need to do to get away from him.

He came behind me and was about to untie my hands when he thought better of it. "You can just climb through now," he offered instead of untying and retying my ropes. At least he held onto me, so I could keep my balance while I stepped through the hole my arms made.

I took a look at the building and saw it was unlikely that I would be able to escape through a window while he was outside waiting. For starters, the window couldn't accommodate more than my arm, and Jim was suddenly intent on coming in with me.

"I can use the sink while you…I won't look," he said, and although I believed him about not looking, it was still wrong on so many levels.

Once my hands were in front of me, I pretended to stagger, knowing he would instinctively come closer so I wouldn't fall. As soon as he was within my reach, I put my arms around his head, using the rope pressed against his neck to pull him into me. He struggled, but hanging on the rope gave me leverage, so within a minute or so, he went limp and I let him fall to the ground. In the car, he had mentioned finding prohibition a lot more fun than people would expect, so I was pretty sure I hadn't killed him for good. Not that it made me feel any less like I just murdered someone, nearly with my bare hands.

I heard flushing and remembered that one of the men would be walking out of the restrooms any second now, so without putting much thought into it, I ran off into the field behind the gas station.

. . .

As I got further away, I could hear shouts and running, so I knew they were following me, but I'd had a head start, and the field was overrun with tall grass and corn stalks. My school athletics wouldn't help against someone with Gabriel's speed, and the vegetation wasn't going to keep me covered forever, but I was convinced that if I could make it to the other side of the field, if I could find someone -anyone- then I would get free.

It rained recently, or they had bad irrigation, because there were puddles along the sides of the rows. Some small enough that I could run over without even jumping, while others looked so deep and wide that I considered hiding in one, as an absolute last resort, if they closed in before I reached what sounded like a highway.

I could see the edge of the field in the distance and sped up to reach it, but I tripped on the uneven ground and fell. Luckily, I managed to put my bound hands out to break my fall, but I still landed with most of my upper body in a puddle.

I tried to use my elbows and feet to push myself off the ground, but my ankle did not appreciate the weight I put on it. I paused and took a deep breath before trying again, this time with less foot and more knee. The ankle was able to bear my weight, and the pain was more like those twists that go away quickly than an actual sprain. I limped a few steps, then used all of my willpower to keep running, knowing they were right behind me. They were gaining on me, and as much as I tried to push the thought out, I knew that it was almost impossible for me to get out of this. I needed to stop a car on the highway and get them to drive off with me before the minions caught up, or I was done for. I was now all wet, in addition to bloody, so even if I found somewhere to hide, I would most likely freeze to death overnight. It was hot summer weather during the day, but I could feel the autumn chill coming once it got dark at night.

I reminded myself that Sam would have died for absolutely nothing if those guys caught up with me, and used it as extra motivation to push myself harder and keep going. No matter what, I couldn't give up.

CHAPTER TWENTY-EIGHT

I turned my head to look behind me and see how close they were, but I ran right into something solid, yet relatively soft. At first, I just saw the T-shirt, which was black, and I froze. I didn't know if I ran the wrong way or if one of them drove to the highway to catch me from the other side, but I felt so defeated. I could feel the tears coming and pushed them away, preparing myself to at least go down fighting, but all I got from my opponent was a shush. I looked up, recognizing the voice but unable to believe it until I saw his face and knew I wasn't dreaming. I had been so sure it was one of the guys from the other car, but it was Embry I crashed into.

I hugged him, and tears of relief formed as I tried to catch my breath, before Embry gently put me to the side and pulled out his sword. It would have been better if we had both made a run for the highway, but I obliged. I found a wet log on the ground behind me and hoped I wouldn't have to use it.

The minions were only expecting me, a little girl by their standards, running for her life with no weapons and her hands tied behind her back. This gave Embry the advantage, so although my teeth were clenched and my knuckles white from holding onto the log so tight, he managed to cut down the three men who came at us with hardly any effort. The Gifted who were acting against their will had all dispersed when Donovan died, so Embry didn't hesitate to use deadly force. I had to look away, but it was a relief to know that it would take some time before any of them got up and came after us.

"Is that all of them?" Embry asked me once Slick, Muscles and their friend were all lying on the ground.

"No, there was another car full." I strained, but couldn't hear a thing. "Where's Gabriel? I thought he would...did he not wake up?" I fumbled for words. I had been worried about Embry and Gabriel, but it was with the assumption that they couldn't die. And dying was supposed to break any previously established bonds. Meaning they would come back to me better than new. I was so worried they wouldn't find me in time that it hadn't occurred to me that one of them wouldn't find me at all.

Embry opened his mouth to say something. I was terrified, not sure I wanted to hear his answer, but then I heard Gabriel's voice.

"I took out four of them on the other side, but I think I saw one..." Gabriel didn't get a chance to tell us what he saw one doing. As soon as I heard his voice and knew he wasn't lost to me, I ran to him. I collided with Gabriel like I had on prom night, and with Embry tonight, only this time it was on purpose. Gabriel took me up so my feet were off the ground, dangling for a few moments before he put me down and let me go. He looked about as surprised as I was by my hug, and his own reaction to it.

"I'm sorry, I thought we lost you for a minute," I tried to shrug it off like it wasn't a big deal.

"Cutting off my oxygen won't kill me for good, but I'd rather not have to go through with the coming back to life again so soon," Gabriel made a joke and gave me a smile.

"I'm really glad you guys found me." I tried to keep my emotions in check, but my relief was threatening to come out as tears.

"You're not getting rid of us that easily," Gabriel assured me, straightening up and fixing his jacket.

I gave him a smile before something rustled in the field to my left, making me jump as Donovan broke through the tall grass. "There you are." Donovan looked at me with hatred and determination, so I froze like a deer caught in the headlights, then fumbled my way to the log I had dropped when I ran to Gabriel.

Luckily, Donovan was slow from recently being dead, and the guys weren't as surprised as I was. There was a fierce anger and precision to their moves, as Gabriel expertly karate-chopped Donovan in the back of the neck, which let Embry slice off his right hand once he fell to his knees. I had expected a threatening curse, but Donovan let out a blood-curdling scream instead.

Embry and Gabriel had both killed all the men they'd come up against, except Donovan. They left him to bleed out on the ground, clutching his right arm. It was better to keep him weak and wounded than to let him come back to life in a few hours. I wondered if limbs grew back as good as new when you were resurrected.

Embry put away his sword and came over to me, pulling me into his arms while Gabriel made sure no more men were hiding in the grass.

"The Onstar was genius," Embry told me with an encouraging smile, trying to distract me from Donovan and his stump.

"I knew I told you that I keep having to call them because I lose my keys, but I didn't know if you would be able to figure it out, or convince them you were Sam or..." I said it fast, because my brain still hadn't registered that I was safe. Or at least relatively safe at the moment. But no matter how fast I said Sam's name, it still hit me like a punch to the gut. "I didn't know how else you would find me," I finished, feeling absolutely defeated.

"We've got you now," Embry assured me. He took me in his arms, thinking it was the fear and the adrenaline dropping that made my shoulders collapse.

"He'll never stop until he has her," Donovan told us, laughing to himself and clutching his stump.

My saviors turned to him like they wanted him to take it back, as if that would make the words untrue. I was more preoccupied with his use of the third person.

"He?" I asked. It was one thing to always refer to himself as a collective 'we', but 'he' usually referred to someone else. "Donovan isn't the one we've been running from?" My heart beat faster against my chest.

"Me?" Donovan laughed, a cackling sound worse than his earlier scream. "I am nothing compared to him. None of you would stand a chance if he was here right now. He has powers you couldn't even imagine."

I suddenly understood that all of the 'we's weren't Donovan's grandiose view of himself, but his linking himself to the one with all the power. Donovan was nothing but the weak sidekick to the almighty powerful evil. The thought made me shiver.

"Let's get you out of here," Embry guided me towards an old station wagon they left running at the edge of the field, off the highway I'd tried so hard to get to.

"You won't save her. Just like you couldn't save Annabelle. Like you couldn't save any of them," Donovan called after us like a curse.

EPILOGUE

T his time it was Embry who drove. Gabriel let me have the passenger seat so I wouldn't be alone in the back. I was grateful to see one of them had managed to get my bag for me, but the only thing I wanted from it was my blankie, which I couldn't touch when I was covered in mud and blood. I turned up the heating instead.

Embry kept one hand on the wheel, but the other was on the armrest between us so he could hold my hand. The rhythmic rubbing of his thumb on my skin slowly calmed me down.

"We can't defeat them, can we?" I asked eventually, looking to Embry for honesty. If the lowly sidekick was enough to take us down, how could we ever face the real Big Bad?

"Defeating them was not our goal tonight; it was just keeping you safe. We thought we gave you enough time to get away, but then the keychain when we came back told us they had you," Embry explained.

"You gave me enough time," I said quietly, turning to look out the window.

"What?" Embry was confused, and I could feel his eyes on me, meaning they weren't on the road anymore.

"You're driving," I pointed out.

"How did they take you if you had enough time?" Gabriel asked me. I didn't look back, but I knew the vein in his forehead was pulsing.

"I got out through the window and climbed one of the trees to hide. I had just made it up to the leafy part when a woman came through. None of them ever looked up, so…you gave me enough time."

"Why didn't you run and get away from them?" Gabriel asked from the back.

"It wouldn't have worked. That is exactly what they thought I did. They immediately ran off, looking around, but they wouldn't have found me up the tree." I gave them the logical reason before the more honest one. "And I was not leaving you guys." I remembered how unfathomable that concept had been for me, but thinking of Sam brought an overwhelming tightness into my chest.

"But they did find you. Do you not realize that we just died so that you could escape, not so you could hang out and wait for us?" Gabriel was angry and upset with me.

"You don't think I know what everyone has been sacrificing for me?" I asked, the tears burning my eyes. "I saw your dead bodies at the motel, okay? I saw them and even though I knew you were coming back, I still knew it was because of me. And I saw them slit Sam's throat because I said no to joining him. I was there, and I held him, and I know that he died so I wouldn't have to—" I tried to keep talking, but the words became muffled in the tears and I couldn't stop the sobs as I relived Sam's final moments in my head.

"Sam is dead?" Gabriel asked more gently, his anger taken over by the realization of what I was going through.

"Because I said no," I nodded as a fresh batch of tears

rolled down my cheeks. I explained to them what Donovan wanted with me, what he planned to do, and how I said no, knowing it would cost Sam his life, but it was a price he was prepared to pay. I told them how I hadn't even realized Donovan was dead because Sam was my main priority, how I hoped Embry would remember that the keys had a computer chip in them, how I tricked Jim into taking me to the bathroom, and killed him so I could run away. They were impressed that I had managed to stab Donovan and kill him, but I couldn't bring myself to show the proper enthusiasm.

"Didn't you see him when you woke up?" I asked, Sam's dead body so vivid in my mind. "We should go back and get him, so we can..." I wasn't sure what I wanted. To have a proper funeral, to bury him, to bring him home to Deanna... all I knew was that we couldn't leave him at the motel, alone.

"I didn't see him," Embry told me, shaking his head before the two of them shared a look.

"Didn't you look?" I asked, figuring they would have gone around to find me before commandeering a car.

"Not long after we woke up and found the keychain, one of the minions drove up in this." Embry nodded to the station wagon he was driving. "We saw him grab one of his fallen friends by the boots and drag him towards the trunk, so we knocked him out to get the keys and came after you."

"He meant discard people," I understood what Slick had been referring to back at the motel. I brought my hand to my mouth when it hit me that Sam was one of those people, the thought making me sick. I closed my eyes and tried to block the images out of my mind before turning to look in the back of the car. I knew it was irrational, but I wanted to see something that would either confirm or disprove my thought. Instead, Gabriel moved so his head blocked my view. I tried to look past him, but he made me look into his eyes.

"Why did you leave the tree?" he asked, changing the

subject for me, but also because he wanted to know the answer. I could tell Embry wanted to pull over so he could take me in his arms and try to comfort me, at least a little, but we had to get as much distance between us and them as we could. The hand that wasn't holding mine was gripping the steering wheel so tight that his knuckles were white.

"I fell," I admitted. I knew he was trying to distract me, but I wanted to play along. This wouldn't have been my favorite subject of conversation either, but it was better than what my brain kept replaying.

"You?" Gabriel was skeptical. Once, when Embry had left me alone with him, before I understood that he was quiet, not evil, I had spent almost an entire day hanging out in a tree, watching him search the house and the grounds for me. Embry had found it hilarious when he got back.

"My little monkey?" Embry asked as well. That was the nickname he called me for the rest of the summer, to taunt Gabriel more than anything.

"I had another dream," I said, causing them to exchange a worried glance.

"Who?" Gabriel asked.

"Beth," I admitted.

"What did you see?" Embry pressed, knowing it had to be bad, or at least shocking, if it made me fall out of a tree.

"The prophecy," I admitted, leaving her pregnancy out. For some reason, I felt like now wasn't the time to share it with them. "The reason they're after me and they killed Sam and you guys keep dying and all the ones before me and..."

"It's not your fault," Embry said pointedly.

"Did you guys know that's why he wants me? Because I have the birthmark?" I asked.

For a moment they were quiet, then they looked to each other. I tried to read what their eyes were saying, but had no clue, before Embry answered. "No. We knew that your line was important to him."

"But Annabelle did, I think," Gabriel spoke up. "I don't know if she knew her line would have replicas of her with identical birthmarks, but she was relieved and incredibly happy when she told me that Margaret's only birthmark was a simple brown spot on her knee."

"Why would Donovan's master fight so hard to find Margaret if she didn't have the birthmark? She would have been useless to him as far as the spell was concerned," I asked.

"I don't think he knew Annabelle didn't pass the birthmark on to her daughter," Gabriel admitted. "Maybe he thought it was something that would come to her when Annabelle died, or when she turned a certain age."

"If Annabelle knew, why didn't she warn you?" I asked, beginning to think Annabelle kept a lot of things secret when she should have shared them, or written them in her diary. "I could have removed the birthmark through surgery, or dyed my hair? He never would have known I was a replica if…"

"I think she thought it ended when she let them burn her," Gabriel ventured, cutting me off so I would stop accusing the woman he loved.

"If ever a miracle happens, and I do make it out of this alive, I think I'll adopt," I said, getting a smile from Embry, but it was a sad one, and he knew that mine was fake.

"You're making it out alive," Embry told me like it was the only option.

WE DROVE until we crossed state lines, at which point we brought the station wagon into what I could only assume was a chop-shop, where they would strip it down and repurpose every single piece. Instead of finding new wheels, we walked a couple of miles in the hopes of finding a place to stay for the night.

"Want to kill two birds with one stone?" Embry suggested when we got to railroad tracks with a cargo train pulling out. It looked like the cars were made out of wood that hadn't been updated since the 1920s. It was still in that slow, building up energy phase, the perfect time to jump on board if we were to be reckless.

"You can't be serious." I looked at them, but knew better than to doubt them after spending days in a moving chicken coop.

"Quick, before it gains speed," Embry recommended, so I ran behind them.

Gabriel got to the train first, but he let Embry get in, then waited for me to catch up. Embry put out a hand to sort of pull me in when I got close enough, then Gabriel joined once I was in.

"Any idea where this train is going?" I asked, pulling Gabriel's jacket tighter around me. I was freezing when we gave up the car, so I put on a sweater from my bag, and Gabriel gave me his leather jacket. It did a much better job at blocking out the wind. I went to sit under the one tiny light in our compartment and took out the Chronicles.

"Home." Embry came to sit across from me, while Gabriel explored the wooden crates that surrounded us.

"The plantation?" I asked.

"We can stop by the beach house on the way," he offered.

"We can't." I wanted so badly to go home over the past month, but now I wanted to be as far from the manor and telling Deanna what happened as possible. I still wanted to take Clara in my arms and be comforted by Deanna, but I couldn't stand them hating me. And I would never forgive myself if my death magnet struck again. "It's too dangerous," I only gave them my second reason.

"We have a bit of a breather now, while Donovan recruits a new army. We'll get warnings before he comes back," Gabriel explained, sitting on one of the crates.

"Like last time?" I asked.

"We won't sit around and wait for him to come for us again. We're going to go home and regroup, get some stuff from the bunker, then…" Embry turned to Gabriel, uncertain about the rest of the plan.

"Maryland has an old army base with a secure underground facility. Even the president can't get into it, but I have a friend who…" Gabriel offered a new location, but I didn't want another prison-like tomb to wait in for the real Big Bad to find me.

"No," I argued, shaking my head before he even finished.

"No?" he asked like he didn't understand the word.

"I don't want to run to a new place to hide. Then wait for him to get close so we can try to run away again." I wrapped my arms around myself. "I don't want any more people dying while I escape, or hide in a not-so-safe house."

"What do you suggest?" he asked like he was humoring me and had no idea what I was talking about.

My current emotional state made it hard to think straight, but I knew exactly what I needed to do. "I want to learn how to take care of myself. Not self-defense against regular guys, but…I want to stand a chance against Gifteds. We need to be ready for *him*."

"How do you plan to do that?" Embry asked delicately.

"I'm going to find out everything I can," I said simply, opening the Chronicles to the section on Beth, since I had finished Cassie's.

"On the prophecy?" Embry asked.

"The prophecy, Donovan's master, the Gifted…anything I can find out."

"Are you looking for something in particular?" Gabriel questioned.

"Anything I can use to defeat him," I said simply. "You've been running for centuries, but now we need to get ready to fight."

DESTINY
THE OWENS CHRONICLES
BOOK TWO
AMANDA LYNN PETRIN

CHAPTER ONE

The light I was using to read the Chronicles in the cargo train went out once it got dark outside. Silly if you asked me, but I guess they weren't used to people riding with the merchandise in the cargo crates. I put the book back in my bag and tried to get some sleep, but my head was spinning.

I started the summer off full of excitement, ready to get away from the house I grew up in and start a new life in college. I never expected to end it on the run for my life with Embry and Gabriel.

My heart felt like it hadn't slowed down since Donovan found us and broke it into a million pieces. I tried not to think about Sam, my surrogate big brother, but he was the reason I wasn't sleeping like Embry and Gabriel. Every time I closed my eyes, all I could see was Sam. How I left him on the cold, hard asphalt to bleed out and be discarded somewhere, probably never to be found. How I let him die.

Letting it happen would have been bad enough, but I went one step further and caused his death. Donovan wasn't going to kill Sam until I said no. Until I fought back, knowing that someone like Sam would pay the price.

I shook my head to get the images out, but Embry must have been watching me rather than sleeping like I thought. "You should get some sleep," he told me.

"I'm not tired," I lied, struggling to keep my eyes open.

"You're safe for now Lucy. We won't let anything happen to you," he gave me a reassuring smile, but I knew he couldn't promise that. They would both give their lives to protect me, but they were out of their league. "Come here," he interrupted my thoughts.

"I'm not really..." I tried to come up with a lie about how fine I was.

"Come here," he repeated, his Italian accent more pronounced when he was tired. I crawled over to where he was sitting and leaned into him while he wrapped his arms around me. "I've got you," he kissed the top of my head. While Gabriel had always kept his distance, at least emotionally, Embry had been a constant source of love and support.

"I know," I assured him. It just wasn't enough.

"Donovan is weak right now. Every time we come back, it takes a while for our Gifts to return at full strength. Everyone who was following because of him has to be recruited all over. We can go to the plantation, get some supplies and find somewhere safe so we can be prepared to face him when he comes back." I knew the only way he would let me fight Donovan was over his dead body, but it was still a likely scenario.

The compartment was quiet, other than Gabriel's occasional snore. I tried to concentrate on that, but the longer we sat in the dark, the more I felt the pain and fear I had been burying rise up.

"What did the Chronicles say?" Embry asking about the book of stories from my ancestors, pulling me from my thoughts.

"I didn't get very far," I admitted. "I think Beth is why Grams made soul cakes for Halloween, though." One of Beth's first entries was a recipe for them. "And why we jumped into the creek to celebrate the solstice," I ventured. It sounded like something she would do.

"Beth had some superstitions." I could hear the smile in his voice.

"She didn't grow up at the plantation like the rest of us. Or the manor. She moved to New Orleans when she was little, and never came back. From what I gather, that kind of stuff is accepted there."

"It's definitely a place where magic feels possible," he agreed.

"Says the guy who's turning 347." He and Gabriel both looked like they were in their early twenties, but I now knew that they were Gifteds who had spent the past few centuries protecting my family.

"The whimsical kind of magic that amazes and amuses, but doesn't harm or curse," Embry elaborated.

"The kind that doesn't actually exist?" I fished for stories.

"There has to be a balance somewhere," he argued.

I didn't remember falling asleep, but I woke up to Embry gently shaking me.

"Wake up, *bambolina*," he used one of his Italian terms of endearment for me.

"What's wrong?" I asked, feeling my heartbeat rising. The darkness was gone, and the sun was shining in through the door Gabriel wrenched open, but my fear was ever-present.

"Nothing's wrong. We're getting off before the end of the line," Embry assured me with a smile that didn't quite meet his eyes.

"What station?" I asked, putting my backpack on and slowly waking up.

"We can't wait for the station. People would see us getting off, we'd have to explain ourselves…"

"Then how are we getting off?" One look at them told me the answer, but I was not ready to accept it.

"We jump." Gabriel gave me a smile. It was his genuine, excited smile, which only made it worse.

GABRIEL WENT FIRST. He lowered himself until he was almost touching the grass, then used his supernatural speed to hit the ground running. I wouldn't say that I was panicked, but it was more than Embry reassuringly touching my arms that got me to actually jump. I didn't like Embry using his Gift to manipulate my feelings, but it was better than the alternative of him pushing me out a moving train against my will. As it was, I landed in Gabriel's arms as softly as could be expected, with my eyes shut tight and possibly not breathing. Once I opened them, Gabriel was no longer running, and Embry had landed on the grass a dozen feet ahead of us.

"That wasn't so bad, was it?" Gabriel asked, putting me down cautiously. He didn't take his arm off me until we walked a few steps with my legs holding me up, rather than buckling from the shock.

"I never want to do that again," I argued, going over to make sure Embry was okay.

"There will be a bruise in the morning, but I'm fine," Embry assured me, brushing a twig out of his sandy blonde hair.

"Which way is home?" I asked, looking from one to the other. I couldn't even tell you which state we were in.

"This way," Embry said confidently, putting his arm around me and leading me in the direction the train had just taken.

∽

"I'LL HAVE the three-egg western omelet with sausage, bacon, and ham on the side. Whole wheat toast is fine. Hash browns, beans, and seasonal fruit would be great, with an order of pancakes and black coffee," Gabriel ordered from the diner's waitress while I stared at him in disbelief. He was occasionally hungry enough for an egg, a piece of toast or a bit of oatmeal, but his usual breakfast consisted of black coffee with nothing else.

"I'll have the same, but French toast instead of the pancakes and espresso rather than coffee," Embry told the waitress, who raised her eyes to him in surprise.

"I'll just have…" my stomach growled as if I hadn't eaten in days. I looked to the guys and realized we were starving because none of us had eaten anything but the protein bars from my backpack since before we got to the motel. Plus, they both fought in multiple battles, died and came back to life. "I'll have pancakes with bananas and Nutella, and all the meats they're having." I chose to forego the fruit and granola yogurt bowl for something more substantial.

"Coming right up." The waitress gave us a smile before moving on to her next table. There was a man sitting alone at it with four stacks of pancakes, each with different toppings. We weren't the first customers to order large amounts of food.

"I didn't even realize how hungry I am." I had to look away when I got the urge to stick my fork into one of the man's pancakes and eat it.

"It comes in waves," Embry explained, as his stomach made the same growl as mine.

"How are we getting to Boston from here?" I asked. The diner menu told me we were in Missouri, which was still a ways from home.

"I saw a used car dealership down the road. Depending on how legit he is, that could be an option," Embry tried to make it sound like a fun prospect, but I had no interest in riding in a car from a shady salesman that would likely fall apart on us.

"We could also hitchhike across the country if staying under the radar is more important than staying alive," I said it in an optimistic way that had Embry shaking his head at me. "I thought we had a breather now, which is why we're going home. If they're still looking for us and ready to pounce, I'm not going anywhere near my family." The guilty feeling in the pit of my stomach intensified when I mentioned Deanna and Clara, Sam's wife and daughter. How could I call them 'family' when I sacrificed Sam so the bad guys wouldn't get me?

"I would never take you in a car that wasn't completely safe, *Tesoro*," Embry assured me. "But we don't want to be obvious about where we are, or where we're going."

Gabriel's main focus was on the other patrons in the greasy spoon. Aside from the man with the mountains of pancakes, the diner had two other occupied tables. One with a man in a suit reading the newspaper while drinking black coffee, and another with a young family dressed like they came from church. The parents looked exhausted, while the children were as excited about their brunch as I would be for Disney World. "Can I have bananas and strawberries on my pancakes?" the little boy asked.

"And blueberries!" his younger sister exclaimed.

"You can have whatever your heart desires," the dad said, ruffling the little girl's hair.

I got lost watching them, thinking how Sam would never be able to ruffle Clara's hair like that again. Because of me, the only happy family I had ever known was broken.

"If you could go anywhere in the world, where would you choose?" I was surprised when it was Gabriel who asked such a silly question, but I saw concern when I brought my attention back to our table. He'd been watching me watch them.

"Italy," I gave my standard response. "England," I remembered what felt like centuries ago when my best friend Keisha's mom said we could visit her there for Thanksgiving. "Everywhere," I shrugged, my heart no longer in it. I still wanted to see the world, but home was the first place I thought of. My main problem was that home wasn't home anymore.

"I'm sure we'll knock a few places off your list." Embry gave me a smile as the waitress showed up with three plates that went to Gabriel. She came back multiple times to bring two plates for me, three for Embry, as well as some sides she left in the middle of the table.

"Could we go to a library at some point?" I asked, trying to swallow the ginormous bite I took.

"Missing homework?" Embry raised an eyebrow at me.

"Research. If I only read what they wrote, I'll never know more than they knew." I swallowed and took a piece of bacon from the plates in the middle.

"I doubt any of it will be in a library," Gabriel said.

"Libraries have internet," I pointed out as the mother's phone from the other table went off with the Imperial March. I was momentarily distracted by how cute it was that the little boy hummed along. Once she answered, it only took him a few notes to turn it into a song from Mary Poppins. "And there are biblical references and Latin words I want to confirm," I came back to our conversation as if I hadn't left it.

"My Latin is excellent," Embry volunteered. "But we can still check out a library at some point."

The conversation took a lull while we savored our meals. I had my doubts about the hole-in-the-wall diner we encountered by the train tracks, but the pancakes were big and fluffy, the bananas were overly ripe, and they were generous with the Nutella.

"Ready to hit the road?" Embry asked once our plates were mostly empty and he finished his third espresso.

"I'll use the restroom, then I'm ready to go." I stretched as I stood, picking up my backpack with the Chronicles inside and handing it to Embry to watch while I was gone.

"We'll get the bill," Gabriel told me, motioning the waitress over.

THE WASHROOM WAS BETTER than I expected. It was old and stained and falling apart, but you could tell that it had been cleaned recently. That didn't stop me from really lathering my hands when I washed them afterward.

I shook my hands to get rid of the excess water, as the young mother from the other table walked in and headed straight for the other sink.

"Is that one empty too?" she asked me when her soap dispenser came up dry. She held her hands out like they were covered in something gross and sticky.

"Nope, it's all yours," I told her with a smile, going to the paper towel dispenser to dry my hands.

"You're nicer than the last one." Something about her voice made the hairs on the back of my neck perk up.

"The last what?" I turned over and looked into her eyes for the first time. I knew exactly what made me uneasy. "You're one of them." She was wearing blue contacts, but they only made the darkness underneath stick out. "How did you find us?"

"Some wounds heal, but they always leave a scar." She kept her eyes on me as she moved closer.

"What do you want?" I took a step back, only there was nothing but wall behind me. Not even a window to escape from.

"What I want is to get back to my grandkids and enjoy a nice Sunday brunch." Like Embry and Gabriel, she was clearly a lot older than she looked. "But Donovan doesn't believe in coincidences, so the two of us in the same room is apparently too good of an opportunity to pass up on," she sounded bitter. "Everyone's gotta have something to live for," She sighed, giving me the impression that she didn't think too highly of the Big Bad's quest.

"What's yours?" I asked, my voice shaky. "Have you done it yet?" I scoured the room but didn't see anything I could use as a weapon. Everything was either bolted down or innocuous. I could try some of the self-defense Caleb taught me earlier in the summer, but she was almost a foot taller than me and looked like she could be a personal trainer.

"That is so cute. Worried you'll hurt me and I won't come back?" she mocked me.

"We can't all be villains intent on destroying humanity," I tried to hit a nerve.

"Don't let my grandbabies fool you. I've killed infants with my bare hands and still sleep soundly every night."

"Lucky you." I swallowed, taking one last look around. I still felt guilty for the Gifted I strangled so I could escape at the gas station, and the guy who evaporated at the plantation, even if he was trying to kill me at the time.

"Listen, we can do this the easy way, or I can carry you out in a bag. It's up to you." She stood with her hand on her hip.

"You can't hurt me," I said with a conviction I didn't feel. I knew my death was what they all wanted, since my heart was an ingredient in a ritual they had to perform, but I was pretty sure Donovan's master, the real Big Bad, had to be the one to do it.

"I can't kill you," she conceded. "But there are lots of ways to get you to him without taking all the life out of you."

"My friends are right outside. If I scream, they'll…"

"They'll die," she said simply, with a lot more confidence than I had earlier. "And I'm not sure if they'll come back from this." She touched the sink to her left without taking her eyes off me. The stained ceramic went grey as she turned it to stone.

A chill went through my entire body. For a moment I thought about how she must have been a cold-hearted monster in her first life to get a Gift like that, instead of how she was about to do the same to me. On the bright side, unless she could reverse it, turning my heart to stone meant no one could use it to complete the ritual.

I saw her take a step towards me and froze. I closed my eyes so I wouldn't see it coming and put my hands up as if that could somehow protect me from her.

I waited for the blow, but it didn't come. There was a gust of wind and a loud bang, then nothing but a faint ringing in my ears and tingling in my palms. When I opened my eyes, the woman was gone.

The sink slowly turned back to white ceramic and my heart dropped into my stomach. I stood there, frozen, before looking down at my hands. They still felt tingly, but looked completely normal, without a scratch on them. I cautiously took a step forward, to see if she was hiding somewhere, but the sink reverting to its former self told me I wouldn't find her. The only thing different from before I closed my eyes was a small pile of what looked like sand on the floor where the woman had stood.

"Is everything okay?"

"What happened?"

Embry and Gabriel burst into the washroom, probably expecting an explosion based on the noise. All they got was me, standing alone and in shock.

"We need to get out of here," I said, snapping myself out of it. There was an explanation for what happened, I just couldn't think of it with the ringing in my head.

"Are you alone?" Gabriel looked around to see what had me so frazzled.

"Yes." I looked to the pile of sand that was most likely her ashes.

Embry and Gabriel were looking for answers, but I knew it was only a matter of time before her husband came to see what was going on, at which point he would either finish her mission, or call the cops on me.

I ignored their questioning looks and went to leave the washroom, relieved when Embry beat me to the door and opened it for me. I was half-expecting an army of Donovan's men to be waiting for us, knowing what I did and ready to exact their revenge. Instead, the hallway leading to the washrooms was empty.

"Let's go this way," I suggested once I saw that Embry already had my bag on his shoulder. I brought us to the back door that opened to a row of dumpsters. I could see the road off to my right, but every other direction had tall grass covered in dew. It would be great to hide in, but we wouldn't get very far, at least not very fast. There was a car parked on the other side of the dumpsters, probably older than me, covered in rust with a duct-taped plastic sheet covering one of the windows. It was falling apart, but would serve our purpose as long as we ditched it before the owner reported it stolen and the cops caught up with us. I was about to make sure one of the guys could hotwire it when I heard the unmistakable hissing of a large bus using its brakes. "Do you have cash?" I asked instead, hurrying towards the road. There was a guy my age walking around the front of a city bus, wearing headphones and looking down at his feet instead of the world around him.

I looked back towards the diner and saw the husband was no longer sitting at his table, but standing in the middle of the restaurant, looking upset. We did not have time to argue over not having bus fare.

"I think I have a twenty," Embry fished it out of his pocket. They followed me into the road but looked at me with confusion and fear. I wondered if my face was as red as it felt, if they could see, maybe not what happened, but that I caused something terrible, without meaning to.

Luckily the bus driver, a plump woman with tight curls, waited for us to get on.

"You're new, child," she said, looking me up and down as I walked by.

For the first time today, I looked at myself. It was hidden by the table at the diner, but our adventures from last night were now on full display. Gabriel's jacket covered most of Sam's blood, but the mud was everywhere.

We took our seats and the bus took off. I looked back at the diner through the window and saw my victim's husband rush through the doors and look around outside. I could almost feel his anger as he kicked the ground and took another look in each direction before going back inside. I let out the breath I didn't know I was holding and sat back in my chair. He wasn't coming after us. At least not for the moment.

The guys waited for the adrenaline to die down and for my breathing to go back to normal before they both looked at me with all of their worried intensity.

"What happened in there?" Gabriel's tone demanded an answer.

"The woman who came in after me, she was Gifted. One of Donovan's willing participants," I swallowed and noticed that Gabriel clenched his fists.

"Why didn't you scream, or call for us?" Embry asked.

"She said she would kill you," I said simply. "I believed her. She touched the sink and it turned to stone," I cut them off before they could defend their fighting skills against lone assailants.

"And she left you?" Embry was confused.

"The sinks were normal when we came in," Gabriel pointed out.

"She died," I said in a whisper.

"How?" I felt like the guilt must be written all over my face, but they were waiting for an answer.

"She was coming at me and I couldn't find anything to stop her with, so I closed my eyes and raised my hands and... and pouf."

"And pouf?" Gabriel asked.

"There was something that sounded like an explosion and when I opened my eyes, she was gone. The sink went back to normal."

"The pile of sand," Embry realized.

"Ash," Gabriel corrected. Neither of them took their eyes off me.

"Looks like you've got powers," Embry said with a sad smile, sounding worried more than anything. He wrapped his arm around my shaking frame while I kept my hands glued to my sides, terrified of what they might do.

CHAPTER TWO

We didn't get off the bus until the end of the line, at which point our driver told us of some nearby hotels, and showers we could use. We got the hint.

"Child." She stopped me when I was on the steps, with the guys on the ground, clocking our surroundings. "I don't know if they're the bad situation, or if they took you away from it, but there's a women's shelter two blocks that way. Tony will be on the bench, ready to step in if they give you trouble." The look in her eyes told me she had been there before.

"Thank you." I was touched by her concern. "But they're the ones keeping me safe."

"It's always open," she called after me when I stepped off.

"Where to?" I asked the guys, looking around the busy street. If I had managed to convince someone to bring me here last summer, I would have admired the Gateway Arch that towered over their skyscrapers and spent hours watching old boats pass by on the Mississippi River. As it was, the hustle and bustle of the city put me on edge, with every person we crossed a potential threat to be avoided and feared.

They gave each other a look, then reached a decision with head tilts and shoulder shrugs. Keisha's parents used to do that while she narrated for me in a whisper. She usually diffused any tension with her wild imagination, but the conversation I pictured them having in my head wasn't very funny. It went something like:

> "Will it kill her?"
> "Maybe."
> "Do we go anyway?"
> "We don't have a choice..."
> "She'll probably die either way."

"This way," Embry ushered me over once they were on the move. We went from the main streets to the side streets until we reached back alleys that, while creepy, made me feel less out of place.

"Tip Top Body Shop?" I asked when we stopped. Gabriel stayed with me while Embry went to see if it was open.

"This was Eli's place, once upon a time. It shut down over a decade ago, but as far as we know, he still owns it, and it's really old, so they can't tear it down."

"The guy who lost an ear and was half-deaf for decades?" I asked of Eli, getting a nod. There was a blue circle plaque beside the door, so I went closer to check it out. "He was from here?" I asked. "Established 1905 by Elias Nettle, oldest garage and gas station in Missouri," I read out loud.

"First life and everything," Gabriel agreed. "I think by the end he was pretending to be Elias Nettle the Eighth or something. Family-run since the day it opened," he smiled.

"Why did it close?" I asked.

"His line died out." His tone was simple, but I could tell from his face that it was anything but.

"You were close?"

"We all were."

I made a mental note to ask Embry, who motioned us over once he got the front door open.

"You've done this a lot?" I asked.

"Eli had a lot of qualities, but he was never going to be the one to help you in the middle of the night."

"Because of his ear?" I asked. It might be hard to hear if you were sleeping on your only ear.

"Even before that." I got a tiny smile from Gabriel.

"He just wouldn't come?" After Terrence and Caleb who selflessly housed us while we were on the run, risking their lives in the process...I had trouble picturing a friend of theirs that selfish.

"He couldn't hear you over his own snoring. It was horrendous. The phone, knocking, sirens, nothing got through to him once he fell asleep. He would wake up every morning at six, without an alarm, but good luck if you needed him before then," Embry shared.

"This is how you would sneak into his shop in the middle of the night?"

"Exactly."

"We once spent hours trying to wake him up after we kidnapped him for his bachelor party. We were not as careful as we should have been in transporting him, and we started drinking long before we tried to wake him," Gabriel admitted.

The inside looked like an abandoned garage. Usually, when a business closes, the owners liquidate their inventory, selling whatever they can to recoup their costs. They would also go through the normal steps and procedures to close down a business, at least on a daily level. This place looked more like everyone got up mid-workday and left. There was a car up on the pillars with two tires off, tools and paperwork all over, a desk calendar with future appointments... The only sign that it wasn't a working garage were the lights being off and the inches of dust coating every surface. When Gabriel said Eli's line died out, I got the feeling it was all at once.

"We can stay here tonight and head out in the morning," Embry suggested.

"We can't go home anymore," I pointed out.

"Where do you want to go?" he asked me.

"Far away from Boston." I was horrified at the idea of going anywhere near the people I loved. "You said we had a breather now, that we were safe for a while, but Donovan knew we were at the diner. He called that woman and told her I was there."

"That phone call could have been anything." Gabriel argued.

"But it wasn't. Maybe everyone out there knows what I look like, but she wouldn't have come after me if Donovan didn't make her."

"I'm sorry," Embry said like he had failed me, yet again.

"I don't understand how they keep finding us." Gabriel was angry. "We knew they would come to the plantation, but we were careful after that. The safe house, the motel...we did everything right."

"Wounds heal but they sometimes leave a scar," I admitted. "I asked her and that's what she told me," I shrugged, not sure what she meant by it. I had a lot of emotional scars that were never going to heal, but physically I was fine.

"That doesn't make any sense," Embry voiced what I was thinking, then looked to Gabriel, to see if he had any ideas.

"It wasn't like they followed us, we ditched our phones, we traveled in a chicken coop and...you died," I said when it hit me, but they both looked at me like I was crazy.

"We both died, but that wouldn't help them find us. It's not like sparks go up and light the sky." Embry didn't understand.

"She said some wounds heal, but they always leave a scar.

That's true for normal people, but when you guys come back, the wounds are gone, right?"

"Like it never happened," they agreed.

"You once told me you always buzz at the airport because there's shrapnel in your shoulder from…"

"The wound healed, but the scar is on the inside. They put something in me when they found us at the plantation," Gabriel realized.

My excitement at figuring it out died when I understood the implications. "That's my theory, but it sounds too high-tech for him, so it's probably not…"

"Don't underestimate him. He's not alone. Even if he is as clueless as you would expect from someone his age, which I don't think is the case, his followers are kids your age. Some of them probably work at Google or Facebook," Embry warned.

"We need to take it out before we leave here." Gabriel gave Embry a look and a subtle nod in my direction.

"Later tonight," Embry agreed.

"We can take care of it later, because we need supplies, and a clean environment to do it in, but from now on, I'm not being the kid who has to be protected from the truth. I know you want to protect me, so you can keep all the evil people away, but I will be right beside you when Embry digs around inside you to get it out," I warned Gabriel.

"Not offering to do the honors?" he gave me a sad smile.

"I would if there was no one else," I assured him. "I'll be there to hold your hand and help in any way I can, but I would rather not cause you pain if I can help it."

"Luckily for you, Embry enjoys it." Gabriel gave me a smile while Embry rolled his eyes, not dignifying the accusation with a response.

"Let's get you cleaned up," he said instead, showing me to the apartment above the garage.

. . .

I was expecting a messy bachelor pad, with stuff lying out as if the owners left in a hurry, like the garage below, but it was empty. Or I should say devoid of anything personal. There were fresh sheets on top of the night table and neatly folded towels on the sink's counter, along with a pack of hotel toiletries. There were no photos, no knick-knacks, absolutely nothing to even hint at who Eli was.

I took the shampoo, conditioner and body wash, then put the water as hot as it would go, which still left a lot to be desired. At first, I let the water rinse off the dark brown crust, telling myself it was only mud, determined to keep it together. The blood was caked onto me, so it was indistinguishable from the crusted mud, until I looked at the stained water circling the drain.

It brought me back to the plantation, to watching Gabriel's blood swim down the drain, but at least he came back. I was traumatized then, but this was so much worse. Sam was gone. Forever.

Once I was as clean as could be on the outside, I put on a pair of shorts and a t-shirt, with Gabriel's jacket on top. The chill wasn't letting me go.

I found Embry in the kitchen, making mac and cheese. All I could smell was cheese and butter.

"We also have a healthy salad," Embry assured me without turning away from the pot he was stirring.

"Thank you." I took a seat and filled my plate with salad. His 'healthy' salad had a dressing made of olive oil, balsamic vinegar, and honey over a bed of mixed greens, cashews and raisins.

"Is it ready?" Gabriel asked, coming in with his shirt off,

looking like he'd been lifting weights, with his headphones in and sweat glistening.

"Pretty much." Embry turned around and saw his attire. "Trying to look pretty for me?" he teased.

"I don't know how butchered I'll be by the time you're done with me. This might be the last time I can do anything," Gabriel defended himself.

"Until the next time you die," I said dryly.

"This smells delicious. Thank you," Gabriel said after a slight pause, where we all sat in silence. I didn't mean to be bitter and make things unpleasant, I just couldn't help it.

"It's perfect," I seconded.

"Gabriel also picked up some dessert," Embry cautiously smiled once we were done with the meal. Gabriel went up to the freezer and came back with cookie dough ice cream.

"Will the Big Bad be intimidated if I weigh three-hundred pounds?"

"No, but we feel better about ourselves when we supply you with comfort foods and tell ourselves they make you feel better."

"All better." I gave them a smile and took a spoonful of ice cream.

THE GUYS GAVE each other looks again, then both got up and walked out of the room. They looked at me with confusion when I followed them.

"No more keeping things from me, remember?" I pointed out, walking past them into a room with a table ready for surgery. There was a garbage bag under the ledge of it to catch the blood, and a tray with the instruments Embry would need.

Gabriel shrugged at my determination, then took his place on the table.

Embry looked at me, then to Gabriel, and sighed. "Hold him down," he let me take part. He took out a scalpel and hand sanitizer and moved with purpose. I wanted to ask what he was doing with this stuff, but I had to prove myself if I wanted them to stop leaving me out. By the time I figured out how I was going to control Gabriel without getting in the way, Embry had spread the sanitizer and put the scalpel on the skin.

"You're going in blind?" I asked, shocked.

"Do you have an ultrasound machine lying around?" Gabriel countered, like I was the one being ridiculous.

"No anesthesia or anything?" This was going a lot faster than I expected. Embry pressed hard enough on the scalpel that he drew blood, but didn't cut yet.

To answer my question, Gabriel took out a bottle of Jack Daniels and downed a few gulps of liquid courage. "Go," he told Embry, who nodded to me.

I did my best to hold Gabriel down, but he was used to pain, and mostly gritted his teeth through it. He barely moved while Embry dug around inside him, but I kept one arm and my body weight across his chest, in case. My other hand found his and held it throughout the procedure.

My biggest fear was that I was wrong, and Embry wouldn't find anything inside him. That he would poke around and cause immeasurable pain before giving up and bringing us back to square one. Fortunately for my guilt, after some very pointed looks from Gabriel, Embry eventually pulled out a tiny black device. If that didn't confirm my theory enough, there was a flashing red light at the end of it. "We got it," Embry told his patient, holding it up so Gabriel could see. He handed it to him before grabbing a needle and thread to stitch him up.

"Our first clue," Gabriel showed the tiniest bit of enthusiasm before finally passing out from what must be unimaginable pain.

"That's not normal thread," I pointed out, a poor attempt at distracting myself. It looked a lot thicker than the one Mrs. Boyd used on my clothes, once upon a time. "You had this lying around?"

"We left the garage as is, maybe as a shrine, maybe because it was hard, but Eli asked us to turn the apartment into a refuge. In our line of work, that requires a very elaborate first aid kit," Embry explained.

"You should splurge on an ultrasound machine next time." I got a smile as he stitched Gabriel's skin back together. "What happened downstairs?" I felt him tense up.

"Nothing." I got the feeling Embry was just as close to Eli as Gabriel. "Eli's Gift was to see the future. Sometimes he could make it happen, other times the visions came to him. He would share if he thought it could help you, but didn't see the point in hurting people before bad things happened. There was a man who didn't like what he saw and kept trying to convince Eli to change it. One day, the man went to the market and shot Eli's wife, as well as his three remaining descendants. Eli was working in the garage when he heard, so he ordered everyone out, threw a chair into the apartment window and never came back."

CHAPTER THREE

We didn't leave in the morning as planned. Gabriel spent the next twenty-four hours or so going in and out of a comatose-like sleep. Embry insisted the wound would heal and he would be fine, but we didn't have real painkillers, so Gabriel spent a lot of the time he wasn't knocked out asking us to kill him so he could come back without the pain.

Embry's face did not betray any emotion as he convinced Gabriel to go back to sleep, but I had to turn away and bite my lip every time he woke up. I couldn't stand the agony in his voice, but I wasn't going to cry over it in front of him. I once suggested that maybe we should consider listening and putting him out of his misery. That's when Embry decided I could only stay in the room with Gabriel if I promised not to say another word about it or interact with Gabriel when he was like that.

I spent most of my time holding Gabriel's hand, wishing this wasn't so painfully familiar, but I also spent time looking into the tracker.

We assumed they knew where we were by now, even though we were pretty sure we deactivated the tracker when the red light went out. Embry let me use an old laptop from the garage that weighed twenty pounds and still used dial-up to do some research.

"Any leads?" Embry asked, drawing my attention away from Gabriel, who moaned in his sleep. I bit down on my lip and tried not to react.

"There's a serial number on it, so I did some googling and it was apparently sold as a way to track wild animals for conservation projects, using this website." I brought the laptop over so he could see the map. "It only gets updated every few hours, but that's us right there." I pointed to the screen. All the other dots were in clumps, but there were none anywhere near us.

"Could we use this to see where they are? Maybe know ahead of time when they're coming for us?" he asked.

"I have no idea," I admitted. "I think we could probably figure out where they are when they're actively tracking him, but...I was able to figure out this much because it was easy, but even when they're on TV shows talking about tracing IP addresses and all of that tech stuff, I have no idea what they're talking about. Which means that even if it is something we could do, it will take a long time for me to figure out how to do it."

"And I thought I had completely embraced the twenty-first century when I let you convince me to buy a smartphone." He gave a half-hearted smile as we heard Gabriel waking up again.

"I think you need to use it for more than phone calls to qualify," I teased. It was easier than watching Gabriel in pain.

"The OnStar woman taught me how to use the maps too," he boasted before I gave in and turned over to Gabriel.

He was obviously still in pain, but he asked for water instead of a mercy killing, so I happily obliged.

By that evening, Gabriel was getting up and slowly moving around, so I made dinner. It wasn't that Embry and I hadn't been eating while Gabriel was out, we just didn't make it a priority. I was also pretty sure that getting cut into and slowly repairing yourself, cell by cell, might make you as hungry as dying and coming back to life.

I made us grilled cheese sandwiches with bacon and apples. I was checking to make sure the cheese was melted when Gabriel walked in, buttoning up his shirt so I could see the white bandage on his chest.

"You're up!" I was unable to contain my enthusiasm, but I stopped myself from taking him in for a hug like I wanted to. I had to assume the wound was still painful, and the last thing I wanted to do was cause him more pain.

"I've had worse." He saw where my eyes went, and only winced a little when he sat down.

"I don't ever want to have to see you like that again," I admitted, putting the food on a plate in front of him.

"Embry said you found out how they've been tracking us. Does that mean we know where they are too?"

"We don't, but I found a hacker who insists they can find anything or anyone, so that's an option." Even if I didn't have the computer skills, I was still reluctant to get anyone else involved. I didn't trust anyone at this point, and I couldn't have another death on my conscience.

"Do you mean a tracker?" he asked.

"No, like a computer hacker."

"We're relying on computers now?" Gabriel raised an eyebrow at me.

"It's how they've been finding us," I reminded him.

"Touché." He bit into the grilled cheese and closed his eyes for a second, savoring it. "Maybe instead of letting some stranger behind a screen keep tabs on them, you could do it with a spell," he suggested.

"I'm pretty sure you need magical powers to do that," I turned him down. He'd said it like he was trying to be helpful, but Embry had also tried to bring up what happened in the bathroom. I was severely in denial and not interested.

"Luce—"

I didn't have to shoot down his next argument, because we heard glass breaking from downstairs before he could get it out. We looked at each other in silence, both of us knowing Embry was in the bedroom, and this was the last location the bad guys had for us.

"Get your bag and the books. Now," he whispered to me before Embry came into the kitchen, only partially dressed after his shower, but holding some kind of axe, with a spare one for Gabriel.

"Get her to the car, I'll hold them off as long as I can," was the last thing I heard Embry say before I rounded the corner into the bedroom.

I shoved all my clothes into the backpack, with the Chronicles and Book of Shadows, then went to find Gabriel in the kitchen.

"Come on, we'll take the fire escape." Embry must have gone downstairs, because it sounded like a battle was going on.

GABRIEL OPENED the window though it clearly hurt him, and climbed onto the fire escape. It was the kind where the ladder didn't go all the way down; you had to hang on it and wait for it to lower itself.

"Are you okay?" I asked Gabriel when it got stuck and he had to use his body's momentum to propel it down.

"It's easier than getting it down when you're at the bottom," he assured me, but I could see he was in pain, and when the movement brought his shirt open, his white bandage was turning red.

The ladder finally budged and made a clinking sound when it hit the asphalt below. Gabriel waited at the bottom for me, but as I grabbed on to the rusted railing to follow, I was pulled back. The air was knocked out of my lungs as I hit the ground.

"There she is." The man who spoke looked like he was at least seven feet tall and didn't loosen his death grip on me. The world started spinning, so I tried to pry his fingers away from my throat, but there was nothing there. *Not now*, I lamented as the alley disappeared, and I was brought into a memory from one of my ancestors.

"I assure you sir, I have nothing. No money..." I was Annabelle, on the side of the road, trying to appear calm and reason with the man who found her there, alone. I could feel how afraid she was, but there was also surprise. She was someone who had traveled great distances before, and never been so accosted. Then again, she'd never been without a male companion. Her father was with her on the crossing to America, and every time she ventured away from home in the years since then, Gabriel or Embry were always by her side. Men looked at women on their own completely different than when they were properly accompanied.

"That ain't true, lass. You've always got something we want," the old man said with a toothless smile. It did nothing to dissuade me from my first impression, that he was planning on kidnapping and possibly having his way with her.

"Please sir, I mean no trouble..." Annabelle pleaded with her

eyes, which had worked in the past. She then looked around to see if there was anyone there who could help her, or at least ensure she was relatively safe from being taken away. All I saw were three younger, well-built working men, whose smiles didn't allow any confusion. These were definitely not nice men, and they were not going to help her.

"Where are you heading sweetheart?" one of the new arrivals asked, sizing us up.

"My husband will be along shortly. I'm sure he would be happy to help you with whatever..." she tried to sound as convincing as she could, but I could hear her voice faltering. Lying wouldn't work any better than the pleading had.

"You don't got no ring," one of them smiled, knowing he had her. No one was coming to our rescue.

She looked away from the man who was making her uncomfortable to see if there was a branch on the ground or a rock, anything she could use to defend herself. I saw nothing.

"Darling, I'm terribly sorry I'm late. I promise it will never happen again. Have these gentlemen been helping you out?" At first it was just a voice with a British accent, like Annabelle's father's, until she looked up and I saw a dashing gentleman who smiled as he extended his arm for her to take. He could be another brigand, looking to take advantage of her like the other men, but right now he was the lesser of two evils, and she didn't have a choice.

"I was telling them you were on your way." She tried to steady her voice and sound like she believed it. "We should get going if we want to get home before dark." The other men's faces dropped, angry they lost their plaything, but her good Samaritan was a foot taller than their tallest and looked strong and sturdy.

"We should," he agreed, so she accepted his arm and walked with him. She kept her head high and exuded confidence, while inside she was gripped by terror. She was waiting until she was far enough away from those men to thank this one and leave, at which point we would find out if he actually saved her or took her for himself.

"I apologize for the impropriety, but I didn't get the impression that you knew those men," he said as we walked along, his voice soothing. "I'm Henry," he put his hand on top of hers like Gabriel used to, making her blush. Soon enough her heartbeat slowed, and I was more and more convinced he was not going to kill her.

"No, thank you so terribly much for saving me. At first, it was just the old man, but then they were everywhere," she admitted, trying to shake away the fear they left her with. "I'm Annabelle."

"A pleasure," he assured her. "There are some exceptions, but I do believe most of us gentlemen would prefer to save the damsel in distress rather than be the ones distressing her. Not that you were in distress, of course."

"Of course not," she smiled at him. "I believe I can find my way home from here."

"As you wish." He released her, so she was free to go. "I don't mean to impose, but it would put my mind at ease if I could walk with you until you truly were at your home, or at least no longer roaming the countryside on your own. Beautiful women should never wander on their own in foreign lands."

"I'm afraid it's only me," she admitted. "I probably shouldn't tell that to someone I just met, but you'll never stop following me if you wait for me to be properly accompanied."

"I wouldn't mind." He looked into her eyes, and I could feel her cheeks redden as she swallowed hard. He was obviously flirting, but unlike the other gentlemen, he was not making her uneasy. If it weren't for the fact that her heart and love life were in shambles, she would have been receptive to his advances. "That is very independent of you." He went back to being polite, looking ahead instead of at us.

"Or incredibly foolish," she acknowledged.

"There's a fine line between foolishness and bravery. For example, I can't tell if it is rather brave of me or completely foolish to ask if I could call on you tomorrow."

I watched him nervously rubbing his fingertips together while

Annabelle debated his proposition in her mind. Her first instinct was to apologize and tell him she was taken. It seemed like less of a lie than the truth, that although her heart belonged entirely to another, she was currently without attachment. Hadn't she come here in an attempt to move on with her life? To find someone who was neither Gabriel, nor Embry and try to be happy. "I believe it would be both foolish and brave of you," she said as he was about to turn away again. "Lucky for you, I am choosing to reward bravery today. I would love for you to call on me." I could feel her heart break a little as she said it, but I knew she wasn't going to end up with Gabriel, and I liked Henry so far.

"Then it shall be my pleasure." He smiled and she tried to dismiss the sinking feeling in the pit of her stomach, the voice that screamed for her to stay away, that he was not the one she should be with.

"This is me." She stopped at the gate to her a little cottage.

"My task is done. I bid you a wonderful evening and look forward to our next encounter." He tipped his hat before continuing along the path, as Annabelle let herself into the house that still felt like someone else's, though it had nearly been a year...

I WOKE up to find the man who'd been holding me was now unconscious at my side, with the battle raging in the kitchen rather than the garage downstairs. I knew the guys would want me to keep going and find a car or something, but I had no means of contacting them, didn't know where we were going, and was convinced I would fare better with them than alone.

Everyone was preoccupied with their own battles, so I was able to climb back into the apartment through the window, carrying a broom from the balcony like a weapon.

"What do you think you're doing?" Embry asked, knocking one of the assailants out with the blunt end of his ax.

"Helping."

"You need to figure out how to control those things," Gabriel said of my tendency to relive memories from my ancestors. He wasn't happy with me, in the way Mrs. Boyd would get upset when I snuck out the window and she couldn't find me.

"You're preaching to the choir," I sighed, shoving my broom into someone's stomach, letting Gabriel knock him out once the man doubled over.

A woman who'd been on the floor got up and rushed at me. My first instinct was to put my hands out to somehow brace myself or stop her, but I barely lifted them when I remembered what happened last time and felt the tingling start. I froze, paralyzed with the thought of killing someone else, when Embry hit her on the temple with his elbow. He shot me a look I had never seen on him before, at least not directed at me, where his nostrils flared, before I hurriedly picked up my broom handle. I stood at the ready, like I hadn't been about to let that woman get to me so I wouldn't have to relive her death in my nightmares.

Soon, there were five bodies on the ground, with the three of us still standing. "They won't be out long," Embry warned, exchanging a look with Gabriel. All I could tell was that they were worried, and we needed to leave fast. My guess was that more people were coming, and Gabriel was nowhere near ready for another fight. He barely made it through this one.

Embry went first to get the ladder back down to the street, and I went second to ensure no one would grab me from behind. Once the three of us were clear, Embry took off through the alley, gently guiding me while keeping a brisk pace. We rounded three corners and I felt like we were in a maze before we finally stopped in front of a residential garage. It was white once, but the paint was so cracked that it was more of a moldy brown now.

"Eli kept a getaway car?" I asked when Gabriel took the

keys out of his pocket rather than breaking a window to get in.

"He wanted it to be a refuge, but sometimes the bad gets in," he shrugged.

CHAPTER FOUR

We drove to a train station, at which point Embry used cash to buy three tickets. There was half a dozen scheduled stops along the way, but Florida was our final destination. He did it as three separate transactions, with three different tellers, at least fifteen minutes apart.

"What's in Florida, other than Disney?" I asked Embry while we waited for them to call us for boarding.

"I don't know," he raised his shoulders before casually looking around, as opposed to Gabriel, who was actively scouring the room for threats.

"We're going to wing it?" I was pretty sure that wasn't in their DNA.

"There will be a stop somewhere along the way where we will get off so someone else can take our places. Three people who could pass for us, at least from a distance. They are the ones who will enjoy Florida," he said under his breath.

"But you won't tell me where we're going?"

"Nope." He crossed his arms.

"Way to make me feel like a child." I pulled Gabriel's jacket closer around me. I could see how floating in a grownup's jacket made my statement ironic, but I was eighteen years old, not six.

"Compared to me you are very much a child," he pointed out. "If it makes you feel any better, I'm not telling Gabriel either. You'll both see when we get there," he assured me before they called us to board our first train to Lincoln, Nebraska.

THE PASSENGER TRAIN was an extreme upgrade from the cargo crates we rode to Missouri in. We switched trains three times before taking an overnight train to Georgia. I lasted that long without taking a nap, but once we were in our own cabin, with the lull of the train, I couldn't resist anymore and finally surrendered to the exhaustion. Gabriel was the only one of us who got enough sleep over the past few days, but I doubt any of it was restful.

I tried to get comfortable with my head against the window, thinking how this train was a lot faster than the old steam ones, but there was still the same flow that carried you to sleep…

"GABRIEL," Rosalind said, her breath catching in her chest when she saw him walking over. I could tell she hadn't seen him in a while, but he had definitely crossed her mind many times.

He paused before masking a look of disappointment, that she might not have noticed, but I did. "Rosalind," he said, taking her hand and kissing it.

"It's been a while." Gabriel turned quickly, and Rosalind followed his gaze to see Embry in the doorway with a little girl, who rushed right over to jump into Gabriel's arms.

It melted Rosalind's heart to see the way Gabriel held Molly close, but she tried to hide it from him. Gabriel didn't even look at us before turning back to the doorway. "Embry," he said through gritted teeth, nodding his head.

"I understand now," Rosie said, looking back to Embry.

"I'm glad you found each other." Gabriel forced a smile for us, but it disappeared the moment he looked away.

"We're not together," Embry told him as if it meant something, but Gabriel didn't react.

"How long are you here for?" Rosalind asked him, but it was Molly's big grey eyes looking up at him that held his attention.

"Maybe a week or so. I was in town and wanted to make sure the both of you were okay. Now that you know," he said.

"If Embry hadn't come and told me the truth, what would your pretense have been?" Rosie unashamedly called him on his lie, getting a smile in return.

"I might have developed a limp or injured myself on the way," he smiled in spite of himself, with a softness she found as unexpected as I did.

"I would have seen right through it," she said with a smile before Molly tugged on his sleeve and he agreed to accompany her to the meadow. Rosie nodded to let him know it was okay. Her heart dropped to watch him walk away, but Molly's joy at being reunited with her friend was everything to her.

THE SCENE CHANGED but I was still Rosalind. She was walking towards the stables that used to be behind the plantation, long before I was born. Gabriel was there, taking care of some horses, looking like he'd been there a while, long enough to get comfortable.

"Thank you." Rosalind put her hand out so the horse could sniff it. She didn't react to the way the horse's breath tickled, but she avoided looking into Gabriel's eyes.

"What for?" he continued to brush the horse's mane.

"Molly. Losing Roger was very difficult on her, and I haven't seen her smile so much as she does when she is with you."

"She's a brilliant little girl. It's my pleasure," he assured her. He was polite, but distant.

"Gabriel..." she gave up pretenses, stopped petting the horse and turned to him. "I know you have seen how Embry looks at me, and I want you to know that I do not return his affections. Even before you came back, I couldn't love him, because I loved my husband until the day I was sure he was not coming back, and then...then I fell for you." She took a step closer to him, but he put his hands out, as if to stop her, and took a step back.

"Rosalind..."

"Gabriel..." she looked right into his eyes, staring him down like I did sometimes, but I wouldn't have been able to stay there with the way her heart was pounding in her chest. "You can't pretend there isn't something there. You can't bury it by avoiding me, and..."

"I see her," he cut her off, looking away so he wouldn't see the pain in her eyes, but it was clear in her voice as she asked, "What?"

He brought her to a bench and took her hand in his, sending heat and shivers to her spine. "You look exactly like Annabelle. The clothes are different, but other than that, as far as looks are concerned, the two of you are identical. Every time I see you, my heart breaks because I have to actively remind myself that you are not the woman I am in love with. And I want you to be happy and safe and I want to protect you. I want to love you like you want me to, but I can't, because I am still in love with the girl I met when I was a boy, who stole my heart and never gave it back. You look like her and I am sorry, but I love Annabelle, not what she looked like." I could tell he didn't say it to be mean, that he just wanted her to understand that any looks of affection he accidentally sent her way were simply him forgetting he lost Annabelle, but I could feel her heart breaking when he said it.

"Gabriel..." she wanted to argue, to tell him it couldn't simply be because she looked like Annabelle, that he obviously had genuine feelings for her...

"*You can't talk me out of this. You should accept Embry's advances, find happiness.*" His words cut into her heart like a knife.

"*I wasn't going to,*" she said, her anger the only reason she was able to hide how much it hurt. "*I understand that I can't talk you into loving me, but I am not a lovesick child. And you can't talk me into loving Embry instead of you either.*"

"*Then what did you want to say?*" he asked, looking heartbroken as well.

"*Don't leave because I made the mistake of falling for you. I promise that I will never bring it up again, if you could just stay,*" she tried to appear strong, and I gave her so much credit for that, but her pain and vulnerability were screaming at him.

"*That would not be a good idea. For either of us,*" he was apologetic. Even if he didn't love her in that way, I don't think he wasn't unaffected either.

"*But it's what's best for Molly. I understand if you have to leave, I have no claim on you, but I'm a mother first, and that girl, who is my world, she loves you. And I would hate to think I was the one who cost her the only person since her father who can make her laugh like that.*"

He looked into her eyes, but all I could hear was her broken heart pounding in my ears. He considering it for the longest time, what felt like an eternity. "*I'll stay,*" he agreed. "*I'll stay for Molly.*"

"*Thank you,*" she gave him a sad smile before getting up and going about her day as if nothing had happened...

I WOKE up to find Gabriel watching me, with a kindness he didn't usually show, especially not during the day. He usually kept his distance, but got more vulnerable at night, when he possibly thought I wouldn't remember what he said to me. I had been longing for another one of these late-night conversations, ever since the night I wore the lace dress that reminded him of Annabelle, and he told me about his brother.

"When you look at me, do you see me, or do you see Annabelle?" I asked, snuggling into Embry, who was asleep beside me. I knew I looked like her, but what he said to Rosalind made me wonder.

"Do you want the truth, or a bedtime story with a happy ending?" he reverted to his carefree, bored self, but I didn't feel like he was trying to protect me from an ugly truth, more like he was the one who didn't want to admit to it.

"The truth." I closed my eyes a bit like I was falling back to sleep, so he would put his guard down. It was wrong of me to manipulate him like that, and I knew it, but it was also mean of him to be really nice to me and tell me things when he thought it wasn't registering.

"I always saw her," he admitted. "When I woke up in Rosalind's arms, I thought I died and went to heaven, to Annabelle...but then I saw the differences. Some were big, others were small, but none of them were Belle. I never got used to it. Every time I saw them, 'Annabelle' was always my first thought." I could hear the pain in his words like I had seen on his face in the memory. "My heart believed it until I saw, or rather reminded myself, that it wasn't her. It was like losing her all over again, every single time," he shared. I opened my eyes a crack and saw he was talking to himself now, assuming I was asleep. I kept my eyes closed and concentrated on the rhythmic breathing that fooled him all those years ago in the East Wing.

I wanted to apologize for the pain it caused him to look at me. I knew he still loved her, but I didn't realize he still forgot, even after all these lifetimes without her.

I thought he was done, but his next words shocked me so much I forgot to breathe. Not just breathing slow to pretend like I was sleeping, but breathing altogether. "Until you. I came for your eighteenth birthday and you ran to me, so relieved and happy to see me, wearing this pink dress... and I thought 'Lucy'. Not Annabelle like every time before...and it broke my heart," he admitted, pausing a moment during which I felt his gaze on me. "I couldn't be near you anymore after that, not until all of this," he sighed before getting up and telling Embry he would go make sure everything was good in the other compartments.

IT WAS ONLY when Gabriel shut the compartment door behind him that I realized I was holding my breath. I kept my eyes closed, but wasn't fooling anyone.

"You weren't asleep," Embry reproached now that we were alone.

"Neither were you," I tried to turn it on him. "He doesn't talk when he knows I'm awake," I relented.

"Be careful with him Luce, he has a dark side," he warned before we heard Gabriel making his way back. "Get some sleep," he recommended, kissing the top of my head. I looked at him, remembering how hurt he was watching Rosie choose Gabriel, and did as I was told.

I cuddled into Embry and tried to fall back asleep, but it was hard when the two of them were talking. Eventually, Embry kept watch while Gabriel got some sleep, but my mind was too stuck on what he said to sleep. What did he mean that seeing me broke his heart? I opened my eyes, thinking maybe I could convince Embry to talk it out with me in the hallway, but once my eyes were open, they immediately locked with Gabriel's, who was on the other seat, facing me, his eyes open and staring at me. I rationalized it by reminding myself it was their job to protect me, but he didn't stop when he saw me looking. We kept our eyes locked, without acknowledging each other or moving, until sleep finally made my lids drop and I drifted off to sleep.

· · ·

WHEN EMBRY SHOOK ME AWAKE, the train was still moving, but there were three extra people in the compartment with us. The two men had the same hair colors as Embry and Gabriel, both dressed in black. The girl, however, looked nothing like me. She had a mess of curly brown hair, like mine, but she wore it up in a bun and was almost a foot taller than me. Her dress either came from my closet at the manor, or she happened to buy the exact same style.

"This is Tristan, Benjamin and Delia," Embry made the introductions. I remembered Delia's name from the chalkboards at Caleb's safe house, but no one ever mentioned the other two.

"It's nice to meet you Lucy." Tristan, the one with dark hair like Gabriel's, had a warm and welcoming smile, while Benjamin looked...not quite miserable, but this was one of the last things he wanted to be doing right now.

"We've heard a lot about you." My decoy was older than me, but not by much. There was something about her eyes, even without the darkness, that told me she had lived many, many lives.

"All of it terrible," Embry smiled, but Delia shook her head at him.

"He brags about you constantly," she told me. "And you're an Owens, you have no choice but to be kind and selfless and perfect." She rolled her eyes, but was smiling at me.

"Is that something we're known for?" I asked.

"According to these guys," she nodded to Embry, then to Gabriel.

"You should wear your hair down," I told her. I didn't feel so perfect, and wasn't looking forward to letting the Owens reputation down.

"We know their disguises won't hold if they see them up close," Embry defended.

"If it's someone new, they might not know exactly what I

look like, but I think they'll all know about my birthmark," I pointed out. It was the whole reason they were hunting me.

Embry nodded, but Delia turned around to show me her neck. It was a near-perfect replica of my crescent moon birthmark, complete with the freckles in the middle that looked like stars. "Etta was going by memory when she drew it, but I think it'll hold up if it isn't someone who knows one of you." She got a sad look on her face. I had yet to meet Etta, whose husband Caleb had housed us at the beginning of the summer, but I knew she was incredibly close to Cassandra, the version of me from the eighteen hundreds.

"Which one?" I asked, touching the back of my neck as if I could feel what it looked like.

"Mostly Cass, but I think I've met all of them, except for Annabelle," she looked to Gabriel for confirmation.

He nodded, so Tristan, his decoy, asked, "We're just going to Florida and chilling, right? There's nothing you need us to do once we get there?"

"That's it. You can work on your surf or meet Goofy. We just need enough time for them to lose us," Embry assured him.

"Oh, we brought these for you." Tristan took a bunch of brightly colored garments out of his backpack and handed some to each of us.

"You're enjoying this too much," Gabriel warned, putting a Hawaiian shirt over his black t-shirt.

"I would enjoy it a lot more if I had a camera to take pictures back to everyone else," Tristan argued.

"These don't go together," I said of the long black coat and baseball cap they brought me. The guys were used to dressing in black, but I was usually in colors.

"We're not aiming for fashion, just something you wouldn't usually wear," Embry said as the train slowed to pull into the station.

"Thank you." Gabriel took Delia in for a hug, while Embry shook the guys' hands.

"Come by when this is all over. We miss you," Delia told him.

I FOLLOWED Embry and Gabriel out of the compartment and through the busy train, careful to keep my head down.

"They're Gifted, right?" I verified, knowing they would be hunted if their disguises passed the test, possibly killed if they didn't.

"Of course," Embry assured me.

"And they haven't done what they were supposed to do?"

"We wouldn't let them do this if they had." Gabriel guided me to an exit.

I nodded, thinking that I should have been raised by people like that, instead of Sam, Deanna and Clara.

WE WENT to a beat-up Volkswagen in the parking lot, that Embry somehow had the keys for. It was so old that he had to actually put the key into the lock and turn it to unlock the doors, then lean across to unlock Gabriel's door, and the one behind him for me.

"Can you tell me where we're going now?" I asked, taking the middle seat.

"Not too far," Embry said, giving me no actual indication of time or place

"And we're currently in…" I looked around for a sign since I hadn't been paying attention at the station.

"Right now, we're in Atlanta."

I tried to pretend this was a road trip vacation so I could forget every horrible thing that happened in the past few days.

CHAPTER FIVE

It was two fast food stops, one gas station and approximately seven hours before we arrived in a very secluded neighborhood of New Orleans.

There were gates and wide-open spaces, but not a lot of houses. Embry drove up to a villa surrounded by fields and stables on one side, with trees and swampland on the other. The house wasn't nearly as big as the ones I grew up in, but it was at least two to three times the size of a normal house.

"Who lives here?" I asked, looking around at the beautiful expanse of land. It was like a cross between an Italian villa and New Orleans charm.

"I do." Embry got out of the car and looked around at the property. "At least sometimes," he amended.

"How long have you had it?" I wondered if it was a new acquisition, or part of his life I knew nothing about.

"1922," he looked at the house like he could see the first time he saw it, with the memories alive in front of him. They made him smile, but it was a sad smile. Beth, the last copy of Annabelle before me, lived in the early nineteen-hundreds and grew up in New Orleans. I wondered if she might have something to do with it.

"There is absolutely no security here," Gabriel declared after a few minutes of observation, unimpressed.

"It wasn't designed for something like this, but we can manage," Embry assured him. "If anything gets out of hand, we can send Lucy to the panic room."

"You put a panic room in this house?" Gabriel raised his eyebrows.

"I made a fireproof room to protect things." There was a finality to the way he said it that dissuaded Gabriel from any further arguments about the location.

"Your plan is to lock me in your bunker with your favorite things?" I asked.

"If things get out of hand." Embry smiled at me, so I rolled my eyes before smiling back at him. I knew better than to complain about tight spaces or not being able to go outside. Others had given up way more than that to keep me safe. Plus, I grew up exploring a manor with secret passageways that I sometimes got lost in. I also had my own bunker I've locked myself in before, not that I wanted to repeat that. But I didn't want the guys to keep shutting me out whenever things got dangerous.

EMBRY TOOK a key from under a flowerpot and let us into the foyer, which wasn't as dark and dusty as I expected.

"A flowerpot? Seriously?" I asked him. Gabriel was fuming, but kept it inside for the moment.

"Locks are easy to break if you really want to get in," Embry said simply before bringing us to the kitchen.

"When's the last time you were here?" I asked. There were eggs and milk in the fridge, along with other very perishable items. The pool in the backyard was spotless, with the jets running, and all the bushes perfectly manicured.

"I want to say months, but I think years would be more accurate." He saw my look and elaborated, "I have someone who takes care of the place and he knew I was coming."

"How?" Gabriel perked up as if ready to relocate me immediately.

"You're not the only one with top-secret messaging systems," he defended.

"What's in here?" I asked, continuing the tour in an effort to diffuse the situation.

The room in front of me looked oddly familiar. There was an oak table covered in books and papers, an antique chair with extra cushions, an old gramophone...it looked like Embry hadn't changed anything in the room since he got the house.

"This is storage; we don't have to go in." Embry hurried in front of me and shut the door before walking us through the laundry room, wine cellar, and his study.

Next, he brought us up the stairs. "Don't worry about these rooms," he said of the first two, that he didn't even look at as we walked by. "This is a bathroom, and some spare rooms," he said of the next ones. "And if anything happens, this is how you get to the panic room."

He brought us through the master bedroom and pressed his hand to the wall to reveal a walk-in closet. It would have been a fashion enthusiast's paradise, but other than one rack in the corner, there weren't any clothes.

"Is this where you hide all the corpses?" I asked of the trunks.

"Just treasures," he still had that sad smile. "I even have some first editions if you get bored," he pointed to an ornate bookshelf, filled with incredibly old, yet pristine volumes. He had all the works of Jane Austen, J.D. Salinger, Ernest

Hemingway, Shakespeare, some Italian playwrights, and a bunch of books whose authors I never even heard of. There were four books at the bottom that looked brand new compared to the others, all written by Laurel Haynes.

"Hopefully this is the first and last time I'm here," I told him, walking out. I touched the carvings in the bed frame before everything disappeared...

I COULD TELL I was in the same room, but while Embry's closet looked dark and a bit like a shrine, this one was warm. I knew I was Beth, even before I caught a glimpse of her in the mirror, but her eyes were focused on the reflection of the closet, rather than on herself. She was in a red silk negligee, with her hair cut a few inches below her ears. She looked so happy. Happier than I had seen any of the girls in any of the memories.

"When are you coming to bed?" she called to the closet, where I could hear someone rummaging around. This must be the house she shared with her husband, David. It explained why the room downstairs was so familiar; it was the room Beth had been researching the prophecy in.

"Got it!" I was shocked to hear Embry's voice exclaim, before he came into the bedroom, positively triumphant.

"You have less than ten pieces of clothing in there. What took you so long to find?" she asked, stretching around in the bed.

"This," he said, hopping into the king-sized bed beside her, a small velvet box in his hands.

"You spoil me," she said it like he should stop, but she was smiling. She kept her eyes on him, not even noticing the gift box.

"You deserve it," he said, giving me a kiss on the forehead. I don't think I had ever seen him so happy, or with so little clothes on, which was slightly awkward. I was used to Sam prancing around in his boxers back home, so it wasn't a big deal, but if things went any further, we would have a problem. "Happy Anniversary," he kissed

her shoulder. Luckily, I wasn't the one controlling her, because it tickled, and I would have burst out laughing.

Beth, on the other hand, chose happy tears as her response to the kiss and the ring with four stones that she found in the box. Birth stones by the looks of them, but I didn't know enough to know which was which, and she closed the box before I got a good look. "These have been the happiest five years of my life," she kissed him on the lips. It was incredibly strange to be kissing him like this, when I couldn't control my actions, and could feel what she felt for him. I knew what was coming and willed myself to come out of the memory, but I was saved when knocking on the door made them stop.

"Come in munchkin," Embry called, laughing.

A little girl ran into the room and climbed into the bed between me and Embry. I recognized her as an older version of Helen from my last Beth memory.

"I had a nightmare," she said, cuddling into Embry. "There was a monster in my closet."

"Do you want me to go make sure everything is safe?" he offered.

"No Daddy! He'll hurt you!" Helen looked up at him. "Can I sleep with you and mommy tonight? Please?" she begged.

"This is why we needed the bigger bed," Beth smiled before they lifted the covers so Helen could get under them. Beth and Embry looked into each other's eyes over Helen's head, holding hands, and fell asleep like that.

When I came back to the present, Gabriel was holding me up and Embry's eyes were locked on mine, like in the memory. Instead of love, his eyes showed fear for what I could have seen.

"Oh my God, did I..." I remembered what I was doing in this memory, and my tendency to act them out.

"No, you passed out. We didn't know if it was a memory

or..." Gabriel kept his arms around me, even though I was able to hold myself up.

"It was just a memory," I swallowed, exchanging a look with Embry, while Gabriel looked at me with concern.

"From who? What happened in it?" he was ready for clues.

I fumbled for an answer, but was saved from lying when an old man with white hair and kind eyes walked in.

"I was hoping it was you," he said, his voice full of southern hospitality.

"Charlie." Embry relaxed his shoulders and rushed over to the newcomer. He took the man in for a hug like they were old friends. "This is the man who watches over the place when I'm gone."

"I had help this time," Charlie assured me. "Eric!" he called into the hallway.

"Yes grandpa?" a voice drifted up the stairs.

"Come on up," Charlie called. Eric was tall and tan with golden locks and his grandfather's kind eyes, only the blue in his was piercing rather than calming like Charlie's. He looked strong in a rugged way, like he helped run the stables and lifted barrels of hay. "You remember Embry, and his friend Gabriel." Charlie paused for them to shake hands. "And this must be Lucy." He reached over and shook my hand with an endearing smile.

"Which one did you know?" I figured Charlie was yet another Gifted.

"I'm old, but not that old," he said with a wink. "Your grandmother and I used to run around and ride the horses here before she moved away. She became a treasured pen pal who sent a lot of pictures after that."

"I didn't know she had any friends," I said before realizing how that sounded. "I mean, outside of the house. She mostly kept to herself."

"She wasn't always like that," he told me.

"They were little troublemakers," Embry cut in. It was weird to picture him running after younger versions of Charlie and my grandmother.

"I believe I have more than made up for it," Charlie didn't argue with Embry's assessment. "We came over to make sure it was you and to invite you to dinner. It's just a little barbecue, but---"

"We would love to," Embry surprised me with his acceptance, and by the looks of it, Gabriel as well.

"I'll give you a moment to get settled in, but we'll be in the yard when you're ready," Charlie smiled at each of us before leading his grandson out. Eric shot me a smile and I could feel myself blushing, which was not something I was used to.

"YOU THINK it's wise to leave the house and parade her around?" Gabriel asked Embry once our guests were gone.

"We share the land and no one else comes out here," Embry defended. "She's as safe there as she is here, and Charlie makes the best crawfish I've ever had. Ever."

Gabriel still didn't look happy, but he went to change out of his colorful outfit and came downstairs in dark jeans and a black t-shirt.

I changed into the last clean outfit I had, a dress. In hindsight, I should have packed more adventure clothes and less vacation ones. I made a mental note to do laundry when we got back, so I would have something to wear in the morning.

Embry was the last to come down, wearing black pants and a button-down shirt, that he rolled up at the sleeves. "Off we go," he said with a smile that reached his eyes. The best description I had for his mood was that he was finally home after a really long and hard journey, so he delighted in and appreciated every inch of it.

. . .

WE WALKED out the kitchen patio doors and went past the pool, to one of those really long picnic tables. Twenty people could sit at it comfortably without touching elbows.

"Blanquette de Limoux." Embry walked over to where Charlie was working over a huge pot and handed him a bottle of wine.

"Thank you," Charlie looked touched.

"Can I get you something to drink?" Eric came out of nowhere and offered, making me jump slightly.

"What are you having?" I asked of the amber drink in his hand.

"Iced tea. Well, my grandma's version. It's a combination of sweet tea and lemonade with a hint of secret ingredients."

"Secret ingredients?" I asked, raising an eyebrow, but he just smiled. "I'll try one."

"Excellent choice," he told me before going over to a pitcher in a bed of ice and pouring me a glass, which he topped with a slice of lemon. I watched him with curiosity, but Gabriel watched like he was making sure no one slipped anything into my drink.

"Do we trust them?" I asked Gabriel in a whisper, leaning closer to him.

"I trust Charlie." He didn't take his eyes off Eric.

"Eat, eat," Charlie insisted, even though he was still busy cooking. I was fine with waiting, but Eric brought me the iced tea and led me to the food table.

"Have you been to the south before?" he asked me.

I considered it before saying, "Not really." He didn't need to know about our recent adventures, running for my life through a tropical jungle and passing the border from Mexico on a truck filled with poultry. It wasn't like I was introduced to any new foods, at least none that looked like the spread in front of us.

"Do you like seafood?"

"I do…" I tilted my head and bit my bottom lip, trying to figure out if I should trust him, which made him laugh.

"Everything is amazing, so you can try it all and let me tell you what it is after, or I can tell you now and you might miss out," Eric shrugged, showing a clear preference for the first option.

"Those are my only choices?"

"They are," he was apologetic, even if it was mockingly so.

"In that case let's try it all," I laughed in spite of myself. Tonight was in such a crazy contrast to everything we had been through lately, that none of it felt real.

Eric scooped up things that were deep fried, some that were boiled, and a bunch of sides I thought I recognized, but on closer inspection, did not. There were none of the barbecue staples like hot dogs and hamburgers. Instead, there was gumbo, jambalaya, po-boys and various types of crawfish. My favorite was the deep-fried crawfish with a spicy mayo sauce, until I tried the jambalaya. It was a smorgasbord of sausage, seafood, rice and the perfect amount of heat. Everything was delicious.

I WAS LAUGHING along with Eric's story about a rogue crab when Sam's face flashed in front of me, so proud when he finally caught the lobster Clara briefly adopted as a pet. For a second, I had forgotten that I was being hunted and caused my brother's death. I was just a girl at a crawfish boil with a cute boy, trying new things.

"You okay?" Eric looked concerned, but he kept his smile.

"I'm fine." I made an effort to smile back, hoping he didn't see how fake it was.

"How long are you guys staying here?" he asked.

"I have no idea," I admitted.

"Are you from New England also?"

"Boston," I agreed. "Have you ever been?"

"I checked out MIT my senior year. And stopped by Harvard for fun," he smiled at the mention of the Ivy League.

"Where did you end up going?"

"I'm at Louisiana State," he shrugged. "Where do you go?"

"I was supposed to start Harvard in September, but I had to defer," I tried to make it sound unimportant rather than admit that life changing events made me doubt if I would even survive to go to college at all.

"Harvard, huh? That's pretty fancy."

"I had a boring and sheltered childhood." It was how I usually explained away my good grades, or lack of friends, but now I could see there was nothing boring about the way I grew up. I would give anything to go back to that sheltered life instead of this one, where I see the world from different hiding places and lose the people I care about.

"Mine was noisy," he said after considering it. "I have three brothers and three sisters."

"That sounds intense."

"It can be," he agreed. "I contributed to the problem, so they sent me here one summer and I loved it. I got my act together, then come spring, I had a full-on regression until my mom told me I could come here for the summer even if it wasn't as a punishment."

"What did you do?" I asked.

"Loads of things. Muck out the stables, repair the fences, lift heavy things, clean Mr. Embry's pool..."

"Sounds like the ideal summer," I teased.

"You're missing the part where as soon as my chores were done, I got to ride the horses and swim in the pool and..."

"Jump the fences?"

"We tried, but my horse didn't have it in him. I was too afraid to try it again with a different one."

"Sounds traumatic."

"It was," he agreed. "But I didn't let it stop me."

"I always wanted to go riding." There were stables on our property, but I don't know the last time they held horses.

"I can take you some time, if you want," he offered.

"That would be amazing!"

"Lucy!" Embry called over before I could thank Eric for the offer. Gabriel and Embry were already standing and ready to go, with neither of them looking happy.

"I'll see you around." Sam was a hugger, so I didn't think anything of it when Eric took me in his arms to say goodbye.

"Come by anytime, Lucy," Charlie told me with a hug as well.

"What's wrong?" I asked as we walked to the villa.

"Nothing," Embry assured me in a way that told me that was not the case.

"Are we leaving again?"

"No, we're going to stay here a while." I was surprised it was Gabriel who endorsed it.

"Get some sleep, *Tesoro*, there'll be lots to do in the morning." Embry kissed the top of my head once we got inside the villa, both of them setting off to their own rooms. I went up to the spare bedroom I'd changed in and wondered what they had in store for me.

CHAPTER SIX

Henry had clearly stuck to his promise, as he was there beside me, walking through the countryside, making Annabelle laugh. She felt a familiarity towards him that told me he hadn't only called on her once, but many times. Still, it wasn't the all-encompassing, can't eat, can't sleep, can't breathe without him love she had once had with Gabriel, nor was it the surprising but steady love she had found with Embry. Being with Henry was doing little to make her forget the men she had loved before, and still did, judging by the thoughts swimming around in her head. At the same time, Henry was someone she could see herself caring about. Especially if Gabriel was no longer an option.

The more we walked, the more I got the feeling this was Henry's property rather than a countryside. He had lovely gardens, just like Annabelle's father's, that you could walk in for hours. I saw lots of exotic flowers, as well as the most gorgeous roses. Some of the plants did not have much going for them appearance-wise, but they smelt heavenly. Every once in a while, Henry would stop so we could smell them, or regale her with all of the cooking uses and healing properties of a particular plant. "I've never seen eyes like yours before," Annabelle said after a few minutes in silence, with him smiling *down at her. It didn't make her uncomfortable per se, but it scared her, because it was the way Gabriel had often looked at her.*

"Is that a good thing, or a bad thing?" Henry inquired, looking into her eyes. They caught Annabelle off guard because she wasn't used to it; how very dark they were. It was like the iris surrounding the pupil had simply absorbed its color, so the entire middle part of the eye was black. I spent the past fifteen years watching Embry and Gabriel's eyes go darker and darker, so it was the knowledge that Henry was Gifted that shocked me.

"I'm not sure yet." She looked closer, trying to figure it out. The darkness didn't scare her, but it wasn't welcoming either.

He sighed before telling her a story. "It was an accident. Years ago, I was playing with my nephew and ran into a woman who was carrying a pot of some chemical that got into my eye and turned it black." I wondered how much of it was true and how much he came up with to answer such questions.

"That's terrible," Annabelle said, wondering what kind of chemical could change the color of one's eyes. Both eyes. "Can you still see everything?"

"It was a long recovery. Eventually everything healed, although the black remained."

"They say that eyes are the windows to the soul." I don't know why she said it, but the idea seemed to intrigue him.

"And what do you see in mine?" he said it low, like a whisper, only there was something excitingly dangerous in it.

She looked carefully before admitting, "All I see is myself." She laughed, but he looked happy with her answer.

"And I pray that is how it always will be."

I woke up from another memory dream and couldn't get back to sleep. It was earlier than the teenager in me on summer vacation wanted to, but it was hopefully early enough that I could talk to Embry about the memory I saw yesterday.

. . .

He was alone at the kitchen table, sipping an espresso. There were two slices of toast with peanut butter and sliced bananas at the spot beside him. But Embry hated bananas.

"I heard you getting dressed," he told my confused look.

"You knew I was coming?" I sat down and took a bite, savoring my toast and discovering a hint of cinnamon.

"I wondered what you would see once we got here. It's one of the main reasons I chose it, but I knew you would eventually see other things as well."

"I don't only see them," I reminded him.

"Hence the apology breakfast," he told me, getting a smile. I could tell he was hesitating to ask, possibly not wanting to scar me any further, but he also wanted to know.

"It was your anniversary," I shared, making his eyes go wide.

"Which one?" he asked. Part of me wanted to know what elaborate plans he put into action over the years, but I did not want to live through them, so I didn't ask.

"Fifth." I picked up the second toast.

For a moment he was lost in the memory, then he smiled. "Helen had a nightmare and slept in the bed with us." He got up to make himself another espresso, relieved.

"Which is the only reason I can still sit here beside you and look you in the eyes."

"How is it when it happens? Do you hear their thoughts and know all their secrets, or..."

"It's weird," I tried to find a way to explain it. "I don't have access to all of their thoughts and memories, just from those moments. I'm still me, but I see what they're seeing, and feel what they feel..."

"I'm sorry..."

"That too, but I meant emotions. Like I didn't know who

she was waiting for in the closet, but I knew she was excited to see them more than annoyed that they were taking so long, and that whoever it was, she loved them. With all her heart. I haven't seen any of them that happy yet."

"Thank you," he said like it meant a lot, but I don't think he needed me to tell him how she felt. I looked at him expectantly, but he was satisfied with the conversation and ready to move on. "What?" he asked when I looked at him with a mix of guilt and curiosity.

"I didn't see you naked, but I still have a million questions."

He nearly choked on his coffee before looking at me with a huge smile, "I forgot about that part."

"The part where you never told me you were married to Beth?" I put it plainly.

"Keep it down," he warned.

I looked at him with confusion before I realized, "Gabriel doesn't know?"

"He might suspect there was something. He knows we were close, but no, he does not know the full extent of our relationship."

"Five years," I pointed out.

"When Beth's husband died, we both came to David's funeral. Gabriel stayed a couple of weeks, but it was his turn to be the guardian of the new safe house. I offered to stay and help her get things settled, and...we fell in love. When Gabriel came back to check on her, I was still there, so he stayed away."

"You guys are ridiculous. Do you even know why you're fighting?"

"Time heals things when you move on, not when you spend your life being reminded of it and waiting for her to come back." There was a sadness to him as he said it, but he wasn't talking about himself.

I could tell he didn't want me to push, so I moved on to the big question I was holding back, ever since I saw the memory of Beth discovering the Prophecy. "I saw something else a while ago that I didn't know how to bring up, but…"

"What is it?" he reassured me that I could ask him anything, but I knew my question would break his heart, whether it was his baby or not.

"In the memory that made me fall out of the tree, Beth…"

"Did you tell her?" Gabriel walked into the kitchen and silenced me. My heart stopped, wondering how much he heard.

"Tell me what?" I asked once I realized he was talking to Embry about something completely unrelated. Embry looked guilty instead of relieved as I would have expected.

"We discussed it, and since you don't want to be left behind, we're going to train you," Gabriel shared.

"Really?" I perked up and finished my toast.

"Don't get too excited," Embry warned.

"I don't know what happened in the washroom," I caught on.

"Annabelle could do magic," Gabriel admitted, looking at me with guilt in his eyes.

"She was a witch?" I tried to remember exactly what he told me at the plantation. "You said she was burnt at the stake, but she was innocent."

"Of the crimes they were accusing her of. Not necessarily of witchcraft," he used a technicality, but it was still a lie. "The night before she died, she did a spell to track the men who were after her, to see how close they were to finding us."

"And…" I wondered if she fought them with her supposed powers, but Embry was looking at Gabriel as expectantly as I was.

"They were close, so she turned herself in," Gabriel said like that was the end of it.

"One spell doesn't mean anything," I decided. "Have any of

the Bearers since Annabelle demonstrated any kind of magical ability?"

"No one has tried," Gabriel gave me a look. He wasn't mentioning it, but we both knew what happened in the wash-room either meant I was Gifted or a witch. Since I didn't die, the obvious answer was that I take after Annabelle in the magic department.

"I don't want to try either," I turned them down. "Why don't you teach me how to fight with weapons, and then we can see how it goes?" I offered.

"You feel more comfortable getting close to people with weapons?" Embry asked, surprised.

"I can control the weapons." I couldn't say as much for my hands.

"You can learn to control the magic too." Embry put his hand on mine, showing me he didn't fear them like I did. "We're no match for the people that are hunting you, but if you can control your powers, you might be."

I did want to learn to fight back against Donovan and his master, to make sure they couldn't hurt anyone else the way they hurt Sam, but I couldn't imagine I would be a match for them. "Are you going to teach me?" I raised my eyebrows at Embry.

"I can show you how Annabelle did her tracking spell, but we don't have that kind of magic." Gabriel handed me a book he'd brought from upstairs. "But that is why we have her Shadow Book."

"Book of Shadows," Embry corrected, but I focused on Gabriel.

"If you're uncomfortable, we can stop, but there has to be a reason you have this, and wouldn't you rather be able to control it next time?" He kept his eyes locked on mine in earnest, until I had to look away.

"Okay," I reluctantly agreed. I never wanted my hands to

betray me like that again. It would also be nice to get ahead of the bad guys for once. To actually stand a chance at defeating them without losing even more people.

"We can go out into the yard and try some easy, simple spells. Work our way up, okay?" Gabriel offered.

"Okay," I repeated, following him when he got up and headed for the patio doors. "You're not coming?" I asked Embry when he stayed back, bringing our dirty plates to the sink.

"He has even less experience with it than I do," Gabriel assured me with an encouraging smile, but nothing about that statement made me feel better.

"I'll be around," Embry nodded for me to go.

"What exactly am I doing?" I asked Gabriel when we got to a blanket on the grass. It was like a picnic, only there were maps, crystals and a book instead of food and wine.

"I saw her doing a tracking spell, so I figured we could start with that." He sat down cross-legged and took out a map.

"Who am I looking for?" I asked.

"We could look for Donovan to make sure he isn't anywhere near us," he suggested.

"Would that mean he could track me?" I was not a fan of that scenario.

"According to Annabelle, there's map tracking and essence tracking. As long as we only do map tracking, you'll be fine."

"Couldn't Donovan trick a tracking spell? With a cloaking spell?" I asked.

"Is that something you read in the books? Or saw on TV?" he was amused by the question.

"There's no magic in the Chronicles and I haven't read the Book of Shadows," I gave him the answer. "Even if it was on TV, it still makes sense."

"I'm sure you can, but I doubt they would be using one. We have never hunted them back, or posed any kind of threat," he pointed out.

"You think this will work?" I asked, eying the candles he lit and placed around a map of the world. "Even if I have no skills whatsoever?"

"The way Annabelle explained it, magic wasn't a skill she had to practice or cultivate to use. If you had it in you and did the right thing, or said the right words, something would happen." As he spoke, he took a piece of paper and started drawing on it with a pencil, fast strokes with a sure hand. It wasn't until he handed it to me that I saw it was of Donovan, accurate enough to give me chills.

"Don't get your hopes up," I warned, following the book's instructions by tying a string around one of the crystals and holding it in my right hand. The roughly drawn sketch of Donovan's face was on my left palm. "Inveniet Donovan."

I closed my eyes and repeated the words, picturing him in my head and feeling the hairs on the back of my neck tense up. I felt like an absolute idiot and was terrified of what I might find out.

"It's okay, relax your mind and think of Donovan," Gabriel encouraged. He sounded supportive, not at all upset it wasn't working, but I did not have his confidence.

I tried to clear my mind, but every time I pictured Donovan, I either saw him giving the order for his man to slit Sam's throat, or threatening to cut off every one of Clara's freckles...one time I saw Donovan, surrounded by darkness, but he had such an ominous look that I completely shut down and needed to start all over again.

After at least a half an hour of trying with no success, Gabriel decided we should attempt a different spell, and flipped to one of the first pages in the book. The entire spread was covered in writing on how to make objects float.

"Can I have a water break?" I asked, feeling overwhelmed. I wasn't used to being bad at learning things, or to accepting magic as a real thing.

"I'll go get you a glass. Try and relax. Don't put so much pressure on yourself," he gave me an encouraging smile before going to the house.

"How's it going?" Embry came over from the stables, where he'd been watching us from for the last fifteen minutes.

"Terrible. I think we made a mistake and it wasn't actually me who made her disappear."

"Or it came to you when you needed it, but you haven't figured out how to get it when you want it," he argued. "Unless you don't want it?"

"No, I love turning someone's grandmother into a pile of ash during their Sunday brunch," I hid behind sarcasm. He raised an eyebrow when I said grandmother, but otherwise saw right through me.

"I know it's scary. Beth told me she was terrified the first time it happened to her," he shared, expecting my shocked reaction.

"Did she ever figure it out?" I asked. It made sense that free-spirited Beth who wrote of superstitions and lived in New Orleans would have inherited the magic as well.

"Of course. You will too," he nodded to reassure me.

"What did she do?"

"Lots of research," he gave me a smile. "Once she was making things happen rather than having things happen to her, it was a lot less scary."

"This isn't something I can read a book to solve," I argued with his logic.

"Maybe not any book, but the Book of Shadows can definitely help. It will teach you spells that you can master, to help you control your magic instead of it controlling you."

"Mind over matter?" I brought my hand to my head, applying pressure to relieve the beginning of a headache.

"Or practice makes perfect."

"I'm trying to practice but nothing's happening."

"It helps if you're not convincing yourself you can't do it."

"I'm not convincing myself; my incapability is convincing me," I argued. He raised an eyebrow at me and waited. "I also don't want to find him. When I think of him…all I feel is fear, and then I think of Sam, and I have to get out of there."

"Maybe you should try finding someone you actually want to find," he suggested. "And believe you can do it. I do."

"Gabriel is taking over because Annabelle kept her powers from you, and he saw her do one spell…but I feel like you're sitting on a lot more experience," I eyed him expectantly.

"We didn't have secrets from each other. And she didn't just dabble when she was in trouble. It was a way of life in the Quarter."

"She was a full-blown witch?" I asked.

"She helped people," he didn't label it.

"About the other memory…"

"It's okay," he assured me, as I struggled over not wanting to hurt him, but needing to know.

"Beth was pregnant," I shared. "I thought it was with Helen, but she was there too."

"Our son, Jackson," he gave me a smile, but his eyes were focused on a memory from the past, not on me.

I had a million more questions, but Gabriel came back, so Embry retreated to the stables.

"Ready?" Gabriel handed me the water.

"I want to try the tracking spell one more time first," I told him, taking a sip.

"Of course," he set everything up for me.

Instead of Donovan, I pictured Clara laughing and smiling, running around the orchard. I said the words to myself, with my heart yearning to see her and take her in my arms and protect her from all the bad things I brought into her life. The hand that wasn't holding the string rubbed the plastic ring she gave me for my last birthday.

All of a sudden, the string tensed so the crystal was no longer dangling, but pointing at a specific location. I looked up from the map, that showed Cape Cod, and saw the horror in Gabriel's eyes.

"I have people there, but I'll send word..." I could see him struggling to find a way to protect them without putting me at risk and realized I should have filled him in on my plans beforehand.

"It's okay," I put my hand on his. "Part of my problem is that I don't want to see Donovan, so I looked for Clara."

"Clara's the one on the east coast, at the Beach House?" He verified.

"Looks like." I couldn't help but smile that it worked.

"Not Donovan," he relaxed a little.

"I don't know where he is, but hopefully not."

"That's really smart," he beamed at me.

"I had help." He followed my gaze and saw Embry looking over at us.

"He does get you," Gabriel said.

"I think he might also get this stuff more than you give him credit for." I was hoping that somewhere along the way, the two of them would be able to put their differences, or similarities, aside and forgive each other.

"That's often the case," he surprised me. "Don't get excited," he warned, noticing the smile that was spreading on my face before I understood he was just stating a fact.

"Unbelievable," I shook my head.

"A three-hundred-year-old habit is hard to break," he defended himself.

"Are you even trying?" I brought my palm to my forehead and ran my fingers back through my hair, sighing out my frustration.

"I'm here, aren't I?"

"Because you have to be."

"You should have seen us with Rosie." A shadow passed his face, but was gone as fast as it came. "And Cassie, before she sat us down and gave us a severe talking to," he smiled at the memory.

"But it didn't change anything?"

"We have been incredibly civil ever since," he assured me.

"Maybe try nice and friendly from now on. See how that goes?"

"I can try," he said with a shrug.

"He's pretty awesome," I looked over to Embry, who was now sitting on a bushel of hay with Charlie, both of them laughing.

"I remember," Gabriel said with a smile, but I could see a hint of sadness over what he lost.

I rolled my eyes before we worked some more on my tracking spells. We went through all the people I wanted to see, finding them exactly where they were supposed to be, before I finally tried Donovan again. I still didn't want to see him, but at least I knew it would work if I put myself through the fear.

I kept my eyes closed, even after the crystal moved.

"California," Gabriel checked the map.

"Then he isn't coming after us," I breathed a sigh of relief.

"Not yet," he said with an edge. It was only a matter of time.

CHAPTER SEVEN

Working on spells left me exhausted by the time I got to bed every night, but at least I felt like I was accomplishing things. I couldn't spend my days reading the Chronicles anymore, so I tried to wake up early and read them over breakfast.

"Anything interesting?" Embry asked, walking into the kitchen. He put a cup under the Nespresso machine for his morning shot of caffeine. He looked more at home here than anywhere else, even if he said he hadn't been back in years.

"Haven't you read them before?"

"I have, but you and I have very different interests. I could spend hours poring over a handwritten grocery list from Beth, which would bore you to tears."

"Fair enough," I considered his question. "We all have different handwriting. Even though we're identical replicas or whatever. Like this note was slipped in Beth's section, but it was clearly written by Cassie."

"Clearly," he agreed with me, but I got the impression he had no idea. "I could tell it wasn't Beth," he shared.

"And Beth decides out of nowhere to leave blank pages, or

ones that have nothing but pictures of teddy bears and imaginary flowers."

"You sound upset by this," he smiled, the pictures making him a lot happier than they made me.

"Cassie and Beth had the most interesting sections, full of adventures and remedies and potentially useful information. I thought I had pages and pages, but out of her last twenty, ten of them are blank," I explained.

"You were gypped."

"Exactly."

"I can't defend her ways, although that is a beautiful work of art that deserves to be admired," he said of the six-legged horse we landed on. "I might have something to make up for it, for you at least."

"A museum?" I teased.

"An apothecary."

"Like a pharmacy?"

"It's time you meet Ingrid," he decided, finishing his espresso and going upstairs.

BY THE TIME I came down after getting dressed and ready for a potential adventure, Embry and Gabriel were both at the bottom of the stairs.

"Family outing?" I asked.

"If you're leaving the property, we're both coming," Gabriel explained, giving Embry a warning look.

"Are we going far?" Excitement mixed with fear to form a ball in my stomach. Adventures were exciting when I thought protecting me was a ridiculous precaution, but I was coming to enjoy the protective cocoons that made me feel slightly safer than the world at large.

"Just the Quarter," Embry said like it was nothing at all, so I pretended to know exactly where that was. Gabriel, for his part, was ever-alert, as if we were heading right into a war zone.

WE DROVE to a parking lot where they gave me a sunhat to keep me slightly disguised, with my long hair falling down my back to cover the birthmark. Embry walked ahead of us on the pedestrian street to show the way, while Gabriel stayed back with me. The Big Bad wasn't currently on our tail, but he was going to be looking for the three of us together, and we didn't want to make things too easy for him.

"Have you been here before?" I asked Gabriel. We were keeping a leisurely pace to not draw suspicion. I was grateful that I didn't have to half-run to keep up, but I could tell he wished we were going a lot faster.

"New Orleans and the Quarter many times, but never to the apothecary."

"But you stayed with Embry when you came?" I found it weird that Eric met him, since the guys avoided each other if it wasn't to protect me.

"I've met Charlie loads of times over the years. I met Eric once when he was very little. Charlie asked for Embry's help when he was away somewhere, so he sent me."

"What kind of help?"

"Neighborly stuff," he shrugged it off, which could mean they didn't want me to know, or he didn't want to make a big deal of whatever he did.

"Where do you go when you're not with me?" I asked. "Before this summer, when you weren't visiting me at the manor, where did you live?"

"Why do you ask?" he looked to me with a slightly raised eyebrow.

"I've been realizing how little I knew about you and Embry before this. How much I still don't know."

"You weren't supposed to know," he said simply, but part of me was hurt.

"Not even where you live or what you do? I can't believe I never asked."

"If we had shown up when you were older you would have asked all the questions, but you were so young when we met you. By the time you cared about those things, we were no longer new, or strangers, we were just there."

"I was also afraid of you," I admitted.

"Of me?" he sounded surprised, so I looked at his face to see if he was joking. It was as dark and intense as ever.

"Sometimes there were glimpses of what I assume is the you from your first life, but most of the time you were this stoic presence that kept his distance and dressed entirely in black."

"What changed?" he asked me with a smile, since I mostly described what he was like to this day.

"I saw glimpses," I admitted, nervous under the very different intensity of his current gaze.

"Of what?" he pressed.

"Of someone who cared," I shrugged. "Mostly about Annabelle, but sometimes about me too."

"Only sometimes?" he asked.

I could feel my face blushing until Embry came out of an alley we hadn't seen him turn into.

"Over here," he ushered us in.

"I.V. Strauss Apothecary?" I read the sign. It was old and musty, like it hadn't been changed in centuries, but the window dressings made it look like the inside was a Pottery Barn.

"I think you'll enjoy it." Embry had the same look on his face as when he handed Clara her birthday present and waited impatiently for her to discover the chef's hat inside.

Wind chimes went off when I opened the door, but they

were coming from somewhere deeper inside the store. The first fifteen feet were exactly like an Anthropologie or some fancy home decor and knickknack store. Different sized jars lined the walls, fauteuils were covered with soft throws, antique tables housed assortments of crystals...there were minimal items on the shelves and lots of open spaces. It had much more of a one-of-a-kind vibe than most stores this size.

The next few aisles were covered in pots and jars and bags of ingredients and spices. It smelled like a combination of cinnamon, vanilla, and pepper, with a vintage register at the end.

The rest of the store was separated by burgundy curtains that looked like a wall until you got close enough to see the sheer section that served as a doorway.

"Ing?" Embry called once we were the only patrons.

"Em?" A voice came from behind the curtains a second before they parted to a cloud of smoke. A little girl rushed to us and nearly jumped into Embry's arms. She was wearing a burgundy dress with an olive colored shawl, her long blonde hair cascading down her back.

I raised an eyebrow before she looked around and saw they weren't alone.

"Oh...I didn't know you brought company, I would have kept..." she was incredibly nervous, with her eyes darting to the curtains like she wanted to run back inside.

"They're friends," Embry assured her.

"Beth!" she exclaimed when she finally looked at me. She came close and took my hands in hers. "Is this Marilyn's daughter?"

"Lucy," Embry agreed.

"He warned me, but you look just like her," she told me.

"Except for the hair," Embry pointed out.

"No, you're what? Eighteen? Nineteen?" she asked, getting a good look at me.

"Eighteen," I said.

"She kept it like this until her twenties. I told her she shouldn't cut her beautiful hair, that no man would ever look at her..." she looked from Embry to Gabriel and changed her mind on what came next. "But she looked gorgeous with the bob as well."

"You're the Ingrid who was like a sister to her?" I asked, having seen the name in the Chronicles many times recently.

"They were inseparable," Gabriel agreed, letting me know that although he hadn't been to the apothecary, he still knew Ingrid, or at least of her.

"We were the same age, once upon a time," Ingrid told me. "The day she moved here I decided we would be best friends and we stayed that way until the day...until the end."

"I'm sorry," I said of her loss, before the wind chimes went off somewhere above us.

"I'll be right back." I could tell it was Ingrid, but she now looked to be about thirty.

"What happened?" I asked Embry.

"I tricked her into showing you her true self, but she normally presents herself as older, so people don't assume they can take advantage of her, and child services don't get involved."

"Is that her Gift, or..."

"A spell?" Embry finished for me. "I believe she was a 'witch' in her first life, but her Gift is to alter your perception of reality. I would not want to get on her bad side."

"She looks so young..."

"Eight," Gabriel shared. "They were both thirteen when I first met them, but Beth had been living here since she was four." Which meant Beth was there for Ingrid's death, and coming back to life, before she found out about Gifteds and what she was. Unless Ingrid kept it from her, but I didn't think that was the case.

"Where were we?" Ingrid came back to us and waited until the customers left the shop before reverting to a woman roughly my age.

"I brought Lucy here to see if you had anything useful to teach her, or wisdom to impart as she follows in Beth's footsteps."

"I could feel it the moment you walked in," she told me.

"Feel what?" I asked before the chimes rang out again, a warning for her to assume a different appearance.

"Mr. Fraser, how can I help you?" the thirty-year-old version of Ingrid asked a man in his fifties who slowly made his way to the register, shaking his head.

"They got Frankie too." He sat in the antique chair like it was too hard for him to stand with the weight of his news.

"Who got him?" Embry asked.

"Who are they?" Was Mr. Fraser's response.

"Friends," Ingrid assured him, but he looked at us with suspicion, before I felt like a huge hand was trying to push its way into my skull. I aggressively shook my head and grabbed my temple, making Embry and Gabriel turn to me before Mr. Fraser cried out, "Ow!" and they all turned to him.

"I said they were friends!" Ingrid got upset and slapped the back of his head, which made him cry out again.

"What did he do to you?" Gabriel came to stand between us with a look that could kill.

"I don't know," I looked to Ingrid.

"Mr. Fraser can read minds. Usually, he's in and out with none the wiser, but I've seen that happen once before..." Ingrid was smiling, which told me the last time she saw it was with Beth.

"Is everyone in New Orleans Gifted?" I asked.

"He's not Gifted, he just pays a heavy price to age very slowly." She put a green ceramic pot on the counter for him.

"You trade in secrets that you steal," Gabriel accused, the vein in his forehead pulsing.

"She's a friend," Embry stood between Gabriel and Ingrid.

"Who got Frankie?" I asked, bringing us back to before everyone was defensive and on edge.

"We don't know," Mr. Fraser admitted, looking like he trusted me even less now that I blocked him out. Or maybe he could see that I looked like Beth.

"Frankie is the fourth person to disappear in the middle of the night. There's no sign of forced entry, no struggle, nothing to make the cops take any of it seriously."

"Did they maybe just run away?" I ventured.

"One of them was a six-year-old boy. He didn't run away," Mr. Fraser was upset.

"He was kidnapped?" I asked, my heart tightening with thoughts of Clara. "Cops would investigate that."

"They think his father took him, so they put out an Amber Alert, but they're looking for the father, not the child."

"Isn't that the most likely scenario?" I asked.

"Not when the father was a violent SOB who is buried in the backyard," Mr. Fraser said under his breath.

"He read it off the mother, he didn't participate," Ingrid assured us.

"Was everyone who disappeared a patron?" Embry asked with concern, putting his hand protectively on Ingrid's arm.

"No, just Frankie and Billy's mother," Ingrid defended herself. "We see the missing posters all around town."

"Do you think it's…" I started to ask the guys, but Embry and Gabriel both shook their heads, even though it was one of their signs for danger being close by.

Mr. Fraser didn't look like he would be leaving any time soon, so Embry and Gabriel exchanged a look. "We have to head out, but we'll try to stop by another time," Embry told Ingrid.

"Bring her by on Wednesday. It's usually quiet, so I can show her a few things," she said before grabbing the middle book in a stack she was using as a table for a vintage Tiffany lamp. "In the meantime, a little light reading," she smiled as she handed me the large volume and brought Mr. Fraser behind the curtain.

ON THE WAY BACK, Embry walked with me and Gabriel went off on his own.

"What's up?" he asked me.

"How much do you trust her?"

"Beth made her godmother to Helen and to Jack," he said simply.

My mom chose Mr. and Mrs. Boyd for me, because she didn't have anyone else she trusted, and you couldn't be baptized without godparents. I considered this a moment, then asked, "Did you ever think of Gabriel for godfather?"

"He was my first choice," he gave me a sad smile. "Why don't you trust Ingrid?"

"She's basically paying a man to invade people's minds and tell her their secrets," I pointed out.

"He's an unsavory character, but he's harmless. And it's more like she pays him not to tell anyone else what he finds out when he hears people's thoughts," he defended her.

"He was pushing hard to get into mine." I could still feel a pressure, although that might be the wall my mind put up to keep him out.

"If every door you came across flew open when you walked up, wouldn't you try a few things if you suddenly found one that was closed?"

CHAPTER EIGHT

My next lesson was making things float, which evolved into seeing how much I could move before I lost all accuracy and safety went out the window. I got nervous when floating heavier or dangerous things over people, or anything involving breakable objects, which usually made me lose concentration and drop them. I managed to lift a really big rock, but a mole ran out from under it, so I panicked and dropped it. Thank God it wasn't on the mole

"How is this useful?" I asked, rubbing my hands together to stop the tingling.

"Patience, padawan," Embry teased.

"What's next, Master Yoda?" I asked instead.

"I appreciate the enthusiasm, but I think that's enough for today."

"We have things to take care of, but Charlie will be next door if you need anything," Gabriel sounded reluctant, but looked resigned.

"Is this the kind of thing where you leave me for days?" It wasn't that I hadn't enjoyed spending time with Terrence and learning to knit when they abandoned me last time, but I didn't want to be left behind again.

"We're looking into those disappearance, making sure it doesn't have anything to do with you," Embry assured me.

"But you'll be back today?" I verified.

"Take the rest of the day off and we'll be back in time for dinner." I looked into Embry's eyes and decided I trusted them to come back to me.

"Just don't leave the property," Gabriel amended.

"And let us know where you are at all times."

"Of course." I rolled my eyes at their predictability before going to my room to get the Chronicles. I probably would have secretly explored the house, looking for clues on Helen, Jack and Beth, but I would never snoop when there was a possibility Embry could find me.

I BROUGHT the huge book to a garden swing deep in the yard and got comfy. I was half-hoping and half-terrified that Beth would use the Chronicles as a diary, but she only wrote about noteworthy adventures, remedies, potions, and some spells. So far there was absolutely no mention of Embry as more than her protector. Helen was the only child in evidence, from drawings and scribbles rather than actual mentions.

I was reading about a celebration Beth did with her friend Ingrid, when Charlie walked up to me. "I'm sorry, there isn't usually anyone here when I take my afternoon stroll," he apologized.

"I can go if you..."

"No, I was rejoicing at the company," he corrected, taking a seat beside me on the swing.

"Company would be nice," I agreed.

"Isn't school out for the summer?" he asked, nodding to the Chronicles.

"Stories from my ancestors." I closed the volume, not sure I wanted him to know about any spells or magic it might mention.

"Don't stop on my account. I spent sixty years with a woman who always had a book in her hands," he said fondly. "She died last spring, but there wasn't a single idea that she shared with the world before sharing it with me first." He must have noticed my reaction, wondering why he was such a controlling and restrictive husband, because he elaborated, "She wrote books, and I always got to read them first."

"What kind of books?" I asked.

"Mostly on science, but she wanted them to be understood by the masses. People like me, not just the ones with PhDs. That's not to say I'm not smart, but it's a different kind of smart than she was."

"You're Mr. Haynes," I realized, remembering when Embry told me about Laurel Haynes, whose husband was Gifted in the sense that he was the one who convinced her to publish her books. She would have written them no matter what, but shared them on a much smaller scale if he wasn't around.

"No, Laurel kept her maiden name for the books, that way no one bothered us out here. It's Mr. Finch, but friends call me Charlie." His hand was callused from a lifetime working outdoors, but when I shook it, I was surprised to find it was still soft.

"Did my grandmother know her too?"

"Your grandfather introduced us," he shared, smiling at my surprise.

"I never met him," I admitted.

"Of course you didn't. But I think you would have gotten along wonderfully."

"All I know about him is that he liked vintage cars and died when my mom was in high school."

"That's a shame," he looked genuinely hurt over it.

"Grams died when I was really young too," I told him. I have memories of my Grams where she is kind and loving, but also a bit paranoid and removed from the outside world. Mr. and Mrs. Boyd would tell me she was different once, but the only example they had was that she used to have parties and visitors and go out all the time before my grandfather died. "You could tell me about them, if you're not too busy some time."

"I would love to," he beamed. "I have a million stories. I wouldn't know where to start."

"At the beginning?" I suggested.

"The beginning of her? Or of us?" he asked.

"When did you first meet her?"

"I can't remember not knowing her," he tried to think. "Her mom brought her here every summer, even after they moved to Boston. I met her before I could walk or talk or any of that."

"Did you two ever…" There was something about the way he said it that made me wonder if they were more than just childhood friends.

"First love and first kiss," he agreed. "I still get nervous around Embry sometimes."

"He was overprotective?" I smiled.

"Very," he agreed. "It was a weird dynamic if you didn't know what was going on."

"Probably weirder if you did," I pointed out.

"Arguably, yes."

"Who broke who's heart?" I asked.

"It wasn't like that," he brushed it off. "She was amazing. This fierce girl from the North who didn't let anyone tell her what to do. It was usually just the two of us, but anyone who met her fell for her. I was lucky enough to be her favorite person in Louisiana," he said, which sounded exactly like what I was asking.

"When did you meet my grandfather?" I asked.

"The summer we turned sixteen, we drove to Nashville to see Johnny Cash at the Grand Ole Opry. I won't lie and pretend I wasn't hoping something would happen, but Grant came over to say hi to her, and the way she looked at him, I knew she would never be mine."

"She broke your heart," I concluded.

"She would have," he agreed. "But by the time she admitted to liking him as much as I knew she did, Grant had spent quite a few weekends in New Orleans, most of them with his best friend, Laurel."

"Were they like you and my Grams?" I asked.

"I am told it was like kissing her brother, so she was relieved when he told her about the girl he met at a concert, and she orchestrated most of their trips."

"For him to see Grams, or so she could see you?" I called him on it.

"Her motives grew more selfish as the summer went on," he smiled.

"Did Grams still spend every summer here after she got married?"

"Once she went to college, she had to go home to Boston in the summers, but we were all at Louisiana State together, so I still got to see her."

"What did they study?" I asked. I had no idea what Grams did other than be rich and take care of me.

"Grant was in the science department with Laurel. Astrophysics and space stuff," he shrugged like it was all Chinese to him. "And your Grams was the only lawyer I have ever trusted. She refused to take on clients who were guilty and deserved to pay for their crimes."

"I don't think you're allowed to do that," I argued.

"Not technically, but she did."

He went on to tell me about her entire process once she

had her practice set up, where she would interview potential clients. "If the crime was one she found reprehensible and they were guilty, she sent them away. If it was a crime she might have committed if she were in their shoes, she would defend the innocent and the guilty alike."

"A lawyer with a moral code," I shook my head. It was hard to picture Grams as a powerful lawyer.

"And how many times did she get you out of something?" Eric came over, wearing dark blue jeans and a green plaid shirt with a cowboy hat, which would have made me laugh my head off, only it somehow worked for him.

"Only the things she got me into."

"I'm sensing a story," I smiled, hoping Charlie would share.

"Lots of them, but I believe my grandson came over for a reason."

"I'm down for stories," Eric assured his grandfather. "But if Lucy would like to accompany me, I was going to go riding."

"We've got time to finish this later," Charlie told me.

"Then I would love to go horseback riding with you. I'll change and be right back," I told Eric before heading inside to put the Chronicles away and change into a pair of pants.

When I got to the stables, Eric had a beautiful, butterscotch colored horse saddled and waiting for me.

"This is Donner," he introduced him to me.

"And who is this?" I asked of the chestnut mare he had for himself.

"Rudolf," he looked embarrassed. "We were very young when we chose their names, and it was December, so…"

"Reindeer," I let him know I understood. "Do you guys get snow here?"

"No, we don't. My oldest sister convinced us that horses were reindeer who lived in warmer climates."

"I'm sensing a lot of these tricks."

"My entire childhood," he agreed. "But now they're having kids and I'm their older and wiser uncle, so I'm making up for it."

"I didn't know you were the vengeful type," I remarked.

"It's not revenge so much as my duty," he argued.

"You're close?"

"Not like when we were all living together, but they come out here every summer, we get together at Christmas... I try to make it to all the birthday parties, but there are lots."

"How many nieces and nephews do you have?"

"Eighteen and a half."

"Missing body parts, or someone's still pregnant?" I got him to laugh.

"Franny married a guy who already had a four-year-old daughter, so she calls herself my half. As far as I'm concerned, it's nineteen, but the nickname makes her happy."

"My niece likes to introduce me as her sister-aunt to kids at school."

"But she's really your niece?" he asked.

"I was orphaned when I was four and the couple that took me in had a son. We grew up together, so I feel like his daughter is my niece, but I also still live with them," I tried to find a less tragic way to explain that every member of my family died, so I won't ever have a sister or a niece, technically speaking. He also didn't need to know that I'd lost Sam too. Maybe I was cursed.

"Sister-aunt," he agreed with Clara's title for me.

"I guess so," I rolled my eyes.

HE TOOK us through a path in the wooded area, toward the swamplands.

"Not a fan?" he asked when I kept slapping myself to kill the bugs.

"It's beautiful, but I'm being eaten alive."

"Zombies or cannibals?" he asked.

"Mosquitoes. They're not bothering you?"

"Guess your blood is sweeter," he smiled. "This was my favorite place to play as a kid, until grandpa freaked out."

"Is it dangerous?"

"The mosquitoes carry a deadly virus," he teased. "I think people might drown in the swamps sometimes, or there's alligators, but it had more to do with me bringing half the swamp back to the house with me."

"That could be upsetting."

"Now the horses play in the mud and I can outrun the bugs."

"I doubt that," I argued as he started slapping himself as well.

"Come on." He brought me around the property, which was beautiful, but also very different from our land in Boston.

He told me more about his family and his childhood with Charlie while I shared stories about life with Sam and Deanna, as if this was just a summer trip and everything would be back to normal once I went home.

WHEN WE BROUGHT the horses back to the stables, he showed me how to take the saddle off and let me brush Donner.

"Out of all the reindeer, why Donner?" I asked as I brushed. "I get Rudolph, but Comet, Cupid, Blitzen, Dasher, Dancer, Prancer, Vixen…"

"He came seventh," he shrugged.

"You're the youngest?" I guessed.

"They would never say unwanted, but my siblings were all born very close together, and I came as an afterthought."

"Maybe they missed having a baby."

"I'm Charlie's favorite now, so that's good enough for me."

"You liked it here because you got to be an only child," I understood.

"And there is nothing wrong with that," he laughed at being caught.

"Nothing at all," I assured him. I had wished for siblings, in the sense that I wished my parents had been around long enough to have more kids, but I was perfectly happy when I had Sam.

"Same time tomorrow?" Eric asked me.

"I have no idea what they have planned."

"Are you their prisoner?" he asked, mostly teasing, but I could tell he was curious.

"I thought you knew them?"

"Embry comes sometimes, but it's more like I know his house really well."

"I have yet to explore it."

"Most of the fun stuff is behind locked doors."

"It usually is," I agreed.

"Not a prisoner?" he verified.

"It depends on your definition." I considered it, but he looked concerned, so I backtracked, "They're looking out for me. I'm ninety-nine percent sure they're the good guys."

"Well, with that glowing recommendation..." he laughed, and I did too, until we ran into Gabriel. Literally, because it was getting dark and he was standing in the shadows, dressed in black.

"Where were you?" he asked, not exactly reproachful, but concerned.

"We went riding."

"We told you not to leave the property." The vein in his forehead was pulsing again.

"We didn't. I know the limits and we went nowhere near them," Eric assured him.

"Thank you." It sounded difficult for Gabriel to get out.

"I'll maybe see you tomorrow?" Eric asked me with a smile.

"Maybe," I agreed, smiling back. Eric went to Charlie's and I headed to the villa, leaving Gabriel outside to do god-knows-what in the shadows.

CHAPTER NINE

"Aim for the pads," Sam told me, holding them up to his chest so I could practice my jabs, my cross, and my hook, like Caleb taught me at the beginning of the summer.

"You have to follow them ladybug, the enemy won't stay still for you." He brought his arms out to the side and above my head, so high that I couldn't reach.

"I'm not tall enough," I argued, jumping as high as I could, but not touching him. Not even close.

"Find something to help you then. You won't always be evenly matched, and I can't be there to help you."

Of course not. You died. The thought came into my mind, but I pushed it away. Sam wasn't dead, he was right in front of me, training me like they should have my whole life, to prepare me for what we were up against. "There's nothing here," I said instead. We were in a field with tall grass. It was the perfect summer day, with not a cloud in the sky...but there wasn't any sun either. The light was white and artificial.

It felt like he kept getting taller and taller, so his head was further and further away from me. I looked around again, but couldn't see anything I could use to get higher, until Beth showed up out of nowhere.

"Beth!" I exclaimed. "Do you have a spell or something I can use? Maybe a ladder?" I asked, showing her how tall Sam was.

"You have everything you need," she said with a smile and a wink before walking over to me and crouching down, so I could get on her shoulders.

"Are you sure?" I asked, knowing I must be pretty heavy.

"I've got you," she said with confidence.

I climbed on and let her straighten up, which gave me a few extra feet, but it wasn't enough. I looked down, about to tell her we needed more height, but I recognized Cassandra walking over and crouching down, like Beth had. I was sure I couldn't stay on, that there was no way the three of us could stand on top of each other without toppling over, but we did. I was almost there, so I tried extending my arms, but I couldn't reach.

By now I was expecting it when Rosalind ran over and crouched down. I wasn't even surprised when Annabelle came and managed to carry us all on her shoulders, making me at least four heads taller than Sam, who smiled.

"You figured it out."

"I had help," I argued, bringing my gloves to his pads, as he slowly regressed to his normal size.

The world was beautiful from up so high, and I felt like I could do anything, but as 'our enemy' grew smaller, the girls relieved their charges, one by one. Once I was on solid ground, back to my own height, my ancestors smiled at me and walked off into the field they came from.

"Wait!" I called after them, but only Annabelle looked back at me and smiled, none of them even slowing down.

"They did what they needed to," Sam shrugged, taking off the pads.

"Will they come back?"

"I guess if you need them to."

"I need all the help I can get right now."

"You're living the adventure we dreamed about."

"Not like this," I argued. "It was supposed to be scary and thrilling, with magical creatures and pirates and happy endings."

"You can't tell if the ending is happy until you reach it," he reminded me.

"When did you start talking like this?" I asked instead of telling him that the ending couldn't be happy if he wasn't there.

"When I became a grown-up," he ruffled my hair.

"I miss how easy it was when the manor was my playground and I was cute, so you followed me around and played all my games. Your mom made us cookies and ice cream, both if I was sad..."

"You were an annoying little monster," he was clearly lying and couldn't keep a straight face.

"You loved me."

"Still do," he assured me, as the clouds moved overhead. I looked up to see if the sun was still there, but when I came back down, we were in the parking lot at the motel.

"Sam, we need to go." I felt a chill and knew in my bones that something terrible was about to happen. I looked around in fear for Donovan and his followers to pounce on us. "Sam!" I turned and his throat was slit, with blood pouring out of it.

"Lucy," he struggled. "What did you do?"

"No, I didn't want this to happen, I tried to..."

"How could you?" he asked, clutching at his throat before falling to the ground.

"Everyone you love dies," Donovan came out of nowhere and spat, less than an inch from my face.

. . .

I SCREAMED and woke up in a room I didn't recognize, with sweat pouring off me. I pulled the covers up to my chin and tried to breathe, reminding myself I was in Embry's house in New Orleans and it was just a nightmare. My breathing came back to normal as Gabriel rushed in, but the pain in my heart remained. The part that made the dream a nightmare was the part that really happened.

"Do you hear that?" I asked as Embry ran into the room, holding a baseball bat. I saw that Gabriel had discarded a fire poker when he saw I was alone in the room.

"It was just a nightmare," Embry said, sitting on the bed with me.

"I know. I'm sorry I woke you, but...that's my name." I wasn't sure at first, but I could hear it as clearly as Embry's words. Someone outside the window was calling my name.

"Is Charlie's..." Gabriel sounded like he was ready to have some very unpleasant words with Eric if he was the cause of my nocturnal turmoil.

"No, it sounds like..." I stopped myself. It didn't make any sense. They would think I was crazy.

"It sounds like what?" Embry asked, but the sound was already growing faint. With the lights on and the guys there, I could almost convince myself I imagined it.

"It sounded like Sam calling me," I admitted, hating the look they exchanged, full of pity and concern.

"You don't hear it anymore?" Gabriel asked gently.

"Not as clearly."

"What was the nightmare?" Embry asked, his hand still on mine to help me calm down.

"It was just a weird dream with Sam." I knew how it sounded. "But then he died, and it was my fault, and he was so hurt."

"Sam knows it wasn't your fault and doesn't blame you," Embry told me.

"No, the real Sam doesn't know or feel anything, because he's dead." I knew he was trying to help, but this wasn't something I wanted to feel better about.

"Pancakes?" Gabriel asked, making Embry and I both look at him like he was crazy. "Unless you would rather go back to sleep, but it's 4 a.m., I'm up and I'm hungry."

Embry looked at me to assess how I was feeling, so I shrugged, "I'm not getting back to sleep any time soon."

"I'll get them started."

There was one other time Gabriel made me pancakes in the middle of the night, although if memory served, they were actually crepes. Clara had this freak fever and I can't remember where Embry was, but Sam wanted someone to stay with me at the plantation so I wouldn't catch it, and Gabriel was the one who showed up. I was not happy and wanted nothing more than to be back with Sam and Deanna, helping them take care of Clara. I would sing to her until she fell asleep, and hold her hand, so I spent the night on the couch, convinced they were going to call for me. When Gabriel realized I wasn't sleeping, he made crepes and we had one of those rare times where it's the middle of the night and he talks to me.

Part of me expected Embry to go back to bed so it would be like last time, but I knew that wasn't going to happen when I was this upset.

It was hot in the house because Embry didn't believe in air conditioning unless it was so hot there was a chance we would melt. Still, I felt a chill, so I brought the quilt from the bed down with me.

"Do you want to take out the toppings?" Gabriel asked me while he worked the griddle.

"I'll set the table," Embry volunteered.

I took out peanut butter, Nutella, cinnamon, sugar, bananas, strawberries, lemon, cheese, and apples, then got chopping and slicing.

"What kind of toppings are these?" Embry asked once the table was set.

"It's the middle of the night so I didn't know if dessert pancakes or apple-cheese pancakes were more appropriate," I explained.

"You're adorable." Embry shook his head and started chopping the strawberries for me.

Soon enough we had a pile of crepes and a table covered with possible toppings.

"DELICIOUS," I said once I bit into my apple-cheddar crepe. I coaxed Gabriel into letting me put the toppings on while it was still in the pan, so my cheese was all melty.

"I thought you were starting with your savory one?" Embry asked when I put maple syrup on it.

"Don't knock it until you've tried it," I warned.

"Why are you wasting your time being smart when you could be a chef?" Gabriel had copied me, and clearly approved.

"You're both crazy," Embry stuck to lemon and sugar. He sometimes splurged on a strawberry Nutella one, because he knew how good it was, but he was a traditionalist.

"Speaking of weird dreams..." Gabriel brought it back to what had us all awake at this ungodly hour.

"We weren't," I argued.

"Is that the first one?" Embry ganged up with him against me.

"I haven't had that particular dream before."

"But..." Gabriel caught on.

"But the ending is what I see all the time. Sometimes it plays over and over again and I can't make it stop," I admitted, using all my will to keep the tears in my eyes without letting them fall. I tried to sound like it was a minor annoyance, rather than something that kept me from sleeping most nights.

"You're right that we can't speak for Sam..." Embry said delicately, like they did every time they used his name around me. "But both of us would gladly give our final lives to keep you safe, without blaming anyone but the asshole who did it."

"My brain knows that. But he didn't give his life to save mine. He gave it because I chose not to go with Donovan. His death didn't change anything. They still kidnapped me and then I got away. Maybe if I had gone willingly, I still would have escaped, but I wasn't brave enough to take that chance."

"You had no way of knowing what would happen. The potential consequences of giving Donovan what he wants are much greater," Gabriel insisted.

"And now that I have this magic thing that came out of nowhere...maybe I could have saved him. Instead of being selfish and scared for my own life, I could have tried to protect his. Instead of killing a woman to save myself, I could have evaporated Donovan to save Sam."

"This is why you don't sleep at night?" Gabriel was full of empathy, which somehow made it worse.

"I sleep," I argued. "Just not easily and not well."

"I wouldn't want you to be feeling this bad over it for me," Embry tried to reassure me with more things Sam could no longer do.

"Even if you had a wife and a daughter who didn't get to say goodbye, who would never see you again?" I admitted what weighed on me the most. My brain understood that Sam knew what would happen and still told me to go for it, but

Deanna didn't expect to lose her husband for me. I was the reason Clara would grow up without her father.

"Sam didn't die because of you, Lucy, he died because of the kind of person he was. The kind who insisted on being your guardian and refused to let us take you, even when we told him all of the dangers it entailed," Embry said with such conviction that I nearly believed him.

"That's another thing that scares me. I might not get the chance to have them yell at me and hate me, because they could be the next targets the Big Bad decides to use against me." I was failing to keep the tears from falling, but I fervently wiped them away as if that would prevent anyone from knowing they were there.

"They're safe," Gabriel assured me.

"Just because we know they're at the Beach House doesn't mean they're safe," I argued.

"I don't just know where they are, Luce. We have codes and signs to keep in touch. There's something Deanna can do that would alert people we trust if something was wrong. Help would be there within minutes of her doing it. We have people watching the house, watching the town. And she checks in every three days to let us know they're okay."

"Every three days?" I asked.

"Without fail," he agreed. "It's not like a phone call where we talk and ask questions, but the last one was yesterday, and everything was good."

"And you know for sure that it was her, not someone trying to keep up appearances?"

"I do."

"Have you read the book Ingrid left you?" Embry asked me, completely changing the subject.

"The first few pages," I played along.

"If it's the book I think it is, that's the one that tells you how to track essences, rather than a location on the map. You could see what they're doing rather than where they are."

"The one you said was dangerous?" I asked Gabriel.

"For Donovan, yes, but we can work on it today for people you care about," Embry took the lead.

CHAPTER TEN

We lasted until 10 a.m. before I fell asleep on the swing with Ingrid's book, not long after Embry tipped his hat over his eyes and drifted off in the field. Luckily, my dreams were just dreams, that didn't make sense, but didn't upset me either.

When I woke up, I was lying on the swing with a blanket over me and Ingrid's book on the table beside me. I looked around, confused because Embry fell asleep before I did, but then I saw Gabriel a few feet away, keeping guard.

"Do you always take turns sleeping?" I asked, not ready to be awake yet.

"I'm not tired," he held in a yawn, which made his face look ridiculous and revealed his lie. "At night, inside the house, we take precautions so there's at least an overlap, but outside, when the rest of the world is awake and plotting, I would rather not chance it," he tried to say in a nonchalant way so I wouldn't feel like I was in danger, but it was ever-present.

"I can keep watch if you want to take a nap," I offered, yawning with a stretch. I wasn't sure if I was ready to face the day or to go back to sleep.

"I'm good," he assured me with a smile.

"I know I'm not useful yet, but I can definitely manage to wake you if someone shows up," I defended myself.

"You're incredibly useful Lucy, don't sell yourself short."

"True, an entire league of super soldiers wants to use me to take over the world."

"You're useful alive too," he told me. "There's more to you than looking like Annabelle."

I wanted to ask him what the more was, but he was looking at me in that intense way that made my heart beat faster and my cheeks flush. "I'm thinking I should get a tattoo and cut my hair in a really weird way," I said instead.

"They know what you look like. A haircut won't trick them," he argued. "Unless you were planning on a face tattoo?" he kept his distance and would lean back as if he wanted to end the conversation, but then he would lean in again.

"Face and neck," I played along. "That way I'm unrecognizable from the front and the back."

"Not the craziest idea I've heard," he leaned back and got comfortable. "What would you get?"

"The face is hard, because it has to be big, and my mouth and eyes have to fit into it, but I feel like skeletons and spiderwebs are overdone..."

"People actually do that to themselves willingly?" he stopped me, leaning close.

"They do," I laughed. "And in the back either a rainbow or a skull with crisscrossed bones."

"Please elaborate," he asked of me.

"Depending on the face, I either need the rainbow to tone it down, or the skull to ensure no one will ever approach me."

"I'm not sure a face tattoo would be enough of a deterrent."

"Paired with my personality?" I used self-deprecation because he wasn't teasing anymore.

"You don't stand a chance at scaring people away once

they actually get to know you." I swallowed, feeling my heart pound before he went on, "You need to scare them away before they can get close." His eyes lingered on me.

"Hey, you're awake!" Eric interrupted, causing Gabriel to retreat, the moment gone.

"You saw me sleeping?" I asked, putting on a smile, but I couldn't help but wish he had come by a few minutes later.

"I saw you out here earlier. I wanted to see if you were up for a ride, but you were snoring."

"I don't snore," I argued, though I didn't have a clue if I did or not.

"Don't worry, it was cute," he smiled before looking awkwardly to Gabriel, kind of nervous. We weren't technically kids, but the guys gave off a vibe that told people to stay away from me.

"Don't mind me, I was just leaving." Gabriel got up, but he looked at Eric in a way that made him even more nervous.

"I think we were supposed to work on stuff," I argued, nodding towards Ingrid's book.

"Embry can help you with that when you get back. You two should go have fun!" Gabriel walked off, but it was weird. I felt like I did something wrong, or I upset him, and I didn't like it.

"Did you not want to come?" Eric looked at me expectantly.

"A ride sounds perfect," I assured him, heading for the stables.

I CHOSE Donner again and got him saddled, then Eric mostly let me lead. I think he felt that I was in a weird place and needed to clear my mind, because there was a lot of galloping and I was out of breath by the time we got back around mid-afternoon.

"It's like you've been riding your whole life," Eric smiled while he unsaddled Rudolph and I brushed Donner.

"I had an excellent teacher and an amazing horse."

"You can also take credit."

"I do, when it's deserved," I assured him.

"You're pretty special, Lucy Owens."

"Thank you, Eric...Finch?"

"Finch," he agreed.

"I didn't even know your last name."

"Don't sweat it, you know the important stuff."

"Like your favorite Care Bear?" I brought up one of the random things I knew about him. Daydream Bear for him, Grams Bear for me.

"It doesn't get more personal than that," he teased. "Although it's a lot easier to find people with last names."

"Find them..." I pressed, my brain going straight to the people hunting me.

"You know, after you go home, when you realize you miss me," he got a huge smile that I couldn't help but reciprocate.

"Yes, last names would help at that point."

I shook my head at him before Embry walked over, smiling at the two of us.

"Ready to try some stuff?" he asked me, holding Ingrid's book.

"Time for your daily homework I guess," Eric sounded disappointed. He always called it my homework. We never openly discussed magic or the Gifted or any of that stuff around him, so I couldn't tell if he was oblivious and really thought we were doing quizzes and science experiments every day. The guys were overprotective and could be overbearing, but I doubt either of them really cared how well I did in school. Especially since it was highly unlikely I would ever be stepping foot in a Harvard classroom. I winced, trying not to think about what this year was supposed to look like.

"We won't be too long. You can probably have her for supper."

I turned to Embry, not sure what was going on, but he gave me a head nod and something resembling a wink.

"Then I guess I'll see you later, Miss Owens," Eric said before heading to Charlie's.

I FOLLOWED Embry to the other side of the barn, where the blanket was already laid out on the ground.

"What do we need for this one?" I asked, seeing nothing but the checkered picnic blanket.

"Nothing but you," he said simply. "Even for the other tracking spell, all you really need is the crystal, the string, and the map. The rest was to make you feel like you weren't on your own, but you just need a clear picture of the person you're scrying for. Most of the words to these simple spells become superfluous when you know what you're doing. It's all about intention."

"I will things to happen?" I severely doubted his assessment of my skills.

"There's a little more finesse to it. It's not like you can will yourself to win the lottery or fly, but things don't happen because you channel a candle's energy or say something in Latin...they happen because you set the intention for them to," he explained.

"Ingrid's book has pages of instructions. It would be way lighter if all you needed was intent."

"There are methods to help channel your intentions. I'm not knocking them. I'm saying the way it worked for Beth, and seems to work for you, is that you don't need that extra boost."

"No pressure," I sighed.

"I don't want you to be somewhere and need to use a spell but hold back because you don't have the right crystal," he explained.

"Didn't it also say I needed something from the person I was tracking?" I asked, mentally going through the pages on tracking people. I saw them in my head like chemistry labs; a set of ingredients and the steps you take to combine them into something better. It was pretty easy to figure out what ingredients were used to boost the magic signal, but I felt like the object of the person you're tracking was essential to not track the wrong person.

"You have your ring, so we can start with Clara." He sat on the blanket. "But I'm pretty sure it will work without objects for people you have a strong emotional connection to."

"Only love, or fear and hatred too?" I thought of Donovan, not wanting any kind of connection to him.

"I wouldn't use this version for someone you didn't feel positively towards. My car broke down when I was driving back from a trip to see Caleb and Etta, so Beth got worried. She used this tracking spell and... I don't have powers, so I didn't know exactly what was going on, but it was like I could feel her in my heart and all around me. Not in an over-whelming way, but I think that if I was someone who did have powers and wanted to hurt her, it could have been dangerous."

"What exactly am I doing?"

"Why don't we try with Clara, then you can tell me if you want to use it for other people, or Donovan," he suggested.

"Is it safe?" I was nervous now.

"For Clara, it should be," he said reassuringly. I trusted him more than anything in this world, but the magic...not so much.

We opened Ingrid's book to the appropriate page, and I

closed my eyes. I slid the ring into the palm of my hand and held it, picturing Clara laughing as she dragged me through the garden, wanting to show me some creature she discovered, or a fort she built us in the trees. It was all so real that I could hear her laughing outside my head, then everything changed. It was like I suddenly zoomed in on her from outer space. She was building a sandcastle on a somewhat deserted beach, wearing a bright yellow swimsuit with an overly large sunhat.

"It's not a real cake because it's made out of sand," Clara explained, checking on the mounds she laid out on the rocks behind her to cook in the sun. "Maybe we can make real ones after supper, with sprinkles, and I can lick the spoons?" she asked.

"Only if you eat all your food," Deanna warned, but she was smiling.

"We can keep some for daddy and Lucy," Clara tried, keeping her head down, but bringing her eyes up to see Deanna's reaction.

"It's not like we can eat all the cupcakes ourselves," Deanna agreed, but I felt like her smile was forced. Thinking of Sam broke her heart as much as it did mine.

"So?" Embry asked when I came back to him.

"It was like I was there and felt her. She was making sandcastles and... I could feel the sand, and the warmth of her sun." It sounded crazy, even to me, but crazy was relative these days.

"That's how Beth described it," he agreed. "She said it was like---"

"Like a part of me went to her," I finished for him.

"She said a part of her essence, but yes."

"I would never want to do that for Donovan." I shivered just thinking about it.

"That was my assumption."

"How does it feel for Clara?" I asked, not wanting her to freak out as he had described for himself.

"Like a hug."

"From me, or from someone?"

"I felt like it was from Beth, but I might have made the assumption based on the limited number of people who felt that way about me and could do magic."

WE DID IT A FEW TIMES, so I got to see Deanna making brownies with Clara, and Keisha working on a research paper before Embry called it a day.

"What are our dinner plans?" I asked when he said I was free to go.

"I didn't have any, but it sounded like you and Eric…"

"He's nice, but I don't know how much he knows about me, if I can trust him, or if getting close to him just puts him in danger," I admitted.

"Charlie knows. And it's not like we hide when we practice," he pointed out.

"Why are you so invested?" I asked.

"Because you're a Bearer of the Crescent Moon, but you're also a teenage girl who just graduated from high school and deserves to have some fun with someone her own age and be reminded what she's fighting for."

"Why are you acting like we're safe here? Just because we got rid of Gabriel's tracker…"

"Because of Beth," he sighed, another memory making him sad. "She made sure this property was safe for her friends, for me, and in case someone ever came after her family. Cloaking, warnings, places where magic doesn't work…she thought of everything."

"I thought magic disappeared when the person who did it…" I couldn't say the words to him, but I could vividly see the sink going back to its original state when the woman died.

"Some of it does," he agreed. "Donovan's control, my mood

swings...they end as soon as we do. But if Etta heals you, you're healed. Some magic lingers..."

"How do you know which is which?"

"You don't. But then again, once she heals you, the wound is gone. I need proximity to alter your mood, and Donovan needs a bond to control someone...they're temporary in nature."

"But the protective spells are permanent?"

"The important ones are," he assured me.

I BROUGHT Ingrid's book back to my room, but when I came downstairs, Embry and Gabriel were having a heated argument in the kitchen.

"What do you know about it?" Gabriel's voice carried with anger and indignation. "Just because you inserted yourself into her life doesn't give you the right..." I tried to mind my own business and not listen, but I could feel that this fight was a long time coming and there would be consequences. I debated walking in and interrupting them, but waited in the living room instead. Hopefully, it was the type of thing you had to get out, so you could get over it.

"You don't understand, Embry. You have no idea what you're talking about."

"I love her, and I will not let you—-" Embry fumed.

"Let me?"

It wasn't that I was eavesdropping, because I tried to tiptoe to the door, but it was hard not to hear their angry whispers. They were talking over each other, so I got the tone more than the words, until Eric showed up and they stopped, leaving an awkward silence until Eric asked if he should come back later.

I hid behind the staircase a second before Gabriel barged in and stormed off through the front door. I heard the car start and wanted to run after him and beg him not to leave, but all I could do was hope he would come back. I got that it was upsetting to have your best friend fall in love with your girlfriend when the two of them thought you were dead, but it happened over three centuries ago. It was time to move on.

Gabriel eventually came back, but he and Embry avoided each other like the plague. As soon as one of them walked into a room the other was in, they would look really annoyed, then leave.

I tried talking to both of them individually, to make them see how ridiculous they were being, but the daggers their eyes shot told me to mind my own business.

It was a relief by the time Wednesday came and Embry said I was still going to Ingrid's shop. I was hoping they would put aside their differences and go together to protect me better, but they made up some excuse as to why it was smarter to take two separate cars. I rode with Embry, and Gabriel followed us incognito-style, so it was like he wasn't even there.

"You know you can tell him about Beth and the fight would be over. You guys could kiss and make up for centuries of—"

"It isn't about Beth," he argued.

"Not directly, but…"

"Maybe it's time he gets off his high horse and sees that my mistake doesn't give him the right to go around for centuries hurting people and toying with their emotions," he said before taking a breath that was full of regret. "I didn't mean that, I'm just upset."

"I think it's also a mistake that you were married at least five years and didn't tell him. Whether it was to an Owens woman or some random girl out there, if I was him, I would be hurt about that," I pointed out.

"He stopped being my best friend centuries before my wedding."

"How did you guys manage to raise Margaret together?" It felt like they mostly survived my childhood by spending limited amounts of time together, running off to do their own things once the big moments were done, and only talking to each other about me.

"It was like when parents stay together for the kids. Regardless of how we felt, Maggie needed us, so we were there for her."

"But I'm not a kid anymore?" I asked of the sudden change in their behavior.

"No, you're not." He looked pointedly at me, then shook his head and let out a breath.

"Funny how you can make me a child or an adult at whim, depending on which way you need the conversation to go."

"You're not a kid who can be fooled by us getting along. By the time Margaret was sixteen, we would take turns going on business trips, and she knew exactly why."

"She knew why you didn't like each other?" I doubted it.

"She knew it was to avoid each other, but we managed to keep the why out of it. For all of his hating me, he never wanted her to."

"Yeah, he definitely hates you," I said sarcastically, looking out the window to try and see Gabriel in my side mirror.

When I gave up and looked back at Embry, he had a tiny smile.

"We've been through a lot," he sighed. "And even though we've spent way more time not liking each other than we did as best friends, that's still how I see him."

"But..." I saw it coming.

"But this won't be fixed by an apology. It's not just him who is mad at me this time. He has things to answer for as well."

"And will you tell him that?"

"No," he told me.

"That's why I still meddle, even when you tell me not to," I pointed out.

"I know," he assured me.

THE STORE WAS CLOSED when we got there, but Embry knocked so Ingrid, looking about my age, could come and let us in. "Perfect! You're just in time," she said, ushering me in. "You can come to get her around four o'clock," she added for Embry.

"We don't leave her alone," he argued.

"This is why children rebel and hitchhike across the country," she warned him.

"I'll take my chances," he assured her.

"TV's upstairs, but don't touch my peanut butter squares," she held out a finger at him.

"Wouldn't dream of it." He took a staircase behind a wall of beads I would never have known was there.

"Just in time for what?" I asked. She ushered me to the back room she came out of the first time I met her. I hesitated a bit in the doorway before following her in. At first, I couldn't see with the dim lighting and the smoke that made me cough, but my eyes adjusted so I could see the large iron cauldron over a fire in the middle of the room.

"Seriously?" I asked. If Embry didn't trust her so much and I hadn't seen her magic with my own eyes, I would have assumed she was a fraud who watched too many movies.

"A friend brought her kids, so I put on a little show for them. It's a genuine cauldron, but there's nothing but spaghetti sauce inside."

"Genuine cauldron as in..."

"As in it's ancient, from Salem, but ninety-nine percent of the witches there couldn't do magic to save their lives, so in this case genuine means it's really old."

"Do you know which ones could?" I asked of the Salem witches, wondering if there was a secret directory or something in the Wiccan community.

"Annabelle was, wasn't she? At least that's what Beth told me. Most real witches knew better than to get caught, and if they did, they could get out of it."

"You weren't..." I let the thought linger, but her smile told me she understood.

"I was born the same year as Beth. I just find it fascinating," she got a dreamy look. "There'll be time for questions later; I want you to see the bloom." She brought me to another room that was like a greenhouse with special lighting, misters and temperature controls. It looked more like an illegal drug operation than the back room of an apothecary.

She brought me to the end of the room, where a large potted plant had a single bulb in the middle.

"Take this and hold it here." She handed me what looked like a miniature pewter cauldron, filled with a foul-smelling orange liquid.

"Are you sure it's blooming today?" I didn't see any sign of movement or growth in the bulb.

"Any minute now," she smiled, with scissors in her hands. "Keep it steady," she warned, eyeing the mini cauldron.

I did as I was told, though I didn't see the point, until the bulb suddenly came to life. The green pulled back, petal by petal, slowly revealing a beautiful flower of deep red and magenta. It was mesmerizing, but just as it reached what I felt was its full potential, Ingrid used the scissors to cut the flower off and let it fall into the mini-cauldron I held steady.

"What was that for?" I was upset that she killed it before it even had a chance to fully bloom, after making such a fuss about it.

"The potion you are holding takes a month to mature and is good for less than three days before you need a new one. The Cereus Labilis blooms once every year for mere seconds, but the flower is the pivotal ingredient in the potion. The fuller the better, but if I cut after it starts to close, I have to start all over and buy a new plant," she explained.

"What does the potion do?" It sounded like a complicated one.

"Numbs the heart," she said dismissively.

"That doesn't sound good." They said Etta could heal everything except a broken heart, which told me there was a reason why that shouldn't be done. You have to let time slowly fit the pieces back together.

"It isn't. But when you lose a child and still have another one to take care of, you need something to get through the day."

"Do you usually sell ingredients, or full potions?"

"Most of my clients dabble for fun, so they get the ingredients and the cauldrons and the crystals and they feel more in control of their destinies. A lot will come here to replenish their stores of particular items, while others will only come to me for something incredibly complicated, with dire consequences if they mess up."

"Like this one," I understood. "Potions are your strong suit?"

"I can alter what you see better than anyone, but my other magic is amateur at best. Beth usually did the spells and let me mix the potions."

"You were in a coven together?"

"We were best friends. We did everything together," she gave me a sad smile.

"Do you know what it is you're meant to do?" I asked delicately. While some might see it as a chance to live forever and be invincible, I got the feeling Ingrid was anxious to move on.

"Rule the world," she teased, unaware that it was not a laughing matter for me. "There are people who are in the right place at the right time, while others have skills and a drive that compels them to do something. For me, that's potions. I assume I will invent a formidable potion someday. Or use a normal one to save someone formidable."

"But you won't know if you got it until you don't come back."

"I'll know when I turn nine," she argued.

"What do you mean?"

"In my very limited experience, dying before you achieve your purpose brings you back and stops time where your body is concerned, preserving you to that moment in time. I believe that once you do what you're supposed to, time starts again and you live the normal life you should have."

"You start over?" I asked, thinking of Gabriel and Embry.

"I'll be me, with all my years and experiences, but I'll be able to turn eighteen and date a man who can actually see me, rather than what I imagine I would look like at that age."

"Do all your customers know…"

"Most don't," she shook her head. "I age until I turn thirty or so, mention a niece or a daughter, take some time off to 'die', then come back as someone new," she used air quotations when she said 'die', like it was a dirty word.

"Is Ingrid your..." I knew it was what Beth called her at least.

"My real name," she agreed. "Most people call me Ivy currently."

"I.V.," I remembered the sign. "But Mr. Fraser—-"

"It's nice to have someone you can be yourself with. When we're alone, I call him John," she assured me.

"This is for the mother of the boy who disappeared?" the potion turned a deep purple.

"Aye, but they found Billy."

"I can't imagine what she's going through." I was used to losing people, but that didn't make it any easier. And I'm not sure I would recover from losing Clara.

"Someone drowned him in the swamps. It was so shallow that a person would have to choke you out or hold your head under," she shivered and wrapped her shawl tighter around her body.

"I'm so sorry," I told her.

"Not as sorry as whoever did this will be." I didn't necessarily feel unsafe, but there was a dark focus to her actions. I wouldn't want to cross her. "How did you like the book?" she changed the subject.

"Very interesting. I had this weird dream, so Embry suggested I use your tracking spell to make sure my family was okay. I liked that."

"What kind of weird dream?" she perked up.

"I saw someone die, so I see it happen when I close my eyes sometimes," I tried to make it not sound weird and depressing, but she looked at me like she knew it wasn't only sometimes, or just someone.

"What was weird about it?" she stopped what she was doing with the potion to look at me.

"I felt like he was calling me," I shrugged. It was less weird than the human pyramid, but it was Sam's voice in the middle of the night that stayed with me.

"In your dream?" she asked, going to a bookshelf.

"More like after I woke up," I admitted. "No one else heard it." I felt fairly confident she wasn't going to lock me up for hearing things.

"They aren't usually this active..." she said, mostly to herself.

"What are we talking about?"

"The fee follet," she finally looked up to me.

"Of course." Like that made any sense.

"You're staying at Beth's?"

"Yes, but what are fee follet?"

"They're fairies," she brought the book over to me. "Louisiana's version of a siren. They appear as a floating light and call out to you. Instead of luring sailors into the rocks, they lure people into the swamps."

"This happened before?" I asked.

"It's usually one or two people every decade, although they're more active during great wars or epidemics."

"Did a big tragedy happen recently?" I asked.

"No, which is why I didn't consider them before. But if you heard them calling you..."

"I did."

"I'll look into it," she assured me.

"Is there anything I can do?" I offered.

"Whip me up a sleeping draught."

"Are you having trouble sleeping?"

"For you," she corrected. "To learn, not take, unless you feel like you need it. Some potions require more than mixing the right ingredients in the proper way. Others, like this draught, demand finesse. I have half a dozen we should get through before Embry takes you back."

. . .

BY LATE AFTERNOON, Ingrid had guided me through the steps of making a sleeping draught, truth serum, an antidote to most common poisons, a love spell, a focusing draught, and one that burns through things like acid, but doesn't hurt skin.

"A love spell?" Embry asked while we drove home and I gave him a recap of my day.

"She says it's temporary. It lasts six hours if ingested, but you can get ten minutes or so if you throw it at them."

"How would that help anyone?"

"It wouldn't if my goal was for them to love me forever, but if someone bad captured me, I could maybe convince them to let me escape. It would at least give me a couple of minutes head start."

"She's...special, but she knows what she's doing. I've seen her get out of impossible situations with mostly her wits," Embry said fondly.

"And magic."

"No, I think she was worse during the summer she chose not to use magic. Helen was eight, and just lost her mother, so Ingrid thought it would be fun to really bond with her goddaughter. I think she wanted to stop hiding for a while as well. She was a force to be reckoned with."

I finished off by telling him about the fee follet, and how worried Ingrid seemed to be about them, before we pulled into the driveway, closely followed by Gabriel. I wondered what he did in town all day, or if he was only with us for the drives.

CHAPTER TWELVE

On Friday morning, Embry left early under the pretense of running errands. I'm pretty sure he was just spending the day at Charlie's so I could have some time with Gabriel. It was like an unpleasant reminder of Keisha's life when her parents were getting divorced and figuring out an arrangement that worked for everyone. My vote was still for them to forgive each other, especially after Keisha's parents ultimately chose to have her dad live hours away and hardly ever see her.

Gabriel got back from his run as I was putting my cereal bowl into the dishwasher.

"Would you like some coffee?" I asked after he took off his headphones. Running turned me into a sweating mess, where my hair went frizzy and my skin got blotchy; it wasn't pretty. Gabriel, on the other hand, was glistening and tan from the sun, so he looked like the statue of a Greek God, rather than a hot mess. It was unnerving.

"I would love some, thank you," he said before going up the stairs, presumably to shower.

I used the French press and ground some beans to be

fancy, while making myself an Earl Grey tea. I made a lot of it, and I made it strong, in the hopes of adding ice to it later. The sweet tea here was amazing, but I was craving something with less sugar.

"Are you ready?" Gabriel asked, coming over and taking a sip of the coffee I made. He ran his hand through his hair, shaking it to remove the excess water.

"Coming." I took my tea and followed him to the blanket we always practice on.

"What am I learning today?" I asked. I was able to track people on a map, make small objects float, and make things temporarily catch fire, even without a candle. Luckily, it was a safe fire that didn't burn you when you touched it, because my instinct the first few times was to send it away from myself, which usually meant throwing it straight at Gabriel.

"I thought we would try a few of these." He opened the Book of Shadows to pages with dark borders. I had ignored them ever since I saw the picture of an invisible hand choking a woman on the first one.

"Or we could see if I can levitate."

"You can," he motioned to the rock I overturned.

"Myself," I argued.

"That would definitely be very cool, but I don't think it would be useful," he pointed out.

"Probably not against the Big Bad, but for day-to-day chores, grabbing things off high shelves...very useful."

"Cute," he assured me. "But I thought you wanted us to train you, so the next time they find us, you won't be defenseless."

"That's true," I agreed. "But if I never use them, what's the point in learning them?"

"Why wouldn't you use them?"

"Because I don't really trust the magic yet, and those spells look like something I don't want to accidentally use on the wrong person or go too far."

"We can start small then, see if you get comfortable, and stop whenever you want," he offered.

"Okay."

HE WENT through the book and found a page he thought fit the criteria. It had ropes drawn around the text, but closer inspection revealed that it would immobilize someone, as if they were held in place by ropes.

"Useful but doesn't harm," he waited for my reaction.

"What should I practice on?" I looked around for a bag of potatoes or something. "The scarecrow?" I asked of the tiny, doll-like figure out in the distance of Charlie's yard.

"You won't know if it works unless you try it on something that moves."

"We can go to the swamps Eric takes me to. They're full of mosquitoes," I suggested.

"You can practice on me," he turned my idea down.

"What if I do it wrong and hurt you?"

"I trust you," he assured me, but I was still nervous. "I'll just come back," he teased, trying to make me smile, but I wasn't there yet. "You've got this, Lucy. I promise." He took my hands in his to support his claim, but I could feel my heart beating faster and my cheeks going red from his touch.

I reread the page in question, which didn't have an incantation, just advice on things I could to say to focus my powers, and the intention I needed to have. It was great that Annabelle and Beth had so much faith in their powers and intentions, but what if I was distracted or my mind wandered, and I did something terrible? What if I ended up doing one of the other things from those pages, with much scarier images of missing limbs and storm clouds.

"Are you okay to try it once?" he asked after a couple of minutes.

"Sure," I said, feeling anything but.

Gabriel walked towards me, slowly, so I concentrated on stopping him. I imagined invisible ropes around his arms and legs, keeping him in place.

"I'm sorry," I said when he reached me without anything happening.

"You don't have to apologize."

"I tried," I told him.

"But…" he said like he already knew the answer.

"I don't want to hurt you. I don't want to concentrate too hard and stop more than your limbs, or think of something or someone else and…"

"I get it."

"You're upset."

"I'm not," he assured me.

"You wanted me to learn all their magic and I'm not making it easy."

"The magic isn't for me," he said, taken aback.

"Embry?" Now I was confused.

"You say you want to fight Donovan and the Big Bad next time they come…"

"We can't keep running and letting them surprise us and take Sam," I agreed.

"How did you expect to do that? Martial arts and weapons?"

"It can't hurt, compared to not knowing anything to defend myself."

"I have seen Caleb go against them. I've had help from someone with blades at the end of their arms…Cassie was strong and fierce, and she had knowledge and weapons…"

"She gave up," I pointed out, which was clearly the wrong thing to say, because he glared at me like I was the one who murdered her.

"She gave her life to protect her daughter," he argued. "And it was after a long time spent running away from them, and a terrible defeat."

"You let her fight them?"

"We didn't have a choice. He surprised us and we were never very good at getting Cassie to do anything she didn't want to," he got a sad smile as he remembered her. "The point is, I could train you in every weapon and every martial art I know, but I don't think any of that will make a difference. Because the real Big Bad, he doesn't need to touch you to kill you. He might not even need to be in the same room...I'm not saying this to scare you..."

"But I'm dead no matter what?" I let him know I understood.

"No," he was upset. "Weapons and combat won't defeat them, but you have something Cassie didn't. You have Annabelle's magic. The only reason I am pushing you to learn how to use it is that if I have to let you defend yourself against them, I need to give you a fighting chance."

"And you think these spells are my best chance to stay alive?"

"I do."

"I can't let them win," I sighed, resigning myself to being uncomfortable.

"I can't lose you." He looked right at me as he said it, with an intensity that made me feel like he could hear how fast my heart was beating. "None of us are willing to accept that outcome." He turned away from me, but it took a while for my heart to go back to normal.

"Let's try again," I relented.

"I don't want to push you if it makes you uncomfortable.

It's no use to us if you *can* do stuff to them but you're never actually going to use it."

"I'm nervous about my powers but you're right. I would rather learn how to use them, so I can focus and immobilize the next person who comes at me, instead of blowing them up," I took a deep breath, trying not to see that woman, or the pile she became when I was done with her.

"If it's Donovan, or the Big Bad, or anyone who is trying to hurt you, you do what you need to stay alive," he waited until I met his eyes, adding weight to each word.

"But hopefully it won't come to that?"

"If I had my way, you would never know about any of this. You would live your life and be happy and none of it would touch you," he got a dark, haunted look.

"Bad things happen even if there isn't a Big Bad hunting you down," I said simply.

"I would protect you from that stuff as well, if I could," his eyes locked with mine in a promise.

"I know. But it's not something anyone can protect me from." I shook my head to snap out of it. "Do I try it on you again?"

"Do your worst. I can handle it," he assured me with an uncharacteristic wink.

He started walking towards me, so I imagined the ropes binding around him and he stopped. It wasn't really like invisible ropes, because other than his eyes, he couldn't move anything. Not even to try and break free.

"It worked!" I said excitedly, but he was still frozen in place, so I imagined him walking to me again, which he did.

"That was perfect," he beamed.

. . .

WE WORKED on that a bit longer, then I tried to build an invisible barrier between us, so whatever he threw at me would bounce off.

"There has to be a way to combine both," I said after we were at it for hours. I could either make one that blocked his high-speed body from colliding with mine, or one that stopped objects he threw at me from getting through. The same barrier couldn't withstand weapons and magic. I had to let one fade away and conjure a new one, which was not an easy feat.

This was the first spell to take a lot out of me. I had to rest a bit between each attempt, or the barrier disappeared as soon as the first assault bounced off.

"What does the book say to do?"

"Imagine a shield for weapons, and a wall of energy for things with magic." I reread it every couple of tries to see if I was doing something wrong.

"Can you picture something in your mind that withstands both?"

"I could try," I shrugged.

"Go for it."

I imagined a wall of blue energy, like water, with a hard shell around it. Once I nodded to say I was ready, Gabriel threw a rock so it would hit above my head, but still within the force shield, and ran at me with his super speed. The rock hit and bounced back, so I closed my eyes to brace against the inevitable collision. I felt it happen, but it was a few feet ahead of me, where I had the shield.

I opened my eyes, ready to celebrate with Gabriel, but he was at least twenty feet away, on the ground and not moving. "Gabriel!" I screamed, my heart in my throat, cursing away tears as I ran over. I shook him when I got there, praying I hadn't killed him.

What felt like an eternity later, but was probably only

seconds, he woke up and coughed. The air was knocked out of him when he collided with my wall and bounced back into a willow tree.

"I thought I lost you. That I killed you." I tried to steady my breathing, holding on to his hand like an anchor.

"I'm fine," he assured me, struggling to get up.

"This is why I don't like the magic," I told him.

"Accidents happen, Lucy, it really wasn't that bad. With a bit of practice you'll be able to--"

"No. You say that I need to practice so I can control it, but I've been practicing and I'm still hurting people."

"You need to give it time."

"No. I'm never doing that again." I crossed my arms, cold now that the fear adrenaline was wearing off.

"Lucy..."

"You said we could stop, and this makes me uncomfortable."

"Okay." He wasn't happy, but he didn't follow me as I went back to the villa, still shaking.

CHAPTER THIRTEEN

Ⅰ woke up early the next morning and went for a jog. Staying on the property made it quite the workout, since I had to run through the wooded trails instead of flat roads. By the time I got back to the villa, I was exhausted and covered in sweat.

"What's with the new look?" Embry asked me, sitting at the kitchen table with his espresso.

I filled a large glass of water and drank it before answering him, "Working on my cardio." My breathing was still labored, but my heartbeat was slowly getting back to normal.

"Because you plan on listening next time we tell you to run?" he asked with the hint of a smile.

"Gabriel didn't tell you?" My legs were killing me, so I wanted nothing more than to take the seat next to him. I knew from experience that I should keep moving, so I walked around the room instead.

"He hasn't," he raised an eyebrow at me.

"I've decided that I don't want to work on the magic anymore. I want you guys to train me like what we did at Caleb's. Kickboxing, weapon-wielding, throwing things…

anything I can use against Donovan's army," I looked him square in the eyes.

"What about Donovan?" he asked after a moment, when his judgmental look didn't make me falter.

"You would never actually let me fight him. I'm not a match for him either way."

"Gabriel agreed to this?" he asked.

"He said I could stop with the magic."

"What happened? You were doing so good," he looked defeated.

"I was hurting people," I reminded him. "I practically set Gabriel on fire, nearly crushed the mole with that rock and almost killed Gabriel when I threw him into a tree."

"None of those actually hurt anybody," Embry argued.

"I killed that woman in the diner. I'm sure she had done terrible things, but there's a reason why we put people in jail and have trials before giving them the death penalty. I didn't even know what I was doing. I raised my arms and she died. I don't ever want that to happen again."

He opened his mouth to say something, then looked at my face and reconsidered, "I won't force you to do something you don't want to do."

"Thank you." I took a seat beside him. "Will you train me?"

"I'll do everything in my power to make sure you get through this," he assured me, putting his hand on mine.

I SPENT my mornings training with Embry, alternating between kickboxing and fencing, then Gabriel would come in the afternoons and do some capoeira or aikido with me. We had just started hand-to-hand combat and it was by far my favorite. I would say I was getting good at it, but learning the equivalent of a choreography with Gabriel was not the same thing as fighting an assailant who took me by surprise.

Last night, Embry had asked me what I would feel most comfortable using if Donovan's people found us again, so I wasn't surprised when he showed up during my training session with Gabriel.

"Why are you hoping I'll be terrible at this?" I asked, knowing how upset he was that hand-to-hand was my favorite.

"Because if you're more confident in hand-to-hand combat, you're going to let them get close enough to use it, which isn't something we ever want to happen." Their faces showed nothing but concern.

"Or I won't panic when someone happens to get close," I argued.

"In a crisis, we don't rise to the occasion, we fall back on our training," Gabriel said like a mantra, upping the speed of the training because I refused to stop and let them talk me down.

"We can keep working on the sticks and swords too," I assured them.

"Fencing doesn't count," Embry argued.

"Then why did you bother teaching it to me?" I called him on it. True, the swords in fencing wouldn't be my first choice if I was attacked, but the skills had to be transferable to real swords.

"In an ideal world, they would never get close enough for you to use any of it."

"You're still planning on hiding me any time someone comes close to us? Spend the rest of my life running?"

"If you're using sticks and stones to fight them, then yes," Embry at least sounded apologetic.

"They won't be unarmed when they come for you, Lucy," Gabriel pointed out. We were in a groove, going faster and faster so I felt completely connected to him. Then he went faster than humanly possible and got my wrists in one hand behind my back, the other arm resting against my neck before I even knew what was going on. "They will either have weapons you can see, Gifts that you can't, or both."

"But you can use this in the future, if there's a weird guy on campus or something," Embry tried to make me feel better as Gabriel released me, his point made.

"Do I even have a future? I either spend the rest of my life outrunning him, or he finds me and I'm dead."

"No," they said in unison, but neither had a plan nor reasoning as to why I would be different from all the Owens women before me.

"I know you think this is useless unless I'm going against a drunk college kid who isn't much taller or stronger than me," I summed up their concerns, "but I would like to have options if ever I am cornered with one of them again."

"You run," Gabriel said with an intensity that left no room for arguments.

"How about we call it a night?" Embry suggested.

"I'll go do some laps," I said, leaving them there and going to change into a bathing suit.

I WAS TRYING to make up for a lifetime of prioritizing book smarts in as little time as possible. My legs protested even light jogging this morning, but the water felt wonderful. I started out with the breaststroke, but mostly swam from one end to the other underwater. Adrenaline would help me go faster and harder, but learning to hold my breath and to control it would help keep me focused. Right now, I needed all the help I could get.

CHAPTER FOURTEEN

"It's a shame you can't see NOLA. You've been here for weeks and you still haven't seen more than this place and one store in the Quarter," Eric said, leaning against the edge of the pool. When he found out about my new goal of 'becoming a fighting machine' as he called it, he offered to teach me a few things from his time on the wrestling team in high school. It gave me a new appreciation of why the guys were so worried about me getting close to someone in a fight. Not that I would ever tell them that, but I had no interest in ever getting close enough to use wrestling. Unless it was a throw, after I got a lot better at them.

Once he ran through what he said were the absolute basics, we decided to go for a swim to rinse off the sweat, escape the heat, and enjoy his last day before going back to school.

"It's not really a sightseeing vacation," I defended.

"There's not sightseeing and then there's not leaving your hotel room," Eric argued.

"I'm sure you've noticed Embry and Gabriel are very over-protective."

"I have," he agreed with that smile. I was pretty sure he had every girl at Louisiana State drooling over him. Charlie either didn't let him out when he was here, or he came to get away from it, because it did not make sense that he was spending all of this time with me.

"What's the one thing I absolutely have to see?" I asked, making a mental list in case I made it out of this alive.

"Cafe du Monde," he said without hesitation.

"Out of all the history and culture in New Orleans, your recommendation is that I have a donut?" I verified.

"Beignets," he argued. "And I was mostly teasing, but they are delicious, and it's not that hard to get in and out of," he defended. "What would you want to see, since you seem to know all about it?"

"Someday, if I come back, I would love to see Bourbon Street and Jackson Square and do some ghost walks...but if you gave me an hour to explore right now, I would choose the library."

"You're one of those?" he asked, shaking his head like he knew it, and couldn't believe I fooled him.

"I am," I agreed. "But that's not why."

"The architecture?" he asked, not buying it.

"For starters, we don't have internet here."

"I can easily fix that," he offered.

"By choice," I stopped him. "But they also have the perfect combination of real books, and ones on fairytales."

"Are you saying fairytales aren't real? Or just the books that contain them?"

"They're real books, just not the published kind of book you would find on amazon." As I said it, I realized that was probably the exact kind of book you would find online, but I wanted a more reputable source than someone dabbling in witchcraft from their basement. I wanted the really old, authentic volumes with only a couple of copies buried in private libraries.

"How do you know what's in our library?" Eric asked.

"Ingrid. She owns the store we went to in the Quarter." I asked her about it during my last visit. It apparently also housed a paranormal cookbook with killer muffins, and histories of witch trials, like the ones in Salem.

"There's a little library less than a mile from here."

"She mentioned one in an old church..."

"At the fork in the road, under the oak trees," he finished for me.

"Have you been?" I asked.

"Not by choice," he smiled at my look of disappointment. "But I wouldn't mind bringing you to see it."

"Oh, you wouldn't mind?"

"Not one bit," he agreed.

"I doubt they'd let me go," I turned him down.

"What if we got lost horseback riding?"

"Are you being a bad influence, Mr. Finch?"

"I'm trying to be the knight in shining armor who gets you to your library," he feigned innocence.

"Where exactly is it?" I asked.

"Across from the old well. If we cut through the woods, it's literally across the street."

"Literally?" I pressed. Most people these days used that word interchangeably with almost. Or figuratively.

"Cross my heart and hope to die."

"Let's not go that far." I bit my bottom lip, considering it. Now that I knew the Big Bad could track us with technology, I was less on board with googling anything even remotely connected to Crescent Moon Bearers, but books could be interesting. Embry and Gabriel hadn't communicated their plans with me, but both of them were gone when Eric came by this morning. "I guess an hour couldn't hurt."

"It's really small. And boring. I would give it thirty minutes, tops."

I rolled my eyes then shook my head at him. He had no idea how long I could spend in a library.

WE LEFT a note in case the guys came back, and took the horses so we could pretend we stumbled on it and couldn't resist, rather than admit that we planned on defying the rules they put in place to keep me safe. We left the horses tied to the well and walked less than five minutes through the woods before we got to a road made of gravel, which told me people didn't often come this way.

I hesitated before stepping past the point that clearly represented the end of the property, then quickly crossed the road to get to the library. Eric was right about it being tiny. I was surprised it was even open, with an actual employee sitting behind the desk to welcome us.

"Oh, hi," she said, looking up from her screen four times before acknowledging us.

"Hi." I looked for a computer or some other kind of index system we could use to find what we were looking for.

"I'm so sorry, you're the first...how can I help you? What are you looking for?" she sprung to her feet, knocking over the plate of samosas she'd been enjoying while playing what sounded like pinball.

"Oh, don't worry about that. Is there an index?"

"We replaced all the shelves last summer, so I can tell you where absolutely peverything is," she assured me.

"Two things, completely unrelated, but umm...We have a school project on witchcraft and prophecies, then I also want to look into Elizabeth Owens. She lived next to his grandfather's place, a long time ago, so if you had some kind of records..."

"Say no more," she assured us, beaming with excitement. "I'll be right back."

"Witchcraft and prophecies?" Eric asked while the librarian ran off through the shelves.

"I have many interests," I said dismissively.

"For what it's worth, I didn't believe grandpa until you made the balls of fire float," he let me know he wasn't oblivious.

"It was a ball of paper that was set on fire."

"But you're not denying it?" he cocked his head.

"Would you believe me if I did?"

"No," he admitted. "But I could pretend if it makes you feel better."

"I would pretend too if I could convince myself."

"Not a fan?" he furrowed his brow.

"It's very new," I tried to explain my reluctance without eliciting the pity I had mostly avoided thus far. "There have been a lot of new things in my life lately, and none of them are good."

"None of them?" he teased, giving me an out.

"Maybe one or two of them," I conceded.

"Much better," he smiled as the girl came back with a pile of books.

"This is the key to the micro-fiche rooms if you want to know about anything that happened in New Orleans in the past few centuries. We should have all the newspapers available," she handed us a key and pointed to a room in the corner. "And these are the best books on the occult that we have. I mean, we have the standards, but these are more...obscure," she told me, but I had no idea what the standards were. "I'm Jessica if you need anything.

"Thank you."

· · ·

ERIC CARRIED the books to a secluded table in the empty library and handed one to me.

"What did she mean by the standards?" he asked, flipping through the pages. He clearly wasn't enjoying whatever he saw on them.

"I have no idea. It's all new to me," I reminded him.

"What are we looking for?"

"Anything that mentions the Bearer of the Crescent Moon." I flipped to the index.

"Sounds fancy."

"Believe me, it's not."

The first book I opened was on magic through the ages. The 'obscure' part of it was a section on spells in the back, which included pictures of their effects, that turned my stomach more than anything. Eric's book was really cool, on witchcraft in New Orleans. I made a mental note to ask Ingrid about it, because I could swear one of the pictures was her.

"What was that?" I stopped Eric as he flipped through a volume on the Salem Witch Trials.

"Inquisition Scandals," he shrugged, flipping back and summarizing it for me. "There's a judge who sent his cousin's wife to burn at the stake, instead of a simple hanging like all the other witches were sentenced to. His great-great-grandson also wrote a book they consider shameful."

I saw the picture and something clicked in my mind; Hathorne was the name of the judge at the Salem Witch Trials. He was the only one who never repented, but I had read the name in the Chronicles as well. I barely had time to grab the book before I was gone...

I WAS ANNABELLE, walking through Henry's property. She was familiar with it, practically showing him the way to a gazebo that overlooked a creek. She thought of it as her gazebo now. He'd told her that no one ever used it, but since she admitted how much she loved the view, he made it a staple of their walks. She pointed out the fresh coat of paint he added to the old wood, but every time they came, something was done to make the place more beautiful and inviting, be it clearing the dead leaves or putting out a vase of fresh flowers.

"I have a surprise for you," Henry said once we were seated. There was a small wicker table between us, upon which there was a candle, some paper, and an inkpot.

"Are you writing me a letter?" Annabelle teased.

"I am actually going to show you a part of me I keep hidden. A secret of sorts, that I believe it is time I trust you with." He was still smiling, so she felt no fear, only curiosity.

First, he dipped his quill in the inkpot, then used his right hand to shield his words from her gaze as he wrote on the paper. She straightened up, ready to read it, but he carefully folded the paper, then put the tip over the candle, until it caught flame. A trick I knew well.

"Why did you do that? How can I read it now?" she playfully reproached, trying to reach for it to put out the flames, but he pulled it away and let go. At first, she was worried it would burn his trousers as it fell, but the paper did not fall. The flames spread so the entire paper was ablaze, then he waved his hands and it floated to her, landing on our side of the wicker table. She reached forward to put it out, but was amazed when she blinked and the paper was whole again, not a mark on it. As if there had never been a flame at all. Her introduction to magic was a lot less traumatizing than mine was.

"How did you do it?" she asked, searching the paper and the candle, looking around to see what could have done the trick.

"Magic," he winked. "Read it."

She raised her eyebrows, hoping to discover his secrets, before doing as she was told.

Will You Marry Me?

"Henry, I..." I could feel her struggle as she wanted to turn him down, but didn't want to hurt him. There really wasn't an appropriate way to tell him she was still in love with someone else.

"What are you afraid of?" he wasn't upset, he was kind. I could tell that he loved her. "Let me love you. Let me take care of you. Be my wife," he proposed.

Annabelle knew Henry would be a great husband, a good father and he would make her happy. But then, part of the problem was that she wasn't sure if she deserved happiness anymore. I wanted to hold her in my arms and tell her everyone deserves love and happiness, but I knew I struggled with the same concerns these days. Henry was waiting for her answer, so she took another piece of paper from the pile, wrote "Maybe someday?", then folded it up and set it on fire as he had.

"What are you doing?" he asked, shaking his head at her ignorance with affection.

"That paper has my answer," she said, putting her concentration into moving the paper, excited more than anything when it also floated instead of falling onto the table. I understood what Embry meant when he said you just had to will it to happen. "What's wrong?" she asked, still enjoying the trick, but Henry's eyes widened, and his brow was furrowed.

"That isn't supposed to happen," he admitted, watching the flaming paper float between us.

"Of course not. It's magic," Annabelle smiled, not understanding what was wrong. Eventually, she saw Henry was truly concerned, and reached for his hand. As she did, the paper landed in his lap, but he had to wave his hand so it wouldn't burn him. He read her answer and looked up, but his smile did not reassure her.

"You wanted me to say no?" she asked, confused by his reaction.

"No," he admitted, shaking his head as if to clear his thoughts. "I

know I'll have to ask a few times before you get there. But that wasn't a trick."

"Of course it was, Henry. You can't light a paper on fire then have it come back as good as new. You also can't make things fly," she used reason.

"You're right, normal people can't."

"But we just did."

"My mother was a part of a long line of witches. When she had a son instead of a daughter, she decided to teach me some of her magic. That is why I could do that with the paper and the fire."

"You can't be magic, Henry. I did the same thing. It's the paper. Or you did something to the fire."

"Or you're a witch." He was worried about her reaction, she could tell, but she also couldn't believe his story. She thought he was confused.

They spent the rest of the afternoon with him giving her little exercises, small magical acts that she had more and more trouble convincing herself were parlor tricks. It reminded me of that first week we tried spells to see what I could do. Henry was throwing challenges at Annabelle to convince her, but he was also impressed by her.

"So, I have magic?" Annabelle asked when she could no longer deny what he was showing her.

"You're very gifted," he agreed.

"And you would still wish to marry me?" she asked. Her mind went straight to Gabriel, and whether he and Embry would still love her, or be afraid of her now.

"More than anything in the world," Henry kissed her temple before leading her back to his house...

"ARE YOU OKAY?" Eric asked me. He and Jessica were both standing over me, looking terrified.

"I'm fine," I tried to stand, but they wouldn't let me.

"Lucy," Eric argued, not believing me.

"I can call an ambulance," Jessica offered.

"No!" I cut her off mid-sentence. "I think I got too hot and I skipped breakfast this morning…" I looked to Eric, pleading for him to get me out of it.

"It's okay, I'll bring her to the clinic," he gave me a look that said he was actually taking me there.

"Are you sure?"

"I am. Thank you so much for your help. I'll try to come back next week," I smiled at her before getting up off the floor and letting Eric bring me outside.

IGNORING MY PROTESTS, he kept an arm around me to cross the street, into the woods.

"I'm fine, Eric, I promise," I told him.

"You're not fine," he argued. "You were, but then you saw something in the book and before you got a chance to freak out you were on the floor. I am bringing you to a doctor or to Embry or something."

"You can't," I argued. A doctor would ask too many questions and I couldn't have him telling the guys that I willingly went off the property. That something happened while I was there, vulnerable and exposed. "It was just a memory."

"What does that mean?" confusion replaced his concern.

"I sometimes get memories from my ancestors. One of them knew the guy in the book, Henry, so when I saw him…"

"You went into her memory of him?" he asked, looking at me like it made no sense, but also like he believed it.

"Sometimes I pass out when it happens and other times I act it out, which led to me almost jumping off a barn," I looked up to him and smiled, to show him I really was okay, but I didn't look where I was going. I tripped on a tree root and instinctively shot my hands up to protect myself, but

Eric's instincts were quick, and he reached out to catch me. Before I knew what happened, a burst of light shot out of my hands, knocking Eric into the side of the well.

"Eric!" I yelled in horror, rushing over to him. "Please don't be dead," I repeated to myself, shaking his limp and lifeless body.

CHAPTER FIFTEEN

"Eric! Oh my God, please wake up, please!" I could hardly see through all the tears, but I felt his neck to make sure he had a pulse. He was still breathing, so CPR wouldn't help, but I needed something to do other than wait for him to wake up.

After what felt like hours, Eric stirred, garnering him all of my attention. I moved the golden curls off his forehead for what must have been the hundredth time in the past few minutes, not sure what else to do.

He opened his eyes and looked around, disoriented and confused, but alive.

"Are you okay?" I asked, keeping my hand on his shoulder so he wouldn't stand up too quickly.

"I'm fine," he said, still trying to get his bearings.

"I'm so sorry. I didn't mean to… I would never want to hurt you."

"I know."

"This is what I was talking about. I can't control it and people get hurt and I am so sorry." The tears were warm as they ran down my cheeks, softening Eric.

"You have nothing to apologize for." His eyes finally focused on me.

"I thought you were dead." The sobs shook me as the adrenaline lost its purpose.

"I'm right here. I'm fine. It was my fault," he took me into his arms.

"I nearly killed you," I moved back so I could see his face, but stayed close enough that his arms were still around me. "I'm a death magnet. Everyone I care about dies." My breathing was back to normal, so I wasn't sobbing anymore, but the tears kept falling.

"I don't even have a scratch on me," he lied. There was no way landing on the wall of the well didn't do any damage, but he looked more worried about me than himself.

"I'll bring you back to Charlie's, then I'll stay away," I decided.

"You don't have to leave," he took my hand in his. I looked to him, so grateful for what he was trying to do, but I couldn't forgive myself if it happened again.

"Let's get you home," I gave him what I hoped was a reassuring smile, then helped him stand.

WE EACH TOOK our own horse, but it was like they knew something was up. They stayed close together, so I could convince myself that I could catch him if he fell.

Eric stayed quiet until we arrived at the stables. He got off his horse and looked at me with the same concern I was looking at him with, only he didn't have my guilt.

"Can we talk about this, or were you planning on pretending nothing happened?" his look gave me the impression Option Two wouldn't be happening.

"You can ask," I said quietly. "But you're sure you're okay? Maybe we should take you to a clinic, just to be safe?"

"I've had way worse. I'm tougher than I look," he gave me a sad smile.

"I slammed you into a stone wall. With supernatural force," I reminded him.

"I touched you without asking," He shrugged.

"To stop me from falling flat on my face," I looked at him like he was insane to compare the two.

"You're more beat up about it than I am," he pointed out.

"I never meant to hurt you. To hurt anyone. It scares me," I explained. Even Annabelle's enthusiasm for the magic died when she realized it was real.

"Do you want to start at the beginning?" he offered.

"My beginning was normal." I never thought I would look back fondly on the days when I was just a little girl whose family kept dying around her.

"Until?" he pressed.

"Prom," I said simply, telling him how I escaped from the window and ran into Gabriel, who whisked me off to the plantation after telling me he promised my ancestor to protect her line until she returned. How he couldn't die until that happened. I told him how the bad guys found us, so we fled, visiting other Gifteds. But the bad guys kept finding us. I struggled to tell him about the motel, how I have a birthmark the Big Bad is after, so he gave me the choice to go willingly, but I didn't. I chose to fight instead, so Sam fought with me and he died. They still got me and took me across the country with them until I escaped by killing someone and the guys found me.

"They said it would be over then, at least for a bit, but it wasn't. This lady found me in the washroom, and she was coming at me, but when I put out my hands, as if they could protect me...she disappeared."

"Into thin air?" he asked, being amazingly quiet throughout my entire tale.

"She was gone, but there was a pile of ash on the floor. We realized they found us with a tracker they put in Gabriel, so Embry took it out and we came here, where the guys decided I had magical powers and now they're trying to train me, so the Big Bad won't get me." I waited for his reaction, but he was taking his time, considering everything I told him.

"I guess I'm glad you only threw me into a wall and didn't turn me to dust." I looked to him, horrified, but he was smiling.

"This isn't funny," I warned.

"I know, but I would rather see you laugh about it than cry."

"What kind of person would that make me?"

"One who made a mistake, because she can't control a new gift she never asked for, but who would never hurt a soul otherwise."

"A gift?" I asked.

"What kid doesn't wish for superpowers?" was his defense.

"It's not all it's cracked up to be."

"But it could be," he shrugged. "You could figure out how to use them and become a superhero. Teleport places. Fly," he gave me options.

"I don't think it works like that," I argued, but he succeeded in making me smile.

It started to rain, so he took my hand as we ran to Charlie's, not stopping until we had shelter.

"What time do you leave tomorrow?" I asked him.

"Early." I could tell there was something he wanted to say, but I wasn't ready for him to make me feel better.

"Take care Eric," I gave him a goodbye hug, letting it last longer than I had intended, before leaving him standing there.

. . .

I WALKED in the direction of the villa, but I was overwhelmed by everything that happened in the past few months. I wanted to run, I wanted to punch things, I wanted to cry…I settled for a run through the trails in the rain, so I couldn't even tell if I was crying anymore. My legs burned and my shoes were soaked through, but I kept going until I had nothing left.

I WALKED BACK from the stables, taking a detour on the way to the villa so I could check in on Eric, maybe see him through the windows. I was walking around to the back patio when Charlie nearly made me jump out of my skin.

"He went to bed early. He has a lunch thing at school tomorrow." He was sitting on a patio chair.

"He told you?" I asked, walking over. He looked concerned, but not afraid of me, so Eric mustn't have told him everything.

"Enough," he agreed. "How are you sweetie?"

"I just wanted to make sure Eric is okay," I told him.

"I'm making some tea; would you like some?"

"I'm okay," I said, looking over to the villa. It was getting dark out, so the guys were either still out and I should be worried, or I was in trouble.

"Eric thought you might need some time," he caught my look.

"They know too?" I asked.

"They were worried when you didn't come back, but Eric was home, the horses were in the stables…"

"I should head over."

"He'll be fine," he assured me. I just wasn't sure I would.

CHAPTER SIXTEEN

Apparently, spending the evening in the same room waiting for me did not mean that Embry and Gabriel had resolved any of their issues. Rather, the fact that they weren't avoiding each other meant they were finally letting it all out without holding back, calling each other on all their pent-up anger from the past three centuries.

I heard the raised voices as soon as I walked through the door. I found them in the living room and tried to cut in to get them to stop arguing, but as soon as I touched them, I was gone. Only it wasn't an Owens memory...

"It really is like losing Annabelle all over again, isn't it?" Embry asked while he and Gabriel sat at Rosie's bedside. It was the middle of the night, but she didn't look like she would make it to morning. She was pale and sweaty, every breath sounding like a losing battle. I was able to walk around the room, rather than being confined to whoever's memory this was.

Gabriel was anything but friendly, practically glaring at Embry. "She isn't Annabelle," he argued. "She has her face, but she isn't her,"

Gabriel cringed, looking to my ancestor like he regretted his words. He and Embry both looked absolutely torn up by her imminent death.

"I'm sorry," Embry looked broken and apologetic. "Do you think there will be another?" he asked.

"There will never be another Annabelle," Gabriel argued.

"I know, but do you think there will be another one like Rosie, who looks like her?" Embry rephrased his question.

"You want one who loves you next time?" Gabriel was harsher than necessary. I remembered the look on his face when he told Rosie he didn't feel the same.

"Annabelle said she would come back," Embry reminded him.

"She said a lot of things," Gabriel turned him down, but whether they admitted it or not, they were both still waiting for her, even in my time...

"It's not like that for me. I love her like a daughter," Embry was saying when I woke up with both of them huddled over me. Someone had carried me to the living room and put me down on the couch.

"You did not love Annabelle, or any of the others, like a daughter. You were looking for your--" Gabriel did not appreciate what he saw as a blatant lie.

"I was looking for Beth," Embry cut him off.

"You're awake," Gabriel spotted me and helped me sit up.

"I'm fine," I assured them.

"What did you see?"

"Nothing useful," I tried to convey neutrality.

"What happened this afternoon?" Gabriel brushed the hair out of my face. He was oblivious, but his attitude in the memory stung.

"I tripped and accidentally knocked Eric into something," I said dismissively, though it was still weighing heavy on my heart. I didn't want lectures on being more careful or needing more practice; I wanted them to make up for once and for all. "You should tell him," I told Embry.

"Tell me what?" Gabriel asked. He looked once to Embry, then tried to read my face.

"I didn't just stay here to help Beth with Helen after David died. Maybe at first, but...we were married," Embry admitted.

"You got your own," Gabriel was upset. The words were meant to cut Embry, but as it was, they caused a pang in my chest.

"No, it had nothing to do with that. I understand what you meant, all those years ago...we had a son," he shared.

"A child?" Gabriel's mouth dropped.

"I got my happily ever after Gabe. It ended, but I am not looking to replace her. I love Lucy like a daughter because she is the daughter of my daughter's daughter's daughter. As far as I'm concerned," he added, since Helen wasn't biologically his. "I'm not looking for anyone else, I'm ready to get up there so I can be with Beth again."

"You had a child and never told me about it?" Gabriel looked hurt.

"It was the first thing I wanted to do," Embry mirrored Gabriel's pain. "It seemed so wrong to not have you there, for you to not be Uncle Gabe...but we haven't been friends since I broke both your hearts."

"Both?"

"I know she loved you. I would never have done anything to take her from you, but you died, and she didn't deserve to be alone. She deserved someone who would love her and still be okay with her being in love with you. When you came back, yes, it hurt that I was going to lose her, but I knew that was the only way things could go. You were meant to be, and I was the placeholder. She left, but if she had stayed, I would have been happy to step aside and let you both have your happily ever after."

"You weren't just holding my place," Gabriel argued, but the fight was out of him.

"Of course not. I loved Annabelle, and I would have fought any man to have her, but not you. You were my best friend and you loved her first and...as much as I do believe she loved me; she could never love anyone the way she loved you. I am so sorry."

"Me too," Gabriel admitted.

They stood there, looking at each other for what felt like forever before they finally pulled each other in for a hug. They slapped each other on the back, as guys do, but I think it was the first hug in centuries for the two best friends who finally forgave each other.

I didn't dare interrupt, but after a while, they pulled apart and Gabriel asked, "You said a son?" looking like he knew exactly what that meant.

"I was lucky," Embry gave a sad smile.

"I'm sorry I never got to meet him."

"Me too."

"How were you lucky?" I wondered if their son was an exception to Caleb's rule, and we had another branch to our family tree.

"Jack was with us for nineteen wonderful years." I knew from the cemetery at the plantation that sons didn't make it past childhood. I think ten had been the oldest one I found.

"I'm sorry," I said. Jack was barely older than me.

"Don't be," Embry assured me. "We never thought we could get pregnant, so that in itself was a miracle. When we knew it was a boy, we assumed we would have a couple of years with him, tops. I got to see him grow up and find his passion."

"Was he a World War 2 pilot?" Gabriel asked suddenly.

"A decorated war hero," Embry agreed with pride, the tears filling his eyes.

"I visited Helen not long after he died. She was torn up, but so vague about who he was to her."

"She doted on him like it was no one's business," Embry said fondly.

"What was he like?" I asked, getting the impression that after all this time spent keeping him a secret, he wanted to share.

"You don't need to humor me."

"I would love to get to know Jack," I assured him.

Embry went up to one of the two rooms he told us to ignore and came out with a large box full of letters, pictures, and rolls of film. When I mentioned that I would love to know about Helen too, he got another box and we spent the rest of the night visiting Embry's past. There were a lot of tears, but also lots of smiles and happy memories about Embry's kids, then about my other ancestors and their kids...all of the people Embry and Gabriel got close to, and then lost.

WE ORDERED pizza around 10 o'clock, which I don't think I have ever done with them, and ate it in the living room while watching old home videos. One of them had a visit from Gabriel, before Jack was born, so one minute we would see Gabriel entertaining Helen, then we would see Embry and Beth stealing a kiss in the background.

"I didn't want to upset you, or have you think I was using her, and she didn't want you to hate her for loving me," Embry responded to the question Gabriel wasn't asking.

"I think I see why Terrence called us stubborn idiots," he smiled.

. . .

After a while, they took out some top-shelf bourbon, so I decided it was time for me to get some sleep. I had spent most of the prior night tossing and turning.

We exchanged goodnights before I went to put my plate away. I lingered in the doorway, watching them laugh and catch up like the old friends I always wanted them to be. Gabriel must have felt me watching because he turned around and we locked eyes before I quickly headed upstairs. Not for the first time this summer, I wished I looked like anyone else.

CHAPTER SEVENTEEN

I was up long before Embry came downstairs the next
morning. He looked like he spent the night partying, but
happier than I had seen him other than in the memory with
Beth.

"Sleeping in this morning?" I called him on it, cradling my
cup of tea. I finished the Chronicles, which was more anti-
climactic than anything. Unlike regular books, this one didn't
have an ending. It went from a homemade remedy for chick-
enpox to a note saying another Bearer of the Crescent Moon
was born on September 20th, 1990 to Marilyn Owens and
Unknown. There were the tiniest of entries marking occasions such as the first time the guys met me, when Mrs. Boyd
died and Mr. Boyd insisted he wanted to raise me, then again
when Mr. Boyd passed away and Sam refused to let them take
me. It brought a tightness to my chest I wasn't expecting.
When people asked, they always apologized for the loss of my
mom, but no one really dwelled on the Boyds. For all intents
and purposes, they were the ones who raised me until Sam
took over, at which point he was more like a brother taking
care of me than a parent.

It was different for Mrs. Boyd, because I had known my mom, albeit briefly, and Grams. She was always an additional motherly figure for me, but Mr. Boyd was the only father figure I ever had. Unknown never showed up, so every Father's Day, Mr. Boyd was the one who received my macaroni flowers and glitter cards. When he died, Sam and I would get together amid celebrating Sam's Father's Day to celebrate the man who raised us. He was everything you needed a father to be.

"Where's Gabriel?" Embry asked after pouring himself a cup of the coffee I brewed for them hours ago.

"He hasn't come down."

"He's not upstairs," Embry argued. A fear came over me before I reminded myself of all the places he could be other than dead or captured.

"Morning," Gabriel came in after I listed all of his potential early morning escapes to myself. Jogging, surveillance, training...

"How are you standing?" Embry asked.

"I switched to coffee after the third shot," Gabriel reminded him.

"How did you manage to sleep?" I chipped in.

"That is why I already did my 10k, showered, got attacked by a dog, and figured out a game plan for today."

"Attacked by a dog?" I asked while Embry inquired, "Game plan?"

"We disagreed over who should eat my last piece of bacon. He won," Gabriel told me. "And I went through the Shadow Book to see what we could work on today," he elaborated on the game plan.

I didn't bother telling him it was a Book of Shadows, as I'm pretty sure he does it on purpose. "I'm not doing magic anymore," I reminded him instead.

"We don't have to work on new stuff. We can use the burning paper thing," he tried.

"No," I shook my head, the image of Eric on the ground all the deterrent I needed.

"Or the floating spell. We can use any of the simple ones."

"I said no," I repeated, not quite storming off, but choosing that moment to get a refill on my tea.

I could hear them whispering about me before Gabriel came over to the kitchen, with Embry hanging back.

"I know your powers scare you, and you don't want to use them," he began.

"I don't," I agreed.

"But not using the powers intentionally doesn't mean you won't use them accidentally," he paused so I could remember what happened to Eric, but he was using it as motivation to learn. "If ever someone invades your personal space or creeps up on you or…"

"I get the picture." Even catching me so I wouldn't fall could be deadly.

"I'm not blaming you, Luce, I'm saying it's new and you can't control it. Yet."

"When I try, people get hurt," I pointed out.

"That's why I thought we could work on that today."

"Using it wasn't helping," I argued.

"We're not going to learn new spells or practice the old ones for the sake of it. I want you to work on actively controlling your magic."

"How?" they kept saying I needed to control it, but never showed me the way, or anything that worked.

"Working on precision rather than power. Flinging your arms without making things happen. I want you to know how to not use them as well as how to master them."

"That sounds great in theory, but I'm not comfortable with any magic right now. I have nightmares of when I threw you into the tree, and Eric into the well, or when that woman…" I shuddered, remembering it, but I didn't want to say out loud that I killed her. "I feel evil when I use it."

"Magic is not inherently good or bad," Embry told me. "It all depends on how you use it. Good people use it for bad things, bad people use it for good things…"

"It's safer if I don't use it," I finished for him.

"If Clara creeps into your room next year on Christmas morning and jumps on your bed…" Gabriel asked me.

"That's not…why would you…" I could see it, because it was what Clara did every year.

"I don't want to scare you, I want to prepare you, so you never get that look on your face again," Gabriel didn't apologize for going there, but he explained himself.

"The more I use it…"

"I will never make you use it if you don't want to, but I think it's important for you to learn how to not use it when you don't want to."

I looked to both of them, terrified of what could happen from using my powers, but even more afraid of what could happen when I didn't mean to use them. "Okay," I reluctantly agreed.

EMBRY MADE US OMELETS, then we headed out to the field with the blanket, a stack of paper, a bag of rice, and a pouch of sand.

"How does this work?" I asked, sitting across from the guys, with our random objects between us.

"We'll use rice first," Gabriel explained, pouring some out into a little pile in front of him. "I want you to make that one float without any of the others."

"Which one?" I asked. There were at least a half-dozen he could be pointing to.

"This one right here," he used a strand of wheat to point to a grain of rice under other grains.

"But not the others?" I verified.

"Exactly."

I took a breath, then got to work. The hardest part was keeping track of which grain I was targeting, but I got it on my first try.

"Impressive," Embry told me.

"Do you think you could lift these three, then lift that one up to here?" Gabriel asked again.

It was easy to get the three grains up, but harder to keep them in place while lifting the other one higher. They faltered the first few times, but eventually, I got them to remain stable while the other one came higher.

"I thought the rice might be beneath you," Gabriel assured me, scooping up the remaining rice and putting it back into the bag.

"Sand?" I asked as he spread it out between us.

"Precision helps with control," he explained.

"What am I doing with the sand?" I sighed, but he was right. I was focusing harder and learning how to single elements out. My magic would be better if I chose to use it now, but I didn't see how this helped me not use it by accident.

"I'm not going to point at a grain in particular, but I want you to lift one."

"Just one?"

"I might not entirely understand all the intricacies of your powers, but so far you seem to need to concentrate and visualize what you're working on..."

"But this is just a pile of sand," I understood.

My first attempt lifted at least a pinch of sand, as did my second and third.

"Try pulling one from this," Gabriel scooped a bit of sand

into his palm, seeing my exasperation.

"Isn't that cheating?"

"We'll come back to the pile," he assured me.

Every time I lifted a few, he took them in his hand, then dropped the excess when I levitated some. This went on until I had a single grain of sand floating between us.

"Again," Gabriel encouraged, but he stopped dropping the excess, so I had to play with the pinch of sand in his hand until I got it down to one.

Once I got that consistently, we tried with the big pile again. After two tries, I levitated a single grain every time.

"Should I separate atoms now?" I asked, taking a sip of the iced tea Embry brought us.

"Now we play with paper," Gabriel smiled.

"Play?" I asked.

"You know how the paper catches fire, you float it to me, then the fire disappears?" he asked of how it usually works.

"We spent the afternoon passing notes," I agreed.

"This time, don't let it burn."

"Protect the paper?" I was confused. Being the one who set the fire meant if I didn't want it to burn, I just had to not set it on fire.

"No, start burning it, but keep it contained. Don't let the entire thing be consumed."

"Do I still float it to you?" I asked.

"If you can," he smiled, making it a challenge.

It turned out that making it float to him was the least of my problems. Unlike the rice and sand, I didn't have to isolate a grain, I had to set the paper on fire, then control the flames that were moving of their own accord. I had to prevent them from engulfing the rest of the paper, which was what they tried to do.

It took me at least a dozen tries, with varying amounts of scorchedness, before I finally passed.

"I get that I can be more precise when I use my powers now, but I don't know how that stops me from hurting people," I asked after another morning spent working on the minutiae of simple spells. I appreciated that the magic was focused on objects for now, but I didn't know how long that would last.

"You don't feel like you have more control over what you're doing?" Embry asked, waving in the distance.

"I was told you needed living targets you wouldn't feel bad for hurting," Ingrid walked over, wiggling her fingers at me.

"I thought the goal was to not hurt people?" I argued.

"To not hurt them accidentally," Embry agreed. "But we don't want you to be afraid to use your powers on real threats."

"Why are you so bent on making me use my powers when your plan is to keep me as far away from everything as possible?"

"Since you insist on not running next time they find us…" Embry paused, waiting for me to change my mind, but I didn't. "Our plan is to keep you as far away from the danger and die protecting you."

"That's not a plan, that's a suicide mission," I argued.

"We're not opposed to you helping out mystically from the shadows," Gabriel relented.

"You want me to hide away from the danger and what? Will them all to explode?" I asked. "If that's something I'm capable of, shouldn't I do it now, from here? Wouldn't Beth and Annabelle have tried if it was that easy?"

"We don't know what you can do, Luce. We can tell that you're powerful and not the damsel in distress one would assume you are…"

"But we won't know anything if you refuse to try," Embry finished for him.

"Do you have a Big Bad for me to practice on?" They were being ridiculous.

"I do," Ingrid shrugged.

"It's…you don't know what he can do. You don't know how he would retaliate, or…"

"We can at least see what you could do to his army," Embry suggested.

"We can try," I rolled my eyes, not really wanting to do this.

INGRID WAITED for me to say I was ready, then closed her eyes. For a moment, everything was calm and quiet, but then a huge black cape jumped out at me from nowhere. I instinctively put my arms up to protect myself and the hooded figure burst into nothingness.

"Very cool," she told me.

"Not when it's a person," I argued. Maybe it wouldn't bother me so much if blowing it up had been my intention, rather than completely unintentional.

"Do you want to try again?" Gabriel offered. I didn't think

practice would help, but I didn't know what else to do to not accidentally hurt people I cared about.

"Can they look more like people?" I asked, bracing myself.

"Of course," Ingrid gave me an encouraging smile.

EVEN THOUGH I knew what was coming, I still blew up the first three illusions she attacked me with. They definitely looked human, but also large and intimidating, brandishing weapons so I would recognize them as threats. I eventually managed to stop exploding them, but I still sent them flying in a way no human would survive.

"How about we take a quick break?" Embry suggested.

"Maybe if I exhaust myself the powers will go away?" I asked hopefully.

"If you're anything like Beth, I'll burn out before you do," Ingrid told me. "And I don't burn out."

"I'm trying to concentrate, but they come at me and my head goes blank," I lamented.

"Maybe think of the force shield?" Gabriel suggested.

"That still hurts people," I argued.

"Then let's go again." Ingrid sent illusions my way without waiting for me to be ready.

Again, I blew up a number of them, then produced a shield they bounced off of at an alarming speed, before one finally froze less than a foot away from me.

"That's awesome," Embry praised once Ingrid paused the attacks.

"Think you can do that again?" Ingrid asked me.

"I can try," I said, taking a deep breath.

FOR THE REST of the afternoon, I successfully froze all of her hooded and menacing figures rather than exploding them.

"Maybe I can do it because my subconscious knows I'm not really in danger," I ventured.

"Not in danger?" Ingrid asked.

"You're sending illusions at me."

"Very powerful ones," she was offended.

"They're scary, but they're holograms." I didn't want to be mean, but I wasn't at risk for a heart attack, and that was the most damage they could do to me.

"I beg to differ." She conjured one and made it run into a bushel of hay, that exploded from the impact.

"That's what would have happened to me if I succeeded in putting my hands up and doing nothing?" I questioned her sanity.

"I get that you don't want to blow up an innocent kid who spooks you on Halloween, but the idea is also to not let you die if a scary person literally throws himself at you," she said, shrugging her shoulders.

"I didn't know they were real," Gabriel assured me, putting his hand out to stop me from reproaching him. "But she is right as far as our goals."

"Unless they destroy my heart with the impact," I sighed.

"Your heart is remaining intact," Gabriel pointed a finger at me.

"Every heart breaks at some point."

"I'll break the boy or girl who does that to you," Embry winked at me.

We went again with me knowing the threat was real, even if it was in my imagination, and I managed to freeze anyone that came between my hands.

WHEN IT GOT DARK, Embry accompanied Ingrid to her car while Gabriel walked back to the villa with me.

"Dying won't bring him back," Gabriel said delicately as I rolled the band Clara gave me through my fingers.

"I know that," I slipped it back on. Embry was usually the one who called me out on bad thoughts.

"I mean it, Lucy. If the Big Bad comes for you and you do nothing...forget the fact that we've been protecting your family for over three hundred years...your death is the absolute worst-case scenario that makes everything else no longer worthwhile. Them getting your heart would mean the end of the world, but we have never once considered destroying it beforehand to prevent that."

"Maybe you should."

"Lucy." There was venom in his tone.

"If I had a nuclear bomb in my chest that was ready to go off at any moment, but killing me permanently deactivated it, I'm pretty sure every government would vote to neutralize me."

"But you're not a bomb. You're not a thing to be neutralized. You're a human being with hopes and dreams and a heart of gold who deserves to share it with the world, not hide it," he paused for the words to sink in.

The tears stung my eyes, so I brought my hand to my temple and tried to shake it off. "Aren't you tired?" I asked him quietly. I had been running for a few months, but this was what his life looked like for the past few hundred years.

"If you die, we die, like we should have centuries ago. But I will spend every last breath I have making sure you get out of this and have a happily ever after."

"What difference do you really think I can make?"

"We'll never know if we don't try. But I believe you can do anything you set your mind to. Not just because you were a genius before this, but you have aced every obstacle the world has thrown at you."

"It was fake," I argued.

"The threats might be sometimes, but the magic isn't. I didn't know about Beth's powers, and Annabelle felt the same way you do about it, but I would imagine that if you let yourself be what you were born to be, you can do it all."

CHAPTER NINETEEN

On Sunday the guys gave me a rest day as far as magic was concerned, so we worked on my self-defense. I was getting better at controlling what magic came out of me, but I still felt more comfortable with physical attacks. Much to the guys' detriment.

"Your jab needs work, but you've got a good right hook," Gabriel gave me a smile while we walked back to the villa for lunch. It was an exhausting morning, but I loved almost every minute of it.

"Sweet tea?" Embry asked, grabbing a pitcher from the fridge. I could see Embry's eyes go wide as someone grabbed me from behind. I turned to see who it was, instinctually raising my arms in defense. I was paralyzed with fear, but it was a little girl standing in front of me. She looked confused and so innocent that I panicked before realizing that I didn't blow her up or send her into the wall behind her. Nothing happened.

What the hell?" I asked when the girl disappeared. I was on high alert with my heart pounding out a marathon in my chest.

"It's okay, you're okay," Gabriel came over and took me in his arms.

"She would have turned into a rainbow if you'd done something, so you would know she was one of my holograms," Ingrid defended herself, rounding the corner.

"Am I broken?" I asked in reference to the fact that I braced my arms and nothing happened.

"When you saw she was a kid, did you want to hurt her?" Gabriel asked.

"No, but that hasn't mattered any other time," I pointed out. Ingrid had slowly been making her illusions less threatening, but the best I could do was freeze them when they came at me.

"It isn't that you're broken. You were able to control your powers enough that they're triggered by you, not by your fear," Ingrid explained.

"You tricked me into possibly destroying Embry's kitchen…"

"To show you that you don't need to be afraid of your powers."

"One time."

"But you felt it," Ingrid called me on it. "You decided not to hurt her, so you didn't."

"Maybe warn me next time?" I asked of her, my heart slowly going back to normal.

"You don't always get warnings," she said simply. "And it would have put a damper on the party if we didn't give you a practice round."

"What party?" I asked before Charlie and Eric came out of the living room, holding up a handmade 'Happy 19th Birthday!' banner.

"For she's a jolly good fellow…" they started singing, reminding me of my graduation party as I realized that today was my birthday.

"I completely forgot." I wasn't sure if I was more shocked that I forgot, or that they remembered.

"We thought you might," Embry agreed, coming over to give me a hug.

"There's so much else going on," I pointed out.

"There is," Gabriel agreed. "But you need to celebrate the small stuff."

I raised my eyebrows. That was not the advice I expected to hear from him of all people.

"You've been through a lot and we don't want you to burn out," he downplayed it.

"Taking care of my mental health?"

"Reminding you that it's not just the fate of humanity you're fighting for. You yourself are worth saving," Embry told me.

"I have a shop to get back to, but I am leaving you this," Ingrid handed me a package wrapped with a shawl instead of wrapping paper.

"You really didn't have to," I argued. I was never good at accepting gifts.

"I wanted to," She assured me, putting her forehead against mine with a smile, before she headed off.

I removed the shawl to reveal a surprisingly modern book on the history of magic. I was expecting spells or a potion book to help me defeat the Big Bad, but reading the back cover revealed it was a study on where magic comes from, its limits, and its affinity for good and evil. Mental health was clearly the theme today.

"You came back for this?" I asked Eric, really happy to see him.

"Of course. It's your birthday," he smiled. "Come on," he took my hand and brought me to the living room, where balloons were on the floor, the walls, and floating in mid-air.

There was also a table with a bunch of finger foods and a bowl of some purple-colored punch.

"You got me something?" I asked, surprised when he took out a box roughly the size of a mini ruler.

"Made it," he smiled confidently.

"Oh," I said, expecting to find something with lots of glue and construction paper, because that's what Clara usually gave me. "You made this?" He didn't seem like the type to lie to impress me, but I had serious doubts that he made me the beautiful fountain pen I found in the box.

"I maybe slightly exaggerated that statement. I found the pen and made adjustments."

"Adjustments?" I asked instead of confirming that 'found' meant he stole it from Charlie.

"Don't do it now, because you'll either pop a balloon or hurt someone, but when you twist off the cap and press this button on the end, you get one of these," he lifted a flap in the box to show me tiny, needle-like inserts.

"Poison?" I asked, wondering what kind of people I was hanging out with.

"A toxin," he corrected.

"The difference would be..."

"It's not a poison that kills people, it's a toxin that should knock them out for maybe an hour. Which is long enough for you to get away."

"And you made it for me?" I couldn't believe how sweet it was of him to offer me an alternative to killing or using magic.

"It's your birthday," he shrugged, but his eyes told me it had everything to do with me, and nothing to do with the date.

"I love it," I tried to be serious, but had to suppress a laugh. I never would have imagined myself being this touched by a tranquilizer dart-shooting pen.

"I'm glad," he smiled before Charlie motioned me over to the couch.

"They're not new..." he warned, taking a big box from beside him. "But these will be a lot better than your hiking shoes."

"I can't take these," I argued. I had no idea how much riding boots cost, but the ones from the box looked like they hadn't been used more than once or twice, and they were gorgeous.

"Of course you can. Some of my granddaughters are less into nature than others."

"Thank you," I told him, sensing 'no' wasn't an option. "Not just for the boots, but for everything you've done since I got here. For this." I looked around the villa, that he and Eric turned into a birthday explosion for me. I had completely missed Deanna's birthday back in July, and I wasn't sure if I wanted to be back in time for Clara's, or let her have one more year before finding out about Sam. I'm sure they had their doubts, but if I hadn't seen it happen, I would have convinced myself he somehow managed to get away.

"It's what you do for family," he told me like it was nothing.

"I'm a stranger," I pointed out.

"You're anything but. For as long as I can remember, your family has been mine."

"You can never have too much family," I smiled instead of arguing.

"I've always believed you choose your family. Sometimes you're lucky enough to be born into it, but sometimes you have to fight for them," he shrugged at the last part.

"I'm very glad to have you as mine," I thanked him again, this time with a hug, before he ushered me to the food table.

He gave me a description of all my options and filled a plate of things for me to try. "I'll be right back," he put his hand on my arm before going to deal with an alarm that went off in the kitchen, announcing more food.

"I'M sorry we couldn't bring you to them. Or them to you," Gabriel apologized when he found me holding the overstuffed plate, playing with my ring and staring into space.

"I can't lose anyone else," I let him know it was okay to keep them as far away from me as possible.

I could see he wanted to say something, to remind me that none of this was my fault, that Sam knew what he was getting himself into… a million things that wouldn't make a difference. Instead, he took a tiny pouch from his pocket and handed it to me.

"Happy birthday," he said with a shy smile, which was intriguing more than anything. Embry was an expert at presents. He always got me exactly what I never knew I always wanted, from rare books to microscopes to online classes…it was always out of the box and always perfect. Gabriel, on the other hand, usually gave me something Deanna picked out and wrapped for him, a gift card, or nothing.

The way he watched me open it made me nervous, as I fumbled with the knot tied in the string. "Wrapped it yourself?" I tried to lighten the mood.

"I think we all went a little homemade this year," he agreed.

"What is it?" I asked, finding a thin stone the size of my palm hanging from a delicate silver chain.

"A necklace," he smiled, getting me to roll my eyes.

"You know what I mean."

"It's moonstone," he admitted, then continued when I failed to react to the name. "It's supposed to help you channel and control your energy. And it brings protection."

"You believe in that stuff?" I wasn't judging or making fun of him, but I was curious. He was surprising me a lot this summer.

"I trust people who do, and I figure it can't hurt. Plus, being the Bearer of the Crescent Moon, if any kind of rock was going to help you, it would have to be moonstone."

"That's a good point," I gave him a smile, taking a closer look at the stone. It was beautiful, whether it protected me or not. It wasn't quite blue, but there was a bluish sheen to it. It had a smooth, oval-ish shape, but there were scratches on the back. I didn't want to point out the flaws of his defective stone, but I was wondering if they would have an effect on the stone's power, when I realized the scratches were deliberate. "What's on the back?" I asked, staring at the stone in my hand to try and make it out.

"I tried something, but I'm not sure it turned out," he took the stone and held it up to the sunlight coming in from the window, with the scratches facing me.

"You did this?" I asked, trying not to, but I could feel my eyes water. He somehow carved Sam, Clara, and Deanna into the back of the stone, so I could carry them with me always. I didn't wait for his answer, I rushed forward and hugged him. I held him tight, waiting until the tears stopped and I wiped away the remnants before pulling back. "Thank you," I said, looking into his eyes, failing to convey how much I meant it.

"Of course," he looked at me in a way that gave me butter-flies, like when Eric did, only my heart joined in, beating faster than it was supposed to.

"Would you mind?" I asked, pulling my hair to one side and giving him my back.

His hands were warm on the back of my neck as they fumbled with the clasp, but they still sent shivers down my spine. I smiled at Embry when he looked over, hoping I wasn't as flushed as I felt.

"I'll let you enjoy your food and get back to your party," Gabriel gave me a smile. I wanted to argue that he wasn't bothering me and could stay, but instead I let him go talk to Charlie, who seemed to have a million stories to tell him and Eric.

AFTER A WHILE, Embry suggested everyone get fresh air and sunlight, so the party moved outside.

"I don't think I can top everyone else," Embry apologized, taking a seat beside me in the yard.

"You've got ten years on them," I assured him. "And no one had to get me anything. It completely slipped my mind."

"Because you feel like you don't deserve to celebrate, which is absolutely not the case," he waited for me to look over and acknowledge it, so I rolled my eyes at him.

"Remember this when your birthday comes around," I warned, but also hoped we wouldn't still be on the run come March.

"Oh, I expect cake and singing and streamers," he teased.

"Your wish is my command," I smiled.

He smiled back before handing me a red leather photo album. There was only one picture per page, but as soon as I opened it, I knew the perfect-gift-giver struck again.

"It's perfect," I told him. There was something about pictures of my mother I had never seen before that made me feel like I was getting another piece of her.

"I put a few pictures of the Boyds near the end, for when you're homesick, but most of them are of her."

"Thank you," I told him, flipping through the first pages. "Is that...."

"A much younger Charlie," he agreed. "And this one is Eric's father if I'm not mistaken."

"Six boys?" I asked, sensing a pattern of large families.

"Only five of them were Charlie's. It was where all the kids ended up every weekend. I only gave you the pictures with Marilyn."

"I appreciate that," I told him before spotting Gabriel across the pool, letting Eric use him for some kind of demonstration in his story. It was surprisingly action-intensive for the smiles they were sharing. I definitely hadn't seen him smile this much, ever.

"It's okay to choose him," Embry brought me back to the conversation.

"Choose him for what?" I asked, surprised by how serious he looked.

"To love Gabriel," he said bluntly, his unwavering stare forcing me to be the one to look away.

"I love both of you." My eyes were focused on a tiny spot in the corner of the photo album.

"Not the way you love him," he argued.

"I'm just trying to survive at the moment." He looked at me like he didn't believe a word I was saying. The flushed cheeks from earlier probably weren't helping my case. "Even if I did, it wouldn't matter, because he loves Annabelle and no one else. You should have seen how heartbroken Rosalind was when Gabriel turned her down." I remembered the memory from the train. "Beth was lucky she fell for you and got to have a bit of a happy ending."

"Luce..." Embry looked at me with...not pity, but possibly compassion, like he knew what I was going through.

"There is absolutely nothing that says I have to fall for one of you. I can break the cycle like Cassie and fall madly in love with someone else. Like Eric, or a stranger who has no idea about any of it," I argued with his empathetic look.

"You definitely can," he agreed. "I'll be happy with whatever you choose, as long as it makes you happy."

"He loves Annabelle. Not the way she looks," I reminded him. I didn't want to get into it, but I had to shut him down.

"But he also loves you. Not because you're a Bearer who looks like her, but because you're you. And I was there when he said he saw you," he reminded me.

"And it broke his heart," I pointed out.

"I'm just saying it's okay if you choose him. You can do what you want with it, but I will love you forever, no matter what," he assured me before Eric motioned for us to come join them. I gave Embry a hand and we went back to the party, which lasted long after the sun went down.

CHAPTER TWENTY

I tried to clear my mind and focus. I held the moonstone in my hand and thought of why I was doing this. Why it mattered if I lived or died. I didn't want to die, of course, but no one wants to. I thought of Clara and Deanna, who didn't deserve to lose anyone else. Then I thought of Sam, knowing I was the reason they lost him. It filled me with guilt and made me think everyone would be better off if we destroyed my heart, and me along with it. But Sam would never forgive me. We were raised to be anything but selfish, or weak, which is what sacrificing myself would be. I would be taking the easy way out to let someone else be hunted. More importantly, if I died without defeating the Big Bad, or living a long and happy life, then Sam died for nothing. Even the guilt at causing his death wouldn't let me make his death be in vain.

I took a deep breath and nodded to let Ingrid know I was ready, opening my eyes just as her illusions came for me, one after the other. Some were dressed in black with swords and guns in their hands, a few looked like Clara, while most of them were more ambiguous.

Ingrid was right, that fear was usually the driving force

behind any magic I did. This time I buried the fear and used intent, the element I made fun of when this all began. Instead of reacting out of fear, I evaluated what was coming for me, even anticipating them. I blasted the ones looking to hurt me, and froze the ones I wasn't sure about, time after time, until Ingrid suggested we take a break.

"I can keep going," I assured them, sweating as if I just ran a 10K.

"I can't," Ingrid argued. "You're destroying them faster than I can conjure new ones."

"I'm sorry." I took a seat beside her on the lawn chairs.

"Don't be," she assured me. "You're doing amazing."

"But we still don't know what his powers are actually like."

"We don't," Gabriel agreed. "But you can definitely take on his army."

"From behind us, preferably in a reinforced steel room that only your magic works in," Embry amended.

"I think I need to see them for it to work," I argued.

"We'll cross that bridge when we get there," they assured me.

We tried it a few more times, with bigger, more powerful illusions rather than a constant flow of them. I was still feeling in control of myself and my powers, but the confidence was only slightly stronger than the fear.

"I would definitely not want to get on your bad side," Ingrid encouraged.

"You're going?" I asked when she grabbed her purse from the lawn chair.

"I left Mr. Fraser in charge of the shop, but I need to go close up and make sure he hasn't burned the place down. It's been busier with yet another disappearance last week."

"Someone you knew?" I asked.

"Only by look." She gave me a hug before going to see Charlie next door.

"How are you feeling?" Embry asked me.

"Okay," I said after considering it.

"Don't hate us too much?" he asked.

"Only a little bit," I was mostly joking.

"Are you both good if I bail on dinner and help Ingrid with something?" he asked.

"Of course," I assured him, while Gabriel nodded.

"It shouldn't take all night," Embry assured me before heading off.

"Have fun," I called after him, then turned to Gabriel, "I need to remove this magical exertion, but I can make pasta or something when I'm done?"

"I'll cook. You've done more than enough today," he gave me a smile before going to the kitchen as I headed for the stairs.

After my shower, I found a tight white tank top, then wrapped the shawl Ingrid gave me for my birthday around my waist, turning it into a skirt. I wanted to take advantage of our time in New Orleans, before we went back to chicken coops and tiny boats, which had to be coming soon. The shawl was a deep burgundy color that, paired with the moonstone necklace, made me feel like Esmeralda from the Halloween costume I wore when I was six or seven. The Boyds gave up on most of Grams' traditions, although I did convince Mrs. Boyd to make us all soul cakes before we went trick-or-treating around the block.

I came downstairs and found Gabriel at the stove, stirring what smelled like a pesto-parmesan sauce. Part of me had been worried he would make up some excuse like 'securing the perimeter' to avoid me, while part of me wanted him to. Which might have something to do with Embry telling me it was okay to love him.

"Johnny Cash?" I asked of what sounded like a record from the scratchiness.

"Embry was storing the record player with the pots and pans, no idea why, but I haven't found any other records yet," he defended the selection.

"Can I help with anything?" I offered.

"You just sit, relax and read the Book of Shadows or something," he assured me.

"Thank you." I went over and got Ingrid's book on magic. It was weird because it looked like the newly published, commercial witch stuff that was the trend of my elementary school days, but I couldn't see Ingrid giving me a capitalist account on magic, from people who had no idea whether or not it even exists.

I wasn't reading every page, definitely not as thoroughly as I should, but I was learning a lot about magical theory. Like how it travels but never dies, how some people can have it in them but be unable to do anything, while others can draw on the magic of people around them...apparently, those people can not only 'borrow' powers when they have none of their own, but go so far as to steal it if they do.

It was in the third chapter, called 'Other Magical Beings' that I found a section on 'The Gifted' that explained why Ingrid chose to give me this particular book. I almost skipped it, because it listed faeries and goblins and other creatures that had no place in the real world, even if witches apparently did.

"The Gifted are a subset of humans with supernatural abilities that manifest in their second lives, although there have been rumors of first life manifestations. The Gifted stay alive, even in death, until a specific task, unique to them, has been completed," I read to myself. The book wasn't clear on all of the intricacies of coming back to life, but it did mention instances where the body was too far gone for the Gifted to come back, such as in nuclear explosions, being entirely dissolved in acid, and meticulous dismemberment.

Apparently, some Gifted never figured out what they were meant to do, especially the healers and first responders who rarely know which patient did the trick. Others, like Embry and Gabriel "become Gifted by making a promise the fates decide they deserve to keep."

A lot of it I already knew, but the book went into oddly specific details on some aspects. There was a list at the end of it, of 'Notable Historical Figures Rumored to be Gifted' which included Nostradamus, Leonardo da Vinci, Queen Victoria, Carl Jung, Adolf Hitler and George Lucas. Each of them was said to have suffered terrible incidents, like car accidents, plagues, and assassination attempts no one thought they would survive before accomplishing incredible feats.

The most shocking to me was the part on scientific studies; "The Gifted become paranormal beings once they enter their second lives, so biological functions such as aging, menses and reproduction become impossible." There were tables of scientific evidence to back it up, but I had Embry's word that disproved it.

"How's the book?" Gabriel asked me after covering a wok-style pan and putting something else in the oven.

"Part of it makes me think it was written as a ploy to make money off suckers who want to believe in magic, but other parts make me wonder if the author wasn't a Gifted witch who saw it all happen," I shrugged.

"I don't think that's a good thing."

"It mentions that Gifted can't have kids." I thought about

Terrence's daughter Angela, Embry's son...I knew many exceptions. "Is it only Gifted women, or is the book wrong?" I asked.

"The book is right. It causes a lot of heartbreaks. Etta was devastated when she found out."

"How do you explain Angela and Jackson?" I asked.

"Angela was born before Terrence died, and the twins were adopted," he reminded me. "And as far as Jackson...maybe your line is different."

"We can have kids with dead people?" I asked, instantly regretting it. "I don't mean it like that, but after you first die, your life is put on hold until you accomplish your purpose."

"It's a fair question," he assured me. "It might be because of the Prophecy. There also seems to be a lack of certainty involving Gifteds. Some get to live out their lives when they finish their task, others fade away. Death gives you new powers or takes old ones away...I really don't know," he got pensive.

"The book has a whole section on controlling your magic instead of letting it control you. I've only skimmed it so far, but they do suggest moonstone," I changed the subject for him.

"There's hope for me yet," he smiled before a timer went off. He took cheesy garlic bread out of the oven, then went to scoop some pesto-parmesan tortellini onto two plates.

"It smells like an Italian restaurant," I breathed it all in.

"I figured you just had your birthday and you didn't get any pasta, so..."

"It's perfect," I assured him.

"How was it today?" he asked, bringing the plates to the table so we could eat.

"Which part?" I blew on my tortellini before tasting it. It would be wrong to say I could die happy now, but the sentiment was there.

"Did it tire you out, were you weakened by it... I guess all of it," he looked down into his plate.

"It's weird," I tried to find a way to explain it. "When we stopped, I felt like I ran a marathon, as you could see," I referenced the sweaty mess I became. "But at the same time, it was like my body was used to running marathons and I could do more. It was sort of outside of me, but inside me at the same time."

"I guess it's like my speed," he mostly said to himself, taking a piece of the garlic bread.

"How does your speed work?" We had never discussed it.

"I run in the mornings, to stay healthy and clear my head, but eventually I need to stop, because my legs are on fire. I need to rest and eat and give it a day. If I'm not consistent, my legs will be sore for days when I get back into it."

"That's just regular running," I pointed out.

"I know. When I'm using my speed, it's the same muscles, and I'm using them more intensely, but I could keep going for as long as I need to, without getting tired, and my legs will be fine."

"That's really weird."

"The only time I can't sustain my speed like that is after I die, before it recovers completely."

"I guess this is a stupid question, but did you run away a lot as a kid?" I got a smile while he finished his bite.

"My family was not wealthy, so if I wanted to impress others, I had to work twice as hard and get more done in the same time frame than anyone else. I was incredibly hard on myself and always pushed to be faster, so I could earn the respect others were born with."

"It wasn't about the running."

"Nope," he agreed. "I can't outrun a bullet, or flick it out of the way, but it is a bit like time slows down around me when

I'm in it. I could write or swim or start an assembly line with it instead. The running just comes in handy."

"To save the damsel in distress."

"I believe you've more than proved that title inaccurate."

"Don't hand in your plate of armor just yet."

"I'll always be there for you Luce," he assured me.

"Until we defeat the Big Bad," I agreed. A shiver ran through me.

Gabriel smiled instead of telling me it wasn't ever likely to happen.

"This is delicious," I told him.

"I very briefly worked in a restaurant," he shared.

"Really?" I did not buy it.

"I was tired of all the stress and wanted something insignificant for a change."

"So you decided to be a chef?"

"I was supposed to chop vegetables, a mindless task I could do in my sleep. Chopping vegetables turned into pressing garlic and peeling potatoes and making pesto and... restaurants are a lot more stressful than you would think."

"Of course they are. How long did you last?"

"A little less than two weeks, but I learnt their pesto and alfredo sauces..."

"And mixed the two together," I understood how he got his pesto so cheesy.

"My Gift should have been sharing it with the world," he teased.

"Definitely," I agreed. "What other jobs have you done?"

"Way too many to count. I migrate around the same general idea, but you can't stay too long when you look like this," he shrugged. I wanted to ask more, but didn't get the feeling he wanted to talk about it.

"I see nothing wrong with the way you look," I teased.

"Some people managed to look past my appearance and

see my worth, but they were few and far between. Probably my fault though. I wasn't very trusting."

"A bit of a lone wolf?" I tied my hair into a messy knot at the top of my head. The oven, the stove, the pasta, and the summer air were all contributing to make the kitchen very hot.

"Not on purpose. One of my first jobs outside of the family was as a day laborer in a factory. All the other men got close, eating lunch together, drinking at night...making friends. I, on the other hand, spent my lunches getting ahead on work, and didn't need to see them in the evenings because if I wanted someone to drink with, I had Embry."

"Loyal with the one best friend." It was like me with Keisha, only that wasn't entirely by choice.

"It wasn't intentional. I just didn't feel a need to make friends, which seems to be something I actually need to work at to achieve."

"You got Terrence," I argued.

"That was all him."

"You've spent the past three centuries not getting close to anyone because you already had a best friend, even if you weren't currently talking to him?" I verified.

"When you put it that way...some people managed to get in. And it was more subconscious on my part."

"I am really glad you're back to being friends then."

"When did you find out about him and Beth?" he asked.

"I saw it when we first got here. But I was pregnant with Jack when I fell out of the tree. Beth was," I corrected myself.

"That must be weird."

"It is," I agreed. "It's really weird and surreal and terrible and incredibly awesome, all at the same time."

"Do you think there's a point to it?"

"I feel like there has to be, not that I can see it. None of the others had memories like this? Not even once?"

"The only ones with supernatural abilities were Beth and Annabelle. Beth never confided in me...about anything, and Annabelle was the original, so there wouldn't have been memories for her."

ONCE WE WERE DONE with supper, I made cookies. We had all the ingredients, except chocolate chips, so I used a pack of smarties instead.

"Not going to warn me about salmonella?" I asked when Gabriel came over and ate one of the balls of cookie dough I had on a cookie sheet while the oven preheated.

"I think that was a real threat when it started, but things don't go bad anymore, they last forever. If Gaston eats five dozen raw eggs for breakfast, what can it hurt if you add some milk, sugar, and flour?" he asked, discovering the much larger quantity of dough I left in the mixing bowl.

"Was that a Beauty and the Beast reference?" I was shocked. "I wouldn't peg you as the fairytale romance type."

"Are you kidding? I was the hopeless romantic who wanted nothing more than to settle down and raise a family."

"That was your dream?" I asked.

"Still is. I just stopped believing it would come true a couple hundred years ago," he shrugged with a sad smile.

"I thought you were waiting..." I was leaning with my back against the oven, but I don't think that was why the room felt like it was a hundred degrees. Gabriel hadn't stepped back since his last dough venture, so I was acutely aware of how close he was.

"I've known a long time that she wasn't coming back," he argued. "It's probably the first rule in your magic books."

"You can't bring the dead back," I agreed, more from movies than the books.

"I grew up and understood that the things I wanted back

then, that I would want now...getting married, having kids, raising a family and being happy...they're not real. They're fairytales."

"You've got a pretty good heart from what you accidentally let show. And you're not horrible to look at. I mean, you might have to adopt, but it could still happen," I told him nervously, putting my hand on top of his.

"I'm broken, Lucy," he argued, looking into my eyes with that intensity only he could bring, where it felt like he could see down to my very soul. "You wouldn't want me," he cut through the subtext of our conversation, but didn't look away from me.

"You don't have to be," I looked right back into his eyes, the black eyes that still managed to have depth and kindness to them. My heart was beating a mile a minute and he was so close...it was like time was frozen, with just the two of us in the kitchen, and nothing else mattered. I could hear my heart as he came closer, the electricity tangible, before he pulled away and walked off without another word.

CHAPTER TWENTY-ONE

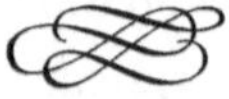

Gabriel didn't come back, so I went upstairs and got ready for bed. I caught sight of my reflection in the mirror and wished I didn't look like her. But then I wouldn't look like me either.

I read a few more chapters of the book on magic, learning that emotions, like love, were the most powerful, and that love, hatred, and fear could deeply impact spells and potions. Which was great for me, because I happened to be feeling all of them at the moment.

I really wanted to track Clara and Deanna, or even Keisha, just to feel them and know they were okay, but this wasn't an emergency, and I wouldn't want people peeking into my life when I thought I was alone.

I stared at the ceiling, unable to sleep for the longest time, finally deciding to open my window to get a little fresh air. That helped, but it would be a long time until I got to sleep.

"You're killing it, Luce." Sam was sitting in the corner of the room, his face beaming with pride.

"How are you here?" I asked, looking around for Ingrid. She hadn't haunted me yet, but I had often wondered why she wasn't constantly hounded by people asking her to bring back their loved ones, at least for a little while. It might drive her crazy in the long run, but she could have an imaginary Beth hang out with her all day, looking, feeling and sounding like the real thing.

"I'm always here for you. Until the end of time," he brought up the promise he made me after his dad's funeral.

"I'm dreaming," I understood, wanting to run to him and take advantage of him being there, even in a dream, but dreams tended to turn into nightmares when Sam was in them lately.

"He can't get us here," he said, reading my thoughts.

"He can. He does all the time," I argued.

"Not tonight," he assured me.

"How would you know?"

"Because I've got you. If anyone bad shows up, you can freeze them or blow them up...you've got this," he smiled.

"I appreciate your confidence."

"But you don't trust it."

"I want to."

"But you don't want to be responsible if someone gets hurt. You would rather freeze or fail at some other kind of self-defense."

"You're acting like I would rather die..."

"Wouldn't you?" he called me on it.

"If I could go back and take your place..."

"I would never let you."

"I would do it. A million times," I said over him.

"I know you would, but I'm the big brother, so I couldn't let you."

"They were after me. They wouldn't have been anywhere near you if it wasn't for me."

"But I was always going to do whatever I could to protect you."

"You had a family. Deanna and Clara will never forgive me."

"And you're mad at me," he called me on it.

"I'm not..." I looked at him and knew he was right. "Of course I'm mad at you. You left me here and... you died for me."

"I didn't just die for you," he tried to downplay it.

"You fought and died so they wouldn't get me. Now I have to go home and tell your wife and daughter that I'm the reason you're gone..."

"And you can't give up," he said, a big reason why I was mad at him. "I died protecting you, so if you die, it's like I died for nothing. You can't give up when things get hard or refuse to do the spells that scare you, because I died so you could live, and now you have to live."

"I hate you," I said, my eyes full of tears.

"I love you too," he opened his arms so I could go in for a hug.

"Are you only okay with this because you're a figment of my imagination?"

"No, I'm pissed off as hell," he said, his red hair glistening in the moonlight, but I saw a hint of his mother's fierceness in his eyes.

"I'm sorry," I said, mostly for causing his demise, but also for asking and upsetting him.

"The difference is that I'm not mad at you. I don't blame you for any of it."

"Not a single thing?" I called him on his lie.

"Silly things that don't matter anymore, like you and Deanna watching that doctor show without me when you know I can't admit that I like it. For growing up so fast and making me feel old. For those times when Clara asks you to read her the bedtime story instead of me," he put his hand under my chin to make me look at him. "But I don't lose sight of who I'm really mad at. I died because if Donovan got what he wanted, he was going to kill Clara and Deanna, and everyone like them. He's the real bad guy. That's who I'm mad at for a lot of things."

"I miss you. So much." It didn't need to be said, but I needed to tell him.

"I miss you too," he agreed. "Do you think you can forgive me for leaving you alone and not letting you take the easy way out of this?"

I sighed and paused, considering it. "I don't really have a choice, do I?"

"Not really," he agreed.

"Then you're forgiven," I gave him a sad smile, knowing he wasn't the one who needed forgiveness.

"Then I can give you your birthday present."

"You really don't have to," I told him, pretty sure I couldn't take things with me from my dream. "Just seeing you...this is perfect," I said of the hug.

"The present's better," he assured me, leading me back over to the bed, where he proceeded to tuck me in, securing the corners like he hadn't done for me in years. "Are you ready?" he asked, sitting on the edge.

I wanted to say no, because I knew he would be leaving as soon as he was done, but I was worried he would have to leave anyway, so I nodded.

"I forgive you," he said, looking into my eyes so I could see he meant it. "For everything you have or will ever do. I forgive you," he kissed the top of my head, then stepped back, out of the light, and was gone.

· · ·

I woke with a start and recognized the room, but it suddenly felt empty without Sam in it. Or I guess I felt empty. I saw on the alarm clock that it was 2 am, so I tried to get back to sleep. Then I heard it.

"Lucy!" It was Sam's voice, as clear as when he was sitting in front of me in the dream, but it was coming from outside the window.

"Sam?" I got out of bed and went to see for myself. It was one thing to talk to him in a dream, but another to hear him when I was awake.

"Come on!" he called with a smile, standing beneath the window.

"You can't be here," my brain tried to process what was going on.

"But I am. Why don't you come see for yourself?" he suggested.

"Let me see your eyes," I called down, knowing the guys would kill me if I fell into a trap.

"Green, like yours." He stood under a porch light and opened them wide, so I could see.

"I'm coming," I told him, putting on the riding boots from Charlie and a sweater, because that was all I had at the door.

"Took you long enough," Sam sounded and looked exactly like himself.

"This is one of those things where you wake up but you're still dreaming," I called him on it as if he were the one who tricked my brain into thinking I woke up.

"That does happen sometimes," he agreed.

"You should visit like this more often," I told him.

"How will you miss me if I never go away?"

"I don't want to miss you."

"Come on," he put out his hand. I followed him over to the stables, but then we walked around them towards the woods, and the swamps.

"It's faster by horse," I suggested.

"I've never been a fan," he argued.

It was true. He was super allergic to any kind of animal. When Deanna found an abandoned puppy in the yard, we had to hide him from Clara and find a new home, because there was no way we'd ever be able to keep him.

"What adventure are you taking me on now?" I asked, glad I chose the boots. It would have been hard to keep up otherwise.

"It's a surprise," he smiled, daring me to figure it out.

"I'm not the biggest fan of surprises."

"You'll like this one." He picked up the pace and I started to see how much easier it was for Donner to hop over obstacles, like overturned trees, than it was for me to climb over them.

I wiped my muddy hands off on the back of my boxer shorts, where I usually dried them.

Sam was unusually quiet, helping me over fallen branches and pulling others back so I could get through, but the deeper we went, the more I started to think this maybe wasn't exactly what it seemed.

"Just a little bit farther," Sam said like he sensed my uncertainty.

"Can I get a hint?"

"It's something you've wanted a lot lately, but haven't told anyone," he said after considering it for a long time.

"But I didn't want it before?"

"Never even crossed your mind."

"I want it right now?" I questioned.

He paused, then looked at me like he wasn't so sure anymore. "You will," he told me.

We got to the clearing where Eric and I stopped the first time he took me riding. We usually avoided this place now, trying not to slow down so the bugs couldn't get to us like they were right now.

"I don't usually get eaten alive when I'm sleeping," I worried, slapping my thigh, yet again.

"Who says you're sleeping?" Sam asked, stepping into the muddy swamp.

"What are you doing?" I didn't like where this was going. At all.

"It's just past those trees there, in the bog," he pointed to a spot where I could see a light, but not much else.

"What is it?"

"Do you trust me?" he asked.

"Of course." Even as I said the words, I knew they were a lie. I trusted Sam more than anything in the world, but this wasn't my Sam.

"Then follow me," he put out his hand again, but this time I didn't take it.

"Why don't we go back to the house now. I can make us some tea and..."

"Don't you want us to be together?" he cut me off, looking so upset, before pushing me into the swamp. I landed where it wasn't too deep yet, but he dragged me further into the water, his hands like claws around my arms.

CHAPTER TWENTY-TWO

"What are you doing?" I screamed at the man who looked like Sam, struggling to keep my head above water.

"It's okay Lucy, don't fight it, I've got you," he assured me.

"This isn't you," I argued, trying to get up.

"It's okay," Sam repeated, then came close to take me in for a hug.

He let himself sink to the bottom, which brought me down as well. I fought to stay up, but he was holding on to my arms, and my legs could only kick so much. I looked for something to grab onto, but we were in the middle of the swamp, which was surprisingly deep. I could swear I saw Gabriel coming for me in the distance, but I chalked it up as wishful thinking. Obviously, my mind would go there.

My head bobbed under for a moment, but I could clearly see Gabriel fifty feet away from me once I resurfaced. He had his hand out in front of him, like he was following someone I couldn't see.

"Lucy!" Gabriel spotted me in the swamp and called out, giving me hope that he wasn't a figment of my imagination.

"Gabriel!" I struggled to stay on top long enough to call out to him. I saw Embry step into the swamp, looking like he was in a daze, before I was pulled to the bottom again.

By the time I fought my way back to the surface, Gabriel was getting closer to me, but he kept having to pull something, or someone off his back to do it. I tried to swim to him, but my sweater was caught on something. When pulling didn't work and the material wouldn't rip, I took a deep breath and willingly went under to untangle myself. When I came up, it was dark and I couldn't see Embry or Gabriel anywhere. I was wishing I'd brought a flashlight when the white light Sam pointed to earlier moved towards us. It lit up the swamp, but it also made me wish I could go back to the dark, when the ominous orb was farther away.

Fake Sam was gone, but there were still hundreds of what felt like winged mice trying to pull me down, so I used magic to get them off.

Fresh air never tasted so sweet, but I only let myself take two deep breaths before I called out to Embry and Gabriel. I still couldn't see them, but there were bubbles not far from me, so I swam over and pulled, which was enough for Gabriel to get his head above water.

"I can't." I could see him try to use his speed to get to me, but a gargoyle-like creature was digging its nails into his neck. I concentrated very hard on the creature and froze it not trusting myself to do anything else when it was so close to Gabriel. "They're all over," he told me, struggling to get them off and stay above water.

No matter how many I blew up, more kept coming, trying to use my clothes and my hair to pull me down.

"You need to get out of the water," Gabriel shouted over.

"I'm trying," I yelled. "Where's Embry?"

Gabriel ignored the creatures clawing at him and managed to swim close and take a few off me. He pulled me through the water, closer to the edge, which seemed so far away.

My heart nearly stopped when Embry burst out of the water a few feet away from Gabriel, but he went down as quickly as he came up. I could see more now that their numbers were growing, but it was more terrifying than reassuring.

I targeted individual creatures underwater, trying to help Embry, but I didn't trust my aim when he was squirming like that.

"Focus on you," Gabriel warned, knocking the creatures off me while they dug into him.

"He's drowning, and you're barely staying up," I pointed out before one of them tugged on my leg. Embry and Gabriel's immortality wasn't an exact science, which meant there was a possibility that if the creatures killed them, they wouldn't come back.

Gabriel struggled harder to help me to a large branch while I blasted any that were close, until I had my arms around the thickest part.

"Don't move," he warned before going under, I think intentionally, but it terrified me all the same.

I DID what I could with my powers, but there were so many of them, all over the guys, that by the time I could concentrate enough to target one, another replaced it.

"Embry!" I exclaimed when Gabriel grabbed hold of him, but they weren't out of the woods yet. The white, orb-like structure above the bog seemed to be a hive with millions of them, waiting to come after us.

I tried to reach out, to give them my hand so they would have something to hold on to, but the creatures hadn't let up on me either. If I didn't have a good hold on the branch, I couldn't stay above water. I also couldn't get close enough to them without completely letting go.

Embry struggled to help Gabriel when he went under. When Embry went down as well, I decided it wasn't worth me being safe if they drowned on me. I let go of the branch and tried to swim to them. If I could get close enough, I could blast the creatures around them.

I GOT SWARMED as soon as I was out of the branch's reach. It was like they knew I was the one who attacked them, so they attacked me with a vengeance to ensure it wouldn't happen again. I quickly changed course and got back to the branch, but this time I had an idea.

I climbed up a little higher on the tree-like structure, until my body was no longer in the swamp. The little creatures followed me, clawing into my skin, but at least I had a better view of what I was dealing with.

I took a deep breath and concentrated as hard as I could on levitating Gabriel and Embry, lifting them out of the water so they wouldn't drown. They came out coughing, which I took as a good sign, but I couldn't break my concentration.

"Just do it," Gabriel suggested when I tried to figure out a way to blast the creatures without hurting the guys. I was not going to let them die so I could save myself. Not again.

"I've got this," I argued with a confidence I didn't feel.

Gabriel looked at me like he wanted to argue and tell me to do as I was told, but he wasn't going to discourage me from saving them with magic.

The creatures were everywhere, attached to every inch of Embry and Gabriel, as well as my legs. I tried to focus on them, like I had with the sand, but there was no way I could get all of them at once.

I took another deep breath and held my moonstone necklace tight. I imagined all of the little creatures as warm fireflies, giving light on summer nights, rather than leading mourning innocents to their deaths in the swamps. I pictured it with all my might until I slowly felt the claws leaving my body. I knew I was imagining the buzzing, but I heard it and felt warmth all around me, like the energy from a million fireflies.

I was terrified to look, because I didn't know if I would be able to turn Embry and Gabriel back if they were fireflies now. They definitely wouldn't regenerate if they weren't human.

WHEN I SLOWLY OPENED MY eyes, Embry and Gabriel were there, floating in the air, looking at all the fireflies with wonder.

"You did it," they looked as amazed as I felt.

"I thought you might be fireflies too," I admitted.

"I had more faith in you than that," Gabriel said as I floated them over to solid ground.

"No, you didn't," I argued, since his solution had been for me to kill everyone and everything in the bog. I half-waddled, half-swam over to the shore with them.

"What were they?" Gabriel asked.

"Fee follet," I admitted. "They lure people into the swamps and drown them."

"The missing people Ingrid was worried about..." Embry ventured.

"We all fell for it," I defended them.

"You followed someone out here even after you knew this was a thing?" Gabriel was upset.

"I thought I was dreaming." They looked to me like that was nowhere near an acceptable excuse. "I know it was stupid, but Ingrid said they looked like floating lights. I wasn't expecting something that looked like Sam. They've clearly evolved because I wouldn't go anywhere with a floating light, but I would follow my real Sam to the end of the earth."

"You nearly did," Embry pointed out.

"I wasn't alone in that swamp, and it wasn't just because you were rescuing me," I threw it back at them.

"We were. At first," Embry said before they looked guiltily to each other.

"Point is, they shouldn't be bothering us anymore," Gabriel got us off the topic of how we all got duped.

"I don't know if it's permanent," I argued. "I don't know much when it comes to my powers."

"You knew enough to do that," Gabriel pointed back to the fireflies, clearly impressed, as we headed to the house.

"How did you come up with that?" Embry asked. "I don't think I've seen anyone actually turn something into something else. Other than Ingrid's illusions."

"I couldn't get rid of them, there were so many. I figured I wouldn't be able to individually destroy them all, but I could try something that would free you, but not kill you if it went wrong."

"I'm glad you didn't kill us," Embry smiled, wrapping his arm around me.

"Speaking of…" I confronted Embry once Gabriel was far enough ahead.

"I didn't nearly kill you," he took the defensive.

"No, you nearly killed you," I called him on it.

"I'm pretty sure we agreed that all of us got tricked."

"We did," I agreed. "But Gabriel and I realized something was wrong and fought back. You were down a really long time."

"I wasn't trying to die."

"But you're ready for it." He wasn't guilty or offended enough for it to not be the truth.

"Don't look so shocked." He didn't meet my eyes, but he was sure of himself, "I've lived centuries. Literally. I've fallen in love, I got married, I had children, I watched one of them get married and have a child of her own...I buried all of them. I won't be jumping into any swamps, or intentionally doing anything reckless, but when my time comes and I don't wake up..." he let the thought linger, and even though he made excellent points, I didn't like it.

"Do you think that's likely? I mean, for you to not come back, we either need to defeat the Big Bad, or I have to not be worth saving."

"I'm going with the first one," he told me like the second wasn't an option.

"The fee came to you as Beth?" I asked him.

"Beth, Helen and Jackson," he corrected.

"Everyone you love."

"Not everyone," he pulled me close.

"It would be really hard to not follow that," I let him know I understood.

"It was," he agreed. "But I wouldn't knowingly choose them over saving you."

"I'm pretty sure Lucy saved us this time," Gabriel rejoined our conversation.

"I raised you right," Embry teased.

"No, she would have stayed where I told her if you had."

"And we all would have drowned," Embry defended me.

"Which shows we all make mistakes sometimes," he gave me a look.

"What now?" I asked when we got to the house.

"Now? We sleep," Embry answered like I was crazy.

"What about the fee follet?"

"We'll have Ingrid come over tomorrow after we've all showered and had some sleep."

"Agreed." The smell and the cold were getting to me now that I wasn't dying.

We went upstairs, where Embry walked straight to the master bathroom without even saying goodnight.

"You can go first," Gabriel said awkwardly when we both headed for the common bathroom.

"Thank you." I went in while he headed downstairs, but I called him back, "Gabriel."

"Yes?" he lingered on the top step.

"Thank you for breaking out of it. I know how hard that must have been."

"They weren't real. You are," he said simply.

"Goodnight."

"Goodnight."

CHAPTER TWENTY-THREE

Ingrid came over the following evening to see if the fee follet truly left us. Just to be sure, she came back every night that week, each time with a different group of paranormal beings. Mostly witches and warlocks, but one called herself a seer, one a druid, and another a leprechaun. Gabriel snickered under his breath for that one, but given the company we were keeping, it didn't seem that far-fetched. On the last day, instead of heading out to the swamps, Ingrid handed us a tiny envelope, smiled and left.

"That was odd," Gabriel stated, waiting for me to open the envelope.

"There's a party in the quarter tonight to celebrate the end of the disappearances. She wants us to go, even if we can't be the guests of honor."

"Not a good idea," Gabriel argued.

"It's in the alley in front of her shop, which will be protected by every means possible to meet our stringent requirements," Embry continued reading from where I left off.

"Who else is going?" Gabriel asked.

"Please find enclosed the list of attendees," I handed him a second sheet from the envelope.

"I wish we had more time to make sure it would be safe…" Gabriel struggled with the decision.

"I'm pretty sure that's why she didn't give you any," I pointed out, completely understanding her smile and quick exit now.

"I don't have a choice in the matter, do I?"

"Of course you do. As long as you don't care whether or not we do what you choose," Embry teased.

"We're not staying long and you're not leaving my sight," Gabriel warned.

"Of course," I agreed.

WE LEFT the villa at five so we could be at Ingrid's shop by six. It really wasn't that far distance-wise, but they liked to take precautions. The dress I brought was coming in handy in NOLA. I paired it with Ingrid's shawl in case it got chilly. The last time I got dressed up pretty to go somewhere was prom. I was no longer under any illusions about magic, or life working out for me, but I was excited at the prospect of spending a night out, where we could pretend my life wasn't extremely complicated and dangerous at the moment.

AS SOON AS I walked into the alley, I felt that horrible, yet familiar feeling of someone trying to get into my brain. I pushed him out immediately and heard Mr. Fraser's "Ow!" before Ingrid came over.

"I'm so glad you came," she took me in for a hug. "Come, there's food and drinks and people to meet…" she brought me through the party, where we were the last to arrive.

"This is my niece, Beth," Ingrid winked to me as she lied,

introducing me to a man who lost his father to the fee follet weeks before.

"You're very good at that," I pointed out once we were away from the crowd a bit.

"Talking to people?" she asked.

"Lying to them." Her face went dark, so I made an attempt to get my foot out of my mouth. "No, I mean it as a compliment. You didn't miss a beat when he asked who I was. You said it so seamlessly that I nearly believed you."

"You need to mix a little truth with the lies and commit," she advised. "Always remember what you tell people, because they do. Not all of them, but the day you mess up, they'll remember, and then it's over."

"Is everyone who's here…"

"Gifted? Of supernatural inclinations?" she finished for me. "No, some are friends of mine, others are people who've lost someone to the fee follet…It's not a magic party, it's a community party. It's very important to have friends from all walks of life."

"I'll remember that."

"Beth would be proud," she said out of nowhere. "I'm amazed at how well you've adapted to your powers. From fearing them to controlling them and experimenting…that's no easy feat."

"I wasn't experimenting," I argued.

"You needed to save them," she gave me a knowing smile.

"Thank you for being here and helping me through it."

"Of course. It's not every day you get to nearly go back in time and fix a mistake."

"What mistake?" I asked.

"I was so jealous of Beth when she was figuring it out that I was useless."

"I'm sure you made up for it."

"I think so. She was the best friend I ever had."

"What about Mr. Fraser?" I asked.

"He was a very different kind of friend."

"Who ran his course?" I guessed.

"Are you implying he got old?" she played offended.

"Potion or no potion…"

"I was head over heels in love with that man, and he offered me all of it. His heart, a house, kids…but I knew what I was, what I could never be to him…"

"You turned him down?"

"I let him marry a woman instead of an eight-year-old girl," she still sounded upset by it.

"What happened?"

"He married Mrs. Fraser. Had children. But never stopped loving me."

"Are you together now?"

"Of course not. We keep each other company and pretend there's nothing there." Her words painted a sad and lonely existence of never getting what you want, but she said it in a no-nonsense manner.

"That sounds terrible."

"Love is strange, my dear. And it makes you do ridiculous things."

"Do you regret it?"

"I regret not having a happy ending," she sighed. "But I don't regret letting him have one. I would rather see him happy than sad, even if he isn't with me." She looked out onto the street, where there was some kind of a parade going on. "They have parades for everything here," she sighed after the bride came into view, but I heard a yearning for her own marriage procession before the party slipped away…

· · ·

I WAS ANNABELLE, nervous with my heart beating out of my chest, possibly because of how small my gown was. I looked down and saw it was a wedding dress that bound me so tight.

"It is quite an elaborate affair," Annabelle teased, as the hands fumbling with the back of my dress stopped.

"I'll figure out the corset," Henry said with determination. "I was transfixed by this," he ran his fingers over the back of my neck, sending shivers down my spine.

"It's a birthmark. I'm told it is a perfect half-moon," she said, trying to look back, to read his expression. All I saw was the top of his head, the perfectly coiffed hair suffering from the sweat and exertion of unlacing the dress.

"A half-moon crescent," Henry agreed, kissing the mark before going back to the dress.

While he unlaced the dress, occasionally planting a kiss as he worked his way down my back, Annabelle's hands twisted the wedding band around her finger. I could feel her excitement at starting a life with Henry, and her gratitude that he loved her in spite of her magic and other flaws. But there was a feeling in the pit of her stomach that was telling me this was a terrible mistake. I couldn't tell if it was her heart or mine that beat faster at the thought of Gabriel, but Annabelle struggled to push all other thoughts from her mind as the dress finally fell free, and she turned to face her groom...

"ARE YOU OKAY?" Ingrid asked, her hand on my shoulder when I woke up.

"Did I pass out?" I asked.

"No, mostly stood there playing with your hands," she shared as I looked around to make sure people weren't staring. "You had a memory?"

"The wedding dress triggered something," I agreed, grateful I didn't have to explain it to her.

"It was a beautiful wedding," she gave me a smile, thinking I saw Beth with Embry, before Mr. Fraser came over. "I'm sorry about earlier. I've been scanning everyone to make sure you would be safe. I didn't know it was you."

"It's okay," I assured him, his earlier intrusion the last thing on my mind. "I'll go check out the food." I made my exit so they could keep each other company.

I WENT over to the food table, sorting through my thoughts to figure out what the memory was for, or if it was a fluke brought on by the dress. I decided Henry noticing the birthmark was worth a mention to the guys, before someone came up behind me and said, "Charlie brought the crawfish, so it's to die for, but the scallops have sand in them."

"I wasn't expecting to see you here," I turned to face Eric and took him in for a hug.

"Charlie and Ingrid go way back," he shared. "And he loves parties."

"I was referring to you being in school."

"Oh, that?" he shrugged it off.

"I was under the impression you only spent the summers in New Orleans."

"Usually," he agreed, getting me to blush again.

"Did you already eat?" I brought the attention back to the food.

"I did. But the crawfish..." he brought his fingers to his lips and kissed the air.

"Is to die for," I repeated his words back to him.

"You get it," he smiled.

"Is this your first of Ingrid's parties, or can you tell a newcomer what to expect?" I looked around, trying to see if anything other than eating, drinking and talking was going on. Gabriel was laughing with Charlie and Embry, the three of them looking like they didn't have a care in the world, until Embry used two fingers to point to his eyes, then back to me. I rolled my eyes at him before coming back to Eric.

"I've been to a few," he told me. "One was in the streets and absolutely crazy, and the other was above her shop, with maybe five people and twenty courses of fancy dishes with food."

"So no idea what to expect tonight," I concluded.

He sighed before looking at me and shaking his head slowly. "Not with the party."

"But with other things?"

"I maybe have an idea," he sounded more resigned than excited.

"Of something bad?"

"For me, yes. For you...I'm not sure yet," he tried to figure me out.

"Is it something with Charlie?" I looked over to the three men again, but they all looked like they were having the time of their lives.

"I think you're awesome Lucy. You're probably the fiercest, most badass woman I have ever encountered, and I like you. As friends, sure, but also as a lot more than friends. If I didn't think Embry and Gabriel would kill me for it, I would want to kiss you right now."

I could feel myself flush and got nervous. Terribly nervous. At first because I thought he was going to kiss me and I wouldn't be good at it, but then because I didn't think I wanted him to. That's when I looked at him and realized he had no intention of kissing me tonight.

"I would want to, except that I have no interest in kissing a girl who doesn't want to kiss me."

"I think you're amazing Eric. You're nice and funny and helpful..."

"But I don't make you swoon," he understood.

"You do..." I remembered how much I blushed when he took me riding for the first time.

"Not like he does." It was a weird role-reversal where I felt like he was the one letting me down easy. "And it's okay... I see the way you look at him, mostly when you know he isn't watching, how jealous he gets about us hanging out, that fight he had with Embry..."

"What fight?" I was about to argue with his previous comments, to defend myself, but the guys were finally friends. I didn't want to have to wait another three hundred years for them to make up.

"The big fight that had them refusing to talk to each other for at least a week."

"That was about Annabelle. Gabriel thought Embry was trying to insert himself in based on loving Annabelle, but it was because he loved Beth," I explained, but Eric looked at me like I look at Clara sometimes when she doesn't understand things that are so obvious to everyone else.

"Maybe Gabriel was upset about that, but the storming off was because of you. Embry saw it too, so he told him not to hurt you like he hurt Rosie, and Gabriel said he didn't understand, and it wasn't like that."

"You remembered all that?" I tried to process what it meant.

"It didn't make sense until you told me about the ones that came before you."

"None of it makes sense," I argued, getting a look from Eric to stop arguing on this. "I'm sorry," I said, for not liking him like that, for liking Gabriel, who I'm pretty sure will break my heart...

"Don't be. Proximity doesn't equal love. It doesn't even guarantee friendship."

"But we are friends, right?" I asked, worried it might be cruel, but I couldn't deal with the alternative.

"If you want to be."

"I do."

"Then we're friends."

"Is that mean?"

"If you had let me kiss you and I had to wait for you to come clean about your feelings, that would have been cruel," he said, but he was smiling.

"You're really awesome. You know that?"

"I do," he assured me. He took one of the crawfish from my plate and ate it with a huge smile that told me we were going to be okay.

CHAPTER TWENTY-FOUR

We stayed at the party another hour or so, which included some dancing and a heartfelt rendition of My Way from Charlie, that garnered a standing ovation. He and Ingrid insisted the party couldn't possibly go on without us, but we weren't even done saying goodbye before they got right back to partying.

Eric smiled at me from across the tables before we walked to the car.

"What was that about?" Embry asked me while Gabriel drove.

"What?" I asked like I had no idea, but I knew exactly what he was referring to.

"Did something happen between you and Eric?" Embry raised an eyebrow and tried to read me.

"He's back at school now," I shrugged, pretty sure I was blushing, but I didn't want to talk about it with Gabriel in the car.

"What does that mean for the two of you?" he pressed.

"That we're friends. And we'll see each other less often.

Possibly never again, or every summer for the rest of our lives." Embry rolled his eyes. "Is that the plan if they never find us? To live in the villa forever? Because so far whatever Beth did seems to be working, or they're planning something big and scary and luring me into a false sense of security, which is not cool," I voiced some of my fears.

"I'll make sure to tell them next time I see them," Gabriel assured me.

"I am partly serious," I argued.

"We want to keep you safe for as long as possible, so we can train you and hone your skills."

"To give me a chance at surviving the next encounter."

"And live happily ever after," Embry smiled back at me before a man ran across the street, right in front of our car like he didn't even see it.

Gabriel slammed on the brakes, propelling me forward. I would have gone through the front window if I wasn't wearing my seatbelt. Thankfully, I don't think the impact was strong enough to kill anyone.

"Are you okay?" Embry poked his head out to address the man once he made sure I was unharmed, but Gabriel was fuming.

"I'm so sorry, I wasn't thinking. I just saw..."

"A car coming, and thought you would run in front of it? I could have killed you, we all could have died here," Gabriel pointed out.

"I know, of course..." the man was apologetic and frazzled until he spotted me in the car. For a moment I thought it hit him how many lives he put in danger, but he looked right into my eyes, and I could see something clicked for him.

"Gabriel..." I tried to tell him to leave, that I had a bad feeling about this, but I could see the black in the man's eyes, and knew it was too late.

Without taking his eyes off me, the man put his hands on the hood of our car. I thought it was a means of preventing us from running him over on purpose, but the black hood turned red, spreading from his hand to cover the rest of it in melting metal. It wasn't long until the engine was smoking, outside at first, but then through the vents, as the car overheated.

By the time we got out of the car, part of the hood was melting. The man had one hand up, palm facing us in a way that suggested he might be able to blast the heat out of it and incinerate us.

"Lucy Owens. Fancy running into you here," he said cockily while the guys glared at him and I stood frozen in fear. "You must be her faithful lapdogs, Embry and Gabriel?"

I kept thinking how the guys were weaponless. It didn't even occur to me that the man was outnumbered by us or that I had magical powers. Not until Embry, who was standing with Gabriel between me and the man, reached his hand back to take mine and said, "You've got this."

My magic hadn't occurred to me because this was a person, not a creature or a monster without a face. The man kept talking about how excited Donovan would be, while I took a deep breath and prepared to use my magic against him. Freezing him would be hard to explain if anyone came by, but it wasn't like I was going to blow him up either.

"Daddy!" I jumped, as did the man, when a toddler ran out from a driveway and rushed into the man's arms.

"Hey buddy. I thought I told you to wait for me at the corner, before crossing the street," he kept his eyes on me while talking to the boy, daring me to proceed with my attack.

"Lucy…" Gabriel said through clenched teeth.

"I can't."

"He's bigger than the rice," Embry pointed out.

"I can't do it in front of his son," I argued.

"He doesn't look like he cares," Gabriel nodded to the man, who had his hand out, ready to fire at us even with his son in his arms.

"I can't…" I was still shaking my head when the man shot a blast of magma in our direction. I put my shield up before it reached us, but it was a very close call.

"We need to get her to the villa. Preferably the panic room," Embry voiced.

"We can't leave and let him make contact," Gabriel argued.

"What about the kid?" I asked, but they both looked at me before exchanging a look that made me feel like a naïve child.

"I don't want to lie to you," Gabriel said delicately.

"Then don't."

"Whatever it takes, Lucy," he sighed, not meeting my eyes.

"Can you keep this up while we move?" Embry asked me.

"I'm not leaving," I argued. No children were dying on my behalf.

"Lucy…" Embry used his paternal tone on me.

"How long would it take you to get to him" I asked Gabriel.

"What are you doing?" he asked as I took the pen Eric gave me from my purse.

"If the man gets knocked out, will you be able to get to the boy before he hits the ground?" I rephrased my question.

"Of course," Gabriel looked at the tiny needle in my hand with concern.

I wasn't sure how much I trusted my aim at this distance, so instead of shooting it as intended, I used one hand to keep up my force shield, and levitated the needle so it nearly skimmed the ground, unnoticed, until it was less than an inch from the man's foot.

"Ready?" I asked Gabriel, who nodded. "Now," I said, stabbing the man with the toxin-filled needle. He looked down with a slight jerk of his leg, like he'd been stung by a bee, before he fell. Gabriel was barely a blur before the man was on the ground and Gabriel was standing there with the crying boy in his arms.

WITHOUT A WORD, Embry went over and took the child, who stopped crying immediately, resting his head on Embry's shoulder like he'd known him forever. Gabriel knelt to the ground and went through the man's pockets, finding a driver's license. "He lives two streets that way," he pointed off in the distance.

"What are we going to do with him?" I asked, hoping there was a mother or someone at the house who could take care of the kid. Maybe we could keep injecting the man with the toxin until we got away from here. I was about to interrupt their exchange of looks with my suggestion, but Gabriel's eyes grew wide as he pulled something out of another pocket.

"Did he reach anyone?" Embry asked, recognizing it as a pager before I could.

"Can you even tell?" I asked, getting a head shake from Gabriel in return.

"We need to get out of here as soon as possible," Embry decided.

"If he knows we're here he'll go straight to your place," Gabriel warned.

"I didn't bring my bag," I admitted. I got too comfortable here and prepared for tonight like I was any other girl going to a party. "Do you have a map?" I asked, doing the mental math to see how long it would take someone to get here from California. They both shook their heads.

"You can't go there," Embry argued, accurately reading my determination.

"We need to know if he's on to us, right?"

"What is she doing?" Gabriel asked before I clutched the moonstone necklace and closed my eyes, picturing Donovan's face. I embraced the fear and the chill in my spine, hoping I would see him thousands of miles away, unaware that anything happened.

"Richard's new, but I trust him," I zeroed in on Donovan, who seemed to be in a garden.

"New Orleans is risky on their part, but not entirely unexpected," a voice answered from behind a vine. It was oddly familiar.

"Does that mean you'll be joining me?" Donovan asked, his head slightly bowed in deference to who must be his master.

"You're going yourself?" There were very few people I knew with British accents. Most of them were movie stars, but I could feel my heart tighten in my chest as I placed this one.

"I want to be the one to bring her to you, my lord."

"There's no need. She'll find us eventually." He stepped out from behind the leaves and my heart stopped. The expression was different, but the face was otherwise unchanged from the last time I saw it, smiling at me in my wedding dress.

"We might not have time for her to figure it out," Donovan argued with as much respect as the words would allow. "I'll take the jet and keep you informed."

"Unharmed," Henry warned, looking straight at me. It was impossible, but...he saw me.

"Are you okay?"

"Are they coming?"

Gabriel and Embry looked at me with concern, but I couldn't reassure them. I couldn't breathe. It felt like my heart was breaking.

"Did he do something to you?" Embry asked.

"Donovan is taking a jet from Salem," I felt the street going blurry and fought it long enough to tell them we were momentarily safe, before I slipped away...

. . .

"*WHAT IS THIS?*" *Annabelle asked Henry, holding very old pages in her hand. I wanted to warn her when she said it with curiosity rather than suspicion, but then I saw the look on his face. The smile he looked up at her with had gone dark, the sparkle disappearing from his eyes as his jaw set.*

"You weren't supposed to find that," he said, coming closer. With every step he took in our direction, I got more afraid, until he got close enough to take the paper from her. She flinched, and though she didn't know what she was afraid of, I did. Henry reacted to the flinch as if she slapped him.

"A few words on a piece of paper and already you're afraid of me?" he asked, hurt.

"A few words combined with a lot of secrets, long absences and I question how well I know you," she argued, taking a step back. "The heart of the Bearer of the Crescent Moon?" she pressed.

"An ingredient in the ritual I was put on this world to complete," he admitted.

"A ritual for what?" she asked. Annabelle was disgusted more than afraid, but I was terrified.

"To become more powerful than anyone else on earth," he said with a hint of hope, like this might entice her.

"Like a king?" she asked, but she knew that wasn't it. With the magic Henry was capable of, he was already more powerful than the men who held powerful positions in this country and every other.

"More powerful than all the kings and rulers and everyone else put together," he said with a gleam in his eye, which had never looked so cold before.

"All it takes is my heart?" she asked, remembering the first time he mentioned it, after the wedding. Annabelle wondered the same thing I did; had he perhaps glimpsed the birthmark on that first day, before he decided to intervene on her behalf?

"Don't look at me like that Annie, this ritual is why I am here on

earth," he pleaded, so unlike what I expected from Donovan's master.

"You've always had these grand ideas, always needed more instead of being happy with what you have."

"I don't want more, I need it. I need it, or I die trying. That's the way it has to be."

"Says who?" she asked. We were nearly in the doorway now.

"Death shall not claim me while I am on the chosen path," he admitted.

"What?" It sounded like he was repeating a passage from a book rather than giving an answer.

"There are people put on this world to accomplish certain tasks. I was put here to complete the ritual, and as long as I am still working on it, until I have achieved it, I cannot die. You can pierce my heart as many times as you like and tomorrow, I will wake up as if nothing happened. I've done it at least a dozen times before."

"You've died?" she asked, trying to process this new information, that went far beyond the little bits of magic he did with her. I was shocked it wasn't hundreds of times, based on how dark his eyes had become.

"You'd be surprised how many people choose to stand in the way of others accomplishing their dreams, rather than helping them along the way. Not to mention those who have the same dream and are jealous because I am the only one to find a way."

"A way to do what?" I noted the fear in her voice, as she failed to recognize the man she married.

"To rule the world. Once the ritual is complete, nothing will be able to stop me."

"And my death is a price you are willing to pay?" I could feel her heart breaking as if it were my own.

"Your death would most likely be temporary, my love. I would be so powerful that the laws of heaven and hell, death and resurrection would mean nothing to me. I could bring you back."

"Your eyes. I should have known as soon as I saw your eyes," Annabelle realized.

"They sometimes get a little darker when I die, but it is hardly anything to..."

"A little darker? It was no accident, Henry, not a small price to pay for coming back to life. The darkness is spreading, and evil is devouring your soul. That is what is happening to your eyes. You're becoming a monster!" She was in the middle of the last word when his hand shot up and collided with her cheek. I felt the sting before she brought her hand up, more as a reflex than from the pain. All Annabelle felt was numb.

"Watch your tongue," he warned, the hatred in his voice doing nothing but prove her right.

"Or maybe you already were a monster, and I was too blind to see it."

"I am offering you the world on a silver platter. You dare question me when you should be showing gratitude and promising me your everlasting devotion? I will be a god," he believed it, but he also knew she wouldn't feel the same; it was evident on his face.

"You will be a demon. Some vile creature that sacrifices whatever it takes to stay on top, a sad excuse for a human being, let alone a god." She turned and headed for a room to our left. I could hear the baby crying.

"Where are you going?" Henry yelled after us.

"I am taking my daughter and getting as far away from you as I possibly can. You dare come after us, or I see you anywhere near her..." She called out of the room, stuffing piles of cloth into a bag while trying to soothe the tiny infant in the crib.

"You can't leave me. You were nothing when I found you. About to be raped by common thieves. You leave now, and you can never come back," Henry threatened. *"You are shocked, this wasn't how I planned to tell you, but if you walk out that door, you are no longer my wife, you are just the Bearer of the Crescent Moon..."*

I could feel a chill down my back, knowing what those words meant, but Annabelle pushed the fear aside and lifted Margaret from the crib. "I assure you; I want nothing more than to be rid of you," she told him once we were out of the nursery, heading for the door without even looking at him.

"You misunderstand me, Annabelle. I will let you walk out the door, because that part of it is a test, but I won't let you leave." We froze and I could feel my heart pounding in my ears, but I could have sworn it stopped altogether.

"You come anywhere near my daughter and I will kill you," we turned to face him, Annabelle standing her ground now that her daughter was involved.

"She is my daughter as well," Henry fumed. "I have just told you that you can stab me or do what you want but I will not stay dead. I will come and find you."

"You might not be able to die, but I can," Annabelle threatened, taking out her dagger.

"I don't need you to be alive to rip your heart out," Henry warned.

"But I'm guessing it puts a damper on your plans if the heart in question has a dagger in it." I envied her bravery more than anything as I felt the tip of the cold blade on my chest. There wasn't a doubt in my mind that she would go through with it.

"You wouldn't kill yourself," he argued.

"Try me," she kept his stare. "Take one step closer and I will drive this through my heart."

"I will find you. I will hunt you down and then I will cut your heart out of your chest while you still breathe," he threatened, shocking her with his hatred.

"Haven't you already done that?" Annabelle asked before walking out of the house.

She kept the point of her dagger against her breast, right above her heart. Once we were a few houses away, she brought the dagger to her side, but she kept it out until we were safely at a church. I was amazed at how calm and confident she was when she told the priest she needed a carriage to get to Boston, even more so when he lent her his personal one. Once we could no longer see the church in the distance, Annabelle broke down and let the emotions out. "Until the next town," she said under her breath. That was how long she gave herself to dwell on it before she was going to gather herself, make a plan, and be strong, like her daughter needed...

CHAPTER TWENTY-FIVE

I woke up with tears pouring down my face and no idea where I was. The crash occurred only a few streets from the villa, but I was still surprised I was out long enough for them to bring me back to what I assumed was Embry's. The closet of the master bedroom by the looks of it.

I went to the door and pounded on it, but nothing I did moved it in the slightest. I took the moonstone necklace in my hand and tried to see Embry, or Gabriel, but it was like something was blocking me. I could make things float inside the room, but the metal doors did more than keep the outside world from getting in.

I tried not to panic, telling myself the guys wouldn't just leave me in here. I had been so curious about Embry's 'treasures', but at the moment I didn't really care. If I let my mind wander it went straight to Henry, who seemed so sweet, but was actually the Big Bad who has been hunting my family for centuries. I wanted to believe that the guys didn't tell me because they didn't know, but I wasn't that naive.

I tried to find some kind of secret passage, or an alarm I could pull to let them know I was awake. I pulled every single book on the shelves, but I guess that only works in movies. If Donovan wasn't on his way to us, I could have spent hours reading each of the antique books, but I needed to find a way out.

There was a sheet covering what looked like frames in the corner, but I lifted it, to be sure. The first one was a life-size portrait of Annabelle, with Embry's initials in the corner. He used to bring me paintings when he would visit, or an easel and canvas he could fill while I read by the creek. He tried to get me into it as well, but it wasn't long until we discovered that painting was not something I excelled at. I could make really advanced kindergarten-level paintings that never went outside the lines, but that was about it. Embry, on the other hand, made Annabelle completely life-like, in every aspect. I would guess that he painted it from memory, or before Annabelle left for Salem, because there was no way she could keep such a carefree smile after finding out she was married to a monster.

I could sort of see what Grams meant about the smiles letting you tell my ancestors apart. The next frame held Rosalind, but I could tell it was her even before I recognized her dress. Cassie was next, looking absolutely elegant, but also fierce. The last painting was of Beth, looking at the world with as much love and happiness as on her fifth anniversary with Embry. I wonder if she knew who we're all descended from.

There was nothing else there besides a few landscapes. When I grabbed the sheet to throw it back onto the frames, I knocked over some papers, revealing a red panic button. Since I was already in the panic room, I would assume it was designed to alert the authorities. Knowing Embry and the type of dangers he might need the room for, I didn't think his worked the same.

. . .

I PRESSED THE BUTTON, expecting an alarm to go off, but nothing happened. I pressed again and was beginning to think it wasn't connected to anything when the metal door opened to reveal Gabriel.

"Good, you're awake," he tried to come close, but I took a step back.

"I've packed your things and we're ready to go," Embry started talking as soon as he got close, before finally looking at me.

"We're not leaving," I argued.

"You told us Donovan was on his way. That gives us six hours, tops," Gabriel reminded me.

"He's on his way here, where he will find Charlie and Eric, defenseless. We can't keep running away and letting other people deal with the consequences." My hatred wasn't exactly directed at them, but I wasn't going to let Charlie and Eric join the ranks of Terrence, Caleb, and Sam so I could get away.

"I understand that you're upset, but sacrificing yourself doesn't protect anyone," Embry said gently.

"It actually protects everyone, but I wasn't planning on dying. Considering Donovan is coming alone, I was under the impression we were going to stop running. To stay here and fight. Or was that a lie too?"

"What did you see?" There was a hint of fear in their voices. I wondered if they knew exactly what I found out or were trying to figure out which of their many lies I was referring to.

"Lucy…" Gabriel pressed.

"Don't Lucy me," I warned.

"What happened?" He didn't back down.

"The Big Bad."

"He's here?" Embry was horrified.

"Part of him." There was venom in my words, and in my

blood, as the anger coursed through me. The fear didn't leave their faces until they understood what I meant, and even then, they didn't own up to it.

"We don't…"

"You know exactly what I'm referring to. You've known all along," I reproached. "I've been seeing her memories. Annabelle's. After she left you guys, she moved to Salem on her own, where she eventually met this guy, Henry, who saved her from a group of thugs on the side of the road. He was the one who showed her that she had magic. He taught her how to use it and eventually, he married her." By now there was no denying it.

"Luce…" Embry tried, but he couldn't meet my eyes.

"Did it slip your mind that the evil man we're running from, who hunts my family, and caused Sam's death was my great-great-many-times-great-grandfather?"

Embry opened his mouth and tried a bunch of excuses before deciding to reason with me. "How would that help you?" he asked.

"You didn't think I deserved to know?" I asked instead. "What kind of person…I never met my dad, so I don't know if this is standard father-daughter behavior, but there has to be something entirely messed up about us if we come from that. He has to be a psychopath, and that stuff is genetic," I was angry at everyone who kept it from me, at Annabelle for not seeing through him, at him for being evil… I felt dirty.

"There is nothing wrong with you Lucy. Henry is a horrible man. Annabelle realized that and brought her daughter away from him to keep her safe. He is Margaret's father, yes, but I raised that little girl, and there was nothing evil or psychotic about her, just like there is none of that in you," Embry said with an intensity I usually associated with Gabriel.

"How could you not tell me? When I started having the

dreams, you had to know I would eventually find out," I felt betrayed and heartbroken. I wanted to get angry, to have any other emotion overwhelm the pain that kept making me cry.

"It's not like he had any paternal instincts towards you. Bringing up the connection would not have made him treat you any better. It would just make it harder for you to do what you have to in order to get away from him."

"Because I'm weak?"

"Because you have a heart. You care about people. We couldn't risk you coming face to face with Henry and letting him kill you because you couldn't harm a twisted kind of father figure," Embry corrected.

"Is that why Annabelle let herself die? Because she couldn't fight him, and she couldn't let him have her?"

"Annabelle would have killed him if she had the chance," Gabriel sounded so sure of himself, but I don't think he ever actually saw them together.

"Annabelle didn't fight the conviction, and she let them burn her at the stake because she knew it was all done on Henry's orders. If she fought it, or waited for a trial, it would give him enough time to come find her and Margaret. She admitted her guilt and let the flames take her so he would not get what he needed. I think she thought it ended with her." Embry looked to Gabriel for confirmation on the last part, and he nodded with conviction.

"Not even close," I shook my head, biting my bottom lip.

"Let's get in the car and talk about this," Embry suggested.

"There's nothing to talk about. You've been lying to me my entire life and it never ends. I don't need to hear your lies because I don't believe them. I don't trust either of you anymore." They'd both stepped towards me, but I crossed my arms and took another step back.

"Lucy, everything we have ever done was to keep you safe," Embry pleaded.

"That's what you tell yourself," I shook my head. "But you were just lying and hurting me." I couldn't even look at them. "I need to clear my head, and then we are going to face Donovan and stop acting like cowards." I tried to channel Annabelle's confidence as I walked past them to exit the panic room, but my insides felt seconds away from a meltdown.

CHAPTER TWENTY-SIX

I wandered around the property for a bit before finding myself in the stables. I got some treats from the bucket and was feeding Rudolph when I heard someone come up behind me. I knew it wasn't Donovan yet, so I debated whether I should yell at Embry and Gabriel to go away or hear them out. When I turned around, it was Charlie.

"I'm sorry, I didn't mean to scare you," he said when I jumped. "You're not planning on riding out in the middle of the night, are you?"

"Of course not. I was wandering around and found myself here," I tried to give him a convincing smile. "Trouble sleeping?"

"I came to turn off the lights. I was going to leave when I saw you, but you looked like you could use some company. I've been told I am excellent at listening, if ever you want to talk."

"Not really," I admitted, but I didn't want to be alone either. "You could tell me more stories, if you don't mind?"

"Are we trying to avoid talking about something else?" he asked.

"Yes," I chose honesty.

"I know all about these. I'm supposed to find a way to tell a story that perfectly reflects what is going on with your life now, so by the time the story is over, you know what you need to do."

"That would be quite the skill," I gave him a small smile. "I don't think there's much I can do about the fact that the people I trusted the most lied to me." I didn't want to talk about it, but the pain and anger were so close to the surface. It wasn't even that I was mad...I felt betrayed and alone, like I didn't know anything anymore.

"One lie doesn't erase a lifetime--"

"Of lies," I cut off Charlie's words of wisdom. "They would come and visit me and make me feel special. I thought of Embry as family, but they've been lying to me since the day I met them. They're here to protect me, but if it comes down to it, they would rather stop him than save me, and I don't blame them, considering what's inside of me." The thought had been gnawing at me since Donovan mentioned it in the motel parking lot, but I had refused to believe it until now.

"I can't vouch for Gabriel, but Embry would give anything to see you safe and happy. He loves you more than anything else in this world."

"Love and duty are not the same thing," I argued quietly.

"He wouldn't spend fifteen years talking my ear off about how wonderful you are if you were just an obligation," he argued. "Every spelling bee and class award, when you climbed to the top of the oak tree, when you made the best chocolate chip cookies he's ever tried...He has spent the last fifteen years telling me how proud he is of you, and showing me how much he loves you."

"Maybe both are true," I suggested.

"Maybe," he agreed.

I looked at him, trying so hard to help me without

knowing what was going on. I took a deep breath and admitted, "The Big Bad who is hunting us and has been trying to kill my ancestors for generations was actually married to Annabelle. The first one," I added in case he didn't know. "We all come from him."

He nodded his head, digesting the information, before he said, "Maybe they kept it from you because they love you and didn't want to hurt you, or risk you getting hurt?"

I was surprised by his reaction. "It's still lying to me," I pointed out. "About everything."

"About a tiny detail that only feels like everything because you just found out about it. I don't think your ancestry changes anything."

"It's the entire reason we're here. People are literally dying because of it," I argued.

"Because you're a strong and fierce Owens woman. Not because one asshole slipped his way into the family tree." I was surprised by the bluntness of his language. "I don't know if you're worried this means you're a bad apple, or have something dark and dangerous inside you, but I knew your Grams her whole life, and there wasn't an ounce of evil inside her, regardless of who her great-great-grandfather was."

"You don't think that giving someone superpowers to stay alive until they kill me means something?"

"You don't know what his purpose is," he reminded me, knowing way more about everything than I ever gave him credit for.

"I know what he thinks it is."

"Villains often get confused about what they're supposed to do," he said with a smile and a wink that got me smiling too. "Would you still like that story?"

"I would love a distraction," I agreed, needing time to process my feelings before going back to the guys.

He looked off like he was consulting his bank of

memories, then got into a story that painted my grandmother in a completely different light than when I knew her; the Evelyn only Charlie told me about. I loved how he made Grams strong and fierce, always standing up for people.

"She chained herself to a tree? Literally?" I verified after his third story, this one about her protesting so they wouldn't cut down a tree on their university campus.

"She was part of a nature conservation group and tried to make it a landmark, but the truth of it was that she couldn't care less about what kind of tree it was or how long it was there. Your grandfather just passed away, and when we were at school together, he carved their initials into the tree and vowed to love her forever."

"She was saving the memories," I understood. "I guess that's when she started being a shut-in?"

"She was as carefree and headstrong as ever," he argued. "Laurel and I were in town when it happened, so once the tree was safe, we took her out to dinner, and she was every bit as sharp and full of plans and ideas as she ever was."

"I thought she became afraid of people and leaving home after my grandfather died?"

"No, that was months later."

"When it hit her?" Grief had many stages before acceptance.

"No, it didn't have anything to do with Grant, I don't think," he said of my grandfather.

"Was there anything else to explain it? Or did she wake up one day and decide she didn't want to go outside anymore?" I found the whole thing ridiculous, but I understood that loss made people do crazy things.

"No one ever told you?" he asked, shifting awkwardly for the first time since we started talking, probably an hour ago.

"Told me what?" I asked.

"She stopped going out right around the time your mom had you."

"It was because of me?"

"It had nothing to do with you, sweetie, Evelyn loved you to the moon and back," he assured me.

"But…" I pressed.

"Your father," he admitted.

"You know who my father is?" I was shocked. Every time I asked, it was implied that my mom and dad weren't all that serious, she never brought him home, and he bailed as soon as he found out she was pregnant.

"Maybe this isn't the right conversation to be getting your mind off things."

"I don't mean to put you on the spot, but no one ever talks about my father. I didn't think anyone knew who he was," I admitted. My father was listed as Unknown in the Chronicles. Even Henry was named as Margaret's father, although it didn't mention his exploits.

"It really isn't my place to tell you," Charlie was apologetic, but wasn't giving me any answers.

"And the people whose place it is would rather keep me in the dark and pretend they're protecting me." We were back at square one. "I'm sorry, that wasn't aimed at…"

"Are you okay?" Charlie asked, leaning in and putting his hand on my shoulder when I suddenly stopped talking.

"I'm fine," I assured him, feeling the hairs on the back of my neck stick up. "Do you think you and Eric could stay somewhere else tonight? Like maybe Ingrid's?" I asked.

"Eric's already on his way back to his dorm. What's going on?"

"Someone is coming here looking for me, and I don't want you to be here when he finds me."

"Why are you still here?" he asked me.

"Because it'll never end if I keep running."

He looked like he wanted to argue, but the look in my eyes must have convinced him. "I'll see you in the morning," he set his jaw, but I could see his eyes tearing up.

"Thank you. For everything," I told him. I was hoping I would make it through, but this time I planned on being strong like Annabelle, if ever it came down to it.

"Be careful," he told me before going home, while I headed for Embry's villa to prepare them for battle.

CHAPTER TWENTY-SEVEN

Embry and Gabriel were sitting in the kitchen with a rather large sword and an axe on the table between them. You could cut the tension with a knife, but for once it wasn't aimed at each other.

"Can I get you anything?" I expected them to yell at me for running off when Donovan was on his way, but Embry showed nothing but concern for my well-being.

"I'm fine," I said, looking from one to the other.

For a minute, the three of us stood there, no one really knowing what to say.

"I'm sorry," they both blurted out at the same time.

"We never knew that he cared about your birthmark. We always assumed he wanted you because you were his descendants," Gabriel came clean, honestly answering the question I asked months ago, when I found out about the Prophecy.

"Did the other Bearers of the Crescent Moon find out who was hunting them?" I asked.

"Cass…" Embry said before they exchanged a look. I gave them one as well, so they decided to share. "She came face to face with him and he made her think he didn't want to hurt her, or her daughter, because they were his blood. She didn't tell us everything he said, there wasn't time, but he used it to trick her."

"Wouldn't it make sense to warn me ahead of time, so I wouldn't fall for his tricks?" I suggested.

"In retrospect…maybe. But I saw what it did to Beth when she found out, and I couldn't put that on you," Embry put his hand on mine, seeking forgiveness, while Gabriel's eyes widened with the knowledge that Embry told Beth. I was glad he meant it when he told me they had no secrets.

"Donovan is in New Orleans," I brought us back to the matter at hand.

"The car is packed…" Embry tried one last time, but I shook my head.

"If you absolutely want to take our chances against Dono-van…" Gabriel paused, his eyes pleading for me to change my mind. "We have weapons," he said, taking the axe.

"You need to listen to us though, Lucy. If I tell you to run to the panic room, you need to run to the panic room," Embry warned.

"I'm not going to abandon the two of you to face him when you wanted to take me away," I argued.

"Will you at least hide?" he tried instead.

"What's your plan?" Gabriel asked, giving me a chance.

"From what I gather, you guys keep coming back as long as your body isn't damaged beyond repair. There are cases of severed heads being sewn back on…" I blinked hard to get the image out of my mind. "But you can't come back from what I did to that woman."

"You want to blow him up?" Embry raised his eyebrows at me.

"I want to stop him from hurting more people I care about. If we can tie him up and lock him in the panic room for all eternity, I'm good with that too."

"What if things get out of hand? He brings an army and we can't handle it?" Gabriel asked with a warning look, as if he knew my plan.

"I'll run to the panic room," I partially meant it. Depending on what Donovan came at us with, it might be better for the two of us to be locked in the panic room. Powers work on the inside, but they can't get out to hurt anyone else.

THE GUYS HAD both spent time as soldiers, so they seemed perfectly content to wait for Donovan to show up. I, on the other hand, was a pack of nerves. I felt like I should be practicing or learning more techniques or...anything would be better than nothing. I had the vials of potion I made with Ingrid, but wasn't sure what would be useful. Donovan could control other Gifteds, and I assumed he had magical powers, but it wasn't like he was going to be poisoning me or drinking anything I gave him. That left me with the focusing draught. I held the tiny bottle up to the light, wondering if potions went bad, when the guys stood up, alert.

"Someone's here," Embry explained as they positioned themselves between me and the door. There was a loud noise, the screech of metal on pavement, before we all recognized Ingrid's voice in the backyard.

"He's close," she gave an involuntary shudder, coming into the kitchen and giving Embry a hug.

"How do you know?" Gabriel asked.

"Charlie came to my place and said you might need some help," she explained. "And I can feel his magic," another shiver. I thought it was because I did the tracking spell earlier, but if she felt it too...

"Can you tell how powerful he is?" Embry asked before his eyes darted to the ceiling, but I didn't hear anything.

"A lot stronger than I am," she hugged herself, then shook it off. "That was him?"

"He's on the property," Embry agreed.

"It's now or never my dear, he's here," Ingrid nodded encouragingly to the vial, so I knocked it back and braced myself.

I WAS grateful Embry chose to bring us out to the yard instead of waiting in the house for Donovan. It felt good to move. Even if we were exposed out here in the open, it was better than feeling caged inside.

More than anything, I wanted to wrap a force shield around the four of us, but Donovan might not know about my powers, and I didn't want to show him all my cards.

"Pretty brave, choosing her house," Donovan walked over to us as calmly as if we were old friends meeting in the park.

Embry, Gabriel and Ingrid stood facing him like statues while I felt like I was made of Jell-O. Or something crumblier.

"Where's Richard?" Donovan sounded bored.

"You didn't stab him with a tracker as well?" Gabriel stepped forward, more so he could adjust his position to cover me than out of bravery.

"His went dark." Donovan didn't look the least bit concerned about Richard's well-being, but the lack of knowledge was a mild annoyance.

Embry must have heard my breath catch in my chest because he reached a hand back to take mine. I hadn't asked about the jogger because I didn't want to know what 'whatever it takes' meant.

"Lucy," Donovan's focus turned to me. "I have a proposition for you."

"Do you want me to rule by Henry's side again?" I asked, using his name but getting no reaction.

"Oh, I think that ship has sailed," his smile was downright jovial, which terrified me. "This one might be better suited for you."

"You had my brother killed. If I didn't take your offer when his life was in the balance, there is nothing you could say or do to make me willingly consider your offer now." I knew I was stalling, but I had a sudden appreciation for why villains always shared their evil plans before putting them into action on TV.

"I admit I was wrong in assuming you would sacrifice yourself to save someone you love," he paused to look at me, his words making my blood boil. "But what about saving yourself?"

Sam's death replayed in my mind, and Donovan's implications brought an anger like I had never felt before. I tried to steady my breathing, but it was no use. "Argh!" I screamed, making a guttural sound that shocked me, as I sent a blast of energy at him.

He was caught off guard for a moment, so the blast pushed him back a couple of feet before he tossed it to the side, barely even losing his footing.

"My, how the generations have diluted your magic," Donovan chuckled to himself before sending a green orb at us. I conjured a force shield, but instead of bouncing off, the green orb pushed against my shield, digging its way in like Mr. Fraser tried to do to my mind. It took Ingrid putting her hand on my shoulder to help me push the orb off.

I HAD BEEN PRAYING Donovan would come alone, without an army, because I truly thought we could defeat him. We outnumbered him, and everyone insisted my magic was powerful, so I believed them. Even holding on to the moonstone and to Ingrid's hand did nothing more than put dents in

Donovan's metaphorical armor. I threw everything I had at him, trying to protect Embry and Gabriel as they faced him with their medieval weapons. If we managed to coordinate our attacks, he would go slightly off-balance, but I was the only one who could get close enough to him without risking being controlled. If four against one was giving us trouble, three against two would destroy us.

Ingrid was the first to fall. She tried altering Donovan's perception of reality, but it was like he could sense the guys once they got close enough, and he had no qualms about half-hazardly sending blasts of energy and sparks in every direction. Even if he couldn't see where we were, he still had a pretty good chance of hitting one of us. And unless something substantial stopped them, his curses were endless, which put everyone in the neighborhood at risk.

Eventually, Donovan sent one of his green orbs at Embry, then immediately sent one at us. I had already conjured a force shield to protect Embry from the brunt of the blast and couldn't conjure another one fast enough. Ingrid tried to use her magic to send the orb back to Donovan, but she only managed to slow it down before it hit her square in the chest.

In the time it took me to get to Ingrid and see that the blow was fatal, Donovan had already frozen Gabriel's axe midair and reached out to touch him. Time froze, or at least I could swear my heart stopped while Gabriel's expression went from shock to a blank slate to determination as Donovan took over his mind. Gabriel turned away from Donovan, set his sights on me and pounced.

I had my hands ready to conjure a force shield, but Embry cut in between us before I had to find out if I could have gone through with fighting Gabriel to save myself.

"Get out of here Lucy," Embry called to me, every blow between him and Gabriel constricting my heart tighter, the

sound of metal on metal so much worse than nails on a chalkboard could ever be.

DODGING orbs and blasts had brought me closer to the stables
than to the villa, with Donovan and Gabriel between me and
the panic room, as well as the getaway car.

I stepped back slowly as Donovan made his way towards
me. He wasn't sending anything at me, but he had his hands at
the ready. I was convinced he would stop me if I tried to run.

"Have you reconsidered?" Donovan asked, wiping a bead
of sweat from his brow. It was good to know that our defense
was exerting him, if nothing else.

"I want nothing to do with you," I told him, calculating my
chances of escaping on horseback to be somewhere below
zero.

"I'm not sure you understand. Turning me down means
you die within the decade. No matter what."

"I'll take my chances," I stood as tall as I possibly could, to
show him I meant it and he didn't scare me, even though
he did.

"Then you leave me no choice." For a moment, he stood
there, palms facing upwards, shaking his head at me. The
next, he had covered the distance between us and wrapped his
surprisingly strong hands around my tiny, fragile neck. I tried
to freeze him, to buy myself some time, but none of it worked.
I couldn't stop him, levitate him, move him away from me, or
bring anything over. I was helpless.

I screamed, using my hands to try and release his grip, but
the weight of him brought me down to the floor. My lungs
were aching for air, but all I could think was that I couldn't let
him take my heart.

Embry had mentioned that there were places on the property where Gifts and magic didn't work. This was either one

of them, or I had exhausted all of my powers. Since Donovan was on top of me, strangling me instead of using his magic on me, I assumed I wasn't the problem. I tried to rip his fingers off my throat or push him away, but it didn't work. Nothing worked, so I dropped my arms. I thought I had given up, but my hands had other plans. They travelled along the ground, searching for something they could save me with, and found a rock. I lifted it up and brought it smashing into Donovan's skull.

I think he was more frazzled than hurt, but it still gave me the chance to get up and run to the big barn doors. He followed me, like I knew he would, but I just needed to get far enough ahead of him for my magic to work. It was the only logical explanation, and if I was wrong, I was dead anyway.

I didn't feel anything when I crossed the threshold, but I turned to face Donovan with my hands on the moonstone necklace. I closed my eyes and channeled everything I had into blasting him into oblivion. I felt like my soul was drained into the magic and fell to my knees, too scared to open my eyes.

I took a deep breath and found the spot where I last saw Donovan, half-expecting him to give me one last menacing smile before carting me off to Henry, but he was gone. In his place, there was nothing but a pile of ash.

"Lucy!" I heard my name, but it sounded so far away. I was cold and damp, which didn't make any sense, until I opened my eyes and saw that I was lying in the dew-covered grass in front of the barn. It was early morning, though I don't think I was out longer than a few minutes. I still felt so tired.

I saw Embry and tried to stand, to run to him, but everything around me started spinning. I would have fallen back onto the grass if Gabriel hadn't appeared out of nowhere and caught me.

"You're friends again?" I verified, judging by the fact that he wasn't trying to kill me.

"You did it, Lucy. Donovan can't hurt you anymore," Gabriel gave me a smile, looking at me with...not quite incredulity, but definitely amazement and respect.

"The ashes…" I turned, pointing to the pile of what used to be Donovan.

"We'll take care of them," Embry assured me. "You're safe."

"We need to get out of here," I argued, walking towards the villa. Henry might not sit back and wait for us to find him if he knew exactly where we were. "We are nowhere near safe."

"No, we're not," he agreed. "But you accomplished something huge, and we need to—"

"We need more magic," I cut him off. "If Henry is more powerful than Donovan, we don't stand a chance. We can't let him complete the ritual. There would be no stopping him." Part of me always thought they were exaggerating, but the four of us barely managed to defeat Donovan, and that was without an army of supernatural minions to contend with.

"We can look into it and figure something out," Embry gave me an encouraging smile.

"Those books in the bunker that you didn't want to fall into the wrong hands…" I pried.

"They might be worth a look," Gabriel agreed.

"Will Ingrid be okay?" I asked once I got to her, kneeling down to bring her head into my lap. With her illusions gone, she looked like a sleeping child.

"She should wake up in a few hours," Embry assured me. "We can bring her to Charlie's so he can keep an eye on her."

"And Richard?" I used the name Donovan gave us, trying to stay composed.

"The child was returned to his mother and Richard spent the night in a very special mausoleum. He'll be back with his family and able to destroy us in no time," Gabriel didn't look happy about it, but I believed him.

"We should leave before that happens," Embry suggested.

THE GUYS WENT to burn Donovan's ashes while I carried Ingrid onto a couch in Charlie's living room. I stayed by her side and held her hand, knowing there was no way I could ever repay what she'd done for me. Or get over the sight of her lying lifeless on the grass.

"Charlie's back. It's time to go," Gabriel came to warn me

as I was running my fingers through Ingrid's hair like I used to do for Clara.

"I'll be right there," I assured him, waiting until he was gone to place a kiss on her forehead.

I ran into Mr. Fraser on my way out and hesitated, not sure if she would want him to see her like that, but someone must have called him.

"I've got her," he promised me, fighting to keep it together.

"Tell her," I paused, trying to find the words to convey my love and admiration for her. "Tell her it has been an honour learning and fighting alongside her."

He nodded, clearing his throat, then went to Ingrid's side. I watched as he tenderly brushed the hair from her forehead before going over to the villa.

THE CAR WAS MOSTLY PACKED, so the guys put their weapons in the trunk, and I took Ingrid's potions. The villa had come to be home over the past couple of months, but we wouldn't stand a chance against Henry if he came after us now. I put everyone here in danger long enough.

"I told you I would see you in the morning." Relief was etched all over Charlie's face as he left Embry to come and take me in for a hug.

"Thank you for the help," I told him, trying not to cry, but something about him was making me tear up.

"I'm always here. Always willing to lend a hand," he assured me as Embry got into the driver's seat, letting me know it was time to go. "This isn't how I would have wanted you to find out, but I know you have to leave, and I don't want to be another person keeping things from you."

"What are you talking about?" I asked him before remembering last night's conversation. It felt like lifetimes ago.

"This is all I know about it. But sometimes it's better to

leave good enough alone." He put an envelope in my hand, then covered it with both of his. "You take care now."

"You too." I took him in for a hug, then took my place in the back seat.

I waved to Charlie as we pulled out of the driveway, looking back until I couldn't see him or the property anymore. Our general direction was home, but the home from my memories was gone. Nothing in my life would ever be anything like it was before. But in spite of our crushing near-defeat, I felt hope. Yes, it took everything from us to defeat Donovan and we barely made it out alive, but Gifteds weren't invincible and hopefully, neither was Henry.

LEGACY

THE OWENS CHRONICLES
BOOK THREE

AMANDA LYNN PETRIN

CHAPTER ONE

Tears blurred my vision, but I didn't want to see the scene playing out around me. Embry was a dozen feet away from me, face down on the wet, muddy ground. I couldn't tell where he got hurt, but the overwhelming amount of his blood mixing into the puddle beneath him told me I lost him. Gabriel was fighting with everything he had, gaining the advantage as he returned the attacks blow for blow, even though there were four of them and only one of him. I knew he was exhausted, but he wouldn't show it until I was somewhere safe. Or he died.

A hatred like I had never known overcame me as I rushed to attack the man in front of me. He had introduced himself as Henry, but as far as I was concerned, he was the devil incarnate. I had the dagger in my hand, but my arm froze in midair, barely an inch from his chest.

"I admire your tenacity, but there really is no need for all of this bloodshed," his tone was conversational, which made my blood boil. He had stood back and watched his men fight, waiting for me to be exposed. Embry's death was the opportunity he was waiting for, but I was not in the mood for conversation.

"You could have fought us yourself instead of sending your

slaves." I struggled with all my strength, but my arm wouldn't budge. My strength should have included magical powers, but the lack of them, and the gown I was wearing, reminded me I was Cassie. She had been reluctant to fight at first, because she knew Henry's Gift was controlling the other Gifteds, making them do despicable things against their will. It wasn't until the choice was killing strangers or watching Embry die that she jumped in. Not that it made a difference.

"There would be no need for any of it if you just came willingly."

"So you can kill me?" Henry was staying alive to complete a ritual that would allow him to take over the world. That would be enough to resist him, but as the Bearer of the Crescent Moon, my heart was the crucial ingredient in his ritual, and I much preferred my heart inside my chest. I shot up my knee, aimed at Henry's crotch area, but like my arm, it froze before reaching its target. Instead of keeping it there, he slowly lowered it back to the ground, with my arm following suit, landing at my side. It felt like a bucket of ice water poured over me as everything tingled for a second, then went numb.

"Death is only temporary, Cassandra. And as you are the blood of my blood, I would never allow any harm to befall you."

"Is that part of your ritual? Blood of my blood?" she spat at him, but I just felt sick inside.

"Once upon a time, Annabelle was my wife. Margaret was my daughter. The last thing I want is for anything to happen to you. Or Corinne." The way he said Cassie's daughter's name, I couldn't tell if it was a threat or a promise. Either way, it sent a shiver down my spine.

"You're attacking us. Hunting us for miles," Cassie shook her head, struggling to figure out if she believed him. Having seen how this scene eventually plays out, I wanted more than anything to show her my thoughts and memories. To warn her.

"Only because they won't let me get close to you," he blamed my guys. I turned to see where Embry was still lying on the ground, but

I couldn't see Gabriel. My heart stopped as I searched through the bodies in the mud, but Henry was halfway through saying Cassie's name before he collapsed onto the ground at my feet.

"Are you hurt?" Gabriel asked, as the feeling returned to my body. I nodded, looking down to Henry, who was unconscious. He wasn't dead, but even his death wouldn't have been permanent. As a Gifted, he would keep coming back until he got what he wanted. Me.

I WOKE up in the passenger's seat with a jolt. *It was just a dream*, I reminded myself, holding on to the door of the old station wagon while I waited for my heart to slowly regain its usual rhythm. I was used to these dreams from my ancestors, and much preferred the ones that happened when I was already sleeping, but these memories feel just as real as my own.

"Tennessee," Gabriel told me before I could ask. He ran his hand through his mess of black hair, though I think it was more about the uncertainty we were facing than the hours spent in cars. Over twenty-four hours since we left New Orleans, and we were only two states over, which would make sense if we were stopping to check out the sights and enjoy sit-down meals, but we barely stopped long enough to go pee and change drivers. With this kind of non-stop driving, we should be home already. Instead, we took forever so the army of Gifteds loyal to Henry couldn't find us; bouncing around Points C to Z. If someone was following us, they would attack us out of sheer annoyance from all the detours, without waiting for reinforcements. Unless their Gift was saint-like patience.

Since Gabriel was at the wheel, it meant Embry was sprawled out across the back seat, napping until we stopped for gas or to change cars at some hole-in-the-wall. The guys took turns driving so we wouldn't have to spend the night in any sketchy motels and risk what happened last time. I wasn't up to losing any more people, so I didn't argue.

"Do you want me to drive for a bit?" I offered, knowing the answer would be no. Gabriel enjoyed having a plan and being in control, so our current lack of a concrete plan was making him hold tight to anything he had control over. Not that I blamed him. We were going up against the man that they stay alive to protect me from, and our only plan was to get more magic. Hopefully from the books locked away in my bunker. It was less than encouraging.

"I don't mind driving," he assured me. "Keeps me alert." His hair was sticking up a bit in the back now, which made him look younger than he usually did. More vulnerable somehow.

"How much longer until we get to the plantation?" I asked, switching positions to get comfy, but there wasn't much I could do after this long in cars. I knew how far we were distance-wise, but they could easily extend it into next week.

"We could be there by tomorrow evening," he said with a shrug.

"You want it to take longer?" I asked.

"No, I'm good with the pace and eager to get you somewhere easier to secure," he checked his mirrors, all three of them, more to make sure no one was following us than for road safety, "but we have no control over Henry's followers. If there's a car that exits when we do, or takes the same turns, we have to lose them before moving on."

"We could also stop so you guys can rest. Maybe eat some food that doesn't consist of microwaved grease?" I suggested.

"That may be pushing it," he smiled at me, more like an equal than when the summer began and I was an intolerable teenager he had to keep his distance from, "but if we find a safe enough location, maybe."

"I was kidding. Constant driving is great," I tried to sound convincing, but he still turned to look at me, not buying it. So far, every 'safe' place we went to ended with someone getting hurt. Usually it was a Gifted who would come back to life, as long as their life's purpose wasn't accomplished yet, but not always.

"Should I be like Embry and tell you all about how hard this journey would have been in a carriage pulled by old horses, with the blistering sun beating down..." he did an excellent job of pointing out how much worse this could be. Embry and Gabriel would both fit in with me and my friends if I ever made it to college, even if they were closer in age to the founders of Harvard than the current students.

"I'll check the sarcasm," I sighed. I was grateful he made a joke about it instead of the annoyed silence he would have given me at the beginning of the summer.

"Don't worry, I can handle it," he assured me, smiling to himself as he checked his blind spot. I looked out the passenger-side window so he couldn't see me blushing. We had a long road ahead of us, and my feelings for Gabriel were the least of my worries.

CHAPTER TWO

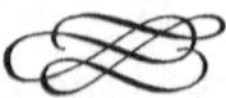

The sun was setting as we crossed through Virginia into Maryland, a mix of purple, red, orange and pink. It was beautiful, but Embry had used 'the sunset' as his i-spy the last three rounds. We were entertaining ourselves in the back seat while Gabriel was at the wheel, again.

"I'm sure there are rules against using the same thing each time," I complained after it took me over twenty-one guesses to ask if he was spying the sunset again.

"I think it makes it easier for you," he argued. "And that's how you played."

"I used a different tree every time," I argued, remembering how annoyed Sam would get with me. My surrogate big brother would play along and was nice about it, but even as a child I could see him rolling his eyes. Sam got his payback when it was my turn to entertain his daughter, Clara. Embry was the only one I believed was having as much fun as I was, even after playing for hours. I should have known then that he was a master at hiding things.

"That should have been against the rules," Embry shook his head as we came up to a slowdown in traffic. It was long past rush hour, but I could see smoke up ahead. I craned my neck to see what was going on and saw a car go up in flames. The sirens were blaring from somewhere behind me, and I knew they were coming closer, but the sound was getting lower and lower, until I couldn't hear it at all…

I was Beth, as she and Embry got ready to go to the theatre, reminding me so much of Sam and Deanna. They touched each other every time they passed by; hand grazes, running her fingers along his back, wrapping his arms around her and snuggling into her neck to get something in front of her instead of just reaching for it… They were young, happy and in love. Which was saying some-thing with Helen and Jack constantly demanding their attention. I couldn't help but smile every time Jackson had a story to tell me in his toddler babble, and I could feel Beth's heart melt when Helen asked if Daddy wouldn't mind being the one to braid her hair.

Once everyone was ready, the four of us took a car into town. It appalled me that their version of a car seat was letting the kids roam around the back seat, with Beth putting her arm out if ever there was a sudden stop. Thankfully, Embry drove the smoothest drive I have ever been on, considering the unpaved roads we took. He parked on the street and we walked to the theatre. Jackson fell asleep in the car, so I carried him in my arms, something I haven't done since Clara. Beth and Embry were in step, holding hands and looking up to smile at each other continuously, while Helen skipped along a few feet in front of us.

"Helen wants to bring you to show and tell tomorrow," I said when we rounded the corner, letting go of Embry's hand long enough to get the theater tickets. It was September 5th, 1926.

"For my magician act? Does she want me to sing?" Embry teased, but Beth was serious.

"They're supposed to talk about their hero," she explained.

Embry processed the information, then asked, "What about you, or… wasn't she going to talk about David?"

"David was a kind man and he would have been an incredible

father... but he died. You're the one who has raised her, the one she looks up to. She wants to be like you."

"Nothing would make me happier," he said before leaning over to give his wife a kiss.

Once we entered the theatre, Beth insisted that we sit in the front, so they could be close to the action. Embry laughed at her, but agreed, and got two seats in the front row. Jackson chose his father's lap, but Helen sat in her mother's.

It was halfway through the play that it started. It was hot in the theater, but not stifling, so I had no reason to think this was anything other than a happy memory, until I smelled smoke. Beth stood up and looked towards the doors, where there was smoke coming from the lighting room. As the flames became visible, everyone rushed for the exit.

Embry was ahead of me with Jackson, while I held on to Helen, my hands on her shoulders as the crowd pushed into us. She was holding onto Embry's coat as I tried to protect her from the people rushing for the door, but somewhere in the shuffle, someone let go.

"Beth!" Embry called when he realized I wasn't following. I could hear him yell, again and again, getting farther and farther away as the crowd pushed against us, so many people making a wall between Beth and everything she cared about.

"Get the children out. Save them," Beth called.

"I'm not leaving you," Embry argued, having to yell really loud for me to barely hear him.

"Get them out. Then you can come back for me, but they're what matters," she called, as they pushed him towards the exit and I lost sight of him. We tried to get to the doors too, but someone pushed me, and I fell. Everyone behind me kept coming, none of them looking down. I tried so many times, but I couldn't get up. Every time I did, all I saw were flames, before someone knocked me back down to the floor. It looked like hundreds of people blocking the exits, so even if Beth kept going, she wouldn't make it out. I clutched the ring Embry

gave Beth, then closed my eyes and let the flames come. Just like Annabelle had...

"What did you see?" Embry asked with concern, bringing his hand to my arm when I screamed. I didn't mean to push it off, but I still felt like I was burning, choking on the smoke.

"I am so sorry." I could feel the tears pouring down my face and my skin was in agony, but it was my heart that broke for his. "Why didn't she use her magic?" I had tried, knowing I had no control over what happened in the past, but I couldn't understand why Beth didn't. She was a favorite of mine, especially after staying in her house and finding out her secrets. We both had magical powers in common, and she seemed like she had so little fear and was always up for a challenge. Centuries after Annabelle died, I still wear my hair the same way as all of my ancestors, except Beth, who defied cultural norms and cut it like a boy. I saw her in my mind as a brave trailblazer, not someone who sits back and lets awful things happen to her.

It took Embry a moment to understand what I was talking about, but I saw his face drop, the pain written in every line once he did. "I don't know," he said, pulling me as close as he could with my seatbelt. Gabriel was quiet in the front seat, but his eyes locked on my reflection in the rearview mirror, full of concern.

It was my second time dying as one of the Bearers of the Crescent Moon, but I also saw Rosie the night she passed. I always knew it wasn't me, that I was just having memories from women who looked exactly like me, but they felt so real to all the senses. Cassie and Beth were obviously a few years older than me, but not that many. Probably around Sam's age.

I never thought much about it, because they always looked to be roughly the same age in all the memories, but this was the third death and none of them looked older than thirty. If I assumed Annabelle died not long after returning to Boston with Margaret, we were four for four on Bearers dying young.

I was about to ask Embry how young Beth was, when I remembered Annabelle's tombstone from the cemetery at the plantation. I did the math of 1692 minus 1664, which told me she died around twenty-eight. I couldn't remember the exact dates for the others, except for Beth dying in 1926, but I knew where to find them.

"What's wrong?" Embry asked when I reached for the backpack at my feet.

"I need to check out something in the Chronicles," I dismissed him. I could find out a lot easier if I asked them, but looking it up in the written account of my ancestors' lives would let me prepare for answers I was pretty sure I didn't want to know. Embry went back to his seat behind Gabriel, but kept an eye on me.

Annabelle's entry in the Chronicles confirmed the dates I used. Rosalind's death in 1778 also put her at twenty-eight. Which could be a rather weird coincidence… only Cassandra lived from 1822 to 1850. I wasn't surprised, but my heart rate that had finally gone back to normal was becoming erratic again.

I shut the book but kept it in my lap, holding on to it so my hands wouldn't shake. It felt like I was suffocating again, only this time it wasn't from smoke. I could see both the guys staring at me from the corner of my eyes, but I wasn't ready to confront them yet. There had to be an explanation.

I bit my bottom lip to push away the anger and tears so I could think. It was looking like each of the previous Crescent Moon Bearers died before reaching their twenty-ninth birthdays. In distinct ways. Some predictable, but others not. Henry had a hand in both Annabelle's and Cassie's deaths, but I don't think he would intentionally give Rosie tuberculosis without taking her heart, especially when she was so weak.

And setting an entire theater on fire was definitely overkill to get to one person, considering how many of them escaped. Still, they couldn't all be coincidences.

"When was Beth born?" I asked Embry, trying to sound like it was simply curiosity.

"May sixteenth," he answered without hesitation, but gave me an odd look. We both knew I wasn't into horoscopes, and it wasn't like I would need to wish her a happy birthday on the day.

"The year?" I asked, trying to look on the bright side. The odds were that I would survive another nine years, but all I could focus on was the fact that I would die. If I was right, even if we defeated Henry and somehow made it through, it would only be temporary. Sam's sacrifice would be for nothing.

"1898," Embry finally admitted, furrowing his brow while attempting to figure out what I was getting at, but I felt like someone grabbed my heart and was crushing it. Beth was twenty-eight.

"Is there anything you would like to tell me about all the Crescent Moon Bearers?" I asked, focusing on Gabriel.

"What?" he sounded confused.

"Is there something about Annabelle, Rosalind, Cassandra and Elizabeth that one of you should have told me by now?" I rephrased my question, turning to Embry. He used to be the one to tell me things, once upon a time. My eyes were glistening, but I refused to blink and let the tears fall.

"We have centuries of knowledge on your family, Lucy, we obviously can't have told you everything," Embry said, getting worried, but neither of them seemed to know what I was getting at.

"How old was Annabelle when she died?" I asked Gabriel.

"Twenty-eight," he shared. It sounded like it stung.

"And how old was Beth?" A shiver went through me from

the memory, still so fresh in my mind, and my skin. I skipped the others and stuck to the two that affected them the most.

"Twenty-eight," I could see Embry's brain working, doing the same math for Cassie and Rosie. "But that's..." he tried to reason it away.

"It's not a coincidence that Beth was trampled, suffocated and burnt alive at the same age as Annabelle," I argued. "Cassie and Rosie were also twenty-eight," I handed him the Chronicles.

"We knew they died young, but... no one gave Rosie tuberculosis, Annabelle chose to sacrifice herself for Margaret and no one could have predicted the lighting room would catch fire. It's just a coincidence," Embry tried to convince himself.

"I thought the Universe sent you guys to protect me, not that I would die either way," I shook my head and stared out the window.

"No, there is no curse on you, no other prophecy, nothing that implies the same will happen to you," Gabriel argued like he wouldn't accept the alternative.

"Except for precedence and the lack of a single exception," I argued. I wanted to throw up. "Stop the car." I said evenly, clenching my jaw to stop the tears.

"Luce," Embry tried to talk me down.

"I need some air," I pleaded. "Whether or not you accept it, there's a distinct possibility, that even if Henry never gets to me, some force out there will make sure I never make it to thirty, and right now I can't breathe." I aggressively rolled down the window. "You guys make sure I survive and make it through all the attempts to kill me, but maybe you're just here so he can't complete the ritual. Because that's the endgame. You help me survive as long as I can, then make sure Henry doesn't get my body when it happens?" I felt sick.

"That's not how it is," Embry argued.

"Neither of us is resigned to you dying. And if his plan

wasn't to kill you, I would rather you be with Henry than be dead," Gabriel said, the vein in his forehead pulsing as he tried to control his emotions and the car.

I would call him on his lie by telling him I knew they would kill me themselves rather than let Henry do what he had to with me, but when his eyes met mine... I believed him.

"Whether you like it or not, I will die when I'm twenty-eight, won't I?" I stopped being angry and turned vulnerable, which felt worse.

"It's a possibility," Embry said after considering it.

"But we will do absolutely everything in our power to make sure that doesn't happen," Gabriel assured me.

"Please stop the car," the numbness in my voice scared me, which is probably why Gabriel pulled onto the shoulder. The child lock was still on the doors, so I looked over to him. His eyes were pleading with me not to go, but he still pushed the button to let me out. I shut the door and walked towards the wooded area beside the highway.

I looked back to see them looking after me before I kept going, past the tree line, into the dense parts where the remaining bits of sun struggled to get in. It was only once I could no longer hear the cars that I truly let the implications hit me. No matter what anyone did, within ten years, I would be dead. I brought my hand up to run my fingers through my hair, an attempt at self-soothing, but ended up pressing my hand to my forehead as a searing pain shot through my skull.

CHAPTER THREE

It was like Mr. Fraser, only a million times worse. Instead of the pressure of a hand trying to get into my brain, this was like a hot iron of electricity burning its way in. Even if I tried to stop it, there was nothing I could do.

"You've discovered the curse," Henry's British accent filled the surrounding forest, as it felt like all the heat and light disappeared, leaving nothing but darkness.

"Where are you?" I asked, turning around in circles. My head was in agony, but I couldn't let him kill me without a fight.

"You're cute, pretending you don't know what I'm talking about," I could hear the smile in his voice, but couldn't see him anywhere, "You only have to hold out ten more years to make sure I can't complete the ritual."

"How do you know?" I asked.

"Donovan may have been your target, but someone should have told you the dangers of soul magic," he warned. "It was brave, but terribly foolish."

"There's a fine line between foolishness and bravery," I shot his own words back at him. At the time I found it endearing, how nervous he was to ask Annabelle out. It was before I knew he was a Gifted who's purpose was to rip her heart out.

"Touché," I sensed a sadness in his tone, but how would he know about the memory dreams? "You don't have to die like the others."

"I won't come willingly," I argued.

"I'm not offering to spare you, Lucy. I still need your heart, but I have a spell, taken from a grimoire, that can save you," it sounded too good to be true, which meant it probably was.

"You're trying to kill me, remember?"

"I am. But a long time ago, the one I was trying to kill was my wife," he almost sounded sorry. "I had to resign myself to doing that, but I never stopped looking for an alternative. Eventually, I found a solution."

"Congratulations," I turned around again to make sure that he and his minions wouldn't jump out at me.

"At the moment, it's more of a success for you than it is for me. I have hidden somewhere very safe, a spell that restores you back to your life as you left it. A complement to the ritual that would have saved me centuries had I found them at the same time."

"What do you mean by restore me?" I asked, curious in spite of myself.

"I mean, there is a spell that will bring back one of those marked by the crescent moon. Unlike your companions or myself, who come back exactly as we were the first time we died, without aging, this spell would fully restore you, as if you never died at all. You could live a full life, get married, have children and forget all this nasty business ever happened."

"That's impossible," I argued, but all I could remember was Annabelle's certainty that she would be back. What if this was it? What if she knew there was a spell, and she thought the guys would use it to bring her back?

"I assure you it isn't."

"Show it to me," I asked with a confidence I didn't feel.

"Join me and the spell is yours. No more limits on your life, no one chasing you… you would be free."

"I don't trust you." I wanted to run away to show him I didn't want anything he had to offer, but since he was in my head, he would most likely follow.

"You don't have to trust me, because you already know I'm telling you the truth, and as honorable as it might sometimes seem, you do not want to die," he said with an edge that filled me with anger. True as it may be, his price wasn't something I could live with, even if it gave me a happily ever after. "You know where to find me if you change your mind," he said before the pain in my head disappeared and I knew he was gone.

"Are you okay? What happened?" Embry was the first to reach me in the woods. He put his hands on my arms and checked me for wounds as Gabriel came over.

"He's gone," he said, having probably run around looking for Henry.

"We heard your scream, but by the time we got to you there was some kind of barrier and we couldn't get in," Embry shared.

"The essence tracking I did to find Donovan was soul magic. He wasn't really here," was my way of explaining that I gave him a way into my head. I could remember the chill I felt when it seemed like Henry saw me through the tracking. Turns out I wasn't being paranoid.

"What did he want?" Gabriel asked me, staying close, but his head turned at every sound, analyzing it to see if the maker was a friend or a foe. It was nearly pitch black now, so far from streetlights, with the trees blocking the stars.

"He tried to get me to go with him again," I admitted.

"After they killed Sam?" He knew that wouldn't happen.

"He knows that we all die at twenty-eight," I admitted.

"It could be a coincidence," they both argued.

"But it's not," I told them, apologetic even though it was my life we were talking about. They wanted so badly to believe that it wasn't true. That the other Bearers' deaths were nothing more than a series of unfortunate events at the same point in their lives.

"How do you know? Did he explain it?" Gabriel asked.

"Not really," I waited until they both looked up at me expectantly. "He said he could save me."

"By bringing you back with magic after cutting out your heart." I could see Gabriel's anger and lack of trust for Henry.

"No, he said it was a spell from a grimoire. One so I won't die when I'm twenty-eight. If I give him my heart, he'll give me the spell that brings me back like nothing ever happened. I can grow old and have kids... the whole nine yards."

"A spell?" Gabriel was skeptical.

"I know we obviously can't trust him, but I also don't think he's lying. There's always a cost with this kind of magic, and it'll probably be one we are not willing to pay, but it can't hurt to look into it, right?"

"Why would he even have something like that?" Embry asked.

"He said that once upon a time, the heart he needed was his wife's, so he tried to find a way to keep her alive," I said like it was a ridiculous idea, but part of me believed him.

"That alone would make me not trust him," Gabriel pointed out. I nodded, not wanting to show how badly I wanted to. "But if there's even a possibility of a cure, then we'll find it," he decided. "We save you and destroy Henry." It was optimistic and overly ambitious, which was weird coming from Gabriel, but he was so sure of himself that he nearly convinced me.

They started talking about logistics, and different people they could ask about the cure, but my mind was on the spell, and its potential price.

"Ready to go, Tesoro?" Embry asked when he saw they'd lost me.

"I'm sorry, I wasn't paying attention," I apologized. "I was just thinking that if the spell needs me to cut someone's heart out, I would rather die. Unless it was Henry's. Maybe."

"You don't have to worry about that," Gabriel said without meeting my eyes, as if my shoes were interesting enough to capture his attention.

"Even if I'm not the one who has to cut it out," I amended.

"We don't know what the spell entails. Life and death spells are a big deal, but since your death would result from some kind of curse, maybe it won't be that heavy. If it's some horrific spell that requires baby sacrifices, then we'll find another way. But if it's a line the two of us are prepared to cross, then you don't have to worry about it," Embry assured me.

"And you two never heard anything about this?" I verified.

"No, but we haven't been asking around and searching for it either," Gabriel reminded me.

"What if Annabelle knew?" I wondered. "What if when she told you she would be back, she meant that spell? Henry said he took it from a grimoire. What if it was hers?"

"I am sure she would have told us if she had a spell she expected us to recite to bring her back to life. Otherwise, we failed her miserably," Embry pointed out.

Gabriel looked to Embry and sighed, probably thinking, like me, that my ancestors kept a lot of things from them. "Have you figured out a way to zoom in on a single memory, to get them at will? Or are you still getting them whenever they want to come to you, like when you're sitting in a tree or about to jump off a balcony?" he asked, his hands bound tightly into fists at the memory.

"I don't control it, but there are triggers. My first Henry memory happened after I saw his picture in a book, being in her bedroom let me see Beth, sometimes I get memories from other people when I'm touching them... It could be coincidence, but I think I can influence it," I shared.

"I don't think we have anything of Annabelle's," Gabriel turned to Embry.

"I might have had something at the villa, but most of her stuff is back at the plantation," Embry agreed.

"No jewelry, a family heirloom... nothing?" I pressed, but Embry shook his head for each one.

"We don't really have much of hers either way. Clothes don't keep for centuries, she was wearing the jewelry that really mattered to her... apart from the Chronicles, it's mostly just a few things back in Boston..." Embry was dissuading me, but Gabriel was hiding something.

"What did you think of?" I asked him, not waiting for Embry to finish.

He looked to me like he wanted to deny it, but I initiated a stare down that he eventually had to turn away from. "The dagger you used on Donovan at the motel... it belonged to Annabelle's father," Gabriel admitted.

"But..." there had to be a reason he was so reluctant to share.

"It was her father's, not hers, and they've been passing it down for generations. Not to mention you stabbed Donovan with it, so his blood was the last thing it came into contact with."

"That ship has sailed," I assured him with an involuntary shudder. "Let's do this," I said with as much conviction as I could muster.

CHAPTER FOUR

We had to find a safer place than in the middle of the woods with the car parked on the side of the highway, so Embry drove us to a college campus and sweet-talked the librarian into letting us use one of the 'quiet study' rooms.

I knew the chances were slim that it would work, since I really didn't have a handle on the memories. At all. I still didn't know if they were to help me or to kill me. Or if Annabelle even knew anything for me to find. I based this theory entirely on her habit of keeping things from people, so it wasn't a lot to go on.

I took the sapphire-encrusted dagger in my hands and thought as hard as I could about Annabelle, and a spell to bring her back.

I could feel the guys watching me, wondering if it would work. I was about to give up and tell them it had been a ridiculous idea of mine, when the room faded away...

"Are you sure you know how to use that?" The Gabriel standing in front of me was maybe twelve years old, and though he was questioning Annabelle's skills, he was looking at her like she was God's gift to mankind and could do absolutely no wrong.

"Of course I do. My father taught me how to take care of myself." *Annabelle was holding the dagger in her hand, but I could sense her fear, both that her father would find her in his study, and that the sharp blade would cut her.*

"I'm sorry I doubted you," Gabriel smiled and looked at her in a way that made her heart beat faster, but she knew it was forbidden.

"Look..." she pulled away before the moment could go too far, twirling the dagger like she had seen the men by the docks do whenever they wanted to impress the ladies. Twirling was going better than she expected, but she got overly confident and threw it up in the air. She caught it in her left hand without a problem, but when she tried to throw it back to her right hand, it spun too much, so she caught the blade instead of the handle. It sliced into her right palm, which as long as I was in the memory, was also mine.

"Ow!" She muttered it under her breath, knowing they would be discovered if she cried out any louder, but boy did it sting.

"Are you alright? I'll go get your mother..." Gabriel offered, taking a step towards the door.

"No, you can't!" Annabelle bit her bottom lip and let out a sharp breath.

Gabriel looked at her, considering it, then sighed. "The bandages are still in the cupboard?"

"Top shelf," she agreed.

"I'll be right back," he shook his head at her before quietly exiting the room.

Once Gabriel left, Annabelle dropped the act and cradled her injured hand to a chorus of "Ow, ow, ow, ow, ow!" until she heard him coming.

"You should sit down and keep it above your heart," Gabriel suggested, helping her to her father's chair.

She bit her bottom lip the whole time he wrapped the white bandage around her palm, holding her hand in his as he did. She took deep breaths against the pain, but also because he was so close and touching her in a way he hadn't before.

"There. All better," Gabriel kissed her hand before looking up at her, and in the moment that his lips were on her soft, damaged skin, the pain went away. Or at least she didn't notice it over the excessive beating of her heart...

"It didn't work?" Embry and Gabriel were by my side when I came back.

"Not the right memory," I argued, trying to ignore the spark I felt when Gabriel touched my hand. I told myself it was the remnants of the memory and tried to push the thought away.

"There has to be something..."

"What about the empty pages?" Embry perked up.

"What?" Gabriel asked.

"The blank pages Beth left in the Chronicles?" It took me a minute to clue in, but Beth left a bunch of empty pages right in the middle of her section in the Chronicles. Not to mention random drawings from her daughter, which were cute, but not what I was hoping for when reading all about her outstanding adventures.

"I'm just thinking out of the box."

"It's worth a try, but I don't know how I could reveal something she hid in there..." I grabbed the Chronicles and riffled through the pages as I spoke, eventually stumbling on one of the blank ones, before I got a flash of Beth transcribing something from a frayed piece of parchment.

"Was that another one?" Gabriel asked. It wasn't a full memory, so I didn't pass out, but he was right by my side.

"Just a flash. I don't know who originally wrote it, but Beth copied it in here."

"It could be invisible ink," Embry suggested, but even he didn't think it was likely.

"I doubt this is a 'lemon juice to a candle' type of operation," I argued.

"Guess you'll have to intend it into revealing itself," Gabriel tried to make me laugh, getting a tiny smile.

I closed my eyes with my hands on the page, visualizing the flash of Beth writing it down.

"That's amazing," Gabriel prompted me to open my eyes as ink formed its way into words across the page, like an invisible hand was writing it.

"It's magic," Embry teased, but I was too busy scanning the page to make sure I didn't have to kill anyone.

"Kiara's Cure," I read the title.

CHAPTER FIVE

"The herbs and powders will be easy to find, but I don't know where we'll get some of the other things on this list," Embry said once the invisible hand finished writing out a list of ingredients that had to be combined under the light of a waxing crescent moon. "We can manage something from each of the Crescent Moon Bearers who came before you, but stuff from your mother and father... I don't even know who he was."

"I thought you were friends with my mother?" I looked from one to the other.

"I checked in on them, but your Grams only wrote to me after you were born, and he was already out of the picture by then," Gabriel explained.

"I knew he broke her heart, but she didn't want to talk about it," Embry added.

"Charlie knew," I admitted, pulling the envelope from my backpack. "My grandmother kept in touch and wrote letters to him."

"I'll go find us a car while you read it," Gabriel decided after a student looked in to see if the room was occupied.

"We'll meet you out front," Embry said, nodding for me to open the envelope.

INSIDE WAS a collection of letters between Charlie and my Grams. I read them while we walked to the front of the building to wait for Gabriel. The first one was sent a couple of years before I was born. "It's just my Grams explaining to him that my mom wouldn't be visiting him that summer as planned."

"When is it from?" he asked, coming closer to put a hand on my shoulder.

"Two years before I was born," I checked the date again to confirm.

"She needed to stay home and get more chemo," he said, like it still hurt.

"She only got cancer after I was born," I argued, even though it was there, blue on white, in my Grams' handwriting.

"Who told you that?" he was genuinely confused. "Your mom was dealing with leukemia since she was a kid. She was the bravest little girl I ever met, fighting it with everything she had, beating it, then starting all over again when it came back."

"I always assumed it was new; that she wouldn't have a kid if she knew she was dying," I explained. It was weird, talking about her like this. I tried to distance myself, to talk about her like she was someone I didn't really know or care about, but at the same time, I didn't. She was my mother, and I loved the idea of her, of what she would have been for me. Her death left a terrible void in my life and in my heart, but I didn't know her at all.

"I think we were all surprised, but it also made sense. I went to see her in the hospital when she was maybe twelve, and she told me the one thing that really sucked about dying young was that she wouldn't get to be a mother."

"The one thing?" I raised an eyebrow at him.

"She got good at resigning herself to the other things," he defended her statement.

"This one mentions a boyfriend," I said of the next letter. "It sounds like Charlie knew him. Grams is worried because no matter what, someone's heart gets broken."

"Does he have a name?" he asked me.

"Brian. No last name," I handed him the letter.

"Brian Sherwood?" he suggested, scanning it.

"Who is Brian Sherwood?"

"He moved in with his grandparents on the other side of the swamp when he was eleven. He worked for me a few summers, trying to get money to cover his grandmother's hospital bills. When Charlie and I found out what he needed the money for, we covered her hospital expenses, and he kept working as a thank you. One day he said he didn't need our help anymore and I don't think I saw him again," he shared.

"Why would you think of him? Is it just the name or do you think he could be my father?" I asked.

"I know he met your mother when she came to stay one summer. He's in some pictures from the album I gave you," he remembered. "They got along, but she had to leave mid-July because they accepted her into a drug trial."

"Did it work?" I asked of the trial, getting a nod. "Was he nice? A good guy?" I wanted him to say yes. "But I guess if he was nice he wouldn't be my dad, because no good guy would abandon his pregnant girlfriend, then not see his daughter after her mother dies of cancer." I crossed my arms and huffed. I wasn't sure what I was hoping to find out, because the outcome would be the same. Good guy or bad, he wasn't here.

Embry looked at me like he was surprised I had this pent-up anger at my father. I didn't seem like I had daddy issues. The truth was, I had so many other issues to worry about that my heartless father wasn't usually worth mentioning.

I grabbed the next letter, but only had time to make out the first tear-smudged line in my mom's handwriting, asking if Brian's family still lived nearby, before I was back at the manor...

"Can I see her?" a man, roughly my age, was standing in front of me, holding my blanket. It wasn't monogrammed, so I couldn't be positive, but it had a pink heart in the corner. There was so much pain and regret on his face, but every fiber of my being, of my mother's body, was tense. She was both on high alert in case he tried to get past her to the bassinet in the corner, and to make sure she stayed strong instead of falling back into his arms. Looking at him, I did not understand how he could have left her.

"No. If I have my way, you will never see her. Ever. So when she asks about you, I can pretend it didn't work out and you left without knowing about her instead of having to tell her the truth; that you never wanted her. That you asked me to get rid of her."

"Will you let me explain?" he pleaded like it was the one thing in the world he had to do.

"I don't want your lies and trying to get me to forgive you."

"You will hate me a lot more than you'll want to forgive me," he admitted.

"Then why bother?" she asked. I could hear her thinking that she didn't know if she could handle another heartbreak from him.

"Because you need to know," he said with an intensity that had her nodding even though she didn't really want another reason to hate him. "My mom had this friend, a guy who would come by and see me every once in a while, even after she died. When you went back home that summer, he came to me and offered to bring me here with him. He said I could work for him and pointed out that I needed to get out of the house, away from death and watching her suffer and... I couldn't do it anymore," he said, knowing she wouldn't

be happy with him because she was dealing with cancer like his grandmother had.

"I never asked you to come."

"He did." I could feel that her heart was breaking more than ever with those two tiny words.

"He did?" she repeated, hoping she had it wrong, or that he was referring to his heart in the third person. Anything other than what he was confessing to.

"My mom's friend. When I went to work for him, he told me it wasn't necessarily a real job, but that you really enjoyed your summer, and as long as I hung out with you, he would cover my tuition and an apartment down here for school."

"He paid you to spend time with me? Who the hell was he?" she let the anger take over so she wouldn't start crying.

"I didn't know who he was, but at first I thought it was sweet that he wanted to take care of you like that."

"You liked the money, and it was pathetic, not sweet." I could tell that she didn't believe the first part, no matter how much he hurt her, but he was looking at her like it got worse.

"It was neither. It was selfish and despicable and horrible," he admitted. She was about to ask what he meant, but he launched into a confession. "When I found out why, I wanted to stop. To leave, but I was in it too far by then. Not just because of the money I owed him, or the threats he started making, but I cared about you, and I knew that if it wasn't me, he would find someone else."

"I'm a human being, Brian, I don't just like people because some guy wants me to. And why would he care who I hang out with?"

"He didn't. He wanted you to fall in love with me," he looked disgusted with himself, but he said it anyway.

"Why?" she asked.

He explained, starting with Annabelle, about the copies, about one of her descendants being crucial for some ritual, how Henry hunted them through time and didn't have what he wanted yet.

"I don't get why he sent you. Did he want me to trust you so you *could kidnap me and take me hostage?" I could tell my mom was only pretending that this was all news to her. Grams must have shared bits and pieces with her about the two guys who stopped by every once in a while.*

"No, he wanted me to make sure you would continue the line," Brian said, the guilt plain on his face, but he didn't look away from her. He looked us straight in the eye and took what was reflected at him, knowing he deserved it.

"He sent you to sleep with me?" she was horrified, and I didn't blame her. I felt dirty, betrayed and disgusted, not just because she was, but because my dad just admitted that someone paid him to impregnate my mother...

I was sitting on a bench outside the library when I came back to the present.

"What did you see?" Gabriel asked, kneeling in front of me.

"My mother," I admitted.

"And?" Embry asked. He was sitting beside me on the bench, his arm around my shoulders, probably to hold me up when I passed out, but I wiggled away from him. I didn't want anyone touching me right now.

"The blanket I packed... it was my father's," I only told them what they needed to know.

"That's it?" Embry pressed.

"The blanket was his," I repeated, handing him the letter to put in my backpack, that he was now carrying, before walking out to the parking lot.

"Lucy..." they called after me.

"I don't want to talk about it," I turned and put my hands out, grateful I didn't accidentally blast people anymore.

They looked at me, then at each other. They must have decided the conversation could wait until later, because they shrugged and followed me out.

Gabriel got us a black SUV, so I tried to go into the back row where I could be alone.

"I'm exhausted, if you wouldn't mind navigating," Embry asked me, a clear ploy to prevent my solitude, but I was too drained to argue.

"Sure," I sighed, taking the passenger's seat. I could feel both of their eyes on me, even as Gabriel watched the road and Embry pretended to sleep, but I couldn't face them right now. My insides were in knots and all I felt was shame. It wasn't just the Henry parts; all of me was rotten.

CHAPTER SIX

I stared out the window even though I couldn't see past the headlights. My father's confession was heavy on my mind, and my heart. I thought it was bad that Henry was Margaret's father, but it hurt a lot more when it wasn't just a distant ancestor, but the man who fathered me. At Henry's urging.

"Am I still heading for the plantation?" Gabriel asked, interrupting my thoughts. Embry never would have let the silence last that long, but Gabriel understood keeping it all inside.

"Isn't that where the books are?" I asked without looking at him.

"It is," he agreed. "But if we're tracking down things that meant stuff to your ancestors, the best place for Cassie..." he let the thought linger, waiting for me to catch on.

"I can't," I argued.

"Can't, or won't?" he asked. "And why?"

"Because I can't face them. Until I see them, they get to live in a world where they're worried about us, but they still think Sam and I will come home to them. Once we go to the Beach House, I won't be able to lie to them, so I'll have to tell them

Sam is dead because of me. They'll never be happy again, they'll hate me, and I will lose what's left of my family," I said simply, though it was anything but.

"First, you will always have me and Embry." He waited for me to look at him before going on, "And second, the girls aren't there anymore."

"What happened? Where are they?" My heart raced, pounding against my chest.

"It's October," he shrugged.

"What does that mean?"

"Clara had to go back to school. They're staying with Deanna's dad and being careful. With increased protection," he told my horrified look.

"You're letting Clara go to school?" It was reckless. What if Henry made good on Donovan's threat and went after them to get to me?

"Clara isn't the one they want, and I told you she is being watched."

"I guess you never promised to protect her," my blood was boiling. I wanted to call Deanna and warn her to run and hide and never let Clara out of her sight, but I didn't have a phone, and had no idea where I could send them to be safe.

"You're upset, so I will let that one slide, but we would never do anything to put Clara or Deanna in danger. There are people who have put their lives on hold to guard them, 24/7, and make sure nothing happens to them."

"I'm sorry," I mumbled.

"I know. And I know it's hard, not knowing how to keep them safe, but you have to trust that we're doing everything we can."

"Of course."

"So, the beach house..." he tried after a few minutes of silence.

"If they're not there, we might as well. That's where most

of Cassie's stuff ended up, right?" I didn't know how real these women were when I would go to the Beach House every summer, but there was a room above the garage that held wooden chests, crates and luggage from way before even Grams was born. I only went inside once, but their age and the bright yellow color of it all suggested it might be hers.

"After she died, Corinne couldn't stand the Beach House or any of her mother's gadgets, so she left it all behind before moving back to the manor."

"She didn't miss her?" I asked, thinking of how often I had bribed Sam to bring me to my mother's room so I could play with her things and feel like I was close to her again. "I mean her things."

"She did. After a few years she came back to the Beach House, eventually bringing her daughter and telling her all about Cass... but to her, the Beach House was where she waited in fear to find out her mother died, filled with the things that got her killed."

"At least the manor had a lot of happy memories for me."

"The family summered at the Beach House, so I imagine she had a lot of those too, but in the winter Cassie and her band of saviors used it as their base of operations to fight crime. I don't think Corinne knew anything about her mother's vigilante activities until she was locked in the house with nothing else to do but explore. Alan defended her, but he didn't want Corinne to know that they might hunt her too, so he let her think her mother died for getting involved in other people's problems."

"It was her lair?" I focused on my ancestor's activities rather than her daughter's pain. She never mentioned that in the Chronicles.

"It was less of a secret lair and more of a place of business," he made it sound less cool, but when you were in the business of defending the helpless, your coolness was a given.

"Did they have a sign on the door with their team name?"

"It was more of a word-of-mouth operation, but they got stuff done."

"I read," I agreed.

"That book was a fraction of what she and her friends accomplished. If she thought it was paranormal or was likely to happen again, she put it in the book, but they accompanied women home late at night, rescued children from abusive homes, housed the poor and desolate..."

"Cassie was a saint," I summed it up.

"She was... sometimes."

"Sometimes?" I raised an eyebrow at him.

"Don't get me wrong, she was amazing, with a heart of gold, but she would never turn the other cheek, or a blind eye to suffering. She ruffled more than just a few feathers in her day."

"And still managed to be the perfect eighteenth century woman."

"Only because she had money and a rich and influential husband who loved her unconditionally, just the way she was," he warned.

"Sounds like a badass role model to me," I sighed and turned to look out the window. I hated being that teenager, who is all sighs and woe-is-me, but this wasn't about silly high school things.

"That she was," he smiled nostalgically. "What's on your mind?" He picked up on the sigh.

"Maybe we're wasting our time," I shrugged.

"Maybe," he agreed. "We don't know how powerful Henry is, or if anything will work, but I could never forgive myself if we didn't try."

"But maybe we shouldn't," I pressed.

"Are you afraid?"

"What if I'm not supposed to live because I'm not a good person?"

"That's ridiculous."

"Not in a silly way. In the 'we created a man whose mission in life is to kill you and we believe so strongly in this that we will make sure he can't die until he accomplishes it,'" I shared.

"He told you his mission is to complete the ritual, not to kill you," Gabriel argued.

"The ritual involves ripping my heart out. That doesn't sound good."

"Just because it's his mission doesn't mean it's right. You've seen it yourself. Some Gifted are downright evil. That's why there's debate on the name, because a lot of us consider it a curse, and we can't reconcile God giving these Gifts for evil people to use in terrible ways."

"You're proving my point," I told him, but I also made a mental note to ask him about his beliefs some other time. I never thought of him as religious, but they said his mother was devout.

"Some of us are evil, Luce. There's a balance. Sometimes terrible things happen to ensure better ones will come. Some missions get misinterpreted, some never come true. Maybe Henry is here to complete his ritual, but Embry and I are here to protect you and make sure that doesn't happen. Two to one sounds like the odds are in your favor."

"Maybe you're just supposed to protect me so I can continue the line, or die at the right time."

"I don't believe that."

"Maybe I was supposed to be stronger, and I failed."

"You didn't fail anything. Nothing that happened was your fault."

"I know that in the big scheme of things, you're right. I didn't ask for any of it to happen, and I was an innocent bystander when it started. Only I wasn't. I am the descendent of the man who married Annabelle for her birthmark, so he could kill her, and has hunted his daughter and granddaughters ever since. All so he could be powerful. A man who not only does terrible things, but makes innocent people do terrible things to other innocent people, when there's nothing they can do to stop it."

"I never pegged you as someone who so deeply valued nature over nurture," he said, like I disappointed him.

"Sometimes nature wins," I stood my ground.

"How can you say that when you are nothing but kindness and warmth and generosity?" He asked. "It isn't our DNA that defines who we are, it's our choices. The things we do time and time again, day in and day out."

"You're trying so hard to protect me, but maybe I shouldn't be saved."

I turned to look out the window and pretended I couldn't feel him looking at me with even more concern than before.

CHAPTER SEVEN

I used to love coming to the Beach House in the summers. There's an old photograph of me on the beach with my mom, where she's bundled up in blankets with a mustard print scarf on her head, but my most vivid memories are of building sandcastles with Sam when I was little, then with Clara once I got older.

We parked in the garage at the bottom of the hill and made our way up the wooden boardwalk, with Gabriel in the lead. When I was little, it felt like a secret entrance to a magical land, because you couldn't even see the house through the tall grass until you got a few minutes into the path.

It was a long walk to the house, even with the boardwalk Grams put in for my mom's wheelchair. I can't imagine how they did it before, walking fifteen minutes through the sand and jagged rocks. Sam told me they used to come by the water if they had lots of bags, or if mom wasn't in the best shape. There was a dock right outside the house that only we could use.

The Beach House didn't have a key hidden under a flowerpot, but it usually had a lockbox under the porch swing, to the same effect.

"It's not here," I let them know after extensively feeling around. I even got on my hands and knees to look better, but there was no box.

"It doesn't take a key anymore," Gabriel pointed to a little grey box, like the ones from the plantation.

"Of course, technology," I sighed before putting my thumb on the screen. "Ow!" I brought my finger to my mouth and sucked where the needle poked it.

"Your fingerprint, DNA and heartbeat match," Gabriel read off the screen.

"That's way more secure than the plantation," I pointed out.

"The Beach House was remodeled later," Gabriel shrugged before putting his finger on the screen and stepping inside once the house cleared him.

He said they remodeled it, but everything on the inside looked the same as it had last summer. It was a mixture of seaside escape and old-time sophistication, which made sense now that I knew more about Cassie.

"We can stay the night and get back on the road in the morning," Embry suggested, walking around with Gabriel to make sure we were alone.

"I'll check out the garage," I headed for the door.

"Wait, we'll come with you," Gabriel followed me. I was about to argue and remind them I could manage it on my own, but he had a look of determination, not concern. This was more about me choosing an object that represented Cassie than about my safety.

TO GET TO THE GARAGE, which held our boat, you could either walk outside or go through the basement that had a tunnel to connect the two structures. It was apparently the safest place in case of an earthquake. Sam and I would explore it, pretending it was a cave because of all the treasure trunks at the end.

This time, the guys went first, with less adventurous exploration, more making sure none of Henry's men were camped out waiting for us.

It was no longer a pressing concern when we saw the entire path was covered in a thick layer of dust. If I had to guess, I would say it hadn't been used since the summer I was six. Sam and I found a rat in the tunnels and decided to never go back.

There was a door at the end to get to the garage, but it hadn't been updated with the exterior, so all you needed to get in was a key.

"Did anyone grab the key from the hook?" I asked, knowing I hadn't. Considering Henry has been after us since before Cassie bought the Beach House, it was ridiculous that we used to protect ourselves with a lock box under a swing and all the other keys on a rabbit foot keychain in the kitchen.

"I'll be right back," Gabriel disappeared, leaving me alone with Embry.

At first, we both stood in silence, waiting for him. I still wasn't big on talking, but he kept opening his mouth like he wanted to say something.

"Can you feel feelings too?" I asked him, realizing I should have figured this out ages ago.

"I can't read thoughts, but I can sense moods," he admitted. "Although I don't need powers to read you. The amazing little girl I met at a funeral, whose heart is bigger than anyone I know, who has gone through so many hardships, but still smiles at strangers..."

"I haven't been that girl for a while," I argued, wondering if I ever was. "What's that?" I changed the subject, focusing on the burgundy bag he had in his hand instead of on my pity party.

"This is your piece of Beth," he looked at it a moment before handing it over, like it really was a piece of the woman he loved.

The pouch had a clear jewelry bag inside, with a velvet box I recognized immediately. "Are you sure?" I asked him, handling it like it was made of the most delicate porcelain. I opened the box and saw the slightly charred ring Beth was holding when she died. It was damaged beyond repair, but I completely understood all the preservation measures he used on it.

"The more it meant to her, the stronger the spell will be," he said simply.

"Thank you."

"I don't know what you saw about your father, but you're not evil or broken Lucy."

"I know," I assured him.

"Got it," Gabriel rounded the corner and showed us the rabbit foot keychain.

They had me wait on the stairs while they went to make sure the garage was safe.

"It's clear," Gabriel came back for me after a few minutes.

I followed him into the garage. It surprised me that the boat was as big as I remembered, even if I was significantly taller. 'Beloved Lyn' was etched on the side of it, named by my grandfather for his wife and daughter, Evelyn and Marilyn. Grams never sold it after he died, or even when my mom did. I guess the Boyds had been waiting for me to grow up to do something with it, but there wasn't much point to it now.

I went upstairs to the room of chests and old luggage. The colors were faded, but the smells of salty air, moth balls and adventure had me smiling. I took it all in and knew I could spend days going through it all and still have more to see.

"Is it stronger if she wore it often, or loved it lots?" I asked when the guys joined me. Part of the discoloration was from the cobwebs that covered nearly every inch of the room, so I grabbed the wooden handle of an old mop and got to work.

"Emotional attachment. Unless it's something like a brush that has her hair on it; some piece of her," Embry shared.

"Bonus points if it fits in a Ziploc bag and doesn't weigh twenty pounds," I argued with the brush idea, remembering the intricate grooming set in my great grandmother's room at the manor. It was silver with diamonds encrusted in the handle. Perfect to pawn for a ride or food if you were down on your luck, but not something you would want to carry in your bag while walking for days in the desert or wherever this wild goose chase would bring us.

The old suitcases weren't locked, but they were closed tight and hard to open, so I let the guys do the honors.

The first one held clothes, perfectly pressed and folded as if she were going on a trip with them. Beautiful and bright colors in the softest fabrics... but not what we were looking for.

The second chest we opened had piles of books on history, geography, etiquette and politics. In the middle of the two piles of textbook-like volumes was a well-read copy of Mary Shelley's Frankenstein.

"Was she a fan of horror?" I asked.

"Not so much as when the second edition credited a woman as the author," Gabriel shook his head with fondness for my ancestor before opening another suitcase full of pamphlets and essays attempting to give women equal rights.

"She was quite extraordinary."

"They all were," Embry agreed, but you couldn't quite compare the richness of Cass' life to any of the others.

"Cass just got a lot more done," Gabriel understood.

I DISCOVERED a little more about my ancestor with every box. The most interesting one was filled with gifts from Alan. I couldn't tell you what half of it was, but nothing was as it seemed. Shoes had spikes or knives that sprung out, purses had secret compartments, necklaces held pepper and bracelets acted as rape whistles. Every piece I picked up was more interesting than the one before.

"Driving gloves?" I asked of a pair of creamy white gloves at the bottom of the chest, preserved in their own box.

"Cass was more of a walker," Embry argued.

"Try them on," Gabriel suggested with a knowing smile.

"They're very stiff," it wasn't like she never used them… they were quite worn in that respect, but it was as if there was a spine to them.

"Now put them on again while pushing into the top of them…" Both Embry and I looked at him like he lost his mind, before I did as I was told.

"What the…" blades came out of the fingertips like claws, and there were gems on the knuckles to put more oomph in punches.

"That's why she was so upset when I brought the black ones…"

"And there should be padding at the knuckles for when she uses the ornamental birth stones…"

I could hear the guys were still talking, but I was drifting off to a memory, alone in a dark alley. There was a chill in the air that made me shiver, but Cassie ignored it and wiggled her now clawed fingers from inside the driving gloves. She focused on every sound, and I could tell that she wasn't afraid to be walking alone at night.

She was hunting something. There was a dripping sound coming from a nearby roof and she followed it instead of running away or waiting for backup.

"Hello?" she called once we reached a dead end. If ever I had any doubts about Cassie's courage, it disappeared as I felt how calm her heart was as she stood in the alley with no escape, hunting an unknown monster without magic or reinforcements.

The wind answered her call, carrying drunken laughter from somewhere close by, and the faintest whimper of a woman who sounded like she was close to giving up.

Cassie took off on a run, taking turns faster than I saw them coming, before we rounded a corner and found a man in a travelling cloak standing over a woman. I couldn't make out much in the darkness until the moon shifted and revealed bright red blood staining her blue dress.

The man froze when he heard Cassie running towards him, clumsily swinging a cane to protect himself. Cassie stopped the blow from reaching her and used her hand like a cat uses its paw, managing to scratch his face. He roared out in anger and we struggled over the cane before Cassie used her knee to get him in the groin. Cassie had hoped the woman would get up and run away while she fended off the man who assaulted her, but her injuries were much worse than expected, and there was no way she was getting away without a lot of help. The man was winded for a second or two before he charged at Cassie, pushing us into the brick wall to our right. Cassie reacted before my mind recovered from the push, shoving him off and grabbing his arm with her gloved fingers, causing him to cry out in pain. He looked at her face, which I imagined was terrifying to behold, because all I could feel from her was determination and anger, not a drop of fear. He seemed to consider it before running off down the alley.

We ran after him, but the woman whimpered again, and there was no way she would last the night if left to bleed out on the sidewalk. Cassie made the split-second decision to help the woman instead of pursuing her assailant and got to work like she was a trained nurse rather than a homemaker. She applied pressure to the wound and fished what looked like a very primitive flare gun out of a small satchel I hadn't noticed she was wearing. I wasn't sure the woman would last long enough for someone to see the flare and find us, but almost as soon as the flares were in the sky, Gabriel showed up.

"What's wrong?" he asked, worried before seeing the woman.

"We need to help her." For the first time, I heard fear in Cassie's voice, as she looked into the fading blue eyes of the woman, before I was back in the room with Embry and present day Gabriel...

I could tell that this was one of the times I acted things out from the slits in the curtain and the way the guys were holding on to things I must have knocked over.

"Did you get him?" Embry asked, looking shocked.

"He ran away, but Cassie stayed to help a woman. She was bleeding so much I don't know if you could do anything other than make sure she didn't die alone," I shared, looking to Gabriel.

"She died in my arms a few hours later," he agreed somberly. "But they caught the man who did it from scratch marks on his face and puncture wounds in his arms."

"These are badass gloves," I tried to give them a smile, thinking of Cassie instead of the woman in the blue dress. My ancestor was the type of woman who wore such delicate gloves to conform to society, yet fitted them with deadly weapons.

"I believe they were her wedding gift from Alan," Gabriel pointed to the Roman numerals at the wrist, then opened another chest, steering me away from Cassie's failed rescue attempt.

The chest was full of jewelry, and there was an entire box filled with pictures in frames that must have been too painful for them to keep in the house after she died.

.   .   .

We unanimously decided on the gloves, which both represented her family and the fighter in her. We found a Ziploc bag to carry them in, and I snatched a few of the weapons that looked like they would still work.

After we ate a dinner of leftovers from the freezer, I went upstairs to the bedrooms. I walked past my room and paused outside Clara's. I was used to knocking when the door was closed.

It looked just like I remembered, with a few extra teddies and trinkets from the beach. She didn't know I would come here, so it wasn't like she left me a note or a clue to tell me she was okay, but physically, it calmed me down to be close to her. I grabbed her biggest stuffed animal; a giant panda with a cape and held him in my arms before lying back on the bed. As I looked up at the ceiling Sam decorated with glow-in-the-dark stickers of the solar system, my heart stopped pounding, my breathing slowed, and the tension I hadn't realized I was holding all over released.

We used to sit like that on rainy days, telling stories before her dad would inevitably come up, pretending to be the tickle monster, and tell us we had to seize the day, even if it was dark and cloudy outside.

"I nearly had a heart attack when you weren't in your room," Gabriel's voice pulled me from a memory as he came into Clara's room and sat on the bed beside me.

"I'm sorry."

"You need to stop apologizing," I could hear the smile in his voice, but we were both looking at the ceiling.

"That'll probably never happen," I sighed.

"Lucy..." he was tentative, which made me feel like I didn't want to know what he was about to say.

"Yeah," I gave him the permission he was waiting for.

"Sam didn't die so you could give up."

My first instinct was to turn and look at him in shock and anger, but I could feel the burn of tears and did not want to let him see that. Instead, I took a deep breath and let it out slowly, trying not to make a sound. I didn't know if Gabriel had more to say or if that was the extent of his attempt, but I stayed there, staring at the ceiling, trying to breathe.

I knew he was right, that I had to stop blaming myself for the things I did to save myself, and for the people I came from.

I was taking another deep breath when Gabriel reached over to take my hand in his. There were a million things he could have said, but none of them would say more than he already had.

CHAPTER EIGHT

We left at the crack of dawn, but I was up long before
then. I switched some clothes from my bag for the
ones from my closet, mostly pants instead of shorts and
dresses, and added some warm sweaters. I snuck into the
master bedroom to take one of Deanna's scarves, then waited
for the guys downstairs.

We walked along the boardwalk in the dark, with the sun
coming up as we drove away. I had taken a pair of Sam's
sunglasses, so I matched the guys in that respect, although
none of us needed them this early in the morning. It garnered
me a smile from Embry, who turned on the radio and sang
along. I wasn't there yet, but I was trying.

THEY DID THEIR DETOURS, which I will never understand, so it
was late afternoon by the time we got to the plantation. We
stopped by the meadow, where the burnt line of grass and
trees greeted us.

"I guess no one's been since I burnt it down?" We all stared
through the windows, trying to assess the damage.

"I believe I was the one who threw the Molotov cocktails. You can claim the forest, but the plantation house is all me," Embry took a shot at me and got a smile in return. I would never have imagined smiling over arson before, especially not burning down a house that had been in my family for generations.

Gabriel drove slowly over the lawn, stopping in front of the garage, where the crispy remnants of the grey box told me the security system was down. The house looked slightly damaged from the outside, where you could tell it caught fire, but most of it looked like a layer of reinforced steel stopped the flames.

"You were right about the tungsten," Embry told Gabriel.

"It's not steel?" I asked.

"A combination. It held up pretty good in some places," he took a critical eye to the structure, assessing whether it was safe for us to go in. "Careful," he cautioned.

"Do you guys have anything in mind for Rosie? Something she treasured?" I looked from one to the other. Gabriel still looked guilty over not returning her affections, but no matter how much Beth was Embry's true love, there was no doubt in my mind that he had loved Rosalind, and still felt the sting of his unrequited feelings.

"I think her stuff is in the bunker," Gabriel ventured.

"I thought the bunker was only for people and dangerous books?"

"It's like Embry's," Gabriel shrugged.

"Understood," I nodded. It was a room for things they didn't want to lose.

"A lot of the paintings and original decor were hers, but there was a box with her jewelry and trinkets that we moved to the safe as soon as they put it in," Embry shared.

· · ·

WE WENT DOWN to the basement, which was the least affected part of the house. The guys watched while I tried at least four times to get into the bunker. It required my blood, the code, and turning the knob a bunch of different ways, even without the computer system.

Once we got in, Gabriel went straight for a small, wooden box with carvings of roses on the sides, and 'My Darling Rosie' etched on the top.

I judged our potential items based on how easy they would be to carry, but they were trying to find a balance between things that meant the world to Rosie and nothing to them. We didn't know what would remain of the objects once the spell was done with them.

"How about this?" I asked of a brooch wrapped in a lace handkerchief with 'R.G.' stitched into the corner of the fabric.

"It was her husband, Roger's. He gave her the brooch as well," Embry told me, but there was a look to him.

"You see something better?" I asked. I wasn't alive anywhere near the same time as her, so none of it meant anything to me, but I saw her wearing the brooch in a memory.

"One night when I was here, there was a fire. It was in the kitchen and we put it out quickly, but just to be safe, we evacuated everyone from the house. Molly took a picture of Roger with her, but the only keepsake Rosalind took was that," Embry pointed to a piece of black fabric that felt like silk and held something heavy.

"A pebble?" Rock would have been my first guess, but it was much too smooth.

"I never knew Rosie to carry rocks," Gabriel cocked his head to the side, as curious as I was.

I removed the silk and found a clear block of what looked like a dandelion floating in... plastic?

"A flower?" I turned to Gabriel to see if he shared my

confusion, but he was holding the stiffest upper lip I'd ever seen, his eyes focused on the block until he turned to Embry. The look he shot him was reminiscent of the previous centuries when they hated each other. If it meant this much to the two of them, it was probably emotional gold for Rosalind.

I brought it close to Gabriel, half-offering it, half-asking if I could use it, before the rest of the world slipped away…

I was in the plantation's foyer, but they set it up as a makeshift hospital for wounded soldiers of the war of independence, including Gabriel who was lying in a bed watching Rosalind. It was weird because I wasn't inside anyone. I was intruding on the moment, like a fly on the wall.

Gabriel wasn't observing Rosie as a stalker, or as someone infatuated with her would; he was trying to solve a mystery. He perked up and strained to see when she moved her hair to rub her neck, but he slumped down, disappointed, when she let it fall again. He was trying to see if she had the crescent moon birthmark, and she wasn't making it easy.

I moved over to sit on the edge of his bed, taking advantage of my non-existence in this moment to take in every detail. His eyes were less dark than the Gabriel I knew, but every bit as intense. There was something hopeful about him, like he knew this wasn't Annabelle, but maybe she could be.

It was either a while after he first arrived, or he died here and regenerated, because his wounds were non-existent as he crept to the windows. Molly, Rosalind's daughter, was in the yard, picking flowers and placing them in a small wicker basket.

Gabriel was back in the bed before a doctor came in to check on him, but no one questioned him when he lied and said they changed his bandages this morning. He was an excellent liar, but something about the way he pressed his lips together told me it wasn't the truth.

"I got them!" Molly rushed into the room, looking absolutely

enthralled to be spending time with Gabriel, especially to be of use to him rather than an annoyance he tolerated.

"These are beautiful, Molly. Absolutely perfect," he beamed at her and her entire face lit up. I could tell he had experience with children, probably from Margaret, but there was also something holding him back. Some apprehension he was trying to hide, that Molly did not pick up on, but I did. It was like he was afraid of her.

"How do you make them stay together?" Molly asked, trying to tie a knot between two flowers.

"Like this." Gabriel demonstrated, folding the stems as I had only ever seen with palm leaves. He finished a necklace, then let Molly put it over his head.

"You can't take it off now," she warned.

"I wouldn't dream of it," he assured her. "Now you try."

She made a solid attempt, Gabriel made an adjustment, then she quickly figured it out.

"You can start one for mama," she suggested when he was just watching her.

"Excellent idea." He worked slowly so Molly could help add the finishing touches once she was satisfied with her own.

"Can you tie mine?" She asked.

"It would be my pleasure."

He finished tying the stems together like a clasp just as Rosalind came in to check on him, or more likely make sure her daughter wasn't bothering him.

"Mama!" Molly ran over to show her mother the necklace she made.

"Wow, that's beautiful sweetheart," Rosie looked from her daughter to Gabriel, wondering what kind of man enjoyed making flower necklaces with a little girl. I could tell that she liked it. A lot.

"It was Gabriel's idea. We made you one too."

"This is for me?" Rosie asked, her hand pressed to her chest and her eyebrows raised. It was the way I overreacted to things for Clara, but I think she was genuinely touched.

"Don't worry, I didn't see any bugs in it," Gabriel gave her a smile as she turned around and pulled her hair out of the way, letting him tie the necklace for her. His breath caught and I don't think he could help himself as he traced the mark with his fingers. It was exactly like mine, like the dolls, down to the freckles in the crescent that looked like stars.

"Is something wrong?" Rosalind asked, snapping him out of his reverie and reminding him of his task. It would thoroughly creep me out if some guy caressed the back of my neck like that, but she looked like she was just as lost in the moment as he was.

"No, of course not," he gave no explanation for touching her in what definitely looked like a sensual way, but she didn't ask for one either...

"THE FLOWER IT IS," I tried to get up and act like it was normal for me to pass out and wake up on the ground, which it kind of was lately.

"Where did you go?" Just like the bedroom in New Orleans, this time it was Gabriel's turn to be nervous about how much I saw.

"When you gave them to her."

"And she felt..." Gabriel tried to find the words to ask what he wanted to know, but it was mostly to torture himself for hurting her.

"I don't know what she was feeling," I admitted.

"You were in me?" His eyes widened in horror.

"No, it was weird. I was just in the room. Like I tapped into the moment rather than a memory."

"You saw it all from above, or..." Embry was curious.

"No, I could walk around. It's just weird in the ones when I can see myself instead of being myself," I tried to explain.

"It happened before?" Gabriel asked. "You saw another moment?"

"The other one was a memory, I think." I based my assumption on how this time it happened when I touched the flower block, whereas last time I was touching them. I wrapped the flower into Roger's handkerchief instead of the silk, thus representing her husband, her daughter, and Gabriel; the three people she cared about most. The guys were looking at me expectantly, so I shared more. "It was of the two of you arguing. It happened when you were fighting and I tried to separate you, so I don't know whose memory it was. Maybe both."

"You get them at will then," Embry concluded.

"No, I did not want to see what I saw," I argued. "Is this all the spell books? We should grab them and get to the manor before dark," I suggested when it looked like they were both going to ask for more details about their memory.

"I was thinking we should get something smaller than the dagger for Annabelle. Preferably something that never belonged to someone else," Gabriel put his own curiosity aside for me.

"Like what?" The plantation was her family home once upon a time, so there were lots of family heirlooms and things that must have belonged to her, but it went through many renovations and I wasn't aware of any secret jewelry boxes of hers. Then again, I never knew about Rosie's.

"It is October," he looked pointedly at me, then down to my neck.

"What do... the locket?" I clued in, bringing my hand to the moonstone necklace I was wearing instead of the locket my grandmother used to make me wear around Halloween.

"Evelyn didn't tell you?" Embry read my confusion.

"She did not," I agreed. A common theme for everyone and everything in my life these days.

"It was Annabelle's. She had it with her when she died."

"She was wearing it when they burnt her?" I involuntarily

recoiled. It was one thing to have Beth's old ring in my bag, but I wore the necklace that touched her searing flesh for months over the years, if not more.

"It was untouched by the flames. We were told to give it to Margaret, and your ancestors have passed it down ever since."

"Is it something Henry gave to her?" I asked, even though the answer might make my skin crawl.

"No, she had it the first day I met her. Minus the rope and hair," Gabriel assured me.

"Is that why it smells so bad?" I understood that the rope and hair were inside the seal.

"You're exaggerating. It's a little musty, but hair and twine don't smell like rotting flesh."

"Did all the others wear it too?" I tried to remember if I wore it in any of the memories.

"We had more control over that when they were children. As in Margaret wore it and made her daughter wear it and so on. It would disappear for a generation or two, then Henry would resurface and it wasn't just a silly superstition anymore."

"So my mom never wore it," I understood.

"Not that I saw, but Corinne wore it every single day until she passed it on to her daughter."

"I'll go get it," I relented.

"I'll pack up any books or things that might be useful," Embry picked up one of the magic books we hid down here when we left. The things we were originally coming here for. Magic books were more useful when you had someone who could do magic, and we needed all the help we could get.

GABRIEL FOLLOWED me upstairs in case someone showed up or the building collapsed on me, but I also got the feeling he wanted to say something.

"It wasn't the fight that made you guys ignore each other this summer," I told him. Eric had filled me in that their fight was about feelings Gabriel might have for me, rather than Embry's feelings for Annabelle, as I had assumed.

He looked at me, surprised I knew where his mind was. There was a flash of him wanting to find out what I knew about that fight, but I didn't want to talk about that, and his face told me he didn't either.

"Give me a decade. Or a century," he teased. The smile implied he wasn't so concerned, at least not now that he knew it wasn't the one about me.

"1770s," I shrugged, going through the hooks on the wall of my closet. I was a lot less good at wearing the locket consistently now that Grams and Mrs. Boyd weren't reminding me. Sam would say something when he saw it, but he had an out of sight, out of mind mentality when it came to Grams' eccentricities, so I kept it at the plantation instead of the manor.

"We fought all the time back then."

"Are you afraid of all children, or just Molly?" I brought us back to my most recent memory, rather than the one where he tells Embry we only look like a woman we can never live up to.

"Afraid of her?" He raised an eyebrow, but played along.

"The entire time you were making necklaces with her, you were trying to bury your fear, or…"

"Pretend I didn't care," he understood. "Margaret was easy, I could just pretend she was mine. I'm sure Embry did the same, but I never wanted to get close to another child like that. I watched her grow up, but no matter how old she got, when she died, she was still… I didn't want to go through that again. But Molly was… I pretended I couldn't care less, that I was giving her projects to keep her out of my hair, but after generations without letting anyone in… she was curious and caring and innocent and everything I didn't know I needed."

I digested the information, of him sharing his vulnerability with me, and took a chance. "It's caring that you're afraid of?" I teased with a smile instead of dwelling on how lonely it must be to watch everyone you care about die, then have to keep going.

"Terrible things often happen when I do. People get hurt," he agreed, choosing to keep it honest, rather than the out I gave him. "With Rosalind, I was so focused on pointing out how she wasn't Annabelle that I didn't notice the dozens of ways she was amazing in her own right. She was strong, self-less in caring for her patients, a devoted mother... she would light up a room no matter how dark it appeared to be..."

"Why are you telling me that?" His eyes were looking at me with that intensity that made my heart beat faster and my cheeks blush.

"Being afraid doesn't stop me from caring. It stops me from letting the other person know, which ultimately causes more pain for everyone," he found my eyes and his guilt told me he knew exactly what memory I saw.

It was just the two of us in the closet, and he was being vulnerable and looking at me in a way that made me want to move closer, but my heart was beating a mile a minute and I was terrified of what might happen if I was wrong.

Just as I moved my hand closer to his, the locket shifted, and I was pulled away...

My heart sank at being ripped from the moment, but I was definitely not expecting to be Annabelle, wrists tied to a post behind my back as the ground beneath me was burning. Inside I was screaming, but Annabelle stood tall and looked ahead, not letting it get to her, even as the flames licked her feet. Gabriel and Embry were in the crowd, with Gabriel holding a little girl in his arms, both of them taking it a lot harder than Annabelle was. It burned, and I wanted to struggle to get free, to use my magic to freeze the flames... anything. Instead I stood there, stoic and strong, the locket around my neck the only thing that wasn't on fire...

"WAS IT THE LOCKET?" Gabriel asked, horrified.

There were a million memories the locket could hold, but he knew which one it would bring. I nodded and shivered, not because I was cold, but I needed to get the feeling of being burned alive, for a second time this week, out of my skin.

"Come on, let's bring you home," he wrapped an arm around me and led me back outside.

CHAPTER NINE

I stayed in the car with the doors locked and the key in the ignition while the guys went to make sure the manor was safe. I knew it looked exactly the same from the outside, but it felt empty and cold. It always seemed like that on the surface, because we were four people living in a ginormous building with old heating systems, but the inside was nothing but warmth and coziness.

After about thirty minutes of reading a book on the laws of magic, Embry came out to escort me and the car inside. He had me activate all the alarms while he carried the rest of the books from the bunker into the kitchen.

"Should we go to my mom's room?" Part of me wanted to stay as long as it took for word to get out that we were here, so Clara and Deanna would come and I could see them for real, but the bigger part needed us to get what we came for and leave as soon as possible. I couldn't be responsible for any more dreadful things happening to them.

"I'll start supper," Gabriel offered.

"I'll go on the adventure," Embry whisked me upstairs. I

spent my childhood with people bribing me with trips to her room, so calling it an adventure was accurate.

Once inside, all I could see was my father telling her he was basically paid to impregnate her because Henry was worried a teenager dying of cancer would let the Owens line die out otherwise. I shivered at the thought.

"Did you have something in mind?" Embry asked to bring me back to the task at hand.

"Everything I found in here as a kid was magical and meant the world to me, because it belonged to her."

"I think I remember you carrying around a doily for days until Mrs. Boyd told you what it was."

"I blame everyone who didn't give me more to go on," I meant it in the sense that I wish I knew more about her. I didn't blame the Boyds.

"I'll tell you as much as I know about whatever you find," he gave me free rein, but I didn't know where to start, or how much he knew about her.

"If you had to pick something in here, what would you choose?" I turned it on him.

"You," he smiled. "You were what meant the most to her in the entire world."

"I would rather not use human sacrifices, but I'm open to other suggestions..." I looked around. "None of this is familiar except from my own memories of exploring the room when I was really good, or when bad things happened to me," I pointed out.

"How do you picture her?" He asked.

"I have the actual memories of a woman with a scarf around her head, who is scared and weak, but also fighting. Who smiles whenever she knows I'm looking. Then I have the ones I make up from pictures of her when she is young and happy and alive. The thing I had that most reminded me of her was the blanket, which I now know was Brian's."

"Marilyn didn't wear fancy jewelry, and I don't remember many trinkets. She had a lot of stuffed animals when she was in the hospital, but she usually gave them all away before she came home and got new ones for her next stay."

"Did she wear not-fancy jewelry? A Cracker Jack box ring would do if it meant something to her." The plastic ring from Clara was the object I was most attached to at the moment. I fished around without going deep, feeling like I was intruding this time, rather than discovering more about my mom.

"She made jewelry," he got one of those sad smiles from when he remembered something about someone he lost. "The last one she sent me was one of those wish bracelets that you tie around your ankle."

"And when it breaks the wish comes true." I made them with Clara once.

"I don't think that's how it worked," he argued.

"Did it have beads?" I could vaguely remember a picture of me eating something from my mom's ankle.

"She put my initials on mine. Her wish was to keep everyone safe, so she told me it would protect me as long as I wore it."

"Do you still have yours?" It didn't belong to her, but she probably put a lot of herself into it.

"I wore it every day for years, while Gabriel left his in a box at Terrence's. I lost mine, and it was like I committed a terrible offence. I don't think she ever forgave me."

"At least he still has his," I gave him a smile.

"If memory serves, hers was always pink or purple."

"Let's find it."

We looked on all the exposed surfaces, then ventured into drawers and boxes. I was familiar with the lower drawers of her standing bureau, the only ones I could reach as a tiny kid. I was exploring the top ones when Embry exclaimed, "Found it!"

"M.E.O.," I read. "Elizabeth?"

"Helen and I might have told your Grams a few stories," he agreed.

"Any thoughts on Suzanne?" I asked of my middle name.

"She liked the name?" He let me know it didn't ring a bell for him, then dropped the bracelet in my hand so I could add it to the other objects, but the moment it touched me…

"Are you making a wish?" Brian asked as my mom tied the bracelet around her ankle. We were in a hospital, but she didn't look sick like I remembered her, just a little tired.

"I never use those rules," she argued.

"The conventional rules that apply to all wish bracelets?" He came over and took her in his arms, looking at her like she was his entire world, though the setting definitely made him uncomfortable.

"If it needs to break to release your wish, you would just be super rough with it until it did, which is stupid."

"What are your rules?" He kissed the top of her head and she closed her eyes, her entire body relaxing.

"Well," she took out another bracelet and tied it around his wrist, "as long as you're wearing this, it will keep you safe," she gave him a smile. She knew how unrelated the two were, but this wasn't her first rodeo, and little kids were quick to believe in magic bracelets. Especially if they got to go home while other kids in the ward never made it out of the operating room.

"Then you are never allowed to take yours off."

"Why not?" She bit her bottom lip, but he didn't play along to her fishing. He got serious.

"Because I can't lose you," he said with an intensity that had me taking a closer look at his eyes, but they were green. Like mine.

"I'm not going anywhere," she took him in her arms…

"Bad memory?" Embry asked when I woke up in his arms.

"Happy memory. Evil person," I brushed it off and stood up with a sigh.

"Care to tell me exactly what you saw?" He asked. All I had told them up to this point was that my dad was not a nice person.

"Not particularly." I wrapped my arms around myself and walked back to the bureau, more out of habit than anything else. "I'm trying to focus on nurture over nature. And who knows, maybe my mom--" I picked up a picture as I was talking and recognized it from the blurry one I've always had of my father, only this one was perfectly clear, of Brian holding me in his arms and smiling so much he was crying...

"How did you get in here?" my mom asked Brian.

"Sam let me in," he admitted, looking guilty and heartbroken.

"How cunning of you. Manipulating a ten-year-old," he was upsetting her, but she made no effort to get him out.

"I brought this for you. Well, for the baby. I don't know if it's a boy, or a girl, but my grandmother made it for me when I was born, and she insists it was blessed and will keep the baby safe. I figured it can't hurt," he tried to hand her my blankie, but she didn't take it.

"What do you want?" she used her vulnerability as a weapon to get him to leave.

"I need to tell you what happened," he pleaded like his life depended on it.

"Yes, well, since you told me to have an abortion, I don't really care what you have to say. Which is why I told you never to come back here." I could feel how much she loved him, still, but she didn't know what I knew yet.

"I need you to know why I said that."

"Because you were young, you had your whole life ahead of you and you didn't want to waste it being tied down to some girl you

slept with a few times." Her words were like a slap in the face for both of them.

"Even if you don't believe a word I say to you today, even if you want to continue to believe that I wasn't ready to be a father, you have to know that you were so much more than that to me. That you meant the world to me. I will love you until the day I die," he promised.

"How could I know that when you told me to kill our baby? Knowing that it was probably the only chance I would ever get, and that the thing I have wanted more than anything my entire life was to be a mom?"

"I had to try and convince you not to. You should have had an abortion," he didn't even try to deny it. "But you were the one who decided that my telling you not to have the baby meant that I wouldn't want to stick around if you did."

"I didn't want you anywhere near her." She had tears in her eyes, but she looked at him with pure hatred.

"Her?" he asked. I could see his brain working, trying to imagine what I looked like, whose nose I had, what colored hair...

"I would love to tell you you have a daughter, but she's mine." I think the hurt in her voice affected him more than her words.

"Can I see her?"

I was forced to watch the part of the memory I heard at the campus library. As if once wasn't bad enough, I got to listen to my father tell my mother about the man who paid him to hang out with her, who was so happy when she got pregnant, because it meant she would continue the line before her cancer killed her.

"He sent you to sleep with me?" My mom was horrified, and I was more than ready to get back to the present, away from this conversation.

"He only told me after he realized that we were. It's not like he told me to do it, he was just happy when we did. That's when he explained it all to me. He told me he was worried because you had cancer, and you didn't go out much, and he thought you might die without leaving a child to ensure there would be more copies," each word he said disgusted him more than the last. I think he hated himself as much as we did.

"Then why did you tell me to have an abortion? Was it some mind game to free yourself and make sure I would keep her?" My mom was way more clear-headed than me, actually taking the time to process what he was telling her.

"When he told me why I was doing it... I couldn't. I mean, yes, he paid for my school and dorm and asked me to hang out with you, but you weren't some stranger... I didn't mind because I liked you. And then I really liked you. And then I loved you. And that's when he told me the truth. As soon as I knew why he was so interested in you, I came here to tell you, but then you told me you were pregnant and I know I should have handled it better, or explained why, but... The point is, I told you to have an abortion not because I don't love you or wasn't already in love with that baby, but because some day, that little girl, or her little girl, will be used in his messed up game, and I wanted to protect you from that."

"This is crazy. You're not making sense," my mom argued, not wanting it to be true.

"I know, it sounds crazy. It's ridiculous, and maybe it isn't true, but he believes it. And some day, he will come after you and our daughter," he emphasized the 'our' to let her know he hadn't given up on it.

THEY WENT TO FIND GRAMS, who not only believed it, but looked destroyed by it. She told Brian to leave her house, then went to make phone calls.

"Her name is Lucy," my mom said once they were in her bedroom to get his coat. "Lucine Suzanne Owens."

I thought he might be upset about the Owens, but his face lit up. "Suzanne?" he asked.

"Your grandmother was sweet and strong and wasn't afraid to tell it like it is."

"The last thing I have ever wanted to do is hurt you, Marilyn. You are my heart."

"I want to believe you, but I don't know if I can trust you," she looked torn.

"I'll just have to spend the rest of my life proving it to you."

"Your blanket," she said when he left it on her bureau.

"It's Lucy's now," he argued. They shared a look that broke my heart.

"Do you want to hold her? Just once," my mom offered.

"More than anything," he followed her to the bassinet, beaming when she put me in his arms. He held me close, like he wanted to protect me from everything.

A camera flash made him turn to my mother, who was shaking a Polaroid. "Smile in this one," she requested, so he obliged.

"What was that for?"

"One day she'll ask about you, and I want to have something to show her."

"Hopefully she won't have to ask." There was a moment where they looked to each other, both of them wanting that, but my mom couldn't admit to it, and he could see he had a long way to go to get there...

"Have you considered hanging out around beds and chairs rather than open spaces?" Embry must have caught me, because I was on the bed rather than on the ground, but the memories never came so close together before.

"He wasn't evil," I ignored his suggestion.

"Your father?" he asked, going off the picture in my hands.

"I mean, he was very flawed and made some awful decisions, but he loved her."

"Everyone did," he gave me a sad smile.

"Back at the library, the memory I saw made it seem like Henry paid a boy to woo my mom and sleep with her so she could continue the line."

"That's disgusting."

"I know."

"What really happened?"

"Henry saw that my mom liked him, so he offered him a job, and to pay his tuition and stuff. It was all just a ploy for him to be close to her. He tried to tell my mom as soon as he found out, but she was pregnant and didn't take it well when he told her to have an abortion."

"I'm sorry," Embry was horrified.

"You're upset at how close he was to us, how involved he was when you had no clue Henry was behind it… I'm relieved that he didn't orchestrate my birth, he just facilitated it."

"Is that why you were so convinced you were evil and didn't deserve to be saved?" he asked.

"One of many reasons," I agreed. I put the picture back in the bureau and found a faded newspaper clipping about a young man drowning when his car drove off a bridge. They were unable to identify the body, but given the fact that my mom kept it, I had a pretty good idea who it was.

EMBRY FOLLOWED me closely on the staircase, ready to catch me if I slipped away again, but I remained in the present. We had a surprisingly okay supper, but it was an emotionally exhausting day for me, and I was ready to go to bed.

"Now we have all the things…"

"Let's stay a couple of days, make a game plan, then go off on your suicide mission?" Embry suggested.

"It's not really suicide if it's inevitable. And the purpose of the mission is to prevent it from happening."

I could tell he was about to argue, but we all froze as the

kitchen door opened behind me. I brought my hands up as I turned, terrified but ready to go down fighting. Thank God my instinct was to freeze rather than explode, because not only did I recognize the man frozen in front of us, I loved him with my whole heart.

"Sam?!?"

CHAPTER TEN

"I have to unfreeze him," I said for what felt like the millionth time this evening. The guys tied Sam up using zip ties so he couldn't hurt us using human means, but they were reluctant to see what magic he might have.

"Not until we know what he is and have a plan," Gabriel argued.

"He's Sam," I repeated. This certainty was probably why they didn't trust me to unfreeze him. "And if he isn't, our best way of finding that out is to talk to him."

"Or to whip up a truth serum." I'm pretty sure Embry was joking, but it was one of the potions Ingrid taught me over the summer.

"I know we all learnt our lesson with the faeries, but I don't think you could hurt someone who looked like Sam, no matter who he is," Gabriel said delicately.

"I could freeze him again."

"We're not getting anywhere with him like this," he reluctantly agreed, exchanging a look with Embry. "I want you to freeze him the second he says anything that gives you the slightest hesitation," he warned me.

"Okay," I agreed, waiting for him to nod before unfreezing Sam.

I wasn't worried, because this had to be him, but if it wasn't, the guys were right. Something evil that looked like Sam was better than no Sam at all, as long as he didn't try to kill us.

"Lucy!" His greeting sounded like he was upset with me, until his brain caught up to his new physical predicament and he looked down at his zip-tied hands and feet. "What the…" Confusion and anger mixed into his unfinished question, which was unlike Sam from before, but fitting for someone who was on the run and recently died because of me.

"We tied you up so we could make sure it's you," I explained, trying to take a step towards him, but Gabriel put his arm out to stop me. He and Embry were standing on either side of me, but slightly in front, so they just had to take a step towards each other if things went south and they would form a wall between our presumed enemy and me.

"Because I died," he let out a breath that held a million emotions, but every single one made me feel guilty.

"We've had our share of fake 'you's, so we have to be cautious," I tried to act normal, but every inch of me wanted to run into his arms.

"Fake 'me's?" He had the tiniest trace of his crooked smile. He understood this wasn't an interrogation for knowledge. It was to see if my big brother was in there somewhere.

"There's a fairy in New Orleans that lures people who are mourning a loss into the swamps. We didn't know they did it by looking like the person you've lost," I explained.

"I tried to kill you?" he was concerned, even though I was clearly alive and well in front of him.

"You did," I agreed.

"I'm so sorry Luce. I wanted to contact you and let you

know, but I didn't know how to do that without risking your safety."

"Because it really is you, isn't it?" I could tell the guys weren't convinced yet, but I was ready to untie him and celebrate.

"That or I'm dreaming."

"What happened to you?"

"I remember dying, and you rushing to me before everything went dark. I was dead, I guess, but I wasn't anywhere until I woke up. Like a zombie, only I was me. I was starving for actual food, not blood or brains or anything, but my main priority was finding you."

"Where did you wake up?" Gabriel tested his story.

"In a large pit. There were claw marks that told me I wasn't the first to climb out, but there was still a body at the bottom when I left. By the time I figured out where I was and got to the motel, police officers and caution tape surrounded it. I couldn't just go up to them covered in blood and ask about their investigation, so I found a squad car and hid in the bushes behind it until I made sure on the radio that they hadn't found any teenage girls."

"Why didn't you go home?" Embry asked.

"They found me once, so I didn't want to risk them coming after my girls. I've been trying to keep an eye on them while keeping my distance. I've been here since they moved in with Deanna's father."

"How are they?" I asked.

"Deanna's doing a good job of making it seem like a fun adventure, but Clara's getting to be too smart for her own good. They're safe, but they're worried."

My entire body was stiff from holding my arms by my side and preventing myself from going to him. I looked to the guys in an 'are you satisfied?' way, but they weren't convinced yet.

"Ask something only Sam would know," Embry suggested.

"What's the secret ingredient in your mom's French toast?" I asked.

"Vanilla."

"What was your dad's favorite color?"

"Orange."

"What did Clara call me before she could say Lucy?"

"Lala."

I fired all the questions in quick succession and Sam answered them without missing a beat, so I turned to Embry, who nodded. I think he just meant for me to go close, but I used my powers to break the zip ties so Sam could wrap his arms around me and hopefully make me feel safe, like this summer hadn't happened.

"What was that?" Sam asked when he realized that although his instincts kicked in and he was holding me now, he'd been tied up a moment ago.

"I really haven't been okay," I said before burying my head in his chest.

I COULD TELL that the guys wanted to give us a minute to catch up, but they also weren't one hundred percent certain they trusted Sam to be alone with me, so they let us sit at the table while they made tea and coffee for everyone.

"Did you know you were Gifted?" I asked, no longer taking anything for granted.

"I had no idea. I thought I was in hell, or purgatory at first, until I realized there was a more likely explanation."

"Do you know what your Gift is?" I focused the conversation on him, though I could tell he wanted to ask a million questions about me.

"I think I was overlooked..." he showed me his hand that disappeared when he willed it to.

"Invisibility?"

"I was hoping for flying, but I'll take it," he teased. "Speaking of superpowers..."

"I'm not a superhero," I argued.

"Did we fail?" He asked of his worst fear being realized.

"No, I'm a witch. Apparently. Annabelle and Beth were too."

"That's..."

"Not as fun as it sounds," I said before he could tell me how awesome it was. "I found out about it when I accidentally pulverized someone, then it took forever before I could control it enough to not attack anyone who got close."

We discussed it further before the guys brought us warm beverages and we had a lighter conversation to catch up on more pleasant topics.

SLEEPING in my own bed didn't make me feel like I was safe and at home, it felt weird. So, when I woke up at 5 a.m. with a splitting headache, I gave up on sleep and went down to make myself a tea.

It was steeping on the counter when Sam walked in, looking apprehensive at first, but then his entire body relaxed.

"I was worried it was a dream," he came and took me in his arms. We weren't necessarily a hugging family before, at least not every time we saw each other, but I mirrored his sentiment.

"I didn't want to ruin last night, but... how's the big bad?" He asked, turning on the coffee machine.

"He's..." I let out a deep breath, searching for the best way to explain it all to him. "The Big Bad's name is Henry, and he was married to Annabelle, which makes him my ancestor. She found the Prophecy and left him, so he has been hunting us down ever since."

"At least you have some answers," he offered me the tiniest of silver linings.

"I can also promise that Clara's life will be back to normal before she graduates high school," I said it like it was another positive in this messed up situation.

"What do you mean?" Sam didn't get it.

"I only have to avoid Henry for the next ten years, because no matter what we do, the Bearers of the Crescent Moon die at twenty-eight."

"That's… there has to be something we can do," he argued.

"There's a spell. So far it looks like we only have to collect a few objects and random ingredients, nothing scary, but I feel like there has to be a catch."

"If there's a spell to make you not die, we're using it," he left no room for discussion.

"That's the plan, I just don't think it can really be as easy as putting rings and flowers in a bowl."

"Rings and flowers?" he asked.

"I need objects from my mother, my father, and all the bearers of the crescent moon who came before me," I sighed.

"How are you going to do that? You don't know who your father is and—"

"We got the last piece last night," I cut him off, not ready to get into that story. "I have my father's baby blanket and my mom's bracelet, then I have Annabelle's locket, Rosalind's flower block thing, Cassie's weaponized gloves and Beth's family ring."

"You found your father?" He was more concerned than excited for me, probably wondering why I didn't mention it last night.

"He was this guy named Brian Sherwood. I'm pretty sure he's dead, though."

"He taught me the Thriller dance," he told me after

thinking about it. I forgot that in the memory, he convinced Sam to let him in.

"He was a nice guy?"

"I liked him. He came over a lot for about a year, and then he came back once. Your mom had told me he was never coming back, so I was thrilled when he showed up, but it was just the one time."

"Yeah, he… it's complicated," I brushed it off, but when he gave me another concerned look, I reluctantly agreed to tell him later.

"How did you get stuff from the others?" he poured himself some coffee.

"What others?"

"The other Bearers of the Crescent Moon," he used my language. "Unless you only need the last four?"

"Annabelle was the first," I said, realizing I had absolutely nothing to back that statement up.

"She was the first that Gabriel and Embry met, the first to come to America… but she wasn't the first."

"I only have four dolls," I pointed out, but even as I said it, I remembered the references to the Prophecy implied it started long before Annabelle. Like five hundred years before she was born.

"I commissioned the dolls," Embry came down, his eyes on Sam, making me think he was listening in from the staircase. A thought confirmed by Gabriel coming with him.

"Who told you there were others?" I asked Sam, who looked surprised that the guys didn't know.

"Genevieve."

I looked at him expectantly, but Embry and Gabriel clearly knew her.

"She kept a diary?" Embry asked.

"Letters to her husband," he argued.

"Who are we talking about?" I waited for one of them to fill me in.

"Cassie's mom died when she was very little, so her father hired Mrs. Lovell to take care of her. Her daughter, Genevieve, and Cassie were like sisters..." Embry started.

"She's the Gen who fought crimes with Cassie," I remembered her name popping up frequently in the Chronicles.

"And she's my ancestor," Sam emphasized the 'my' as if to show that his family was interesting and went back generations as well.

"When your mom said her family had been looking after mine for a long time, she didn't mean just you and your dad," I realized I had it wrong all these years.

"Martha's family has been linked with yours since roughly 1830," Gabriel shared.

I looked to Sam, wondering how many people I needed to hunt down now, but also feeling betrayed by yet another thing he kept from me.

"I've had a lot of time in the house and I wanted to find out more about being Gifted, so I went through my mother's old things. I don't know if I was nostalgic or if I needed to make sense of things, but Gen's letters were the only things that mentioned anything supernatural."

"What did she say about us?" I asked, counting myself as one of the Bearers.

"I can get the letters for you, but basically she and Cassie went to England before Cassie's wedding and they stumbled into someone who knew her. Or, you know, someone who looked like her."

"How many were there?" Embry asked.

"Cassie wanted to stay to find out, but she had the wedding."

"Go get the letters," Gabriel sighed.

"It didn't even occur to me about the other Bearers," I

clenched my teeth and shook my head as Sam rushed up the stairs. We had nothing from anyone before Annabelle and her parents.

"How much do you know about them?" Embry asked me.

"There was a brief passage in a book Beth was reading. The oldest mention of someone being marked by the Crescent Moon was in 1148, and again with Talina and Zeke, who ruled from 1385 to 1460," I shared, knowing it wasn't much to go on. "What do we do?"

"If there were others… you saw the spell, we need something from every Bearer who came before you."

"In England?" I asked. "How do you know anything would even be there anymore?"

"We have to try," Gabriel had a lot more determination and confidence than me.

Sam came downstairs with a stack of letters, but they were fifty percent Gen missing her husband, forty-five percent praising Europe and its beautiful sights, with maybe five percent of it relevant to us. She never gave specifics, either because she didn't think he would care, or because she was keeping it a secret.

The letter with the most details was her second, sent a couple of days after their arrival. I was reading it out loud when I found myself living it instead…

"Judith! Judith!" A man ran across the street, trying to flag Cassandra and another woman down. He looked so happy to see her that he forgot himself and tried to take her in his arms, but as soon as he got too close for comfort, she hit him in the stomach with the rounded end of her umbrella. "You don't remember me," he said, doubled over to clutch his stomach.

"No, I do not," she said. He intrigued her more than he scared her. "How do you think you know me?"

"My name is Alaric," he paused to see if it would jog her memory. "I was at your wedding."

"You're mistaken, Sir. I'm not from here and my fiancé--" Cassandra tried to be polite, but exchanged a glance with her friend, probably Genevieve.

"It was in 1560," he added.

"And what did you call me?" she asked, having only met a handful of people who knew another Bearer, but none of them had mistaken her for someone else yet.

"Judith. But you're not her," he said sadly.

"I'm not. And I'm terribly sorry, but we're expected for dinner and..."

"Of course," he assured her. "Meet me tomorrow for lunch. My estate is just outside of London, one of those old ones that everyone knows where to find since it's been in the family for ages."

"I don't think I can, we're very busy," Cassie was nervous, but it wasn't about the stranger.

"Please?" the look he gave softened her.

"I'll see what I can do," she decided.

"Dawes Estate. I'll see you tomorrow," he gave her a smile, full of nostalgia, then let her continue on her way...

"Her name was Judith," I shared when I came back to them.

"Anything we can use to find her?" Embry asked.

"The man who recognized Cassie had an estate outside of London. He said it's been in his family for generations, so he might still be there."

"I guess we're going to London," Embry gave me fake enthusiasm.

. . .

THE GUYS PUT in a few calls to arrange our travel while I stayed back in the kitchen with Sam.

"I don't think I renewed my passport since the baby moon fell through," he told me.

"We probably don't need those. Last time I crossed the border with them, I was in the back of a pickup, surrounded by chicken and roosters."

"You must have loved that," he laughed at me.

"We do what we have to," I shrugged before getting serious. "You can't come with us."

"I'm already dead, Lucy. And I can do this," he made his body disappear to prove his point.

"Exactly. I've been living the past few months wracked with guilt because I thought I killed you. There is no way I could get over it twice."

"I don't think it's up to you."

"I think you got to be invisible because it lets you keep an eye on Deanna and Clara without getting them in danger. That's where you need to be."

"And who will make sure you don't follow fairies into ponds over there?"

"I learnt my lesson. And you know Gabriel and Embry won't let anything happen to me."

"They're a lot friendlier than they used to be," he pointed out instead of agreeing to not come.

"They had a huge fight and eventually made up for everything."

"I'll make a deal with you. Promise me you'll come home and be at my daughter's graduation and I'll let you go without me."

"Only if you promise you'll save my seat," I turned it on him, since neither of us could really promise such things.

"I promise," he looked into my eyes, and even if it was fueled by hope, I believed him.

"I promise too."

"I'll hold you to it," he warned before we went to pack.

I SPENT the rest of the day sifting through all the magic books, trying to find anything that could help us become more powerful before confronting Henry and his army. A lot of the books were more theoretical, but there were also a lot of spells with graphic images of what they did. If the goal was to torture Henry into admitting something, we would be golden, only I couldn't even look at the pictures without wanting to throw up, and it said it wasn't enough to hate someone, you actually had to want to see them in pain and suffering. Embry told me the books were mostly for research, or gifted to them by friends trying to be helpful, but I was really glad we found Kiara's cure, because the books were a major disappointment. There was a tiny passage in one book stating that the Bearers of the Crescent Moon are strongest during the Crescent Moon, but I felt like we could have figured that out for ourselves.

We left before dawn the following morning, with Sam driving us. He could make anything he touched invisible, which was awesome, but also terrifying when the other cars couldn't see us. He only used it from the manor into town, where we could get lost into the crowd, but it was not an experience I wanted to repeat.

We drove into a secluded entrance of the Logan International Airport, with passports bearing other people's names. Sam took me in his arms and said, "I'll see you soon," before I watched him drive away, praying to God he was right.

I had most of my stuff in my backpack, except for Cassie's gloves and Annabelle's dagger, which Gabriel was holding on to while I went through the security line. We were away from prying eyes with no one but airport employees around us, but that also meant it would be very hard to get anything past them.

"When you guys said you were making arrangements, I thought you found another crop duster in a nearby field, not that we were flying on a private plane," I told

Embry while returning my tiny bag of liquids into my backpack.

"Those aren't designed for transatlantic flights, and we're on a time crunch," he reminded me. It wasn't like there was anything that said we had to perform Kiara's Cure under the upcoming crescent moon, but since it was the only supermoon this year, we figured it couldn't hurt to aim for sooner rather than later. "But we're not on a private plane, this is just to avoid the crowded airport and board in anonymity."

"But it's a passenger plane?" I verified.

"You'll have a seat," he teased. Given previous modes of transportation, I wasn't reassured.

I looked back to Gabriel, to see how he was getting through with all the weapons we were bringing, but after a few words with the security guys, he handed them something I couldn't see. I tried to read the expression on the guard's face, but he brought Gabriel to a partitioned area.

"Did Gabriel just get arrested?" I asked Embry in a whisper, as a man in a suit went into the room as well. I was expecting him to buzz at the metal detector because of the shrapnel in his shoulder. He told me it was a hassle because he didn't have the scars that should go with that kind of wound, but Embry digging the tracker out of him should provide enough plausibility to let him through this time. He never mentioned anyone detaining him for it.

"I don't think so," Embry wasn't concerned.

"He just tried to bribe a security guard," I pointed out.

"When?" He looked back as if the moment would play out again for him.

"He opened his jacket and handed them something I couldn't see... how did you guys get us in here?"

"He just showed them his badge," Embry reassured me, but it didn't help.

"He thought he could get the dagger through with a fake

cop badge?" I whispered, not wanting the government to overhear me if Keisha was right and they bugged airports with microphones. That might explain being brought into a different room. I knew Gabriel had been a soldier in lots of wars, and he did a short stint in a restaurant, but neither of those should allow him to board a plane with weapons.

"His badge is FBI, and it's real," Embry said like it wasn't a huge deal.

"And what, you're CIA?" I asked.

"Wouldn't you like to know," he teased before they let Gabriel out of the isolation area, shaking hands with the man in a suit who went in after them.

"What happened?" I asked him.

"We're good," he assured me.

THEY BROUGHT us to the plane on one of those trolley things and we boarded from a door in the back. There were two seats in that row for us, and another one in the last row, with the flight attendants.

"See you on the other side," Embry, who got on first, told me before making his way to the single seat, leaving me with Gabriel.

He put his seatbelt on, placed his arms on the armrests and settled in for the flight. I put my seatbelt on, and was going to sit there quietly, but I wasn't good at keeping my curiosity to myself.

"You're FBI?" I turned to ask him in a whisper.

"A long time ago," he said loosely, looking around to make sure no one was listening to us. All the other passengers were following the safety briefing. "I've done lots of things," he reminded me.

"Was this during my lifetime?" I couldn't picture him wearing a suit with the earpiece, going to an office every day.

Then again, it might explain some of his reluctance for talking and sharing. "Or did the guard just not look at the date?"

"Recently enough that I still have friends there who don't mind supplying the occasional badge for me. They'll also vouch for me whenever I get into one of these situations. They know I'm not about to bring a plane down, and they're used to not asking questions, so they'll cover for me with a fake op or justifying my need for personal protection," he said like it wasn't a big deal.

"You must have been really good at it," I shrugged, putting my backpack under the seat as the flight attendant came over. I doubted high-ranking FBI officials had that many people they would lie like that for.

"It became something different from what I signed up for, but the guys who joined with me... even though I would never go back, I would do anything for them," he shared.

"You'll have to tell me about them some time. Or we can have them over for dinner once all of this is settled. You can share war stories and I can learn your deep, dark secrets..." I teased.

"You are my deep, dark secret," he looked at me with the intensity that made me weak in the knees, then smiled like he was just teasing me.

"What else have you done?" I asked, steering away from his comment, even though I wanted more than anything to push him while he couldn't get away.

"Lots of things," he said dismissively, but I was looking at him expectantly, so he went on. "When I was young, Patrick got sick, so a physician came and made him better. I thought he was God and made it my goal to become a physician, so I could help people like he had. I worked long, hard hours as a laborer to afford medical school, and convinced our local physician to teach me everything he knew in the meantime. Then I died and lost everything, then we were raising

Margaret… we were slightly overprotective, so she was my sole priority," he explained why having a child would prevent him from pursuing his career. "When she got married and didn't need me anymore…"

"That's when you went to war for the first time, right?" I asked because he was trying to explain that after Margaret died, he didn't see the point anymore, so he stopped caring and spent his time trying to die.

"The Seven Year's War," he agreed.

"Were you a medic?" I asked, knowing he taught Terrence how to do that job during the Second World War.

"Not officially. The first time I enlisted, I didn't really care where they put me. When I inevitably died, I couldn't just go back to my unit as if nothing happened, so I kept finding new ones. If someone got injured, I used what I knew to help them. Some units made me their medic, but I wasn't recognized for it."

"Have you practiced since I met you? More than just stitching up friends?"

"I've always dabbled in it. Every few decades I go back to med school…"

"Is that necessary?" I cut him off. "Couldn't you just forge a new diploma, or edit the year on yours?"

"It was. When I started practicing, the United States didn't even have official medical schools. I went to Harvard when it opened and loved it. Graduated top of my class," he had a proud smile that made me smile too.

"A Harvard education wasn't good enough for you?" He basically lived my Ivy League dream. I was supposed to be at Harvard enjoying my first year of pre-med. We had bigger concerns at the moment, but a part of me needed to mourn the life I should have been living.

"It was incredible, but medicine is a field that is constantly improving and expanding. I usually wait a lifetime, then register as the son or the grandson of my previous self. Fraternities allow for legacies, so…."

"You were in a fraternity?" I raised my eyebrows. There were so many things I was learning about him, some of them completely unexpected.

"My roommate brought me in when I first attended, and it truly is a brotherhood that lasts forever. I would use the fact that I was a legacy to get recruited, but once initiation was over, there were higher levels of alumni who knew about me. Some of them were equally Gifted, which made things a lot easier for me."

"Are there support groups for Gifteds?" I imagined secret societies made up of people like him.

"More like friend groups," he considered it. "Embry established a group in Italy that he goes back to every few years. I have the fraternity whenever I go back to school, or who reach out sometimes for favors, but they're not exclusively like us. Sometimes we just run into people who wake up after dying, or who talk about the Great War like they were there… we make friends."

"Did you warn your friends I was coming to Harvard?" I realized what his fraternity ties implied.

"I was thrilled when you got in. Had things not gone… upside down, they would have invited you to join our sister sorority. I personally thought you were better than that, but they felt it would be incredibly rude not to ask."

"I can't picture you as a preppy frat boy," I shook my head at the idea.

"I wasn't. I was in a fraternity, but I made sure I was a legacy, or there is no way I would get an invitation."

"Did Embry ever go to school with you? He's always had weird jobs whenever I ask."

"He's been a soldier, a barista, a few years of law school, but I don't think he finished…"

"His painting is just a hobby, like your drawing?"

"How do you know about my drawing?" he asked.

"I always suspected it, but this was the proof," I showed him the moonstone necklace he gave me for my birthday, with an image of Sam, Deanna and Clara that he scratched into the stone.

"I dabble," he dismissed his artistic side. "We both have properties and investments from so long ago that we don't need income, but we get bored sometimes. He likes to try new things, like ice cream shops and dog walking. I never know what he'll be doing," he smiled.

"What was your most recent job?"

"I've been working events more than job recently."

"Like concerts and festivals?" It didn't seem likely.

"No," he smiled at me and shook his head. "I got called in to work the Oklahoma City Bombing by an old FBI friend, then I volunteered as a doctor after 9/11..." he explained what he meant, and how he knew about the fertilizer bombs I made at the plantation.

"You help people," I summed it up.

"I try to," he agreed.

"What will you do when all of this is over?" I asked. For me, the likelihood was that it would never be over. I would either die because we lost, or because of the curse. For him, he had a deadline of ten years before he could do whatever he wanted for a few decades.

"Keep checking in on you, make sure you're okay and you get your happily ever after," he raised his shoulders like it was the same thing as always, but his eyes lingered on me before he looked out the window as we took off.

"What if everything goes right and we defeat him, and you guys get to live normal lives... don't you think you would want a break? To not worry about protecting someone else, but live your own life for a change?"

"I would definitely enjoy a stress-free vacation once we defeat Henry," he agreed, not really believing that was likely. "But no matter what happens, or where I am, you can always count on me. I will forever be there for you." We locked eyes and I could feel my cheeks burning before the seatbelt signs went off.

"Okay," I breathed, letting the moment linger a bit longer before looking at the screen in front of me. "Want to watch a movie?" I asked.

"Sure," he cleared his throat and adjusted his position before we settled in to watch an in-flight movie. It was a comedy that neither of us got into with all the other things on our minds, but it was nice to just sit there and pretend we weren't on our way to find things to help break a curse that would kill me if we didn't reverse it, and stop the Big Bag who wanted to rip my heart out.

CHAPTER TWELVE

"That was so much smoother. No offence," I told Gabriel once the plane taxied into its spot and the seatbelt sign went off. I'm sure he was an excellent pilot, and it wasn't like we crashed, but the crop duster he flew us to Terrence's in was near the bottom of my favorite modes of transportation list. Barely a step above boats.

"It's a very different plane," he pointed out.

"My first real plane ride," I smiled despite the terrible circumstances. "Again, no offence."

"None taken," he assured me, grabbing his bag of weapons so we could make our way through the crowded airport.

Embry joined us not long after, with one of the flight attendants smiling at him. It wasn't a flirtatious smile, more like she was grateful.

"I take it you had a pleasant flight?" I asked him.

"She's going through a very hard time. She's flying all over the place while her son lives with her parents and she's trying to pay her way through school so she can support him, and… it was an interesting flight," he stopped himself from sharing her entire life story, but I understood that he made her feel better, if only for a while.

"What do we do now?" I asked once we were outside. There was a line of taxis waiting to bring passengers to hotels, buses to tourist destinations, rental car services... "Do we just go to his place and ring the doorbell?"

"I had an old friend look into it. As far as the government is concerned, the property is owned by a Ric Dawson, who's been there since 2000," Embry shared.

"Does that mean we don't know how to find him?" I asked.

"It would. Only Ric inherited it from a great uncle, so he might just be a Gifted who is on top of his paperwork."

EMBRY USED a fake driver's license to rent us a black sedan, so Gabriel used the map they gave us to locate Dawes Estate. I knew I was naïve and too trusting, but I really didn't get the impression that the man from Cassie's memory would ever want to hurt me.

It was a three-hour drive before we stopped at a bed-and-breakfast. It was charming and rustic, giving the impression that there was no internet and probably not even cable, but it was welcoming and felt safe. Not to say that I trusted it, but it was a lot better than the motel.

Embry used his fake name and got us two adjoining rooms, which he paid for in cash.

"How far are we from the estate?" I asked Gabriel while Embry had a conversation with the woman who owned the B and B about the history of the area.

"Five or ten minutes. There are a couple more houses, then it's the property, but he has as much land as you do."

"What's your feeling about him?" I asked.

"I haven't met him yet."

"But we're here, in England, for no other reason than…"

"Than to get things from your ancestors so we can save you. If he can help us, great, but I won't be trusting him."

WE WALKED UP to the front door with the two of them standing in front of me, forming a wall in case he wasn't friendly. His manor was a lot like ours, in the sense that it seemed cold from the outside, but I heard laughter when we got close, and wondered if it was just as warm as my home used to be.

"How can I help you?" A woman in her thirties opened the door, covered in glitter, still smiling from whatever adventures we interrupted.

"We were looking for—"

"Ric!" As soon as she spotted me, she called into the room on her left, where all the laughter was coming from.

Embry and Gabriel both put their arms out to hold me back. I could feel the tension in their bodies. Friend or foe, we were definitely in the right place.

"What is it?" Ric asked, a little blonde girl giggling over his shoulder while another was wrapped around his leg. I could tell it was him, but there were wisps of gray in his hair that definitely hadn't been there in the memory. He smiled at the guys before his eyes landed on me. I tensed up, knowing he would react, but I relaxed when he looked at me like I looked at Gabriel when he showed up in the field behind the gas station after I thought he died. "You're not Judith, or Cassie," he gave me a sad smile.

"Lucy," I agreed.

"Come on in," he handed the smaller of the girls to the woman and lifted the one from his leg up into his arms.

Gabriel and Embry exchanged a look before following him into the house.

The inside looked like a real estate agent staged it. Then a mini tornado ran through it. The decor was elegant and beautiful, but there were books and pictures and teddies and things that turned houses into homes strewn all over. Not that it was messy, just... lived in.

"You are Alaric Dawes, right?" I asked once we got to the kitchen. He motioned for us to sit, then put a kettle on the stove.

"Older than you expected?" He asked me, still smiling. The constant happiness would worry me, but I didn't have to be Embry to know it was genuine.

"You've done pretty well since I saw in you in 1840, but I was under the impression you wouldn't age."

"I didn't. Until one day I did," he looked over to the woman, probably his wife, and they exchanged a smile that reminded me of Sam and Deanna.

"What were you supposed to do?" I asked.

"All I thought I had was money, so I've spent many lives running charities, doing aid trips to Africa, sponsoring children and rainforests and doing everything I could imagine that would be helpful to the world. I long ago resigned myself to living forever alone, but then I met Sarah," he smiled over at her. "I had no intentions of falling in love, so I kept my distance until one night, I selfishly accept her offer for pizza and a play at the Globe with some friends who worked with us. By the end of the night, I knew I was done for, but I had no idea how to tell her. Not even five minutes after I left her house, I came across a mugging. A pregnant woman. The guy had a gun, she was terrified, he looked like he might use it... I couldn't die anyway, so I stopped it and then, suddenly, I had grey hairs," he shared.

"Who was she?" I asked, noting that both my guys were apprehensive, not at all ready to trust this man spilling his guts in front of us.

"I don't know, but some day, either she or her son will do something hopefully wonderful, and I just had to be in that place at that time."

"When you say you just got grey hairs…" I let it linger, hoping he would elaborate on the process. "I've never met anyone who was Gifted and isn't anymore," I admitted.

"I don't think it's the same for everyone, but I was given a choice. The light was there, and I knew I could walk into it and be reunited with everyone I loved… but Sarah was a few blocks away, and the way my heart skipped a beat at the thought of her, I knew I had to see where it went," he explained. "You call us Gifted?" he asked.

"You don't?" I turned it on him.

"Jude always called people like me supernaturals," he shrugged.

"Jude being Judith?"

"She was brilliant, in every sense of the word," he agreed before the kettle sang. "Tea?"

"Thank you."

The guys declined, so he poured milk into three mugs, added tea, then handed one to me, one to Sarah and kept the last for himself.

"I'm here because I need to find something of hers. I don't know how well you knew her, but I was hoping you could help." It wasn't exactly true. I knew from Cassie's memory that he knew her very well, but I wasn't going to tell him that.

"Why do you need something of hers?" he asked.

"It's a long story," I dismissed his question.

"Forgive me if I see you and talk like you're her. I imagine saying you can trust me won't mean much?"

"Not really," I apologized.

"How did you know her?" Gabriel asked.

"She was my wife."

I could tell that the guys were just as shocked as I was.

"That makes you…"

"Your ancestor," he agreed. "Jude was my best friend and my first love. I was ready to marry her the day I met her, this beautiful and insanely smart woman who didn't take no for an answer… but she had no intentions of settling down until she conquered the world. I waited through school, her crush on an asshole from her class, even her running away to study under a private tutor in Spain. She wrote, but I didn't know if being her friend was worse than being nothing, so I never responded. When she came home, she was furious, and after telling me so, she proposed to me."

"Very progressive," I commented.

"She knew what she wanted and usually went after it," he explained. "It was only a few months after we got married that I died on a hunting trip with my brother. I was just as shocked as my nephew who shot me a second time, this one on purpose. Jude came immediately, did hours of research, sat by my side while my brother, a physician, ran test after test without figuring out what was wrong with me. I told her to leave me, that she deserved a husband, not an abomination, but she told me she just wanted someone who would love her and her child, and really hoped that person would be me," he was beaming. "They were born a few months later, and we lived happily ever after for a few years, until we lost her."

"When you say 'they' were born?" It was Embry who asked. I also wondered if there was a whole other branch to my family tree, another me out there that needed protecting.

"We had twins. Josephine and Oliver, after my father," he shared.

"Did they take your last name?" I asked, since all my ancestors after Annabelle took their mother's name.

"They did," he agreed. "We lost Oliver to measles when the

twins were eight. Josephine never quite got over it, but she insisted on doing all the things he made her promise she would do. We had many adventures before I had to let her go."

"You didn't keep track of them?" Gabriel asked, with a slight accusation to his tone.

"I did, until Esther told me they were moving to the colonies. I wanted to come with her, but my little Esther said it was her adventure and promised she would write. Which she did, but her daughter, Annabelle, didn't know me and didn't carry on the tradition," the guys perked up at the mention of Annabelle.

"How old was Judith when she died?" I asked, trying to be delicate, because I was pretty sure I knew the answer.

"Almost twenty-nine," he shared. "Cancer."

"I'm so sorry," I told him.

"Thank you," he said, though the words were meaningless. "Why do you ask?"

"All of us who looked like her... we've all been dying at the same age. That's why I need something of hers."

"For a spell?" He asked.

"Judith was a witch?"

"Sometimes. She had an unpleasant experience before we got together, so she mostly stayed away from it, but the twins got sick when they were barely a year old and she did some kind of protection spell that required something from each of them."

"This is like that," I agreed.

"I have her portrait in the attic, which would be how my wife recognized you," he answered a question I was definitely going to get to. "But as far as something that belonged to her..." he brought his hand to his chin, trying to think of something. "I gave her ring to John when he proposed to Josephine, who got all of her jewelry... I have a box in the attic, but it's mostly papers… I'll go get it," he went off, leaving the three of us with his wife.

"You're taking this really well," I said to her after a minute of us sitting there awkwardly.

"It was difficult to believe that he used to wake up every time he died and was alive when my great-great-grandparents were born, but he's worth it," she told me. "I asked about the painting when he showed me the attic. He explained that she was his wife, who died, but he ran into one of their descendants who was the spitting image of her and nearly had a heart attack."

"At least you were prepared."

"Oh, nothing surprises me now," she assured me.

ALARIC CAME DOWN with a round hat box that held their marriage license, partially disintegrated letters, and an old pair of glasses.

"Were these hers?" I asked hopefully.

"Oliver's," he said sadly, picking them up. "But this was hers," he found a handkerchief underneath them. "Her something blue," he smiled.

"Do you mind if I take it?" I asked. "I don't know if you'll be able to get it back after I'm done with it," I warned.

"A decade ago, I might have held on, but I'm good now," he looked over to Sarah.

"Thank you. You have no idea what this means."

"It means someone else won't have to lose you like I lost her," he let me know he understood.

"Daddy, we're hungry," one of the girls came in and tugged on Alaric's sleeve.

"Is that so?" he asked her.

"Yes, and it's nearly supper time, and Poppy was thinking we could maybe have chicken nuggets."

"Poppy thought that?" he questioned her.

"Yes," the girl lied, but she was committed.

"Would you like to stay for supper?" Sarah offered.

"We wouldn't want to impose," I argued.

"It would be our pleasure," she told me. "We don't entertain nearly enough, and Ric always makes industrious quantities of chicken nuggets."

"We can stay," Embry assured me.

"DID YOU KNOW JUDITH'S PARENTS?" I asked Alaric once he put the nuggets in the oven. Sarah was making a salad, and the guys were talking in hushed voices.

"I did," there was a question to his answer.

"We thought Annabelle was the earliest one who looked like me. I'm wondering if there was another one before Judith."

"When I met Cassandra, she wondered the same thing," he admitted.

"Did she find out?"

"She left before we could do any research, but I tried to look into it for her."

"What did you discover?"

"This was centuries ago, so I was working with a very limited paper trail, but I found a few generations at the County Records Office in town."

"That's really helpful. I'll check it out in the morning," I told him.

"Do you already have a place to stay?"

"We do, but thank you for the offer."

"You're always welcome here," he assured me.

. . .

THE NUGGETS WERE DELICIOUS. Alaric's daughters, Poppy and Violet, were hilarious and adorable with their British accents. I could tell the guys were uncomfortable and only said we could stay to let me find out more about Judith's ancestry, so I declined Sarah's offer of cake.

"Thank you so much for everything," I told Alaric, giving him a hug. It was nice to find out about a decent male ancestor of mine for a change.

"It was my pleasure," he smiled. I believed he meant it, even though I brought up so many sad moments of his life. "And Lucy, I hope you succeed," he told me.

"Me too," I agreed.

GABRIEL DROVE us back to the bed-and-breakfast, with neither of us talking much.

"How many do you think we have left?" Embry wondered as we climbed the stairs.

"I don't know, but we'll have to make sure before we attempt the spell. It said all of them, and I don't want to see what happens if we only have some," Gabriel was concerned.

"Ric says there were records at the County Records Office. We could go there and trace back from Judith, like researching a family tree," I suggested.

"Keep going back until we can't go back any further," Embry shrugged, which didn't sound good to anyone.

"I also have the dreams... hopefully they can help steer us in the right direction."

"We'll head out first thing in the morning," Gabriel decided.

"After breakfast?" I asked with a smile. "The brochure says that her clotted cream is the best in the country."

"We can grab a quick bite," Embry smiled and ruffled my hair before we went to the rooms. The guys were sharing one with two double beds, while I got the king to myself. I closed the adjoining door while I changed and got ready for bed, but left it open for the night, in case anything happened.

It was weird, because everything was still scary, and I was hunting down an unknown number of needles in a field of haystacks, but Sam being alive and finding Judith's handkerchief made me feel like somehow, I might get through this.

The following morning, we drove into town to get a look at the records. The three of us walked into the building together, but Gabriel and I stayed back while Embry used his Gift to make the woman behind the desk trust him.

"They're public records. You can't take the books out, but anyone can access them," she assured him.

"Thank you."

He nodded for us to follow him to the second story of the building, which was set up like a very small library, only all the books were basically ledgers and registries.

"Is there an index?" Gabriel asked, but I was already going through the cards by the desk. It was empty, and by the looks of it, no one ever worked there. It was more for people consulting the books.

I found Judith and Ric's marriage certificate, then used that to track down her birth certificate. "They hold death, marriage and birth certificates in the blue books. Now that I know Judith was born in 1540 to George and Irene, I can look up when her parents were born and find their parents and so on," I explained what I was doing.

"I'll look into her father," Embry went to get the right year for him, while Gabriel went to get her mother's, and I scribbled down everything about Judith that might eventually be useful.

"I THINK I'VE FOUND ONE," I ventured, stumbling upon an ancestor with a mother named Kiara. "You needed parental consent to marry before twenty-one, but her mother was deceased," I showed them the marriage certificate.

"Kiara?" Embry asked. Thanks to 'Kiara's Cure', the name itself was enough to tell me we had to look into it.

"According to Saoirse's birth certificate, she was born in Ireland," I handed it over.

"Meaning we have to find the building like this in Ireland to go any further?" Gabriel verified.

"We also have the place Saoirse was born. If it was a family home they had for generations…" I let the thought linger, not sure what I was hoping to find other than memories. Unless a relative of mine was still living there, it was very unlikely that I would find any kind of paperwork in an old house.

"Haven't they digitized all of this yet?" Embry asked, putting the books we were no longer using back on their shelves.

"Not anywhere that I can find without raising suspicions," I turned him down. I wanted to google all this recent information to find out more, but if they were using computer chips to track us, I was not going to chance it.

"What's on your mind?" Gabriel asked when I stared at the word 'deceased'.

"Do you think Henry had anything to do with it, or he just started hunting us with Annabelle?" I asked. "Do either of you know how old he really is?"

"Older than us, but I don't know more than that," Gabriel told me.

"I wonder if he knew all of them." I thought back to my memories of him. "He didn't look like he knew Annabelle when he saved her, but he might have spotted her from a distance and approached her because he knew she was one of them. But he seemed genuinely surprised when she could do magic…"

"You can check his memories after we kill him," Gabriel didn't appreciate my intimate knowledge of him. He worried that the more I knew about Henry, the harder it would be for me to harm him, or allow them to, once we got to it. He underestimated how much I despised the man.

"I'll find us a boat," Embry sighed.

"A real one, or…"

"They have ferries to Ireland, I'll do my best," he told me before we followed him outside.

We already had all of our possessions, so we drove the rental car back to one of the company's locations and made our way to the ferry on foot. Embry took us through a shortcut to avoid the larger crowds.

"Have you lived in the United Kingdom?" I asked him. He hadn't used a map since we landed.

"Not exactly. I've visited many times, stayed for longer stretches, but never long enough to buy a place to call my own."

"You stayed with…" I let it linger. I knew they were both in love with Annabelle and utterly devoted to her, at least until Embry met Beth, but I couldn't imagine that they never even entertained the thought of any other women for those three centuries.

"Other Gifted, mostly."

"Delia is from here, originally," Gabriel shared. "Still has family in the area, but I couldn't risk contacting her. Or them."

"Are they okay?" I asked. I last saw Delia when she, Tristan and Benjamin travelled to Florida to be decoys for me, Gabriel and Embry. She had told Gabriel she missed him, but I didn't think there was anything there. Or maybe I didn't want there to be.

"They left word that they made it safely. I haven't heard that they asked for help, but such a request wouldn't have come to us. It would have gone to someone else in the network who was closer and not busy protecting you."

"Is she who you stayed with?" I asked Embry.

Before he had the chance to answer, a man with long black hair and an eyebrow ring walked over from the street and stopped right in front of me. My breath caught in my chest as I brought my hands up, waiting to see his eyes, or for him to make a move to tell me if he was just a tourist, or someone trying to kill me.

"You came," he said as five other people arrived and stood around us. I had yet to master 360° freezing, so I couldn't take care of everyone at once, but I also wanted to know what he was talking about.

"How did you find us?" I asked the man who, for the moment, seemed more intent on scaring me than killing me.

"We've been waiting for you."

"In this alley?" I looked around to see if there was something special about it, but came up short.

"Don't play innocent," he warned. "You won't get it."

"Get what?" I asked, but he had already pulled out his weapon, as did all of his friends. I knew I couldn't freeze them all, but I wasn't prepared to blow them into smithereens either.

I put up my shield when he came at me and sent him flying back into some garbage bins. The guys each took on two of the assailants, meaning I didn't have a clear shot until they stood still. I grabbed a discarded piece of wood from the pile of trash nearest me and hit one of the men attacking Embry. I thought I got him on the head and incapacitated him at least a little, but he turned around and faced me with nothing but anger and annoyance.

He charged at me, sending some kind of blue light ahead of him, so I quickly put up my force shield. He bounced back, but not nearly as far as people usually did. This angered him further, but Gabriel was down to one attacker, so he stabbed him in the stomach with the dagger and came to my defense. His speed was the only thing that put him on somewhat of an equal footing with the man, who had the build of a lumberjack and seemed unfazed by most of our attacks. When I got a clear shot, I froze him, which allowed Gabriel to knock him out for good.

"Follow me." Embry called out once all of our attackers were on the ground, though I wasn't naïve enough to believe they would stay there. We ran through a couple of alleys, to the busier streets, and didn't stop until we got to the docks.

"WE'LL TAKE three tickets to Ireland," Embry told the woman, charming her with his Gift while we tried to look normal.

"They're boarding in a few minutes," she gave him a smile as she handed them over.

"What were they doing there?" I asked, looking worriedly back to the city, but no one was following us as we headed for the line at the end of the dock.

"How would he know we would be here? Judith lived hours from here, and those men weren't following us. They were waiting for us," Gabriel was upset, but I appreciated him thinking out loud instead of in hushed voices with Embry once I was no longer around.

"Do you think they have another tracker on us?"

"No, I think there is something here that Henry expects us to be after," Embry argued.

"Do you know exactly where we were when they found us?" I asked.

"A tiny alley."

"I know that, but was there anything nearby? A museum with relics from Crescent Moon Bearers, a magic shop with grimoires… he told me there was a spell, but I don't think he would know we found it…" I was thinking out loud.

"We can't assume he doesn't know everything we do. We need to act like he has spies following us every step of the way," Gabriel argued.

"There's an old bookshop but I don't think it has any occult origins. There's business buildings close by, a church, shopping…"

"A church might make sense. You said Henry's people couldn't go into churches, which could explain why they were waiting in an alley," I suggested.

"It's an old church, I don't even think they have a museum or anything. It's not a tourist attraction," Embry argued.

"What's it called?"

"Sacred Heart."

We got to the end of the line and stood behind a girl who looked to be about fourteen, travelling with an older woman in a wheelchair, doing patchwork by the looks of it.

"Excuse me, is that a pamphlet for Sacred Heart?" I asked, noticing the paper in her hand. It was like a newsletter, only it had the name of the church and an enormous picture of a cross on the front of it.

"It's just the weekly catholic newsletter or something. It's hers," she told me before bending down closer to the older woman, who reacted when she heard the name of the church. She said something to her in a language I didn't understand, before turning to me, "She says they have mass at 7 every evening, but you wouldn't make it back in time," she dismissed the older woman.

"Is it worth checking out on our way back?" I asked, sensing something from the way the woman looked at me.

"She says their old priest now lives in Rome, and he brought the Lignum Crucis this week to celebrate the church's anniversary or something," the girl translated.

"What's the Lignum Crucis?" I asked her.

"The true cross," she told me. "Any authentic fragments of the cross Christ was crucified on are known as Lignum cruces."

"Thank you so much," I smiled at the teenager, who took out headphones and put them in before I could ask her any more questions.

"That's Emmanuel's Betrayal," I turned to the guys and whispered, using the spell's term for the Cross Jesus was crucified on. "That has to be it."

"Why would Henry think we were going after the ingredients to the ritual?" Embry asked.

"He already said he has all the ingredients except for you, so it's not like we can collect them first and stop him," Gabriel shared.

"And the coalescence is a ritual only he can do, right?" I looked from one to the other, but they both shrugged.

"Not necessarily. We are here to protect you, but that doesn't mean that someone else can't stand in the way of you getting hurt. Your destiny is shaped by many things," Gabriel explained.

"We can complete the ritual instead of him?" I confirmed what he was saying, momentarily disregarding the fact that it involved ripping out my heart.

"I don't know enough about the ritual to answer you as far as magic goes, but I know that even if he is staying alive to complete it, that doesn't mean that someone else couldn't."

"But Henry definitely thinks we're going after the ritual's ingredients."

"Which means we could stay under the radar by not going after them," Embry understood what I was hinting at.

"But if we're supposed to be getting them, shouldn't we?"

"Do you think it can help us?" Gabriel wasn't so quick to turn me down, but he didn't look convinced either.

"Even before I knew that magic was real, I knew that you can't bring people back to life. If Annabelle and Beth had the spell but never used it, I'm thinking it can't be so easy as putting some things in a bowl and saying a few words."

"You think only someone who has completed the ritual can use the spell?" Gabriel turned to Embry to see what he thought of it.

"That would explain why he thinks we're going after it. The ritual ingredients were in public books, and lots of people tried to complete it. But Kiara's cure, based on the name, was probably tailor-made for my family."

"Is this something you want to do?" Embry asked me, resigning himself to it.

"I don't want to, but I would much rather have one of you cut my heart out and have undying power than Henry."

"Then it's settled. We're getting all the ingredients," he sighed, neither of them happy about it.

CHAPTER FOURTEEN

"It's so beautiful," I said, mostly to myself, but Gabriel was beside me, so he took a break from watching the other passengers to take in the scenery. The ferry to Ireland was better than a boat, but I still preferred land travel. We were nearing our third hour, and I was ready to get off.

"It's green," was his response.

"It's luscious green. I have never wanted to run through a field and roll around in the grass, but I want to do that now."

He looked at me like he was suddenly struck by how young and immature I was.

"Nothing excites you anymore?" I asked, turning to face him instead of the view.

"I guess I'm letting the context get in the way. You look at it as a silver lining, but I'm looking at all the places people could hide, marred by memories..."

"What memories?" I asked him.

"I have happy ones, like spending weeks with Terrence's family when I was best man at his wedding, but there have been wars and famines and escaping dangerous people...."

"With Cassie?"

"Sometimes I help other people," he admitted.

"With the FBI?" I whispered, but more to tease him than to keep it a secret.

"There are amazing people in the world who see someone in need and go out of their way to help them. There are other people who see a weakness and exploit it. Who see something they want and take it, whether it belongs to them or not. When those people have Gifts, they believe the normal rules don't apply to them. We have the safe houses for those types of situations, but sometimes it's safest to be constantly moving."

"We have time, if you wanted to give me an example of these people," I pointed out. It would be at least another hour until we arrived in Ireland.

"Maybe forty years ago, there was a Gifted who decided his task was to liberate all the child soldiers of the world. It was a beautiful dream, and his Gift was that he could open anything, so he could easily free them once he found them. He got some hired guns for protection, but it cost a lot of lives, both from him and from the children he wanted to rescue. He recuperated at the safe house a few times when a friend of Caleb's was the guardian, and the conversation turned to Etta and her Gift. The guy saw this as his solution to save all the kids, but instead of bringing the injured to her or asking if she could help, he kidnapped her, chained her to the back of a van and forced her to fix people for him."

"That's... he was trying to do a good thing in a terrible way," I tried to translate my thoughts into words.

"Our callings can drive us mad. Especially if you don't have an end in sight. Was it one particular child he had to save, or did he have to keep saving them until there were no more child soldiers? I'm sure he started out with the best of intentions, but he eventually built his own army of unwilling soldiers."

"Did you just rescue her, or did you take care of him too? Are there prisons for Gifteds?" I asked, so many questions floating around my mind.

"There is one prison that has a section to contain Gifteds. There are rooms and devices that can contain Gifts, but before that they would cater the room to the Gifted. When I was a government man, there was a block of cells we visited, where the guards wore hazmat suits tailored to the Gift. As long as they couldn't touch you, you couldn't hear them or look into their eyes, you were safe."

"That seems like..."

"A lot of trouble. There are Gifteds who, although they're not bad people, don't like being locked up, or held accountable for the things they do. A lot of them will hang themselves to get out, but if you stumble upon someone who knows what you are... it's not like we did that for every Gifted who got arrested, but if the crime was violent, we kept them contained."

"Which prison?" I asked. "Guantanamo, Alcatraz..."

"Rikers," he shared. "But don't tell anyone I told you, because it is way above your clearance level."

"My lips are sealed," I assured him with a smile.

I convinced him to tell me more about his times in Ireland, finally getting him to admit that the Emerald Isle could be beautiful if you weren't on the run or fighting for your life, before Embry came back with food.

"What did I miss?" He asked, handing me a chicken and pesto panini.

"I'd say we're about an hour out, but I can see it and it's gorgeous," I filled him in.

"Half an hour according to the screens inside, but I'm glad you're enjoying this boat ride," he smiled.

"Enjoying is a stretch, but it's the best I've had yet."

"At least you've got delightful company?" Embry tried.

"And time to go over the Chronicles, the Book of Shadows, and everything we know about Henry's ritual."

"Did you come to any conclusions?" Gabriel asked me.

"We know of six ingredients needed to complete it. The kindling from Emmanuel's Betrayal is what those men were trying to stop us from getting. They can't possibly be watching every single piece of the cross, because there are thousands. But then again, none of them can prove their authenticity. The church recognizes some as more likely, but that's it."

"Our best bet would be to collect all of them and hope at least one of them is real," Gabriel said like it was a plan rather than an impossible setback.

"The soul of his untouched child just means a virgin, which sounds sketchy, but since my life is at stake either way, I might as well risk my soul," I swallowed, aware that my face was burning red at that admission. "Tears of Isis are the easiest, because you can buy vervain pretty much everywhere."

"The arms of Yggdrasil?" Embry pressed.

"That's where it gets complicated. Yggdrasil is an imaginary tree that connects the Nine Worlds in Norse mythology."

"What does that mean?" Gabriel furrowed his brow.

"It means I have no idea where we can find it because it's a mythical thing and no one knows where it is."

"Henry said he had everything except for your heart," Embry pointed out that it couldn't be imaginary.

"We'll figure it out," Gabriel stated.

I wanted to argue with his optimism, but I could tell it was determination and he would get it done. "The blood of the incumbent means whoever does it has to prick themselves," I moved on to the next ingredient. "And we all know about my heart," I finished.

"Which he will never get," Embry assured me.

"Fingers crossed," I agreed, getting him to roll his eyes at me. "I've also been trying to figure out how Beth got Kiara's cure. I think she and Cassie knew more than they let on," I bit my bottom lip and looked to Embry for his reaction.

"We didn't keep any secrets," he gave me an intense stare that could rival Gabriel's, then sighed, "But she liked to research and look into things on her own. She might have found something she was waiting to get more information on before sharing with me."

I gave him a smile before looking back out at the expanse of our destination. He seemed convinced, but there had to be a reason no one ever mentioned a spell that could save us to the men responsible for protecting us. Maybe we were right, and it didn't work unless you completed the ritual first. Perhaps it came with terrible consequences that they weren't prepared to pay. Either way, I hoped Ireland held the answers we were looking for. But I had a bad feeling about what we would find.

CHAPTER FIFTEEN

When we finally docked in Ireland, I was more than happy to set foot on solid ground, even if I still felt wobbly. We used a tourist map to find the address Saoirse was born at in 1462, not expecting to find much, since we knew she ended up in England, but I was expecting more than a literal pile of rubble.

"The parish church should have some records," Embry put his hand on my shoulder.

"Maybe they'll have a family plot in the cemetery," I was staying optimistic, but I was no genealogist, and the farther back we went, the harder it would be to track my ancestors down. Not to mention we had no way of knowing when the first one of us appeared.

It was a short walk to the parish cathedral made of large stones. I took the 'est. 1225' as a good sign for finding information on Kiara, but we wouldn't be able to go much further than that.

"Good morning," a priest walked over and whispered as soon as we opened the doors. "Are you here for the mass?"

"No, we're..." I looked back to the guys, but it was a small building, and everyone looked busy at the moment. "Yes, we are," I decided.

"Wonderful, it's just starting," he ushered us over to some pews near the back. I made sure to kneel and do the sign of the cross before taking my seat.

I hadn't been in church for ages. Mrs. Boyd used to bring me with her, but after she died, Mr. Boyd didn't see the point in it. *'God is everywhere. Why should I have to go to church to talk to him?'* was his answer the one time I asked about it.

I only said yes to put us in the priest's good graces and not disturb the mass, but being back in a church brought me so many questions. I always believed in God and Jesus Christ in a very compartmental way. When they taught us about the Big Bang in school, I listened and accepted it as fact. But I also knew that God created the earth and man and woman and everything I read in the Bible. Both facts existed in my brain simultaneously, as long as I never tried to consider which was right.

I spent most of the service trying to figure out what I believed in, given my new knowledge of Magic and Gifted and the upheaval of everything I took for granted. By the end, I decided I needed a third compartment to make sense of it all and allow magic, religion and science to co-exist in my mind.

We followed the dozen or so congregation members towards the exit, but the priest who let us in stopped us before we could talk to the priest who said mass.

"Are you interested in a tour as well?" he asked us. He was a plain man in his forties, but he had a smile that made his eyes twinkle.

"That would be lovely," I said, speaking for the group again.

"I'm Father Dunn," he extended his hand to shake mine, then did the same for Gabriel and Embry. "What brings you to Killaloe?"

"I've been working on my family tree, and one of my ancestors was born a few minutes from here back in 1462," I gave him a partial answer.

"That's exciting!" his enthusiasm seemed genuine, but misplaced for someone his age, in his profession. "I grew up not even ten minutes from here. What's the name?" he asked.

"Saoirse Muldoon," I shared, reading his face for any sign of recollection. The guys were staying close, but so far letting me handle it.

"Don't know any Muldoons in town, but we have records going back to the late fifteenth century, if you want to know more about it," he offered.

"That would be brilliant, thank you."

HE BROUGHT us to a small office in the back and went through stacks of black volumes before he found the one he was looking for. "We've been digitizing the records to make them more comprehensible. Faded ink and elegant handwriting are not helpful when trying to decipher names and dates," he shared.

"This is incredible, thank you," I flipped through the printed pages representing church records of the time.

"You can't search by people, but if you know when in 1462, you can find the entry that records her birth."

"January 1st," I found her faster than I would have expected. "If her mother was born here, would she also be in the book?"

"This is the oldest book we have. It goes all the way back to 1425. We lost anything before then in a fire."

"Deaths too?" Embry inquired.

"Anything a priest would have presided over," he agreed. "Can I fetch you all some tea?"

"Thank you," Gabriel told him.

It surprised me that he left us alone in the office, but it seemed to be a pretty small town.

"You're going to go through every page?" Embry asked me.

"We know she died before 1480, so it's just eighteen years," I said, flipping through the pages. "Kiara Muldoon died in 1468," I showed them. "They found it shocking, probably because she was only twenty-eight."

"Can you remember anything?" Gabriel tried.

"Maybe if I touched her tombstone, or we can go back to the pile of rocks later?"

"Let's see how far back we can go, then we'll ask Father Dunn about her grave," Embry suggested.

I KEPT SEARCHING when Father Dunn came back with the teas, scribbling names and dates onto a post-it while Embry and he discussed World War One. I wouldn't have pegged him as such a war aficionado, but Embry recognized a medal on the desk and the conversation was never-ending.

"Did you find what you were looking for?" Father Dunn asked when I closed the volume. Kiara was either first generation, or her parents were born before the fire.

"This was really helpful," I agreed. "Do you think you could point us to where she was buried?"

"Let me see," he came over to see her death entry that I bookmarked, but got uncomfortable as he read the information. "She's not in our plot," he told me delicately.

"What do you mean?" I asked, going back to the book. I saw nothing wrong with her entry, other than a few symbols underneath her name, but every death notice had a variety of symbols.

"This symbol here means she'll be in the Cillin," he waited for me to understand, but I didn't.

"What's a Cillin?" I asked.

"It's a special burial place for stillborn babies, and the ones that die before we can baptize them," Gabriel filled me in, but he directed it at the priest, since Kiara was neither.

"It's for anyone who didn't have the right to a proper catholic burial."

"As in she wasn't catholic?" I pressed.

"It says she committed suicide."

"She killed herself?" I was shocked, and by the looks of it, so were Embry and Gabriel.

"I'm sorry," he apologized. "The closest one isn't that far, but they're unmarked graves."

"Might be worth a look," I tried to smile in gratitude. It wasn't that she killed herself that bothered me; it was the idea that she did it because the bad guys were closing in, and they buried her as a sinner because she sacrificed herself to save the world.

"Here, I'll write down the directions for you, and if there's anything else I can help you with, just let me know," he handed me another post-it, so we thanked him for the teas and headed out.

We left by the back of the church to follow the Father's directions and encountered a colossal statue of the Virgin Mary in the courtyard.

"Henry definitely had something to do with it," I bit my bottom lip and looked up at them. I still wasn't sure I believed that he was evil from the start of his relationship with Annabelle, but I couldn't face the idea that Kiara just gave up. Especially when she's the one they named the Cure after.

"Or someone like him," Gabriel agreed, which surprised

me. He was the last person I expected to hear defending Henry, of all people.

"That's probably why they moved to England."

"It would have been quite the scandal," Embry agreed.

I absent-mindedly ran my fingers along the bottom of the statue, but as soon as my hand touched the smooth rock, everything went blurry...

From what I could tell, I looked exactly like myself, and all the other Bearers, but I was someone new. I'd been through it with Beth, but it was still a shock to feel the baby kick my bladder. The woman whose memory I was in, probably Kiara, didn't even notice the kick. She was staring up at the Virgin Mary statue, with tears pouring down her face and a war between guilt and determination in her heart.

She left the statue and scurried through the streets, looking over her shoulder like she was being followed and expected an attack at any moment. She turned down a street where it seemed like the sun vanished. As if the clouds of smoke from the chimneys all converged together to block out any light. I shivered and, though she stood tall and kept walking, she pulled her shawl tighter around herself.

When she got to a rather large wooden shack with dead animals hanging beside the doorway, she paused and took a deep breath. She brought her hand to her bulging stomach and rubbed it protectively, taking more deep breaths to stop the tears that had been threatening to fall ever since this memory started. One more and she knocked.

"I was hoping you wouldn't come," the woman said as a greeting. She left the door open, but that was the only welcome Kiara got as the woman went back to chopping something putrid-smelling and purple.

"If there were any other option, I wouldn't have," Kiara looked right into the woman's eyes, her jaw set.

"This is dark magic, love. Not the kind you can take back," the old woman softened, but still looked disappointed. Her hair was just as curly as mine, but much longer and blonde. Her face had many

wrinkles, but I would have bet money she got them from smiling more than frowning. Except today.

"I know."

"Are you sure about this Kiara? Curses come with consequences that no one can predict. Putting a curse on yourself doubles the danger."

"Saoirse is far away and safe with her father, but if they get me, it won't matter where they are or what we do. The power they would gain is unimaginable. They would be unstoppable, wreaking havoc on the world, immune to any manmade weapons, resistant to most magic... if one life can save millions, how can I not?"

"But it isn't just one life, is it?" the woman eyed Kiara's stomach, which she cradled protectively.

"They're still a few days out and he's nearly ready."

"You'll wait?" for the first time, the woman was hopeful.

"I will do everything in my power to keep him safe," my voice shook and the tears slowly rolled down my cheeks. But Kiara's determination did not waver.

"God help you," the woman shook her head before grabbing two pieces of paper from a small wooden chest, and a handful of powders.

"You couldn't have called it Kiara's Brave Sacrifice?" she asked, reading the title of the first paper while the woman crushed the powders together. Kiara's Curse sounded intriguing until you realized it was Kiara's Curse on Kiara.

"I call it as I see it, not as you wish it to be."

"And this reverses it?" she asked of the second sheet.

"It ends the Curse. As long as you haven't done the unspeakable, it will be like this never happened."

"It won't be in my lifetime," Kiara said it to herself, reading the Cure I'd already seen in the Chronicles. "Is all of this necessary?"

"It's a simple list of items you have in your chest at home," the woman sounded exasperated with Kiara's being difficult, but Kiara knew she wouldn't be the one using the Cure. It was nice of her to

realize that her descendants wouldn't find the list as easy to track down, but she might have considered preparing us for it.

"Of course. Is it ready?" the powders she had been mixing were producing a yellow cloud of smoke that moved like it was alive, unmolested by the wind, smelling out its environment.

"Give me your hand," the old woman sighed. I would have thought she was annoyed, or bored, but there was something in her eyes that made me think she cared so much that this was the only way she could get through what she was about to do. As soon as I gave her my left hand, she sliced it open with a tiny blue blade. The drops of my blood sizzled once they touched the powder, turning the smoke to a rust-like color.

"Warning would have been nice." I said, but the woman put her finger on top of the wound and used my blood to paint a crescent moon on her forehead.

"If I give myself the chance, I will change my mind," she explained her abrupt manner. "Have you memorized it?"

"I have."

"Then take my hand, sister, let ye be damned," her steely gaze broke as her glassy eyes watered. We held hands and started chanting in a language I didn't understand. The Curse was long, but they repeated it over and over, so it no longer sounded like words, but like a melody; dark and ominous, but also beautiful. The powder caught fire and the rust-colored smoke filled the room.

When the chanting stopped, we lifted our hands to the sky, and the fire exploded, but it was like the smoke and the flames, all the energy in the room shot into my nose and mouth, hitting me right inside my chest. I was still standing, but I wouldn't be surprised if you told me Kiara died then and there.

"I told you it wasn't to be taken lightly," the woman warned, but there was more kindness to her now that it was done. She went to get a cup and filled it with boiling water and herbs, ushering me to take a seat.

"Is this a part of it?" Kiara asked of the Curse.

"This is for your nerves, your heart and protection."

"I've never seen anything like them, Nell. There are hundreds of them, each driven mad with this quest for power. I've watched them die and come back to life, seen them murder without a second thought. If they unlock the powers, it will be hell on earth."

I finished my hot water and stood, taking a cylinder from my bag and handing it to her.

"I don't want payment for this one," Nell argued, pushing it away.

"Take it as payment for the Cure then. Or as a thank you for always being there for me."

"I'll take it when you use it," she decided.

"Thank you, Nell. You're a loyal friend."

"Not a good one," she argued, but she still let me take her in for a hug.

I LEFT the wooden shack and walked along the road back to the church, but the world went fuzzy again, until I was in a stony cottage, my heart racing with fear. I also felt overwhelming pain, not from any wound that I could see, but from a primal place that tore through my heart and soul. I was holding a dagger in my right hand, while the left one rubbed my still-pregnant stomach. I took so many deep breaths, but nothing calmed me down in the least.

I stood in the middle of the room, facing the front door, ready. I couldn't hear anything other than my own heartbeat, pounding in my ears, but I could feel them. It was like when Donovan got to Embry's villa. I couldn't feel any individual person, but there was so much magic, more than I could even imagine, coming at me from all sides.

The closer they got, the more panicked Kiara got, her breathing more difficult, until the magic got closer than she was comfortable with. It moved faster, rushing at her. I looked out the window and saw an army of men, women and creatures, ready to strike. My *breathing calmed. I let out one last deep breath, then drove the dagger through my heart.*

I WOKE up and heard screaming, before understanding that it was me.

"Kiara?" Embry asked, looking worried, but I was in Gabriel's arms, and he looked downright horrified. "What happened?"

The look in Gabriel's eyes told me that this was one of those times where I didn't just pass out, I acted parts of it out, so he knew exactly what happened.

"They were coming, and I knew I couldn't stop them. No matter how hard I fought I was alone and there were so many of them, and they would do terrible things to so many people and I didn't have any other choice," I said, Kiara's thoughts mixing with mine.

"Let's get you somewhere safe," Gabriel decided, lifting me up in his arms as if I weighed nothing. I wanted to tell him I was fine, that I could walk, so he really didn't have to... but I felt so safe in his arms that I let him.

CHAPTER SIXTEEN

We rented a room at another bed-and-breakfast. I think the guys liked their non-digitized check-in systems, but I worried that if anyone found us, the somewhat nosy proprietors might interfere and get hurt more than the minimum-wage employees at a chain hotel.

There was a coffeemaker on the bureau, so Embry made me some tea. I took a sip, feeling a chill despite being all bundled up on one of the double beds. My head was killing me, but I tried not to show it, keenly aware of their eyes on me.

"I'm sorry I reacted like that. I've seen worse," I tried to figure out why it hit me so hard, but I knew. Kiara not only gave up the fight and took her own life, she took her unborn child's.

"Seeing things isn't the same as living through them," Gabriel assured me.

"I was Kiara, obviously, and she knew people were after her. She went to a witch who gave her both Kiara's Cure, and Kiara's Curse. The witch, Nell, she wasn't happy about it, but she cursed her. She said there would be unexpected consequences, but Kiara was prepared for that."

They gave me a moment to compose myself and keep going, but when I didn't, Embry asked, "What did the curse do?"

"I'm not sure, but she called it a sacrifice. The room filled with smoke and it shot into me. I thought it killed me, but it didn't."

"But you did die, right?" Gabriel had the same look in his eyes from when I woke up in his arms.

"Not exactly. I could feel them coming, like Ingrid felt Donovan. They were so powerful and there were so many of them. She didn't have Gifteds protecting her, so when they got close enough," I took a deep breath and closed my eyes before continuing, "she put the dagger through her own heart."

Gabriel put his hand on mine like he didn't really know what to say, but he could see there was more. They also knew that calling it her heart might be accurate, but I was still inside her when she did it.

"Your dagger?" Embry asked the least invasive of all the questions he must have.

"I don't think so," I shook my head. I was more concentrated on what was going on inside. "I know it's a long stretch, but I could bring us to the witch's place tomorrow in case there's anything." I didn't expect Nell to still be living there, but magic seemed to be something passed down through generations, so her grimoire might be there somewhere. Otherwise I might get another memory, preferably of when Kiara asked for it, so I could know what the smoke did that was so terrible, compared to killing two birds with one dagger.

"First thing in the morning," Embry said, but they were both looking at me like I might break at any moment.

"I... she was pregnant," I admitted, wiping the warm tears that fell as I did. I didn't mean to be this affected, but I couldn't help it. I kept thinking of Cassie, who lost so many babies, and how broken Kiara was when she did it. "She said it was a boy, but I don't know how she would know..."

Gabriel gave my hand a squeeze and looked at me like he wanted to wrap me in his arms and take the pain away, but he couldn't. Embry let in a sharp breath and couldn't meet my eyes. I knew he was thinking of his son, Jackson, that they never thought they'd be able to have, who died before having a family of his own, like all the sons in my family.

"That was the consequence, wasn't it?" I asked, but it was mostly rhetorical. Kiara killed her son, so her descendants were cursed to endure heartache after heartache, as a reminder.

"You said she didn't have a choice," Gabriel emphasized the 'she' to remind me that although I was holding the knife and did it, I was just reliving a memory of something someone else did roughly five centuries ago.

"I don't know. She didn't think she did, but I don't know if she even tried running or fighting or if she just..."

"Gave up," Gabriel finished for me. I made the mistake of looking into his dark eyes, which were so intense that I nearly got lost in them. "You said it yourself that she didn't have us," he reminded me. "I will not let that happen to you. We will fight, we will run, and I will keep you safe."

"What if you can't?" I asked quietly, wanting so badly to believe him.

"That isn't an option," he said simply, but looking into those eyes, I believed him.

"Why don't you get some sleep and we'll start again in the morning?" Embry suggested, coming over to take the empty mug from me. He pulled down the bedsheets so I could climb in, then placed them back on top of me, along with the blankets I'd been bundled up in since we arrived.

He put his hand on mine and gave me an apologetic smile, but a calm washed over me. I knew exactly what he was doing, but for once I didn't mind. The headache disappeared, and I got so tired that I couldn't keep my eyes open. It was scary how quickly his Gift sent me into dreamland, but I prayed I wouldn't have any.

CHAPTER SEVENTEEN

I slept in the next morning, either naturally or because of Embry's Gift. I replaced my shock and sadness with a determination to sort this out and reverse the Curse before we lost more innocent lives. Not that I planned on getting pregnant and continuing the line while Henry still walked the earth, but if the Gifted taught me anything, it's that some things are predetermined and there isn't much you can do to stop them.

I LET Embry lead the way to the church's courtyard, then followed the path Kiara took, basing my directions off of which way I had to turn rather than landmarks, because nothing looked the same. I still had the directions Father Dunn gave us, but now that I knew why she was denied a proper burial, I wasn't sure I wanted to see it.

A cozy little tearoom with a chalkboard announcing the specials replaced the wooden shack from my memory. I stopped dead once I spotted it, causing Embry to nearly walk right into me.

"I think we're in luck," I said soberly.

"Which one is it?" they asked.

"The tearoom," I pointed, waiting for them to see it.

"Or that's a scary coincidence," Embry said of the crescent moon logo above the shop's door. It was an exact replica of the one on the back of my neck, only it was sideways. You could argue it was the outline of a mug with three marshmallows inside, but I wasn't that naïve.

WIND CHIMES ANNOUNCED OUR ARRIVAL, but the tearoom was empty. This was a small town with few tourists, and we were hours early for afternoon tea. I was surprised by how small the room was, given the size of the building. I was looking for something supernatural or out of place, but I felt like there was more to the little shop.

"Welcome to the tearoom. Can I get you a cream tea, afternoon tea or just regular tea?" the girl who came up to us was younger than me and clearly not the owner. We were interrupting her from whatever she'd been doing on her cell phone while walking over, and she was eager to serve us and get back to that.

"Cream tea has scones with jam and clotted cream, but afternoon tea has all the mini sandwiches and desserts," Embry told my confused look because the waitress wasn't going to.

"Afternoon tea," I decided. The original plan was just to come by and ask questions, maybe look around a bit, but we had to eat anyway, and I doubted this girl knew anything.

"Is this a family business?" I asked after the guys ordered the same.

"Not mine," she told me. "Miss Duncan is in the kitchen baking."

"Do you think I could ask her some questions? Once she's done baking."

"I'll tell her you asked," she assured me before going to put in our orders.

"I haven't had afternoon tea in at least a century," Embry looked excited, but it was possibly just for my benefit.

"Delia likes to drag me to these whenever I'm in town," Gabriel looked around the room, both like he was comparing it to the other tearooms and scoping out the security threats.

"I always thought it looked like the pinnacle of sophistication. I loved the idea of drinking tea and having an excuse to try every dessert they put in front of you."

"That's because you chose not to do cotillion," Embry stopped me from feeling sorry for myself.

"Have you been to those things?" I asked, but Embry shook his head. "I looked at the pamphlets. You learn how to do things like a proper lady, which sounded fun, but then you get introduced to society as the daughter of so and so, accompanied by so and so. I had one guy who talked to me in high school, but not so much that he would escort me to something like that. And Unknown just doesn't have the right ring to it."

"I would have proudly claimed you, as I'm sure Sam would have," Embry told me. I caught Gabriel in the corner of my eye, looking down at his plate. The realist in me figured he was trying not to hurt my feelings by not volunteering to do the same, but the optimist wondered if he would want to be the one to escort me, should the opportunity come up again.

"I doubt it would have helped with anything now," I shrugged it off.

"Here's your tea," the waitress put a large teapot in the middle of the table, where there was a small ceramic milk pot and a bowl with cubes of sugar inside. "Miss Duncan said she'd be happy to come 'round later."

"Thank you," I gave her a smile before pouring out the tea. I added one of the brown sugar cubes and milk to mine. This was one experience I had looked forward to when reading about them or watching movies, but real life wasn't measuring up. The tea was delicious, so that wasn't it, but even though this was nothing like the wooden shack, I still felt very uneasy here. The entire purpose of the trip also put a damper on any sightseeing or experiences we were having.

"Is any of it familiar?" Embry caught my mood.

"No, everything is different. When I came it was a wooden shack; every surface had jars or vials with powders and liquids… there was a big fire over there, but it wasn't any bigger than that," I used my arms to designate a corner of the shop.

"Which means the crescent is new."

"Or the coffee cup," I agreed. "Do you know any Gifteds named Duncan?"

"I know a guy whose first name is Duncan, but no one from around here," Gabriel shared.

"What can Duncan do?" I asked, mostly as a distraction.

"He took voices," there was an edge to his voice.

"Like Ursula in the Little Mermaid?" I asked.

"Maybe?" Gabriel looked unsure, as if he hadn't seen the movie.

"This wasn't a friend," I read his look. Not to mention, Duncan's Gift implied he took advantage of people.

"He was a slaveowner in his first life and a scream trader in every life after that."

"Scream trader?" I pressed.

"I never asked," he looked away, giving me the impression he was lying.

"Here are some scones with our homemade clotted cream and fig jam," the waitress gave each of us two scones, then went back to the kitchen and her cell phone.

I watched Gabriel put his clotted cream first, then a spoonful of fig jam to each half, while Embry spread the jam on one half and clotted cream on the other. Embry put the whole thing together like a sandwich, but Gabriel savored one half at a time, so I followed his lead.

"This is delicious," I said of my first bite.

"They're pretty good as far as scones go," Embry agreed.

"AFTERNOON TEA FOR THREE," the woman who carried out the multi-tiered plates was about fifty years old with the same long, blonde curly hair as Nell, only she had it all tied up in a bun. "I heard you had some questions?"

"My… my grandmother came here a long time ago, so I was wondering if this has been in your family for a long time," as I said it, it occurred to me how unlikely it would be that she was related to the woman who owned a wooden shack here centuries ago, but I still had that feeling.

"Since the sixteenth century," she agreed with a warm smile. "It hasn't always been a café though. We just used to sell trinkets and souvenirs, but this isn't the most touristic area."

"I like the logo," Embry mirrored her smile, so it sounded like a compliment, but he was fishing.

"Funny story," she smiled to herself, "the old shop used to have this moon and stars logo, which was ridiculous when we sold nothing related to astronomy. Or astrology. I can never tell those two apart, but we didn't have either of them here. Anyway, on the day the shop became mine, the sign fell. Only one end came loose, so it was hanging sideways above the doorway. I thought it looked like a coffee cup and this place was born."

"That's interesting," I said it with a smile, but the idea that my birthmark was their shop's logo gave me pause. "When you say the shop became yours…"

"Oh, my parents died in a car crash after my grandparents retired, so it all came to me," she said it fast, in that way I sometimes did so people wouldn't pity me for my tragic life story.

"I'm so sorry," I said.

"It was a long time ago, dear," she assured me. "Did your grandmother want you to pick something up for her?"

"I was hoping to find out more about this place in the sixteenth century," I shrugged, not sure how to find out where she stood on the supernatural without scaring her away.

"My grandmother could have told you all about it. I have some city stills of life back then if you'd like," she offered.

"City stills?" I asked.

"I don't know what else to call them, but I have five or six paintings upstairs, each one is just people living their day-to-day life."

"Painted now, or..."

"Then," she answered for me while heading to a staircase. She looked surprised that the guys followed, but didn't stop them. "My ancestor used to brew homemade remedies and stuff, with her customers paying in trades. One of them gave paintings and poems, though I'm not sure if they were all for remedies or just gifts."

"Is this that ancestor?" I asked, the portrait of Nell sticking out among all the cityscapes.

"This is the one that makes me think they were friends," she agreed.

"You say she brewed home remedies?" I probed.

"Remedies, potions, spells... whatever the people needed," she agreed.

I turned to her in shock, but she brought over a large volume to show me a handmade drawing of Kiara. "You're one as well?" I asked.

"Very minimally, but I felt it as soon as you came in. I

wasn't sure you were her until I checked the book," she explained.

"What do you know about me?" I asked, looking back at the guys who both tensed up, not as trusting as I was.

"You're in the grimoire that's passed down through the generations of my family. Nell wrote ninety percent of it, with a few spells added in along the way."

"What does it say?"

"It has Kiara's Curse and Kiara's Cure," she said, flipping through the pages. "But you're not Kiara, obviously."

"Lucy," I agreed. "Does it say what the Curse was?"

"Have any of the Bearers lived past twenty-eight?"

"No," I shook my head.

"When Kiara died, Nell added a paragraph with the drawing. The 'Curse' bound Kiara's Coalescent powers so the people hunting her couldn't get them, but provided a failsafe in case they did."

"How come she stabbed herself if the spell would have killed her?"

"The Curse works however it needs to. And from what I understand of the Prophecy, if she hadn't pierced through her heart, as long as they showed up within a few minutes, they would have been able to use it."

"Would you have anything of hers?" I asked, not needing her to confirm that our lack of male heirs was also because of the curse.

"Just the paintings," she shrugged, looking around at all the cityscapes.

"These are all hers?" I looked around as well.

"There's also a canvas in a preservation tube upstairs. It was payment for the Curse, and Nell refused to open it until Kiara used the cure. I never had that much self-restraint, but it felt wrong to hang it up," she shared. "It's yours if you want it."

"I would be eternally grateful," I told her as Embry took money out.

"That's not necessary," she told him. "We've spent generations trying to get rid of it without Nell cursing us for it, but I think she would approve. I'm guessing it's hard to track down objects belonging to women who died centuries ago."

"It is," I agreed. "But this really helps."

"You look like you've got a few years to figure it out," she tried to reassure me.

"Of course." She didn't need to know that I had doubts about making it through the week these days. "You wouldn't know how many Bearers came before Kiara, would you?" I asked, eyeing the volume that was open to the Cure page.

"I would guess... two," she said after counting under her breath. "Nell's spells all have ingredient counts at the bottom and this one has nine. That's daffodil, sage, aloe, bezoar, honeywater, something from her mother and her father, which leaves two for the Bearers that came before her."

"What's that?" I asked, noticing a scribble that wasn't on my copy either.

"It's Nell's handwriting... it just says veil with a question mark."

"Did she often scribble on spells?"

"It probably has something to do with Kiara, but I couldn't tell you what," she shrugged.

"Thank you so much. You've been incredibly helpful."

"It's what we're here for," she gave me a smile.

"Is there a reason the logo was a crescent moon with stars?" I asked as we were heading out.

"The crescent symbolizes life and death, fertility, womanhood... old Nell thought it represented her skills, since most people those days came here to get pregnant, to get rid of an unwanted pregnancy, or to poison people. I don't think she actually helped those last ones, but historically, that's what people asked for,"

"Thank you again," I told her before following the guys outside.

I got a flash of Kiara spotting the symbol painted on a rock outside the wooden shack and knocking with a smile, convinced she found a kindred spirit.

CHAPTER EIGHTEEN

We waited until we were at the hotel before opening the preservation tube, as she called it. It was a lot newer than the one Kiara had given Nell, which told me they took care of it, even if they wanted nothing to do with it.

"Should we leave it inside to protect it?" I asked, feeling nervous as Embry slowly removed the canvas from its casing. As the painter among us, we figured he was best suited for the task.

"This is the best we're likely to find for Kiara, but it might have a clue or something to point us in the direction of the first Bearers, if we are to believe Mrs. Duncan," Embry pointed out.

"And we need the object, it doesn't matter if it falls apart," Gabriel reassured my nerves as Embry started unrolling it.

At first, I thought it would be another city still, because I could only see the side of a stone house. But as he gently unrolled the canvas, it revealed a family. I would bet money that the laughing little girl was Saoirse, and the man her father.

"I think home would definitely mean a lot to her," I said,

since my primary concern for the painting was whether it meant something to her.

"But it doesn't tell us anything about the women who came before her," Embry sighed, disappointed.

"If we're down to two, it's just the ones mentioned in Beth's book; the one that told me about the Prophecy."

"Any idea where we find them?" Embry asked me.

"I hoped we would figure that out by working our way backwards, but I still have no idea who Saint Malachy or Talina and Zeke are," I looked from one to the other, who both shook their heads.

"Remind me exactly what the book said?" Gabriel asked.

"Something about the first mention of the Prophecy was in 1148 by Saint Malachy, talking about the miraculous light of angels," I tried to remember the exact words, but other than the names I wrote down, all I had were bits and pieces. "Then the actual spell was written in the part about Talina and Zeke, who apparently ruled from 1385 to 1460."

"Let's find their kingdom." Embry decided, guiding us to the local library.

THE KINGDOM of Talina and Zeke turned out to be a rather large island off the coast of Spain. It was known as La Isla de la Luna Encantada, or the Island of the Enchanted Moon, which told me we were definitely headed in the right direction. According to the one book we found that referenced it, a tsunami destroyed a large part of the island a couple hundred years ago, leaving only a small part of the majesty it once was. The book was from the sixties, so probably not the most accurate information, but it said there were still over twenty thousand people living on the island.

We flew a commercial flight to Spain, then took a boat to the island. I didn't want to take any chances with the Ocean waves, so I slowly sipped water with crushed ginger and lemon, keeping my eyes on the land in the distance.

"It'll help calm your stomach," Gabriel explained, handing me a pack of saltine crackers.

"Thank you," I gave him a grin, feeling ridiculous to be so affected by seasickness. "I'm sorry you can't hide me away from lurking eyes in one of the cabins below deck."

"As long as they wait until we're on dry land to attack, we should be good," he gave me a teasing smile.

"This is another time where levitating myself would have come in handy," I pointed out.

"I think I'd rather have you seasick than have to explain to everyone on this ship how come you're floating above them."

"Now you're just being difficult," I warned.

"My apologies, please continue with your marvelous plan."

"Thank you," I said graciously, but that was the extent of it. "Are you going to tell me this is also a plain landscape full of awful memories?" I turned the focus on the island that was coming a lot quicker than Ireland had.

"No, this is my first time in Spain. It reminds me of a cross between Italy and New Mexico."

"Warm and colorful with Latin influences?"

"Exactly," he agreed. "I would love to draw it."

"Why don't you?"

"I'm working," he said dismissively.

"We're traveling. And although Embry is sitting with the bags, he's diligently staring at me and checking everyone out."

"I don't have my pencils," he argued.

"All I'm hearing are excuses."

He looked at me, considering it, before going to get some paper from my backpack.

"That's bold," I said of the pen he chose to draw with.

"Your mechanical pencil was too thin and barely had an eraser," he explained.

We kept up a stream of conversation, with lengthy pauses whenever he was concentrating hard. I could tell because his forehead creased, and he bit on his bottom lip. I found myself staring when he was looking down, but caught myself before he looked up at the scenery again.

"Oh, that's just beautiful," a woman said, stopping to look over Gabriel's shoulder. If I were him, my first instinct would have been to cover my work and close myself off, but the woman had Grams' smile and Charlie's kind eyes.

"Thank you," Gabriel gave her a shy smile. I could swear he was blushing.

"We've been watching you from over there and we think you make the loveliest couple," she looked over at me while her friend came to join her. Both women were nearing their nineties, but while the first woman had white hair, the second's was dyed flaming red.

"We're not a couple," I corrected her when Gabriel stayed silent.

"Shouldn't be too long," Embry interrupted, coming to stand beside me. I saw him watching from afar earlier, but I guess he felt the need to come close when the women lingered.

"Oh, I'm so sorry, I was sure..." the first woman apologized, looking from Gabriel to Embry with confusion.

I wanted to tell her it wasn't like that with Embry either, even less actually, but the two women walked off as our ship got close to shore. The closer we got, the more a weird feeling overcame me. It wasn't like when someone powerful was close... it was like the whole island was made of magic.

Our first stop was the island's museum, since we were coming here mostly clueless as to who Talina and Zeke were. The rest of the island inhabitants, on the other hand, honored them on every street corner. The manhole covers all featured an elaborate intertwining of 'T&Z'.

"It's $12.50," a girl my age was sitting behind the desk when we walked in. She looked like she was falling asleep while working on some math homework.

Embry took the money out of his pocket and paid for the three of us.

"Is there a guide or something we can get as well?" I asked when she handed over the change.

"We have a coloring guide we give to kids when the schools come, but you mostly just walk around and read the stuff on the walls."

The museum went through the entire history of the island, with a 'step into the past' theme. Which meant we started with the present-day politics and economics, going further and further back in time.

"We're getting close," I pointed out when we reached the painting of the Island's first democratically elected President, a Spanish woman who came to the island as a child when they hired her mother to teach here. The book Beth was reading said Talina and Zeke ruled before her, from 1385 to 1460, which had to be a mistake.

"While a majority elected her, it took a long time for some of the elders to warm up to her, as she was the one who encouraged the Crowned Princess Ilana to travel to the mainland, where she fell in love and never returned," Embry read the description.

"You're emphasizing the last part instead of how exceptional it is that this island, in the fifteenth century, introduced elections into their system."

"Talina gave up her crown when she lost Zeke, training her replacement before living out a quiet life in her country house," Gabriel suggested as a possible location to find things.

"I think everything valuable is in here," I argued, moving closer to the glass cases in the middle of the room. They held objects that showed how people lived under Talina and Zeke's rule, but the star of the show seemed to be a large, faded brown book open to a page full of squiggles I couldn't really make out, even if I had understood the language.

"Who's Ioanit?" Gabriel asked, reading over my shoulder.

"Their historian," I shared, still feeling his breath on the back of my neck.

"Nothing here actually belonged to them."

"Except for that," I nodded to the coronet they forged specifically for Talina. Apparently, instead of passing down the crown, a new one was made for each ruler, with the previous one keeping theirs. It was more surprising that the position seemed to be passed on when the current ruler chose to step down rather than upon their death, as in every other country throughout history.

"Nothing smaller?" He asked.

"I think they'll notice if we leave with the crown," I argued when I caught on to their plan.

"Coronet. Because it's smaller," Embry pointed out.

"Not that small. We can't take it," I whispered, looking around to see if the place had any security cameras.

"It's not stealing, it's borrowing. If the spell doesn't destroy it, we can bring it back," Embry reminded me.

"We'll have to come back tomorrow morning," I reluctantly agreed to their plan.

"And not right now because…"

"I think going to jail will put a huge damper on our plans," I said.

"You're a witch," Gabriel reminded me.

"Yes, but once we leave the museum, we have to hide out on the island until the next boat that leaves at 10 am tomorrow."

"I'm glad someone read the ferry schedule," they gave up on trying to make the heist happen tonight.

CHAPTER TWENTY

Embry told us he had some potential leads he wanted to look into, so Gabriel and I were alone for supper on a gorgeous island. I knew he would want to keep me locked up in a hotel room to be safe, but I had a plan.

"We can pick up burgers or a pizza on the way to a hotel," he told me. He was clearly paying more attention to the people than the buildings because I hadn't seen a single American food chain. Even restaurants were few and far between; all mom and pop shops from what I could tell.

"Or we can try to find an alternative to stealing the most valuable item in that museum," I suggested.

"Do you have a suggestion where we should look?" he asked.

"All the guidebooks suggest that if you want to get to know a place, you ask the locals."

"We're trying to lie low and not let everyone on this island know that we're travelers from America looking into Crescent Moon Bearers and a long-forgotten dynasty," he argued.

"We stick out like a sore thumb. As soon as we got off here

instead of the party island, we became gossip. If someone was going to know we're here, they know."

"Can you sense anyone?" he kept leaning in and speaking softly, which I knew was an attempt to prevent people from overhearing him, but every time his fingers accidentally brushed mine, I had to ignore the urge to hold them.

"This entire island is giving off some mega-vibes, but they seem peaceful, if that makes any sense."

"Not really, but let me know if that changes," he gave me the tiniest of smiles before we walked towards where the royal house used to be. The majority of it was destroyed along with most of the island, but there was a tiny part of it that still stood at the northernmost end. History books had led me to believe that kingdoms comprised a castle surrounded by their city, with the whole thing encompassed by impenetrable stone walls. According to movies, the only way in or out was some kind of drawbridge, because water always surrounded them.

This kingdom either didn't have enemies, or they trusted the outer layer of tiny walls to keep their attackers out. Or at least slow them down when they hopped over it.

"Anything?" Gabriel asked when I sat on the wall that barely reached my waist and put my hands on its stones.

"Nope," I shrugged, looking around for talismans or discarded jewels on the ground, knowing neither was likely.

"It's beautiful, isn't it?" he said of the waves crashing on the beach.

"It must have been paradise once upon a time," I ventured.

"I always knew you came from a line of strong, capable women."

"You never thought it went this far," I called him on it.

"No, but I am not at all surprised to find that your ancestors ran a matriarchal kingdom that saw centuries of nothing but peace and prosperity."

"It's a lot for anyone to live up to," I thought of Kiara's mother, Ilana, and wondered if it was more than love that made her want to leave the island.

"This is where you come from, Lucy. This light and strength and greatness; that's who you are."

I gave him a smile instead of answering. I knew what he meant, and I definitely came from some impressive women, but you couldn't just forget about the other contributions.

The wind blew my hair into my face, so I brought my hand up to tuck it behind my ear. When I brought my hand back to the stone wall, I accidentally put it on Gabriel's hand instead. I was going to take it away and apologize, but he didn't move his hand away. He said nothing, so I left my hand on his and for a moment, we just sat there, staring out at the ocean, almost hand in hand.

THE SUN WAS SETTING, so we walked back towards civilization, choosing a pizza place for our dinner, but it was nothing like the delivery pizza he'd originally suggested. The crust was paper thin, covered in olive oil, spinach, mushrooms and tomato. I added cheese to mine and Gabriel had sun-dried tomatoes on his.

"Interesting," I commented, biting into my heavenly slice.

"Embry's mother used to preserve tomatoes by leaving them out in the sun, but every time she did it, squirrels took at least a quarter of them," he was the face of innocence.

"She knew it was you."

"You never even met her," he argued, more because he wanted to hear my argument than because he thought I was wrong.

"She would have put something on top to prevent it, or added spices to them ahead of laying them out. She let it happen because she knew it was you. Mrs. Boyd used to smile at Mr. Boyd and say the birds came through the window and ate the cookies she had on the counter, but she knew he was the one who took them."

"Mrs. Dante was a very honest woman," he defended her with a smile.

"Sometimes you tell yourself lies to make the people you love happy," I shrugged.

"Or keep things from them," he tried.

"Lie to them, you mean?" I knew we were talking about us now. "I understand lying to people when the truth is something that will hurt them, but not when it's vital information that determines whether they live or die and who they can trust and..." I cut myself off, but put my hand out so he wouldn't respond yet, "It hurt me that you didn't feel you could trust me with the truth. That even after everything, you still see me as a child who can't deal with the hard things, but I am not. I passed middle-age years ago," I tried to make it less serious with a joke about my impending doom.

"We will fix that," he told me like there was no other option, but I knew it was far from being the case. The lie was more for him than to me, so I let it slide. "And I know you're not a child, Lucy. I wish I didn't. I wish I could tell you to stay back and hide, and that you would listen and be safe. Not that I don't trust you with the truth, it's that I want to protect you from it. To save you from whatever pain or sadness that I can. Not because I think you're too young to handle it, but because you lie to make the people you love happy," he went back to eating his slice of pizza like that wasn't a heated declaration that gave me butterflies. I don't think Gabriel had told me he loved me before. Ever.

"I thought your job was to keep me safe, not happy," I don't know why I felt the need to prod instead of taking the win, but I had a bad feeling that Henry would catch up with us soon, and I didn't want to have regrets when we failed.

"You're right," he agreed. "I'm here to protect you. Rather your heart. Which I think means more than not letting someone cut it out, or stopping you from running a dagger through it."

"I'm not planning on that," I argued, going back to my pizza.

"No, but you're willing to. If we get to a point where you don't think we'll win, you're prepared to sacrifice yourself."

"Better than sacrificing someone else for my curse."

"Who are you to tell us who we're allowed to give our lives up for?"

"Who are you to tell me?" I countered.

"I come back," he pointed out.

"How are the pizzas?" the man who ran the kitchen chose that moment to come out and talk to us.

"Delicious," I gave him a smile, but Gabriel was still looking pointedly at me.

"How long are you in town for?"

"We leave in the morning," I shared.

"Short visit," he shook his head, pressing his lips together like he found this to be a shame.

"It's a quick trip, but I wanted to find out more about Talina and Zeke," I gave him an opening.

"You saw the museum?" he asked.

"We did," I agreed.

"Then you know the official stuff."

"Is there unofficial stuff?" I asked, leaning forward in my chair, causing him to make a big-bellied chuckle.

"I was born here, then went to school in London. Instead of retiring, I came back here and opened a pizza parlor because this is the only place in the world where I wouldn't lock my doors, would lend a stranger my car and have never felt unsafe," he shared.

"The museum mentioned a low crime rate," I agreed, feeling guilty about our plans.

"It's not just low, it's nonexistent. I don't know if it's the island or the lifestyle, but we honor Talina and Xiomara and all the ones who turned us into this instead of that," he pointed across to the ocean, toward Europe.

"I need to live here to know the unofficial stuff," I understood.

"Tonight might be a good start," he nodded to the sky, where a firework had just gone off.

"What's tonight?" Gabriel asked.

"It's Luna Creciente," he shared.

"The Crescent Moon?" Gabriel translated, although I would have guessed it even if I didn't speak Spanish.

"Not for a few days, but tonight's the opening of the festival. There'll be fireworks and dancing... it lasts all week, if you can stay a little longer."

"No, we really need to leave, but thank you."

WE SETTLED our bill and headed off to the hotel to meet Embry. Islanders crowded the streets for the festival, so Gabriel took my hand and brought me through a quieter alley instead.

"I think it's the island," I suggested. "I mean, not to take away from my ancestors, but the energy I'm getting from it is like... it feels very wholesome," I tried to explain it. I don't know if it was the magic or my ancestors I was feeling.

"I was going to say hopeful," he agreed instead of telling me I was crazy. "You're enjoying it, but it terrifies me."

"Being hopeful?" I asked, very aware that he hadn't let go of my hand yet. Recent events had me uncomfortable in crowds and in dark alleys, so I appreciated it for more reasons than one.

"Hope can be dangerous," he pointed out. "I feel like I can do things I would normally stop myself from doing."

"Things you would regret?" I asked.

"No, but I probably should," he looked over at me, his black eyes piercing in the moonlight, making me catch my breath.

"You think everyone on the island gets along because they all feel buzzed?" I had never been drunk, so I didn't know what it was supposed to feel like, but I was pretty sure this wasn't it.

"No, it's not like being drunk. Alcohol lowers your inhibitions and prevents you from thinking things through. I can see all the consequences my actions could have, all the implications… but they seem worth it. Like a weird optimism that has me believing that good things can happen, and I deserve them. It's very strange."

"What actions?" I asked. He was looking at me in a way that told me I knew what he was referring too, but he was sharing so much that I couldn't believe he would be that open about something we'd only ever mentioned in subtext before.

"I can't tell you that, Luce," he said, but his eyes told me everything.

"You can tell me anything, remember?"

"I'm supposed to protect your heart," he argued.

We weren't walking anymore. We were both standing in the alley, looking straight into each other's eyes, lit only by the moon. My heart was pounding in a way that made me want to scream, or to reach out and kiss him, but the only thing worse than not acting on these feelings would be if I did something and lost him for it.

"Sometimes keeping things from the people you love doesn't make them happy," I warned, biting on my bottom lip, hyperaware of how he was now holding both of my hands, and how he kept looking down at my lips.

I could see the battle going on in his mind, his head against his heart. I was rooting for his heart with every fiber of my being, trying to act normal while I was screaming inside.

"It's funny, I never realized I was getting over her, never felt my feelings dim or the pain grow smaller, but one day, I just saw you walking towards me and I knew."

"You knew what?" I asked, feeling nervous, even though this was Gabriel, and I had dreamed of this moment so many times over the summer.

"That I loved you," he admitted. He said it simply, not like he expected anything in return, but I knew he didn't mean it like I loved Sam or Embry. He meant the way he had loved Annabelle. "I was broken long before you smiled at me on your eighteenth birthday and took my breath away. For the first time in what felt like forever, my heart came alive and I wanted those things I thought I would never get to have. But I knew that I shouldn't, that you deserved better. That's why I stayed away, hoping the feelings would disappear, but as soon as you crawled out of the bathroom window and barreled into me, it all came back. I tried to be distant, to stay in the woods at the plantation so I wouldn't betray myself and lose you, but... I love you." Suddenly, before I realized what was happening, Gabriel leaned in, his hand pulling my face closer to his. Our lips were inches away when he paused, giving me the chance to back away if I wanted to, but I didn't. I moved closer just as he did, so our lips touched. I felt the tingling all the way down to my toes. It was like I didn't know I was drowning until he pulled me up and I could breathe again.

A new string of fireworks surprised me with their loud bangs, closer to us than they had been earlier, but as soon as Gabriel made sure it wasn't a danger to us, he laughed at my reaction. It was a childish laugh, full of innocence that made me smile before leaning in and kissing him back. I half-expected him to push me away, like every other time I got close, but he caressed my cheek and looked at me like he never wanted me to go.

EMBRY HAD ALREADY RENTED the rooms for us; two with an adjoining door. Gabriel didn't let go of my hand the entire walk there, which included lots of detours, sparks and fire-works. When we got to the room, he stopped and pulled me close, kissing me one last time before knocking so Embry could let us in. It felt like I lost a part of me when he let go of my hand, but later, when we brushed our teeth side by side, he gave me a smile, the kind where as hard as you try, you can't stop smiling. I could tell this wasn't a one-time thing. It was the start of something wonderful.

CHAPTER TWENTY-ONE

W e checked out the next morning and headed straight for the museum. Our plan was to have Embry distract the person behind the desk while Gabriel and I got the coronet. Whatever Embry had done last night told him that the museum had no security guards or cameras, which made sense with what the man told us at the pizzeria. The information slightly lowered the fear factor of the mission, but greatly increased the guilt factor.

"It was definitely blue," I told Gabriel as soon as we walked into the museum, my entrance fee already in my hand. It would have been more realistic to try and get in for free to check out one tiny detail, but I felt better paying something for the coronet rather than just taking it.

"It was green. I know because I thought it was an emerald at first," Gabriel played along to perfection, but I tried not to look surprised. I knew the guys could lie, but wasn't aware they could act.

"Then maybe you're colorblind," I told him before turning

to the girl, who was still working on some kind of homework. "Us again. Two tickets, please. It'll be worth it to see your face when you realize that I'm right," I said the last part to Gabriel.

"Um, sure. Go on in," she looked equally surprised that she had visitors, and that it was us. Again.

"This is what the entire trip has been like…"

I could hear Embry being his charming self, but I focused on our part of the mission.

"I'll get rid of the glass for you, but if anyone catches us, you need to leave me behind," I told Gabriel.

"Not happening," he argued.

"I can talk my way out of whatever happens, especially with Embry, but we won't have another chance at the coronet, and that's what we're here for," I reminded him it wasn't about me sacrificing myself, it was just logic. "It's not like they can do much to us if you have the evidence."

He looked like he wanted to point out all the ways that wasn't true, but didn't want to worry me, so he nodded and took my hand to bring me to the room with the coronet. We both pretended we were looking for the stone on the spine of Ioanit's book.

We put a lot more into the cover story than we needed, but I chose the perfect place where I would have an unobstructed view of the coronet's display case, but they couldn't accuse me of stealing it from so far away.

"See, I told you it was blue," I said, my voice shaky. Gabriel looked at me to see if I was ready, then gave my hand a squeeze. I didn't have as much confidence in myself as I implied, but a few moments after I held the moonstone necklace and concentrated on the case, it disappeared. One second I was smiling with pride for accomplishing a new spell, and the next the coronet was gone. I let out a breath I didn't realize I was holding, then let the glass materialize back in its place.

"It was a trick of the light," Gabriel gave me a reassuring look before heading to the exit.

His version of leaving me behind consisted of walking two steps ahead of me and not stopping once we got to the front desk.

My heart was beating a mile a minute, but I tried to appear calm, cool and collected in case Embry was wrong and a delayed alarm went off. It would have been smarter to get a forgery, because they would find us out the second someone else visited the museum. I wondered if I should tell someone it was missing, or ask what happened to it, just for plausible deniability.

Embry was waiting by the doors, so I took another calming breath before joining him.

"He was wrong," I explained Gabriel's quick exit.

Embry and I were about to walk out when the girl behind the desk called out, "Miss!"

I froze, terrified. There had to be some kind of morality code against using magic to steal things, which meant I definitely couldn't use it on this girl to save us from being caught.

I took a deep breath to steady myself before turning to face her. "Yes?" I asked, every inch of me stiff from trying to appear normal.

"I found one of the coloring guides we give the kids, if you still want it," she offered.

"Thank you," I swallowed before retracing my steps to get the guide from her.

"Have a great day," she sighed, getting back to her homework.

I waited until we were outside to let the breath out, but for someone who never even skipped school or stole so much as a chocolate bar, I felt like I may have just had a heart attack.

· · ·

Gabriel was standing across the street with the coronet safe in his jacket pocket. "Everything okay?" he asked me, putting a hand on my arm.

"We made it," I tried to smile, but I wasn't there yet. I was guessing it would take being back on American soil before my heartbeat went back to normal. It was crazy how stealing got me this nervous after all the magic stuff I had done in the past few months. Then again, stealing has always been wrong in the world I grew up in, whereas being hunted and nearly dying is so far-fetched I sometimes have trouble wrapping my head around it.

"We need to get out of here and board the ship before anyone notices the coronet is missing," Embry stated, looking back at the museum, where I half-expected a SWAT team to be rushing out at us.

"Here you go," Gabriel came close to hand me the coronet, away from any potential prying eyes, but he held me extra close, as if to reassure me that I didn't just imagine last night. I was grateful, because as soon as I wrapped my hand around the little crown, I felt myself slipping…

My hair was longer than I had ever seen it, cascading down my back, all the way to my hips. I felt like a Greek goddess, amplified by the incredibly fine, empire-waist silk gown I was wearing. There was a woman standing in front of me with a smile on her face, and a crowd of people surrounding us. Most of them were smiling too, some with the same love I felt from her, while others with some sort of curious excitement.

"Today my baby girl Talina turns eighteen," she addressed the crowd, but finished with a warm smile to me. "When I was little, my mother raised me to be strong and fierce. To be the best warrior, because you should never expect of your people something you wouldn't expect of yourself."

I recognized the coronet in her hand, shinier than the current version from the museum, but recognizable nonetheless. This one also seemed to have carvings in it, though I couldn't make them out from this far away.

"She was a force to be reckoned with," a very tall man added with a laugh, looking at the woman speaking, Talina's mother, in a way that suggested he might be her husband.

"True. But she was also warm and vulnerable. Because we are not just warriors, we are the mothers of our people. We tend to our sick, we comfort our dying, and we nurture our children to be kind and compassionate above all else. These are traits the world has convinced us to hide, but it is not weakness to fall apart. It is a chance to rebuild yourself and grow stronger, though most won't understand. When you put your heart in the game, others will see it as weakness, but it means you will fight harder and longer than anyone else. If something matters to you, my love, be all in," she told me with a fierce determination. "Courage isn't blindly running into danger without fear. Courage lies in seeing the danger, knowing what can happen, and going in regardless. Because there are things worth fighting for," she looked to the man who had interjected earlier. "But there are also things worth laying down your weapons for, and a queen must recognize the difference. This crown does not make you better than anyone, it marks you as the heart and soul of the kingdom."

I listened with fascination, but all I could feel in Talina was love. For her mother, for her people... her heart was bursting with it.

"I promise to rule justly, as a voice of reason when needed, but mostly, to be one of you. To be a friend and neighbor, through good times and bad, so we all may prosper and live happily ever after," as Talina said the last words, she looked to a man in the crowd who smiled at her in a way that made her heart flutter and her knees go weak. I would guess it was Zeke, but he didn't take part in the ceremony today. He was just one bystander among many. Talina smiled to him, then accepted her crown without fear, or even a trace of

imposter syndrome. She didn't see it as her birthright, but as an honor she couldn't wait to begin. She made eye contact with every person in that crowd, giving each one her love and respect. Her eyes landed on the man who must be Zeke, and I could hear in the back of her mind, her mother warning her it was okay to want someone at your side, that the right person will strengthen you, but you should never need to have anyone else there....

CHAPTER TWENTY-TWO

"We have got to stop meeting like this," Gabriel smiled down at me once I opened my eyes.

"Where are we?" I tried to get up, not recognizing the street corner I had passed out on.

"Two men carrying an unconscious young woman wouldn't look good, so Embry went to get us tickets before the cutoff and we are in an alley waiting for you to wake up," he explained.

"Passing out on the street was too risky, but a man with an unconscious woman in a dark alley seemed safe?" I questioned his logic.

"People expect shady things to happen in alleys. They don't question it as much," he looked at me like he was taking it all in and definitely had me blushing.

"Thank you for catching me," I swallowed, smiling both because I was shy under his gaze, and because the nearness of him made me smile.

"Anytime," he brought me back up to a standing position but kept me close, leaning in for a short, sweet kiss.

"The boat leaves in twenty minutes," I checked my watch. I

wanted to ask him what this was, to figure out what we would tell Embry, but I didn't. He looked at me like there wasn't even an ounce of him that regretted his decision, but I couldn't help but worry the island really did put everyone on it under some magical spell of love and optimism that would all disappear once we reached the mainland.

"We have time then," he teased. He leaned in but let me bridge the last inch before a kiss that made me weak in the knees. From now on, that was the only reason I wanted to be fainting into people's arms. "We should board. Like Embry said, I don't want to be here when they realize it's missing."

"Always the voice of reason," I said it teasingly, but as I finished the last word, I felt a negative energy, like when Donovan had come to New Orleans. It was much weaker, but it was like the entire positive vibe of the island got upset at it.

"Get behind me," Gabriel pulled me behind him as the sky went dark and four people appeared in front of us. "Go to the ship," he told me.

"What's missing?" the person closest to us was a woman, but she was wearing a trench coat, with a hat covering most of her face. It was jarring to see Henry's army in anything other than black.

"Who are you?" I asked, stepping out from behind Gabriel. I put my hands up with my palms facing them, ready to use my powers if they made a move.

"Is 'Your Worst Nightmare' too much of a cliché?" she asked the person to her left as I felt a chill behind me. I turned to see four more people show up, blocking the exit Gabriel wanted me to take.

"If it's accurate, I say go with it," her friend had a look in his eyes like he wanted to rip us to pieces, and I could tell he would enjoy it.

I was pretty sure that the way they were making jokes meant that they were here of their own free will, not being manipulated by Henry, but I didn't know the logistics of his control, and so far, only two of them were talking.

"We'll take the girl and no harm will come to you," the woman told Gabriel. Something about her voice felt like a hammer against my skull, but I tried to shake it off.

"Over my dead body," he said through clenched teeth.

"It would be my pleasure to arrange that for you," she braced herself with her arms mirroring mine, only when she moved them, icy air surrounded us, like she was summoning a blizzard.

I could see her bring her arms down and although I didn't know what she was throwing at us, I knew it wasn't good, so I put up my force shield. It kept us safe from the avalanche she poured on us, but the weight was going to crush me if I didn't push it off.

"The first chance you get, I need you to run," Gabriel looked me in the eyes with that look of utter intensity, laced with fear.

Instead of answering, I shot my arms up to push off the snow, but they were expecting it. As soon as I lifted my force shield, jets of hail, sparks and weapons flew at us from different directions, causing Gabriel and I to separate to avoid being hit.

Gabriel pulled knives out of nowhere and got to work, brandishing one and throwing the others. I tried to freeze as many assailants as I could, but it was like they knew the limitations of my magic and operated around them. Instead of coming at me from one direction, they came from everywhere, making me constantly have to defend myself instead of being able to take the offensive.

I had two of them frozen, but the third one's Gift seemed to be popping in and out of places, so one minute he was behind me, the next he was beside me and so on. His weapon felt like a baseball bat, but he wouldn't even stay still long enough for me to confirm what he was hitting me with.

Every time I turned around to find him, I could see how Gabriel was doing fending off his five attackers. I watched the number drop to four, then three… He was down to the two talkative ones when one of the men on the ground got up and came at him from behind. Gabriel was concentrated on the front with nothing but a knife in his hand, leaving him nothing to throw. I ignored my fight and blasted the man away from him.

If Gabriel hadn't noticed the man before, he definitely reacted to him being thrown into the garbage can beside him. I wasn't even thinking about my bat-toting disappearing act when he popped in out of nowhere and gave me his best whack yet, right in the stomach.

I doubled over and fell to my knees, catching the anger in Gabriel's eye just as he threw his knife into my attacker, who'd had his arms raised to incapacitate me more permanently now that I was down. This left Gabriel weaponless with two Gifteds ready to take their shots.

I forced myself to move past the fact that I was winded, and tried to blast the woman into the wall, since she was closest to him. Just as I shot my arms up, Gabriel reached for something sharp on the ground and stabbed her with it. I shifted to the guy coming at Gabriel from his right. He made a noise when he hit the wall, before falling to the ground.

I was expecting Gabriel to yell at me for my carelessness, his standard response to nearly losing me, but we were both silenced by an elderly man who came out of nowhere, holding a box. "Come," he said, opening a door to the building behind Gabriel.

"Who are you?" I asked, sensing that he was not a part of Henry's army. He felt… ethereal. Like he was a lot older than he looked.

"My family took care of the Bearers of the Crescent Moon for centuries. You need to get on the boat," he held the door open behind him, but kept walking.

"How do you know…"

"I know lots of things, Gabriel. I know that coronet won't help you if you get arrested, and I know that you are missing generations of Bearers from your line," he said while walking, not looking back once.

"How do we find them?" I asked, but Gabriel looked skeptical. Nell's book implied we were only missing one object, not generations worth.

"This is all you need," he lifted the box above his head, but held on to it as he brought us through corridors. "Kiki entrusted me with it before she…" he cut himself off and slowed the pace for a tiny moment, "it contains something from every bearer that came before her."

He was like a human Rafiki, bringing us through an underground maze with no ending, but I could almost taste the salty air before he opened a door I hadn't even seen in the pitch-dark hallway. The sun nearly blinded me as we stepped onto the top deck of the ship. I could see Embry below at the ticket counter, searching for us.

"How did you do that?" I asked the man.

"Remember where you came from Lucy. Not just the pieces, but the whole picture," he put his hand on my sternum. My first instinct was to pull back, but his touch made my headache go away. It was warm and full of light, not that I understood it.

He put the box in my hands, then bowed. When he stood up straight, he got this smile on his face, like he had accomplished something he'd been working on forever. Then he faded away. I don't know how else to describe it, except one second he was standing in front of me, and the next he was blowing away like dust in the wind.

"Wait!" I tried, but he was already gone.

Gabriel, who kept his head on in all situations, went to the edge and called out to Embry, who was heading back to town in search of us and would have missed the ship.

"What was he?" I asked Gabriel, before noticing that as shocked as he was, anger was his dominant emotion. And it was directed at me.

"You nearly died," he pointed out.

"What?" I asked, more focused on the guy with secret doorways onto ships who disintegrated in front of us than on what happened in the alley.

"You put your own life at risk to save mine," he was fuming. He was trying to hold it in so he wouldn't yell at me and cause a scene, but also talking fast so Embry wouldn't witness it.

"He was going to kill you," I argued.

"It doesn't matter, Lucy. I don't matter."

"You matter to me." I took a step towards him, but the look in his eyes stopped me dead. His hatred and disgust were reflected back at me.

"This is another reason I shouldn't..." he cut himself off, shaking his head. "I'm Gifted. So if he had killed me, I would come back. And even if that wasn't the case, I am here to protect you. I meant it when I said I can't lose you Lucy, and it isn't just because of the prophecy or your birthmark or a promise I made centuries ago," for a moment, his anger deflated and I thought this was one of those times where he was yelling at me because he was scared, but he would realize that we were both okay now, and clearly stronger together. Instead, his eyes went cold as he said, "This was a mistake."

"Coming here, or..." I knew what he meant. A part of me had been expecting it from the very beginning, but hearing him say it... I couldn't breathe.

"I never should have kissed you. I'm sorry, it was my

mistake to lead you on and… let's just go back to not talking," he wouldn't meet my eye as he went over to find Embry and tell him what happened. I felt like I'd been whacked in the stomach with a baseball bat all over again, only this time I couldn't catch my breath. I felt the warm tears welling up and roughly wiped them away. I didn't want to give him the satisfaction of seeing it, but he was breaking my heart.

PEOPLE WERE CROWDING onto the top deck, so I put the box in my backpack and watched the island disappear. I held onto the steel railing, bracing myself for a couple of hours of seasickness, but as I stared off into the distance with my heart breaking, I got flashes of someone else going through the same thing…

I knew I was Judith from the shawl I was wearing, the same one from her portrait at Alaric's estate. It was a different island that she was staring at, thinking of all the reasons why she was leaving, reminding herself of all the excuses why she shouldn't, but she still closed her eyes and looked inside her mind, into her own memories…

"Oh, Judith, you have perfect timing, my son should be here any minute," a woman said excitedly. She had ebony hair that was going gray, and I would guess her to be the owner of the apothecary-like shop Judith just walked into. It was more established than Nell's, but nothing compared to Ingrid's.

"Darling, come, I want you to meet a friend of mine," I heard while browsing through different herbs and roots.

"Mother, I don't have time for this," he argued.

I froze and felt a shiver run through me when I heard his voice, but Judith had an entirely different thought when she recognized him.

"Henry," his mother sounded stern, but he laughed at her.

"Fine, I'll say hello, but I have somewhere to be," he bent down to kiss her cheek. The nearness of him paralyzed me with fear, but

Judith was nervous with excitement, her heart reacting to him the way mine did to Gabriel.

"Henry, are you ready?" a female voice called from the doorway.

"Coming!" he responded. "I promise I'll meet your friend another time," he told his mother. "Nice to meet you," he called out through the shop on his way to the door.

"Oh, that boy... he drives me crazy sometimes," his mother was shaking her head in the direction he took while Judith walked over to her.

"Boys can be oblivious sometimes," Judith shrugged while the woman went to put the shop sign to 'closed', ushering her to a back room.

"He will wake up one day and realize there is more to life than parties and loose women, but until that happens..." she let out a deep breath, then took out a book. "Where were we?" I looked at the pages and recognized them as spells, before the memory changed...

I was sitting at the very back of a classroom, trying to be invisible in the all-male university. Henry sat in the row in front of me, occasionally turning back to talk to the person beside me. He was quick to put his coat on and head out as soon as class let out, so I hurried to bundle myself up and followed him.

"Henry!" I called, catching up to him on the stairs outside.

"Do I know you?" he asked.

"I'm Judith. Ric's friend. I sat behind you in class."

"Oh, of course," he was friendly and charming, like in Annabelle's first memory of him.

"I heard you asking about cosines. If you'd like, we could study together before the exam. My father was a professor, so..."

"You've been doing this for years," he understood.

"I'm studying on Saturday either way, so if you wanted to stop by, we could go through things. I'm sure you understand tangents way better than I do."

"Oh, I doubt that, but a study partner sounds nice. Judith, right?"

"Yes," I could feel that her cheeks were on fire, though it probably

looked like they were red from the cold, not from finally talking to him one on one...

All of a sudden, I was waiting at home for someone who was never showing up, wearing something I would be more likely to wear to a ball than to a study session. I heard the door and could feel her excitement bursting as she ran over, then took a moment to compose herself before opening it.

"Alaric," she said, confused.

"May I come in?" he asked. "It's freezing out here."

"I thought you were at the early Christmas party," she asked, stepping aside so he could warm himself up by the fire.

"I was, but then it got boring."

"Is boring code for Henry showed up?"

"For what it's worth, I think he had every intention of coming here before Anya showed up at his place."

"Not much," Judith took the pins out of her hair.

"I know you think you know him, and he was perfect that night, but the way he's treated you since..."

"I know," she assured her oldest friend, but I could feel her pain and reluctance. "I would have forgotten him and moved on, but he keeps showing up all over the place. I mean, what are the odds he would be in the only mathematics class they allowed me to attend?"

"What about Mrs. Hathorne's son? She thinks he's perfect for you," he reminded Judith, but she just looked at him over the bridge of her nose. "No," he argued.

"Henry. I heard his voice and nearly died," she admitted.

"What are you going to do?"

"Ace the exam, graduate top of the class, find my happily ever after," she shrugged, pretending she wasn't heartbroken, but the smile she gave him was genuine.

"You're amazing, Jude," he said, and I could tell how much he loved her, though I don't think she saw it. Yet.

"You're the only one who thinks so, but I plan on changing that," she didn't let it bring her down...

CHAPTER TWENTY-THREE

Once we got to the mainland, we immediately headed for the airport, where a man in a suit was waiting to bring us through a private security checkpoint. He then brought us to a small waiting room with half a dozen chairs, all spaced out in groups of two. I didn't think I could handle sitting next to Gabriel or having to answer Embry's questions about it. They were both acting like nothing happened, or that they didn't notice that something was off, but I could tell Embry knew. And more than once I caught Gabriel looking at me in a way that made me bite my bottom lip to keep from reacting.

We each ended up taking a seat with an empty one beside us. I felt Embry itching to say something, so I took out the box the old man handed me. I still wasn't sure what happened to him. My best guess was that he was Gifted, waiting to give the box to a Bearer before he could move on, but no one said anything about them disintegrating into sand once their task was done.

The box was old, probably red once upon a time, but it was now a faded pink. I lifted the cover and saw nothing but white tulle with what looked like pearls. I reached for one to see if it was attached, but wasn't surprised when I was pulled away…

I was Talina, surrounded by a group of women who were weaving the veil into my hair with pearls. They used large needles, with my hair as their thread, each woman placing a single pearl, adding to the ones that were already a part of the veil.

"Why are there so many people?" A little girl asked, holding tight to her pearl.

"It's a mother's love," Talina's mother, Xiomara, said in the voice my Grams used when she was telling me a story.

"But Talina only has one mother," the girl argued.

"My mother died years before I got married," Xiomara pointed out.

"No one was there?" she looked like she was about to cry.

"On the contrary. This ritual isn't meant to make the bride feel loss, but to show her that a mother's love comes in many shapes and sizes and colors. My aunts all came together to put in my pearls, then my father took over at the end with my mother's pearl, as he had taken over after my mother passed."

"How many pearls are there?"

"One for every woman that came before Talina, for as long as time can tell," Xiomara winked at her, before some women left, letting others take their place.

The newcomers helped Talina slip into the dress that looked like it had also been passed down throughout the generations.

"You used to ask me if you could wear the beautiful dress every time there was a grand occasion," Xiomara had tears in her eyes as she smiled at her daughter in the dress.

"You always told me it was for weddings, nothing more," Talina remembered.

"And now it is yours, to give to your daughter, and her daughter after that."

The sun was setting by the time a new woman came, that I soon understood was Zeke's mother. "Not all daughters are made," she said, coming to stand behind me. "Some are found, to be received as a gift. You are mine," she put a delicate necklace around my neck.

I thought it was sweet of her, but Talina was so touched she cried...

"WE HAVE ALL the ingredients for the Cure," I told Embry and Gabriel's expectant looks when I woke up. "This has pearls woven into it from every woman in Talina's line who came before her."

"I've reached out about the Arms of Yggdrasil, but so far everyone agrees that it doesn't exist, and if it does, they have no idea where to find it," Embry shared, having apparently done more research than just checking the museum for security cameras.

"Maybe there's only one," I suggested. "A family heirloom or guarded secret that wasn't advertised so it wouldn't be stolen. I mean, who even knows if any of the remnants of the True Cross are actual from the True Cross."

"But Henry already has everything he needs for the Coalescence, other than your heart," Gabriel was going through all of our options, the vein in his forehead pulsing like it often did when he was mad or concentrating very hard on something.

"We can keep looking for it while running from him and his people every time they find us..."

"Or we can bring the fight to him and use his ingredients," Gabriel understood what I was getting at.

"We don't have enough magic. There's no way we can win against him," Embry argued.

"If we distract him long enough, I can try to complete the ritual. That should give us more than enough power," I suggested.

"I'll see what I can do," Gabriel decided, not at all on board with anyone completing the ritual, given the essential ingredient of my heart.

While Gabriel went off to make calls or send codes or whatever it was he did, Embry came and sat beside me. "What happened?" he asked, wrapping his arm around me.

"I opened the box and had a memory," I shared, having assumed it was self-explanatory.

"I meant between you and Gabriel."

"Nothing happened," I lied, swallowing when he looked at me with disbelief.

"You were practically making googly eyes at each other last night, but now you avoid even looking at each other," he pointed out.

"You're using your---"

"I don't purposely use it on either of you," he cut me off. "I actively try not to, but I know you, Luce, and your feelings are practically screaming at me."

"I'll try to be quieter."

"I can see your heart breaking, Tesoro," he looked to me like he could feel it as well.

"I'm just being silly. It's really the last thing that should be on our minds right now."

"It's not good for anyone if you're distracted," he warned.

"I got hurt. Not bad, but I took a blow to the stomach because he didn't see someone coming at him from behind," I sighed, coming clean. I didn't feel like I had anything to be ashamed about.

"It distracted you," he understood.

"No, I miscalculated how long it would take me to blast the person coming at him before the person I was dealing with could reappear. He had this annoying disappearing act going on."

"Which had nothing to do with Gabriel being in danger."

"It had everything to do with him being in danger, but I

wouldn't have done anything different if it was you in that alley or Ingrid or Sam or anyone. I was okay, but he wasn't, so I helped. And it was a baseball bat. No one was going to kill me."

"But Gabriel...."

"Completely overreacted and told me I was a mistake."

"You?" he seemed confused.

"You know what I mean," I reproached. Gabriel being upset with me and pushing me away because of his stupid overprotectiveness was something I could vent to Embry about. It was the same behavior he'd had at the plantation, only slightly magnified. Last night, however, was not something I wanted to share with anyone except for Gabriel. Not that he would let me get anywhere near that topic now. "One step forward, twenty steps back," I shook my head.

"Sometimes people react emotionally instead of rationally," Embry shrugged.

"Three centuries of life experience does nothing to prevent immaturity?"

"When you've lost a lot of people, some of them to tiny moments of distraction, you don't use reason anymore, you react out of fear, doing whatever you can to keep the people you love safe, and make sure you don't lose anyone else. Especially when you look like someone he has watched die repeatedly," he pulled me close.

"Way to make me feel worse," I sighed.

"I don't want you to feel bad, love, I just thought you might want to understand."

"I'm never not going to be in danger, or not look like a woman he's lost a bunch of times."

"I disagree with the first one, and I think he just has to figure out that it's better to be with the woman you love than to watch her love you from afar. Because it's not like either of you is safer pretending. It's the feelings that get you in trouble, not owning up to them," he was talking about him and Beth just as much as he was talking about me and Gabriel.

I took a deep breath and gave him what I hoped was a reassuring smile before doing my best to zip up my backpack with the veil's box inside. I removed a few things to reorganize it and accidentally dropped a loose sheet of paper. I opened the Chronicles to have a safer place to store it than letting it get all crumpled, then gasped when I picked it up. It was the landscape Gabriel had drawn on the boat to the island, only the scenery wasn't the focus. I completely understood why the two women were confused, because I was holding a drawing of myself. I was staring out in the distance with a smile and the tiniest of dimples. My hair was up in a messy bun with wisps falling and framing my face. It's not like I had always wanted him to draw me, but seeing that he had, even before we set foot on the island of cursed hope...

"I got us a ride to Salem," Gabriel came back and interrupted my thoughts. I quickly closed the Chronicles on his drawing as he handed us each a boarding pass.

"Are you sure about this?" Embry asked me.

"They keep finding us and if we do nothing, one of his men or these memories will do damage we can't come back from," I pointed out. "And this week is the crescent moon," I brought up the cause of last night's fireworks.

"ANOTHER FBI CONTACT?" I asked Embry when we walked across the tarmac to a private jet. He was shaking his head and laughing to himself, but I didn't see what was so funny.

"This plane belongs to Angela's husband," he explained of Terrence's daughter, who was married to a pilot.

"Does he hate you as much as his wife does?" I asked, smiling at the memory of how much Angela disliked Embry for turning her down when she threw herself at him in her youth.

"If he does, he hides it a lot better than she does," he gave me a wink before going up the stairs.

I wasn't sure if I was expecting it to be empty or to have celebrities on it, but I definitely wasn't expecting the group that greeted me once I boarded the flight.

"What's going on?" I asked, turning back to face Gabriel, the one who made our travel arrangements.

"If we're fighting to win, not just to survive, then we need a fighting chance," he said simply.

"We heard you could use a hand," Delia smiled at the shock on my face. I saw Tristan and Benjamin behind her, sitting at a table with a guy I didn't recognize. He hadn't looked up when I came in.

To their left was Caleb, looking unscathed by the flames I had watched engulf his island safe house. I assumed the raven-haired bombshell on the couch with him was Etta, but when she looked up at me, struggling not to react as if I were Cassie, I recognized her.

"Being a badass suits you," Caleb told me with a smile before I could say anything.

"I'm glad you're okay," I returned it. I'd had my doubts while watching the island burn.

"It'll take more than that to get rid of me, but they keep trying. This is my better half," he introduced me.

"Etta," she extended her hand for me to shake, a firm grip where I had been expecting warmth.

"I saw you in a memory..." I tried to find a delicate way to tell her I saw a few moments of the night she died. It would have been better if I hadn't said anything at all. "I saw the night Cassie met you," I swallowed, figuring it got the point across without bringing it up.

"I'm surprised you recognized me," she exchanged a look with Gabriel before Caleb pulled her closer. I definitely wasn't getting on her good side so far.

"Your eyes," I said simply, "they left a mark."

"Not one of my finer moments. But a defining one for her." Etta looked deep into my eyes, then moved from my moonstone necklace down to my running shoes, sizing me up.

"I hope I can live up to her," I said, twisting the ring Clara gave me around my finger. Etta was nothing like how Caleb said she would treat me. Either because I'm not really Cassie, or because I was the cause of the fire on the island that claimed another one of Caleb's lives.

"Try to win," the guy from Tristan and Benjamin's table spoke up.

"I'll try my best," I told him, but he was getting looks from nearly everyone else.

"I'm just saying, Cassie went out in the middle of the night to confront him on her own and sacrificed herself to fix her mistake. I don't want to risk my life if this one will give up the minute it gets dangerous," he defended himself. He looked younger than me, with dark brown eyes and copper hair that looked like it was on fire when the sun reflected it.

I could see the vein pulsing in Gabriel's forehead as he clenched his fist, resisting the urge to punch him. To be honest, I didn't blame the guy for saying what everyone else was probably thinking.

"Is everyone ready?" the flight attendant came over and

asked Gabriel, interrupting the stare-down, though I'm not sure the stranger was aware, or would have cared.

"We're good," he agreed.

"Then if everyone could please take their seats, I'll tell the captain we're ready for takeoff," she gave an awkward smile before shutting the door and going into the cockpit.

"Collin makes earthquakes, but he can't control the Gift and his emotions at the same time, so he often comes off a bit..."

"Like an asshole," Collin finished for Embry, who was trying to find a nicer way to describe his personality.

"This is a suicide mission," I told him bluntly. "I'm not going in blind like Cassie, because I know what he wants and I know we don't stand a chance. But I'm still willing to try, and like Cassie, if it comes down to it, I would rather stab something through my own heart than let him win." I felt the dagger in my chest from when Kiara did just that and winced, feeling like a naïve child now that so many people were risking their lives for me.

"Let's go sit," Embry encouraged, gently nudging me. He brought me past everyone so we could take our seats in the back, while Gabriel stayed in the front with Delia.

"Do we have a plan?" I asked him, buckling my seat belt.

"We will go to the house Henry and Annabelle once shared and hopefully find Henry minimally surrounded. We will keep them busy while you get the missing ingredients for the ritual, and then we all live happily ever after," he gave me a smile, knowing that sounded more like a fairytale.

"Your plan lacks a lot of specificity," I warned.

"It depends how many henchmen he has, and what their skills are," he shrugged, but I was not happy with his nonchalance. "Most of us have been fighting together for centuries. We know each other's skills and weaknesses and know how to work together, even without a plan."

"And you'll let me venture off on my own while you fight a guy whose magic is stronger than anyone we've ever encountered?" I was both skeptical that they would let me out of their sight, into the lion's den, and not sure I wanted to leave them alone and magically defenseless.

"You'll never be alone," he said, like there was no other option. "And you're right, he is stronger than anyone we've encountered, but we know a lot of people who are strong on their own, so if we put them together…"

"I'm getting the feeling we will lose a lot of people."

"Luckily we all come back," he said in a way that told me I shouldn't worry, but he did me the courtesy of not using his Gift on me, and the words didn't do the trick.

"Even Collin?" I tried to lighten the mood.

"He gets better once his sister is around," he assured me.

"Can't you just… calm him down?" I suggested.

"He let me do it once when he was having a meltdown, but I tried to be helpful another time and nearly lost a life because of it."

"I guess no one likes to be manipulated," I ventured. "Were they just hiding out in Spain, waiting for us?"

"They were in France, about to head back to the States, so Gabriel got them to take a minor detour and change their destination."

"That's a big ask," I said. More of the plan that would probably cost them their lives than of the change in travel plans.

"We have this thing where if someone asks you for help, you go without questions."

"Because these are your best friends, or all Gifted?"

"More like family than best friends. We've all helped each other out so many times I don't think anyone knows who owes who anymore. I could gladly go a century without seeing Collin, but if he was in trouble, I would go to him. Without a second thought."

"It's nice that you have that," I said, looking around the plane. It was nice that it wouldn't just be the three of us, but we were nowhere near enough to defeat Henry. I couldn't even sense a trace of magic from any of them.

"More are coming," Embry assured me. I tried to hide how relieved I was, but we needed a lot more people. "The connection in Mexico was not an accident, and I'm sure some will meet us in Salem."

"He knows we're coming, doesn't he?" I asked, but the question was rhetorical. Henry told Donovan his plan was to sit back and wait for me to come to him, and although he hadn't barged his way into my mind since the forest, I got the feeling these headaches were supernatural.

WE'D BARELY BEEN in the air for an hour when we hit a patch of turbulence. I instinctively reached out for Embry's hand, and he gave me a reassuring smile that showed me why he got his particular Gift. It amplified his natural abilities.

"Good evening ladies and gentlemen, this is your Captain speaking. We're experiencing some slight turbulence, but I am told it should clear up momentarily as we make our descent. Please get back to your seats and we'll be landing shortly."

"We're nowhere near Mexico," I told Embry.

"I guess we're bringing Kate," he gave me a knowing smile, but I had no idea who Kate was.

It was getting dark, but I could still make out the landscape from my window. We were approaching an island, probably the same size as the Island of the Enchanted Moon, but all I saw was grass, trees, a river and log cabins. As we got closer, I felt nearly Donovan-level magic.

"Is Kate…"

"A witch?" he asked as the turbulence stopped suddenly, replace by what I can only describe as a tugging feeling, before the plane went silent. I had wondered how we would land without a runway, but I was not expecting this.

I knew we landed because I could see how close we were to the ground, but I didn't feel a thing.

"Sorry 'bout that, Mallory doesn't like visitors." A girl with flaming red hair came in through the side door of the plane, that opened seemingly of its own accord.

"Collin's sister?" I whispered to Embry.

"Jazmin," he agreed. "You'll like her."

She was followed by five women and two men, but only one of them caught my eye. Her pink hair didn't help, but it was the way she looked at me, like she wanted to run over and give me a hug.

They had two bags between the eight of them, and the same resigned look. Within minutes of our landing, a girl with blonde hair closed her eyes and made the entire plane rise into sky, slowly getting higher and higher, until the engines kicked in and we were flying again.

"THE ONE WITH the silver hair is Kate. She tired of hiding her magic and her Gift, so she started a commune on the island with her sister and a few friends. I think they're twenty of them now, but they don't live there all the time, and most of them don't owe us anything," Embry explained before leaning back in his chair. I think the goal was just to rest his eyes, but within minutes he was asleep, his soft breathing occasionally interrupted by a snore.

I took out the Book of Shadows and went through the pages, trying to find something that could help us with what we were about to attempt. I found nothing even remotely useful against Henry, so I sighed and leaned into the aisle, trying to sneak a look at Gabriel. On the off-chance that he was awake while everyone around him was sleep, I could maybe go over and...

"There's something about his intense broodiness that makes my knees buckle too," the girl with the pink hair interrupted my plans as she came and sat beside me. "I'm Jen."

"Lucy," I told her. "I was just stretching." It was none of her business, but I felt the need to defend myself.

"We all know who you are," she rolled her eyes at me. "It's cute that you introduce yourself. Although I guess Rosenberg calls you the new Cassie, but even he knows your real name."

"Is he here too?" I asked, looking around. There were still a few more people I didn't know, but Rosenberg was a name I remembered. Caleb had described him as someone who likes confrontation, in a way that made me feel like I never wanted to meet him. Although I guess beggars can't be choosers.

"He's meeting us there. Which is good, because he doesn't like plane rides, and no one enjoys being near him when he's not happy."

"But he's on our side?" I had to make sure.

"He likes to fight, but it's not like he goes around beating people up or insulting guys at bars to start them. I wouldn't want to spend more time with him than I have to, but if I was in trouble, he would have my back," she assured me. I guess they all were like family, where even if you don't like each other, you're still there for them.

"You both knew Cass?"

"I think he fought with her at some point. She was always running around saving people," she smiled, but it wasn't the way she looked at me when she walked in.

"Eugenia here is way more ancient than that," one of the guys from the commune joined our conversation.

"How ancient?" I asked, regretting my decision to use his wording instead of putting it more delicately. They might be close enough to tease each other, but I wasn't.

"Annie was the one I saw when I walked in," she answered the question I'd been trying to ask.

"That would mean you knew Embry and Gabriel," I turned to Embry, but he was fast asleep beside me.

"I told you he made my knees buckle," she looked over to Gabriel and gave me a knowing smile.

"Who makes your knees buckle?" the guy asked.

"He made. You make," she assured him with a kiss.

"I'm Peter," he extended his hand once they pulled apart.

"Lucy," I shrugged apologetically, but I wasn't just going to assume everyone in the world knew my name. "What about Henry?" I pressed, going back a few questions.

"I died in a very obvious way, so when I woke up, I knew I couldn't just go back to my old life. I did the whole sit in the back pew and listen to my own funeral, then I left town and never came back. I eventually ended up with Delia and was pleasantly surprised when Gabriel showed up for Christmas one year."

Peter introduced me to Lara and Gigi, both of whom had magic in addition to their Gifts, but I mostly sat back and listened to them tease each other and hang out like we weren't about to face my worst nightmare.

"You should get some sleep, Lucy. There won't be much rest once we get there," Jen told me before everyone found themselves a corner and they turned off the lights.

I didn't think I would ever get to sleep with what I knew was waiting for us once we got to Salem, but the roller coaster of emotions from the past few days and my lack of sleep eventually caught up to me.

I WOKE up as a half-dozen newcomers were boarding the plane, which told me we were in Mexico. My sights immediately landed on Terrence, who was being led by a man with dreadlocks. I wouldn't have been concerned, only Terrence was blindfolded and wearing noise-cancelling headphones. Once he was sitting, he took out needles and started knitting what looked like a poncho.

"Is he okay?" I asked Embry, who looked about as alert as I was.

"Terrence will be with us once we get to Salem, but we thought it was best to not let them in on all of our plans," he explained, reminding me that Terrence had been touched by a Gifted who now had access to his mind. He couldn't control it, but he could report whatever he saw inside.

I wanted to check out the new arrivals, but they turned the lights out again and everyone seemed to be sleeping. Except for Gabriel, whose eyes found mine in the dark before he looked away, crushing me. I panicked slightly over the fact that our next stop was Salem, where Henry was waiting, but at some point between the hyperventilating and attempts to calm down, I fell asleep.

CHAPTER TWENTY-FIVE

We landed at a private airport that looked more like a paved backyard than an actual runway and were greeted by at least ten cars. One driver looked miserable, with his hands permanently balled into fists, so I assumed he was Rosenberg.

I spotted Ingrid, looking like her grown-up illusion, and was rushing over to make sure she was okay when I saw, "Sam!"

"Don't sound so happy to see me," he reproached, taking me into his arms.

"This is the dangerous stuff you're not supposed to be a part of," I explained.

"You're not either," he kissed the top of my head, then let me take Ingrid in for a hug. I tried to give him a look like we would talk about this after, but he didn't seem the least bit concerned.

"It's good to see you," she told me once we pulled apart. There was a sense of excitement and fear in the air. It was what I imagined sports teams felt before they went out on the field, but then again, most athletes didn't die if they lost their games.

Watching them come up with our strategy, I realized it was much more like troops preparing for a battle. Gabriel, Embry, Kate, Delia and Rosenberg all huddled together around a map they made on the ground from rocks and sticks, saying things like, "The witches will hang back as long as they can," and "We can use the muscle for that." The only mystery element was me. "What do we do with her?" Rosenberg moved his head to the side in my general direction.

"She'll come with us," Embry decided.

"It'll be game over before half of us show up," Rosenberg argued.

"With Sam?" Delia asked Gabriel. I wasn't thrilled by how in sync they seemed to be, but she was a lot like me. She sat back and listened to everyone, but when she spoke, it was usually whatever I was thinking, right before I could cut in to say it.

"Embry and I will drive together while Sam hides Lucy. I need everyone to stay back as far as possible until we're at the door. Once the fighting starts and everyone is outside, Sam and Lucy will go inside and find the missing ingredients. As soon as they have them, Sam will send up a flare and we get the hell out of there," Gabriel looked around and got nods of agreement from everyone.

"Let's get the party started," Rosenberg clapped his hands, making more than a few of us jump, before everyone headed for a car and we left.

BY THE TIME Embry finally pulled into a driveway, I knew we were in the right place. Even without the garden that I recognized from Annabelle's memories... there was just something dark and ominous about the house. It looked just like all the other ones from the outside, but I could feel it.

I could see the gazebo in the distance, but it was in a state of disrepair, like no one had bothered with it since Annabelle left. The fields surrounding it looked like they were left to their own devices except for a tiny patch right beside the house that was in full bloom.

"It's not too late to change your mind," Embry tried, looking to me and Sam in the back seat. The only part of the plan I wanted to change was me hiding inside while everyone else engaged in battle outside.

"I made up my mind months ago," I assured him.

I was even more sure Henry knew we were here. He was always a million steps ahead of us, and even I could sense all the magic back at the airport. We were hoping mine would be lost in the sea of other powers. Or maybe our magic didn't come anywhere near to even comparing to him, and we were thus less than blips on his radar.

Gabriel opened the back door to take his weapon, but his eyes rested on me. I bit my bottom lip and looked up at him, trying to convey everything I knew I couldn't say to him, especially before a fight. That he needed to be careful, that I loved him, that I didn't think we were a mistake and I couldn't lose him. His eyes tried to be cold and professional, like when he was trying to run from his feelings at the beginning of the summer, but I could tell he also wanted to reach out and pull me close, so I could be safe in his arms. He lifted his hand, but Sam took my arm before he could do anything. We both needed to be invisible to get out of the SUV unnoticed.

Henry opened the door as the guys stepped onto the porch, wearing dress pants and a button-down shirt. This normalcy somehow made him even scarier. He took his time to walk out and join them, while his men stayed huddled behind him. I counted five, but there were probably more waiting inside.

"Can I help you?" Henry asked with that twisted smile, looking behind them, searching for me. I trusted Sam's Gift, but I still pulled him behind the SUV. It was bad enough that everyone in a ten-mile radius could hear my heart racing.

"We came for the spell," Embry said. "The one that keeps her alive."

"You did?" Henry looked amused. "And what gave you the impression that I would give you the spell?" he asked. "Or do you plan on making a trade?"

"No, we plan on taking the spell and keeping her alive," Gabriel said.

Henry tried to read their faces, knowing they wouldn't have shown up blind and unprepared, hoping for a miracle after centuries of running from him at all costs. He started laughing as if Gabriel had just told him the most hilarious joke he'd ever heard, before he stopped, as suddenly as he had started.

I knew he'd already sensed them, like I had, but our reinforcements were coming into Henry's view. He looked more annoyed than worried, but I knew we had a sizeable enough group to at least give him pause. He snapped his fingers and without a word, the men who had been waiting behind him filed past him to fight Gabriel and Embry, who were closest.

Henry had a few more lackeys who materialized out of nowhere, but they were incredibly outnumbered. Not that it mattered much when we had Terrence, whose Gift was taking confessions, fighting against a woman whose arms turned into tentacles that allowed her to choke four people at once.

Most of the Gifts on our side were rather harmless, or at least defensive, while Henry's men were groomed to kill. Still, those with the most passive powers seemed to have trained harder to compensate. Sure, the way Rosenberg made his arms turn into swords, spiked balls and carving knives at will was terrifying, but Etta wielding her whip looked deadly. Everyone was holding their own, except for Ingrid, Kate, Lara, Gigi and the man with the dreadlocks, who were fighting Henry, hands clasped together to pool their powers. Even from where I stood behind the car, I could feel how strong their combined powers were, but it was nothing compared to Henry's. Even with the metal spikes Mallory kept shooting at Henry whenever she had the chance weren't doing much damage. Unless I got the missing ingredients soon, they would not last long. I could only imagine what would happen to everyone else if Henry was no longer distracted.

I couldn't see myself, or Sam, but he followed without question when I brought us towards the house. Henry looked like he was distracted enough to not notice, but a part of me was convinced he could still see us, or at least sense me.

THE HOUSE LOOKED like it belonged in a photoshoot for a magazine, not like anyone lived in it. Everything was meticulously laid out to achieve the perfect look, except for the dining room that had leftover coffee cups and fast food bags all over it. I wondered if Henry had a rotating group of guards at all times, or if he brought his army here around the time he started actively hunting me.

"What are we looking for exactly?" Sam asked in a whisper once we were in what I assumed was Henry's office.

"Splinter's from the cross Jesus Christ was crucified on, vervain, a wooden cup and my heart," I shared, looking for a safe rather than items lying around.

"I found the last one," I could hear the smile in his voice, but he was keeping a hand on me to keep me invisible, even while everyone else was outside.

"This will take forever if you hold on to me," I warned.

"It'll take even longer if you're dead."

"We closed the door and I can sense when his magic is close," I pointed out.

We had a mini staring competition before he decided it was better to get me out of there faster than to keep me invisible while in a locked room, riffling through Henry's things.

Sam took the left side of the room while I scoured the right, which included a mahogany desk and three towering bookshelves. I gently pulled out each book, half-expecting the walls to shift and reveal a hidden passage to his secret lair.

"I found a safe," Sam whispered, pulling me from my menial task.

"Try 0108," I suggested.

"What's that?" he asked.

"The day he married Annabelle," I shrugged. If that didn't work, I would suggest Margaret's birthday, but my hopes weren't high on that one.

I didn't get to find out if I was right. I had barely touched the wooden chalice to move it aside, not even thinking of the cup of Yggdrasil, when I was gone...

"*You're not supposed to see the bride on the wedding day.*" I was Talina, talking to the guy from the crowd of her coronation. His guilty smile immediately mollified her reproach.

"*I asked to spend the rest of my life with you, not to spend twenty-four hours without being able to see you,*" he argued, standing up to wrap his arms around her.

"*You make an excellent point,*" she agreed, burying her head into his chest. "*Is everything ready?*"

"*My mother woke this morning with a fear that there won't be enough food,*" he shared.

"*My father is helping her,*" Talina agreed.

"*Are you sure that this is what you want?*" He brought up the *real reason he came. His concern made others doubt him, Talina knew that, but it was one of the main reasons she decided on the full ceremony, rather than the partial one the women in her family usually performed.*

"If something matters to you, go all in," she repeated her mother's words to him.

"All I can offer is my love," he reminded her, like he was worried it wasn't enough.

"And the purest of hearts. The warmest of smiles. The smoothest tongue to calm the voices inside my head, the strongest arms to hold me when I need to feel safe... you are more than worthy my love," Talina said before giving Zeke a kiss, letting it go further than she'd intended before the ceremony, but she didn't want him to doubt himself.

"There are enough traditions being broken, I'll not let you break another," Talina's mother warned, coming in with a basket that held what looked like a wedding dress.

"And the first rule is to make sure I never upset you, Xiomara," he gave her a warm smile.

"Empty words, Zeke," she pretended to be stern, but her eyes smiled throughout.

"I shall see you both at dusk," he bowed before retreating, leaving Xiomara to give her daughter a look.

"He worries he is not worthy," Talina explained his presence to her mother.

"It won't work if he isn't," Xiomara said simply.

"You told me to marry for love," she was confused.

"You wouldn't love someone who wasn't worthy," Xiomara waved her daughter's comment away.

"Mama," she reproached.

"You can marry whoever you choose. The bonds of the flesh need only the vows, and even then..." Xiomara shrugged like vows were not entirely necessary for that kind of bond.

"Mama!" Talina reproached once more.

"*The Coalescence will not happen if Zeke is not worthy. You choose with your heart, but being worthy of love, and being worthy of your burden are not the same thing.*"

"*How will we know if it worked?*"

"*There will be no doubt in anyone's mind. The legend is that the Coalescence is so miraculous to behold that it bathes the world in light.*"

"*Have you seen it before?*"

"*My grandfather used to say he chose not to steal my grandmother's glory, but we both knew it was because he would fall short,*" was her way of letting Talina know it had been generations since anyone saw it.

"*Zeke is the best man I know. If he is not worthy, no man is,*" Talina shared. "*I've always resented the idea that love makes you blind. I think it gives you a perfect understanding of another human being. I see every fault and every good deed, so I know what kind of man he is.*"

"*Then I look forward to the brightest night in memory,*" Xiomara hugged her daughter before carefully removing items from her basket. "*Are you ready to begin?*"

"*Yes mama,*" Talina smiled, taking a deep breath.

The memory continued with the Mother's Love ceremony I saw at the airport, before Talina followed Zeke's mother outside and went to stand at the front of the crowd, where Zeke was waiting. He took my hands in his and brought me to an altar. The smile on my face unable to express all the happiness Talina was feeling.

"*You are the beat of my heart and the air in my lungs. You are the light in my life and the song in my soul,*" he started, the nerves seeming to calm when he looked into Talina's eyes, mirroring her tears.

"*I take you for the love you hold in your heart, and the goodness in your soul.*"

"*I vow to spend my life caring for you and being true.*"

"You are my priority, giving me strength through hard times and sharing my joy in good times."

"I promise you honesty and patience, to spend each day becoming a better version of myself, and helping you to do the same."

They took turns reciting the vows, before Zeke walked over to a table I hadn't noticed before. There was a wooden cup in the middle of it, and he took a candle to light it on fire. "From the kindling of Emmanuel's Betrayal burns the soul of his untouched child," he said the familiar words with his hands hovering above the flames.

"Let the tears of Isis fuel the flames in the arms of Yggdrasil," he added a handful of vervain, then took a ceremonial dagger and sliced into his own hand, "As the blood of the incumbent quells the fire, may the heart of the Bearer of the Crescent Moon originate the Coalescence."

Talina took the dagger and sliced into her own palm, so by the time Zeke said Coalescence, he pressed his cut hand into hers, locking their fingers together, before a light, brighter than any I have ever seen, burst from my heart and surrounded us all. Everyone except Zeke, who completely disappeared into the light...

I WAS BREATHING FAST when I came back to myself, trying to process what I just saw. So many thoughts were going through my mind. Mostly the fact that those words weren't actually for a ritual to summon power through nefarious means, but also how my heart wasn't so much an ingredient as where the 'coalescence' bursts out from. Then again, the Coalescence looked more like a wedding than anything else.

I turned and excitedly told Sam what I saw, grateful this was one of the times where I acted out the memory rather than passing out. I saw Sam's face light up, but before he could reply, I got a sinking feeling in my stomach and turned to find Henry standing in the doorway.

"Do I even bother offering you the chance to join me, one

last time?" he asked, stepping closer to me. I stepped back, but there was nothing but wall behind me. I could no longer see Sam and hoped he was gone to get help rather than doing something reckless.

"I would still rather die," I told him.

Sam chose that moment to rush at Henry with a letter opener. He was invisible, so I saw the weapon disappear from the table a second before the flick of Henry's hand sent Sam flying into the wall.

"It seems a pity to knock out the last of my line, but if you leave me no other choice..." Henry said as if Sam was nothing more than a fly he swatted away.

"Go to hell," I said, resigned to not let him see my fear. The fact that no one followed him inside the house did not bode well for the men and women who came with me.

"Been there, done that," he said, his smile making my skin crawl before he put up his hand and I suddenly felt paralyzed, unable to move or even scream. It was just like Cassie's dreams, and it turned out my magic was useless too. "Now I promised you I would cut your heart out of your still beating chest, and I am sure you have figured out that I am a man who keeps his promises," Henry said with a gleam before pulling a knife out of nowhere and planting it in the top of my chest, far enough from my heart or any major arteries so he wouldn't damage the coveted ingredient, but also ensuring that I would be alive to feel the pain for as long as possible.

Inside, I was screaming. In agony and for Gabriel and Embry, but I knew I wasn't making a sound, just like my arms and legs were refusing to move as I willed them to. I had just decided to do like Beth had done, to close my eyes and let death take me, but Henry wasn't done with me yet. He stood and stared at me for a moment that felt like an eternity before saying, "It wasn't really you I made that promise to. Your misfortune lies in that you look so incredibly like her. The birthmark is your actual curse, but my Annie, she broke a lot of hearts." The knife was in my chest, but he was taking his absolute time killing me. "You may not believe it, but I loved her once. More than life itself, I thought. I saw her crescent moon on our wedding night. Having it be on her neck nearly took all the joy out of it. I found the last piece of my puzzle, that I had spent over a century trying to complete, yet I couldn't bear to use it. I spent years searching for a way to achieve my life's purpose without losing her. There was a time I hoped that her loving me would be enough. My heart was hers, so if she loved me the same, I might have..." he stopped cutting, and looked away from me. When he came back to me, he was no longer nostalgic. If I didn't know any better, I would think he was hurt. "Unfortunately, she had taken my heart, but given hers to another. I should have killed her then, but still, she was the mother of my child, and I was convinced I could make her love me. I thought the spell in her grimoire solved all of our problems, but she broke my heart all over." The anger in his voice was reflected in his movements, as the knife went farther than it had previously, catching my breath.

CHAPTER TWENTY-SIX

The thoughts were swirling in my head. Henry had me alone, Sam was knocked out, and I didn't know if some of the people outside were still fighting, or if everyone was dead. Either way, there was nobody coming to save me.

But, if the coalescence was a wedding, it seemed like the light came out of Talina's chest. As if the power Zeke gained wasn't summoned from the Gods, but came from her.

The blood loss must have been getting to me, because I kept seeing that dream, where I couldn't reach Sam on my own, so all of my ancestors came, one after the other, and gave me what I needed to get there. The Sam from the dream had told me that they would come if I needed help, but dream-Beth said I already had everything I needed. If it wasn't all in my imagination, then maybe the magic was already somewhere inside me, flowing through the blood of my ancestors that I just needed to unlock.

Everything for Kiara's Cure was in my bag in the car, but the guys insisted my magic was about intent, and I didn't need an object to channel the magic as long as I was strong enough to channel it on my own. Which they seemed to think I was.

Henry was still talking about Annabelle, but I closed my eyes and focused on each Bearer before me. I focused on the moments they shared with me; Cassie being shot and jumping off the cliff to save her daughter, Beth being burned alive, Rosie's heart breaking when Gabriel turned her down, Annabelle seeing Gabriel with that woman, Judith waiting for a Henry who never showed up, Talina's joy on her wedding day... I focused on all of their emotions and pleaded for their help. I asked for the powers of my ancestors to defeat the man who took so much from so many of us...

It wasn't a burst of light so much as a ball of warmth that formed in my chest, radiating through my entire body. I could feel it building, filling me up, but it wasn't until Gabriel and Embry barged into the office that I realized I could move again.

HENRY TRIED to send them against the wall like he had Sam, but my hands shot up and Henry was knocked backwards instead, as if something bumped into his shoulder.

"I thought I made you stay put," Henry turned to face me, sending shivers down my spine. I could feel the magic trying to hold me in place as he turned back to the guys, but this wasn't because he forgot to immobilize me, it was me fighting back.

Embry and Gabriel both stood in front of me, putting a barrier between Henry and I.

"How cute. Ready for another round?" Henry asked, cocky in the knowledge that they had never won against him.

Embry took his sword and rushed at Henry, but he was thrown up in the air before he could get close. I saw Henry bring his hands down as if to smash Embry into the ground, and put my hands out to slow his fall.

Gabriel looked to me, shocked by what I did and by the

dagger in my chest, but I was oddly calm. Henry wasn't panicking, so I must look normal, but every one of my nerve endings was firing with warmth and electricity.

"What did you do?" Henry asked me, his smile fading as he realized I was no longer the weak teenager he was up against earlier.

"Asked for a little help," I put my hands in front of me, ready for him to throw something at me, but he looked like he was calculating his next move.

"I still have the True Cross, you can't have completed the ritual," he warned.

"The ritual only gives you access to my birthright," I pointed out.

"I guess I'm a few cuts away from sharing it then," he said with a confidence I didn't buy.

"If you prove yourself worthy, which I don't think is likely," I argued.

"It's my birthright," he was getting angry, which made him look like a child.

"It was. A long time ago. But I think we both know you're not that boy anymore."

He looked at me like I was crazy before creating a great big ball of energy between his hands. His smile, though much less confident, was back. He rightfully guessed that although I was suddenly more powerful than him, he'd had centuries to figure out how to use his powers, and I barely had a summer.

I stood there and waited for Henry to strike, grateful that the guys each took a step back so I wouldn't have to worry about them being in the crossfires. Henry split the great ball of energy into three smaller ones and shot them at me, one after another. I could deflect them with my force shield, which was clearly much stronger than it was when I threw Gabriel against the tree. Henry's power balls shot through the house and landed in the gazebo out back. I could only tell because the fire was visible from the window.

Eventually, Henry used his mind instead of his skills and shot his energy balls at the three guys I would give my life for. I deflected them all, but wasn't quick enough to stop the one he shot at me. It caught me in the stomach and I doubled over; the wind knocked out of me. I took a second, looked at Henry with all the hatred I was feeling, and released a devastating gust of wind that knocked him off his feet.

Apparently, even without practice, my ancestors gave me the skills I needed to kick Henry's butt. We went back and forth with the powerful air strikes, before Henry switched to lightning. It was a horrible idea because anything he did; I did so much better. Unlike the air, that seemed to be a temporary inconvenience, the lightning I shot sent Henry fifty feet into the air, before he landed with a horrible crunch of breaking bones.

"IF YOU KILL ME NOW, they die too," Henry warned as I walked over, about to strike him with some more lightning.

I finally felt like I had the upper hand, but his words stopped me. His smile was gone, and he resorted to pleading for his life, but the words struck me to my core.

"Protecting you from me was the only thing keeping the two of them alive," he said, making me turn to Embry. He nodded like a goodbye, resigned to dying. I knew their deaths were the most likely outcome after defeating Henry, but to be honest, I never thought we would get this far.

"As long as you can never hurt her again, I'm okay with that," Gabriel locked eyes with me, giving me permission to do what I needed to do. I held on a few moments, then took a deep breath and released some kind of laser-like energy that made Henry glow for a few seconds before the light turned into fire and he erupted into flames. It was a brilliant spectacle until all that remained was a pile of ash.

I stared at it, having trouble believing it was really over, not ready to look over to the guys, terrified they would drift away like the old man on the boat.

I had been ignoring the wound in my chest, but it hurt so much now that I wasn't fighting for my life. My bleeding had slowed while I was under Henry's control, but the fight exacerbated it. The blood loss was getting to me, making me so woozy that I fell to the ground. I was vaguely aware of the guys rushing to me, but I felt like my death was a decent price for the world to be rid of Henry.

"Lucy!" Embry said frantically, lifting my head into his lap while trying to put pressure on my wound. "Gabriel went to get the Cure, you'll be okay," he assured me, but I felt myself drifting away, and knew they didn't have much time.

Gabriel came back into the room with the backpack and set up everything for Kiara's Cure. "It will be okay," he told me, but the fear I was starting to no longer feel was in every word he said.

They followed all the steps, the two of them getting so blurry that I could hardly tell them apart anymore. I could tell from the tone of their voices that it wasn't working, but they kept rereading the paper and trying again.

"It's okay," I told them.

"We are not letting you die, Lucy. We will find a way," Gabriel told me.

"Take my heart," I told him, having so much trouble swallowing.

"What?" he asked, visibly shocked.

"There," I said, lifting my arm so I could point to Embry's paper, which he figured out even though my hand dropped almost as soon as it went up.

"We can't..."

"Take my heart," I told Gabriel, as authoritative as I could manage.

"We need to complete the ritual," I could hear the reluctance in Embry's voice.

"I can't..."

"Gabriel..." I said, pleading with my eyes because I couldn't find my words. I saw tears in his black eyes as he looked back at me, but I couldn't really keep mine open anymore.

"I love you," Gabriel whispered, or it seemed like he was whispering, because it came from so far away.

"We will bring you back," Embry assured me, though I could barely hear anything at that point. I felt light as a feather, and warm when my eyes finally closed. I knew that unless they completed the ritual and the spell, my eyes would never open again. I thought it would terrify me, that I would be screaming about not being ready to die, but the warmer and lighter I felt, the less I worried about being too young or all of the things I hadn't done.

CHAPTER TWENTY-SEVEN

When Lucy stopped breathing and they knew she was gone, Gabriel and Embry just sat there, watching her inert body. They were both used to death, and they had watched this woman die many times, but seeing it was always hard. It didn't help that Lucy was younger than all the others. Too young. They couldn't process the scene in front of them.

It wasn't until Embry gently closed her eyelids that Gabriel found his voice. "What do we need to do?" he asked, the emotion making it raw.

They split the list in half and went around the property, as well as through their own bag, to find everything they needed to perform the ritual that would grant one of them the terrible power they needed to save her.

Most of the items from the list were scattered around Henry's office, his ego preventing him from properly hiding them. Vervain was one of the few plants still growing in the garden, but the True Cross proved to be a challenge.

"If he knew we didn't have it, it can't just be lying around somewhere. It has to be in the safe or a secure location..." Embry scanned the room for something they might have missed. The safe opened on Margaret's birthday, which was only the third combination they tried, but it only held passports, money and paperwork.

"How could he know we didn't find it somewhere else? There are pieces of it all over," Gabriel tried to control his breathing, but the longer they left Lucy lying there, the less convinced he was that they could bring her back.

"Unless most of them are fake. If you added up all the fragments known as the True Cross you could rebuild a dozen of them," Embry pointed out.

"If I had something like that, I would never let it out of my sight," Gabriel got the words out before a flash went off in his head. It was less of a flash and more of a panicked rush to the pile of ash that Henry had become. Sifting his hands through the cursed remnants, he quickly found what he was looking for; a tungsten vial.

"He put it inside himself," Embry swallowed hard.

"No one knew the cup existed, so he hid it in plain sight, but the coveted True Cross he kept with him at all times," Gabriel subconsciously brought his hand to the scar from when Embry dug inside him to take out a similar object.

They brought everything back to Lucy and set it up, following the instructions down to the letter, with no room for mistakes.

"Are you ready to do this?" Embry asked once they got down to the final element, the one neither of them was ready to retrieve.

"No, but I'm not ready to lose her either," Gabriel pointed out.

They turned to Lucy, with Embry holding the encrusted dagger they were supposed to use to cut out her heart. As soon as he got close enough to see her, to feel her skin that was growing cold, but still felt like she was there, he froze. She looked like she was playing her trick on them, pretending to sleep so she could wake up and surprise them.

"I can't," Embry said, dropping the knife.

"The one who cuts out her heart is the one who gets the power. It has to be you," Gabriel argued, not trusting himself with all of that power. It wasn't something he coveted or was worried he would abuse, but Embry seemed so much more inherently good than he was. The power probably wouldn't have any altering effects on him.

"Then it has to be you, Gabriel. I can't," Embry handed over the knife.

GABRIEL LOOKED at the dagger in his hand, then to Lucy, lying so peaceful in front of him, and couldn't reconcile the two, couldn't accept what he had to do. You would have to be a heartless monster to cut into her, even if she was dead. He had to remind himself that this was the only way to save her, before closing his eyes, mentally preparing himself to make his incision.

Gabriel opened his eyes and brought the dagger to Lucy's chest just as Sam woke up and rushed at him, crying "Stop!"

"Keep him back," Gabriel warned, taking a deep breath. It was hard enough to do this without someone begging him not to.

"The coalescence isn't a ritual to summon magic, it binds two people together so they can share the magic she already has," Sam explained what Lucy had told him earlier.

"But her heart…" Embry argued.

"Is not an ingredient. It's where the magic comes from. To complete the ritual, her heart needs to choose you."

"You don't need to cut it out of her chest because it's

already yours," Embry understood, turning to his oldest friend.

"What do I do?" Gabriel asked, relieved he didn't need to cause more damage, but terrified they were wrong, that this wouldn't work.

"Read this and mean it," Embry said, passing him the paper with Lucy and Annabelle's birthmark on it. Gabriel didn't have trouble meaning it, he didn't even have to pretend that he believed every word, because if this didn't work, then he had lost her.

"You are the beat of my heart and the air in my lungs. You are the light in my life and the song in my soul," he began, looking to Embry for confirmation before looking down at Lucy. This was a confession of love, not a summoning of power. "I take you for the love you hold in your heart, and the goodness in your soul. I vow to spend my life caring for you and being true. You are my priority, giving me strength through hard times and sharing my joy in good times. I promise you honesty and patience, to spend each day becoming a better version of myself, and helping you to do the same. From the kindling of Emmanuel's Betrayal burns the soul of his untouched child. Let the tears of Isis fuel the flames in the arms of Yggdrasil," Gabriel added the vervain, then took the dagger and used it to cut into his hand so his blood could pour into the cup. "As the blood of the incumbent quells the fire, may the heart of the Bearer of the Crescent Moon originate the Coalescence."

"I DON'T THINK IT WORKED." Gabriel said once he said all the words on the paper, thus completing the ritual. He had expected it to wash over him, maybe see a flash of light or fireworks.

"It definitely worked," Embry assured him, as Lucy's chest

glowed bright, before everything around them was bathed in light.

It seemed like Sam and Embry could no longer see or hear him, as they looked around, trying to find him.

"She said there was a test of worthiness," he heard Sam telling Embry. That would have been good to know before they wasted their only chance of saving her on him.

GABRIEL WONDERED if he had to prove that Lucy was worthy of being saved, which would be easy, or that he was worthy of saving her, which might be slightly harder. He waited for the test, or some kind of instructions, but there were none. He looked to see if Lucy was waking up, but she was still on the ground a few feet away, not moving.

All of a sudden, Gabriel found himself in a white room he could only describe as soft. He looked around, wondering how he could prove that Lucy deserved to be saved. Or that he was worthy of saving her. Then he heard it.

"Gabriel..." she said it softly from behind him, but he knew that when he turned around, it would be Annabelle. All the girls' voices were the same. It wasn't even the accent that gave it away, but no one said his name the way she did.

"Belle," he turned around slowly, afraid she would disappear if he made any sudden movements. She was as beautiful as he remembered, her eyes looking at him like they always had, like she loved him more than anything in the world, and in her eyes, he could do no wrong.

"My love," she moved close and put her hand on his cheek. He closed his eyes, thinking he could die now and be happy, but thinking of dying reminded him of Lucy, who was counting on him to save her.

"I came here to save Lucy. She's dying and I need to bring her back," he explained. The woman in front of him had died centuries ago, but he believed in the afterlife, that Annabelle had been up there watching him all those years.

"You have the power to bring her back," Annabelle agreed in a way that told him there was a catch. "But you can only bring back one of us."

"What do you mean?" he asked, not sure if he understood what she was suggesting.

"You can bring back whichever one you choose. But only one. The spell cannot be redone, so… this is your chance."

"That means…"

"That we can be together again, my love," she smiled at him.

"This is how you were going to come back to me?" he asked, taking her face in his hands.

"I hadn't expected it to take this long," she looked up at him apologetically. "I had hoped it would be before there were any others, but I knew you would find a way. Now you can bring me back, so we can be together."

"But Lucy…"

"Lucy is a shadow of the woman you love. I know she was something to look at and I don't fault you for pretending she was me sometimes, but now you can have the real thing. We can be together forever, Gabriel, isn't that what you've always wanted?" she looked up at him expectantly.

"Yes," he agreed. "For centuries, all I have wanted was to be with you," he said, tucking the loose hairs behind her ear so he could look into her eyes. "I never wanted any of the others, not even the one who loved me. She had your face, but she wasn't you," he said, as if not using Rosalind's name would make it less of a betrayal, or make him feel less guilty for all the pain he caused her.

"I'm right here, Gabriel, we can be together, forever, live the life we have always dreamed of."

"I promised Lucy… I need to save her," he argued.

"And I promised you I would be back. You promised me you would love me forever," she was getting upset, which wasn't like her.

"And I will, Belle, I will love you with my very last breath, but I lost you. You died in front of my eyes and I have spent centuries trying to get over it, but Lucy doesn't deserve to die. She is kind and sweet and thoughtful and so much stronger than she realizes. She hasn't lived the life you got to live, finding love and having a beautiful daughter. She was taken long before her time, because I couldn't save her then, but I am going to save her now."

"You think you love her?" she sounded surprised and jealous. "You just love the fact that she looks like me. That's it. That's all you're feeling. We can be together forever. All you have to do is let her go."

"I can't," he argued. "I love her, but it is not because she looks like you, it is in spite of it. It breaks my heart to look into her eyes and see yours, but I love Lucy. And although I will always love Annabelle, you can't be her, because she would never even consider letting me save her over a young girl who has her entire life ahead of her... one of her descendants."

"If you loved Annabelle, it wouldn't have even been a dilemma. You would have chosen her without a second thought," Annabelle said, but she no longer looked like the woman he had spent his entire life loving. Her features got distorted and her anger turned her into a vile version of the woman she pretended to be.

As the Annabelle imposter steamed and grew red, Gabriel said, "I choose to save Lucy." Knowing not only that it was the right decision, but that he never would have been able to live with himself without her. Annabelle, the real one, would have agreed.

· · ·

THE WHITE ROOM DISAPPEARED, and Gabriel found himself back outside the house, with Embry calling after him.

"What is it?" he asked, rushing over.

"She's alive," Embry shared.

The wounds were gone, though her clothes were still bloody. Sam's fingers were at her throat, finding a pulse as they both watched her chest go up and down. Gabriel heard her heart beating and thought it was the loveliest sound he'd ever heard. He looked up to thank God or whatever deity would take credit for it, but all he saw was Annabelle. The real one this time. He was sure of it, because she smiled sadly, as if she was proud of him. Realizing it wasn't really her and choosing Lucy must have been how he passed the test. Annabelle blew him one last kiss, smiled at him, and then she was gone.

I woke up confused and disoriented, with Sam and Embry staring at me while Gabriel looked up to the sky. It was quiet, even for a night in the country. All I could hear were crickets and grasshoppers. They seemed so far away, but also clearer than they had ever sounded before.

"What happened?" I asked, trying to sit up, only to be stopped by Embry, who put his hands on my shoulders and gently put me back down.

"Maybe rest a bit more. Gabriel just brought you back from the dead," he shared, unable to control his smile.

"It worked?" I asked, looking from one to the other as it all came back to me.

"You're breathing, aren't you?" Sam smiled.

"How did you do it? I can't believe... it's gone," I said, bringing my hands to the spot where the knife had gone in.

"How are you feeling?" Gabriel asked, joining our conversation.

"Maybe a little lightheaded, but we haven't eaten in a while," I reminded them. Embry rolled his eyes at my attempt to make light of my dying and being brought back to life, but he didn't argue with my explanation.

"We'll have a feast when you get up, any place you want," Sam looked so relieved to have me back. Gabriel did too, only I got the feeling he paid a terrible price to do it.

"I'm good with getting out of here," I assured them. "Where's everyone else?"

"They crushed us, which is how he got to you," Embry explained.

"Let's get them out of here," I suggested.

The guys told me to wait in Henry's office while they got everyone into the vehicles we came in, but I wasn't a fan of that plan. As soon as they left me alone, I put the remnants from the spell back into my bag and headed outside to join them, only slightly exploring the house on my way. Part of me wanted to look around and hopefully find out more about Annabelle and my ancestors, but the bigger part of me wanted to get as far away as possible from anything even remotely linked to Henry.

By the time I made it to the front yard, Caleb was carrying Peter to a car while Rosenberg was doing the same to Collin. I wondered how many times they'd both died for it to take so little time for them to come back to life? It was perfect though, since they're the only ones who could lift another grown adult as if they were a child.

I saw Etta leaning over Delia, who was lying on the ground with a large gash in her stomach, struggling to breathe. Etta put her hands over the wound and closed her eyes in concentration. A tiny light floated between the two of them before Delia took a deep breath, and I knew her wound was gone.

"That was amazing," I said, walking over to Etta.

"My job is to hide and watch as everyone I love dies, over

and over again, so I can try to save them before the end comes," she shared, looking out at the field of her friends. Mallory looked like she might hold on a few moments longer, but everyone else was dead.

"I've got her," I assured Etta, allowing her to go help Mallory.

She gave me a grateful smile and said, "I'm glad you made it," before running off.

"Did we win?" Delia asked me.

"We did," I agreed, letting out my breath as I realized it was over.

Delia and I helped where we could, carrying people like Ingrid into the cars, until everyone was finally ready to go.

"WHAT WAS IT?" I cornered Gabriel while we walked back to our car. I didn't know where we were going yet, but nobody wanted to stay there a moment longer than we needed to.

"What was what?" he asked, but he was still looking like he had lost something huge, as if a piece of his heart was gone forever.

"What did you have to give up so I could be here?" I said, getting him to stop and look at me, staring right into my eyes.

"Annabelle," he admitted after a moment's hesitation.

"What do you mean?" That was not what I had been expecting.

"She isn't coming back. The spell could only be used once, and I saved you instead of saving her," he explained.

"I'm so sorry," I apologized. "I know how much you love her."

"I love you," he said.

"Yes, I'm the annoying kid you have to keep from dying, but Annabelle has been the love of your life for centuries," I said without bringing up the fact that I had ever been anything more, however briefly.

"You're my heart," he argued. He looked down at my lips, then deep into my eyes, in that terrifying way where I feel like he can see into my soul, but he wasn't looking for anything other than permission. I nodded, subtly, but he seemed to be equally aware of me as he took a step closer and brought his hand to the side of my head, so his fingers were in my hair and his thumb rested on my cheek. He moved close, and I wanted to pinch myself, to make sure I wasn't dreaming, but then I felt his lips on mine and knew that I wasn't. "I'm never letting you go again," he promised.

"Your eyes," I realized. "They're brown," I said with a smile, getting him to smile as well before he leaned in and kissed me again.

"You're not riding with us?" I asked Embry when he stayed standing in front of the house.

"Not this time," he agreed, a weird look on his face. It was like how Sam looked at me before the guys took me to the plantation at the beginning of the summer.

"I'll see you at the manor?" I tried, a sinking feeling growing in the pit of my stomach.

"Luce," he gave me a sad smile and my heart broke.

"You're not coming back with us, are you?"

"I love you to the moon and back, but you have grown into a magnificent young woman and you don't need me to keep you safe anymore."

"I'll always need you," I argued, remembering how Alaric said you could choose whether you wanted to move on or die once you accomplished what you set out to do.

"You'll always want me," he corrected. "And I would stay a

few years for you to get settled, but then I would stay for Clara and you would have kids and…"

"You would just grow old watching me have the life I'm keeping you from getting back to," I let him know I understood. "Is she here?" I asked, looking around as if I could see her. I couldn't stomach the idea of him killing himself to join her, but if she was here, I wouldn't stop him from walking into the light.

"She's been waiting a long time," he agreed.

"Thank her for me," I said, bridging the distance between us and letting him take me in his arms for one last time.

"I am so proud of you, Lucy. You really are incredible."

"I was raised by a collective of really awesome people," I smiled.

"It shows," he teased, squeezing me tight before going over to Gabriel, who was checking the vehicles to make sure we had everyone. I couldn't hear what they said, but Gabriel gave him a sad smile before they hugged. Embry walked off towards the gazebo, lifting his arm like he was reaching for someone's outstretched hand, and then he was gone.

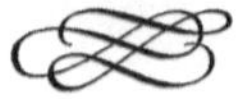

I t felt weird being back at my high school, especially since everything looked the same as it had back when I knew nothing about magic or the world of Gifted. Everything except the students. The freshmen today looked like college students had when I was in school. Or maybe I just felt that way because Clara was the one graduating, and no matter how many milestones I watched her reach, I still thought of her as my baby sister.

"There they are," Gabriel waved over to where Sam and Deanna were saving us seats, his fiery red hair and her platinum pixie making them hard to miss. Gabriel put his hand out to help me up the bleachers, which made me roll my eyes, even if I have been a little clumsier lately. He says I glow, but I'm pretty sure I look like a whale and he's just too in love with me to mention it.

"How was Italy?" Deanna asked of our babymoon once the hugs were out of the way.

"I think I ate my weight in pasta, but it was so worth it," I shared, tickling Ethan who was in his father's lap, giggling at my comment. I don't know what promise or mission had made Sam Gifted, but not long after we got back from Henry's, we noticed him growing older right along with Deanna, as if I hadn't watched him die. I know from Gabriel that you don't lose your Gift when you become human again, but Sam never mentioned it.

"It shows," Sam teased, nodding to my very pregnant stomach and garnering a new fit of giggles.

ONCE CLARA'S graduation was over, we went back to the manor for a celebratory dinner, but my sister-niece spent most of the meal going over all the things she should do on her graduation trip to Europe. She and her friends were trying to cover twelve countries in twenty-one days, and I happen to have been to all of them. Every year, during my summer breaks from Harvard, Gabriel and I chose a different place I had always dreamed of visiting and explored it to our heart's content. He almost always knew someone in the area who could show us how the locals live, but most of the time we just wandered around and stumbled onto amazing little gems off the beaten path. Now that I wasn't going to die from a Curse and Gabriel wasn't going to live forever, we made it a point to live our lives to the fullest.

"And which one was your favorite?" Clara asked me with her best friend, Eloise, hanging on every word. "Italy?" she guessed, since the babymoon was our second time in Embry's birthplace.

"It's very romantic," I explained, looking over to Deanna to gauge her reaction, but she was no longer in the dining room. "It's the perfect place to escape with someone you love, but I've been told it's also a cool place to be wooed by a..."

"For she's a jolly good fellow..." the singing interrupted my suggestion that Clara have an Italian fling, which was probably for the best.

"You still haven't figured out a better song?" Clara asked as we finished our off-key rendition and Deanna put the cake down in front of her.

"Found it," Sam rushed into the dining room with a video camera and pointed it at his daughter. "We're going to have to do the singing over again," he told us.

"Dad," Clara said, making two syllables of the word as she rolled her eyes. It was the standard response from a teenager embarrassed by her parents when her friends come over. But unlike her friends who laughed with her, Clara and I both knew how lucky she was to have her dad there to fuss over her.

"One day, you'll be happy you can look back at how cute you were as a child. All the fun, happy memories," I pointed out as Gabriel came and wrapped his arms around me from behind, resting his hands on my stomach and his head on my shoulder.

"They hardly ever use them to embarrass you," Gabriel added, teasing her and getting a smile. I watched her friends from school stare at him until he caught them, at which point they looked away and giggled.

"Did your dad follow you around with a video camera?" Clara asked me.

"My dad wasn't as cool as yours," I said. She knew my dad wasn't in the picture now, but she assumed he used to be, like Sam's dad. She rolled her eyes at me, not agreeing with my assessment of her father.

"Also, we were born in a time when video cameras were these huge things that you had to lug around, and transfer onto VHS if you wanted to watch them," Deanna shared, with Ethan now perched on her hip. He was trying so hard not to fall asleep because of all the excitement, but it might be a little too much for a four-year-old.

"Can we watch them?" Clara asked, always curious about

the past, probably because we had all decided not to talk about it. Especially not with her.

"Not unless you have a VCR," Gabriel said apologetically, knowing full well that we had one back at the plantation. I went through all the old home videos and photographs when Gabriel and I moved into our newly renovated home. I wouldn't say we had a shrine to the women that came before me, but we had a room that housed all of my ancestor's artefacts. One day I would tell our kids about them, the women who made me who I am, and ultimately brought Gabriel and I together.

"What's a VCR?" Clara asked with a smile.

"Way before your time," I assured her, knowing that she knew and was just trying to make us feel our age.

"You guys must be really old."

"You have no idea, sweetie," Gabriel said, kissing her forehead. He sometimes slipped, and Clara would look at him funny, as if she was about to point out that there was no way he had met JFK, but then she would decide against it and let him backtrack to say he read it in a book or saw it in a movie. She probably knew way more than any of us were giving her credit for, but she was smart, and seemed to understand that it wasn't a happy story we were keeping from her.

After Sam got his video of Clara blowing out her candles and making a wish, he turned the camera on me. I was about to wish Clara a happy birthday on camera, assuming it was some kind of video testimonial, but they started singing again.

"My birthday isn't for months," I pointed out as they put the large cake in front of me.

"It's not a birthday cake," Clara argued, eying my stomach as I read the icing on the cake.

"A baby shower," I turned to Deanna.

"Clara didn't want us to do it while she was in Europe, and today was the only day everyone could show up."

"I love you kid," I took Clara in for a hug. "But this is your graduation."

"And you can tell that to my niece or nephew so they know I love them the most," she gave me a big smile before nodding over to where Keisha, Ingrid, Etta, Delia, Angela, Jen and Sarah were standing with their husbands, and some of my co-workers from the hospital. I was touched, even before Gabriel brought Charlie over, followed by Eric, his wife, and their two adorable sons.

I got up from the table and went to hug them all. It was getting harder and harder with Keisha; who's twins with Tennison were due any day now.

AFTER THE CAKE, Clara went to celebrate with her friends from school, while Deanna hosted an alcohol and guy-friendly baby shower. It was very entertaining watching my husband try to figure out modern-day diapers, since the last time he changed one was probably centuries ago.

I ended up by the doorway into the living room, watching all of my worlds intermingling. Delia and her husband were laughing with Keisha and Tennison, Caleb and Etta were in their glory playing hide and seek with Ethan, Ingrid was using her Gift of illusions on Sarah, who was staring at a painting like it was a television screen... even Alaric was promising Deanna that Clara could come to him if anything happened while she was in London.

I loved seeing the house so full of people, but it's always at the big occasions like these that I get nostalgic, remembering the people we lost, and how far we've come.

It took me a long time to stop blaming myself for some of the things I did, but instead of dwelling on it, I now try to make up for it, by putting more good out into the world than I took away. It means a lot of late nights at the hospital, but it isn't so bad when your husband is there with you. And Clara makes sure we take Sundays off to be there for a family dinner.

We missed a few last year, when Gabriel and I spent six months in Africa. Alaric's charity sponsored a mission to build houses and provide medical aid, so Gabriel and I went as doctors, Caleb brought his muscles and I have a suspicion Etta came in case I needed emergency healing. Luckily, Kiara's Curse was indeed lifted, and I made it to the ridiculous party everyone threw for my twenty-ninth birthday. Many people asked why we were going all out for a random, non-milestone birthday, but most of them understood.

"Where are you?" Gabriel asked me when he came over with a sizeable piece of cake and two forks, waking me from my daydream.

"I'm back," I said with a smile, grabbing the fork and taking a bite.

"Want me to whisk you away from all the celebrating?" He offered after swallowing an abnormally large piece.

"I like it," I assured him. "A wise old man once told me to celebrate everything."

"Embry was right," he smiled sadly at me. "But I'm not sure he would appreciate you calling him an old man."

"There's absolutely nothing wrong with getting old. I happen to be married to a much older gentleman who is waiting for me to catch up."

"Is that so?" he asked, putting the plate down to take me in his arms.

"I have my whole life ahead of me, and I plan on taking advantage of that with you," I said, leaning in for a kiss. When we pulled apart, I looked into his eyes, his beautiful brown eyes, and brushed my fingers through his slightly graying sideburns.

"If you keep obsessing over my gray hairs, you'll give me a complex," he warned.

"You know I love watching you go gray. It reminds me that..."

"That we're all going to die?" he finished for me.

"No, that we get to live. We aren't surviving anymore, we're settling down, having kids and families, then one day, in a very long time, we will die peacefully in our sleep of old age."

"Sounds perfect," he said, kissing me.

ANNABELLE

AMANDA LYNN PETRIN

"I bet I could reach that branch," Embry said while we walked through the forest that surrounded my father's property. We had been over the bridge to play in the part of the creek where it wasn't so deep, so we could splash around a bit to cool off. I dreamed of being able to take off my boots and slip my feet into the icy waters, but I loved my father too much to give him a heart attack.

"I bet I could get as high as that one," Gabriel pointed to a slightly smaller branch a few feet higher than the first. Everything was a competition with those two. They were equally matched in the sense that they each dominated different fields; Gabriel would win any races, but Embry could take anyone in a wrestling match, and so on. Climbing was fair game, though it always made me nervous. Embry was stronger, so he could lift himself up easier, but Gabriel was lighter and could usually go higher if the tree was weaker at the top, such as this one.

"I can outclimb the both of you on that tree," I said, walking past them. They both stopped, looked at each other, then turned to me.

"How high do you think you can go?" Embry asked me skeptically.

"To the top," I said like it wasn't a big deal.

"Really?" Embry asked, sizing me up. "What are we betting?"

"Bragging rights," I smiled. My father had become more diligent about not letting me 'muck around like a child' lately, but I was sure I hadn't lost my old skills yet.

"Loser has to bring the toffee next week," Embry looked so smug that I understood why they were so obsessed with beating each other.

"Deal," I shook his hand.

"Gabriel?" Embry turned to his best friend when he didn't take the bet.

"I'm sitting this one out," Gabriel raised his hands in innocence and surrender.

"Afraid to lose to a girl?" Embry teased.

"More like I know that this particular girl can beat both of us when it comes to trees. My money is on her."

"She won't like you more if you suck up," Embry warned.

"This isn't me sucking up or flattering her ego. I know I can beat you at this, but I also know that she climbs to the top of Old Henderson's steeple and we barely make it halfway."

"Climbed," Embry corrected, looking at my attire, that was definitely more restrictive than it used to be. "Can you even climb in that dress?"

"I can climb in anything," I said defiantly in response to his doubt, rather than because of my confidence.

"Ladies first?" Embry turned to me. "Or no, you said you could outclimb me, that was the bet."

"You have to go first," Gabriel agreed.

"What do I get if I prove you wrong?" Embry asked him, skipping the lowest branch and pulling himself up onto one that was taller than him.

"I'll do your chores tomorrow."

"For a week," Embry leveraged.

"For a month," Gabriel smiled to me.

"We'll leave it at the week," Embry shook his head as he rose higher and higher in the tree. I was more nervous watching him than I was of going up myself.

"Regretting your decision?" I asked Gabriel, mostly to distract myself from watching Embry climb branch after branch on a tree that didn't look capable of supporting him.

"Never. I would bet on you any day."

"Does that make you a fool?" I asked.

"It makes me someone who knows you don't make false claims. If you say you will do something, you will. You're honest to a fault."

"That's a lot of pressure," I couldn't help but smile at the way he was looking at me.

"You're good for it." He smiled and looked up to see Embry pass the point he said he would climb to, then reach the branch Gabriel had said he'd reach.

Embry looked down at us and asked, "Do you think you'll make it this high?"

"Wouldn't you like to know," I called up.

He smiled down at me, his blond hair catching in the wind, then went a little higher, but the branches at the top would not support his weight.

"Do I stay here so we can tell how high I got?" he asked.

"I would have the advantage of using you to climb higher."

"I guess I'll come down then." His smug smile lasted the entire time he climbed down, and only got bigger once he was standing tall at the bottom.

"Congratulations," I told him. "You beat your expectations."

"I did. And I'm okay with leaving it at that," he assured me with a smile that drove the other girls in town crazy. They were the reason my father kept pushing me to act more like a lady, so he could find a nice, strong, powerful, well-to-do man to marry me and take over the estate. I was lucky that my father wanted me to be happy, so he wanted someone who would also love and take care of me...hence the acting, and looking, more like a lady.

"Afraid you'll lose to a girl?" I threw his own words back at him.

"Would you like a boost?" he offered.

"I think that would be cheating," I ventured before lifting my skirts so I could use the lower branch as a step to reach the higher one Embry started with.

I moved slowly at first, but my muscles remembered as soon as I got going. I couldn't do it as effortlessly as Embry, but I had a sure foot and a strong grip.

"There's a nest up here!" I whispered excitedly when I was a few branches below Embry's original target.

"Robins, I think," he agreed.

"They're not just eggs, there's little babies!"

"We've been yelling since we got here, whispering now won't make a difference," Gabriel whispered up. I could tell from his voice that he was laughing at me.

"The chicks are sleeping. Now that I know, I have to be considerate of that," I pointed out, taking one last look before continuing on my way.

The trees grew thinner the higher I got, and from Gabriel's target I could see my home, where my parents would die if they saw me. I went slower from there, testing each branch before I put any weight on it.

"Congratulations, Monkey," Gabriel called up to me.

"You can climb," Embry was impressed.

"You knew that, Embry Dante. You just thought I got old and forgot."

"I thought it wasn't considered ladylike, but I stand corrected."

"Thank you," I pretended to tip my hat down to him, then tested the next branch.

"You can come down now Annabelle, you won," Gabriel pointed out.

"I won against Embry, but I said I could reach the top," I reminded them.

"We believe you," Gabriel called up.

There was some murmuring before Embry agreed, "We believe you can get to the tip of the tallest branch."

"Maybe I don't," I argued before going up a couple more branches. I paused near the top to feel the wind in my face, but it also made the branches sway, which I wasn't entirely comfortable with. There were three branches between me and what I considered the top. I was currently sitting to take in the view, and to make the branches stop moving.

"Come on, Belle!" Gabriel called up to me.

"I'll be down in a minute," I said, smiling to myself at how I said it as if I was simply coming down the stairs, rather than climbing down a tree.

"Do you enjoy causing heart attacks?" Gabriel pressed.

"What do you call cliff diving?"

"Fun," they said in unison.

"I call it a million ways to die of stupidity, so I say we're even."

"What are you even doing up there?" Embry asked, and I could hear the concern.

"You'll see," I was standing as tall as I could without using the top two branches, as they didn't feel secure. I took the long white ribbon from my curly brown hair and tied it around the highest branch I could reach. "Alright, catch me if I fall," I called out before making my way down.

"You better not..." Gabriel warned.

"You can't tell me what to do," I teased, careful not to get overly confident until I was on the ground.

"Can I ask you very politely to please not fall, because my heart would never recover if I didn't catch you, or if you got injured in any way."

"Same here," Embry voiced.

"It sounds to me like men have the weaker hearts."

"Definitely," Gabriel agreed.

"We can do the scary stuff, no problem but my heart... don't ask me to watch someone I love in danger or in pain."

"I would much rather be the one in pain," Gabriel said.

"Pathetic," I teased, passing the nest with the robins.

"You, Miss Owens, are unlike any other lady I've ever met," Gabriel gave me a hand once I got to the last branch.

"Possibly because I am not a lady."

"You are, according to your father."

"Yes, he wants me to grow up and be proper, but until summer is over..."

"You get to be a girl," Embry shrugged, causing me to raise an eyebrow at him. "Which is clearly a very good thing. Have I mentioned my best friend is a girl?"

"I thought I was your best friend?" Gabriel pretended to be offended.

"I have two," Embry assured him.

"Same," I smiled at them.

"Me three," Gabriel agreed.

"Come on, let's get you home before your father sees the state of you," Embry put an end to the moment.

"I'm more afraid of her mother," Gabriel warned.

My father was stern when needed, but I was his beloved little girl who could do no wrong, whose happiness was his main concern. My mother's job was turning me into the lady my father needed and convincing me my happiness lie in whatever was best for the family. My father could decide to allow me a few more weeks of childhood, but my mother had to make sure he got what he wanted when he wanted it. The whole thing sounded exhausting.

"You also have a lot of chores to get through," Gabriel reminded Embry.

"Does the month start now then?" Embry asked.

"A week is fine," Gabriel assured him.

"I guess I better leave…" Embry waited for Gabriel to tell him it was fine, that they would do double or nothing on the next bet.

"I'll see you tomorrow," I told him, as Gabriel was not letting him off.

"It might be afternoon. Late afternoon," he looked to Gabriel for pity.

"Godspeed," Gabriel told Embry, who sauntered off none too pleased.

"You're terrible," I said once we were alone.

"Are you forgetting when he had me muck out the stables for weeks?"

"I think the difference is that he beat you fair and square, whereas today…"

"You were the one who beat him," he finished for me. "But I bet on you, which is no different from…"

"From what?" I asked when he stopped himself.

"It's actually very different."

"From what?" I repeated.

"The time we bet on the rabbits."

"Oh, so I'm a rabbit?"

"Only in the sense that you are someone independent of us, that we bet on, even though neither of us could influence the outcome."

"He could have," I pointed out.

"Not against you," Gabriel smiled as we got to the bridge. My father paid his laborers extra to build it after I spent a summer crossing the divide by balancing on an overturned tree.

"Flattery gets you nowhere," I warned.

"Honestly, I would let him start any other day, but…"

"But what?" This time he didn't stop himself, he let the thought linger, as if I could guess what he meant to say.

"But I liked the idea of being able to walk the rest of the way home with you."

"Without him?" I asked.

"Without him," he agreed.

"I thought you had two best friends, Mr. Black."

"I do. But I have high hopes for one of them."

"What kind of hopes?" I asked. My heart was beating like it had at the top of the tree. My palms were sweaty, but I felt a shiver.

"Well, she's just a girl now, the kind with muddy boots, leaves in her hair and tears in her dresses--"

"Is something wrong with that?" I asked, ready to be offended if that was the case.

"Not a thing. I would have her stay that way forever."

"Just a girl?" For some reason, I didn't like that idea. I wanted all the liberties afforded to me as a girl, but when Gabriel smiled at me, I wanted to be one of those women in the beautiful dresses who go to a dance and fall in love.

"No, a beautiful lady who climbs trees and runs through puddles and laughs in a way that makes me feel like everything will always be okay, because nothing can be wrong when she smiles."

"She sounds nearly impossible to find," I could hear my heart pounding against my chest and had to remind myself to breathe.

"She would be. I can't imagine there's more than one of her in all of creation," he stopped on the edge of the forest that lines our property and turned to face me. "Luckily, I have found her, and she is standing right in front of me."

"She is," it came out as a cross between a question and a statement, as I got lost in his beautiful brown eyes. "I'm not..." I tried to come up with something clever.

"You're perfect," he said before leaning in so our lips were so close that I could nearly taste the strawberries we ate earlier. He wasn't coming any closer, so I bridged the distance. His lips met mine in a fabulous millisecond of magic.

CHAPTER 2

I had never been kissed like that before, so I had nothing to compare it to, but I was certain that no kiss could ever compare. Gabriel and Embry were both my best friends, but I had been in love with Gabriel for as long as I could remember.

"Annabelle!" my mother yelled from the front porch of our plantation house.

Technically, we were still hidden by the trees, but I nearly jumped out of my skin before stepping away so there were feet of distance between us.

"Don't worry, she can't see us," he assured me. He was smiling from ear to ear, like he just couldn't help it. "I've been wanting to do that forever," he admitted.

I swallowed hard before smiling back at him. "Me too," I agreed, but there was a sinking feeling in the pit of my stomach. Because he was my best friend, and that kiss was going to change things. For us, for Embry, for my parents…it changed everything.

"Come on," he put out his hand to bring me through the woods to the house, but I kept my hand to myself, shaking my head and motioning to where I knew my mother was standing, waiting for us. "Of course. Don't worry, I'll win her over," he winked before leading the way to the house. There was a bounce in his step that made my heart flutter.

"Good evening Mrs. Owens. How is the picnic coming along?" he asked once we got close. My mother was staring at us like she knew exactly what just happened. While I was a bunch of nerves, Gabriel attempted to normalize the situation.

"Will your father be at the picnic, Mr. Black?" my mother asked with the utmost politeness, though she held her head particularly high.

"He's been preparing for weeks," Gabriel assured her. "My mother's even made me a suit, in case there's dancing. It's very smart, quite like your husband's from last year's picnic," he was clearly trying to win her over, as he had promised, and I found it adorable. My mother, on the other hand, was not so impressed.

"You should be heading home," she told him, making it a point to look out at the setting sun. "It's getting late."

"Of course. Have a lovely evening, Mrs. Owens," he bowed to her before turning to me. "I'll see you tomorrow?" he asked with a smile.

"I'll see you tomorrow," I couldn't help but return his smile. I could feel how red and flushed my face was.

"Go wash up, Annabelle," my mother told me when I got to our porch. I looked back to Gabriel, who turned as he was walking to give me one last smile.

"Of course, mama," I gave her a kiss on the cheek before going inside and trying to remove any evidence of climbing the tree and splashing adventures in the creek.

CHAPTER 3

My father's partner and his wife, whom I called Uncle Robert and Aunt Elena, were invited to dine with us, so most of the dinner conversation revolved around them and their business ventures, leaving me to sit in my own world, trying to think straight while I could still feel the imprint of Gabriel's lips on mine.

I thought I was doing a wonderful job of participating just enough in the conversation that no one would get suspicious, but Aunt Elena found me in my room once the adults went to the sitting room for a night cap.

"Is everything okay?" she asked, gently knocking on my door, not waiting for my response before letting herself in. She and Uncle Robert had three boys who were all grown up, so she had always treated me a bit like the daughter she never had. I'm fairly certain it bothered my mother, who got jealous whenever Aunt Elena did something motherly towards me, but I didn't mind.

"Of course," I gave her what I hoped was a convincing smile, but she sort of squinted at me before coming to sit beside me on the bed.

"Anything on your mind?" she pressed.

"The picnic is coming up. And the summer's almost over."

They were trivial events. We were literally talking about the weather, but she nodded in understanding.

"Is this about climbing trees, or the boys you do it with?" My shocked expression made her laugh. "You shouldn't go so high if you don't want to be seen," she reproached.

"I had to," I said with utter conviction.

"Because…" It wasn't that she didn't believe me, but she could tell it was more arbitrary than a gun to my head that forced me to do it.

"Embry thought I couldn't do it," I admitted, aware that wasn't a good enough reason to defy my parents.

"What about Gabriel?" she asked.

"What about him?"

"Did he think you could do it?"

My feelings were either written on my face or she could read minds, something I had often suspected of her.

"He did, but I had to prove it to Embry, and to myself."

"You needed to defend your own honor," she said simply.

She didn't say anything else, but she sighed and looked over to me, waiting with a small, compassionate smile.

"He kissed me," I admitted, feeling the flush in my cheeks and the smile that I couldn't stop.

"Gabriel," she said like there was no other option.

"How do you know?"

"Your face lights up when you talk about him. If Embry kissed you, there would be less smiling and more dread."

"Embry is my best friend," I argued.

"Oh, he's wonderful. But I'm sure even he knows you're in love with Gabriel, and to do anything like that would mean destroying his two most important friendships."

"You're saying everyone knows?" I asked.

"Everyone who pays attention," she agreed.

"My mother?" I asked.

"What's wrong?" she asked instead of answering.

I sighed before coming clean. "When he kissed me, it was like…fireworks," I smiled, bringing my fingers to my lips and remembering it.

"The best ones are," she agreed.

"But then I realized that it changes everything," I continued, her smile not helping. "We can't stay best friends who occasionally kiss. And as soon as we tell Embry, things will be weird…"

"And more importantly…" she pressed when I didn't.

"My mother doesn't approve. At all. My father hasn't said anything, but I doubt he feels differently," I admitted.

"What do you want in all of this?" she asked me.

"Gabriel," I said simply. "But I also want things to stay the same. To climb trees and run around with both him and Embry, until I'm older and we get married and live happily ever after," I added, not expecting it when she laughed at me. "It isn't funny."

"No, but it is familiar," she assured me.

"What did you do?" I asked.

"I waited for him to grow up," she shrugged.

"I don't think it's his age she has a problem with," I argued.

"No, I think it's a boy being interested in her little girl."

"Growing up won't change that. I hope," I added the last part worriedly, but even the thought of Gabriel not being there for me seemed ridiculous. He'd been there the first day I set foot on American soil and hadn't left my side since. No matter what I was going through, or what happened in the world around us, he always felt like home. A strong, stable, solid presence that made me feel safe, yet also gave me butterflies. I brought my hand to the scar on my right palm, remembering the day I got it, trying to impress him in my father's study. Gabriel bandaged it and kissed my broken skin, setting my world on fire. But that was Gabriel. Taking care of me and knowing exactly what to do. I remember thinking I would take another wound if it gave me another kiss.

"I don't think so either," Aunt Elena smiled. "But right now Gabriel is a boy your mother knows as the reason you come home with tousled hair, torn stockings and muddy boots."

"It's not his fault. Or Embry's. I know she wants me to be prim and proper, but she has no idea what it is like at the top of the trees, or how good it feels to splash around in the creek on a hot summer day."

"I didn't know your mother at your age, but I daresay she knows exactly what being young, innocent and carefree feels like," Aunt Elena said, her eyes drifting off as if she was remembering when she was a little girl.

"So once I stop acting like a child, you think she'll approve of Gabriel?" I asked hopefully.

"Once you start acting like the lady she wants you to be, and he becomes the man who deserves you, I'm sure she'll approve."

"She might be more interested in a man who can tame me."

I got her to laugh, but this time it was on purpose. "Give him a chance. I've seen him in town. He's been following Dr. Smith around since he cured Patrick, and I believe he has big dreams. Let them come true," she suggested. I shuddered at the memory of the time we thought Gabriel's little brother was going to die. Gabriel had been reading up and asking questions about everything related to medicine ever since.

"There you are, Annabelle. Stop bothering Mrs. Archer. Your father would love for you to sing for us," my mother barged in and expertly disguised her shock at finding Aunt Elena and I sharing secrets in my bedroom.

"Of course, mama," I went over and kissed her on the cheek before going downstairs.

CHAPTER 4

Once Aunt Elena and Uncle Robert went home, I found myself lingering outside my father's study, pacing back and forth in the hallway. I knew Aunt Elena was right, that the best thing I could do was nothing. Gabriel knew how my mother was, so he would have to understand that we had to stay friends for now, until I could convince my parents he was my perfect match. But at the same time, I didn't want to wait. I loved him, and I didn't care who knew it.

"Annabelle," my father called, just as I brought my fist up to knock on his door.

"Yes, papa?" I asked, trying to steady my heart and slow my breathing. My nerves were making me look guilty, although I knew I hadn't done anything wrong.

"Were you in the hallway?" he asked, crinkling his eyebrows at me.

"I was coming to say goodnight," I lied. He seemed nervous, which couldn't be good.

"I was talking to your mother," he began, coming around to sit at the edge of his desk.

"About the picnic?" I asked hopefully when he stopped

there, but he took off his glasses and pinched the bridge of his nose.

"I know we agreed you could spend one last summer doing things that could be considered inappropriate for a daughter of mine…"

"Until classes start again," I agreed.

"Of course," he smiled, but there was something dismissive about it. I knew a lot of my classmates weren't returning in the fall, as they were going to work or get married instead, but I had hoped I wouldn't be one of them. "But your mother and I were talking, and the picnic is a big event that launches the social season, and…"

"And it's my last summer picnic." I knew where he was going, but it was taking him forever, and I hoped he might lose his resolve.

"You'll have so many summer picnics, my darling." He put his hand out, so I gave him mine, and he pulled me into him. "We had a beautiful dress made for you, and I think it would be nice if I could present you to society without grass stains on your skirts and mud on your cheek."

"I can be careful," I offered. "It's really just races, and…" even as I said the words, I knew it was useless. Reluctant or not, his decision was made.

"You're too old to be running around and gallivanting with those boys, my love."

"Is this about dresses or Embry and Gabriel?" I asked, careful not to show any emotion as I said their names.

"It's about both, as it's about neither. They all represent your childhood, but it's time to grow up, Annabelle. You're not a child anymore."

"Are you saying I can't be friends with them anymore?" I asked, my heart almost stopping in my chest.

"Of course not. You'll see them in town and you can be friendly, but it's not normal for a lady to spend all of her time with boys." For the first time this conversation, he looked at me with certainty. His answer was final.

"Yes, father," I said blankly. "Goodnight." I tried to hold my emotions in until I could get to my room and be alone.

"Goodnight, Annabelle," he dismissed me.

I WENT to bed and stared at the ceiling, thinking how much things could change in a matter of hours, or in an instant. That afternoon I was enjoying one of my last carefree days of summer. Then Gabriel kissed me and it took me out of my comfort zone, into a world of scary possibilities. Now I was alone, my carefree days over, and things would never be the same again. I was dreading the dress I would have to wear and the conversations I would have to fake, but more than anything, I was dreading what this meant for me and Gabriel. Not only was a relationship completely out of the question now, I wasn't even sure we could be friends.

CHAPTER 5

"Miss Owens," Gabriel walked over and did a fancy bow when he ran into Eugenia and I at the picnic. I'd heard my mother telling him I couldn't go out and play with him anymore when he came to the house, but I hadn't seen him since he'd kissed me. My breath caught in my chest at the sight of him in his new suit, but I tried my best not to show it.

"Mr. Black," I overexaggerated my curtsey.

"Miss Monroe," he acknowledged my companion before turning back to me. "I trust you're enjoying the festivities?"

"You'll have to congratulate your brother for me, on his excellent marksmanship," I said, as Patrick had claimed the first-place ribbon. Normally, I would have competed with the boys, never coming close to winning, but still having a wonderful time. My parents were right though; I would have been the oldest girl there by far if I had participated.

"We're all very proud of him," he assured me. I could already feel everything shifting. He was looking at me the way he always had, but his words were guarded, analyzing the optics before saying or doing anything.

"Congratulations to you as well," Eugenia chimed in. "Fastest man in Boston."

"The last sober man at the picnic," he was always modest, implying it had less to do with skill, and everything to do with drinking habits.

"Aren't you ladies a lovely sight for sore eyes," Embry arrived, draping an arm around Gabriel's shoulder.

"Oh, Embry, what have you done to your hair?" I asked. There was a gold ribbon tied in it, as well as what looked like twigs and dead leaves.

"A gentleman doesn't kiss and tell," he smiled to me.

The four of us stood there awkwardly for a moment. Eugenia was trying to weigh her chances with both of my best friends, while I was struggling to resist rushing into their arms. With Gabriel officially apprenticing for Dr. Smith now, Embry working with his brother, and my father's thinly-veiled warning... I doubted I would have another chance to.

"We were on our way home, if the two of you wouldn't mind accompanying us," Eugenia broke the silence.

"It would be our pleasure," Embry assured her, breaking the ice as he fell in line between us, leaving Gabriel the spot on my right.

"Why are you leaving so early?" he asked me while Eugenia talked to Embry about his sister, Maria, who was teaching her how to play the viola, without much success.

"There isn't so much to see when you're not allowed to do any of it," I explained. "Why did you leave?"

"Perhaps I was waiting for you?"

I could feel my cheeks blushing. "That would be quite inappropriate, Mr. Black," I warned.

"In that case we'll say I had business to get to," he said, his brown eyes studying my face like he was trying to see the truth behind my polite exterior. With those eyes, I believed he could.

CHAPTER 6

The next time I saw Gabriel outside of church was a few months later, as I was getting ready for yet another social engagement, where my mother would introduce me to all of the eligible bachelors, and I would do my best to be equally polite and annoying, so none of them would want to stick around. I was walking down the stairs so my mother could help me with the final touches, but instead I found Gabriel in the foyer.

"You look...breathtaking." he said, making me blush more than I already was. My dress was deep green, like a luscious forest. He was in awe, nearly speechless, but his eyes were full of yearning and remorse.

"Are you coming to the dance?" My heart beat faster and my stomach was in knots.

"No, I came to see your father. Purely business," he gave me a smile, that told me it was anything but. His eyes had a sadness to them.

"Purely?" I tried to get his eyes to smile along.

"Perhaps I hoped I would be lucky enough to see you before you left."

"And this doesn't change your mind?" I asked, twirling for him. The words had my usual confidence, but inside I was nothing but nerves. Around Gabriel, of all people. It made no sense, but every time he came close, I was overrun by a mix of emotions that, while confusing, I did not want to stop.

"About attending?" His eyes never left me, going back and forth between my dress and my eyes, both making me blush.

"I am certain you were invited," I agreed.

"I really must speak with your father," he argued. I was so fixated on my own nerves that I hadn't noticed his.

"Is everything okay?" I asked.

"Of course, Bells. Just some boring forms to sign."

"He's in the study. Bookkeeping, I believe, so your forms will fit right in."

"Thank you." There was nothing silly about his bow today, but his eyes did linger on me, taking one last look at my dress before he went down the hallway.

"Who was that?" my mother asked, bringing me the pearl earrings she wanted me to wear.

"Gabriel Black," I said like I couldn't care less. "These are beautiful." The earrings were simple, but I had never seen such big, white pearls before.

"They were my mother's. I never felt comfortable wearing them here, but you look like a princess," she told me proudly.

"The dress is lovely," I was grateful. Tonight was a big event, and I knew how much effort she put into it for me.

"No, you're lovely, and the dress is lucky to be on you," she gave me a smile before adjusting my hair.

"Thank you, mama," I told her.

"One day you'll have a daughter of your own and you'll understand," she told me.

"We should get going," I went over to grab my coat. I was

truly grateful, and did feel like a princess tonight. It wasn't that getting married and having children scared me. I had long ago resigned myself to being the lady and wife I knew I had to become, but I did not want to meet him tonight, which I knew was her dream.

"I'll go get your father," she smiled at me before she went, but it didn't reach her eyes. Our relationship had been strained for years, and I had always been a daddy's girl, but I still remembered when her arms around me were the only thing that made me feel safe. Which was why her polite smile to cover her hurt broke my heart.

"We can drop you off on the way," my mother was offering when she returned with my father and Gabriel at her heels.

"Oh, that won't be necessary. I can walk," Gabriel assured her.

"You're not attending?" my father asked, surprised.

"It's not really my—"

"He can't go wearing—"

My mother and Gabriel both tried to dissuade him, but my father's mind was immovable once he made it up. "Nonsense, you can wear my jacket. If you're looking to establish yourself, you need more than excellent grades, Gabriel. You need to know people, and tonight will be full of people.

"The very best people," I added with a smile I wouldn't have been able to stop, even if I had tried.

"That's the spirit," my father put his hand on my shoulder before Gabriel followed him to get a jacket, leaving me alone with my mother.

"I thought Gabriel was a laborer," she interrupted the silence.

"He's apprenticing with Dr. Smith so he can some day take over and treat people."

"That doctor is a godsend," she said. I could almost see the wheels spinning in her brain.

"I heard Gabriel is a fast learner who has proven to be incredibly helpful." I spent a lot of my time casually bringing up all of Gabriel's achievements in an attempt to get a reaction from her. She tended to focus on any bad rumors about him and Embry, completely ignoring anything that painted them in a decent light.

"Winter months are when help will be needed. It's not even November yet and the cold is already moving in," she looked out the window as if she could see it happening.

CHAPTER 7

My father and Gabriel talked business on the ride, then left to make introductions once we arrived. I let my mother fix my hair one last time before going over to Eugenia and Maria, who were patiently waiting to be introduced to society.

"I was hoping he would be here," Eugenia said excitedly, looking over my shoulder as I sat down beside her.

"Who?" I asked, turning to where she was looking. "Gabriel?"

"Gabriel Black makes me weak in the knees. I nearly trip over my own feet every time he's near me."

"I had no idea," I said, looking around at the other girls my age. Some of them had grown up with us, while others I had never seen before, but they all noticed him. Most looked at him like he was a delicious piece of cake they wanted very badly, but couldn't have, while the new faces were intrigued, whispering amongst themselves about who he might be.

"Embry is adorable as well, but there's something about tall, dark and handsome that I can't resist," Eugenia defended herself.

He is irresistible, I thought to myself. But I always hoped the other girls wouldn't notice.

EUGENIA WAS the first of us onto the dance floor, with Mr. Roosevelt, one of the rich merchants from the city. He'd just bought the property across the grounds from ours and, while he was at least a decade older than us, he had a kind smile and bright green eyes that gave him a youthful air. I also knew, from occasionally wandering where I shouldn't, that he was an absolute gentleman when he found women on their own in the middle of a forest.

"I'm starving to death," I confided in Maria. I usually ate before coming, but Gabriel had shown up and distracted me. I could practically feel my stomach digesting itself.

"Surely you won't die?" she asked with concern.

"Of course not. I just mean that I'm hungry," I assured her. She had a tendency to take me literally, which I assumed came from her having to translate everything into Italian in her mind. Embry had moved here when he was a little boy, but his older siblings had joined after my family was already settled.

"I'm certain I saw a table with some –"

"That's quite alright, Maria, I'll eat when I get home." I knew that no matter what was on that table, my mother would not approve of me eating it here, in front of everyone.

She looked at me with confusion before Eugenia returned to us from the dance floor.

"Escorted home by Embry Dante and asked to dance by Mr. Roosevelt, what is your secret?" Maria asked her.

"He reminds me of my brother," Eugenia did a face that implied she had no interest in the wealthy Mr. Roosevelt, before her eyes found Gabriel across the dance floor. He was still talking with my father and a group of men whose daughters were on the dance floor.

"Miss Owens," a voice I didn't recognize said from behind us, summoning me away from Gabriel. "My name is Bartholomew Mayweather. I was hoping I could have this dance," he asked, extending his hand to help me to my feet.

I looked over to Gabriel, who was busy talking to Uncle Robert, then to my mother, whose smile urged me to accept him.

"It would be my pleasure," I nodded.

He moved gracefully and followed the music perfectly, but he didn't talk. Nor was he very forthcoming when I asked him questions, getting nothing more than he was new to Boston and renting a small cottage while his estate was being built.

"Are you with any family?" I asked. He didn't look much older than me, so I doubted he moved to town on his own.

"My parents. We came tonight for my sister." He nodded over to a timid girl of maybe thirteen, who tried, unsuccessfully, to hide her red hair with a dark brown bonnet.

"And what is it you do?" I asked him.

"We own ships."

"Sounds interesting. What kinds of ships?" I tried my best to be polite and interested, but he made it incredibly difficult.

"We lease them."

"To pirates?" I teased, hoping to get a smile. He had a foot and a half on me and was staunchly looking ahead. He was either bored or distracted.

"Pirates are not a laughing matter," he warned. "And they would never pay for a ship. By their very definition, they take them."

"Of course. I'm sorry, I don't know much about ships and was—"

"No one would expect you to," he assured me in what felt like a very condescending manner, before he put his concentration back on the dance.

· · ·

I WAS INCREDIBLY grateful when the music finally ended, so I could bow out of that encounter. I was heading back to Eugenia, to warn her to stay clear of Mr. Mayweather, when Gabriel was suddenly in front of me, smiling.

"I see you've managed to escape my father's companions," I returned his smile while doing a slight curtsey.

"Just in time, by the looks of it," he nodded off to my previous dance partner, who was now talking to Maria. "May I have the honor of escorting you to the dance floor?" he asked of me.

"I assure you, the honor is mine, Dr. Black."

"Let's not get ahead of ourselves," he warned, trying to disguise his smile. "Your father has been most helpful."

"He loves helping people," I assured him. "Plus, it's good for him if years from now, he's in the good graces of the town's very prominent doctor."

"He knows he would never have to worry about that."

"He can be cutthroat in business when he has to be."

"He's still your father," he argued. "No matter how he treated me, he would always receive the utmost of my capabilities, because of what it would do to you to lose him."

"Well, you've certainly garnered an audience," I changed the subject, focusing on the people around the room rather than on his words.

"Where?" he looked around like he didn't even see them.

"You must have noticed. Every girl in here is looking at you like you're—"

"I'm too busy looking at you," he cut me off.

"You were busy putting yourself in the good graces of every member of high society my father could spot."

"I don't know if it will be enough, but it certainly won't hurt," he agreed, sounding surprised. As was I.

"What were the forms for?"

"Are we really going to talk about your father's business?"

He twirled me around the floor with a skill I did not expect him to have. My heart was beating a mile a minute, and this wasn't helping.

"What else did you want to talk about?" I was nervous, which I attributed to the inner battle I was going through, of wanting more than anything for him to kiss me, while also knowing that I would die if he did it here, in front of everyone, including my parents.

"All of the eligible bachelors vying for your affections this evening, how beautiful you look in this dress, how easily one could get lost in your eyes..."

"Normal, everyday conversations," I summed it up.

"Always," he agreed with his smile, the one that feels like home and melted all my nerves away.

"You have no competition here," I assured him of all the eligible bachelors. "Mr. Mayweather is a bore who believes I am too simple to comprehend too many words."

"I'm sure one of them will be charming and respectful and check all the boxes your mother has for you." The words weren't meant to be comforting. He knew it was only a matter of time before my parents found me someone worthy of carrying on my father's legacy.

"Even then," I locked eyes with his, seeing mostly sadness reflected in them.

"Bells..." He kept an appropriate distance from me, but just the heat of his palm on mine sent shivers down my spine.

"You're going to be a doctor, Gabriel. No one could say you aren't worthy."

"Your mother still sees me as the boy you snuck out in the middle of the night to chase fireflies with."

"Are you turning me down or warning me not to get my hopes up?" I asked.

"What are you proposing?" He grinned, but there was a sadness behind it.

"To wait. As long as I make myself undesirable enough, you'll go to medical school and become a doctor, at which point my parents would be crazy to do anything other than welcome you into the family with open arms."

"See, right there, that's a terrible plan."

"Why?"

"How in the world could you ever make yourself undesirable?" he asked before the music ended, and my father summoned him once more, either for further introductions, or because of the way he was looking at me.

"I'M sorry about all those things I said earlier," Eugenia said once I followed her to the gardens for some air.

"What did you say?" I asked, wondering if she had complained to Maria about me when I wasn't paying attention.

"About Gabriel."

"I don't remember you saying anything rude about him," I argued. Everything she said just told me that he could have his pick of women if he didn't still have his eye on me.

"Nothing rude, but I didn't realize the two of you were—"

"We're not," I stopped her before she could go any further, but she just looked at me with the compassion Aunt Elena usually gave me.

"I saw the way you danced together."

"We're old friends," I argued.

"Take this from someone who has spent the entire evening watching him; he has not taken his eyes off you. Whether he was talking with old men or fending off flirtatious smiles, his eyes always found you."

"I hadn't noticed."

"He mostly waited until you were no longer staring at him," she gave me a smile.

"I'm sorry," I apologized to her.

"Don't be silly, Annabelle, he's my tall, dark and handsome, but he's your soulmate," she said with certainty.

"Embry is incredible," I offered with a smile.

"You're not the first to say it," she assured me.

"Really?" I asked.

"He has quite the following." She raised her eyebrow suggestively and I couldn't help but giggle. "But I think I'll give Mr. Roosevelt a chance.

"I didn't think you liked him."

"Not when I thought I had a chance with Gabriel, but he's…he's kind," she decided, and I knew exactly what she meant.

"You have my full support if he's what you want, but you deserve someone who isn't just kind to you. You deserve someone who sets your heart on fire. Or at the very least, makes you smile," I told her.

"So do you," she replied, looking over to where Gabriel was talking to my Aunt Elena. "You should go to him," she told me as Mr. Roosevelt approached us.

I WAS MAKING my way to Gabriel, but was surprised to see my father in the courtyard with who I believed to be Bartholomew's father. I had no idea that they knew each other.

"When you asked me here, I thought you had a business proposal," my father did not sound impressed.

"Not in the strictest sense of the word, but I do have a proposition," he paused to gauge my father's interest, but I could picture my father's stony business face, which usually revealed nothing.

I don't know why I didn't walk over and let them know I

was there, but I hid behind a rose bush and eavesdropped instead.

"I wanted to ask you for Annabelle's hand in marriage. For my son," he said as simply as if he were purchasing a loaf of bread. I was shocked, having assumed Bartholomew found me as boring as I found him.

"You want him to marry my daughter?" my father sounded confused. "Have they even met?"

"Yes, they danced earlier, and I spoke with your wife. I am told she is an accomplished singer who speaks multiple languages."

"My daughter or my wife?" my father made a joke, giving himself the chance to process the question. Mr. Mayweather's expression remained unchanged.

"We have a very lucrative shipping business and though he will be required to travel back to England on occasion, this will be his home base. Your daughter is beautiful and pleasant to talk to, and he would like to marry her."

"While I am flattered by the interest," my father paused, in complete control of the conversation. "I'm afraid there have been many libations this evening, and you'll have to wait for an answer in the morning."

"Of course, Mr. Owens, take your time." Mr. Mayweather's words did not match his tone. "Bartholomew will be in your neighborhood tomorrow afternoon, if that's suitable?"

"That should be fine," my father was non-committal, but it was clearly the end of the conversation.

I hurried back to the garden just in time to watch Mr. Mayweather return to the music inside, followed a few minutes later by my father.

. . .

"THERE YOU ARE," Gabriel found me still leaning against a tree, with my hand pressed to my heart. "I grew worried when Eugenia returned and you were—"

I silenced him by wrapping my arms around his waist and holding him close, something I hadn't done so openly in years.

"What's wrong? Did someone hurt you?" he asked.

Everything I needed to know about him I could hear in those words; his concern and love for me, what he would do to anyone who dared hurt me, and the promise that I would always be safe with him.

"It's nothing. I just needed a moment." I stepped back from him and tried to smile like everything was okay, but this changed everything. We couldn't just wait for Gabriel to become a physician so he could be an acceptable prospect for my parents. I had to do something now.

"Are you sure?" he asked me, knowing I was lying, but giving me the benefit of the doubt.

"It will be," I assured him with a more convincing smile this time. "You're working with Dr. Smith this week?"

"As soon as I'm done at the factory," he agreed.

"What time do you usually finish at?"

"Eight or nine, it depends how many patients he has to see. Though he always takes Wednesdays off," he volunteered.

"Can you meet me on Baker street as soon as you're done work on Wednesday?"

"Should I ask what this is all about?"

"Will it change your answer?" I turned it on him.

"I will see you on Wednesday," he shook his head like he found me impossible.

I tried to tease him back, even sticking out my tongue when no one was looking, but it felt like my heart was being compressed by a ton of rocks, and the whole structure was about to crumble on me.

"Everything will be okay," he assured me, reaching for my hand and giving it a squeeze.

"Of course it will."

He knew I wasn't convinced, just like I knew he had no way of knowing anything would be okay, but when he held my hand, I felt like it would be.

CHAPTER 8

The following morning, I got up early and made myself a tea, then waited at the kitchen table until I heard my father's footsteps on the stairs.

"Would you like some tea?" I called up to him.

"You're up early?" he said, coming into the kitchen.

"I couldn't sleep," I chose honesty, but didn't tell him why.

"I would love some," he decided.

"Shall I bring it to your office?"

"I think I have time to enjoy breakfast with my daughter," he assured me, taking a seat at the table.

I poured him a cup of tea, then made a plate of scones and biscuits, with some homemade jam.

"You spoil me," he said when I put it down in front of him.

"It might be a bribe," I admitted, taking a seat.

"You know I can't say no to you, sweets or not."

I waited until he put half the scone in his mouth before saying, "I heard you and Mr. Mayweather last night."

"Perhaps *I* should have made *you* breakfast," he gave me a sad smile.

"You're going to say yes?" I asked, not expecting how

heartbroken it made me feel that he cared so little about my happiness.

"Ultimately the decision would be yours," he told me. "I spoke with your mother and we were going to give him our blessing, but I would never force you to accept a proposal you didn't want to."

I believed him. He would never force me to say yes. But I was raised better than to go against him, so as soon as he gave his blessing, my fate would be sealed.

"Could you ask for more time?"

"Time for what?"

"As soon as he asks me, with your blessing, I would say yes." He gave me the courtesy of not pretending it wasn't true. "I'm not asking you to say no, papa, I understand that he's wealthy and powerful and I'm sure mama could tell me all about him," I smiled so it didn't seem like I was blaming her for organizing this. "But I don't know him. I barely spent five minutes with him last night, and I would love it if you could ask for more time to make your decision, so that I can get to know him," I rambled and lost the rehearsed speech I'd been reciting in my head all morning.

"How much time?"

"A couple of months?" I asked. It wasn't nearly enough time for what I had planned, but it was more than he would be willing to give me.

"I'm sure a month would be sufficient to know his character," he countered.

"A month then," I agreed.

"And when this month is over, you'll say yes and be happy with him?" he verified.

I didn't want to lie to him, so I chose my words carefully, "If, at the end of the month, you give him your blessing, then I will say yes to Bartholomew's proposal and try my best to be happy."

"Then I'll see what I can do," he assured me.

"Thank you, papa." I gave him a kiss on the cheek.

"Can we still have breakfast, or was it really just a bribe?"

"I would love some breakfast." I smiled at him before grabbing a scone and smothering it with jam.

"What's happening here?" my mother asked when she walked in and found us giggling.

"Nothing, my dear. Just telling Annabelle that Bartholomew will be coming over this afternoon. It should be an excellent opportunity for her to get to know him," he winked at me.

"He's a wonderful young man," she sat beside me at the table and took my hands in hers. "I met him on the way home from picking up your dress last week. He was heading into town and found me right after we got stuck in a mudslide. He asked if he could help and I told him yes, once you get to town, please tell my husband to send someone for me—"

"I heard nothing of this," my father cut in.

"Yes, I told you last night."

"You told me you met him, but I did not hear about a mudslide."

"I didn't need to tell you, because Bartholomew took care of it. He got out of his carriage and used his own hands to push us out."

"As opposed to someone else's hands?" I asked.

"What?" she was confused until my father laughed, and she understood what I had said. "Oh, you laugh, but he saved me from spending hours waiting for someone else to come by. Most men in his position would have just gone to your father, or sent someone else to take care of it."

"You're right. That was very nice of him," I said apologetically. "I'll be sure to thank him for it this afternoon."

"Give him a chance," she urged me.

"I will," I promised.

BARTHOLOMEW WAS BROUGHT straight to my father's study when he arrived. It took all of my self-restraint not to wait outside the door and eavesdrop as I had last night, but I trusted my father, and my mother was already suspicious enough.

"Miss Owens," Bartholomew said when he came out what felt like an eternity later.

"Mr. Mayweather," I greeted him.

"I have heard that your father's gardens are like a work of art. Would you care to show them to me?"

"It would be my pleasure," I assured him, but my mother was the only one whose smile was genuine.

On Wednesday I waited for Gabriel outside of Mr. Cole's shop. They were closing soon, but he agreed to stay a bit late to take some measures for me, although I'm not sure how much longer he was going to wait. My mother certainly kept him occupied, but he was the best tailor in Boston.

"Is this an adventure or a conversation?" Gabriel asked from behind me. Even before he spoke, there was an electricity in the air that gave me shivers.

"Both," I said, turning around to face him. "You're late."

"One of the guys in the shipping yard cut himself, so his buddy thought he would be funny and brought him to me instead of the foreman," he gave his excuse.

"How did you do?" I asked. As far as excuses went, his was pretty valid.

"I don't think he'll lose the finger, and the foreman said I had a physician-like precision."

"Makes sense, as you're a future physician," I smiled at the exhilaration on his face, from the adrenaline that hadn't quite died down yet.

"Hopefully," he agreed. "What are we doing this evening?"

"Our first stop is Mr. Cole," I explained, letting him inside the shop.

"This is your friend?" Mr. Cole asked me, eying him up and down.

"Yes, this is Gabriel Black," I introduced him.

"I know the Blacks," he assured me. "Is this for any particular occasion?"

"Just something he can wear day to day while assisting Dr. Smith. Perhaps something that could be used for important house calls as well as dinner parties."

"What are you talking about?" Gabriel asked me.

"I have the latest fashions from Paris," Mr. Cole tried to entice me.

"Leave those for my father. We're looking for something more traditional here. Elderly people with weak hearts, you see," I turned him down.

"Of course, Miss Owens. I'll be right back." He ran off to a back room.

Gabriel's eyes were still on me, waiting for an explanation.

"This is the adventure part."

"I can see that. What I don't see is how I am going to pay for a new wardrobe on a laborer's salary while also saving for medical school and—"

"It's my treat," I said, even though he was looking at me like his next words would be about his plans to marry me and provide me with the life I deserved.

"I can't accept that," he argued.

"Of course you can," I assured him.

"I never realized it bothered you," he was offended.

"It doesn't," I said, bridging the distance so I could put my hand on his arm. "At the ball, someone asked my father for my hand in marriage."

"Congratulations," the hurt in his eyes destroyed me, while the rest of his face tried to look happy for me.

"I convinced my father to give me a month. I said it was so I could get to know my suitor, but…"

"But what, Annabelle?" he was so close, and his eyes were locked on mine.

"When you kissed me in the woods…" I said, very aware of my voice shaking.

"Before your parents decided we were no longer allowed to 'run around' with you outside of school," he let me know he hadn't forgotten.

"I told you to do it again someday."

"That wasn't some veiled way of turning me down without crushing my feelings?"

"No, it was me trying to find a way to save you from my parents without losing you."

"You'll never lose me, Annabelle. No matter who you marry or where you go, you will always have me."

"I know," I brought my hand to his cheek and gave a weak smile. "But I don't just want you as my best friend. I don't want to dance with you on the side while my husband talks to his friends, or spend the rest of my life wishing I was with you. Because I do. I want to be with you," I told him.

"But I have to look the part?" he focused on our adventure rather than my words.

"I thought that as soon as you became a doctor, they would have no choice but to welcome you like the son they always wanted."

"It doesn't work like that," he argued.

"No, it doesn't, because my father is only giving me a month, and that is not enough time."

"So you're going to turn me into what they want for you, in the hopes that they'll finally accept me?" he asked.

"The last thing I want to do is change you, Gabriel. As far

as I'm concerned, you're perfect. You have the biggest heart, you're hardworking and smart and my heart beats faster at the thought of you…but I need you to look like them, so they can see it."

"Bells…" he still wasn't convinced.

"Do you love me?" I asked, suddenly nervous.

"With all my heart," he said without hesitation.

"This is my own money that I have saved, and I want to spend it on you, because I will never forgive myself if I didn't do everything in my power to make sure I got the happily ever after I have always wanted."

"With me?" he verified.

"There has never been anyone else, Gabriel. There never will be." I assured him.

"Then I will do whatever you need me to," he promised.

Mr. Cole came back with a large package and the measuring tape around his neck. After confirming a few sizes, he opened the package to reveal three gorgeous suits.

"They were ordered months ago for Mr. Lemming, but they won't be fitting him any time soon," Mr. Cole said delicately. Mrs. Lemming passed away over the winter and Mr. Lemming was not taking it very well at all. He was hardly seen outside of the house they once shared, and every time he was spotted, he was substantially larger than the time before. It was like he spent his days eating to try and fill the void his wife's death left him with.

"They're beautiful," I told Mr. Cole.

"You're a bit shorter than he was, so I'll have to hem the pant a bit, but if you don't mind that they weren't custom made for you, I can sell you the lot of them for a shilling," he offered.

"That would be incredibly kind, and I would be grateful," Gabriel told him.

"I should have them ready by Friday," Mr. Cole assured us.

"I'll bring the money with me," Gabriel promised.

"You can't afford those," I reproached once we were outside.

"I can pick up some extra shifts," he said like it wasn't a big deal, but I knew that it was. "If I want to prove to your father that I deserve you, I can't let you buy me suits to impress him. I don't want to trick him, I want him to see that I am the man for you. That I will love you every single day for the rest of my life, and I will provide for you, so you can live the life you deserve."

"All I want is you," I argued.

"But you deserve the world." He brought my hand to his lips and kissed it, causing a shock right through to my heart.

CHAPTER 10

My father's influence helped, and people started requesting Gabriel for house calls when Dr. Smith was unavailable. Sometimes even instead of him. He was maintaining his hours at the factory, but also accompanying Dr. Smith more and more. He was meeting influential people and showing them his competence, which had me overly confident with my plan, especially now that I knew for sure that Gabriel was on board with it.

Bartholomew, on the other hand, seemed to have taken my father's request for time to heart. He showed up every three days, just before lunch, so I could get to know him better. A combination of his boring personality and his displeasure with the wait resulted in the most dreadful meals in his company. If this continued any longer, I wouldn't be surprised if he turned even my mother against him as well.

I was prepared for another meal in silence, followed by an afternoon of boredom, when Bartholomew walked in with his parents and younger sister.

"You brought your family." I made an effort to smile.

"Yes, your mother recommended it. Although I dare say my mother has been just as eager to get to know my fiancée."

I tried to argue and remind him that there had been no proposal, no blessings given, and I would hopefully never be his fiancée, but my mother came and wrapped her arm around me, ushering us toward the backyard.

"I'm sure Annabelle would love to show your parents our gardens," she volunteered me.

"Oh, that would be lovely," his sister said excitedly.

"I've heard the gardens are a sight to behold," his mother said, louder than necessary, probably in the hopes of summoning my father from his office. He'd been cooped up in there all morning, upset about some accounts. He was being incredibly secretive around my mother and I, who both couldn't care less about his business.

"Why doesn't Annabelle give you a quick tour while I make sure lunch is ready?"

"I doubt a quick tour would be satisfying. I would much rather sit down and catch up so we may enjoy the extent of it after lunch," Mrs. Mayweather argued.

"Of course," my mother nodded to her before going to check on lunch, while I brought everyone into the sitting room. Mr. Mayweather immediately took to examining all of the paintings on the wall, while Mrs. Mayweather observed me like a farmer observed an animal at auction; a little crazy was okay, as long as I had wide enough hips to birth children, and the manners to hide it from strangers.

I sought refuge in his sister, Edith, who was enthralled by our harpsichord.

"Do you play?" she asked me.

"I sing mostly," I said, sitting beside her.

"Mother never lets me sing. Barry loves the viola, so she let me try it once, but she thinks I have no rhythm."

"Maybe you just have your own," I suggested.

"Isn't that the same thing?"

"No. Some things are beautiful, even if the world doesn't agree on it. My father finds me stuffy and out of tune whenever I play sheet music, but some days I'll just play around and do my own thing and he says it sounds beautiful."

"And you believe him?" she asked, looking over to her own father.

"I do," I smiled at her. "He rarely tells me in the moment. Usually it's at the next party, when he'll ask me to play that piece I was rehearsing the other day, and I have nothing to offer."

"Can you play all of these?" she asked, flipping the pages of sheet music, quickly tucking a loose strand of red hair back into her bonnet.

"I've learnt them all, but there are only a very few I can play well."

"Is this you?" she said, making me turn to see a full-page rendition of my face.

"It is," I agreed, hoping my emotions wouldn't betray me.

"It's not a self-portrait," she decided.

"My friend used to draw while I practiced. Sometimes I was the muse," I remembered the hours we spent in this room. Gabriel and Embry would come in while I was practicing. My mother always said I could only leave once my hour was done, so Embry would sing along or tease me while Gabriel would make sketches in a book I gave him one year for Christmas. It wasn't until he gave me this page that I saw most of his sketches were of me.

"I would love to be somebody's muse," she said longingly, bringing her fingers to the lead-covered page.

"It can be intoxicating," I agreed before looking around to make sure no one else was paying attention to our conversation. My mother would immediately know who drew my likeness.

"I'm so glad we'll be sisters soon, and you can teach me all the ways to find a dashing suitor who uses me as his muse," she was smiling to let me know she wouldn't really hold me responsible for her future prospects, but she was also excited for us to be sisters. Which I was under the impression wouldn't happen.

"I'll go check on the food," I decided, getting up and walking out without waiting for a response.

"I thought I had a month?" I asked, barging into my father's study.

"What?" he asked, distracted by a piece of paper he was holding.

"I thought you told Bartholomew you needed time before you could give him your blessing."

"I did," he agreed.

"His sister just told me she can't wait for us to be sisters, and he referred to me as his fiancée," I pointed out.

"You have your month, Annabelle, but it's merely a formality. He knows he'll have my blessing once the month is up, and he knows you'll say yes once he asks. Unless you plan on turning him down, he's only being precocious."

"I didn't think of it like that," I felt like a child reluctant to grow up, but this wasn't about delaying the inevitable. I needed to change it if I ever wanted the chance to be happy.

"He hasn't done anything untoward to you, has he?" he verified.

"No, he's been…a perfect gentleman," I lowered my definition of the word. He was polite and dutiful, but nothing more. I still wasn't sure if he actually liked me.

"Just give him time, my darling. He has a good heart," he assured me.

I nodded, but wasn't comforted in the least. "His father has been commenting on your absence," I told him.

"I'll be out in a minute," he assured me.

The following week, Dr. Smith left suddenly to visit his daughter, leaving Gabriel in charge. He took his responsibilities very seriously, checking on all the patients and making himself available should anyone need him. I was incredibly proud, although I missed seeing him.

"This was his dream," Embry reminded me as he accompanied me in the shops, looking for ribbons.

"He loves helping people," I agreed, smiling at his eternal optimism and belief in the goodness of everyone.

"Reminds me of someone," he teased, showing me a dark red sample.

"That looks like blood," I argued.

"Did you hear about the accident in the forest?"

"What accident?" I asked, not sure if I needed to be concerned yet.

"They were at the lumber yard and little Edwin McAllister came to bring his father some food, but no one saw him, and —"

"Oh, don't tell me," I warned, flinching from the images my mind conjured up.

"He's not dead," he assured me.

"No, but I'm sure he's mangled, and I don't want to hear about it."

"I mean, he'll never be the way he was, but he's a lot better than he could have been. I don't know all the details, not that I would tell them to you if I did, but Gabriel convinced them not to cut off the whole arm, and I'm told he's doing very well."

"Very well considering he only has one arm," I corrected.

"The point is, everyone who has told me the story called Gabriel a hero," he explained why he felt the need to tell me about the horrific accident.

"He is," I agreed, causing Embry to shake his head.

"How's it going with your betrothed?"

"He told you about that?" I asked. I'd made it a point not to mention Bartholomew to anyone, in case they got the wrong impression.

"Maria overheard your mother telling mine," he explained. "I think she fancied him."

"She can have him," I sighed. "His entire family came over the other day, talking like the engagement is secure and the wedding has all but happened," I sighed, trying to focus on the fabric, but my heart was beating fast. Not in the good way it did when Gabriel was close, but in a terrible way where I feared my one chance for happiness was slipping away.

"Have you told your family you don't want to marry him?"

"They know. They're just under the impression I'm reluctant to leave them and grow up or something, not that I'm in love with someone else."

"If they've seen the two of you together, there's no way they don't know."

"We're not that bad," I argued.

"You know, I thought I was in love with you once." He looked up at me with a nervous smile.

"You thought?" I asked.

"Or I was," he amended. "But then I saw the way you looked at Gabriel. I was fine with the way he looked at you, because there's nothing like competition to win a woman's heart, but when I saw you were looking at him the same way, like your heart beat for him alone…I decided I wasn't going to be in love with you anymore."

"How does that work?" I asked, hoping I wouldn't have to do the same.

"Lucky for me I caught it early. And I realized that loving you would break three hearts and destroy any chance of me ever finding happiness, so I had a lot of motivation."

"When was this?" I asked.

"Maybe a month after you arrived in Boston?" he scratched his temple, more to hide the fact that he was blushing than to help him think.

"No one has been in love with me that long," I argued. Not to mention that I had moments up until recently where I was convinced Embry cared for me as more than friends.

"I'm pretty sure you had him under your spell the moment he first saw you."

"That would mean he enjoyed the way I looked, not that he loved me."

"It would. Only the way he explains it, you were there, carrying a doll and a very fat cat, comforting him that this was a nice adventure and the people would be very kind, and you would protect him if they weren't. Promising him that he had nothing to worry about, because you would take care of him."

Gabriel had been alone the first time I met him, standing with his father a few feet away from where I was waiting for my father to ensure all of our belongings would be brought to the plantation for us. I was fairly certain I had moved on to playing with my doll while Maurice chased rats by the time I spotted Gabriel.

"I can't marry Bartholomew," I told him honestly, my heart breaking at the thought of it.

"I know," he said, but there wasn't really much he could do. "If I know Gabriel, I know that he loves you, and there is nothing in the world he wouldn't do to make you happy. He'll win your parents over."

"Or we can run off together."

"The three of us? Or is this a couples thing?" he asked.

"You're always invited Embry. You truly are my best friend." Even now that I wasn't supposed to interact with them, I never found anyone else I could talk to like I did to them. Eugenia was wonderful, and she was my favorite person to talk to at dances and other social functions, but Embry and Gabriel were where I could be myself and come home.

"You're definitely in my top two," he teased before someone pushed through the store's entrance with such speed that we both jumped and turned to look.

"There you are." Gabriel was out of breath, like he'd been running through town searching for us.

I was worried at first, but then I saw his smile.

"What's going on?" I asked as the shop owner lazily swatted at him and returned to the back room.

"Dr. Smith says I am ready to make house calls and treat people without him," he beamed.

"So soon?" I asked, surprised, but relief was already flooding my heart.

"He says he was so impressed with how I handled everything in his absence that, while he would still like to take me with him whenever possible, to give me a more complete education, he feels confident to let me go off and establish my own practice. I already have three families who've requested me, mostly thanks to your father, but..."

"You're like a real physician now," I understood.

"I'll always be learning, but the title is mine to use, and I can start earning an income."

"This is wonderful," I said, taking him in for a hug. I knew it wasn't proper and it lasted longer than it should have, but I felt like I could breathe easy for the first time in forever. Gabriel was now the suitor with prospects that they expected me to marry, so I no longer needed to mislead Bartholomew.

"Congratulations," Embry told the both of us. There was a hint of sadness behind his eyes, but he was genuinely happy for us.

"I came to you as soon as he told me," he explained his state.

"We have to tell my father," I smiled at him, biting down on my bottom lip to prevent myself from kissing him right there in the middle of the shop.

CHAPTER 12

The driver raised an eyebrow, but couldn't really argue with me, especially since we had the open carriage today. The drive to the plantation felt like the longest fifteen minutes of my life, possibly because it was the last fifteen minutes before the rest of my life could begin. We sat apart from each other, and I kept my hands neatly folded in my lap so I wouldn't reach out to grab his.

"You're home early," my mother met me in the foyer. "Did Eugenia not show?"

"She did, but she couldn't stay long. Embry accompanied me until I ran into Mr. Black," I lied, having always intended to see Embry. The words sounded funny, as I only ever used Gabriel's last name to tease him, but I felt the added touch of propriety might please her.

"Mr. Black," my mother's smile dropped when she saw him come in behind me. "How kind of you to accompany Annabelle home."

"It was my pleasure," Gabriel told her.

"Is papa home?" I asked, looking around, wondering if it

was best to ask her to get him, or to walk past her and find him myself.

"I believe he's in his study. What's going on, Annabelle?"

"Gabriel has some very exciting news," I said, suddenly nervous under her apprehensive stare.

SHE FOLLOWED us to the study, where my father had left the door open. This was always a good sign.

"Find what you were searching for?" he asked without looking up from his papers.

"I did," I told him, having trouble containing my excitement.

He looked up quickly to smile at my happiness, but did a double take when he saw Gabriel.

"Mr. Black."

"Mr. Owens," Gabriel was nervous, but still smiling.

"How is the apprenticeship going?" my father made conversation.

"Very well sir, thank you. In truth, Dr. Smith recently decided I was ready to set up my own practice. He would still mentor me, of course, but I have already started building up clients, and—"

"And you would like us to pay to have you on call for us," my father finished for him, like he understood exactly what was going on.

"No sir, there is only one thing I want from you, and it isn't money."

"How can I help you, Gabriel?"

"I would like to have your blessing to marry your daughter, if she'll have me." Any bit of the happiness he'd managed to hide thus far resurfaced with a vengeance. "As a physician I will make decent money. I can build a practice and provide her with a home, status, and all the love in the world to ensure she has everything she needs and more. I know I don't deserve her, no one does, but I would like to spend the rest of my life trying to."

Gabriel took my hand in his at the end, and I smiled at him before focusing on my father. I don't know what made me think that he would be happy for me and smiling as well, but he looked...not quite disappointed, but definitely not happy as he sighed, bringing his hands together.

"I'm sorry, but I can't," he apologized.

"You can't?" Gabriel repeated.

"I know you love my daughter and you will be good to her, but I'm afraid you're too late. Another man has already asked for her hand and I have given him my word. It would be my pleasure to support you in your new career, but Annabelle is spoken for."

"You said I had a month," I reminded him.

"Before I gave the blessing, yes, but he knows he has it. The matter has been discussed and although Bartholomew won't ask for another three days, he is under the impression that he is marrying you, and I can't go against that. I'm sorry Gabriel, I truly am."

"You're going to be late," my mother said, just as I was about to argue.

"Right, I must leave, but I can drop you off if you would like."

"Thank you, I appreciate it," Gabriel said, looking entirely defeated.

I looked from one to the other with absolutely no idea what was going on. My father said no, just like that, and Gabriel was accepting it.

"Papa," I tried to stop him, even putting my hand on his arm.

"I'm sorry, my darling, but I have a meeting I simply cannot miss. I'll be home in a few hours."

"But…"

"I'll be back," my father promised before heading out.

783

"I know this feels like the end of the world, but it isn't. Childhood crushes fade. Bartholomew might not be the most interesting man, but he is kind and caring and he will provide for you. He has a wonderful house that you can turn into a home, a large fortune...you won't want for anything," my mother told me. I just kept staring out the window, at the trees we climbed, the one we carved our names into, all of the dreams I had for my life that would never come true.

"Have I ever told you about Christopher?" she asked, taking my silence as a sign for her to continue. "He grew up on the property beside mine, where his father tended to the horses, and I was so in love with him. I dreamed of marrying him and living happily ever after..."

"And then what? You found Papa, someone of your social class and were much happier?" I asked, hating her more than I had hated anyone before. I was convinced I could have made my father see my side if she hadn't been there. In fact, we wouldn't even be in this position if she hadn't orchestrated the match.

"You make it sound so terrible, but I grew up deep in the country. My parents rarely took me into town, and Christopher was the only person my age. He was my best friend and I thought I loved him, but I didn't have a clue what love was, I just knew that I enjoyed spending time with him. When I finally went to town with my mother and met your father, it was like an explosion inside my chest. I never knew that you could care about a person that way, to want to be with them every minute, to miss them the instant they left the room. I could have spent my entire life thinking I was in love with Christopher, only because I didn't know any better, and never gave anyone else a chance," she said.

"I don't love Gabriel because I never gave anyone else a chance," I argued.

"You've known him since the day you arrived, he's comfortable--" she started, but I cut her off.

"No," I disagreed. "I love him because he is where my heart is. When something good happens to me, he is the first person I want to share it with. When I'm afraid, or sad, he is the person I want to turn to. I could give Bartholomew or any other suitor a million chances, but the only person I want to spend the rest of my life with is Gabriel Black. No one will ever love me, or be better for me than Gabriel. He didn't grow up with as much as us, but he has been working every single day, both at the factory and with Dr. Smith, so he can learn the skills and build a practice to take care of me, to be worthy of your blessing." The very thought of it made my blood boil. "I love you mama, but I have waited my whole life for you to accept Gabriel, to see that he is more than good enough. I thought becoming a doctor would be sufficient, but he shouldn't have to do any of it. You should see that he is worthy simply because he loves me. And I love him," I told her.

She had been looking at me with a growing uncertainty, that turned to horror at some point, when she understood the extent of my feelings for Gabriel.

"He isn't your Christopher," she voiced her realization.

"No, he's my everything," I agreed.

CHAPTER 14

My mother left me alone in my father's study, but it wasn't like I could just stand here while my dreams were crumbling around me. I had to get out of here, to do something, anything to try and hold on to them. My father had taken the carriage, so I was forced to take a horse from the stables. My first thought was to find Gabriel, but I doubt he would agree to run away with me if it meant losing my family and destroying my father's honor in the process. I next thought of Aunt Elena, who always managed to know the right thing to say, but I don't think there was anything she could do. I felt like there was a war raging inside my chest, and I either had to let it out or it would drown me, but I feared that if I didn't keep it contained, I could never get it back in.

I thought of Bartholomew and how I could have lived with his lack of a sense of humor, and maybe even been happy, if I had never met Gabriel. Never fallen in love with him. I always thought it would be the idea of breaking Embry's heart that would stop me from acting on my feelings for Gabriel. I never imagined it would be because I was promised to another man.

Without realizing it, I'd ridden to the cottage the Mayweathers were renting. I saw Edith first, picking flowers from the garden, her red hair so much longer than I'd expected. It was beautiful, now that she wasn't hiding it.

"Miss Owens!" she said excitedly when she saw me.

"Is your brother at home?" I asked, getting off the horse and taking a deep breath. I didn't know what I was going to say to him, but I knew that I had to try.

"He's over there with Miss Dante," she said, nodding over to the fields behind her. "We were together making a bouquet, but this is where the yellow flowers are," she explained.

"Maria?" As I said it, I saw them in the distance, not doing anything improper, but she was looking at him the way I knew I looked at Gabriel, and if I wasn't mistaken, he was looking at her in the same way.

"Annabelle," Maria said, shocked when she noticed me.

"Miss Owens," Bartholomew said, taking a step back.

"I came to confide in you, heart to heart, but I feel like you've just shown me yours," I shared. I wondered if every time I thought he was frustrated I was making him wait, he was really upset that I wasn't Maria.

"There is nothing going on, Miss Dante and I were simply walking with Edith when…"

"Of course," I stopped him from whatever lie he was coming up with.

"How can I help you, Miss Owens?" he asked.

"I wasn't sure what I thought would come of this conversation, but now I am hoping we can all find our happiness."

"You have your answer then?"

"To the question I haven't let you ask?"

"Is that not why you are here?"

"I'm here to plead for you to release my father from his word."

He looked at me, shocked, then for a second I saw anger,

before he stopped and looked to Maria. "Our families are expecting us to marry, Miss Owens. Anything else would be..."

"Better for the both of us," I said pointedly. "Do you even want to marry me?" I asked, and although I think he might have wanted to at the beginning, I believe he hadn't for a long time.

"My father asked, and I—"

"I made you wait," I tried to remind him how frustrating it had been for him.

"Is this because of Ga-- Mr. Black?" Maria spoke up. She had been silently listening to the man she loved trying – unconvincingly – to get me to marry him.

"I love him with all my heart," I agreed.

Bartholomew looked to Maria, then to me, and said, "My father wants what he wants, Miss Owens. Even if I wanted to..." he let the thought linger.

"Why me?" I asked.

Once more, he looked to Maria, as if her reaction weighed more in his decision to share than mine did. "My father has a business deal that risks to ruin us, but if your father's company shows an alliance to us, no one would dare act on it," he admitted.

His words brought an anger that made me want to slap him. Losing Gabriel to protect an innocent man's heart and my father's reputation was one thing, but losing him to be a pawn in a business transaction that uses my father's reputation...it left an awful taste in my mouth. The only thing that prevented me from following through on the impulse was the fact that Bartholomew looked as disgusted at the prospect as I felt. No wonder he'd been miserable for the past month.

"What if my father agreed to show his support for your family's business regardless?" I suggested.

"Why would he do that?"

"I am hoping my father cares enough about my happiness to not let this ruin four lives," I explained, trying to sound confident. My father had sounded like he wanted to say yes to Gabriel, but it was a question of honor that stopped him.

"If you can convince your father to show his support, I can surely convince my father to release you," he said to me, but his eyes were focused on Maria, with a smile I had never seen on him before.

"Thank you," I told him. For the first time since meeting him, I wanted to kiss him.

I rushed back to my horse, keenly aware of Edith following me, knowing she must have listened to every word. "You're still welcome at the plantation any time you'd like," I told her.

"I hope you mean that!" she called after me as I rode off.

"Absolutely," I yelled behind me.

CHAPTER 15

I rode to my father's office, not sure what I could say to persuade him, but willing to try anything. Unfortunately, he wasn't there, and neither was the carriage. I tried Uncle Robert's, but was told they were out of town, so my father couldn't be with him. I went to every place I could think of, but couldn't find him anywhere.

I eventually went home, figuring I would wait for him and plead my case as soon as he got home. I put the horse in the stables and tried to steady my nerves. I was about to go into the house to get cleaned up when I saw the carriage in the distance. I ran over with my dress hiked up, not even caring that my mother wouldn't approve. It took a moment for the driver to notice me, before he stopped the carriage and my father stepped out.

"Is everything okay?" he asked.

"No," I admitted, trying to wipe away the tears before I gave up and let them fall. "I lied, papa, when I said I would marry Bartholomew, I didn't mean it. Or I did, but I was hoping that you would come around and see how incredible

Gabriel is and give him your blessing instead. That's all I've wanted for as long as I can remember."

"Annabelle—"

"No, you have to listen, papa. I can't marry Mr. Mayweather, and I don't think you want me to. I know you don't want to go back on your word, but I spoke to him, and as long as you don't mind taking his company under your protection, he would be happy to release me and marry someone else. I don't know what the details of his business are, but I know that it would destroy me if I had to be without Gabriel. He is literally the best man I have ever met, and he will love me and be good to me, which I know is what you really want, deep down."

"Is that so?" my father asked while I regained my breath.

"It is," I said, determined.

"I was asking Gabriel," he explained.

I was surprised to see Gabriel climb out of the carriage, followed by my mother. I had thought my father was alone, with my mother still inside the house, wondering where I went.

"Yes, sir. I would give the very heart in my chest if it meant I could spend the rest of my life with her."

"And if she married another?"

"Then I would be her friend, and be there for her if ever she needed anything. Forever." Gabriel didn't say it, but it was clear that although he meant it, his heart would break in the process.

"Okay then," my father sighed.

"Okay then what?" I asked.

"If you love him and believe he will make you happy, then I will speak to Mr. Mayweather. I'm sure we can come to an arrangement."

"You won't give Bartholomew your blessing?" I verified.

"In light of your declaration, your mother's insistence, and

Gabriel's eloquent defense, I am giving it to him."

"In that case…"

Gabriel came forward and brought me to the edge of the field, under the oak tree we'd carved our names into. I could feel my parents watching as he went in front of me and got down on one knee, but at least they couldn't hear.

"Bells, you are the love of my life. I knew it the first moment I saw you, and I fall more in love with you every day. My heart can hardly contain how happy you make me just by being near. I know I can't offer you everything you grew up with, but I will spend every day for the rest of my life loving you. Will you do me the honor of being my wife?" Every word was grounded in the certainty of his feelings, but with the weight of his question as well. Like my answer to it was all that mattered.

"Yes," I told him, looking into those deep brown eyes I loved so much. "A million times yes, with all my heart."

He took a ring from his pocket and slipped it on my finger, but I didn't even have time to get a good look at it before he took me in his arms and twirled me. I wrapped my arms around him and he kissed me, like he had done once before, just a few feet from where we were now standing. This time, even though I knew my parents could see, I had absolutely no fear.

The End
***

Lucy's story may be over, but the Gifted adventures continue in First Life , the first book of The Gifted Chronicles…

To get your bonus Gabriel chapter and Lucy's family tree, be sure to join my mailing list!
www.amandalynnpetrin.com/chroniclesbonus

ABOUT THE AUTHOR

Amanda Lynn Petrin grew up on the South Shore of Montreal with a big and supportive family. She studied Psychology and History at McGill University, then went into acting once she graduated.

In 2017 she moved to Toronto, Ontario, in the hopes of finding more opportunities. Instead, she discovered that you need to create your own. She has written, produced and starred in multiple short films, including Get-Together, All the Things, and Touched. Being an author was a dream she thought would never come true until she started doing the things that scared her. Her debut novel, Shards of Glass, was released in August 2019, and she is just getting started.

Find her at: https://www.amandalynnpetrin.com